RISE OF THE EMPIRE

RISE OF
THE EMPIRE

FEATURING TWO NOVELS—
STAR WARS: TARKIN AND STAR WARS: A NEW
DAWN—AND THREE ORIGINAL SHORT STORIES

DEL REY
NEW YORK

A Del Rey Trade Paperback Original

Copyright © 2015 by Lucasfilm Ltd. & TM where indicated.
All rights reserved.
Excerpt from *Star Wars: Battlefront: Twilight Company* by
Alexander Freed copyright © 2015 by Lucasfilm Ltd. ® & TM
where indicated. All rights reserved.
Excerpt from *Star Wars: Aftermath* by Chuck Wendig
copyright © 2015 by Lucasfilm Ltd. ® & TM
where indicated. All rights reserved.

All rights reserved.

Published in the United States by Del Rey,
an imprint of Random House, a division of
Penguin Random House LLC, New York.

DEL REY and the HOUSE colophon are registered
trademarks of Penguin Random House LLC.

Star Wars: A New Dawn and *Star Wars: Tarkin* both originally
published separately in hardcover in the United States by
Del Rey, an imprint of Random House, a division of
Penguin Random House LLC, in 2014.

This book contains the following short stories
originally created for this edition. Copyright © 2015
by Lucasfilm Ltd. & TM where indicated:

"Mercy Mission"
"Bottleneck"
"The Levers of Power"

This book contains excerpts from *Star Wars: Battlefront: Twilight Company*
by Alexander Freed and *Star Wars: Aftermath* by Chuck Wendig.
These excerpts have been set for this edition only and may not
reflect the final content of the forthcoming editions.

ISBN 978-1-101-96503-0
eBook ISBN 978-1-101-96506-1

Printed in the United States of America on acid-free paper

Starwars.com
Delreybooks.com
Facebook.com/starwarsbooks

1 2 3 4 5 6 7 8 9

THE DEL REY

STAR WARS®

TIMELINE

I — THE PHANTOM MENACE

II — ATTACK OF THE CLONES
THE CLONE WARS (TV SERIES)
DARK DISCIPLE

III — REVENGE OF THE SITH
LORDS OF THE SITH
TARKIN
A NEW DAWN
REBELS (TV SERIES)

IV — A NEW HOPE
HEIR TO THE JEDI
BATTLEFRONT: TWILIGHT COMPANY

V — THE EMPIRE STRIKES BACK

VI — RETURN OF THE JEDI
AFTERMATH

VII — THE FORCE AWAKENS

CONTENTS

A long time ago in a galaxy far, far away. . . .

For over a thousand generations, the Jedi Knights were the guardians of peace and justice in the Old Republic. Before the dark times . . . before the Empire.

—Obi-Wan Kenobi

MERCY MISSION

Melissa Scott

"THIS JOB IS PREPOSTEROUS, and you know it!"

Hera Syndulla winced as the voices from the commons echoed through the freighter's central corridor. Ever since they'd left Rishi with the load of gattis-root extract intended for Twi'lek civilians on Ryloth, Trae Baratha had been protesting the mission.

"Your Karthakk Group thought it was sensible enough to take our credits. And if you want the final payment for your people, Clinician, you have to deliver the medicine." Goll, a former leader of the Free Ryloth Movement, sounded as though he'd reached the end of his patience.

For a second, Hera considered retreating, but *Eclipse* was a small freighter, and there were few places where you weren't practically on top of everyone else.

"I'll deliver the medicine if it can be done safely," Baratha retorted. "Only then."

"Your people won't be happy if they don't get paid," Goll said.

Hera heard footsteps behind her and saw the *Eclipse*'s Nikto gunner, Ul'ligan, coming down the corridor. He cocked his multihorned

head at her, but before she could say anything, Baratha's voice rang
out again.

"They'll like it even less if we get caught and the Imperials seize the
cargo."

Hera squared her shoulders and stepped through the hatch into
the commons.

"The Karthakk Group agreed to take the job," Goll said, his voice
hardening. He was sitting on the padded seat that ran along the forward bulkhead, his lekku, the heavy head tails that curled down to
his shoulders, stiff with irritation. Hera hoped the human clinician
couldn't read the level of annoyance that would be clear to any
Twi'lek. "You were outvoted."

That was inarguable, but Baratha waved a hand in dismissal anyway. *Eclipse*'s engineer, a slim, lavender-skinned Sephi named Eira
Tay, sat at the little table, hunched low over her plate, trying to pretend the others weren't there. Ul'ligan made a sympathetic noise and
patted her on the shoulder as he made his way to the caf dispenser.

"They didn't know whom you'd hired," Baratha snapped. She was
tall, and very thin, her graying hair cut short around her sharp face.
When they had first met, Hera thought the hair looked like the downy
feathers of a very young chick, but now Baratha reminded her of a
carrion bird. "This thing—no offense, Engineer, but this ship isn't
going to stand up to anything bigger than a two-shot blaster."

Tay's pointed ears swiveled and flattened. "Mostly we try not to get
caught . . . or shot."

"We've been doing this a long time," Ul'ligan said, his voice low
and grating. He spoke so rarely that Hera was still unsure if he was
annoyed or if that was his natural tone.

Tay nodded vigorously. "And look! We're still here."

"They're the best available," Goll said. If he was aware of the ambi-
guity of the statement, he gave no sign of it. "Plus, your people knew
how serious our situation was when they agreed to help. The price for
the gattis reflected it."

"Bybbec fever is unpleasant," Baratha said, "but only rarely fatal."

"It's fatal to Twi'leks." Hera couldn't stop herself. The cargo was
intended for a settlement of Twi'lek elders, who had come together to

preserve their culture in the face of the Imperial conquest. But when Goll asked her to join the mission, he had told her to keep the extract's real destination a secret. He didn't trust any of the others well enough. "And the symptoms are more severe—fever, bone ache, weakness."

"True," Goll said. "And that's not the only problem. The Empire is rationing treatment—oh, they're offering the gattis extract for free, but to receive it, you have to register with the distributing clinic. Then they use that registration to sniff out false identities. Even worse, they're forcing many of the jungle settlements to reveal themselves to the Empire in exchange for treatment. They're demanding that entire communities relocate, all under the guise of making it easier to get the drugs."

"What we're carrying is a drop in the bucket," Baratha said.

"It'll help thousands of people avoid Imperial control," Hera said.

Baratha ignored her. "Come on," she said to Goll, "you have to see the problems here."

"We're not going up against Star Destroyers," Goll said. "The Imperials on Ryloth have V-wing fighters, and we can handle that. If we even have to."

"We could handle it, but I like to think our plan is a little smarter than that."

Hera turned to see *Eclipse*'s captain, Krysiant Rheden, standing in the hatchway. She was perhaps a few years younger than Baratha and a head shorter, broad-shouldered and unremarkable except for the blaster at her hip. Hera wondered if she carried it on all her jobs.

"Hera—" Rheden stopped, grimacing, and Baratha flung up her hands.

"So much for security!"

Baratha had urged them to use titles instead of names. Hera thought the idea was silly.

"Copilot," Rheden corrected herself, with angry precision. "And Engineer," she said, turning to Tay. "We're about to exit hyperspace. I want you both in the cockpit."

Hera followed the others forward and settled herself into the copilot's seat. Outside the reinforced canopy, hyperspace flared electric blue; between the two pilots' stations, the navigation computer was chattering to itself, lights flashing as it signaled the approaching transition. She belted herself in and gave Rheden a cautious look.

"I don't mind if you call me Hera. I trust you."

"You probably shouldn't. Baratha may be right," Rheden said.

"Except we already know each other's names," Tay said.

Rheden grunted in agreement, and Baratha's voice crackled from the intercom.

"Captain. Are you planning to crew the turrets?"

Rheden's mouth tightened. "I'm keeping weapons at standby unless we get into trouble."

"We'll take positions just in case." Goll sounded calm enough, but Hera guessed his lekku were stiff with annoyance.

"Suit yourself," Rheden said. "Ul'ligan, take the stern pod."

"Will do," Ul'ligan answered, and Rheden shook her head, covering the intercom pickup with one hand.

"What a pain in the neck that woman is."

Before Hera could decide how to answer, the nav computer beeped insistently.

"Stand by, we're coming up on the transition." Rheden glanced at the nav computer's screen. "Three, two, one—cut in sublight, Tay."

The sound of the ship's engine shifted subtly, the vivid blue of hyperspace fading to lines that suddenly blurred and shortened and became stars. Hera's lekku tightened: She'd been on missions before, some easy, others complicated. But it seemed as though she'd never get used to making the first step. There was a ping, and a series of blue lights flared at the top of Hera's board. "I'm picking up a small Imperial cruiser, but it's just scanning us."

Tay looked up sharply. "Since when does the Empire scan ships on approach? That's unusual."

"It's fine. As long as that's all they're doing." Rheden kept one hand on the control yoke as the ship fed false data to the Imperials.

The communications system pinged. "FT-2991 *Tirion,* you are cleared to enter Ryloth system. Follow Beacon Tivik, channel 81, to planetary orbit and hold there for further instructions."

Rheden flicked a switch. "Roger that. Beacon Tivik to orbit, and hold for instructions." She flipped the switch off again and gave Hera a crooked smile. "Here we go."

The flight into the Ryloth system was uneventful. After the first hour, Rheden announced that the guns didn't need to be crewed any longer. Ul'ligan and Goll returned to the commons, but Baratha said that she would stay in the starboard turret. "Suit yourself," Rheden said, and looked at Hera. "Take a break, kid. And when you come back, bring us some caf?"

Hera nodded, glad of the chance to stretch her legs, and slipped out of the cockpit. As she reached the commons, the hatch slid open, revealing Ul'ligan, who scowled over his shoulder. "I really don't care what happens as long as our ship comes through intact."

Hera stepped back as he stomped away, then she entered, letting the hatch slide closed behind her. "Is everything all right?"

Goll sighed. "Fine. It's all fine."

From his tone, there was no point in pursuing the question. Hera poured herself a cup of caf and settled across from him at the narrow table. "Captain Rheden is annoyed with Baratha."

"So are we all." Goll showed sharply filed teeth. "But the Kar-thakk Group had the gattis extract, and so we're stuck with her. We keep everyone moving along as happily as possible. Even if I'd like to—" He stopped, shaking his head. "We keep moving. It's what leaders do."

Hera finished her caf and made up cups for Rheden and Tay, waiting for Goll to elaborate, but he didn't. She was glad she wasn't in charge. She wasn't sure she could have kept from snapping at Baratha. "Feels strange to be going back to Ryloth, doesn't it?"

"Feels strange doing it without your father. Cham would have . . ." Goll shook his head again, and Hera knew there was no point in asking questions. Goll wouldn't even tell her where he was. *He'd be angry enough if he knew I let you volunteer for this,* Goll had said the last time she asked. She nodded instead and turned to leave.

She returned to the cockpit with the mugs of caf and took her turn at the controls, while first Rheden, then Tay took breaks of their own. By then, Ryloth was swelling in the viewscreens, and Hera adjusted the sensors to magnify the image. She hadn't seen Ryloth in so long that the rust-brown disk was as much a symbol as a remembered home. She sighed, and the engineer reached over to pat her shoulder.

"Must be weird, huh?"

"Better not be," Rheden said. "She's got to guide us in once we're off the traffic-control net."

Hera's lekku twitched in embarrassment. "I can handle it."

Rheden ran a hand through her hair. "Sorry."

To Hera's relief, the control panel beeped at her. "Tivik is signaling." She reached for the comm system, while Rheden slowed the ship. A moment later, a bored voice sounded over the speakers.

"*Tirion.* You are cleared to enter atmosphere. Stand by for your descent heading and auto-control frequency."

"Standing by," Hera answered. The system chattered and flashed a series of numbers that flickered to green. "Received and confirmed."

"Roger, *Tirion.* And a friendly reminder. Any deviation from the reentry corridor or from auto-control will result in the destruction of your ship."

"Understood, Tivik," Hera said. "Commencing reentry. *Tirion* out."

"Charming welcome," Rheden said.

"You're sure your people can cut the auto-control system," Tay said.

"That's the plan," Hera answered. She recited the procedure she had memorized. "Once we're at the designated altitude, we slave the ship to the traffic network. It's supposed to take us all the way into the port at Lessu. After we pass Marker 210, our contact will cut the network broadcast for twenty-five seconds. We drop beneath the net and proceed to the rendezvous."

"So they'll assume we've crashed," Rheden said. Warnings flared as *Eclipse* touched the edge of the atmosphere, and she trimmed the ship for reentry. "Won't someone be looking for us?"

Hera shook her head. "Goll says the Imperials won't care about one civilian freighter. They'll just report it to what's left of the civil authority."

"Lovely," Rheden muttered, and reached for the intercom. "All right, everybody, we're beginning reentry. Stand by for some turbulence, and I'll let you know when we're down."

"Captain." It was Baratha, of course, and Hera saw the captain roll her eyes. "We should be on the guns."

Goll cut in quickly. "That makes sense. We'll be in the turrets, Captain. Give us power when and if you have to."

Outside the cockpit, the stars were disappearing. *Eclipse* bounced once and steadied, Rheden balancing the ship's shields against the atmosphere, melting away velocity.

"What if your people don't cut the power?" Tay asked.

Hera glanced warily over her shoulder. "We can override the system from here—we're not locked in. But that will alert every Imperial patrol in the area."

"If we have to do that, the mission's off," Rheden said. Under her hands, *Eclipse* steadied into blue sky, the broken clouds beneath them revealing flashes of barren orange ground.

"But—" Hera began, and Rheden shook her head.

"Not up for debate. My first priority is to protect the ship."

And what about the people on the ground, the people who were risking their lives to help deliver this cargo? Hera struggled to find words, but the warning from the console interrupted her. "The auto-control system wants to take over. They have us on the standard course for Lessu."

A new bank of lights sprang to life in the center of the control boards. Rheden glared at them but entered the codes to give the autopilot access to the ship's systems. One by one, the lights went from orange to green, and a voice came from the speaker, scratchy with distance.

"*Tirion,* you are now on remote pilot. Do not attempt to adjust your controls. I repeat, do not attempt to adjust your controls."

"Confirmed." Rheden leaned back in her seat, folding her arms across her chest. "Better not fly my ship into anything."

Tay reached up to flick switches on an overhead panel. "Set the tertiary receiver to 93.39, please, Hera."

Hera did as she was told. A smaller speaker crackled, and voices came clear.

". . . V-254 vector Alpha 10. Delta Flight return to base . . ."

Hera's eyes widened as she listened. "That's the main Imperial channel."

Tay shrugged. "It seemed like a good idea to know what they're up to."

It would have been a better idea if the information had been shared. This was part of the problem, Hera thought. Each group kept its assets secret from everyone else. There was no trust.

Minutes turned into hours as *Eclipse* bored on toward the capital, the background chatter of the patrolling V-wings and the steady thrum of the engines blurring into a soporific drone. Hera blinked hard, trying to stay awake, then sat up abruptly as she saw the scrolling map.

"Captain. We're coming up on Marker 210."

"I see it," Rheden said, and flipped the intercom switch. "Okay, people, we're in the zone. Everybody be ready. Hera, do we have patrols in range?"

"Only one, and it's moving off." Hera adjusted the sensors. "No other traffic within a thousand kilometers."

Red lights flashed across all the displays, and a mechanical voice announced, "Auto-control disengaged! Auto-control disengaged!"

Rheden pitched *Eclipse* into a steep dive. Hera disabled the autopilot and silenced all outgoing transmissions, one eye on the clock. The first layer of clouds whipped past the cockpit windows.

"Twenty-two seconds," she said. "Twenty seconds."

"Engines at maximum," Tay said. "Weapons hot."

Rheden didn't respond, all her attention on the controls. Hera could feel the ship shivering, hull and engines straining. They were shedding height, but not fast enough. "Ten seconds."

"More power," Rheden said.

"We're at max," Tay answered, and Rheden swore, the controls jerking in her hands.

"Three seconds," Hera said. "Two . . . One."

The lights on the auto-control console went from red to green, then began flashing yellow, a silent warning streaming across the screen. *Signal present, auto-control disabled. Reengage auto-control.*

Baratha cut in over the comm. "Did we make it?"

The lights in the control room flickered, and instantly the alarms blared. Moff Delion Mors, Commander of the Imperial Forces on

Ryloth, bolted to her feet and leaned over the railing of the mezzanine office that let her literally overlook the nerve center of Imperial control. The main display screen showed a stream of error messages rather than the regional traffic plot, and every console seemed to be glowing red. A dozen different alarms were sounding, and a confused clamor of voices rose from the pit as the technicians shouted for answers. There was a power problem somewhere, she could tell that much just from the pattern of the lights, and she closed her hands on the rails and leaned forward.

"Report! Stations, report!"

There was no immediate answer from the technicians and supervisors bent over their consoles, and her grip tightened.

"Karris! Report, now!"

This time, her voice cut through the clamor, and she saw the frantic movement take on new purpose as supervisors shut off superfluous alarms and technicians began to work together.

"Moff Mors!" That was Karris at last, shouldering past the last row of technicians to look up at her. "We've had a power glitch, several systems are offline—"

"Which systems?" Mors glared down at him, a knot of fear tightening in her stomach. "I need proper reports, Commander."

"Sorry, ma'am. Working on it." He turned to slap the nearest technician's shoulder, ambiguous encouragement, and Mors scanned the control room again. On both ends of the arc of consoles, systems were coming back online. She identified them as base environmentals and the main comm network—a good start, but the tracking systems were still down, and it looked as though the sensor net was only partially restored—

"Moff Mors!" Karris swung away from the pit to look up at her, clasping his hands behind his back to hide his nerves. "Our technicians have traced a fault in power production that led to a five-second general outage. Backup systems are coming online. We have full communications back, sensors report no sign of attack or infiltration, and I am running a full set of diagnostics—"

Mors waved the words away. "What's not working?" She started down the stairs: This was something she needed to see for herself, not watch from a distance. She'd come too close to losing everything during the Emperor's visit to Ryloth a year ago; she was not going to allow anyone the chance to make mistakes on her watch.

Karris's eyes fell. "The traffic-control net was down, but our people are bringing it back up—"

"Commander!" That was one of the technicians in the center of the pit—traffic control, Mors identified, and fear knotted her guts. The Emperor had made it clear that this was her last—her only—chance, and she squared her shoulders. She would not fail.

"Commander, we've restored the auto-control system, but a ship is missing. It was there when the system went out, but now—it's gone."

"Show me," Mors said before Karris could answer, and pushed her way past the other consoles. The man on duty was a stranger, when once she'd prided herself on knowing all the people under her command. "What's your name, son?"

The technician gave her a nervous glance. "Denner, ma'am."

"Tell me what happened, Denner."

Denner took a deep breath. "When the power went, we also lost the auto-control grid, with twenty-eight ships on the beams. We weren't down for more than twenty seconds, twenty-five at the outside . . . Ma'am, we're missing one freighter, inbound to Lessu on Route Alpha, A2.93. *Tirion.* We have one last ping, falling like a stone, then she's below our net. Looks like the pilot wasn't paying attention when the beam went out."

Mors looked up at the main display. He was probably right. The Free Ryloth Movement was broken, destroyed by the Emperor himself, and a part of her was tempted to ignore the missing ship. However. She was on probation, the Emperor had made that clear, but he'd also made it clear that she could redeem herself. She couldn't afford to ignore anything, no matter how trivial it might seem. "Maybe. And just maybe . . . Well, if they did crash, I want to know where and why." She squinted at the display, reading the symbols. *Tirion* had been over the jungle: Luck help the poor devils if they did crash in that, she thought, and looked at Karris. "Commander. Lieutenant Niol's flight is the closest. Have him check it out and report back."

"I thought they didn't take civilian problems seriously," Tay said.

"They never used to," Hera answered. She could see the V-wings on her screen, swinging in an arc that would bring them up on *Eclipse*'s tail. "Captain!"

"I see them," Rheden answered. "Tay, all the power we've got. The rest of you, weapons hot! We've got company."

There was a bank of clouds ahead, and for a second, Hera thought they might reach its shelter before the V-wings found them. But the Imperial ships were too fast, the group of three swelling in her screen, and the sensors pinged loudly as the flight leader located them.

"Jam their transmissions," Rheden said, and Hera obeyed.

"*Tirion*, reduce speed and return to auto-control."

"Not happening," Rheden said. "Let them get close, then take them out."

"Ready," Ul'ligan said, and Goll and Baratha echoed him.

"*Tirion*, respond! Respond, or we will fire."

"Hera, are you jamming?" Rheden demanded.

"Yes—" Hera flinched as the first V-wing fired a warning shot, the bolt of emerald fire snapping past the canopy.

"Respond—"

Baratha opened fire, followed an instant later by Ul'ligan and Goll. Hera saw one V-wing disintegrate immediately, but the other two veered away, one trailing a thin stream of smoke. She twisted the jammer's knob to full power, and the speakers filled with static. *Eclipse* rolled hard left and pulled up, and the first V-wing overshot, airfoils extending as it tried to brake and turn. For an instant, its vertical radiators presented a perfect target, and both Goll and Ul'ligan fired. The radiator disintegrated in a shower of flame and fragmenting metal; the V-wing pitched up and fell off to its right, and Baratha hit it again, blowing it apart.

Eclipse rocked violently as the remaining V-wing came up under her stern, and Hera heard the steady pounding of the cannons as first Ul'ligan, then Baratha returned fire without result. The V-wing swept past, pulling up and over as it tried for a head-on shot. Rheden banked sharply away, but the ship bounced again as the shots went home. A warning flashed on Hera's console—primary communications were hit—and sparks flew from Rheden's secondary console. She cursed, slapping at breakers, but the main panel exploded in her face. She cried out and tumbled from the pilot's chair. *Eclipse* nosed up, and Hera snatched for the controls.

She pointed *Eclipse* down again, and the V-wing rolled as it came around behind for another pass. Goll fired, and the V-wing rocked, shedding parts in a stream of spark and flame, but came on, firing steadily. *Eclipse* shook again, warnings flaring. Hera cut power, and the V-wing shot past, trailing smoke. Baratha fired twice more, and it dissolved in flames. Hera wrenched *Eclipse* sideways to avoid the debris, and the cockpit filled with the sound of alarms. She steadied the ship, though it had an alarming tendency to heel left every time she eased pressure on the yoke. "Status, Tay?"

"Engines took a direct hit." Tay answered. Hera could hear her moving from station to station at the back of the cockpit but didn't dare take her eyes off the controls to see what she was doing. Out of the corner of her eye, she could just see Rheden slumped unmoving against the bulkhead. "I've got creeping shorts in the electrics, too. Still locking them down."

They'd lost long-range sensors and the main transmitter, Hera saw, but she could compensate for that. At least there was no sign of any other patrols, but they'd be on their way. *Eclipse* pitched again, more violently, and there was a heavy thud as either Tay or Rheden fell hard against something.

"I need the gravitics back," Hera said, and a thin thread of smoke rose from behind the environmental display. "Tay—"

"Working on it," Tay said grimly.

Something snapped in the control linkage, and *Eclipse* nosed up again, then fell off to the left. Hera hauled on the controls, got no response, and saw the breaker lights flashing. She flipped the switch, once, twice; the lights went out, and when she pulled again, the control yoke moved, *Eclipse* shuddering under the strain. The jungle was coming closer, but she concentrated on the pressure of the controls against her hand, waiting for the gravitics to stabilize. More power, and turn into the spin: She pushed the yoke hard left. Trees filled the cockpit windows, a flock of insects exploding away from them as *Eclipse* arrowed down. And then the spin slowed, stopped, and she hauled back on the yoke. *Eclipse* groaned and lifted, the stern turret just brushing the top of the forest.

She leveled out a dozen meters above the treetops, scanning her panels for any more damage. Everything seemed stable for the moment, and she risked a glance at the captain. Rheden looked only half-conscious, clearly in need of help. "Tay . . ."

"The captain needs help." Tay moved closer, dropping to her knees to open another panel. "And the ship needs proper repairs. We have to land."

"Not here," Goll said from the hatch, and Hera jumped. "The jungle life is more dangerous than being chased by V-wings." He went to one knee beside Rheden's crumpled body, his face tightening, and reached for the intercom. "Baratha, get up here. Captain's injured!"

"On my way," Baratha answered. *Eclipse* wobbled again, and Hera caught it, then freed one hand to extend the secondary sensors to their maximum range. The screen was empty so far, but she doubted that would last.

"I can't fix this if we don't land," Tay said. "Whatever's down there, you can hold them off."

Goll shook his head. "They're lyleks—armored insects, with stabbing limbs and poisoned tentacles. They hunt in packs, and they'll travel for days to get fresh food. We might kill the first wave, but we couldn't keep them back for long."

"Lovely," Baratha said under her breath. Hera flinched at the raw burn that covered Rheden's face from her forehead to the left side of her chin, but at least the captain seemed to be conscious.

"Tay." Ul'ligan appeared in the hatchway. "Repair droids are deployed, but I don't know how much they can do on their own."

"Let them work," she said. "I've got bigger things to worry about."

For an instant, Hera wished she'd been able to bring Chopper. But Goll had been certain there was no place for another droid on the ship, especially not one with Chopper's notable eccentricities. A warning light flashed on the sensor display, and her heart sank. Another flight of V-wings was coming in fast from the north.

"Goll."

"I see them. Can they see us?"

"Not yet." Hera turned *Eclipse* south and increased power, losing altitude so that they were barely skimming the treetops. If she could stay out of range—yes, there were the mountains, and she angled her course westward, aiming for the Bypass Notch. If she could get through that before the V-wings were fully in range, the mountains would block their scanners.

Tay flung herself to the floor plates beside the nav computer and yanked open an access hatch. There was a puff of smoke and the smell of burning, and she blasted the compartment with an extinguisher. "Okay, rerouting that. We've got to at least slow down, I can't keep giving you full power."

"We have to get through the mountains." Hera looked at the map unscrolling on her screen. "Ten minutes."

"The mountains? We have to abort," Baratha said to Goll.

"That'll put us right in the path of the V-wings," Goll answered.

Tay tore open another panel and began shifting cables. Hera heard a fat snap, and the ship lurched again but steadied.

"The captain can't fly," Baratha said.

"I'm—" Rheden hissed in pain. "I can handle it."

"You can't see out of that eye," Baratha said. "And you're in shock."

"I've studied the landing," Hera said. "I can get us in and out."

Baratha shook her head. "Look, I'm sure you think you're a good pilot—"

"She can do it," Rheden said. "The ship, though—" She broke off again as Baratha wrapped a bandage around her face, her hands more gentle than her words.

"I don't know." Tay's hands were busy inside another console. "If we can't put down—we could lose the ship. Maybe Baratha is right."

"What about the V-wings?" Goll asked.

Hera glanced at the scanners. "Just coming into range, but they haven't spotted us yet." The mountains weren't far ahead, their gullied orange slopes rising jagged out of the jungle. She could see the gap between Mount Foreth and Mount Maali that would hide them from pursuit. Or at least from these pursuers; there would be other patrols out looking for them. She tipped *Eclipse* into the turn that brought them into Foreth's shadow. "Clear."

"The droids aren't making much progress," Ul'ligan said to Tay, who shook her head.

"Either we set down, or we need to get out of here."

"Can we make hyperspace?" Ul'ligan asked.

Tay shrugged, ears flat. "If we go now, if there's no more damage—"

"We have to make it to Lessu," Hera said. Goll shook his head in warning, but she ignored him. If they didn't trust the rest of the team with the real purpose of the mission, how could she expect them to trust her with their lives? "This medicine is earmarked for a settlement of our elders. They're the foundation of our culture. If they die, we die."

No one said anything, and Goll turned to the comm. "I'm contacting the rendezvous." He adjusted the secondary transmitter, and a light flashed green. "Dianthy, this is Goll."

"Goll!" The connection was scratchy with static, but the words were clear. "Goll, all the rendezvous points are being watched—"

"Calm." Goll flattened his hands in the air as though Dianthy could see him. "All the fallbacks, too?"

"Everything close to Lessu."

"Stand by." Goll cut the channel, frowning.

"That's that," Baratha said. "I'm sorry about your elders, but we can't risk losing the gattis extract. Abort and try again."

"We don't have time," Hera said. "Is there somewhere else we can land?"

"Weren't you listening?" Baratha glared. "All your fallbacks are being watched."

"There was another one," Rheden dragged herself upright, Baratha supporting her. "To the west?"

Eclipse was stable enough that Hera risked manipulating her maps, then saw that Goll had called up a different file. "If you mean Rho-vari, that's too far. It'll be too hard to distribute the medication from there."

"That's better than not having it at all," Rheden said. She swayed and sat down hard on the floor plates.

"It's too much of a risk," Baratha said.

Hera pushed the voices away. Goll was right, they had to get through, but Baratha was also right, much as she hated to admit it. And Rhovari really was too far west . . . She looked at the map display again, symbols scrolling past as the system laid out a course to Lessu, possible landing sites marked with blue diamonds. There weren't any between the mountains and the jungle's edge, and the next were all too close to Imperial observers; the rendezvous and fallback sites formed a rough crescent in the badlands west of the city, but if the Imperials had them under surveillance, there wasn't much chance of getting *Eclipse* out again even if Tay could finish the repairs. A new mark caught her eye, on the southern slope of the cone that con-tained the city, and she quickly queried the system. It was a commer-cial landing zone, originally intended to serve a local factory, now disused; it was small, and the original approach lane had been nar-rowed by two new towers, but there was just enough room to set *Eclipse* down.

"Goll. What about here?"

Goll leaned over her shoulder. "Too small."

"There's about ten meters clearance each way," Hera answered. "I can do it."

"Ten meters?" Baratha rose to her feet. "Are you crazy?"

"It's tight," Hera said, "but we can drop straight in on the field. *Eclipse* can handle it."

Goll shook his head. "It's close to Dianthy's territory, but—"

"It can't be done," Baratha said.

Tay hauled herself to her feet. "We'd fit, but we're in no shape to try. We have to abandon."

Ul'ligan tipped his head to one side, and Rheden stretched out one hand to catch Tay's sleeve. "Can we make it into hyperspace?"

Tay hesitated. "Yes. I think so."

"No," Goll said. "We are going to deliver the medicine. That's what I paid you for, all of you."

"I'm not losing my ship for this," Rheden said.

"And I'm not letting this medicine fall into Imperial hands," Baratha snapped. "That's final."

Hera looked from one to the other. They'd never been anything like a team, but now it was all falling apart. She took a deep breath, remembering what Goll had said before: The leader's job was to keep everything moving, however they had to do it. "Whatever we do, we need to finish the repairs. If someone directs the droids, the work will go a lot faster."

There was a moment of silence, Tay's ears twitching, but it was Ul'ligan who spoke first. "She's right."

Hera hurried on before anyone else could argue. "Once we get the repairs finished, we make one attempt to deliver our cargo, and if that doesn't work, we bail. But we have to try once."

Goll nodded slowly. "If Dianthy can get her people there . . ."

Rheden leaned over the map display, blinking hard as she tried to focus. Hera could smell the bacta on the bandages and saw her grimace as she made sense of the display. "You're sure?"

"Yes." Hera nodded.

"I'm not," Tay said, and Ul'ligan laid a hand on her shoulder.

"One try. She'll hold together for that."

"And if she doesn't, we're in bigger trouble anyway," Rheden said. "I'm in."

Tay sighed. "All right."

"One try," Baratha said. "Nothing more. And only if they complete the repairs in time."

"We'll do that," Tay said. She looked at Goll. "I'll need your help out on the hull. Ul'ligan needs to be on guns."

"Let me update Dianthy," Goll said, "And I'm all yours."

Hera turned *Eclipse* onto the new heading, watching the jungle thin out beneath them as the ship drew closer to the city. Behind her, Baratha was mercifully silent, tending Rheden with quiet competence; the monitors showed Goll and Tay busy on the hull's starboard side, while the droids worked along the tail, patching conduit and cable. She could still feel the damage—sluggish response to the control surfaces, a definite lag when she asked for more power—but she'd flown worse. In the background, she could hear V-wing chatter on the Imperial circuit: So far, they were concentrating on the spot where the patrol had caught *Eclipse,* but sooner or later they were going to start looking toward the capital again. The short-range sensors showed a couple of flights at the edge of their range, but no one had spotted them yet.

"Hera." Tay's voice crackled from the intercom. "Gravitics are repaired. We're good—oh, damn it."

"What?" Hera scanned her controls, but nothing seemed to have changed.

"We've got a break in the secondary power conduit on this side," Tay said. "Not a problem now, but we need it fixed before we jump to hyperspace."

"How long?"

"Twenty minutes."

Hera checked her readings. That was just enough time to finish before she had to begin the landing. "All right. We're going in."

"But they're still out there!" Baratha demanded, and out of the corner of her eye, Hera saw Rheden grab the clinician's arm.

"We're committed. Sit down and be silent."

Astonishingly, Baratha obeyed. Hera banked *Eclipse,* chasing the ship's shadow south and west across the broken ground. They were still safely under the Imperial sensor net, but they were entirely too visible from the surface. The Imperials were still searching, and it wouldn't take much to draw their attention—and if she did, Goll and Tay were still on the hull, utterly exposed. She chose a vector that kept them well clear of an Imperial monitoring station and dropped *Eclipse* lower still.

The cone that was the city of Lessu swelled on the horizon, and the nav computer chimed, offering a new heading. It would take her around the old industrial district, keeping clear of the maze of chimneys and drop towers that broke the steep surface, but anyone watching from the main traffic tower would have trouble missing a star freighter. She keyed the intercom.

"Goll. How are the repairs coming?"

"Almost done," Goll answered, sounding strained.

In the monitor, Hera could see Tay lying flat on the hull, reaching into an open compartment, the harness that tethered her to the ship stretched taut. Goll crouched beside her, a toolkit open at his knee. "We're coming up on Lessu."

"Five more minutes," Tay said.

"We'll be landing then," Hera said. But they had to get that conduit repaired if they were going to escape. "Ul'ligan, call in the repair droids, get them stowed."

"Right." The Nikto's growl was strangely reassuring.

The nav computer's beeping was getting louder, but Hera ignored it, aiming for the heart of the factory district. "Hold tight."

Eclipse streaked across the barren ground—mercifully, there was no one in sight—and she pulled up as they crossed the ditch and the wall beyond. Hera swung around a leaning drop tower, lights strobing along its side, and flung *Eclipse* instantly to the right to avoid a shorter chimney. On the monitors, she saw Goll brace himself, one hand pressing Tay into the hull, the other clinging to an exposed strut. A pair of towers loomed ahead, rising from the same base and connected at the top by a rusted walkway. To go over would put them into the Imperial sensors, and either side led to a tangle of chimneys and turrets, but the space between was impossibly narrow. She tipped *Eclipse* sideways, not daring to tilt more than twenty degrees for fear of losing Goll and Tay, and held it there as she threaded the gap.

"Conduit's fixed," Tay called.

"Confirmed," Hera answered. A landing light flared ahead: Dianthy's people. She hit the air brakes, balancing *Eclipse* against Ryloth's gravity, and hovered above the gap. Checking the monitors, she could see Goll drag Tay to her feet, then both of them headed for the nearest hatch. Hera triggered her landing cameras and winced. Ten meters clearance didn't look nearly as large as she'd hoped. She eased the big ship down, red dust swirling off the buildings. The walls rose around them, so close she felt as though she could touch any of them. And then, at last, the landing gear touched, lights flaring as Ul'ligan and Goll opened the hatch.

She gave a sigh of relief but kept the power up, resetting the controls for takeoff. The Imperials weren't going to overlook a freighter sitting on the city's shell for very long—

"Go!" Ul'ligan shouted, and the hatch indicators flared green. Hera took a breath and let *Eclipse* rise.

"Moff Mors! The unidentified freighter has landed on the outer surface of the capital."

Mors glared at the screen, wishing she could force the V-wing patrols to exceed their maximum speeds. She'd guessed wrong—it hadn't occurred to her that the missing freighter would continue to its stated destination, and she'd wasted time and men searching for signs on vectors that led away from Lessu. "Get ground troops moving. They're obviously smuggling something. Find them and cut them off. Now!"

"Yes, ma'am." The nearest comms officer spoke into his mouthpiece, and a moment later she saw lights flare on secondary screens as Colonel Piik's men turned out from their barracks in the capital.

"Shut the city down. I want every exit sealed." That was all she could do about Lessu for the moment, and she turned her attention to the main display. The freighter was still on the ground, and she turned to Karris. "Signal *Despot*. Tell them to watch for an unauthorized liftoff from Lessu, a YT-209 freighter. Capture if possible, but destroy it if it won't stop."

"Yes, ma'am," Karris said, and turned to his own controls. "*Despot* acknowledges. They're reversing course."

For a second, she thought the V-wings might have a chance, arrowing across the badlands at their top speed, but the freighter began to lift, dragging itself out from among the buildings. As soon as it cleared the roofs, it shot upward, showing a surprising turn of speed, and headed for open space. The main screen switched to an orbital view, and Mors swore as she saw the angles. *Despot* was still reversing course: They'd been caught flat-footed. The captain fired anyway, but the bolts fell short. The freighter seemed to shift slightly, then it was gone.

"They've jumped to hyperspace, ma'am," someone said, and Mors swallowed an angry retort. Of course they'd jumped; it wasn't as though *Despot* had managed to hit anything. She stifled her anger with an effort, knowing that what she truly felt was fear. *One chance.*

"I want the city searched—" She stopped abruptly, recognizing the folly there. They didn't have the personnel to do a proper door-to-door investigation; the best she could manage was a general sweep and hope that something useful turned up.

"Yes, ma'am," Karris said again. "Ma'am, there hasn't been any sign of organized resistance in the capital. Is it possible they're just smugglers?"

It was possible, of course. The Outer Rim produced smugglers who were as dedicated, or determined to earn their full fees, as any Imperial officer. But it was not a risk she cared to take. "I don't care who they are. I want that cargo found. Search the city, first, then inform all our agents that I will pay a handsome reward for information on the freighter, the cargo, and/or its eventual recipients. Keep the city sealed until I say otherwise." That would be hard on the locals, but she couldn't afford to care. She would not be found wanting again.

Hera engaged the autopilot and leaned back in her seat, staring at the blue shimmer of hyperspace. "On course for Manda, Captain."

"Good," Rheden said. She had managed to reclaim the captain's chair, but she was clearly in no shape to fly. "We'll drop the rest of you there. Plenty of transport on Manda."

And who'll fly you wherever it is you're going? Hera swallowed the words, knowing they were pointless.

"At least we made it," Tay said, and pulled herself up out of her own chair. "Come on, Krys, let's get another look at that burn."

Rheden accepted her extended hand, and the two of them made their way slowly out of the cockpit. Baratha rose as well, grimacing, and gave Goll a sharp look. "I'll expect to receive our final payment before we land."

"You'll have it," Goll said wearily. "But not right this moment."

Baratha snorted and ducked out of the hatch. Goll settled himself in the captain's chair, shaking his head. Hera glanced over her shoulder at Ul'ligan, who was sitting in the pull-down seat behind the engineer's station.

"Thank you for supporting me."

The Nikto shrugged. "We are both subject peoples, the Twi'leks and us. I know what it is to lose a culture. It was worth the chance."

And that, Hera thought, was the most frustrating thing about the mission. Yes, they'd made it, delivered the gattis-root extract and escaped, but that was all they'd done. And even when someone recognized that there was common cause to be made, it didn't actually change anything.

"I'm going to eat," Ul'ligan went on, "then sleep. I'll leave food for you."

"Thanks," Hera said, and sighed as the hatch closed behind him.

"You did well," Goll said after a moment. "The gattis extract should make a difference."

"Yes."

"More than the flying. I always knew you were a good pilot. It was a good plan." Goll paused, his face serious. "You have the makings of a good leader. Like your father."

Leader of what? Hera thought. But maybe she could pull together a group of her own, find some way to stand up against the Empire. "I want to," she said, and was mildly surprised by her own desire. "I hope I can."

STAR WARS®: TARKIN

James Luceno

Five standard years have passed since Darth Sidious proclaimed himself galactic Emperor. The brutal Clone Wars are a memory, and the Emperor's apprentice, Darth Vader, has succeeded in hunting down most of the Jedi who survived dreaded Order 66. On Coruscant a servile Senate applauds the Emperor's every decree, and the populations of the Core Worlds bask in a sense of renewed prosperity.

In the Outer Rim, meanwhile, the myriad species of former Separatist worlds find themselves no better off than they were before the civil war. Stripped of weaponry and resources, they have been left to fend for themselves in an Empire that has largely turned its back on them.

Where resentment has boiled over into acts of sedition, the Empire has been quick to mete out punishment. But as confident as he is in his own and Vader's dark side powers, the Emperor understands that only a supreme military, overseen by a commander with the will to be as merciless as he is, can secure an Empire that will endure for a thousand generations. . . .

1

THE MEASURE OF A MAN

A SAYING EMERGED during the early years of the Empire: *Better to be spaced than based on Belderone.* Some commentators traced the origin to the last of the original Kamino-grown soldiers who had served alongside the Jedi in the Clone Wars; others to the first crop of cadets graduated from the Imperial academies. Besides expressing disdain for assignments on worlds located far from the Core, the adage implied that star system assignment was a designator of worth. The closer to Coruscant one was posted, the greater one's importance to the Imperial cause. Though on Coruscant itself most effectives preferred to be deployed far from the Palace rather than anywhere within range of the Emperor's withering gaze.

For those in the know, then, it seemed inexplicable that Wilhuff Tarkin should be assigned to a desolate moon in a nameless system in a remote region of the Outer Rim. The closest planets of any note were the desert world Tatooine and equally inhospitable Geonosis, on whose irradiated surface the Clone Wars had begun and which had since become a denied outlier to all but an inner circle of Imperial scientists and engineers. What could the former admiral and adjutant general have done to merit an assignment most would have regarded as a banishment? What insubordination or dereliction of duty had prompted the Emperor to exile one he himself had promoted to the rank of Moff at the end of the war? Rumors flew fast and furious among Tarkin's peers in all branches of the military. Tarkin had failed to carry out an important mission in the Western Reaches; he had quarreled with the Emperor or his chief henchman, Darth Vader; or his reach had simply exceeded his grasp, and he was paying the price for naked ambition. For those who knew Tarkin personally, however, or had even a passing familiarity with his upbringing and long record of service, the reason for the assignment was obvious: Tarkin was engaged in a clandestine Imperial enterprise.

In the memoir that was published years after his incendiary death, Tarkin wrote:

> After much reflection, I came to realize that the years I spent at Sentinel Base were as formative as my years of schooling on Eriadu's Carrion Plateau, or as significant as any of the battles in which I had participated or commanded. For I was safeguarding the creation of an armament that would one day shape and guarantee the future of the Empire. Both as impregnable fortress and as symbol of the Emperor's inviolable rule, the deep-space mobile battle station was an achievement on the order of any fashioned by the ancestral species that had unlocked the secret of hyperspace and opened the galaxy to exploration. My only regret was in not employing a firmer hand in bringing the project to fruition in time to frustrate the actions of those determined to thwart the Emperor's noble designs. Fear of the station, fear of Imperial might, would have provided the necessary deterrent.

Not once in his personal writings did Tarkin liken his authority to that of the Emperor or of Darth Vader, and yet even so simple a task as overseeing the design of a new uniform was perhaps a means of casting himself in garb as distinctive as the hooded robes of the former or the latter's signature black mask.

"An analysis of trends in military fashion on Coruscant suggests a more tailored approach," a protocol droid was saying. "Tunics continue to be double-breasted with choker collars, but are absent shoulder-boards or epaulets. What's more, trousers are no longer straight-legged, but flared in the hips and thighs, narrowing at the cuffs so as to be easily tucked into tall boots with low heels."

"A commendable alteration," Tarkin said.

"May I suggest, then, sir, flare-legged trousers—in the standard-issue gray-green fabric, of course—accented by black knee boots with turndown topside cuffs. The tunic itself should be belted at the waist, and fall to mid-thigh."

Tarkin glanced at the silver-bodied humaniform couturier. "While I can appreciate devotion to one's sartorial programming, I've no interest in initiating a fashion trend on Coruscant or anywhere else. I simply want a uniform that *fits*. Especially the boots. The stars know, my feet have logged more kilometers aboard Star Destroyers than during surface deployments, even in a facility of this size."

The RA-7 droid canted its shiny head to one side in a show of disapproval. "There is a marked difference between a uniform that 'fits' and a uniform that suits the wearer—if you take my meaning, sir. May I also point out that as a sector governor you have the freedom to be a bit more, shall we say, *daring*. If not in color, then in the hand of the cloth, the length of the tunic, the cut of the trousers."

Tarkin considered the droid's remarks in silence. Years of shipboard and downside duties had not been kind to the few dress and garrison uniforms he retained, and no one on Sentinel Base would dare criticize any liberties he might take.

"All right," he said finally, "display what you have in mind."

Dressed in an olive-drab body glove that encased him from neck to ankles and concealed the scars left by wounds from blasterfire, falls, and the claws of predators, Tarkin was standing on a low circular platform opposite a garment-fabricator whose several laser readers were plying his body with red beams, taking and recording his measurements to within a fraction of a millimeter. With his legs and arms spread, he might have been a statue mounted on a plinth, or a target galvanized in the sights of a dozen snipers. Adjacent to the fabricator sat a holotable that projected above its surface a life-sized hologram of him, clothed in a uniform whose designs changed in accordance with the silent commands of the droid, and which could be rotated on request or ordered to adopt alternate postures.

The rest of Tarkin's modest quarters were given over to a bunk, a dresser, fitness apparatus, and a sleek desk situated between cushioned swivel chairs and two more basic models. A man of black-and-white tastes, he favored clean lines, precise architecture, and an absence of clutter. A large viewport looked out across an illuminated square of landing field to a massive shield generator, and beyond to the U-shaped range of lifeless hills that cradled Sentinel Base. On the landing field were two wind-blasted shuttles, along with Tarkin's personal starship, the *Carrion Spike*.

Sentinel's host moon enjoyed close to standard gravity, but it was a cold forlorn place. Wrapped in a veil of toxic atmosphere, the secluded satellite was battered by frequent storms and as colorless as the palette that held sway in Tarkin's quarters. Even now an ill-omened tempest was swooping down the ridge and beginning to pelt the viewport with stones and grit. Base personnel called it "hard rain," if only to lighten the dreariness such storms conjured. The dark sky belonged chiefly to the swirling gas giant that owned the moon. On those long days when the moon emerged into the light of the system's distant yellow sun, the surface glare was too intense for human eyes, and the base's viewports had to be sealed or polarized.

"Your impressions, sir?" the droid said.

Tarkin studied his full-color holo-doppelgänger, focusing less on the altered uniform than on the man it contained. At fifty he was lean to the point of gaunt, with strands of wavy gray streaking what had been auburn hair. The same genetics that had bequeathed him blue eyes and a fast metabolism had also granted him sunken cheeks that imparted a masklike quality to his face. His narrow nose was made to appear even longer than it was courtesy of a widow's peak that had grown more pronounced since the end of the war. As well, deep creases now bracketed his wide, thin-lipped mouth. Many described his face as severe, though he judged it pensive, or perhaps penetrating. As for his voice, he was amused when people attributed his arrogant tone to an Outer Rim upbringing and accent.

He turned his clean-shaven face to both sides and lifted his chin. He folded his arms across his chest, then stood with his hands clasped behind his back, and finally posed akimbo, with his fists planted on his hips. Drawing himself up to his full height, which was just above human average, he adopted a serious expression, cradling his chin in his right hand. There were few beings to whom he needed to offer salute, though there was one to whom he was obliged to bow, and so he did, straight-backed but not so low as to appear sycophantic.

"Eliminate the top line collars on the boots, and lower the heels," he told the droid.

"Of course, sir. Standard duranium shank and toes for the boots?"

Tarkin nodded.

Stepping down from the platform, out from inside the cage of laser tracers, he began to walk circles around the hologram, appraising it from all sides. During the war, the belted tunic, when closed, had extended across the chest on one side and across the midsection on the other; now the line was vertical, which appealed to Tarkin's taste for symmetry. Just below each shoulder were narrow pockets designed to accommodate short cylinders that contained coded information about the wearer. A rank insignia plaque made up of two rows of small colored squares was affixed to the tunic's left breast.

Medals and battle ribbons had no place on the uniform, nor in the Imperial military. The Emperor was scornful of commendations for sand or pluck. Where another leader might wear garments of the finest synthsilk, the Emperor favored robes of black-patterned zeyd cloth, often concealing his face within the cowl—furtive, exacting, ascetic.

"More to your liking?" the droid asked when its cordwainer program had tasked the holoprojector to incorporate changes to the boots.

"Better," Tarkin said, "except perhaps for the belt. Center an officer's disk on the buckle and a matching one on the command cap." He was about to elaborate when a childhood recollection took him down a different path, and he snorted in self-amusement.

He must have been all of eleven at the time, dressed in a multi-pocketed vest he thought the perfect apparel for what he had assumed was going to be a jaunt on the Carrion Plateau. On seeing the vest, his grand-uncle Jova had smiled broadly, then issued a laugh that was at once avuncular and menacing.

"It'll look even better with blood on it," Jova had said.

"Do you find something humorous in the design, sir?" the droid asked in what amounted to distress.

Tarkin shook his head. "Nothing humorous, to be sure."

The foolishness of the fitting wasn't lost on him. He understood that he was simply trying to distract himself from having to fret over delays that were impeding progress on the battle station. Shipments from research sites had been postponed; asteroid mining at Geonosis was proving unfeasible; construction phase deadlines had not been met by the engineers and scientists who were supervising the project; a convoy transporting vital components was due to arrive . . .

In the ensuing silence, the storm began to beat a mad tattoo on the window.

Doubtless Sentinel Base was one of the Empire's most important outposts. Still, Tarkin had to wonder what his paternal grand-uncle—who had once told him that personal glory was the only quest worth pursuing—would make of the fact that his most successful apprentice was in danger of becoming a mere administrator.

His gaze had returned to the hologram when he heard urgent footsteps in the corridor outside the room.

On receiving permission to enter, Tarkin's blond-haired, clear-eyed adjutant hastened through the door, offering a crisp salute.

"A priority dispatch from Rampart Station, sir."

A look of sharp attentiveness erased Tarkin's frown. Coreward from Sentinel in the direction of the planet Pii, Rampart was a marshaling depot for supply ships bound for Geonosis, where the deep-space weapon was under construction.

"I won't tolerate further delays," he started to say.

"Understood, sir," the adjutant said. "But this doesn't concern supplies. Rampart reports that it is under attack."

BLOWS AGAINST THE EMPIRE

THE DOOR TO TARKIN'S QUARTERS whooshed open, disappearing into the partition, and out he marched, dressed in worn trousers and ill-fitting boots, with a lightweight gray-green duster draped over his shoulders. As the adjutant hurried to keep pace with the taller man's determined steps, the strident voice of the protocol droid slithered through the opening before the door resealed itself.

"But, sir, the *fitting!*"

Originally a cramped garrison base deployed from a *Victory*-class Star Destroyer, Sentinel now sprawled in all directions as a result of prefabricated modules that had since been delivered or assembled on site. The heart of the facility was a warren of corridors linking one module to the next, their ceilings lost behind banks of harsh illuminators, forced-air ducts, fire-suppression pipes, and bundled strands of snaking wires. Everything had an improvised look, but as this was Moff Wilhuff Tarkin's domain, the radiantly heated walkways and walls were spotless, and the pipes and feeds were meticulously organized and labeled with alphanumerics. Overworked scrubbers purged staleness and the smell of ozone from the recycled air. The corridors were crowded not only with specialists and junior officers, but also with droids of all sizes and shapes, twittering, beeping, and chirping to one another as their optical sensors assessed the speed and momentum of Tarkin's forward march and propelling themselves out of harm's way at the last possible instant, on treads, casters, repulsors, and ungainly metal legs. Between the blare of distant alarms and the warble of announcements ordering personnel to muster stations, it was difficult enough to hear oneself think, and yet Tarkin was receiving updates through an ear bead as well as communicating continually with Sentinel's command center through a speck of a microphone adhered to his voice box.

He wedged the audio bead deeper into his ear as he strode through a domed module whose skylight wells revealed that the storm had struck with full force and was shaking Sentinel for all it was worth. Exiting the dome and moving against a tide of staff and droids, he right-angled through two short stretches of corridor, doors flying open at his approach and additional personnel joining him at each juncture—senior officers, navy troopers, communications technicians, some of them young and shorn, most of them in uniform, and all of them human—so that by the time he reached the command center, the duster billowing behind him like a cape, it was as if he were leading a parade.

At Tarkin's request, the rectangular space was modeled after the sunken data pits found aboard *Imperial*-class Star Destroyers. Filing in behind him, the staffers he had gathered along the way rushed to their duty stations, even while others already present were leaping to their feet to deliver salutes. Tarkin waved them back into their swivel chairs and positioned himself on a landing at the center of the room with a clear view of the holoimagers, sensor displays, and authenticators. Off to one side of him, Base Commander Cassel, dark-haired and sturdy, was leaning across the primary holoprojector table, above which twitched a grainy image of antique starfighters executing strafing runs across Rampart's gleaming surface, while the marshaling station's batteries responded with green pulses of laser energy. In a separate holovid even more corrupted than the first, insect-winged

Geonosian laborers could be seen scrambling for cover in one of the station's starfighter hangars. A distorted voice was crackling through the command center's wall-mounted speaker array.

"Our shields are already down to forty percent, Sentinel . . . jamming our transmiss . . .lost communication with the *Brentaal*. Request immediate . . . Sentinel. Again: request immediate reinforcement."

A skeptical frown formed on Tarkin's face. "A sneak attack? Impossible."

"Rampart reports that the attack ship transmitted a valid HoloNet code on entering the system," Cassel said. "Rampart, can you eavesdrop on the comm chatter of those starfighters?"

"Negative, Sentinel," the reply came a long moment later. "They're jamming our signals net."

Peering over his shoulder at Tarkin, Cassel made as if to cede his position, but Tarkin motioned for him to stay where he was. "Can the image be stabilized?" he asked the specialist at the holoprojector controls.

"Sorry, sir," the specialist said. "Increasing the gain only makes matters worse. The transmission appears to be corrupted at the far end. I haven't been able to establish if Rampart initiated countermeasures."

Tarkin glanced around the room. "And on our end?"

"The HoloNet relay station is best possible," the specialist at the comm board said.

"It is raining, sir," a different spec added, eliciting a chorus of good-natured laughter from others seated nearby. Even Tarkin grinned, though fleetingly.

"Who are we speaking with?" he asked Cassel.

"A Lieutenant Thon," the commander said. "He's been on station for only three months, but he's following protocol and transmitting on priority encryption."

Tarkin clasped his hands behind his back beneath the duster and glanced at the specialist seated at the authenticator. "Does the effectives roster contain an image of our Lieutenant Thon?"

"On screen, sir," the staffer said, flicking a joystick and indicating one of the displays.

Tarkin shifted his gaze. A sandy-haired human with protruding ears, Thon was as untried as he sounded. Fresh from one of the academies, Tarkin thought. He stepped down from the platform and moved to the holoprojector table to study the strafing starfighters more closely. Bars of corruption elevatored through the stuttering holovid. Rampart's shields were nullifying most of the aggressors' energy beams, but all too frequently a disabling run would succeed and white-hot explosions would erupt in one of the depot's deep-space docks.

"Those are Tikiars and Headhunters," Tarkin said in surprise.

"Modified," Cassel said. "Basic hyperdrives and upgraded weaponry."

Tarkin squinted at the holo. "The fuselages bear markings." He turned in the direction of the spec closest to the authenticator station. "Run the markings through the database. Let's see if we can't determine whom we're dealing with."

Tarkin turned back to Cassel. "Did they arrive on their own, or launch from the attack ship?"

"Delivered," the commander said.

Without turning around Tarkin said: "Has this Thon provided holovid or coordinates for the vessel that brought the starfighters?"

"Holovid, sir," someone said, "but we only got a quick look at it."

"Replay the transmission," Tarkin said.

A separate holotable projected a blurry, blue-tinted image of a fan-tailed capital ship with a spherical control module located amidships. The downsloping curved bow and smooth hull gave it the look of a deep-sea behemoth. Tarkin circled the table, appraising the hologram.

"What is this thing?"

"Begged and borrowed, sir," someone reported. "Separatist-era engineering more than anything else. The central sphere resembles one of the old Trade Federation droid control computers, and the entire forward portion might've come from a Commerce Guild destroyer. Front-facing sensor array tower. IFF's highlighting modules consistent with CIS *Providence*-, *Recusant*-, and *Munificent*-class warships."

"Pirates?" Cassel ventured. "Privateers?"

"Have they issued any demands?" Tarkin asked.

"Nothing yet." Cassel waited a beat. "Insurgents?"

"No data on the starfighter fuselage markings, sir," someone said.

Tarkin touched his jaw but said nothing. As he continued to circle the hologram, a flare of wavy corruption in the lower left portion captured his attention. "What was that?" he said, standing tall. "At the lower— There it is again." He counted quietly to himself; at the count of ten he fixed his gaze on the same area of the hologram. "And again!" He swung to the specialist. "Replay the recording at half speed."

Tarkin kept his eyes on the lower left quadrant as the holovid restarted and began a new count. "Now!" he said, in advance of every instance of corruption. "Now!"

Chairs throughout the room swiveled. "Encryption noise?" someone suggested.

"Ionization effect," another said.

Tarkin held up a hand to silence the speculations. "This isn't a guessing game, ladies and gentlemen."

"Interval corruption of some sort," Cassel said.

"Of some sort indeed." Tarkin watched silently as the prerecorded holovid recycled for a third time, then he moved to the communications station. "Instruct Lieutenant Thon to show himself," he said to the seated spec.

"Sir?"

"Tell him to train a cam on himself."

The spec relayed the command, and Thon's voice issued from the speakers. "Sentinel, I've never been asked to do that, but if that's what it's going to take to effect a rescue, then I'm happy to comply."

Everyone in the room turned to the holofeed, and moments later a 3-D image of Thon took shape above the table.

"Recognition is well within acceptable margins, sir," a spec said.

Tarkin nodded and leaned toward one of the microphones. "Stand by, Rampart. Reinforcements are forthcoming." He continued to study the live holovid, and had begun yet another count when the transmission abruptly de-resolved, just short of the moment it might have displayed further evidence of corruption.

"What happened?" Cassel asked.

"Working on it, sir," a spec said.

Repressing a knowing smile, Tarkin glanced over his right shoulder. "Have we tried to open a clear channel to Rampart?"

"We've been trying, sir," the comm specialist said, "but we haven't been able to penetrate the jamming."

Tarkin moved to the communications station. "What resources do we have upside?"

"Parking lot is nearly empty, sir." The comm specialist riveted her eyes on the board. "We have the *Salliche,* the *Fremond,* and the *Electrum.*"

Tarkin considered his options. Sentinel's *Imperial*-class Star Destroyer, the *Core Envoy,* and most of the flotilla's other capital ships were escorting supply convoys to Geonosis. That left him with a frigate and a tug—both vacant just then, literally parked in stationary orbits—and the obvious choice, the *Electrum,* a *Venator*-class Star Destroyer on loan from a deepdock at Ryloth.

"Contact Captain Burque," he said at last.

"Already on the comm, sir," the specialist said.

A quarter-scale image of the captain rose from the comm station's holoprojector. Burque was tall and gangly, with a clipped brown beard lining his strong jaw. "Governor Tarkin," he said, saluting.

"Are you up to speed on what is occurring at Rampart Station, Captain Burque?"

"We are, sir. The *Electrum* is prepared to jump to Rampart on your command."

Tarkin nodded. "Keep those hyperspace coordinates at the ready, Captain. But right now I want you to execute a microjump to the Rimward edge of this system. Do you understand?"

Burque frowned in confusion, but he said: "Understood, Governor."

"You're to hold there and await further orders."

"In plain sight, sir, or obscure?"

"I suspect that won't matter one way or another, Captain, but all the better if you can find something to hide behind."

"Excuse me for asking, sir, but are we expecting trouble?"

"Always, Captain," Tarkin said, without levity.

The hologram disappeared and the command center fell eerily silent, save for the sounds of the sensors and scanners and the tech's update that the *Electrum* was away. The silence deepened, until a pressing and prolonged warning tone from the threat-assessment station made everyone start. The specialist at the station thrust his head forward.

"Sir, sensors are registering anomalous readings and Cronau radiation in the red zone—"

"Wake rotation!" another spec cut in. "We've got a mark in from hyperspace, sir—and it's a big one. Nine hundred twenty meters long. Gunnage of twelve turbolaser cannons, ten point-defense ion cannons, six proton torpedo launchers. Reverting on the *near side* of the planet. Range is two hundred thousand klicks and closing." He blew out his breath. "Good thing you dispatched the *Electrum*, sir, or it'd be in pieces by now!"

A specialist seated at an adjacent duty station weighed in. "Firing solution programs are being sent to downside defenses."

"IFF is profiling it as the same carrier that attacked Rampart." The spec glanced at Tarkin. "Could it have jumped, sir?"

"If the ship was even there," Tarkin said, mostly to himself.

"Sir?"

Tarkin shrugged out of the duster, letting it fall to the floor, and stepped down to the holoprojector. "Let's have a look at it."

If the ship in the orbital-feed holovid was not the same one that had ostensibly attacked Rampart, it had to be her twin.

"Sir, we've got multiple marks launching from the carrier—" The spec interrupted himself to make certain he was interpreting the readings correctly. "Sir, they're *droid* fighters! Tri-fighters, vultures, the whole Sep menagerie."

"Interesting," Tarkin said in a calm voice. One hand to his chin, he continued to assess the hologram. "Commander Cassel, sound general quarters and boost power to the base shields. Signals: Initiate countermeasures."

"Sir, is this an unannounced readiness test?" someone asked.

"More like a bunch of Separatists who didn't get the message they lost the war," another said.

Perhaps that was the explanation, Tarkin thought. Imperial forces had destroyed or appropriated most of the capital ships produced for and by the Confederacy of Independent Systems. Droid fighters hadn't been seen in years. But it was even longer since Tarkin had witnessed HoloNet subterfuge of the caliber someone had aimed at Sentinel Base.

He swung away from the table. "Scan the carrier for life-forms on the off chance we're dealing with a sentient adversary rather than a droid-control computer." He eyed the comm specialist. "Any separate channel response from Rampart?"

She shook her head. "Still no word, sir."

"Carrier shows thirty life-forms, sir," someone at the far end of the room said. "It's astrogating by command, not on full auto."

From the threat station came another voice: "Sir, droid fighters are nearing the edge of the envelope."

And a thin envelope it was, Tarkin thought.

"Alert our artillery crews to ignore the firing solution programs and to fire at will." He pivoted to the holotable. A glance revealed Sentinel Base to be in the same situation Rampart appeared to have been in only moments earlier, except that the enemy ships and the holofeed were *genuine*.

"Contact Captain Burque and tell him to come home."

"Tri-fighters are breaking formation and commencing attack runs."

The sounds of distant explosions and the thundering replies of ground-based artillery infiltrated the command center. The room shook. Motes of dust drifted down from the overhead pipes and cables; the illumination flickered. Tarkin monitored the ground-feed holovids. The droid fighters were highly maneuverable but no match for Sentinel's powerful guns. The moon's storm-racked sky grew backlit with strobing flashes and globular detonations, as one after another of the ridge-backed tri-fighters and reconfigurable vultures was vaporized. A few managed to make it to the outer edge of the base's hemispherical defensive shield, only to be annihilated there and hit the coarse ground in flames.

"They're beginning to turn tail," a tech said. "Laser cannons are chasing them back up the well."

"And the capital ship?" Tarkin said.

"The carrier is steering clear and accelerating. Range is now three hundred thousand klicks and expanding. All weapons are mute."

"Sir, the *Electrum* has reverted to realspace."

Tarkin grinned faintly. "Inform Captain Burque that his TIE pilots are going to enjoy a target-rich environment."

"Captain Burque on the comm."

Tarkin moved to the comm station, where Burque's holopresence hovered above the projector.

"I trust that this is the trouble you were expecting, Governor."

"Actually, Captain, most of this is quite unexpected. Therefore, I hope you'll do your best to incapacitate the carrier rather than destroy it. No doubt we can glean something by interrogating the crew."

"I'll be as gentle with it as I can, Governor."

Tarkin glanced at the holotable in time to see squadrons of newly minted ball-cockpit TIE fighters launch from the dorsal bay of the arrowhead-shaped Star Destroyer.

"Sir, I have Rampart Station Commander Jae on the comm, voice-only."

Tarkin gestured for Jae to be put through.

"Governor Tarkin, to what do I owe the honor?" Jae said.

Tarkin positioned himself close to one of the command center's audio pickups. "How is everything at your depot, Lin?"

"Better now," Jae said. "Our HoloNet relay was down for a short period, but it's back online. I've sent a tech team to determine what went wrong. You have my word, Governor: The glitch won't affect the supply shipment schedule—"

"I doubt that your technicians will discover any evidence of malfunction," Tarkin said.

Instead of speaking to it, Jae said: "And on your moon, Governor?"

"As a matter of fact, we find ourselves under attack."

"What?" Jae asked in patent surprise.

"I'll explain in due course, Lin. Just now we have our hands full."

His back turned to the holoprojector table, Tarkin missed the event that drew loud groans from many of the staffers. When he turned, the warship was gone.

"Jumped to lightspeed before the *Electrum* could get off a disabling shot," Cassel said.

Disappointment pulled down the corners of Tarkin's mouth. With the capital ship gone, the remaining droid fighters could be seen spinning out of control—even easier prey for the vertical-winged TIE fighters. A scattering of spherical explosions flared at the edge of space.

"Gather debris of any value," Tarkin said to Burque, "and have it transported down the well for analysis. Snare a few of the intact droids, as well. But take care. While they appear to be lifeless, they may be rigged to self-destruct."

Burque acknowledged the command, and the holo vanished.

Tarkin looked at Cassel. "Secure from battle stations and sound the all-clear. I want a forensic team assembled to examine the droids. I doubt we'll learn much, but we may be able to ascertain the carrier's point of origin." He grew pensive for a moment, then added: "Prepare an after-action report for Coruscant and transmit it to my quarters so I can append my notes."

"Will do," Cassel said.

A specialist handed Tarkin his duster, and he had started for the door when a voice rang out behind him.

"Sir, a question if you will?"

Tarkin stopped and turned around. "Ask it."

"How did you know, sir?"

"How did I know what, Corporal?"

The young, brown-haired specialist gnawed at her lower lip before continuing. "That the holotransmission from Rampart Station was counterfeit, sir."

Tarkin looked her up and down. "Perhaps you'd care to proffer an explanation of your own."

"In the replay—the bar of interval noise you noticed. Somehow that told you that someone had managed to introduce a false real-time feed into the local HoloNet relay."

Tarkin smiled faintly. "Train yourself to recognize it—all of you. Deception may be the least of what our unknown adversaries have in store."

3

COLD CASE

IN SENTINEL'S MAINTENANCE HANGAR, Tarkin paced the length of a high, blastproof partition. The storm had blown through and the base had resumed normal operations, but many of the soldiers and specialists were still parsing the fact that Sentinel had come under attack. For the youngest among them, recruits or volunteers, it was the first action they had ever seen.

On the far side of a series of massive transparisteel panels set into the partition, several hazmat-suited forensic technicians were examining wreckage from the battle and running tests on three droid starfighters grasped in cradles suspended from tall gantries. Elsewhere in the hangar loadlifters and other droids were sorting through piles of debris. The tang of lubricants and flame-scorched metals hung in the air, and the noise level created by the labor droids was grating. As Tarkin had warned, many of the vulture droids had transformed into bombs on losing contact with the warship's central control computer. Regardless, Captain Burque's salvage teams had managed to recover a droid whose auto-destruct mechanism had been damaged during combat.

Hung in walking configuration with its blaster cannon lateral wings split, the three-and-a-half-meter-long vulture looked less like its namesake scavenger than it did a long-legged alloy quadruped with an equine head. With the central nacelle open and the computer brain exposed and studded with instruments, the droid might have been undergoing torture rather than autopsy. The other two dangling captives—three-armed fighters that mirrored the appearance of the species that had designed them—were similarly exposed and quilled with probes.

Tarkin had lost count of how many back-and-forth meanders he had completed, and was standing opposite the vulture droid when a decontamination lock in the partition opened and a tech emerged, removing the hood of his anti-rad suit and wiping sweat from his face and balding pate with a bare hand.

Tarkin spun around to meet him halfway. "What have you learned?"

"Not as much as we'd hoped to, sir," the tech said. "Analysis of data received by the command center's friend-or-foe indicator confirms that the capital ship is a downsized version of a Separatist *Providence*-class cruiser-carrier, modified with modules taken from CIS frigates and destroyers. Ships of the sort made a name for themselves during the war by jamming signals and destroying HoloNet relays. Parts of the ship's sensor array tower, which the Seps usually mounted aft rather than forward, appear to have come from the cruiser *Lucid Voice*, which saw action at Quell, Ryloth, and in a couple of other contested systems."

Tarkin frowned. "How did the appropriation teams manage to miss confiscating that ship?"

"They didn't, sir. Records show that the *Lucid Voice* was dismantled at the Bilbringi shipyards four years ago."

Tarkin considered that. "In other words, some components of that vessel went missing."

"Lost, stolen, sold, it's impossible to say. Other sections of the warship appear to have come from the *Invincible*."

Tarkin didn't bother to mask his surprise. "That was Separatist Admiral Trench's ship—destroyed during the Battle of Christophsis."

"Partially destroyed, in any case. The ship was modular in design, and the modules that survived must have been worth salvaging and putting on the open market. Parts dealers in the Outer Rim are desperate for supplies, so the modules may have ended up in the Tion Cluster or the like." The tech removed his other elbow-length glove and wiped his face again. "The Idellian scanner isolated thirty life-forms—a crew of humans and near-humans—which is in keeping with the practice of placing sentients in command of most *Providence*-class ships. But for a ship of that size and armament, thirty sentients is virtually your definition of a skeleton crew. Sometimes the Seps substituted OOM pilot battle droids, and I'm guessing our skittish warship had some of those as well, because whoever cobbled the thing together retrofitted it with a rudimentary droid-control computer—possibly a redundant comp of the sort you used to find on first-generation Trade Federation Lucrehulks."

"*Whoever*, as you say."

"*Lucid Voice* was built by the Quarren Free Dac Volunteers Engineering Corps—much to the displeasure of the Mon Cals who share their planet with the Quarren. We're checking to see if QFD or their erstwhile partners, Pammant Docks, might have supervised the reassembly. TradeFed and Separatist technology has been showing up lately in the Corporate Sector, so we're also looking into the possibility that the ship was built there. The Headhunter starfighters seen in the holovid could have come from anywhere. Tikiars are produced in the Senex, but it's not uncommon to encounter them in this sector of the Rim."

Tarkin nodded and motioned toward the hangar. "The droids?"

The specialist turned to face the viewports. "Relatively few modifications to the vulture. Same fuel slug propulsion, same weapons system. Alphanumeric identification indicates that this one belonged to a Confederacy battle group known as The Grievous Legion."

"And also managed to find its way onto the black market . . ."

"So it appears, sir."

Tarkin moved farther down the partition. "And the tri-fighters?"

"Unremarkable. But we've no evidence regarding their origin. Not yet anyway."

Tarkin forced an exhalation through his nose. "Were you able to retrieve data regarding the warship's point of origin?"

The specialist shook his head. "Negative, sir. The memory modules of the droids don't log jump information."

"All right," Tarkin said after a moment. "Continue with the analysis. I want every weld and rivet investigated."

"We're on top of it, sir." The tech pulled the hood back over his head, slipped his hands into the long gloves, and disappeared through the lock.

Tarkin watched him enter the hangar, then resumed pacing, replaying the attack in his mind.

Harassment of Imperial installations by pirates and malcontents was nothing new, but in almost all cases the assaults had been hit-and-run sorties, and none had taken place so close to heavily defended Geonosis. The counterfeit real-time holotransmission had been designed to draw ships from Sentinel to Rampart Station, in the hope of leaving the former vulnerable. But the attack was clearly calculated to be suicidal from its inception. Even if he had dispatched the *Electrum* to the marshaling station—even if he had been taken in by the distress call and dispatched half his flotilla—the energy shields and laser cannons that protected Sentinel would have been sufficient to ward off any strikes, let alone from droids. The warship seen in the holovid the attackers had transmitted through the local HoloNet relay had shown up at Sentinel, but where were the modified starfighters, which had to have been flown by living pilots? Despite being crewed by sentients, the mysterious cruiser hadn't discharged any of its point-defense or ranged weapons. If destruction of the base was the goal, why hadn't whoever was behind the attack used the ship as a bomb by reverting from hyperspace in closer proximity to the moon? Planetary bodies larger than Sentinel had been shaken to their core by such events.

Equally worrisome was the question of how the counterfeiters had known about Lieutenant Thon, whose recent posting to Rampart should have been top secret. The creators of the false holovid had been able to improvise by transmitting a real-time hologram of the young officer in response to Tarkin's order that he show himself. Was

Thon involved in the conspiracy, or had the attackers merely doctored existing footage of him, lifted perhaps from the public HoloNet or some other source?

As troubling as it was to accept that the locations of Sentinel and Rampart bases had been compromised, he still couldn't make sense of the attack itself. What would pirates or privateers stand to gain by launching an ill-fated drone attack? What, for that matter, would political dissidents stand to gain?

Was it a case of vengeance?

One group fit the bill: the Droid Gotra, a lethal band of repurposed battle droids with what some considered legitimate grievances against the Empire for having been abandoned after their service during the Clone Wars. But recent intelligence reports stated that the Droid Gotra was still confined to an industrial complex in the bowels of Coruscant, serving as muscle for the Crymorah crime syndicate in robberies, protection, kidnapping, illegal salvage, and extortion. It was possible that the Gotra was branching out—it was even possible that the group had learned about Sentinel Base—but it was unlikely that the droids would make use of obsolete weapons to send a message to the Empire.

Tarkin shook his head in aggravation. In part, the deep-space mobile battle station was meant to put an end to harassments of any sort, whether driven by greed, political dissent, or revenge for acts committed during the Clone Wars or since. Once everyone in the galaxy grasped the weapon's capabilities, once the fear of Imperial reprisal took hold, discontent would cease to be a problem. But just now—and notwithstanding the covert nature of the Geonosis project—the Imperial Security Bureau and Naval Intelligence were continually trying to quash rumors and prevent information leaks. In the three years Tarkin had been commanding Sentinel and hundreds of nearby supply and sentry outposts, as well as administering a vast slice of the Outer Rim, no group had been successful in penetrating Geonosis space.

The chance that that could change shook *him* to the core.

If establishing the identity of Sentinel's enemies was already proving daunting, getting to the truth of the battle station's origin was nearly impossible. Everyone from celebrated ship designers to gifted engineers wanted to take credit for the superweapon. Tarkin himself had discussed the need for such a weapon with the Emperor long before the end of the Clone Wars. But no one outside the Emperor knew the full history of the moonlet-sized project. Some claimed that it had begun as a Separatist weapon designed by Geonosian Archduke Poggle the Lesser's hive colony for Count Dooku and the Confederacy of Independent Systems. But if that was the case, the plans had to have somehow fallen into Republic hands *before* the Clone Wars ended, because the weapon's spherical shell and laser-focusing dish were already in the works by the time Tarkin first set eyes on it following his promotion to the rank of Moff—escorted to Geonosis in utmost secrecy by the Emperor himself.

All the same, he had no compelling reason to solve the enigma of the battle station's beginnings. What bothered him was that, compliant with a strategy that no base commander—Moff, admiral, or general—should have unrestricted access to information regarding shipments, scheduling, or construction progress, no single person was in charge of the project, unless of course the Emperor was considered to be that person. But the Emperor's visits had been few and far between, and it was anyone's guess just how much information was getting past the Imperial Ruling Council the Moffs and others answered to and actually reaching the Emperor's ear. Certainly he was being briefed, but briefings were no longer enough. The project had reached a point where it had to rely on countless suppliers; and though each was being kept in the dark regarding the final destination of their contributions, millions of beings, perhaps tens of millions of beings galaxywide, were now involved with the battle station in one capacity or another. Yes, the project required the on-site presence of a think tank of scientists, weapons specialists, and habitat architects, but what did any of them know about *protecting* the station from saboteurs?

If Tarkin had his way, and at this point it was uncertain he ever would, he would adopt the hegemonic arrangement that was in place on Coruscant and elsewhere, and appoint an overseer to coordinate all construction and defense considerations. A single overseer to whom others would answer—or be damned if they didn't.

If whoever was responsible for the dubious attack on Sentinel was simply hoping to get his attention, then that part of the plan had succeeded, for in the end he was left with more questions than answers.

His restless pacing subsided as his adjutant hurried into the maintenance hangar's safe area.

"A communiqué from Coruscant, sir."

Tarkin assumed that it was Military Intelligence, responding to the after-action report he had filed, and said as much.

"No, sir. Higher up the chain of command."

Tarkin arched an eyebrow. "How high?"

"Nosebleed altitude, sir."

Tarkin stiffened slightly. "Then I'll take the transmission in my quarters."

Where Tarkin's own uniformed holopresence had stood two days earlier, the holotable now projected a towering apparition of Vizier Mas Amedda, swathed in rich maroon robes, the cyan tint of the holofield darkening the Chagrian's natural blue pigmentation. From bulging extrusions of flesh on either side of Amedda's thick neck dangled tapered horns that matched the pair crowning his hairless cranium.

"We trust all is well at Sentinel Base, Governor."

Tarkin couldn't be certain if or how much Amedda knew about the recent attack. On Coruscant information was closely guarded, if only as a means of maintaining one's cachet, and even the head of the Ruling Council might not have been made privy to details known to Military Intelligence and the Admiralty.

"Rest assured, Vizier," Tarkin said.

"No surprises, then?"

"Only the expected ones."

The ambitious amphibian vouchsafed a tight-lipped smile at his end of the duplex holocomm. Obstructive and fault finding during his years as vice chancellor of the Republic Senate, he had become one of the Emperor's most valued advisers, as well as the Empire's most formidable intermediary.

"Governor, your presence is required on Coruscant," Amedda said after a moment.

Tarkin moved to his desk and sat down, centering himself for the holocam. "I'll certainly try to make time for a visit, Vizier."

"Permit me, Governor, but that will not suffice. Perhaps I should have said that your presence is *urgently* required."

Tarkin waved a hand in dismissal. "I'm sorry, Vizier, but that doesn't alter the fact that I have my priorities."

"Priorities of what sort?"

Tarkin returned Amedda's mirthless smile. There was probably no harm in sharing with Amedda information about the expected shipments of matériel from Desolation Station to Geonosis—including vital components for the battle station's complex hyperdrive generator—but he was under no obligation to do so.

"I'm afraid my priorities are on a need-to-know basis."

"Indeed. Then you are refusing the request?"

Tarkin glimpsed something in the thick-skulled Chagrian's pink-rimmed cerulean eyes that gave him pause. "Let's say that I'm reluctant to abandon my post at this time, Vizier. If you wish, I'll provide the Emperor with my reasons personally."

"That's not possible, Governor. The Emperor is presently engaged."

Tarkin leaned toward the cam. "So engaged that he can't speak briefly with one of his Moffs?"

Amedda affected a bored tone. "That's not for me to say, Governor. The Emperor's concerns are on a need-to-know basis."

Tarkin stared into the hologram. What his grand-uncle Jova wouldn't have given to be able to mount a Chagrian head on the wall of his cabin in the Carrion.

"Perhaps you're willing to clarify the need for such urgency?" he asked.

Amedda tilted his massive head to one side. "That's a matter for you to discuss with the Emperor, since it was he who issued the order that you report to Coruscant."

Tarkin concealed a grimace. "You might have said as much at the start, Vizier."

Amedda adopted a haughty look. "And deprive us of such verbal sport? Next time, perhaps."

Tarkin remained at his desk after Amedda ended the transmission and the hologram vanished. Then he signaled for the protocol droid.

"I'm going to need that uniform as soon as possible," he told the RA-7 as it entered.

The droid nodded. "Certainly, sir. I'll instruct the fabricator to begin at once."

Tarkin summoned the uniformed 3-D image of himself from the holotable and regarded it, thinking back to Eriadu and recalling Jova's comment once more.

"It'll look even better with blood on it."

4

A BOY'S LIFE

CYNOSURE OF THE Greater Seswenna sector of the Outer Rim, Eriadu could trace its history to the earliest era of the Republic. At that time, the galaxy's dark age had ended, the Sith had been defeated and driven into hiding, and a true republic had emerged from the ashes. With a member of House Valorum presiding as Supreme Chancellor, a pan-galactic Senate had been created, and the military had been disbanded. Revitalized, the populations of the Core Worlds, ravenous for new resources and not above exploiting every opportunity to enhance the quality of their lives, were eager to expand their reach.

The planet was transformed from just another Outer Rim wilderness to a civilized world worth considering for inclusion in the Republic by adventurous pioneers who had been granted permission by Coruscant to procure and settle new territories, either by cutting deals with indigenous populations or simply by overrunning them, and finally to establish trading colonies capable of furnishing the Core with much-needed resources. It was a scenario played out in many remote regions, and in Eriadu's case the resource happened to be lommite ore—essential to the production of transparisteel—rich deposits of which had been discovered on worlds throughout the Greater Seswenna. Lacking funds to mine, process, and ship the crude, Eriadu's settlers had been forced to secure high-interest loans from the InterGalactic Banking Clan, but in an era when hyperspace travel between the Seswenna and the Core required astrogating by hyperwave beacons—with numerous reversions to realspace necessary to ensure safe passage—shipments of ore were frequently delayed or lost due to one catastrophe or another. As debts mounted, Eriadu risked becoming a client world of Muun bankers until entrepreneurs from the Core world Corulag had intervened, rescuing the planet from servitude. It was likewise through Corulag's influence with the Republic Senate that the fledgling Hydian Way had been routed through Eriadu space and the planet placed on the galactic map.

Corulag's motives, however, were not altogether altruistic; the Core entrepreneurs forced Eriadu to increase the lommite supply and had demanded the bulk of the mining profits. Amplified operations led to rampant growth and an influx of impoverished workers from neighboring worlds. Eriadu's once lush mountains were soon stripped of cover, a pall of pollution hung over the major cities, and the standard of living plummeted. Still, there was prosperity for a few; quick credits to be made in ore processing, local and deep-space transport, and usury.

For the Tarkins, wealth came by providing security.

Their climb to the top had been hard won. Among Eriadu's earliest pioneers, the ancestral Tarkins had had to function as their own police force and defenders, countering attacks first by the ferocious predators that thrived in Eriadu's forests and mountains, then by off-world rogues and scoundrels who preyed on the exposed populations of the struggling settlements. Under Tarkin leadership local militias evolved slowly into a sector military. As a result, and despite his celebrated ancestors having had their start as hunters, freelance pilots, and mining contractors, Tarkin thought of himself as the product of a military upbringing, in which discipline, respect, and obedience were held in the highest regard. Avowed technocrats as well, the family held a view that it was technology—more than Corulag—that had rescued Eriadu from savagery and had allowed Eriaduans to forge a civilization from a murderous wasteland. Technology in the form of colossal machines, swift starships, and potent weapons had helped convert the hunted into the hunters, and it would be technology that would one day usher the planet into the elite of the modern galaxy.

While Tarkin had been raised with all the advantages that came with wealth, it was a curious kind of privilege. In mansions that strived to emulate the architectural fashions of the Core but were little more than gaudy imitations of the originals, the Tarkins and others like them did their best to mimic the customs of the affluent, without ever succeeding. Their hardscrabble roots were far too apparent, and life on Eriadu seemed barbaric compared with life on cosmopolitan Coruscant. Tarkin understood this at an early age, particularly when dignitaries from the Core visited and made his parents feel smaller than he knew them to be; less evolved for living on a wild world whose outlands were racked by seismic quakes, whose rough cities lacked weather control and opera houses, and whose residents were still battling pirates and rapacious nature for supremacy. And yet he felt no need to search outside his own family for childhood heroes, since it was his ancestors who had fought back the wilderness, survived the odds, and brought order and progress to the Seswenna.

Even in relaxed and safe surroundings, then, Tarkin was not the entitled child one might have imagined judging by his tailored clothes or rambling home. As proud as his parents were of their achievements, they were also well aware of their low social standing among people who mattered. They never missed an opportunity to remind their son that life was inequitable, and that only those with an appetite for personal glory could succeed. One needed to be willing to crush underfoot anything or anyone. Discipline and order were the keys, and law was the only unanswerable response to chaos.

At every opportunity Tarkin's parents would emphasize what it meant to live in deprivation. Their sermons were designed to drill into their son the fact that everything they owned was the product of having overcome adversity. Worse, affluence could vanish in an instant; without constant vigilance and the drive to succeed, everything one had could be wrested away by someone stronger, more disciplined, more committed to personal glory.

"How do you imagine we came to the point where we have so much," his father might say over dinner, "while so many outside the gates of this elegant home have to struggle to survive? Or do you imagine that we have always resided in such luxury, that Eriadu was accommodating from the start?"

Early on, young Wilhuff would only stare down at his plate of food in silence or mutter that he had no answers to his father's questions. Then, during one supper, his father—tall and straight-backed, with deep forehead creases that curved down past his eyes like parentheses—ordered the family's servant to remove Wilhuff's meal before he'd had a chance to take so much as a bite from it.

"You see how easy it is to go from having everything to having nothing?" his father asked.

"How would you fare if we now banished you to the city streets?" his mother added. Nearly as tall as her husband, she dressed in expensive clothes for every meal and affected elaborate hairstyles that were sometimes hours in the making. "Would you do what you needed to do to survive? Could you bring yourself to wield a club, a knife, a blaster, if weapons were what it took to keep you from starving?"

In an effort to calculate the expected response, Wilhuff glanced between the two of them and puffed out his chest. "I would do whatever I had to do."

His father only grinned in disdain. "A brave one, are you? Well, you'll have that bravery put to the test when you're taken to the Carrion."

The Carrion.

There it was again: that strange word he had heard so often growing up. But just then he asked: "What is the Carrion?"

His father seemed pleased that his son had finally wondered aloud. "A place that teaches you the meaning of survival."

In the quiet comfort of the family dining room, rich with the heady odors of exotic spices and long-simmered meats, the statement had no meaning. "Will I be afraid?" he said, again because he sensed he was meant to ask.

"If you know what's good for you."

"Could I die there?" he said, almost in self-amusement.

"In ways too numerous to count."

"Would you miss me if I did die?" he asked them both.

His mother was the first to say, "Of course we would."

"Then why do I have to go there? Have I done something wrong?"

His father placed his elbows on the table and leaned toward him. "We need to know if you are simply ordinary or larger than life."

To the best of his ability, he mulled over the notion of being *larger than life*. "Did you have to go there when you were young?"

His father nodded.

"Were you afraid?"

His father sat back into his tall, brocaded armchair, as if in recall. "In the beginning I was. Until I learned to overcome fear."

"Will I have to kill anything?"

"If you wish to survive."

With some excitement, Wilhuff said: "Will I get to use a blaster?"

His father shook his head in a grave manner. "Not always. And not when you'll need one most."

Wilhuff grappled with imagining the place, this Carrion. "Does everyone have to go there?"

"Only certain Tarkin males," his mother said.

"So Nomma never had to go?" he asked, referring to their diminutive, heavily jowled near-human servant.

"No, he didn't."

"Why not? Are Tarkins different from Nomma's family?"

"Who serves whom?" his father responded with force. "Have you ever placed a meal in front of Nomma?"

"I would."

His mother's expression hardened. "Not in this house."

"What you learn on the Carrion will one day allow you to show Nomma how to be content with his station," his father went on.

Wilhuff struggled with the word *station*. "To be happy about serving us, you mean."

"Among other things, yes."

Still on unsure ground, Wilhuff fell silent for an even longer moment. "Will you be taking me there—to the Carrion?" he asked finally.

His father narrowed his eyes when he smiled. "Not me. Someone else will come for you when the time is right."

A more delicate, impressionable child might have lived in fear of that day, but to Wilhuff the threat of sudden change, the abrupt undermining of his effortless life, and the need to forge his own future eventually became a promise: a parable, an adventure on which he yearned to embark, made real in his imagination long before it actually came to be.

The day arrived shortly after his eleventh birthday; Wilhuff was, by then, a shipshape kid burning with desire for bigger things, already something of a dreamer, an actor, an exaggerator. He was seated with his parents for the evening meal. The litany of harsh reminders was about to commence when three men looking as if they had just crawled out from beneath a mine collapse barged through the front door and into dining room. Tracking mud across the polished stone floors, they began to stuff the pockets of their ragged longcoats with food snatched from the dinner table. When Wilhuff looked to his suddenly silent parents, his mother only said, "They've come for you."

But if his parents and the three intruders thought they had taken him by surprise, he had one of his own in store for them. "First I need to get my gear," he said, hurrying up the curving stairway as expressions of puzzlement began to form on the faces of the uninvited guests.

The looks were still in place when he returned a moment later, dressed in cargo pants and a multipocketed vest he had stitched together in secret over many weeks. Dangling from his neck was a pair of macrobinoculars that had been a birthday gift. His gear, his outfit, his uniform for when it would be needed.

Scanning Tarkin from head to toe, the tallest and grimiest of the three launched a short laugh that shook the anteroom chandelier. Then he stepped forward to take the boy by shoulders that would remain bony and narrow throughout his life, shaking him as he said: "That's a beauty, it is. A uniform fit for a future hero. And you know what? It'll look even better with blood on it."

His father stepped forward to say: "Wilhuff, meet my father's brother, your grand-uncle Jova."

Jova grinned down at him, showing even teeth, whiter than Wilhuff would have expected considering his uncle's dirt-streaked face.

"Time to go," Jova announced.

So: whisked from his home without a reassuring embrace from either parent, the two of them standing instead in each other's arms, expressions of sad resolve on their faces. This was something he needed to experience. And through the gate into Eriadu's pitch-black pall, safe for the moment within the uniform, exhilaration stifling the hunger he was already feeling. Whisked not only from the manicured grounds but also from the city itself in an aged airspeeder, on a shaky flight across the finger-shaped bay and up into the hills beyond to follow the meandering Orrineswa River to a region he had never known to exist on his homeworld, one that seemed more the stuff of holodramas and escapist literature: an untamed expanse of flat-topped mesas separated by surging boulder-strewn rivers, and in the far distance volcanic mountains that were perhaps still active. Even more shocking was Jova's explanation that while vast areas of Eriadu were much like this one, everything the boy's wide blue eyes could take in from horizon to horizon was family land—Tarkin land, procured twenty generations earlier and never allowed to fall into the hands of developers, miners, or anyone with designs on the region. A protected place and more: a natural monument, a reminder of what the planet could devolve into should sentient beings lose their grip and surrender their superiority to nature, to savagery. For young Wilhuff, a place of initiation; and central to it all, the Carrion Plateau.

A rickety speeder listing to one side because of a faulty repulsorlift carried them up onto the tabletop summit: Wilhuff, Jova, two other headclothed elders, and a pair of elderly Rodians who worked as guides, caretakers, trackers, all six of them perched atop the ailing machine and Wilhuff's five keepers carrying long-barreled slug-throwers. His hunger partially staved by dried meat almost too tough to swallow, Wilhuff was beginning to have serious misgivings, though he refused to let them be known. This was a much darker and more dangerous place than the one his imagination had conjured. Fixed on masking his unease and on seeing an actual animal in the wild, he sat with the macrobinoculars glued to his eyes as the speeder navigated immense stretches of grassland and forest, passing thick-boled ten-thousand-year-old trees with skinny, near-leafless limbs; monolithic ruins and cliffside petrogylphs ten times older; and shallow seasonal lakes dotted with flamboyant birds.

At length that first twilight he spotted something: a stately quadruped two meters tall, striped in black and white and crowned with graceful, curving horns. *My first animal in the wild.* The others spied it, as well, without the aid of magnifying lenses, and Jova brought the speeder to a jarring halt. But not, as it happened, to gaze on the beauty of the beast. In unison, the antique rifles came up and half a dozen shots rang out. Through the glasses, Wilhuff watched the majestic creature leap up, then fall heavily onto its side. And a moment later they were all hurrying through the sharp grass in an effort to reach their kill before other predators or scavengers could arrive—and also to get to it while it was still warm.

Wilhuff asked himself what the creature had done to deserve such a fate. If it, too, had come to the Carrion to learn the meaning of survival, it had failed miserably.

The Rodians rolled the animal onto its back, and from a sheath strapped to his thigh Jova drew a well-used vibroblade.

"Cut straight up from between the legs to the thoat," he said, handing Wilhuff the knife. "And take care not to make a mess of the innards."

Fortifying himself—worried as much about fainting as about disappointing his elders—Wilhuff plunged the point of the weapon through the creature's fur and flesh and tasked the vibroblade to cut. Hot maroon blood spurted, striking him full in the face. The Rodians seemed almost gleeful as it dripped from the tip of his nose to his chin and down the front of his pristine vest, saturating the seams and pockets he had stitched with such care.

"Good cut," Jova said when the carcass had parted, the smell of the beast's entrails nearly overwhelming Wilhuff. "Now, you reach deep in there"—he indicated a place in the torso—"and follow the rear curve of the breathing muscle until your hands find the liver. Then you pull it out. Go on: Do it. Do it, I said!"

In went his hesitant, shaking hands, maneuvering through squishy bulbous organs until they found a heavy lump rich with blood. He had to yank several times before the liver broke free of its fibrous net of blood vessels and ligaments, and he nearly fell backward when it did. Then Jova took the slippery, uncooperative thing into his callused hands and began tearing chunks from it.

"This one's for you," his uncle said, placing the largest of the pieces in the palm of Wilhuff's already bloodied hand. He motioned with his chin: "Go ahead now. Down it goes."

Once more Wilhuff focused on living up to expectations, and when he had gotten past his revulsion and devoured the chunk, his uncles and the Rodians celebrated his act with a short song in a language Wilhuff didn't understand; celebrated Wilhuff's first step, the opening stage in an initiation that wouldn't conclude until years later at the Carrion Spike.

While Eriadu didn't have indigenous creatures as large as the rancor or as unusual as the sarlacc, it did boast ferocious felines, carnivorous crustaceans, and a species of veermok far more fierce and cunning than others in its primate family. For the next month Wilhuff did little more than follow in the tracks of his elders, observing predators of many varieties killing and devouring one another, and learning how to keep himself from being similarly devoured. There was no denying that witnessing death up close was a far more visceral experience than watching such events transpire in holodramas viewed in the airy tranquillity of his bedroom. Still, he struggled to understand just what he was supposed to be taking away from the close encounters. Could daily brushes with death transform a simply ordinary person into one who was larger than life? Even if that was possible, how could that transformation have an impact on the lives of Nomma and others like him? He might have been able to puzzle out the answers were he less preoccupied day to day with being set upon and eaten by the beasts they stalked.

Gradually the routine changed from merely observing kills to *stealing* them. Frequently the Rodians would use their vibro-lances to drive killer beasts back from their quarries and hold them at bay while Wilhuff rushed in to complete the theft. Other times it would be Wilhuff's turn to wield a vibro-lance, and someone else who would make the grab.

"We're teaching them how to behave in the presence of their betters," Jova said. "The ones who learn, profit from the laws we lay down; the rest die." He wanted to make certain Wilhuff understood. "Never try to live decently, boy—not unless you're willing to open your life to tragedy and sadness. Live like a beast, and no event, no matter how harrowing, will ever be able to move you."

When his uncle decided that Wilhuff had experienced enough stealing, it came time to do the actual hunting. And so Jova and the others began to teach him tactical methods for taking advantage of the wind or the angle of the light. They taught him how to defend against attacks by groups of beasts by confounding them with unexpected moves. They taught him to kill by concentrating all his power on one point. All the while the vest became more bloodied and tattered, until ultimately it was useless except as a rag, and he was on his own, without a uniform or costume to hide within.

The routine of tracking, hunting, killing, and cooking over fire continued as the land surrendered the last of its moisture to the blinding sky. His feet turned raw and his sunburned skin blistered, his mind given over to memorizing the names of the Carrion's every tree, animal, and insect—all of them serving one purpose or another. Late one evening the speeder's powerful forward lamps illuminated a rodent as it leapt from the saw grass, and with a carefully aimed collision Jova sent it flying. Wilhuff was instructed to use his vibroblade to excise a scent gland buried where the animal's thin, hairless tail met its plump body. From that gland the Rodians prepared a musky gel that they then used in their hunts for more of the same rodents. Similarly, they prepared stimulant concoctions from residue drained from the stomach of long-necked ruminants or the droppings of felines that had ingested certain plants. Wilhuff grew accustomed to eating every part of an animal and to drinking blood on its own or mixed with mind-altering plants gathered during treks across the plateau.

Over time he became so inured to the sight, smell, and taste of blood that even his dreams ran red with it. He kept waiting for the adventure to conclude at some log-walled shelter stocked with prepared food and soft beds, but the days grew only more harrowing, and at night half-starved scavengers would circle and howl at the edge of a meager cook fire, their eyes glowing furiously in the dark, waiting for a chance to rush in and steal back what food they could.

The tight-knit band of humans and Rodians didn't always succeed at remaining at the top of the food chain. Jova's cousin Zellit was killed during a nighttime raid by a gang of reptiles whose saliva contained a powerful poison. By midseason Wilhuff knew real hunger for the first time, and came close to dying of an illness that caused him to shake so violently he thought his bones would break.

Sometimes even the smallest of the plateau's creatures would catch them unprepared and get the better of them. One night, when they had been too exhausted to set up a perimeter of motion detectors, he dreamed that something was feasting on his lower lip, and what his numb fingers found there was a venomous septoid, its pincers anchored in his soft flesh. Waking with a start, he hurried through the open flap of the self-deploying tent only to land in a stream of the segmented critters, which were all over him in a moment, hungry to find purchase wherever they could. By then his pained cries had woken the others, who themselves became targets, and shortly all of them were all hopping around in the dark, yanking septoids from themselves or plucking them off one another. When at last they had retreated to safety, it became clear that the assailants comprised only a narrow tributary of the insect river; the principal torrent had gone up and over the tent to where the Rodians had stored pieces of the beasts the group had slaughtered and dressed earlier in the day—all of it now devoured to the bone.

But regardless of whether they had won or lost the day, Wilhuff would be treated to tales of his ancestors' exploits: the lore of the early Tarkins.

"All of Eriadu was similar to the Carrion before humans arrived from the Core to tame it," Jova told him. "Every day, on their own, as pioneers and settlers, they waged battles with the beasts that ruled the planet. But our ancestors' eventual triumph only altered the balance, not the reality. For all that sentients have achieved with weapons and machines, life remains an ongoing battle for survival, with the strong or the smart at the top of the heap, and the rest kept in check by firepower and laws."

Jova explained that the Tarkin family had produced a succession of mentors and guides through the many generations. What made him unique was his decision to make the Carrion his home following his initiation in young adulthood. That was how he came to have tutored Wilhuff's father, and why he might even live long enough to tutor Wilhuff's son, should he have one.

They spent the remainder of the dry season on the plateau, leaving only when the rains came to that part of Eriadu. Wilhuff was a different person when the speeder carried them down from the mesa and back into civilization. Jova had no need to lecture him on what technology had allowed his ancestors to achieve in the planet's handful of cities, since it was evident everywhere Wilhuff looked.

But Jova had something to add.

"Triumphing over nature means better lives for sentients, but dominance is sustained only by bringing order to chaos and establishing law where none exists. On Eriadu, the goal was always to rid the planet of any creature that hadn't grown to fear us, so that we could rule supreme. Up the well, outside Eriadu's envelope, the goal is the same, but with a different caliber of predators. When you're old enough to be taken there, you're going to find yourself faced with prey who are every bit as quick thinking, well armed, and determined to succeed as you are. And unless you've taken the lessons of the Carrion to heart, only the stars themselves will bear witness to your cold airless death, and they will remain unmoved."

Returned to his comfortable bedroom, Wilhuff wrestled with what he had been put through, the experiences on the plateau infiltrating his sleep as vivid dreams and night terrors. But only for a short time. Little by little, the experiences began to shape him, and would become the stuff of his true education. Each of the next five summers would find him on the Carrion, and each season his education would widen, right up until the day he had to endure his final test at the Spike.

But that was a different story altogether.

5

PREDACITY

TARKIN WAITED UNTIL the *Carrion Spike* was in hyperspace to announce an impromptu inspection of the officers and enlisted ratings who were accompanying him to Coruscant. In the starship's austere main cabin, furnished only with a round conference table and chairs for half a dozen, eighteen of his crew were standing smartly in two rows, arms at their sides, shoulders squared, chins held high. Each wore a uniform similar to his, though the tunics were slightly longer and the trousers slimmer and more threadbare than those the fabricator had produced for him. The officers wore brimmed caps studded with identity disks, and displayed code cylinders in their appropriate pockets.

Hands clasped behind his back and looking stylish in his new garments, Tarkin had reached the last crewmember in the second row—a midshipman—when he stopped to peer down at the instep of the junior officer's left boot, where a smudge of what looked like grease or some other viscous substance had left a large circular stain.

"Ensign, what is *that*?" he asked, pointing.

The young man lowered bloodshot eyes to follow Tarkin's forefinger to the spot. "That, sir? Must have spilled some hair product I was applying in preparation for the inspection." His gaze was unsteady when he looked up at Tarkin. "Permission to wipe it off, sir?"

"Denied," Tarkin said. "To begin with, it's obviously a *stain*, Ensign, not some blemish you can simply rub out." He paused to scan the midshipman from head to toe. "Remove your cap." The youth's brown hair was regulation length, but it did indeed have the stiff look that hair gel might have imparted.

"Attempting to train it, are you?"

The midshipmen stood stiffly, eyes front. "Exactly, sir. It can be unruly."

"No doubt. But that blot on your boot is not hair product."

"Sir?"

"One can tell simply by the way it congealed that it is lubricant— lubricant of a type used almost exclusively in the repulsor generator of our T-Forty-Four landspeeders." Tarkin's eyes narrowed as he focused on the stain. "I see, too, that the lubricant is impregnated with grit, which I suspect came from outside Sentinel's auxiliary dome, almost certainly from where the landing platform is undergoing renovation."

The youth swallowed. "I don't know what to say, sir, I could have sworn—"

"One of our landspeeders was recently sent to the repair bay of the vehicle pool after having become fouled by construction dust," Tarkin said, as if to himself. "There are areas in the bay that are not entirely accessible to our security holocams. However, I often tour the vehicle pool to review repairs, and recently have chanced upon envelopes of a sort that have become fashionable for the storage of a particular class of stimulant spice." His gaze bored into the youth's face. "You're sweating, Ensign. Are you certain you're fit for duty?"

"A touch of hyperspace nausea, sir."

"Perhaps. But nausea doesn't account for the fact that the thumb and index finger of your right hand bear yellow-ocher stains, which are often the result of pinching plugs of spice that hasn't been sufficiently processed. I observe, too, that your left eyetooth reveals what appears to be a nascent cavity, such as might be caused by dipping spice. Finally, your record indicates that you have recently been late in reporting for duty, as well as inattentive when you deign to report." Tarkin paused for a moment. "Have I forgotten anything?"

Embarrassment mottled the midshipman's face.

"Nothing to say for yourself, Ensign?"

"Nothing at this time, sir."

"I thought not."

Tarkin swung to a female officer standing at the opposite end of the row. "Chief, Ensign Baz is relieved of duty. See to it that he is escorted to the crew berth and confined to quarters for the remainder of the voyage. I will decide his fate once we reach Coruscant."

The petty officer saluted. "Yes, sir."

"Also, alert Commander Cassel that the vehicle pool has become a rendezvous area for spice users. Tell him to perform a flash inspection of all barracks and personal lockers. I expect him to confiscate all inebriants and other illicit substances."

"Sir," she said.

Dismissed, the rest of the crew scattered with haste, and Tarkin blew out his breath in irritation. The conversation with Mas Amedda had left him on edge, and he was taking his frustration out on his crew. He understood and fully supported the idea of a chain of command, but he took it personally when power plays interfered with his duties. He trusted Cassel to attend to Sentinel's responsibilities in his absence, but he wasn't comfortable with being summoned away at such a critical time, much less without full explanation. If the purpose of the visit was to discuss the recent attack, then perhaps he should have delayed filing the report. If not about the attack, what matter could be so vital that it couldn't wait until after the looming shipments were safely escorted to Geonosis?

What was done was done, however, and he was determined to present the best possible face to the Emperor.

Leaving the main compartment, he walked forward through two hatches to the ship's command cabin, which he had designed to be more spacious than those found on similar ships, as it was here that he spent most of his travel time. Immediately he found himself relaxing, and let out his breath in slow reprieve. If exasperated by Coruscant's demands, he should at least be able to find some solace in the ship.

At just under 150 meters in length, the corvette fit neatly between the old Judicial cruisers and Corellian Engineering's new-generation frigates. Heavily armed with turbolasers, ion cannons, and proton torpedo tubes, and featuring a Class One hyperdrive that made it the fastest ship in the Imperial Navy, the *Carrion Spike* had been designed specifically for him—and to meet many of his personal specifications—by Sienar Fleet Systems. Based on a prototype stealth corvette that had been introduced during the Clone Wars at the Battle of Christophsis to counter Separatist Admiral Trench's blockade of the planet, the triangular-shaped ship was unique in having cloak technology. Powered by rare stygium crystals, the stealth system rendered the ship essentially invisible to ordinary scanners.

Hearing Tarkin enter, the captain—a slim, dark-complected man who had served under Tarkin during the war—swiveled in his acceleration chair.

"Sir, do you wish to assume the controls?"

Tarkin nodded and replaced him in the command chair, running his hands over the instruments as he settled in. The *Carrion Spike's* ion turbine sublight arrays, countermeasures suite, and navicomputer were also state-of-the-art, the latter allowing the ship to make the jump from Sentinel Base to Coruscant without exiting hyperspace to retrieve routing data from relay stations or primitive hyperwave beacons.

Gazing into the nebulous swirl of hyperspace, he decided that, yes, he could take comfort in having such a ship. In many respects the *Carrion Spike* was a sign of just how far he had come, and where he now stood in the Imperial hegemony.

And what Eriadu wouldn't have given for such a vessel in the decades leading up to the Clone Wars! At that point the sector's problems were pirates lured by sudden wealth, privateers hired by Eriadu's competitors in the lommite trade, and resistance factions protesting the unjust practices of shipping conglomerates operating with impunity in the free trade zones. Eriadu would eventually triumph with the defenses it had at its disposal; but a ship like the *Carrion Spike* might have granted the Seswenna the edge it needed to vanquish its enemies with greater efficiency and added flourish.

In the absence of a Republic military, and as punishment for refusing to provide the Core Worlds with profitable deals, Judicials—the Republic's non-Jedi law enforcers—were often withheld from intervening in disputes, leaving the Seswenna little choice but to create its own armed forces. A loosely knit group that came to be known as the Outland Regions Security Force, the sector's response to pirates and privateers had to make do with second-rate ships built on Eriadu or at Sluis Van, and with laser and ion cannons purchased from arms merchants who for a century had been ignoring the Republic's ban on the sale of weaponry to member worlds.

Not six standard months after passing his ultimate test on the Carrion Plateau, sixteen-year-old Wilhuff was sent up the well to begin his training in space combat, his tutelage supervised by an entirely new cast of characters, some of them Tarkins, but others from worlds as distant as Bothawui and Ryloth. Jova had neither a taste nor the tolerance for space, but would sometimes sedate himself with anti-nausea drugs and accompany his grand-nephew, less to offer hands-on instruction in astrogation, combat maneuvering, and weapons training than to make sure that Wilhuff was applying in zero-g the lessons he had learned on the plateau.

"More than fifty Tarkins have lost their lives to marauders," his uncle told him, "and the number of Eriaduans who've been killed is beyond estimation."

To drive home the point, their first stop was a colony world of Eriadu that had suffered a recent attack by pirates. Wilhuff had had ample time to grow accustomed to the sight, scent, and taste of blood, but he had never seen so much human blood spilled in one place. The mining colony had been attacked without warning, thoroughly plundered, and burned to the ground. Those settlers who hadn't died of laser wounds or been incinerated in the fires had been mercilessly butchered and left to be picked over by scavengers or consumed by insects. It was clear to Wilhuff that many of them had been tortured.

Hundreds of settlers had been abducted and perhaps already sold into slavery.

Wilhuff was sickened, physically and spiritually, in a way he had never experienced on the Carrion, and the disgust he felt gave rise to despair and a hunger for revenge.

"This is the way of things among the lawless," Jova said as they moved grimly through the destruction, not so much to defuse Wilhuff's outrage as to anchor the massacre in a moral context. "Pirates, privateers, or activists, they're no different from the vermin and predators we dealt with on the Carrion. They need to be educated, and acquainted with our notion of law and order. So you treat them just like the ones we hunted or forced into submission, striking fast and in full commitment. You make use of asteroid fields, nebulae, star flares, whatever you find, to intensify the havoc. You keep them off balance with unexpected maneuvers, and you let your starfighters function like vibro-lances in the hands of our Rodians. You establish supremacy like we showed you, by concentrating all the force at your command on one point, hammering away like you would with a vibroblade, through armor like you would through scales or cartilage or bone, and you show no quarter. You stay on your quarry until you've found the soft spot that brings death, and you put the fear into the rest by gutting your victim, ripping out his liver, and devouring it."

As he was expected to, Wilhuff took his uncle's instructions to heart, by demonstrating in space the mettle he had shown on the Carrion.

The incident that would garner the most attention in the academies he would later attend was one involving Eriadu's ore convoys and a Senex sector pirate group known as Q'anah's Marauders. Loans from offworld financiers had enabled the Greater Seswenna to create the Outland Regions Security Force, but the militia had far too few vessels to protect every lommite shipment traveling between Eriadu and the Core. Making the most of the shortage, several pirate groups had forged an alliance wherein some would monitor or engage Outland's warships while others preyed on the unguarded convoys.

The titular head of the alliance was a human female known only as Q'anah, whose audacious raids throughout the Senex sector had made her something of a folk hero. A native of the Core world Brentaal IV, she was the only daughter of a former bodyguard for House Cormond, who had accepted a lucrative offer to leave the Core to oversee security for House Elegin on the world Asmeru. Trained in combat by her father and eager for adventure, Q'anah became the mistress of the youngest son of the noble house, who was himself leading a secret life as a pirate and whose group Q'anah eventually joined. Fighting alongside the members of her lover's crew, Q'anah lived a colorful and bawdy life until the young Elegin was captured, sentenced to death, and executed on Karfeddion. Having by then given birth to Elegin triplets, Q'anah dedicated herself to avenging the death of her paramour by targeting ships and settlements strewn across the Senex-Juvex sectors.

At the point she became a nuisance to Eriadu, she had already become the subject of breathtaking HoloNet tales and scandalous rumors, having survived starship collisions and starfighter crashes, blaster-bolt and vibroblade wounds, and countless fistfights and personal duels. Said to be as fast on the draw as a circus sharpshooter and as talented on the dance floor as a double-jointed Twi'lek, Q'anah had chewed off her own infected hand while awaiting rescue on an isolated moon, and was known to wear artificial arms and at least one leg—from the knee down—in addition to an ocular implant and who knew what else. Twice she had been captured and sentenced to lengthy terms in maximum-security prisons, and had escaped from each thanks to daring rescues mounted by her soldiers, who all but worshipped her. Only her link to House Elegin had saved her from execution. But following an encounter with Judicial Forces, during which she destroyed six ships, the Republic also put a high price on her head, and it was that bounty that had landed her in the Greater Seswenna, a sector rarely if ever patrolled by Judicials, notwithstanding repeated entreaties by Eriadu and other harassed worlds.

Lommite convoys typically comprised up to a score of unpiloted container ships slave-rigged to a crewed shepherd vessel, now and then with an armed gunboat trailing. Each container was capable of

jumping to hyperspace, but during those years before the era of af-
fordable and reliable navicomputers, the convoys had to navigate by
hyperspace buoys located along the route, and experience had proved
that jumping in single file was safer than going to hyperspace in clusters, even though the maneuver left the containers vulnerable to attack on their reversions to realspace.

Outland capital ships would ride herd on valuable shipments, but
ordinary convoys frequently found themselves targeted by Q'anah's
flotilla of deadly frigates and corvettes. With the swiftest ships engaging the shepherd vessel, the rest would deliver boarding parties to
some of the containers and separate them from the pack. Once the
slave-rigs of the ore carriers were disabled, the boxy vessels would be
slaved to a dedicated pirate frigate and jumped in line to hyperspace.
By the time Outland could respond to the distress calls, Q'anah's
crews were already selling the stolen ore on the black market or turning it over to the companies that had hired them to carry out the
raids.

The convoys became easier and easier pickings, and Eriadu Mining began to accept that it was more cost-effective to surrender the
containers than to risk having their overpriced lead or follow ships
destroyed in defensive engagements. The company attempted to trick
the pirates by placing empty container ships among the fully loaded
ones, but the dummy ships only prompted an increase in the number
of raids. The company also tried concealing explosive devices and
even, on a few occasions, parties of armed spacers in some of the
containers. Not once, however, did Q'anah's raiders take the bait, and
over time the strategy of including dummy containers and armed
troopers was also deemed too expensive. Attempts were made to predict which containers the pirates would target, but in the end Eriadu
Mining's battle analysts decided that Q'anah was choosing containers
at random.

Just coming into his own as a lieutenant in Outland's anti-piracy
task force, Wilhuff refused to accept the disheartening analysis and
devoted himself to a detailed study of the raids in which Q'anah had
participated—failures and successes both—in the hope of decipher-
ing her method for choosing containers. Her attacks weren't at all like

the hunts he had witnessed on the Carrion Plateau, where solitary predators or prides would select the stragglers, the young, or the weakest of the herd animals, and for some time it indeed appeared that her choices had neither rhyme nor reason. But Wilhuff remained convinced that a pattern existed—even if Q'anah herself wasn't consciously aware of having created one.

The scheme that ultimately emerged was so deceptively simple, he was surprised no one had unraveled it. *Q'anah* turned out not to be the pirate's original name, but rather one she had adopted after her father had relocated the family to Asmeru. In the ancient language of that mountainous world, the word referred to an ages-old festival that always fell on the same day of the planet's complex calendar: the 234th day of the local-year, in the 16th month. Q'anah had assigned each of the five numbers to a letter of her name, and had used that sequence as her basis for choosing targets. Thus on her initial attack on an Eriadu Mining convoy, she had targeted the second container ship counting back from the lead ship; then the third from that one, then the fourth from that one, and so on, until she had grabbed five containers. On subsequent attacks the sequence might commence substituting the last targeted container for the lead vessel. Sometimes she would reverse the sequence, or move forward in the line rather than toward the rear. Occasionally a pattern would begin in one convoy but wouldn't conclude until the next convoy or even the one after that. The numeric sequence itself, however, never changed. Q'anah was essentially spelling out her sobriquet over and over, as if leaving her mark on every convoy she attacked.

Once Wilhuff had grasped the pattern and persuaded Outland's commanders that his months of obsession hadn't driven him completely mad, Eriadu Mining agreed to sacrifice several container ships to the pirates as a means of confirming the theory. Emboldened by the results, the company urged Outland to stock the predicted convoy targets with soldiers, but Wilhuff's paternal cousin, Ranulph Tarkin, proposed an alternative method for exacting revenge by secreting a computer virus in the containers' hyperdrive motivators. One of Outland's most respected commanders, Ranulph—who so resembled Wilhuff's father they could have passed for twins—had designed the ploy years earlier, but Eriadu Mining had balked, based on the cost of having to outfit countless containers with the virused computers. With a lead on which containers Q'anah would target, however, the company agreed to finance the measure, even though the strategy entailed dispatching only one convoy at a time and often operating at a loss.

To make matters worse, the attacks suddenly ceased. It was almost as if the pirates had learned of the ploy, and with increasing pressure from Core buyers for added shipments and wasting funds on attempts to ferret out spies in their midst, Eriadu Mining was on the brink of financial ruin when the Marauders finally struck, targeting precisely those containers Wilhuff had predicted. No sooner did the pirates slave the containers to their frigate than the virus wormed its way into the ship's navicomputer, overriding the requested jump coordinates and delivering it to a realspace destination where Outland warships were lying in wait. Once the frigate had been crippled and boarded, and Q'anah and her crew rounded up and shackled, Ranulph—always the gentleman—insisted on introducing the pirate queen to her eighteen-year-old "captor."

Her sneering expression ridiculed the very idea of it. "Barely a whisker on his chin, but luck enough for a professional sabacc player."

"It was your vanity that turned out to be a laudable substitute for luck," Wilhuff told her. "Your need to leave your signature all over Eriadu's convoys."

Her real eye opened wide and she quirked a grin that told him she understood what he had accomplished, but she followed up the begrudging grin with a snort of contempt. "There isn't a prison that can contain me, boy—even on Eriadu."

Wilhuff offered the sly smile that would later become a kind of signature. "You're confusing Eriadu with worlds that have noble houses and trials by jury, Q'anah."

She searched his youthful face. "Execution on the spot, is it?"

"Nothing so straightforward."

She continued to appraise him openly and defiantly. "There's hardly a part of me that hasn't been replaced, boy. But take my word: I'm not the last of my kind, and your convoys will continue to suffer."

He allowed a nod. "Only if we fail to discourage your followers."

Outland had Q'anah and her crew transferred to one of the stolen containers, whose sublight engines were programmed to send the ship slowly but inexorably toward the system's sun. The plight of the captives was broadcast over the pirates' own communications network, and several of Q'anah's cohorts succeeded in determining the point of origin of the transmission and hastening to her rescue. Their ships were destroyed on sight by Outland forces. The rest were wise enough to go into hiding.

Wilhuff demanded that the container ship's audio and video feeds be kept enabled to the very end, so that Outland's forces and any others who might have been listening could either savor or lament the agonized wails of the pirates as they were slowly roasted to death. In the end, even the notorious Q'anah succumbed to the torture and wailed openly.

"Your task is to teach them the meaning of law and order," Jova would hector his nephew. "Then to punish them so that they remember the lesson. In the end, you'll have driven the fear of you so deeply into them that fear alone will have them cowering at your feet."

6

IMPERIAL CENTER

BRIGHT-SIDE CORUSCANT air-traffic control directed the *Carrion Spike* to the Imperial Palace, and there into a courtyard landing field that was large enough to accommodate *Victory-* and *Venator-*class Star Destroyers. As repulsors eased the ship down through the busy skyways and into the court, Tarkin realized that the Emperor's current residence had once been the headquarters for the Jedi—though practically all that remained of the Order's elegant Temple complex was its copse of five skyscraping spires, now the pinnacle of a sprawling amalgam of blockish edifaces with sloping façades.

At the edge of the landing courtyard, centered among a detail of red-robed Imperial Guards armed with gleaming force pikes, stood Mas Amedda, dressed in voluminous shoulder-padded robes and carrying a staff that was taller than him, its head ornamented by a lustrous humaniform figure.

"How charitable of you to make time for us, Governor," the Chagrian said as Tarkin approached from the corvette's lowered boarding ramp.

Tarkin played along. "And for you to welcome me personally, Vizier."

"We all do our part for the Empire."

With crisp turns, Amedda and the face-shielded guards led him through elaborate doors into the Palace. Tarkin was familiar with the interior, but the expansive, soaring corridors he walked years earlier had contained a rare solemnity. Now they teemed with civilians and functionaries of many species, and the walls and plinths were left unadorned by art or statuary.

Tarkin felt curiously out of step, perhaps because of the increased gravity, the pace, the crowds, or a combination of all those things. For three years the only non- or near-humans he had seen or had direct contact with had been slaves or recruited laborers at outlying bases or at the battle station's construction site. He had heard that one needn't have been absent from Coruscant for years to be startled by the changes, in that each day saw buildings raised, demolished, incorporated into ever larger and taller monstrosities, or merely stripped of Republic-era ornamentation and renovated in accordance with a more severe aesthetic. Curved lines were yielding to harsh angles; sophistication to declaration. Fashions had changed along similar lines, with few outside the Imperial court affecting cloaks, headcloths, or garish robes. By most accounts, though, Coruscanti were satisfied, especially those who lived and worked in the upper tiers of the fathomless cityscape; content if for no other reason than to have the brutal war behind them.

Tarkin's most carefree years had been spent on Coruscant and neighboring Core Worlds before he had been elected governor of Eriadu, with some help from family members and influential contacts. He had a sudden desire to sneak outside the Palace and explore the precincts he had roamed as an adventurous young adult. But perhaps it was enough to know that law and order had finally triumphed over corruption and indulgence, which had been the hallmarks of the Republic.

Someone called his name as he and Amedda were moving down a colonnaded walkway, and Tarkin turned, recognizing the face of a man he had known since his academy years.

"Nils Tenant," he said in genuine surprise, separating himself from the Chagrian's retinue to shake Tenant's proffered hand. Fair-skinned, with a prominent nose and a downturning full-lipped mouth, Tenant had commanded a Star Destroyer during the Clone Wars, and displayed on his uniform tunic the rank insignia plaque of a rear admiral.

"Wonderful to see you, Wilhuff," Tenant said, pumping Tarkin's hand. "I came as soon as I learned you were coming."

Tarkin affected a frown. "And here I thought my arrival would be a well-kept secret."

Tenant sniffed in faint amusement. "Only some secrets are well kept on Coruscant."

Clearly bothered by the delay, Mas Amedda tapped the base of his staff on the polished floor and waited until the two had joined the retinue before moving deeper into the Palace.

"Is that the new uniform?" Tenant asked as they walked.

Tarkin pinched the sleeve of the tunic. "What, this old thing?" then asked before Tenant could respond: "So who let it be known that I was coming? Was it Yularen? Tagge? Motti?"

Tenant was dismissive. "You know, you hear things." He moved with purposeful slowness. "You've been in the Western Reaches, Wilhuff?"

Tarkin nodded. "Still hunting down General Grievous's former allies. And you?"

"Pacification," Tenant said in a distracted way. "Brought back to attend a Joint Chiefs meeting." Abruptly he clamped his hand on Tarkin's upper arm, bringing him to a halt and encouraging him to fall back from Amedda and the guards. When they seemed to be out of earshot of Amedda, Tenant said: "Wilhuff, are the rumors true?"

Tarkin adopted a questioning look. "What rumors? And why are you whispering?"

Tenant glanced around before answering. "About a mobile battle station. A weapon that will—"

Tarkin stopped him before he could say more, glancing at Amedda in the hope that he and Tenant were, in fact, out of the Chagrian's range.

"This is hardly the place for discussions of that sort," he said firmly.

Tenant looked chastised. "Of course. It's just that . . . You hear so many rumors. People are here one day, gone the next. And no one has laid eyes on the Emperor in months. Amedda, Dangor, and the rest of the Ruling Council have taken to dispatching processions of Imperial skylimos simply to maintain an illusion that the Emperor moves about in public." He fell briefly silent. "You know they commissioned an enormous statue of the Emperor for Senate—I mean, Imperial Plaza? So far, though, the thing looks more terrifying than majestic."

Tarkin raised an eyebrow. "Isn't that the idea, Nils?"

Tenant nodded in a distracted way. "You're right, of course." Again he regarded the nearby columns with wariness. "The scuttlebutt is that you're scheduled to meet with him."

Tarkin shrugged noncommittally. "If that's his pleasure."

Tenant compressed his lips. "Put in a word for me, Wilhuff—for old times' sake. A great change is coming—everyone senses it—and I want to be back in the action."

It struck Tarkin as an odd request, even a trifle audacious. But in considering it, he supposed he could understand wanting to be in the Emperor's good graces, as he was certainly grateful to be there.

He clapped his fellow officer on the shoulder. "If the occasion arises, Nils."

Tenant smiled weakly. "You're a good man, Wilhuff," he said, falling back and vanishing as Tarkin hurried to catch up with Amedda and the retinue turned a corner in the hallway.

Tarkin attracted a good deal of attention as the group climbed a broad stairway and debouched into a vast atrium. Figures of all stripe and station—officials, advisers, soldiers—stopped in their tracks, even while trying not to make an obvious display of staring at him. Subjugator of pirates; former governor of Eriadu; graduate of Prefsbelt; naval officer during the Clone Wars, decorated at the Battle of Kamino and promoted to admiral after a daring escape from the Citadel prison; adjutant general by the war's end, and named by the

Emperor one of twenty Imperial Moffs ... After years of absence from the Imperial capital, was Tarkin here to be forgiven, rewarded, or punished with another mission that would send him chasing Separatist recidivists through the Western Reaches, the Corporate Sector, the Tion Hegemony?

He sometimes wondered where fate might have taken him if he *hadn't* entered the academy system after his years with Outland, when a move to civilian instruction had seemed the best strategy for introducing himself to the wider galaxy. Perhaps he would still be in pursuit of Outer Rim pirates or mercenaries, or slaved to a desk in some planetary capital city. No matter what, it was unlikely that he would ever have crossed paths with the Emperor—when he was still known as Palpatine.

It was while Tarkin was attending the Sullust Sector Spacefarers Academy that they met—or rather that Palpatine had sought him out. Tarkin had just returned to the academy's orbital facility from long hours of starship maneuvers in an Incom T-95 Trainer when someone called his name as he was crossing the flight deck. Turning to the voice, he was astonished to find the Republic senator walking toward him. Tarkin knew that Palpatine was part of Supreme Chancellor Kalpana's party, which included his administrator Finis Valorum and several other senators, all of whom were on station to attend the academy's commencement and commissioning day ceremonies. Most of the graduates would be moving on to positions in commercial piloting, local system navies, or the Judicial Department. Dressed in fashionable blue robes, the red-haired aesthete politician flashed a welcoming smile and extended a hand in greeting.

"Cadet Tarkin, I'm Senator Palpatine."

"I know who you are," Tarkin said, shaking hands with him. "You represent Naboo in the Senate. Your homeworld and mine are practically galactic neighbors."

"So we are."

"I want to thank you personally for the position you took in the Senate on the bill that will encourage policing of the free trade zones."

Palpatine gestured in dismissal. "Our hope is to bring stability to the Outer Rim worlds." His eyes narrarowed. "The Jedi haven't provided any support in dealing with the pirates that continue to plague the Seswenna?"

Tarkin shook his head. "They've ignored our requests for intervention. Apparently the Seswenna doesn't rate highly enough on their list of priorities."

Palpatine sniffed. "Well, I might be able to offer some help in that regard—not with the Jedi, of course. With the Judicials, I mean."

"Eriadu would be grateful for any help. Stability in the Seswenna could ease tensions all along the Hydian Way."

Palpatine's eyebrows lifted in delighted surprise. "A cadet who is not only a very skilled pilot, but who also has an awareness of politics. What are the chances?"

"I might ask the same. What are the chances of a Republic senator knowing me on sight?"

"As a matter of fact, your name came up in a discussion I was having with a group of like-minded friends on Coruscant."

"My name?" Tarkin said in disbelief as they began to amble toward the pilots' ready rooms.

"We are always on the lookout for those who demonstrate remarkable skills in science, technology, and other fields." Palpatine allowed his words to trail off, then said: "Tell me, Cadet Tarkin, what are your plans following graduation from this institution?"

"I still have another two years of training. But I'm hoping to be accepted to the Judicial Academy."

Palpatine waved in dismissal. "Easily done. I happen to be personal friends with the provost of the academy. I would be glad to advocate on your behalf, if you wish."

"I'd be honored," Tarkin managed. "I don't know what to say, Senator. If there's anything I can do—"

"There is." Palpatine came to an abrupt halt on the flight deck and turned to face Tarkin directly. "I want to propose an alternative course for you. Politics."

Tarkin repressed a laugh. "I'm not sure, Senator . . ."

"I know what you must be thinking. But politics was a noble enough choice for some of your relatives. Or are you cut from so different a cloth?" Palpatine continued before Tarkin could reply. "If I may speak candidly for a moment, Cadet, we feel—my friends and I—that you'd be wasting your talents in the Judicial Department. With your piloting skills, I'm certain you would be an excellent addition to their forces, but you're already much more than a mere pilot."

Tarkin shook his head in bewilderment. "I wouldn't even know where to begin."

"And why should you? Politics, however, is my area of expertise." Palpatine's relaxed expression became serious. "I understand what it's like to be a young man of action and obvious ambition who feels that he has been marginalized by the circumstances of his birth. Even here, I can imagine that you've been ostracized by the spoiled progeny of the influential. It has little to do with wealth—your family could buy and sell most of the brats here—and everything to do with fortune: the fact that you weren't born closer to the Core. And so you are forced to defend against their petty prejudices: that you lack refinement, culture, a sense of propriety." He stopped to allow a smile to take shape. "I'm well aware that you've been able to make a name for yourself in spite of this. That alone, young Tarkin, shows that you weren't born to follow."

"You're speaking from personal experience," Tarkin risked saying after a long moment of silence.

"Of course I am," Palpatine told him. "Our homeworlds are different in the sense that mine wished no part of galactic politics, while yours has long sought to be included. But I knew from early on that politics could provide me with a path to the center. Even so, I didn't get to Coruscant fully on my own. I had the help of a . . . teacher. I was younger than you are now when this person helped me realize what I most wanted in life, and helped me attain it."

"You . . . ," Tarkin began.

Palpatine nodded. "Your family is powerful in its own right, but only in the Seswenna. Outland forces will soon have the sector's pirate pests on the run, and what will you do then?" His eyes narrowed once more. "There are larger fights to wage, Cadet. When you graduate, why not visit me on Coruscant? I will be your guide to the Senate District, and with any luck I'll be able to change your mind about politics as a career. Unlike Coruscant, Eriadu hasn't been corrupted by greed and the welter of contradictory voices. It has always been a Tarkin world, and it could become a beacon for other worlds wishing to be recognized by the galactic community. You could be the one to bring that about."

As it happened Tarkin wouldn't enter politics for many years, though he did accept Palpatine's help in gaining admission to the Judicial Academy. There—and precisely as the senator from Naboo had predicted—his fellow cadets had initially viewed him as a kind of noble savage: a principled being with abundant energy and drive who had the misfortune of hailing from an uncivilized world.

In part, Tarkin's father and the top echelon of the Outland Regions Security Force were to blame. Eager to impress the Core with their achievements and the fact that they were willing to contribute one of their finest strategists to the Republic, Outland's leaders had personally delivered Tarkin to the academy in one of its finest warships, its glossy hull emblazoned with the symbol of the fanged veermok and Tarkin himself turned out in the full regalia of an Outland commander. His arrival caused such a stir that the academy's provost marshal had mistaken him for a visiting dignitary—which, while certainly the case on worlds throughout the embattled Seswenna sector, carried no weight in the Core. Were it not for Palpatine's influence once more, Tarkin might have been dismissed from the academy even before he had been enrolled as a plebe.

Tarkin understood that he had neglected to heed the lessons he had learned at Sullust and had committed a tactical blunder of the worst sort. Both on the Carrion Plateau and in Eriadu space he had grown so accustomed to flying boldly into confrontation and announcing himself with flourish and dash that he hadn't stopped to consider the staid nature of his new testing ground. Instead of sowing chaos of the sort that had so often served his purposes on land and in deep space, he had succeeded only in rousing the instant scorn of his instructors and the ridicule of his fellow plebes, who took every chance to refer to him as "Commander" or to offer facetious salutes when- and wherever possible.

Early on, the derisive teasing led to brawls, which he mostly won, and also to disciplinary action and demerits that sentenced him to remain at the bottom of the class. That a plebe could be expelled from the Judicials for standing up for himself was something of a revelation, and perhaps he should have seen it as emblematic of the stance the Republic itself would adopt in the coming years, when its authority would be challenged by the Separatists. But he couldn't keep himself from answering fire with fire. Gradually he came to suffer the mockery of his peers without resorting to retribution, though demerits would continue to accrue owing to mischief making and impulsive outbursts. Even so, he refused to allow himself to be cut down to size, choosing instead to bide his time and wait for an opportunity to show his peers just what he was made of.

Halcyon would prove to be that opportunity.

A Republic member world located in the Colonies region, Halcyon was suffering a crisis of its own. A cold-blooded group of would-be usurpers clamoring for the planet's right to manage its own affairs had abducted several members of the planetary leadership and was holding them hostage at a remote bastion. After attempts at negotiation had been exhausted, the Republic Senate had granted permission for the Jedi to intervene and, if necessary, to employ "lightsaber diplomacy" to resolve the crisis. Tarkin was chosen to be one of the eighty Judicials the Senate ordered to attend and reinforce the Jedi.

Never having seen let alone served alongside a Jedi, he was fascinated from the start. His theoretical grasp of the Force was as keen as that of most of his academy peers, but he was less interested in furthering his understanding of metaphysics than in observing the aloof Jedi in action. How adept were they at tactics and strategy? How quick were they to wield their lightsabers when their commands fell on deaf ears? How far were they willing to go to uphold the authority of the Republic? As a self-considered expert in the use of the vibrolance, Tarkin was equally captivated by their lightsaber skills. Watching them train during the journey to Halcyon, he saw that each had an individual fighting style, and that the technniques for attacks and parries seemed unrelated to the color of the energy blades.

At Halcyon the Jedi divided the Judicials into four teams, assigning one to accompany them to the fortress and inserting the others on the far side of a ridge of low mountains to block possible escape routes. While Tarkin saw a certain logic in the plan, he couldn't quite purge himself of a suspicion that the Jedi merely wanted to rid themselves of responsibility for law enforcement personnel they clearly thought of as inferiors.

What the Jedi hadn't taken into account was the fact that Halcyon's usurpers were a tech-savvy group who had had ample time to prepare for an assault on the bastion. No sooner were the Judicial teams inserted into the densely forested foothills than the planet's global positioning satellites were disabled and surface-to-air communications scrambled. In short order, Tarkin's team lost touch with the two cruisers that had brought them to Halcyon, their Jedi commanders, and the other Judicial teams. The prudent response would have been to hunker down while the Jedi attended to business at the fortress and wait for extraction. But the team's commander—a by-the-numbers human with twenty years of Judicial service whose piloting and martial skills had earned him Tarkin's reluctant respect—had other ideas. Convinced that the Jedi, too, had fallen prey to a trap, he got it in his head to strike out overland, traverse the ridge, and open a second front on reaching the fortress. This struck Tarkin as pure arrogance—no different from what he had seen in some of the Jedi he had come to know—but he also realized that the commander likely couldn't abide being stranded in a trackless wilderness with a group of raw trainees.

Tarkin was immediately aware of the potential for disaster. The commander's datapad contained regional maps, but Tarkin knew from long experience that maps weren't the territory, and that triple-canopy forests could be confounding places to negotiate. At the same time, he realized that the opportunity for finally proving his worth couldn't have been more made to order if he had designed it himself. Mission briefings had acquainted him with the local topography, and he was reasonably certain he could follow his nose almost directly to the bastion. But he decided to keep that to himself.

For three days of foul weather, mudslides, and sudden tree falls, the commander had them stumbling through thick forest and bogs, occasionally circling back on themselves, and growing increasingly lost. When on the fourth day their blister-pack rations ran out and exhaustion began to set in, all semblance of team integrity vanished. These scions of wealthy Core families who thought nothing of journeying across the stars had forgotten or perhaps never known what it meant to stand or sleep beneath them, far from artifical light or sentient contact, in an isolated wilderness on a far-flung world. The frequent, intense downpours dispirited them; the hostile-sounding but innocuous calls of unseen beasts unnerved them; the overhead roar of swarming insects left them huddling in their confining shelters. They grew to fear their own shadows, and Tarkin found his strength in their distress.

The chance to show just what he was made of came on the pebbled shore of a wide, clear, swift-flowing river. Off and on for some hours, the team had been moving parallel to the river, and Tarkin had been studying the current, making parallax observations of objects on the bottom and observing the shadows cast by Halcyon's bashful suns. Hours earlier, downstream of a waterfall, they had passed a stretch they would have been able to ford without incident, but Tarkin had held his tongue. Now, while the commander and some of the team members stood arguing about how deep the water might be, Tarkin simply waded directly into the current and trudged to the middle of the river, where wavelets lapped at his shoulders. Then, cupping his hands to his mouth, he yelled back to the team: *"It's this deep!"*

After that, the commander kept him by his side, and eventually surrendered point to him. Navigating by the rise and set of Halcyon's twin suns, and sometimes in the sparing illumination of the planet's array of tiny moons, Tarkin led them on a tortuous forest course that took them through the hills and into more open forest on the far side. Along the way he showed them how to use their blasters to kill game without burning gaping holes in the most edible parts. For fun, he felled a large rodent with a hand-fashioned wooden lance and entertained the team by dressing and cooking it over a fire he conjured with a sparkstone from a pile of kindling. He got his fellow plebes used to sleeping on the ground, under the stars, amid a cacophony of sounds and songs.

At a time when the Clone Wars were still a decade off, it became clear to his commander and peers that Wilhuff Tarkin *had already tasted blood.*

When they had walked for three more days and Tarkin estimated that they were within five kilometers of the usurper's fortress, he fell back to allow the commander to lead them in. The Jedi were astounded. They had only just put an end to the insurrection—somehow without losing a single eminent hostage—and they had all but given up on finding any members of the Judicial team alive. Search parties had been dispatched, but none had managed to pick up the team's trail. Relieved to be back on firm ground, the cadets were at first reserved about revealing the details of their ordeal, but in due course the stories began to be told, and in the end Tarkin was credited with having saved their lives.

For those Judicials who knew little of the galaxy beyond the Core, it came as a shock that a world like Eriadu could produce not only essential goods, but also natural champions. A clique of congenial cadets began to form around Tarkin, as much to bask in the reflected glow of his sudden popularity as to be taught by him, or even to be the butt of his jokes. In him they found someone who could be as hard on himself as he could be on others, even when those others happened to be superiors who shirked their responsibilities or made what to him were bad decisions. They had already witnessed how well he could fight, scale mountains, pilot a gunboat, and succeed on a sports field, and—as crises like the one at Halcyon grew more common—they grew to realize that he had a mind for tactics, as well; more important, that Tarkin was a born leader, an inspiration for others to overcome their fears and to surpass their own expectations.

Not all were enamored of him. Where to some he was meticulous, coolheaded, and fearless, to others he was calculating, ruthless, and fanatical. But no matter to which camp his peers subscribed, the stories that emerged about Tarkin in the waning days of the Judicial Department were legendary—and they only grew with the telling.

Few then knew the details of his unusual upbringing, for he had a habit of speaking only when he had something important to add, but he had no need to brag, since the tales that spread went beyond anything he could have confirmed or fabricated. That he had bested a Wookiee in hand-to-hand combat; that he had piloted a starfighter through an asteroid field without once consulting his instruments; that he had single-handedly defended his homeworld against a pirate queen; that he had made a solo voyage through the Unknown Regions . . .

His strategy of flying boldly into the face of adversity was studied and taught, and during the Clone Wars would come to be known as "the Tarkin Rush," when it was also said of him that his officers and crew would willingly follow him to hell and beyond. He might have remained a Judicial were it not for a growing schism that began to eat away at the department's long-held and nonpartisan mandate to keep the galaxy free of conflict. On the one side stood Tarkin and others who were committed to enforcing the law and safeguarding the Republic; on the other, a growing number of dissidents who had come to view the Republic as a galactic disease. They detested the influence peddling, the complacency of the Senate, and the proliferation of corporate criminality. They saw the Jedi Order as antiquated and ineffectual, and they yearned for a more equitable system of government—or none at all.

As the clashes between Republic and Separatist interests escalated in frequency and intensity, Tarkin would find himself pitted against many of the Judicials with whom he had previously served. The galaxy was fast becoming an arena for ideologues and industrialists, with the Judicials being used to settle trade disputes or to further corporate agendas. He feared that the Seswenna sector would be dragged into the rising tide of disgruntlement, without anyone to keep Eriadu and its brethren worlds free of the coming fray. He began to think of his homeworld as a ship that needed to be steered into calmer waters, and of himself as the one who should assume command of that perilous voyage. The time had come to accept Palpatine's invitation to join him on Coruscant, for his promised crash course in galactic politics.

Entering one of a bank of turbolifts that accessed the centermost of the Palace's quincunx of spires, Tarkin was surprised when Mas Amedda charged the car to descend.

"I would have expected the Emperor to reside closer to the top," Tarkin said.

"He does," the vizier allowed. "But we're not proceeding directly to the Emperor. We're going to meet first with Lord Vader."

MASTERS OF WAR

TWENTY LEVELS DOWN, in a courtroom not unlike the one in which Tarkin had tried to make a case against Jedi apprentice Ahsoka Tano for murder and sedition during the Clone Wars, stood the Emperor's second, Darth Vader, gesticulating with his gauntleted right hand as he harangued a score of nonhumans gathered in an area reserved for the accused.

"Was this where the Jedi Order held court?" Tarkin asked Amedda.

In a voice as hard and cold as his pale-blue eyes, the vizier said, "We no longer speak of the Jedi, Governor."

Tarkin took the remark in stride, turning his attention instead to Vader and his apparently captive audience. Flanking the Dark Lord was the deputy director of the Imperial Security Bureau, Harus Ison—a brawny, white-haired, old-guard loyalist with a perpetually flushed face—and a thin, red-head-tailed Twi'lek male Tarkin didn't recognize. Bolstering the commanding trio were four Imperial stormtroopers with blaster rifles slung, and an officer wearing a black uniform and cap, hands clasped behind his back and legs slightly spread.

"It appears that some of you have failed to pay attention," Vader was saying, jabbing his pointer figure in the chill, recirculated air. "Or perhaps you are simply choosing to ignore our guidance. Whichever the case, the time has come for you to decide between setting safer courses for yourselves and suffering the consequences."

"Wise counsel," Amedda said.

Tarkin nodded in agreement. "Counsel one dismisses at one's own peril, I suspect." Glancing at the Chagrian, he added: "I know Ison, but who are the others?"

"Riffraff from the lower levels," Amedda said with patent distaste. "Gangsters, smugglers, bounty hunters. Coruscanti scum."

"I might have guessed by the look of them. And the Twi'lek standing alongside Lord Vader?"

"Phoca Soot," Amedda said, turning slightly toward him. "Prefect of level one-three-three-one, where many of these lowlifes operate."

Vader was in motion, pacing back and forth in front of his audience, as if waiting to spring. "The liberties you enjoyed and abused during the days of the Republic and the Clone Wars are a thing of the past," he was saying. "Then there was some purpose to turning a blind eye to illegality, and to fostering dishonesty of a particular sort. But times have changed, and it is incumbent on you to change with them."

Vader fell silent, and the sound of his sonorous breathing filled the room. Tarkin watched him closely.

"*The Tarkin heritage will grant you access to many influential people, and to many social circles,*" his father had told him. "*In addition, your mother and I will do all within our power to help bring your desires within reach. But nothing less than the strength of your ambition will bring you together with those who will partner in your ascension and ultimately reward you with power.*"

Since the end of the war, Vader had on occasion been such a partner in Tarkin's life, both in Geonosis space and in political and military campaigns that had taken them throughout the galaxy. Tarkin had long nursed suspicions about who Vader was beneath the black face mask and helmet, as well as how he had come to be, but he knew better than to give open voice to his thoughts.

"Lest any of your current activities infringe on the Emperor's designs," Vader continued, "you may wish to consider relocating your operations to sectors in the Outer Rim. Or you may opt to remain on Coruscant and risk lengthy sentences in an Imperial prison." He paused to let his words sink in; then, with his gloved hands akimbo and his black floor-length cape thrown behind his shoulders, he added: "Or worse."

He began to pace again. "It has come to my attention that a certain being present has failed to grasp that his recent actions reflect a flagrant disrespect for the Emperor. His brazen behavior suggests that he actually takes some pride in his actions. But his duplicity has not gone unnoticed. We are pleased to be able to make an example of him, so that the rest of you might profit at his expense."

Vader came to an abrupt stop, scanning his audience and certainly sending shivers of fear through everyone—Toydarian, Dug, and Devaronian alike. As his raised right hand curled slowly into a fist, many of them began nervously tugging at the collars of their tunics and cloaks. But it was the Twi'lek prefect, standing not a meter from the Dark Lord, who unexpectedly gasped and brought his hands to his chest as if he had just taken a spear to the heart. Phoca Soot's lekku shot straight out from the sides of his head as if he were being electrocuted, and he collapsed to his knees in obvious agony, his breath caught in his throat and blood vessels in his head-tails beginning to rupture. His eyes glazed over and his red skin began to pale; then his arms flew back from his chest as if in an act of desperate supplication, and he tipped backward, the left side of his head slamming hard against the blood-slicked floor.

For a long moment, Vader's breathing was the only sound intruding on the silence. Without bothering to gaze on his handiwork, the Dark Lord finally said: "Perhaps this is a good place to conclude our assembly. Unless any of you have questions?"

The stormtrooper commander made a quick motion with his hand, and two of the white-armored soldiers moved in. Taking hold of the prefect by his slack arms and legs, they began to carry him from the room, tracking blood across the floor and passing close to Tarkin and Amedda. The vizier's blue face was contorted in angry astonishment.

Tarkin hid a smile. It pleased him to see Amedda caught off guard.

"Lord Vader," the vizier said as the Emperor's deputy approached, "we've refrained from requesting that you grant stays of execution to those in your sights, but is there no one you are willing to pardon?"

"I will give the matter some thought," Vader told him.

Amedda adopted a narrow-eyed expression of exasperation and withdrew, leaving Tarkin and Vader facing each other. If Vader was at all affected by the Chagrian's words, he showed no evidence of it, in either his bearing or the rich bass of his voice.

"We haven't stood together on Coruscant in some time, Governor."

Tarkin lifted his gaze past Vader's transpirator-control chest plate and grilled muzzle to the unreadable midnight orbs of his mask. "The needs of the Empire keep us elsewhere occupied, Lord Vader."

"Just so."

Tarkin directed a glance at the exiting stormtroopers. "I am curious about Prefect Soot."

Vader crossed his thick arms across the illuminated indicators of the chest plate. "A pity. Tasked with controlling crime in his sector, he succumbed to temptation by hiring himself out to the Droid Gotra."

"Well, clearly his heart wasn't in it," Tarkin said. "Strange, though, that the Crymorah crime syndicate had no representation in your audience."

Vader looked down at him—blankly? Perturbed?

"We have reached an accommodation with the Crymorah," Vader said.

Tarkin waited for more, but Vader had nothing to add, so Tarkin dropped the matter and they set out for the turbolifts together, with Amedda and his retinue of Royal Guards trailing behind.

Nothing about Vader seemed natural—not his towering height, his deep voice, his antiquated diction—yet despite those qualities and the mask and respirator, Tarkin believed him to be more man than machine. Although he had clearly twisted the powers of the Force to his own dark purposes, Vader's innate strength was undeniable. His contained rage was genuine, as well, and not simply the result of some murderous cyberprogram. But the quality that made him most human was the fierce dedication he demonstrated to the Emperor.

It was that genuflecting obedience, the steadfast devotion to execute whatever task the Emperor assigned, that had given rise to so many rumors about Vader: that he was a counterpart to the Confederacy's General Grievous the Emperor had been holding in reserve; that he was an augmented human or near-human who had been trained or had trained himself in the ancient dark arts of the Sith; that he was nothing more than a monster fashioned in some clandestine laboratory. Many believed that the Emperor's willingness to grant so much authority to such a being heralded the shape of things to come, for it was beyond dispute that Vader was the Empire's first terror weapon.

Tarkin didn't always agree with Vader's methods for dealing with those who opposed the Empire, but he held the Dark Lord in high esteem, and he hoped Vader felt the same toward him. Very early on in their partnership—soon after both had been introduced to the secret mobile battle station—Tarkin grew convinced that Vader knew him much better than he let on, and that behind the bulging lenses of his face mask, whatever remained of Vader's human eyes regarded him with clear recognition. More than anything else it was those initial feelings that had provided Tarkin with his first suspicion as to Vader's identity. Later, observing the rapport the Dark Lord shared with the stormtroopers who supported him, and the technique he displayed in wielding his crimson lightsaber, Tarkin grew more and more convinced that his suspicions were right.

Vader might very well be Jedi Knight Anakin Skywalker, whom Tarkin had fought beside during the Clone Wars, and for whom he had developed a grudging appreciation.

"How is life on the Sentinel moon, Governor?" Vader asked as they walked.

"In a week we'll be back on the bright side of the gas giant, where security is improved."

"Is that the reason you were opposed to coming to Coruscant?"

Vader shouldn't have known as much, but Tarkin wasn't surprised that he did. "Tell me, Lord Vader, does the vizier always share confidences with you?"

"When I ask him to, yes."

"Then he should have qualified his statement. I may have been reluctant to leave my post, but I wasn't opposed to doing so."

"Certainly not when you learned that the request originated with the Emperor."

Tarkin smirked. "Why not simply call it an order, then?"

"It is unimportant. I might have done the same."

Tarkin looked at Vader askance, but said nothing.

"Will your absence affect the construction schedule?"

"Not at all," Tarkin was quick to say. "Components for the hyperdrive generator will be shipping on schedule from Desolation Station, where initial tests have been completed. Work continues on the navigational matrix itself, as well as on the hypermatter reactor. At this point I'm not unduly concerned about the status of the sublight engines or shield generators."

"And the weapons systems?"

"That's a bit more complicated. Our chief designers have yet to reach an agreement about the laser array, and whether or not it should be a proton beam. The designers are also debating the optimum configuration for the kyber crystal assembly. The delays owe as much to their bickering as to production setbacks."

"That will not do."

Tarkin nodded. "Frankly, Lord Vader, there are simply too many voices weighing in."

"Then we need to remedy the situation."

"As I've been proposing all along."

They fell silent as they entered a turbolift that accessed the Palace's primary spire, leaving Amedda and the Royal Guards no choice but to wait for a different car. The silence lingered as they began to ascend through the levels. Vader brought the lift to a halt one level below the summit and exited. When Tarkin started to follow, Vader raised a hand to stop him.

"The Emperor expects you above," he said.

The turbolift carried him to the top of the world. He stepped from the car into a large circular space with a perimeter of soaring windows that provided a view for hundreds of kilometers in every direction. A curved partition defined a separate space that Tarkin assumed was the Emperor's personal quarters. Prominent in the main area was a large table surrounded by oversized chairs, one of them with a high back and control panels set into the armrests. Alone, Tarkin wandered about admiring artworks and statues positioned to catch the light of Coruscant's rising or setting sun, some of which he recognized as having been moved from the Supreme Chancellor's suite in the Executive Building, in particular a bas-relief panel depicting an ancient battle scene. A circular balcony above the main level contained case after lofty case of texts and storage devices.

The Emperor emerged from his quarters as Tarkin was regarding a slender bronzium statue. Dressed in his customary black-patterned robes, with the cowl raised over his head, he moved as if hovering across the reflective floor.

"Welcome, Governor Tarkin," he said in a voice that many thought sinister but to Tarkin sounded merely strained.

"My lord," he said, bowing slightly. Gesturing broadly, he added: "I like what you've done with the place." When the Emperor didn't respond, Tarkin indicated the bronzium statue of a cloaked figure. "If memory serves, this was in your former office."

The Emperor laid a wrinkled, sallow hand on the piece. "Sistros, one of the four ancient philosophers of Dwartii. I keep it for sentimental value." He gestured broadly. "Some of the rest, well, one might call the collection the spoils of war." His glance returned to Tarkin. "But come, sit, Governor Tarkin. We have much to discuss."

The Emperor lowered himself into the armchair and swiveled away from the window-wall so that his ghastly face was in shadow. Tarkin took the chair opposite and crossed his hands in his lap.

As Nils Tenant had reaffirmed, there were as many rumors circulating about the Emperor as there were about Darth Vader. The fact that he rarely appeared in public or even at Senate proceedings had convinced many that the Jedi attack on him had resulted not only in

the ruination of his face and body, but also in the death of the san-
guine politician he had been before the war, betrayed by those who
had served him and had supported the Republic for centuries. Some
Coruscanti even confessed to having fond memories for ex-chancellor
Finis Valorum, about whom they could gossip to no end. They
yearned to see the Emperor strolling through Imperial Plaza or attending an opera or officiating at the groundbreaking of a new building complex.

But Tarkin didn't speak to those things; instead he said: "Coruscant appears prosperous."

"Busy, busy," the Emperor said.

"The Senate is supportive?"

"Now that it serves rather than advises." The Emperor swiveled
slightly in Tarkin's direction. "Better to surround oneself with fresh
loyal allies than treacherous old ones."

Tarkin smiled. "Someone once said that politics is little more than
the systematic organization of hostilities."

"Very true, in my experience."

"But do you even need them, my lord?" Tarkin asked in a careful,
controlled voice.

"The Senate?" The Emperor could not restrain a faint smile. "Yes,
for the time being." With a dismissive gesture, he added: "We've come
far, you and I."

"My lord?"

"Twenty years ago, who would have thought that two men from
the Outer Rim would sit at the center of the galaxy."

"You flatter me, my lord."

The Emperor studied him openly. "I sometimes wonder, though, if
you—born an outsider, as I was—feel that we should be doing more
to lift up those worlds we defeated in the war? Especially those in the
Outer Rim."

"Turn the galaxy inside out?" Tarkin said more strongly than he
intended. "Quite the opposite, my lord. The populations of those
worlds wreaked havoc. They must earn the right to rejoin the galactic
community."

"And the ones that waver or refuse?"

"They should be made to suffer."

"Sanctions?" the Emperor said, seemingly intrigued by Tarkin's response. "Embargoes? Ostracism?"

"If they are intractable, then yes. The Empire cannot be destabilized."

"Obliteration."

"Whatever you deem necessary, my lord. Force is the only real and unanswerable power. Oftentimes, beings who haven't been duly punished cannot be reasoned with or edified."

The Emperor repeated the words to himself, then said, "That has the ring of a parental lesson, Governor Tarkin."

Tarkin laughed pleasantly. "So it was, my lord—though applied in a more personal manner."

The Emperor swiveled his chair toward the light, and Tarkin glimpsed his sepulchral visage; the molten skin beneath his eyes, the bulging forehead. After all these years, he was still not accustomed to it. *"When one consorts with vipers, one runs the risk of being struck,"* the Emperor had told Tarkin following the attack on him by a quartet of Jedi Masters.

There were many stories about what had occurred that day in the chancellor's office. The official explanation was that members of the Jedi Order had turned up to arrest Supreme Chancellor Palpatine, and a ferocious duel had ensued. The matter of precisely how the Jedi had been killed or the Emperor's face deformed had never been settled to everyone's satisfaction, and so Tarkin had his private thoughts about the Emperor, as well. That he and Vader were kindred spirits suggested that both of them might be Sith. Tarkin often wondered if that wasn't the actual reason Palpatine had been targeted for arrest or assassination by the Jedi. It wasn't so much that the Order wished to take charge of the Republic; it was that the Jedi couldn't abide the idea of a member of the ancient Order they opposed and abhorred emerging as the hero of the Clone Wars and assuming the mantle of Emperor.

"I thank you for remaining in service to the Empire and not turning your hand to writing," the Emperor said, "as some of your contemporaries have done."

"Oh, I still dabble, my lord."

"Doctrinal writings?" the Emperor said in what seemed genuine interest. "Examinations of history? A memoir perhaps?"

"All those things, my lord."

"Even with your obligations as sector governor, you find the time."

"Sentinel Base is remote and mostly tranquil."

"It suits you, then. Or is it that you are well suited to it?"

"Sentinel isn't exactly privation, my lord."

"Even when attacked, Governor?"

Tarkin restrained a smile. He knew when he was being goaded. "Is this the reason you summoned me, my lord?"

The Emperor sat back in the chair. "Yes and no. Though I am familiar with the report you transmitted to the intelligence chiefs. Your actions at Sentinel bespeak a keen intuition, Governor."

Tarkin adopted an expression of nonchalance. "The important thing is that the mobile battle station remains secure."

The Emperor imitated Tarkin's affected indifference. "This isn't the first time we've been forced to deal with malcontents, and it won't be the last. From both near and far." He paused. "There is no refuge from deception when adversaries remain."

"All the more reason to safeguard the supply lines, especially through sectors that aren't under my personal control."

The Emperor placed his elbows on the table and steepled his long fingers. "Clearly you have thoughts about how to rectify the situation."

"I don't wish to be presumptuous, my lord." ·

"Nonsense," the Emperor said. "Speak your mind, Governor."

Tarkin compressed his lips, then said: "My lord, it's nothing we haven't discussed previously."

"You are referring to the need for oversector control."

"I am. Each oversector governor would then be responsible for maintaining control beneath him—if only as a means of policing districts without having to request guidance from Coruscant."

The Emperor didn't reply immediately. "And who might assume your position if I were to remove you from Sentinel?"

"General Tagge, perhaps."

"Not Motti?"

"Or Motti."

"Anyone else?"

"Nils Tenant is very competent."

Again the Emperor fell briefly silent. "Are you certain that Sentinel's unknown assailants managed to override the local HoloNet relay station?"

"I am, my lord."

"Have you some notion as to how they achieved this?"

Tarkin wet his lips. "Travel to Coruscant prevented me from carrying out a complete investigation. But yes, I have some ideas."

"Ideas you are willing to share with our advisers and intelligence chiefs?"

"If it will serve your purpose, my lord."

The Emperor exhaled forcibly. "We will see at length just whose purpose it serves."

8

THE EMPEROR'S NEW SPIES

SIMILAR IN DESIGN to the pinnacle room, the audience chamber on the penultimate level of the central spire was a circular space, but without partitions and featuring a ten-meter-tall podium reserved for the Emperor, who accessed it by private turbolift from his residence. Tarkin arrived by means of the more public turbolift, entering the vast room to find nearly a dozen people waiting, all of whom he knew or recognized, loosely divided into three groups that made up the Empire's uppermost tiers. First, and positioned closest to the podium, was the Ruling Council, represented just then by Ars Dangor, Sate Pestage, and Janus Greejatus, all three dressed in baggy costumes of riotous color and floppy hats more befitting a night at the Coruscant Opera. More or less on equal footing, the two other groups were made up of members from the Imperial Security Bureau and the more recently created Naval Intelligence Agency, with Harus Ison and Colonel Wullf Yularen speaking for the former, and Vice Admirals Rancit and Screed for the latter. Feeling like the odd man out, Tarkin gravitated to where Mas Amedda and Darth Vader were standing, off to one side of the podium.

Tarkin acknowledged his military comrades with a friendly nod to each. Some he had known since his academy days; others he had served with during the Clone Wars. Interestingly, the Emperor's advisers were also a kind of clique, having attached themselves to the Emperor since his early years as an untested senator from Naboo. Perhaps their outlandish garb was in some sense a tribute to the sartorial extravagance of Naboo's nobility. Even those who should have known better tended to dismiss Dangor, Greejatus, and Pestage as sycophants, when in fact members of the Ruling Council oversaw the everyday affairs of the Empire and wielded wide-ranging and sometimes menacing powers. Even the Empire's twenty Moffs were obligated to answer to the Imperial cadre.

On receiving a signal from the Emperor, Amedda banged his statue-tipped staff on the floor as a sign that the briefing should commence. First to step forward was white-haired ISB deputy director Ison, who bowed to the Emperor before turning to address everyone else in the chamber.

"My lords, Moff Tarkin, Admirals . . . With your permission, and for the benefit of those of you who may not be fully conversant with the matter at hand, I offer a brief summary. Three weeks ago, one of our intelligence assets reported a startling find on Murkhana."

Tarkin came to full alert at Ison's mention of the former Separatist stronghold world.

"Due to the nature of the find, ISB wasted no time in bringing the matter to the attention of the Ruling Council, as well as to our counterparts in Military Intelligence." Ison glanced at Rancit and Screed. Having lost an eye in the war, Screed was sporting a cybernetic implant. "Normally ISB would have pursued an investigation on its own, but on Vizier Amedda's recommendation we are opening it up to discussion, in the hope of resolving how best to proceed."

Tarkin wasn't surprised by Ison's equivocal introduction. ISB functioned under the auspices of COMPNOR, the Commission for the Preservation of the New Order, which itself had arisen from the dregs of the Commission for the Protection of the Republic, and the deputy director was determined to spearhead the investigation without appearing overly proprietary and ambitious. And so he was generously "opening the matter up to discussion," when it was clearly his hope that the Ruling Council would grant ISB full oversight, exempting the bureau from having to share sensitive information with Military Intelligence or anyone else.

"Please don't leave us hanging, Deputy Director," Amedda said in his most sniping voice, "and come to the point."

Tarkin watched Ison's square jaw clench. The deputy director was surely biting his tongue, as well.

"The Murkhana discovery consists of a cache of communications devices," Ison said. "Signal interrupters, jammers, eradicators, and other apparatus, which, to ISB, suggests evidence of a potential stratagem to incapacitate the HoloNet, as was temporarily achieved by the Separatists during the Clone Wars."

Obviously in the dark about the find, advisers Greejatus and Dangor traded looks of bewilderment. Where Greejatus's dark sunken eyes and puffy face granted him an ominous look, Dangor's long, braided mustachios and broad, furrowed brow imparted a bit of élan to an otherwise surly aspect.

"Director Ison," Dangor said, "perhaps these devices—though recently discovered—are nothing more than a cache left over from the war. They may even have been discovered elsewhere by beings unfamiliar with such devices, and relocated to their present site."

Ison had an answer ready. "That's entirely possible. The cache is so large that our agent didn't have time to inspect every crate and container, much less catalog every component. However, his preliminary report suggests that some of the devices may not have been available to the Confederacy during the war."

"Accepting that at face value for the moment," Dangor went on, "what importance do you attach to this technological trove?"

Colonel Yularen took over for Ison. "My lords, ISB fears that political dissenters may be planning to launch a propaganda operation similar to the wartime Shadowfeeds but directed, of course, against the Empire."

Close to Tarkin's age—though with more gray in his hair and especially in his bushy mustache—Yularen had traded a distinguished career in the Republic Navy for a position in Imperial Security, heading a division devoted to exposing instances of sedition in the Senate. He now served as a liaison between ISB and Military Intelligence. But not everyone in the audience chamber was touched by the colonel's justified concerns. In fact, Greejatus appeared to be *cackling*.

"That's a bit far-fetched, Colonel," he managed to say, "even for ISB."

"Has there been any evidence of HoloNet tampering that might support such a claim?" Dangor asked in a more serious tone.

"Yes, there has," Yularen said, though without explanation or so much as a glance in Tarkin's direction.

Vice Admiral Rancit stepped forward to speak. "My lords, while Naval Intelligence agrees with ISB regarding the possibility of Holo-Net sabotage, we feel that Deputy Director Ison is understating the importance of the evidence and the real nature of the threat. Yes, Count Dooku succeeded in using the HoloNet for Separatist propaganda purposes, but Republic forces were quick to shut down those Shadowfeeds." He looked at Ison. "If memory serves, COMPNOR itself was established as a result of the navy's actions at the time."

"No one in this chamber needs a history lesson, Vice Admiral," Ison interrupted. "Do you actually intend to go down that path?"

Rancit made a calming gesture. Exceedingly tall, he had a full head of jet-black hair and the symmetrical facial features of a HoloNet idol. The fit of his uniform was equal to if not superior to the fit of Tarkin's.

"I'm merely pointing out that Naval Intelligence should not be left out of the loop here," Rancit said. "For all anyone knows, this newly discovered cache is merely part of a much more sinister plot—one that could require military intervention."

Ison shot Rancit a polar look. "You weren't worried about the cache when it was first brought to your attention. Now all of a sudden you're convinced that it's part of a plot against the Empire?"

Rancit spread his hands theatrically. "What became of opening the matter to discussion, Deputy Director?"

Tarkin smiled to himself. His history with Rancit went back even farther than his history with Yularen. Rancit had been born in the Outer Rim, had graduated from the naval academy on Prefsbelt, and served as an intelligence case officer and station chief during the Clone Wars, dispatching operatives to Separatist-occupied worlds to foment resistance movements. After the war, he had commanded Sentinel Base during the mobile battle station's initial stage of construction, while Tarkin had been busy doling out punishments to former Separatist worlds. Replaced at Sentinel by Tarkin—a circumstance Rancit's rivals enjoyed interpreting as a demotion—he had been reassigned by the Emperor himself to head Naval Intelligence. Fond of art and opera, he was a very visible presence on Coruscant, though few were aware of the covert nature of his work.

As the backbiting between Rancit and Ison continued, Tarkin was tempted to raise his eyes to the podium to see if the Emperor was smiling, since it was his policy to encourage misunderstanding as a means of having his subordinates keep watch over one another. A form of institutionalized suspicion, the policy had proven an efficient fear tactic. He recalled Nils Tenant's wariness in the Palace corridors. The competition for status and privilege and the jockeying for position brought to mind the waning years of the Republic, but with one major difference: Where during the Republic era cachet could be purchased, present-day power was at the whim of the Emperor.

"Now who's understating the risk," Ison was saying, "despite abundant evidence to the contrary?"

Rancit kept his head. "We would have been glad to step aside and allow ISB full oversight if not for recent events." He made no secret of looking directly at Tarkin.

"What recent events?" Dangor asked, glancing back and forth between Rancit and Tarkin.

Mas Amedda banged his staff on the floor in a call for quiet. "Governor Tarkin, if you please," he said.

Tarkin stepped out from between Amedda and Vader to place himself where everyone in the chamber could see him.

"As regards the matter of whether ISB, Naval Intelligence, or some combination of our various intelligence agencies should be tasked with the investigation, I offer no opinion. I will allow, however, that the concerns of Deputy Director Ison and Vice Admiral Rancit are warranted. A base under my command was recently attacked by unknown parties. The attack followed the successful sabotaging of a HoloNet relay station and the insertion of both prerecorded and real-time holovids, in an attempt to mislead us into dispatching reinforcements to a secondary base. The details of my after-action report are available to anyone here with proper clearance, but suffice it to say that if a connection exists between the discovery on Murkhana and the sneak attack on the base, then it stands to reason that something more nefarious than anti-Imperial propaganda may be in the works."

Ison nearly groaned, and the Emperor's advisers conferred in confidence before Dangor said: "With all due respect, Governor Tarkin, it is my understanding that this base you go to some lengths to leave unidentified is far removed from Murkhana—on the order of several sectors."

Tarkin gestured negligently. "Irrelevant. Communications devices are cobbled together in one place to be deployed elsewhere. What's more, we've seen incidents of attack in many sectors these past five years."

"By pirates and outlaws," Greejatus said.

Tarkin shook his head. "Not in every instance."

"The Separatist war machines were shut down," Dangor went on. "Their droid warships were confiscated or destroyed."

"Most were," Tarkin said. "Clearly, some escaped our notice or were made available by insiders to a host of new enemies."

Ison glared at him. "Are you accusing ISB—"

"Review my report," Tarkin said, cutting Ison off.

"Furthermore, not every Separatist warship was crewed by droids," Rancit said. "As Governor Tarkin can attest, our navy was still chasing Separatist holdouts as late as a year ago."

Sate Pestage, who had remained silent throughout the meeting, spoke up. "Governor Tarkin, we're curious to know how you knew you were being deceived at your base of operations." With his shaved head, pointed chin beard, and raking eyebrows, Pestage resembled some of the pirates Outland had chased through the Seswenna.

Rancit stepped forward before Tarkin could utter a word. "May I, Wilhuff?"

Tarkin nodded and stepped back.

"Governor Tarkin—*Moff* Tarkin," Rancit began, "back when he was merely *Commander* Tarkin, was personally instrumental in frustrating Count Dooku's propaganda efforts. I know this to be fact because I was the case officer who supplied him with counterintelligence operatives. No doubt he was able to identify specific elements of corruption in the false holofeed—corruption even the Separatists were unable to purge from their intrusion signals." He turned to Tarkin. "How am I doing?"

Tarkin nodded in appreciation. "My lords, that is the long and short of it. I recognized telltale noise in the holovid and knew then that the feed was originating at the HoloNet relay station and not being transmitted from our auxiliary base." He paused to glance around the chamber. "Regardless, my first recommendation to the Joint Chiefs would be to issue an advisory to our base commanders that they should double-check the encryption codes of all Imperial HoloNet transmissions."

Again the advisers leaned toward one another to confer, while Ison exchanged rancorous looks with Rancit and Screed. Tarkin returned to where he had been standing with Vader, who simply cast a downward gaze at him. After a long moment, Mas Amedda's staff struck the floor with finality.

"The Emperor will take the matter under advisement."

AS ABOVE, SO BELOW

"RISE, LORD VADER."

Vader stood from his genuflection and joined his Master, Darth Sidious, at the railing of the central spire's west-facing veranda. Roofed but otherwise open to the sky, the small balcony—one of four identical overlooks, each oriented to a cardinal direction—crowned a finlike architectural projection located several tiers below the spire's rounded summit. The air was thin, and a persistent wind tugged at Sidious's robes and Vader's long cape.

The briefing in the audience chamber had ended hours earlier, and just now that part of Coruscant was tipping into night. The long shadows of distant cloudcutters seemed to reach in vain for the gargantuan Palace, and the sky was swathed in swirls of flaming orange and velvety purple.

When the two Sith Lords had stood in silence for some time, Vader said, "What is thy bidding, Master?"

Sidious spoke without turning from the view. "You will accompany Moff Tarkin to Murkhana to investigate this so-called cache of communications devices. You will report your findings directly to me, and I will decide what if any information needs to be conveyed to our spies and military. I won't have Ison and the others muddying the waters by conducting their own inquiries."

Vader took a moment to reply. "The governor's presence is unnecessary, Master."

Sidious swung to his apprentice, his eyes narrowed in interest. "You surprise me, Lord Vader. You have carried out previous missions with Moff Tarkin. Has he done something to prompt your disfavor?"

"Nothing, Master."

The Emperor exhaled with purpose. "A reply that conveys nothing. Provide me with a satisfactory reason."

Vader looked down at him, the sound of his regulated breathing diminished by the howl of the high-altitude wind. "Moff Tarkin should be ordered to return to Sentinel Base and resume his duties there."

"Ah, so you're arguing on Tarkin's behalf, are you?"

"For the Empire, Master."

"The Empire?" Sidious repeated, miming surprise. "Since when do you put the needs of the Empire before *our* needs?"

Vader crossed his gauntleted hands in front of him. "Our needs supersede all, Master."

"Then why do you contradict me?"

"I apologize, Master. I will do as you have commanded."

"No—not good enough," Sidious snapped. "Of course you will do as I command, and of course Moff Tarkin needs to resume his duties on the Sentinel moon. The sooner the battle station is completed, the sooner you and I can devote ourselves to more pressing matters— matters *only* you and I can investigate and that have little to do with the *Empire*."

Vader allowed his hands to hang at his sides. "Then why is Murkhana important, Master?"

Darth Sidious moved from the railing to a chair snugged up against the spire's curved wall and sat down. "Do you not find it intriguing that both you and Moff Tarkin have ties to the very planet where this newly discovered cache of jamming devices has been found? Tarkin, to quash Dooku's Shadowfeeds, and you—in one of your first missions, I seem to recall—to effect an execution. Or perhaps you feel that no connections exist, that this is mere coincidence."

Vader knew the reply. "There are no coincidences, Master."

"And *that*, my apprentice, is why Murkhana matters to us. Because the dark side of the Force has for whatever reason brought that world to our attention once more—as you should well understand."

Vader turned his back to the railing, and the wind wrapped his cape around him. "Which of us would be in command of the mission, Master?"

A sudden glint in his eye, Sidious shrugged. "I thought I would allow you and Moff Tarkin to work that out."

"Work that out."

"Yes," Sidious continued. "Reach a compromise, of sorts."

"I understand, Master."

Sidious's tortured face was a mask. "I wonder if you do . . . But let us return to Moff Tarkin for a moment. Has it never struck you that all three of us—you and Tarkin and I, the Empire's architects, if you will—hail from worlds that occupy but a narrow slice of galactic space? Naboo, Tatooine, Eriadu . . . all within an arc of less than thirty degrees."

Vader said nothing.

"Come, Darth Vader, you of all people should accept that some are born for greatness. That some are larger than life."

Vader remained silent.

"Yes, Lord Vader—*Tarkin*." Sidious softened his tone. "You are a true Sith, Lord Vader. Your dedication is unerring and your powers unparalleled. Perhaps, however, you are under the misimpression that only Sith and Jedi have trials to pass."

"What trials has Governor Tarkin passed?"

"Have you never been to Eriadu?"

"I have."

"Then you know what that world is like. Venture outside the safe haven of Eriadu City and the land is every bit as bleak and hostile as Tatooine. That land forged Tarkin in much the same way Tatooine forged you."

Vader shook his head. "Tatooine did not forge me."

Sidious stared at him, then grinned faintly. "Ah, I see. Slavery and the desert forged Skywalker. Is that what you mean?"

Vader left the question unanswered. "What trials did Tarkin endure?"

Sidious took a long moment to respond. "Trials that helped transform him into the military mastermind he has become."

Vader was silent for a moment. Then he said, "We will go to Murkhana, Master, as you command."

Sidious tilted his head to regard Vader. "Sometimes there is more to be gained by stepping into a trap than by avoiding it. Particularly when you're interested in learning who set it."

"Are you suggesting that Murkhana is a trap?"

"I'm suggesting that you pay close attention to what you and Moff Tarkin uncover there. Getting to the heart of this matter may require us to peel away layer upon layer of purpose."

Vader bowed his head in a gesture of obedience.

Sidious pressed the tips of his fingers together. "Do you know why Tarkin's ship is named the *Carrion Spike*?"

"I do not, Master."

Sidious looked past Vader to the darkening sky. "You should ask him."

On being informed of the Murkhana mission by Mas Amedda, Tarkin had contacted Commander Cassel to say that he would be delayed in returning to Sentinel Base, and had sent everyone but the *Carrion Spike*'s captain and communications officer back to the moon. For the moment, the crew would be limited to the dozen stormtroopers Vader had handpicked to accompany them. Amedda hadn't said whether he or Vader had command of the mission, and Tarkin was trying to puzzle that out on his own. Vader held an invisible rank. But the *Carrion Spike* was Tarkin's ship, which gave him authority. Tarkin was also a Moff, but the title alone didn't grant him jurisdiction in the sector to which Murkhana belonged. Disdain crept into his thoughts. That Vader was a Sith shouldn't factor into the question of authority, and yet how could Vader's dark side powers and crimson lightsaber *not* factor into the matter?

The whole business had the taint of *politics*.

Twenty years earlier, Tarkin had been on a career track to be appointed provost marshal of the Judicial Department when he resigned his rank and position. Coruscant at the time had been in the throes of an economic upswing for those senators, lobbyists, and entrepreneurs who had placed themselves at the service of the galactic industrial conglomerates. Availing itself of loopholes built into the free trade zone legislation, the monolithic Trade Federation was expanding its reach into the Outer Rim, as well as its influence in the Republic Senate. Against expectation, Finis Valorum's supporters had managed to secure his reelection to the Republic chancellery, but Valorum was scarcely a year into his second term when the citizens of Coruscant began to place bets on whether he would be able to hold on to his office. Palpatine's name was already being whispered as someone who might replace Valorum as Supreme Chancellor.

Tarkin and Palpatine had had only sporadic in-person contact during the years of Tarkin's service with the Judicials, but they had been faithful correspondents, and Palpatine had remained a staunch supporter of legislation that benefited Eriadu and the Seswenna sector. When Tarkin asked to meet with him on Coruscant, Palpatine made the travel arrangements. Tarkin was one of few people to be on a first-name basis with the senator, but out of respect for his elder and mentor of a sort, he most often referred to him by his title.

"You need a new battlefield," Palpatine said after he had listened in silence to Tarkin's tale of disillusionment. "I sensed from the moment we met that the Judicial Department was too insular to contain a man of your talents—despite your having garnered a following superseding the one you attained at Sullust."

They were sitting in stylish chairs in the senator's red-roomed apartment in one of Coruscant's most prestigious buildings.

"The Judicials are at the end of their tenure, in any case, as the Jedi seem to have become the Senate's arbiters of choice." Palpatine shook his head ruefully. "The Order has been given approval to intercede in matters it normally would have avoided. But complicated times beget wrongheaded decisions." He blew out his breath and looked at Tarkin. "As I told you so many years ago at Sullust, Eriadu will always be a Tarkin world, no matter who resides in the governor's mansion. Now more than ever, your homeworld needs the guidance of a leader who is astute in both politics and galactic economics."

"Why now?" Tarkin asked.

"Because something dangerous is brewing in our little corner of the Outer Rim. Discontent is on the rise, as are criminal enterprises and mercenary groups in the employ of self-serving corporations. In the Seswenna sector, several lommite mining concerns are vying for the attention of the Trade Federation, which is determined to forge a monopoly in the free trade zones. Even on my own Naboo, the king finds himself embroiled with the Trade Federation and offworld bankers with regard to our plasma exports."

Palpatine held Tarkin's gaze. "Ours are remote worlds, but what transpires in those sectors of the Outer Rim could very well have galactic repercussions. Eriadu needs you, and, perhaps more to the point, we need someone like you on Eriadu."

Palpatine's use of the plural was more than an affectation, and yet as close as their relationship had become, the senator never spoke in detail of those like-minded friends and allies he frequently alluded to. Not that that had kept his political opponents from speculating. Aside from the cabal of senators with whom he was often grouped— along with a following of devoted aides who had followed him from Naboo—Palpatine was rumored to have wide-ranging links to a host of shadowy beings and clandestine organizations that included bankers, financiers, and industrialists representing the most important sectors of the galaxy.

"I've been away from Eriadu for many years," Tarkin said. "The Valorum dynasty enjoys an influential presence there, and a political victory by me can hardly be assured. Especially given what happened on Coruscant."

Palpatine waved his thin hand in negligence and what seemed annoyance. "Valorum didn't *win* the election; he was merely *allowed* to win. The Senate's special-interest groups require a chancellor who

can be easily entangled in bureaucratic double-talk and arcane procedure. That is how loopholes are maintained and illegalities overlooked. But as regards your doubts, we have sufficient funds to
counter the Valorums and guarantee your victory." He fixed Tarkin
with a gimlet stare. "Perhaps you and I could serve each other, as well
as the Republic, by taking Valorum down a notch." His shoulders
heaved in a shrug of uncertainty. "With the backing of your family,
you may not even need our help, but rest assured that we will bolster
you if necessary." Palpatine quirked a sly smile. "You will be Eriadu's
finest leader, Wilhuff."

"Thank you, Sheev," Tarkin said, with obvious sincerity, and using
Palpatine's given name. "I will do what's best for my homeworld, and
for the Republic—in any manner you deem fit."

Palpatine's words about Naboo and Eriadu turned out to be pro-
phetic.

After the Naboo Crisis and Palpatine's election as Supreme Chancellor, many of Tarkin's former Judicial peers would pin their hopes
on Palpatine to keep the Republic from splintering. But the Separatist movement grew only stronger, and Tarkin and others were forced
to accept that Palpatine, for all his talents, had come to power too
late. Social injustices and trade inequities prompted hundreds of star
systems to secede from the Republic, and local skirmishes became
the norm. And then came war—a war that soon raged across the
galaxy.

Owing to its strategic location in the Outer Rim and its geopoliti-
cal alliances, Eriadu found itself in a thorny situation with regard to
the Republic and the Separatists. Perhaps Governor Tarkin, too,
should have found himself in a quandary. But in fact, there was never
a question as to whose ambitions he was ultimately going to serve.

Dawn the following morning, Tarkin went to the Palace landing field
to ready the *Carrion Spike* for the voyage to Murkhana, only to find
Vader and a contingent of stormtroopers already on the scene. Unen-
cumbered by helmets or armor, most of the bodysuited soldiers were
engaged in overseeing the transfer of a featureless black sphere from
a *Victory*-class Star Destroyer into one of the larger of the *Carrion*

Spike's cargo holds. Some three meters in diameter, the sphere was flattened on the bottom, and evidently made to nestle in a hexagonal base that was also being lifted toward the corvette. Vader was pacing beneath the repulsorlift cranes in what was either agitation or concern. When the stormtrooper operating the equipment accidentally allowed the flattened sphere to bang against the edge of the cargo hold's retracted hatch, Vader stamped forward with his gloved hands clenched.

"I warned you to be careful!" he shouted up at the trooper.

"My apologies, Lord Vader. Wind shear from—"

"Excuses won't suffice, Sergeant Crest," Vader cut him off. "Perhaps you are aging too quickly to remain on active duty."

Tarkin couldn't make sense of the remark until he realized that Crest's was a face he had seen countless times during the war—the face of an original Kamino clone trooper. The bareheaded others comprising Vader's squad were human regulars who had enlisted after the war.

"It won't happen again, Lord Vader," Crest said.

"For your sake it won't," Vader warned.

Tarkin turned his gaze from Vader to the dangling black sphere, unsure about just what he was looking at. A weapon, a laboratory, a personal toilet, a hyperbaric chamber—some merger of the three? Had Vader become reliant on the sphere in the same way he was on the transpirator and helmet? Perhaps the chamber was nothing more than a private space in which he could temporarily free himself from the confines of the suit.

Whatever the sphere was, it lacked a proper hatch, though two longitudinal seams appeared to indicate that the device was capable of parting. Tarkin glanced at Vader again: gauntleted fists on his hips, black cloak snapping in the wind whipped up by departing warships, the morning light reflecting off the top of his glossy, flaring helmet. He was being as short with his men as Tarkin had been with his during the jump to Coruscant. Worse, Vader was clearly as irritated as Tarkin was about having been tasked to head for Murkhana.

Vader seemed to regain his composure as the sphere and its platform were successfully lowered into the cargo hold. A trio of stormtroopers was already uncoiling cables with which to link the device to the *Carrion Spike*'s power plant. Passing close to Tarkin on his way to the ship's boarding ramp, Vader paused to say, "This shouldn't take a moment, Governor. Then we can be on our way."

Tarkin nodded. "Take as long as you need, Lord Vader. Murkhana isn't going anywhere."

Vader stared at him before marching off.

That look again, Tarkin thought—or at least that *suggestion* of a look that always made him feel as if Vader knew him from some previous life.

"*We no longer speak of the Jedi,*" Mas Amedda had said when they had watched Vader issue his warnings to members of Coruscant's underworld. It struck Tarkin now that the Chagrian's attitude wasn't one that was confined to the Emperor's court. In the five short years since the Order had been eradicated—Jedi Masters, Jedi Knights, and Jedi Padawans wiped out by the very clone troopers they had commanded and fought beside—the Jedi already seemed a distant memory.

Despite their refusal to come to Eriadu's aid against pirates, Tarkin had respected the Jedi as peacekeepers, but as generals they had proven failures. The Jedi Master with whom he had served most closely during the Clone Wars was Even Piell, to whom Tarkin's cruiser had been assigned. Brusque and bellicose, the Lannik excelled in lightsaber combat, seeming to have integrated every possible fighting style, but he, too, had his flaws as a strategist. If Piell had deferred to Tarkin during their mission to investigate a hyperlane shortcut into Separatist-held space, they might have avoided capture and imprisonment, and perhaps the Lannik would have survived at least until the end of the war.

The Force had endowed the Jedi with wondrous powers, but their biggest failing was in not having used the Force in all ways possible to bring the war to a quick end. By remaining faithful to their ethical code, they had allowed the war to drag on and spiral downward into a meaningless bloodbath. The conflict's sudden conclusion and the Order's decision to depose Supreme Chancellor Palpatine had taken nearly everyone by surprise. But Tarkin suspected that even if the

Jedi had restrained themselves from rising against Palpatine in his moment of glory, the esoteric Order had doomed itself to extinction. Where their flame had burned bright for a thousand generations, technological might was the new standard.

Tarkin had never been able to make sense of the Clone Wars, in any case. A battle on Geonosis, an army of clones springing up out of nowhere . . . Almost from the beginning he had suspected that an elite outsider, or a group of elite outsiders, had been tampering with or manipulating events; that the battles had been waged in support of a surreptitious agenda. In the meandering prewar conversations Tarkin had had with Count Dooku, the former Jedi had never made a convincing case for Separatism, much less for galactic war. If, as some claimed, Dooku had never actually left the Jedi Order, why then hadn't the Jedi thrown in with the Separatists from the start?

In their final meeting, only weeks before the Battle of Geonosis and the official outbreak of the Clone Wars, Dooku had tried to persuade Tarkin to bring Eriadu into the Confederacy of Independent Systems.

By then Tarkin's homeworld had transformed itself into a major trade center along the Hydian Way. With the Trade Federation monopoly on Outer Rim shipping broken as a result of the Naboo Crisis, and the loss of prestige suffered by Valorum Shipping as the result of scandals and Finis Valorum's truncated term as supreme chancellor, Eriadu Mining and Shipping was prospering beyond the wildest dreams of the Tarkin family. Tarkin himself was just completing his second term as planetary governor and was being urged by many to run for a seat in the Republic Senate, even while many of his academy friends—convinced that a war between the Republic and the Separatists was inevitable—were urging him to leave himself open to the possibility that the Military Creation Act could be pushed through the Senate, and a Republic Navy instated.

Count Dooku of Serenno had been most responsible for bringing the galaxy's disenfranchised worlds under one umbrella. Tarkin had never known him when he had been one of the Jedi Order's most dashing duelists, but they had met shortly after the count's quiet disaffiliation, introduced to each other on Coruscant by Kooriva senator Passel Argente, who would himself go on to become a member of the Separatist leadership. Tarkin was intrigued by the tall, charismatic count, not so much because he had been a Jedi but because he had surrendered a family fortune that would have guaranteed him a place among the galaxy's most powerful and influential beings. During that first meeting, however, they had spoken not of wealth but of politics and the escalating tensions that had been stirred by trade inequities and intersystem conflicts. Tarkin agreed with Dooku that the Republic was in danger of imploding, but he held that a supervising government—even if ineffectual—was preferable to anarchy and a fractured galaxy.

For some eight years following his leave-taking from the Jedi Order, Dooku was scarcely heard from. Amid rumors about his fomenting political turmoil on a host of worlds, most people were convinced that he had gone into self-exile, intent on founding an offshoot of the Jedi Order. Instead he had staged a theatrical return to public life by commandeering a HoloNet station in the Raxus system and delivering a rousing speech that condemned the Republic and essentially set the stage for the Separatist movement. Moving about in secrecy—some said one step ahead of assassins hired by Republic interests—Dooku became the focus of galactic attention, backing coups on Ryloth, meddling in the affairs of Kashyyyk, Sullust, Onderon, and many other worlds, and spurning all opportunities to negotiate with Supreme Chancellor Palpatine.

Chiefly because of its location at the confluence of the Hydian Way and the Rimma Trade Route, Eriadu became something of a contested world early on, and as adjacent and neighboring sectors seceded or joined the Separatists, Tarkin found himself pressured by both sides to declare his loyalties. Dooku went out of his way to meet with Tarkin on several occasions, as if to demonstrate that he had taken a personal interest in Eriadu's future. In fact, having already laid the groundwork for the creation of a southern Separatist sphere by bringing Yag'Dhul and Sluis Van over to his side, he needed Eriadu to seal the deal. If Dooku could achieve in the Greater Seswenna what he had achieved elsewhere, he could effectively collapse the Core back into itself, reversing the expansion that had resulted from millennia of space exploration, conquest, and colonization.

At each meeting Dooku had emphasized that for most of its history Eriadu had either been ignored by or been at the economic mercy of the Core. Having forged its own destiny, it owed no allegiance to Coruscant. But on the occasion of their final meeting, threat replaced persuasion. Recent turmoil at Ando and Ansion had left the galaxy staggered, and Dooku seemed caught up in the feverish rush of events. Still, he had arrived on Eriadu in his usual caped finery, elegant and urbane. At Tarkin's residence overlooking the bay and the glittering lights of the distant shore, they dined on foods prepared by Tarkin family chefs and rare wines provided by the gray-bearded count. Even so, Dooku was restless throughout, ultimately dropping his guise to storm from the long table to the balcony railing, where he whirled on Tarkin.

"I need an answer, Governor," he began. "This is a pleasant evening and I have always enjoyed your company, but circumstances demand that we conclude the matter of Eriadu's commitment."

Tarkin set his napkin and wineglass down and joined him at the balcony. "What has happened to bring this to a head?"

"An imminent crisis," Dooku allowed. "I can't say more."

"But I can. I suspect that you are now close to persuading your secret allies to initiate an economic catastrophe."

Dooku's response was limited to a faint smile, so Tarkin continued.

"Eriadu's friendships are wide ranging. Nothing happens in this or any other sector without our knowledge."

"Which is precisely why your world is so important to our cause," Dooku said. "But sometimes economic pressures are not enough to guarantee success—as you well know, Governor. Or do you believe you could simply have bought off the pirates who harassed this sector for so long? Of course not. Eriadu established the Outland Regions Security Force to deal with them. You went to war."

"Is war what you have in the works?"

Instead of answering the question directly, Dooku said, "Consider

Eriadu's current situation. I realize that you have been successful in shipping lommite through Malastare, and circling around Bestine to reach Fondor and the Core. But where will Eriadu be when Fondor opts to join the Confederacy?"

"Opts to join, or falls to you?"

"Join us and you can continue to transact business in Confederacy spheres—through Falleen, Ruusan, all the way to the Tion sectors." He paused. "Is your friend and benefactor on Coruscant in any position to offer you a similar guarantee, with the Core contracting around him?"

"The Supreme Chancellor is not required to bribe me into remaining loyal to him."

"As a complement to previous bribes, you mean. In allowing your illegal actions in the Seswenna to go completely unchecked since you abetted in the undermining of Finis Valorum." Dooku snorted in scorn. "A strong leader would never have allowed galactic events to reach a point of crisis. He is weak and inadequate."

Tarkin shook his head negatively. "He is hemmed in by a corrupt and incompetent Senate. Otherwise the Republic would have already raised a military to oppose you."

"Ah, but the end of his second term is upon him, Governor, with no one of any merit to succeed him. Unless, of course . . . some crisis results in his term being extended."

Tarkin tried to decipher the count's inference. "One might almost conclude that you're positing an *advantage* to going to war. But how would that work? The volunteer security forces of the Confederate worlds against—what, Judicials and ten thousand of your former Jedi brethren?"

Dooku adopted an arrogant expression. "Don't be too surprised, Governor, if the Republic has access to secret forces."

Tarkin regarded him in open astonishment. "Mercenaries?"

"*Proxies* is perhaps a more accurate term."

"Then you have already committed to war."

"I am committed to the idea of a galaxy ruled by an enlightened leader, with laws that apply universally—not one set for the Core Worlds, another for the Outer Rim worlds."

"An autocracy," Tarkin said. "Guided by the count of Serenno."

Dooku gestured in dismissal. "I am ambitious, but not to that degree."

"Who, then?" Tarkin pressed.

"We'll leave that for another day. I'm simply trying to keep you from finding yourself on the losing side."

Tarkin studied him. "Will there actually be a losing side for men like you and me? I sometimes suspect that this crisis is a mere charade."

Dooku appraised him. "Would you be opposed to being part of a charade if it meant that the galaxy could be brought under the rule of one?"

Tarkin regarded him for a long moment. "I wonder what you mean, Dooku."

The count nodded in assessment. "I may not be able to forestall repercussions, Governor, but should this situation escalate to war between the Confederacy and the Republic, I will do my best to see that no lasting harm comes to your homeworld."

Tarkin's brows beetled. "Why would you?"

"Because in the end, you and I are likely to find ourselves under the same roof."

Tarkin had long wondered why Dooku's prophecy had never come to pass. It was the Separatists who had wound up on the losing side, along with Dooku and, most unexpectedly, the entire Jedi Order, and the Emperor and Tarkin who had found themselves under the same roof.

"The *Carrion Spike* has launched, Your Majesty," 11-4D told Darth Sidious.

The droid resembled a protocol model, except for its several arms, only two of which terminated in what might be considered hands; the rest were devoted to tools of varied purpose, including computer interface and power charge extensions. The droid had once been the property of Sidious's tutor, Plagueis, and had been in Sidious's possession since his former master's death, though in several different guises.

The announcement roused Sidious from meditation, and he took a moment to reach out to Vader, his perturbed apprentice.

"Alert me when the ship makes planetfall on Murkhana," Sidious said.

The droid bowed its head. "I will, Your Majesty."

The two of them were in Sidious's lair, a small rock-walled enclosure beneath the deepest of the Palace's several sublevels that had once been an ancient Sith shrine. That the Jedi had raised their Temple over the shrine had for a thousand years been one of the most closely guarded secrets of those Sith Lords who had perpetuated and implemented the revenge strategy of the Jedi Order's founders. Even the most powerful of Dark Side Adepts believed that shrines of that sort existed only on Sith worlds remote from Coruscant, and even the most powerful of the Jedi believed that the power inherent in the shrine had been neutralized and successfully capped. In truth, that power had seeped upward and outward since its entombment, infiltrating the hallways and rooms above, and weakening the Jedi Order much as the Sith Masters themselves had secretly infiltrated the corridors of political power and toppled the Republic.

Save for Sidious, no sentient being in close to five thousand years had set foot in the shrine. The room's excavation and restoration had been carried out by machines under the supervision of 11-4D. Even Vader was unaware of the shrine's existence. But it was here that they would one day work together the way Sidious and Plagueis had to coax from the dark side its final secrets. In the intervening years he had actually come to appreciate Plagueis for the planner and prophet he had been. Such perilous machinations required two Sith, one to serve as bait for the dark side, the other to be the vessel. Success would grant them the power to harness the full powers of the dark side, and allow them to rule for ten thousand years.

Sidious found himself unable to return to his meditations. Stretching out with his feelings, he endeavored to assess the mood aboard the *Carrion Spike*. Vader had made clear his thoughts about the mission, but Sidious had learned from Vizier Amedda that Tarkin, too, was displeased with the assignment. During the Clone Wars, Sidious had made every attempt to promote a rapport between Skywalker and Tarkin, but the relationship had never prospered to his satisfaction. Then came that business with Skywalker's Togruta apprentice, Ahsoka Tano, which, while it had provoked further disaffection in Skywalker, had also created a rift between him and Tarkin that perhaps had yet to mend. Yes, they had partnered since the end of the war, but—to Sidious's own annoyance—absent a true appreciation for each other's talents.

Well, if they were going to continue to serve him, Sidious thought, it was long past time that they found a way to work out their differences.

The fact that Sidious held Tarkin in such approbation made the matter all the more wearisome. They had met several years after Sidious—still an apprentice of Darth Plagueis at the time—had been appointed Naboo's representative to the Republic Senate. Despite the fact that Naboo and Eriadu were very different Outer Rim worlds, Sidious had recognized Tarkin, some twenty years his junior, as a fellow colonial. And more: a human who had the potential to become a powerful ally, not only with regard to Sidious's political ambitions, but also in helping to implement his true agenda of destroying the Jedi Order.

Toward that end, Sidious had brought Tarkin into the fold early on, even facilitating a meeting between Tarkin and many influential Coruscanti, if only to solicit their opinions of Eriadu's local hero. The more Sidious investigated Tarkin's past—his unusual upbringing and exotic rites of passage—the more he grew to feel that Tarkin's thinking about the Republic and about leadership itself was in keeping with his own, and Tarkin hadn't disappointed him. When Sidious had asked for help in weakening Supreme Chancellor Valorum so that Sidious himself could win election to the position, Tarkin had stonewalled Valorum's attempts to investigate the disastrous events of an Eriadu trade summit, thereby helping to foment and hasten the Naboo Crisis. Tarkin had remained loyal during the Clone Wars as well, enlisting in the military on the side of the Republic, despite repeated entreaties by Count Dooku—which Sidious had arranged as a test of Tarkin's dedication.

Sidious assumed that Tarkin had puzzled out that Vader had once been Anakin Skywalker, under whom Tarkin had served during the war. Tarkin may also have determined that Vader was a Sith. If so, it followed that he accepted that Sidious was Vader's dark side Master. But Tarkin's intuitions were important only in the sense that he never revealed them and never allowed them to interfere with his own ambitions.

For his own sake as much as Tarkin's, Sidious had been careful to keep those ambitions in check. He understood that Tarkin was frustrated with his current position as sector governor and base commander, but overseeing construction of the mobile battle station was too grand an undertaking for any one person, even one of Tarkin's caliber. As powerful as the battle station might become, its real purpose was to serve as a tangible symbol and constant reminder of the power of the dark side, and to free Sidious from having to portray that part.

Darth Plagueis had once remarked that *"the Force can strike back."* The death of a star didn't necessarily curtail its light, and indeed Sidious could see evidence of that sometimes even in Vader—the barest flicker of persistent light. Attacks like the one directed against Tarkin's moon base and discoveries like the one on Murkhana were distractions to his ultimate goal of making certain that the Force *could not* strike back, and that whatever faint light of hope remained could be snuffed out for good.

A BETTER WOMP RAT TRAP

LIKE MANY FORMER Separatist bastions, Murkhana was a dying world. The lingering atmospheric effects of years of orbital bombardment and beam-weapon assaults had raised the temperature of the world's seas and killed off coastal coral reefs that had once drawn tourists from throughout the Tion Cluster. What had been wave-washed black beaches were now stretches of fathomless quicksand, and what had been sheltered coves were stagnant shallows, rife with gelatinous sea creatures that had risen to the evolutionary fore when the fish had died. Battered by relentless squalls of acid rain, the once graceful, spiraling structures of Murkhana City were pitted and cracked, and had turned the color of disease-ridden bone. Even when the rains ceased, menacing clouds hung over the bleached landscape, blotting out light and leaving the air smelling like rancid cheese. Descending through the atmosphere was like dropping into a simmering cauldron of witch's brew.

Below was what remained of the seaside hexagonal spaceport and the quartet of ten-kilometer-long bridges that had linked it to the city; the Corporate Alliance landing field was slagged and tipped on the massive piers that had supported it, and the bridges had collapsed into the frothing waters. Arriving starships were now directed to the city's original spaceport at the base of the hills.

"Governor Tarkin, we have a visual on the landing zone," the captain said as the ship pierced a final low-lying layer of dirty cloud, revealing the ravaged city spread out beneath them from sea to surrounding hills like some terrain exported from a nightmare. "Spaceport control says that it's up to us to find a place to set down, as their guidance systems are no longer in service and the terminal has been shut down. Immigration and customs have relocated to the inner city."

Tarkin shook his head in disgust. "I suspect no one makes use of them. What do our scanners tell us of the atmosphere?"

"Atmosphere is a mess, but breathable," the comm officer said, her eyes fixed on the sensor board. "Background radiation is at tolerable levels." Swiveling to Tarkin, she added, "Sir, you might want to consider wearing a transpirator."

Tarkin watched smoke pour into the sky from fires that might have been burning for six years. He considered the specialist's advice for a moment, gradually warming to the idea of being the only one among the mission personnel to be bareheaded, thus appearing more the commanding officer.

"Looking for an adequate site, Governor," the captain said.

Tarkin leaned toward the viewport to assess the landing field. It was impossible to tell the bomb craters from the circular repulsorlift pits that had once functioned as service areas for the Separatists' spherical core ships. The edges of the field were lined with ruined hemispherical docking bays and massive rectangular hangars, their roofs blown open or caved in. The façade of the sprawling terminal building had avalanched onto the field, and the interior had been gutted by fire. Ships of various size and function were parked at random, though most of them looked as if they hadn't seen space in a long while.

"Twenty-five degrees east," Tarkin said finally. "We'll have just enough room."

Vader entered the command cabin as repulsors were lowering the corvette toward the cracked permacrete.

"A world I never expected to see again," Tarkin said.

"Nor I, Governor," Vader said. "So let us be quick about it."

Tarkin scanned the immediate area as *Carrion Spike* began to settle on her landing gear and the instruments were shut down. Only a handful of starships occupied their corner of the uneven field, including a decrepit forty-year-old Judicial cruiser and a sleek and obviously rapid black frigate bristling with weapons, its broad bow designed to suggest slanting eyes and bloody fangs thrusting from a cruel mouth.

"Charming," Tarkin said. "And very much in keeping with the surroundings."

Wedging a brimmed command cap into the pocket of his tunic, he joined Vader and eight of the stormtroopers as they were filing from the ship. Barely through the air lock, he could already taste acid on his tongue. They had just reached the foot of the boarding ramp when a teetering low-altitude assault transport soared into view, its wing-mounted repulsorlift turbines straining as it dropped from the sky to hover alongside the *Carrion Spike*. Two Imperial stormtroopers in scratched and dented armor leapt from the open side hatch, while well-armed door gunners kept watch over the field.

"Welcome to Murkhana, sirs," their squad leader said, offering a lazy salute.

Tarkin heard stifled laughter from someone inside the gunship. Adorning the vehicle's vaned sliding hatch was the faded insignia of the Twelfth Army.

His posture reflecting obvious displeasure, Vader appraised the noisy gunship. "Are you certain that this relic is capable of carrying us, Squad Leader, or might *we* end up carrying *it*?"

The stormtrooper glanced over his shoulder at the gunship. "Sorry to report that we've no choice, Lord Vader. The rest are in even worse shape."

"Why is that?" Tarkin stepped forward to ask.

"Sabotage, sir. We're not well liked by the locals."

"No one asked them to like you, Squad Leader," Vader snapped. With a swirl of his cloak, he climbed aboard the gunship, followed by his personal stormtroopers.

Tarkin paused to comlink *Carrion Spike*'s captain. "We're leaving four stormtroopers to guard the ship. Keep the comlink open and contact me at the first sign of trouble."

"Acknowledged, Governor," the comm officer said.

Vader extended a hand to Tarkin and pulled him up onto the deteriorated deck plates of the gunship's deployment platform.

"Go," the Dark Lord shouted to the cockpit crew.

The gunship lifted shakily off the landing field and began to wheel toward the heart of Murkhana City. Placing himself behind one of the door gunners, Tarkin grabbed hold of an overhead strap and peered out the open hatchway.

He wasn't surprised to see that most of the city's charred, devastated buildings had yet to be demolished. Facing sanctions, the local government had not been able to grow the economy, and the substantially reduced population had been forced to rely on black marketeers for goods and resources. Rusting remnants of the war, carbon-scored Hailfire, spider, and crab droids stood idle in the desolate streets, picked clean of usable parts by gangs of scavengers. Scattered among them were a couple of burned-out Republic AT-TE and turbo tanks, along with a Trident transport. The hulk of a Commerce Guild warship protruded like a broken tooth close to what remained of the Argente Tower, which was itself a husk.

Breath-masked residents scurried for cover as the gunship raced over glass-littered avenues, past boarded-up storefronts, toppled monuments, and gloomy cantinas. Packs of famished animals roved the alleyways, and nearly every street corner hosted crews of smugglers and hoodlums. Tarkin caught glimpses of limping war veterans—Koorivar with broken cranial horns, Aqualish with missing tusks, and Gossams with crooked necks—along with children stricken with hideous birth defects.

As the gunship veered through a turn, a hunk of twisted metal slammed into the hatch's retracted door, hurled by a young woman who had stepped boldly from a lopsided doorway and stood in the street, hands on hips, as if challenging the Imperials to reply.

"Permission to exterminate, sir," one of the stormtroopers said, his blaster rifle braced against his shoulder.

Vader stretched out his gloved hand to lower the weapon. "We haven't come all this way to instigate a riot."

And yet two city blocks later, catching sight of defaced military recruitment posters and walls vandalized by hand-scrawled insults aimed at the Emperor, he turned to Tarkin to say: "We should put this place out of its misery."

"Too magnanimous," Tarkin said. "Though it may come to that."

The gunship began to shed velocity as it crossed a cratered plaza; it came to a hovering halt in the middle of a broad concourse obstructed by a collapsed coral archway.

"We're here, sirs," the squad leader said.

"Which building?" Tarkin asked, then followed the line of the stormtrooper's extended hand to see a squat structure with rounded corners three blocks away.

"Originally the property of the Corporate Alliance, sir," the squad leader continued. "A medcenter, until it was used to house a deflector shield generator that protected a vital Separatist landing platform."

"And the current proprietor?"

"Unknown, sir. The place has changed hands several times since the end of the war. Identities of the various owners are buried under layers of phony documentation."

"You have been maintaining surveillance?" Vader asked.

"Continuous since receiving orders from Coruscant three weeks back, Lord Vader. But we haven't observed anyone coming or going. The locals tend to steer clear of this entire area."

"Then you have no one in custody."

"No one, Lord Vader."

Tarkin's eyes clouded over with suspicion. "Yes, but who might have been watching you while you were watching the building?"

Vader nodded. "Yes, Governor, it might very well be a trap."

The stormtrooper indicated several nearby buildings. "We've installed rooftop snipers there, there, and there, Lord Vader."

"Are you carrying remotes?"

"We have a couple of AC-ones on board, along with an ASN retrofitted with a holotransmitter."

"Those will do. Prepare them."

The gunship touched down and Vader stepped from the deployment platform, all but floating to the buckled street. When his stormtroopers had followed, he turned to Sergeant Crest.

"Take four of your men and trail the remotes inside. We will monitor the holofeeds from here. Perform a full reconnaissance of the building, but do not enter the room where the devices are said to be located until we follow on your all-clear."

Crest saluted and pointed to four of the stormtroopers. By then the spherical remotes had already been tasked and were whirring off toward the building. The squad leader placed a handheld holoprojector on the deployment platform deck plates and enabled it. A moment later the device began receiving transmissions from one of the remotes. While Vader paced, Tarkin watched as illuminated views of narrow hallways and short staircases resolved above the holoprojector. The squad leader shifted feeds from one remote to the next, but the views and sounds remained largely unchanged: puddled hallways, dark stairwells, dripping water, creaking doors, indistinct noises that may have come from still-working machines.

Almost an hour passed before the voice of Sergeant Crest issued from the comlink of one of his subordinates. "Lord Vader, the building is clear. We're holding at the head of a corridor leading to the device storage room. I've tasked one of the remotes to guide you to our position."

Leaving the local stormtroopers to establish a perimeter outside the building, Tarkin, Vader, and the remainder of the Coruscant contingent entered, glow rods in hand as they trailed the tasked remote through some of the corridors and up and down some of the stairways they had been shown earlier. In short order they had rendezvoused with Crest and the others, fifty meters from massive, retrofitted sliding doors that appeared to seal the storeroom.

Vader gestured for the squad leader to send one of the remotes down the final stretch, then to follow with four of his troopers. Tarkin tracked their wary advance on the sliding doors, which Crest parted just widely enough to allow passage for the remote. When after a long moment the remote exited, Crest signaled for Vader, Tarkin, and the others to proceed.

First to reach the sliding doors, Vader came to a sudden halt.

"The remote found nothing untoward?" he asked Crest.

"Nothing, Lord Vader."

Vader's breathing filled the corridor. "Something . . ."

Tarkin watched him closely. Vader's exceptional instincts had alerted him to a threat of some sort. But what? He began to think through the holotransmissions of the remotes' dizzying exploration of the confused interior of the building. On every level the surveillance droids had reached dead ends similar to the one he, Vader, and the stormtroopers now faced. Did that mean that the storeroom was several stories high? Perhaps it had been an atrium before it became a storage space. Tarkin thought back to the squad leader's description of the building: *"A medcenter . . . Housed a deflector shield generator . . ."*

Tarkin couldn't imagine such an enormous piece of machinery having been assembled in place. Which could mean—

"Lord Vader, this isn't the primary entrance," he said.

Vader turned to him.

"Who would be fool enough to haul communications devices through these corridors and up and down these stairways?" Tarkin gestured upward with his chin. "I suspect they were delivered here through a rooftop access. The sliding doors could lead to an ambush of some sort."

Vader took a moment to consider it, then looked at Crest. "You've failed me again, Sergeant."

"Lord Vader, the remote—"

"The rooftop," Tarkin interrupted.

Vader glanced at him but said nothing.

They exited the building by the same route they had taken earlier. Once outside, Vader ordered the squad leader to call for the gunship, and all of them scampered up onto the deployment platform. On the building's flat roof they discovered a well-concealed and functional turbolift shaft, five meters in diameter, transparent, and safe to use. Surveying the vast room while they were descending, Tarkin spotted the remains of a reception counter centered among stacks of metal shipping containers and exposed machines.

"No one touches anything until I've had a look," he told the storm-troopers. "And take care where you walk. The doors may not be alone in being rigged."

While Vader, Crest, and some of the others moved off to investigate the secondary entrance, Tarkin, feeling as if he were stepping back in time, began to meander through the rows created by the stacked containers and devices.

It had been just nine months after the Battle of Geonosis that Count Dooku's scientists had succeeded in slicing into the Republic HoloNet by seeding the spaceways with hyperwave transceiver nodes of a novel design. The Separatists could have kept quiet about the infiltration and tasked the nodes to gather intelligence about Republic military operations. Instead, Dooku—as if suddenly intent on winning hearts and minds rather than defeating the Republic with his droid armies—began using the HoloNet to broadcast propaganda Shadowfeeds, providing Separatist accounts of battle wins and disinformation about Republic war crimes, and in the end spreading apprehension among the populations of the Core Worlds that a Separatist victory was imminent.

It was, however, Separatist success in jamming Republic communication relays that had brought Tarkin into play. Together with operatives of the Republic's fledgling cryptanalysis department and elements of the Twelfth Army, Tarkin had been sent to Murkhana both to spearhead the invasion and to oversee the dismantling of the Shadowfeed operation.

Running his hands now over S-thread jammers, signal eradicators, and HoloNet chafing devices, he recalled being among the first wave of clone trooper platoons to fight their way into the building that was the source of the Shadowfeeds; then, on overpowering the Separatist forces, torturing the captive scientists into revealing the secrets of their jamming and steganographic technology, and putting to death thousands of beings who had contributed to Dooku's scheme. The mission had constituted the first of Tarkin's covert operations undertaken for then supreme chancellor Palpatine. Murkhana had kicked off a year of similar successes—though it had ended in Tarkin's capture, torture, and incarceration in Citadel prison.

With the Emperor's proclamation of the New Order, some aspects of the HoloNet had come under strict Imperial control, as much to provide the military with exclusive communications networks as to censor unauthorized news feeds.

Tarkin was completing his initial survey of the components when Vader sought him out.

"The sliding doors were engineered to trigger a blast when opened fully," he said. "Odd that the remote failed to register the explosives."

Tarkin gestured to the stacks of devices. "Whoever assembled this array found a way to blind the remotes."

Vader looked around. "Imperial Security's operative made no mention of a rigged entrance."

Tarkin pinched his lower lip. "That could mean that the explosives were only recently installed."

"With the building under constant surveillance?"

"The street entrances, yes," Tarkin said. "Probably not the roof."

Vader absorbed that in silence, then said, "Puzzling, even so. All this merely to lure and murder an investigative team?"

"I doubt that the door trap was meant for us, Lord Vader."

"Intruders of a more ordinary sort? Would-be thieves, black marketeers?" Vader gazed about him in what struck Tarkin as mounting vexation. "Have you found any unfamiliar devices?"

"Not yet," Tarkin said.

"Then it is all too obvious. These devices were deliberately placed where they could be discovered. This is a stage set."

"Perhaps," Tarkin said. "But we're going to need to investigate every container to be certain there's nothing new among the devices. This cache may date from the war, but that doesn't negate that the components appear to be fully functional and capable of interrupting or corrupting HoloNet signals."

Vader was dismissive. "Technology that has been available for nearly a decade, Governor."

"The question is, why are these devices here?"

"Someone found them elsewhere and moved them here for safekeeping until their value could be determined."

"That would explain the rigged doors . . . ," Tarkin said. "But it's also possible that whoever originally found the cache made use of some of the components to engineer the false distress call transmitted to Sentinel Base."

Vader fell silent for a long moment, then said, "I agree. Your proposal, then?"

Tarkin glanced around. "We cam everything and record and transmit to Coruscant any serial numbers or markings we find. Any suspect components should be relocated to the *Carrion Spike* and also returned to Coruscant for further analysis. The rest should be destroyed."

Vader nodded in agreement.

Tarkin glanced around again and sighed with purpose. "We have our work cut out for us."

"The stormtroopers can see to most of it," Vader said. "There is someone I wish to speak with before we return to the Core."

Tarkin showed him a questioning look.

"The Imperial Security Bureau asset who first reported the find."

11

FAIR GAME

AS THE GUNSHIP SPED back toward the center of the city, Tarkin, gazing on the devastation, thought: This might have been Eriadu had he not warned the planetary leadership that supporting Dooku would have meant inviting cataclysm.

Not every member of the planet's ruling body had agreed with him, but in the end he'd gotten his way and Eriadu had remained loyal to the Republic. For Tarkin, though, the stewardship of his homeworld had come to an end. When word of his decision not to seek reelection became known, his aging and by then ailing father had summoned him to the family compound for a frank conversation.

"Politics hasn't been enough of a battleground for you?" his father had asked from the bed to which he was confined, his body punctured by feeding tubes and shunts. The view out the large window took in nearly all of the calm bay.

"More than enough," Tarkin said from a chair beside the bed. "But the immigration issues are solved, the economy is back on track, and our world is now thought of as a Core world in the Outer Rim." The adjoining room of the master suite had been transformed into a kind of intensive care unit, with a bacta tank and a team of medical droids standing by in the event the elder Tarkin should desire resuscitation.

"Granted," his father said. "That, however, does not mean that your work is done. A lot of people worked very hard to get you in office."

"I've done what I set out to accomplish and paid them back in full," Tarkin said more harshly than he intended. "Some more than they even deserve." He fell silent for a moment, then added: "I'm exasperated by having to appease so many separate interests and fight to have laws passed and enacted. Politics is worse than a theater of war."

His father snorted. "This from someone who has always preached the importance of law and rule by fear."

"That hasn't changed. But it has to be on my terms. What's more, Eriadu's internal problems scarcely matter in the present scheme of things. When I met last with Dooku, he made it sound as though galactic war is both inevitable and imminent."

"And why wouldn't he? In his determination to persuade you to throw in with his Separatists, he would make use of enticement, threats, whatever it takes."

Tarkin thought back through his recent conversation with the count, and shook his head. "There was something else on his mind, but I couldn't pry it from him. It was almost as if he was offering me an opportunity to join some secret fraternity of beings who are actually responsible for this mess."

His father seemed to consider it. "What will you do, then? Wait for the Republic to instate a military and enlist?" He shook his head in disgust. "You served in Outland, you served in the Judicial Department. Enlistment would be a backward step just when Eriadu needs you most. *Especially* if this schism leads to war. Who will be able to keep Eriadu safe should it fall to Dooku's forces?"

"That's precisely the point. There's only so much one can do with words and arguments."

"So you'll race to the light of the lasers. Wasn't that what you used to exclaim as an Outland commander?" His father managed a rueful laugh. "You may as well adopt it as a personal motto."

"Death or renown, Father. I am, after all, your son."

"So you are," his father said, slowly nodding his head. "Has the supreme chancellor remarked on your decision?"

Tarkin nodded. "Palpatine is in my corner, as it were."

"I was afraid of that." His father regarded him for a long moment. "I urge you think back to the Carrion, Wilhuff. When a pride's territory is threatened, the dominant beast stands its ground. It doesn't run off to enlist in a larger cause. You must think of Eriadu itself as the plateau."

Tarkin stared out the window, and then turned to face his father. "Jova told me a story that bears on my decision. Long before you were born—long before even Jova was born—a group of developers had designs on the Carrion and all those resource-rich lands the Tarkin family had amassed. Our ancestors initially attempted to resolve the matter peacefully. They attempted to placate the developers with credits. At one point, as Jova tells it, they were even prepared to offer the developers all the lands north of the Orrineswa River clear to Mount Veermok, but their offer was rejected in the strongest terms. For the developers, it was either the entire plateau and all the surrounding territory or none at all."

His father smiled weakly. "I know how this story ended."

Tarkin smiled back at him. "The Tarkins understood that they weren't going to keep their adversaries at bay by posting NO TRESPASSING signs or encircling the Carrion with plasma fences. Giving all evidence that they were prepared to capitulate, they lured the leadership of the conglomerate to the bargaining table."

"And assassinated them to a man," his father said.

"To a man. And that was the end of it."

His father took a deep breath and loosed a stuttering exhale. "I understand. But you're naïve to think that the Republic has the guts to do that with Dooku and the rest. Mark my words, this war will drag on and on until every world pays a price. And I'm glad I won't be around to see that happen."

The ambassador to Murkhana was waiting at the top of the ornate stairway that fronted the principal building of the Imperial compound. A tall, broad-shouldered woman, she was dressed appropriately for Murkhana, Tarkin thought, in that she was sporting stormtrooper armor.

Seemingly unable to decide whether to salute or bow as he and Vader approached, she simply spread her arms in a welcoming gesture and adopted a cynical smile. Murkhana's acid rain and soupy air had taken a toll on her hair and complexion, but she appeared otherwise healthy.

"Welcome, Lord Vader and Governor Tarkin. I was aware that Coruscant was sending an investigative team, but I had no idea—"

"Has the operative arrived?" Vader interrupted.

She gestured to the residence with a flick of her head. "Inside. I summoned him as soon as I received your comm."

"Show us to him."

She spun on her boot heels and made for the reinforced front door, two stormtroopers flanking the entrance stepping aside and saluting Vader and Tarkin as they passed. The entry hall and main room of the residence were sparsely furnished, and the dry air was artificially scented. A Koorivarn male taller than Tarkin and draped in tattered robes stood silently behind a curved couch. His cranial horn was of average size for his species, but his facial ridges were marred by intersecting scars.

The ambassador gestured for Vader and Tarkin to sit, but they declined.

"May I at least offer you something to—"

"Tell me, Ambassador," Vader interrupted again, "do you ever leave this compound of yours, with its high sensor-studded walls and company of armed sentries?"

"Of course."

"Then no doubt you have seen the obscene scrawlings and defacements displayed on every other building between here and this planet's wretched excuse for a spaceport."

She showed him a sardonic look. "My lord, as quickly as I have them expunged, new ones spring up."

"And what of the criminal rabble that cluster on every corner?" Tarkin asked.

She laughed shortly. "They proliferate even more quickly than the defacements, Governor Tarkin. The moment Black Sun moved out, the Crymorah moved in."

"The Crymorah," Vader said.

"Actually a local affiliate known as the Sugi."

Vader seemed to tuck the information away.

"You need to make an example of them," Tarkin said.

The ambassador looked at him as if he'd lost his mind. "You think I haven't tried?"

Tarkin cocked an eyebrow. "Meaning what, exactly?"

She started to reply, then blew out her breath and began again. "I've made appeal after appeal to Moff Therbon for additional storm-troopers, to no avail."

"And if we see to it that you have additional resources, you'll do what must be done?"

She continued to regard Tarkin with skepticism. "Excuse me, Governor, but I don't think you understand the situation fully. Officiating here has been like serving a sentence for a crime I didn't commit. The stormtroopers have a saying, *Better spaced than based on Belderone,* and we're a far cry from Belderone." She blew out her breath. "Yes, I can leave this compound, but my life is at risk whenever I do. Hence, the white wardrobe." She glanced between Tarkin and Vader. "Maybe you two haven't noticed, but Murkhana isn't Coruscant. The population here *hates* me. I sometimes think *Murkhana* hates me. I'm held responsible for every Imperial tax increase and every minor change to the legal system. The smugglers are the only ones who garner respect, because they're the only ones providing goods—even if at exorbitant rates. As for the crime lords, they're the only ones powerful enough to provide protection from the thieves and murderers this planet has bred since the war ended."

Vader took a step in her direction. "I will be sure to let the Emperor know of your dissatisfaction, Ambassador."

She didn't retreat. "I sure as hell wish someone would. I mean, I'm humbled that the Emperor deemed me worthy to serve him, but this assignment—"

Vader thrust his forefinger at her. "Allowing a cell of dissidents to operate under your watch is not what I would call serving the Emperor, Ambassador."

"Dissidents?" She shook her head in genuine bewilderment. "I don't understand."

Instead of explaining, Vader turned his attention to the Koorivar. "You are the intelligence asset?"

"I am Bracchia," the Koorivar said in little more than a whisper.

Tarkin knew that it was nothing more than a code name, but it was the only name Deputy Director Harus Ison had been willing to provide. "You were a Republic operative during the war."

Bracchia nodded. "I was, Governor Tarkin. I assisted in your anti-Shadowfeed operation here."

Tarkin adopted a thin-lipped expression of wariness. "Tell us about the Corporate Alliance building—the former medcenter."

The Koorivar nodded in deference. "Before entering, I watched the building every day for a week, Governor Tarkin. When I determined it to be unoccupied, I entered and made a quick inventory of the devices as directed."

"As *directed*?" Tarkin asked in surprise.

But before Bracchia could respond, Vader said, "You entered how?"

The Koorivar turned to him. "Through sliding doors, Lord Vader. I'm not aware of any other entrance, and the devices were just where I was told I would find them."

"How could you fail to notice the turbolift?" Vader said.

The Koorivar looked at the floor. "My apologies, Lord Vader. I was fixated on investigating the devices."

Tarkin placed himself deliberately between Bracchia and Vader. "Are you saying that you didn't make the discovery on your own?"

"No, Governor, I did not. I was merely tasked with verifying a report sent to me from Coruscant."

Tarkin's brow furrowed. "From Imperial Security?"

Bracchia nodded. "From my case officer at ISB, yes."

Tarkin had his mouth open to pursue the matter when his comlink sounded and he prized the device from its belt pouch.

"We're at the building, Governor Tarkin."

Tarkin recognized the voice of Sergeant Crest. "At what building?"

"Back at the Corporate Alliance building, sir."

"You're not at the landing field?"

Crest took a moment to reply. "Sir, you told us to return here after we'd off-loaded the devices at the corvette."

"Who told you?"

"You, sir." Crest sounded as confused as Tarkin.

"I sent no such orders, Sergeant."

"Excuse me, sir, but the order came by holotransmission from you just after we'd transferred the last of the devices you marked for the ship. Without the gunship, we had to commandeer an airspeeder at the landing field."

"Who is with the ship?" Vader stepped in to say toward the comlink's audio pickup.

"Two of our group, Lord Vader, in addition to the corvette's captain and comm officer."

Tarkin felt blood rush from his face. "Sergeant, return to the ship immediately."

"On our way, sir."

Vader looked at Tarkin while he was contacting the *Carrion Spike*'s captain. "A second feature from the makers of the false holovid transmitted to the moon base?"

"In which *I* am now the principal actor," Tarkin said, trying not to sound too rattled. Checking the comlink again, he added: "I can't raise the ship."

"That happens all the time, Governor Tarkin," the ambassador said. "If it's not the city's power grid, it's the communications array."

He glanced at her with his mouth open, an uneasy feeling beginning to coil in his chest. Fingers dancing over the comlink's keypad, he opened a second channel that allowed him to communicate with the corvette itself, and entered a code that commanded the *Carrion Spike*'s slave system to prevent anyone from so much as approaching the ship. But the system didn't respond.

"Nothing," he said to Vader. "Not from the command cabin, not from the ship itself."

Vader whirled on the ambassador. "Contact Coruscant by Holo-Net immediately."

She spread her hands in apology. "Lord Vader, Murkhana hasn't had HoloNet communications since early in the Clone Wars." She cut her eyes to Tarkin. "The HoloNet was destroyed during the first Republic assault."

Tarkin recalled. The relay had been destroyed as a means of disrupting Dooku's Shadowfeeds to worlds along the Perlemian Trade Route. His thoughts reeled.

"Send a subspace transmission," Vader was saying.

"Governor Tarkin," Crest said from the comlink, "we're back at the landing field." He fell silent for a long moment, and when he spoke again his voice betrayed astonishment. "Sir, the *Carrion Spike* is nowhere in sight."

Tarkin stared at the comlink. "What?"

"It's not here, sir. It must have launched."

"Impossible!" Tarkin said.

"Where are your troopers, Sergeant?" Vader all but snarled.

Again the reply was long in arriving. "Lord Vader, we have a visual on four bodies—two stormtroopers, the captain, and the comm officer." Crest paused, then added, "Shot through and through, Lord Vader."

Vader clenched his right hand. "You've failed me for the last time, Sergeant."

"I get that, sir," Crest said in a somber voice.

Vader turned to Tarkin. "We sidestepped the smaller trap only to fall into the larger one, Governor. If nothing else, we now know the reason we were lured here." Bringing his left hand to the brow of his helmet, he paced away from Tarkin and the ambassador, then swung back to them. "The ship is still in the Murkhana system."

Tarkin didn't waste time asking how Vader knew that to be the case. Instead, he glanced at one of the stormtroopers. "The Judicial cruiser at the landing field."

The stormtrooper shook his head in a mournful way. "Not spaceworthy, sir. We've been waiting on replacement parts for the hyperdrive motivator for three months, local."

"I know where to procure a ship," Vader said abruptly. He swept his arm in a gesture aimed at the stormtroopers. "All of you—come with me." Then he turned and pointed to Bracchia. "And you."

Tarkin fell in among them as they hastened from the ambassador's residence.

Tarkin had his doubts.

At Lola Sayu, when Skywalker, Kenobi, and Ahsoka Tano had participated in rescuing him from the Citadel, Tarkin had taken issue with the Jedi strategy of splitting into two teams. Surrendering group integrity for twice the number of potential problems made little sense, and that was precisely the way the mission had unfolded. Tarkin's general, Even Piell, had been killed, and the rest of them had nearly fallen back into the clutches of the Citadel's sadistic Separatist prison warden. Now, all these years later, Vader had split their forces, and here they were allowing themselves to be herded at blasterpoint into the den of a Sugi crime lord while the stormtroopers were elsewhere in Murkhana City carrying out their part of Vader's plan.

So Tarkin had his doubts.

But with the *Carrion Spike* apparently in the hands of shipjackers, and his captain, comm officer, and two stormtroopers dead, he had little choice but to go along with the subterfuge, in the hope that it would succeed.

"I *still* don't like splitting up the team," he said to Vader as one of the Sugi was shoving him from behind.

Vader glanced over at him, but as ever it was impossible to tell what was going on behind the black orbs and muzzle of his mask.

The headquarters building was in better condition than most in Murkhana City, its graceful swirls of coral and undersea colors having either survived the war or been restored since. Initially Tarkin had taken the Sugi for an insectile species, but in fact they were short bipeds who affected armored powersuits. The suits provided them with a second set of legs and a segmented, barb-tipped abdomen, which gave them the appearance of mythological creatures. The soldiers, at any rate. Others in the dank hall Vader and Tarkin were escorted into stood on their own two feet and wore cowl-like helmets, with power packs of some sort on their backs. The outsized helmets made their large-eyed skeletal faces seem even smaller than they were.

Twenty soldiers complemented the half dozen who were holding weapons on Vader and Tarkin, with several repurposed Separatist battle droids augmenting the hall group. Their apparent leader lounged on a gaudy throne of coral, clicking orders to his minions.

Vader came to a halt five meters from the throne and spent a moment taking in the overstated surroundings. "You have done well for yourself since the demise of your former competitor, crime lord," he said at last.

"And for that I owe you a debt of gratitude, Lord Vader," the Sugi answered in heavily accented Basic. "That is the sole reason I have allowed you entry to my abode—to thank you personally for killing my predecessor and persuading Black Sun to abandon Murkhana for safer realms."

"You are as insolent as he was, crime lord."

"Given that I enjoy the upper hand here, Lord Vader, I can well afford to be."

Vader folded his arms across his massive chest. "Don't be too sure of yourself."

The Sugi dismissed the warning. "I have been apprised by my associates of your prowess, Lord Vader. But I doubt that even you could triumph over so many." When Vader said nothing, he continued: "Now, what is this drivel about commandeering my starship?"

Tarkin stepped forward to speak. "We take your meaning about being outnumbered. But perhaps there's a healthier way to persuade you to do as Lord Vader asks."

The Sugi's large eyes expanded. "I have not had the pleasure . . ."

"Meet Moff Tarkin, crime lord," Vader said. "Sector governor of Greater Seswenna and more."

The Sugi sat back in his chair. "Now I am impressed. That Murkhana should play host to two such luminary Imperials . . . Though many might say I would be doing the galaxy a favor by eliminating you here and now." He fixed his gaze on Tarkin. "But you were saying, Governor Tarkin . . ."

"That in meetings of this nature there are always alternatives to using brute force."

"I can't imagine any alternatives that will convince me to surrender my fanged beauty of a starship, Governor Tarkin."

Cautiously, Tarkin drew a portable holoprojector disk from the pocket of his tunic. "If I may?"

The Sugi waved permission.

"Sergeant Crest," Vader said toward the device. "Are you in the crime lord's warehouse?"

"Yes, Lord Vader. Ready to bring the entire place down on your command."

"Then you have redeemed yourself, Sergeant."

"Thank you, Lord Vader."

The crime lord's expression approximated entertainment. "You can't be serious. Or do you actually believe that I would surrender my ship for a warehouse full of weapons?"

"Your Crymorah associates on Coruscant might encourage you to do just that."

"I'll take my chances, Lord Vader."

"You're right of course," Tarkin said quickly. "But just now your warehouse contains more than weapons. We've arranged for your wives and brood to be present as well." He called up an image of the Sugi's family members huddled in a circle on the warehouse floor and surrounded by stormtroopers with raised weapons. "We understand that you are very attached to them. A product of your genetics, I suspect."

"You wouldn't!" the Sugi said.

His earlier doubts about Vader's plan beginning to fade, Tarkin lifted an arrogant eyebrow. "Wouldn't we?"

The Sugi fidgeted in apprehension. "I can have both of you killed where you stand!"

"We'll take our chances," Tarkin said, grinning slightly. "Your ship for their lives."

After a long moment of rapid clicking and nervous hand wringing, the Sugi broke the tense silence. "All right, take the ship! I will purchase a replacement. I will purchase twenty replacements. Just let them live—let them live!"

Tarkin's face grew deadly serious. "You'll need to furnish us with all the necessary launch codes and order all of your underlings to leave the landing field at once."

"Then I will do it," the crime lord said. "Whatever you ask!"

Vader leaned slightly in the direction of the comlink. "Sergeant Crest, transport the crime lord's family to the landing field and let me know when your troops are in possession of his ship."

"Let them live," the Sugi repeated, rising halfway out of his throne in supplication.

"Take heart," Tarkin said. "They most certainly will survive you."

12

BURYING THE LEAD

OUTBOUND FROM MURKHANA, the *Carrion Spike*'s new pilot and three members of the new crew were gathered in the command cabin marveling at the wonders of the ship. The shipjackers— a human, a Mon Calamari, a Gotal, and a Koorivar—some standing, others seated in the chairs that fronted the curved instrument console, could hardly keep still, having pulled off an act of piracy that had been close to two years in the planning.

The human, Teller, was a rangy, middle-aged man with thick dark hair and eyebrows to match. His long face was perpetually shadowed with stubble, and his chin bore a deep cleft. Dressed in cargo pants, boots, and a thermal shirt, he stood between the principal acceleration chairs, watching as the Gotal pilot and the Koorivar operations specialist familiarized themselves with the ship's complex controls. The bulkhead left of the forward viewports bore traces of carbon scoring and blood from the brief blaster fight that erupted when the shipjackers had had to burn and battle their way through the command cabin hatch to deal with Tarkin's defiant captain and comm officer.

"Getting the hang of it?" Teller asked the Gotal, Salikk.

The twin-horned, flat-faced humanoid nodded without taking his heavy-lidded scarlet eyes from the instrument array. "She flies herself," he said in accented Basic. A native of the moon Antar 4, he was short and dark-skinned, with tufts of light hair on his cheeks and chin. He wore an old-fashioned but serviceable flight suit that left the clawed digits of his sensitive hands exposed.

"It will fly itself, but we're going to tell it where to go," Dr. Artoz told him.

The Mon Cal wore a flight suit whose neck had been altered to accommodate the amphibious humanoid's high-domed, salmon-colored head, and whose sleeves ended mid-forearm to allow passage for his large webbed hands. Pacing the length of the instruments console, Artoz was pointing out individual controls, his huge eyes swiveling independently of each other to focus simultaneously on Salikk and the ops specialist, Cala.

Teller had known all three of them for years, but what with Salikk's sweaty scent and the saline smell Artoz emitted, he was grateful for the spaciousness of the *Carrion Spike*'s command cabin. Then again, from what he'd been told by his nonhuman friends, humans weren't exactly a picnic when it came to body odor.

"Computer-assisted fire control for the lateral lasers and in-close weapons," Artoz was saying, indicating one set of instruments after the next. "Full-authority navicomp, stealth system initiator, sublight ions, hyperdrive."

"State-of-the-art Imperial technology," Cala said. Jutting from a headcloth that fell past the Koorivar's shoulders, his spiraling cranial horn was twice the height of Salikk's conical projections and thicker than both of them combined. He wore pouch-pocketed pants not unlike Teller's under a roomy tunic that reached his thick thighs. "This corvette will easily exceed a Star Destroyer."

"Nothing less than what I promised," Artoz said, though without a hint of self-importance. He gestured to the auxiliary controls. "Sensor suite, rectenna controls, alluvial dampers, reverse triggering acceleration compensator—"

"Which one empties the toilets?" a second human asked as she stepped through the scarred cockpit hatch. Fit and scrappy looking, she had a narrow frame and skin the color of a tropical hardwood. Her short curly hair was naturally black but had been lightened to a mishmash of brown and blond. She wore a white utility suit and ankle-length ship-tread boots. The Zygerrian female who followed her into the command cabin was also slender, though somewhat taller, and distinctly feline in appearance. Pointed, fur-covered ears sprang straight up from the sides of a narrow-nosed, triangular face. Her innate exoticism was enhanced by reddish coloring.

Teller turned to them. "Everything locked down back there?"

The woman, Anora, nodded. "The outer hatch is fully sealed. The air lock, not so much." She gestured with her pointed chin to the Zygerrian. "Hask's going to keep working on it—since it was her blaster that did the damage."

Hask snorted. "When she slammed into me." She spoke Basic flawlessly, but with a thick accent.

Anora showed her a long-suffering look. "You were supposed to keep the safety on."

"For the last time," she said, "I'm not a soldier, and I'll never be one."

"Plenty of blame to go around," Teller said, cutting them off. "The holocams survive?"

Enthusiasm informed Hask's nod. Her head bore a symmetrical pattern of small spurs. "They're in the main cabin. I'll get started slaving them to the HoloNet comm board—"

"As soon as she's repaired the air lock," Anora said, blue-gray eyes bright over her smile.

Hask ignored her. "Nice of Tarkin's stormtroopers to carry some of the storeroom components aboard. I thought we were going to have to sacrifice them."

"We have Tarkin to thank for a lot of things," Teller said. He swung forward in time to catch the end of Artoz's instrument rundown.

"Air lock overrides, blast-tinting for the viewports . . . What else?"

"Do all the Emperor's Moffs rate one of these?" Anora asked, running a hand over the console in appreciation.

"Only Tarkin," Artoz said, "as far as we know."

"A testament to his friendship with Sienar," Teller said.

"Sienar Fleet Systems wasn't the only contributor," Artoz amended. "The company's design sense is all over the corvette, but every ship-builder from Theed Engineering to Cygnus Spaceworks played a part in outfitting it."

"Not to mention Tarkin himself," Teller said. "The Moff was designing ships for Eriadu's Outland Security Force when he was nineteen."

Hask made a sour face. "More Prefsbelt Academy legends."

Anora shook her head negatively. "True by all accounts."

Teller perched on the arm of one of the secondary acceleration chairs. "The way I heard it, Eriadu was losing a lot of its lommite shipments to a pirate group that had fortified the bow of one of their ships to use as a rostrum—a kind of battering ram—after destroying too much cargo with their lasers."

"The pirates weren't acquainted with ion cannons?" Salikk said from the pilot's seat.

Teller glanced at the Gotal. "Seswenna's ships were too well ray-shielded for that—another Tarkin innovation, I might add. Anyway, he designed a narrow-profile ship with cannons that could swivel on pintles to direct all firepower forward. Confronted the rammer bow-on."

"Damn the particle beams, full speed ahead," Hask said, still refusing to buy into the legend.

Teller nodded. "Burned through the pirates' armor like a knife through butter and blew the ship apart." He turned to point to toggles on the control console. "Same system here."

Cala grinned. "Should come in handy."

"We can hope," Artoz said, giving the console a final appraisal with his right eye while his left remained fixed on Salikk. "Proximity alarms, hypercomm unit, Imperial HoloNet encryptor . . ."

"Why is it called the *Carrion Spike*?" Anora said.

Teller drew his lips in and shook his head. "Not a clue."

Everyone fell silent for a moment, gazing through the viewports at the Murkhana system's small outermost planet and the vast starfield beyond.

"I still can't get over Vader being there," Hask said finally. "I mean, why would the Emperor send him to escort Tarkin?"

"Vader paid Murkhana a visit just after the war ended," Cala said. "Executed a Black Sun Twi'lek racketeer, among other acts."

"Still," Hask said. "Vader . . ."

"Stop calling him by name," Anora said harshly; then softened her tone to add: "He's a machine. A terrorist." She looked at Teller. "You took a real risk having him and Tarkin walk right into that sliding door ambush."

Teller shrugged it off. "We had to make the scenario ring true. Besides, their getting themselves blown up wouldn't have affected our plans one way or another."

"The Emperor wouldn't have been happy losing two of his top henchmen," Cala pointed out.

"He's not going to be happy either way," Teller said.

The console issued a loud tone, and Cala lifted his eyes to the display. "Uh, Teller, we've got a starship on our tail."

Teller's dark eyebrows quirked together. "Can't be. You certain you have the stealth system enabled?"

The Koorivar nodded. "Status indicators say so. We should be invisible to scanners."

Everyone crowded around the sensor suite. "Put the ship on screen," Teller said.

Cala's stubby-fingered hands raced across the keypad, and a black ship with forward fangs resolved on the display. "Waiting for a transponder signature . . ."

"Don't bother," Salikk said. "That's Faazah's ship. The *Parsec Predator*."

Teller nodded. "The Sugi arms dealer."

"Murkhana's most wanted," Salikk said.

Cala ran his gaze over the sensor indicators. "Matching our every move."

Teller stared at the screen and scratched his head in bafflement. "I'm willing to entertain explanations."

Artoz spoke first. "Perhaps this Sugi is simply heading for the same jump point we are."

Teller nodded to Salikk. "Put this thing through some maneuvers, and let's see what happens."

The corvette changed vectors, slewing to port, then to starboard before rocketing through an abrupt, twisting climb that delivered them swiftly to the dark side of the impact-cratered planet.

Everyone fell silent again, waiting for the Koorivar's update. "The *Predator*'s still with us, just emerging from the transitor." Cala swiveled to Teller. "And here's something strange: We're not being scanned."

Teller and Artoz looked perplexed. "You stated that it is matching our every maneuver," the Mon Cal said.

"It is," Cala emphasized. "And I repeat, we're not being scanned. No sensor lock, no indication that we're being observed."

Teller traded glances with Artoz. "A homing beacon?" he suggested.

The Mon Cal's confusion didn't abate.

Teller looked at Hask. "It was your job to check for trackers."

"I did," the Zygerrian all but snarled. "There weren't any."

"Or you didn't find any," Teller said.

"Why would this Faazah attach a locator to Tarkin's ship?" Anora said. "Or is that just a Sugi thing to do?"

"Offhand, I can't imagine a reason," Artoz said. "But we can certainly outrace the *Predator* if we have to."

Teller considered it. "That doesn't make me feel a whole lot better, Doc. Not if we've got a faulty stealth system."

"Teller, we are *not* being scanned," Cala repeated. "The stealth system is operating impeccably. Check the status displays for yourself if you don't trust me."

Teller made a placating gesture. "Of course I trust you. I just don't get it."

"Should we contact our ally?" Salikk said.

"No, not yet," Teller said. "We'll be updated soon enough, in any case."

"Unless . . . ," Hask began.

Anora aimed a faint smile at the Zygerrian. "I'll bet I know what you're going to say, and yes, that occurred to me, too."

Teller and the others looked at the two of them. "What am I missing?" Teller asked.

"Vader," Hask said, exhaling. "Vader and Tarkin."

Teller continued to regard them. "What, the Sugi is giving them a ride?"

Anora rocked her head from side to side. "Or they appropriated his ship."

"They could have." Teller plucked at his lower lip. "Still doesn't make sense, though—not if we're invisible to the *Predator*'s sensors. Or are you saying that Tarkin's got some secret way of locking onto us?"

Cala spoke to it. "We disabled the slave circuit when we silenced the stormtroopers' comlinks and the ship's comm."

"Maybe Tarkin is a telepath, along with being a ship designer," Salikk said.

"Vader," Hask rasped. "*Va-der.*"

Teller locked eyes with her. "Vader has a way of neutralizing stealth technology?"

Hask spread her slim, furry hands. "Who knows what's inside that helmet of his? Besides, what other explanation is there?"

"We should have launched sooner," Cala said. "We'd be out of the system by now."

Teller shot him a gimlet look. "A couple of jumps from here, I'm going to remind you that you said that." He glanced at Salikk. "How soon until we can go to lightspeed?"

The Gotal studied the navicomputer display. "As soon as you give the word."

Teller took a breath and let it out. "Let's see them try to track us through hyperspace."

"Is this ship fast enough to close the distance?"

Darth Vader pulled the yoke toward him. "It is faster than most, Governor, but unfortunately not as fast as yours. We need to disable the corvette before it can elude us."

Tarkin despaired. As disturbingly well armed as the late crime lord's ship was, disabling the *Carrion Spike* was easier said than done.

If the ship was, in some sense, a measure of his standing in the Imperial hegemony, then his vaunted reputation just might go down with her.

They were at the edge of the Murkhana system, the eponymous world well behind them, already a memory, and a bitter one. He and Vader were sharing the controls, Vader wedged into an acceleration chair made for a much smaller being, Tarkin strapped into the copilot's chair. Crest and the other stormtroopers were amidships, manning the ship's quad laser cannons.

Never having shared a cockpit with Vader, Tarkin was astonished by the Dark Lord's piloting skills. Though perhaps he shouldn't have been.

The sound of Vader's slow, rhythmic breathing overwhelmed the cockpit as he indicated an area dead ahead and slightly to port. "There."

Tarkin saw nothing but star-studded blackness. Nor did the ship's instruments register the *Carrion Spike,* which was obviously running in stealth mode. He couldn't imagine how Vader was managing to track the ship, but was for the moment content to be mystified.

"Why are they still in system?" he said. "They can't have shipjacked it for a joyride."

Vader glanced at him across a center console. "They were convinced we couldn't follow them. They are merely taking time to familiarize themselves with the instruments."

"Then they must know that we're tracking them."

"Indeed they do."

Tarkin found himself actually warming to Vader, especially after what had happened in the Sugi's headquarters. No sooner had word arrived that Sergeant Crest and his stormtroopers were in possession of the *Parsec Predator* and the codes necessary to launch her than Vader exacted his revenge on the crime lord for having been kept waiting. Tarkin knew merely by the gasping sounds that began to erupt from the Sugi that Vader was performing that thumb-and-forefinger dark magic of his to crush the crime lord's windpipe. By then, too, the ambassador's stormtroopers had rushed into the headquarters, unleashing flash grenades and blaster bolts that had caught

the Sugi's underlings by surprise. At one point Vader had asked them
whether they actually wanted to die for their leader, and it was when
they replied with weapons that Vader drew his crimson-bladed lightsaber from beneath his cape. Tarkin had witnessed numerous Jedi
wield lightsabers during the Clone Wars, but he had never seen anyone put an energy blade to such determined purpose or achieve such
rapid and lethal results. Two stormtroopers had died in the exchange,
but all the Sugi had paid with their lives; Vader's blade had even reduced the repurposed battle droids to useless parts.

"The ambassador owes you a big favor," Tarkin had told Vader at
the time.

Now he said: "Surely we weren't lured all the way to Murkhana just
so the *Carrion Spike* could be shipjacked."

"And why not?" Vader said. "Stealth, firepower, alacrity." He paused
as if he were about to ask a follow-up question, but said nothing further.

"Granted it's one of a kind, but what is their plan? To strip and sell
it for parts? To have it dissected and replicated?" Tarkin heard the
words tumbling from his mouth in a rush and got control of himself.

"A flotilla of *Carrion Spikes*," Vader said, clearly dubious.

Tarkin gestured in dismissal. "Not without the help of the top engineering conglomerates in the galaxy. More to the point, whoever
they are, they now have the corvette, as well as a capital ship."

"You are convinced that the piracy was carried out by the same
beings who attacked Sentinel."

"I am. Anyone with skill enough to create counterfeit holovids of
ships and beings and to interrupt Imperial HoloNet signals would
also have the skill to wrap the *Carrion Spike* in a mantle of silence,
disabling not only the ship's slave system but also her various communications systems, including comlinks and helmet radios." He
paused briefly. "Vice Admirals Rancit and Screed were correct about
the cache being part of a more far-reaching plan. If the cache was
merely the lure, then the plot is still unfolding."

"Then tell me how to disable your ship, Governor."

Tarkin firmed his lips. "There is a weakness. If the thieves can be persuaded to lower the shields, concentrated fire on the spine where the main fuselage meets the aft flare should do the trick. We were never able to resolve the problem of properly safeguarding the hyperdrive generator while the power plant is supplying the ion drives, the deflector shields, and the weapons. It's not so much a design flaw as an accommodation to the ship's size in relation to her armament. Even Sienar Fleet was at a loss."

"I will bear that in mind," Vader said, though mostly to himself.

"Frankly, Lord Vader, I'm more concerned about what the *Carrion Spike*'s weapons can do to us while we're attempting to line up what has to be a very precise laser blast."

"Leave that to me, Governor."

"Do I have a choice?"

Abruptly Vader poured on all speed, accelerating away from the system's outmost planet and taking the crime lord's ship into the starry space he had indicated earlier. But then only to loose a guttural sound of anger and frustration.

"They've jumped to lightspeed!"

Tarkin ground his teeth. The situation was growing worse by the moment. In star systems lacking nearby hyperspace relay stations, a ship's pilot had to navigate by beacon or buoy, unless the ship was equipped with a sophisticated navicomputer of the sort the *Carrion Spike* boasted, which could plot jumps well beyond the next beacon, all the way to the Core if necessary. According to the *Predator*'s inferior device, the Murkhana system had no fewer than a dozen jump egresses, and most of those were into other Outer Rim systems where beacons were still more plentiful than hyperspace relay stations.

Vader broke his protracted silence to say, "They have jumped, but not far." He stretched out his left hand to enter data into the ship's navicomputer.

Tarkin was nonplussed. Then it dawned on him: Vader wasn't tracking the ship; he was tracking the mysterious black sphere he had had transferred to the *Carrion Spike*!

Even so, his optimism was short-lived, undermined by a memory of something Jova used to say when they had turned the tables on a predator, making it the hunted rather than the hunter.

"*Think first when you're in pursuit: Is your prey trying to escape, or is it going for reinforcements? Is it perhaps looking for a temporary hiding place from which to spring at you, or—still driven by hunger—has it decided to search out a more vulnerable target?*"

13

SOFT TARGETS

DARTH SIDIOUS WAS ANNOYED about having been disturbed
from his meditations at the shrine. By the time he ascended to the
pinnacle of the Palace spire to meet with Mas Amedda, he was ready
to take someone's head off.

"Must I attend to every trivial matter, Vizier?"

"I apologize, my lord. But I believe you will want to attend to this
one."

Sidious eyed him for a moment. "Murkhana," he said in arrant
disgust.

The Chagrian bowed his horned head in acknowledgment. "Just
so, my lord."

Sidious took to his tall-backed chair while Amedda readied the
table's holoprojector, then moved to stand silently by the window-
wall. In the hologram that emerged, several members of Military Intelligence and the Imperial Security Bureau were grouped before a
positioning grid in one of the ISB's situation rooms.

"My Lord Emperor," Harus Ison of ISB began, "I'm sorry—"

"Reserve your apologies for when they are most needed, Deputy Director," Sidious said.

"Of course, my lord." Ison swallowed hard and found his voice. "We thought it prudent to apprise you of recent developments on Murkhana."

"I'm well aware that Lord Vader and Governor Tarkin found and investigated the cache of communications devices."

"Of course, my lord," Ison said. "But we have since received a subspace transmission from Lord Vader and Governor Tarkin informing us that the *Carrion Spike* has been seized."

Sidious sat straighter in the chair. "Seized?"

"Yes, my lord. From a landing field on Murkhana—by unknown parties."

Sidious used the chair's armrest controls to mute the audiovisual feeds and swiveled to Amedda. "Why have I heard nothing of this from Lord Vader?"

"Without the *Carrion Spike,* neither Lord Vader nor Governor Tarkin has access to the Imperial HoloNet or other suitably encrypted communications devices. The first subspace message originated from the ambassador's residence in Murkhana City. The second was sent from a starship in the Murkhana system."

"Lord Vader has procured a replacement ship?"

"Yes, my lord."

Sidious re-enabled the holofeeds to the situation room. "Proceed with your report, Deputy Director."

Ison bowed his head once more. "Lord Vader and Governor Tarkin have commandeered the starship of a local crime lord and are in pursuit of the *Carrion Spike.* In their most recent transmission, they stated that they were jumping the commandeered ship to the Fial system, Coreward of Murkhana, though still far removed from the Perlemian Trade Route."

"Do we have a military presence in that system?"

Vice Admiral Rancit stepped forward to address it. "No, my lord, we don't. We do, however, have a presence in the Belderone system, which is nearby."

"My lord, if I may interrupt briefly," Ison said.

Sidious motioned with his right hand.

"My lord, most of the star systems in that region of the Tion Cluster lack hyperspace relay stations. Given the likelihood that the ship Lord Vader commandeered has only a standard navicomputer, he and Governor Tarkin will be forced to navigate buoy-to-buoy."

"Your point?"

"Only that we face a hopeless task in trying to establish a rendezvous while the pursuit is in progress."

Sidious swiveled the chair slightly. "Vice Admiral Rancit?"

"Military Intelligence is even now calculating and prioritizing possible jump and egress points in those local systems, and on into the Nilgaard sector. Ships can be dispatched accordingly, my lord."

Sidious muted the feed once more, steepled his fingers, and brought them to his lips. During his meditations he had tried without success to trace a snaking current of the dark side to its source. What had it been trying to communicate to him?

No doubt Vader was tracking the *Carrion Spike* by focusing his attention on his meditation chamber. But why had he not sensed a disruption in the Force when Tarkin's ship had been taken? In the private transmission he had sent from Murkhana he had dismissed the communications cache as inconsequential; nothing more than misplaced hardware left over from the war. So did his inattention owe to a lingering sense of frustration about the mission? Perhaps he was at odds with Tarkin. Or had he allowed himself to step willingly into the trap, as Sidious had encouraged him to do?

"Tell me, Deputy Director Ison," he said when the audio feed was reestablished, "do you suspect any link between the communications devices and the theft of Governor Tarkin's ship?"

"My lord, we are investigating the recorded evidence and serial numbers in an effort to ascertain the identities of those who gathered the components. At the moment, however, we have no leads."

"There has to be some link, my lord," Rancit said. "Those now in possession of the *Carrion Spike* had to have sliced into the ship's security systems, and are likely the same assailants who launched the attack on Governor Tarkin's base. That means they have now added one of the navy's most sophisticated ships to their arsenal of warship and droid fighters."

Harus Ison was shaking his head. "There's no proof of that. We don't have enough information to establish a solid connection."

Sidious took a moment to consider the options, then said, "Vice Admiral Rancit, instruct your analysts to continue their calculations. You will also inform the Admiralty that their resources in the Belderone system should be prepared to jump to whatever target systems Lord Vader and Governor Tarkin deem significant." He leaned toward the holocam's lens. "Deputy Director Ison and the rest of you are to devote yourselves to unraveling the intentions of our new enemy."

"Imperial Security will not rest until it has done so," Ison said with a stiff bow of his head.

"We will apprehend them, my lord," Rancit added. "Even if that requires repositioning half the capital ships in the fleet."

The *Carrion Spike* reverted to realspace in the Fial system with the eyes of the six shipjackers focused on the main display of the sensor suite.

"Anything?" Teller asked Cala.

"No sign of the *Predator* so far."

Teller waited a long moment, then breathed a guarded sigh of relief and got to his feet. "Time to get down to business." He turned to Salikk. "Coordinates for Galidraan?"

Salikk watched the navicomputer. "Coming up."

The words had scarcely left the Gotal's full-lipped mouth when Cala said, "Teller!"

"I knew it, I knew it," Hask said, pacing through tight circles while Teller hurried back to the sensor suite.

Cala was sitting stiffly in the chair, staring fixedly at the display. "The *Predator*!"

"Right on cue," Artoz said from the far side of the command cabin.

Teller blinked in disbelief.

In a gesture of concern, Cala touched his forehead below the dangling headcloth. "It's the *Predator,* and she's coming for us all speed."

"Not even Vader could do this," Teller said. "There's a tracking device hidden somewhere aboard this ship."

"Or on the hull or concealed in a landing strut or just about anywhere," Hask said. "But unless you want to power down and perform a full EVA search you better come up with a revised plan."

Teller clenched his jaw. "We're not revising anything. Not now, not anytime." He glanced around him.

Artoz and Salikk nodded, then Cala and Anora, and finally Hask.

Teller rolled his head through a circle to work the kinks out of his neck and nodded to Hask. "You've got the comm board." As Cala stood up from the chair, Teller added: "Doc, you and Cala better get yourselves positioned." Then he turned to Salikk to say: "Jump us to Galidraan."

Seated in the copilot's chair, Tarkin watched Vader expectantly as the *Predator* emerged from hyperspace.

"Full ahead," the Dark Lord said.

Tarkin was glad to oblige, though he saw nothing through the viewports but star-strewn space and nothing on the sensor screens but background noise.

One moment Vader's gloved hands were clamped tight on the yoke, then they flew to the navigation console. "They've jumped to lightspeed again."

"Just as I would have," Tarkin said.

Vader fell silent, then lifted his head as if just roused from a nap and swiveled to the navicomputer display, the fingers of his left hand punching the control pad keys.

"Galidraan," he said at last.

Tarkin gave him a moment to complete the request for jump coordinates. "The chamber," he said. "That's how you're tracking them."

Vader glanced at him, as unreadable as ever, but said: "Very discerning of you, Governor."

Tarkin called up a star map of the Galidraan system and began to study it. "An even shorter jump. Two populated planets." He frowned in uncertainty. "Why not jump farther afield? An error in judgment?"

Vader made no reply.

Tarkin retrieved additional information on the system. "An Imperial space station in fixed orbit at Galidraan Three." The onscreen image of the station showed it to be an outmoded wheel with numerous space docks radiating from the perimeter.

"There is little point in alerting the station," Vader said, "as we will arrive long before a subspace transmission."

"The station won't be able see the *Carrion Spike* coming, in any event."

Vader grunted and reached for the hyperdrive control arm. Beyond the viewports the starfield elongated, and the *Predator* leapt to lightspeed.

Tarkin sat back in his chair, allowing his vision to adjust to the mottled corridor the ship had entered. No past or future here, he told himself. Time's blank canvas. And yet he couldn't keep his thoughts from running wild and in all directions.

Reflecting on Jova's sage advice, he could recall countless instances of each scenario playing out during his years of training on the plateau. Animals had escaped despite the team's best efforts to track and hunt them down. Others had hidden and sprung from concealment, on one occasion nearly making a meal of the Rodians had Jova, Tarkin, and Zellit not come to their rescue. Some with braying calls had summoned reinforcements too numerous for the humans and Rodians to compete with, and they had been the ones to go hungry. And yes, there had been numerous instances of hunted animals skulking off to sniff out more vulnerable game, softer targets. In deep space, similar circumstances had transpired. Pirate groups had gone hungry, sounded calls for support, abandoned the Greater Seswenna for less fortified zones, and employed every method of concealment, taking every advantage of the glower of starlight, the glittering tails of comets, iridescent clouds of interstellar gas.

Again Tarkin tried to assemble all the pieces: the counterfeit distress call, the sneak attack on Sentinel, the bait set out on Murkhana, the theft of the ship, and now the flight.

But to where? To what end?

Out of the corner of his eye, he saw Vader prepare the *Predator* for the transition to sublight. The timeless corridor narrowed and vanished and the starlines compacted to pinpoints of light, skewing slightly as the ship reverted to realspace. No sooner had Vader engaged the ion drives than proximity alarms began to squeal and something large and white caromed off the forward deflector shield.

Tarkin quickly captured an image of the object on one of the display screens. It was the mangled and frosted body of a stormtrooper.

In the middle distance, fiery explosions flared at the edge of Galidraan III's atmospheric envelope. Plumes of incandescence, like stellar prominences, erupted into space.

Vader firewalled the throttle and the *Predator* raced deeper into the system, the space station coming into unassisted view, an arc of its silvery rim blown wide open and hemorrhaging gas, flames, objects, and bodies. The source of the destruction was invisible to the naked eye and the *Predator*'s scanners, making it appear as if green packets of bundled energy were being fired from deep space. Even so, particle-beam weapons emplaced along the station's curved outer surface were returning fusillades that streamed futilely into the void. Like some sea creature lunging forward to chew flesh and withdraw before it could be counterattacked, the invisible menace continued to advance and retreat, its lasers opening surgical lacerations along the spokes of the wheel as if intent on separating the rim from the hub. Larger explosions blossomed, along with dense clusters of superheated ejecta.

Tarkin bent to the controls, searching for a heat signature, gravitational flux, evidence of propellant glow, anything that might pinpoint the location of the *Carrion Spike*, all the while well aware that the ship was beyond his efforts to track. She could conceal herself from any sensor, contain her own reflection and heat, accelerate out of danger, maneuver beyond the capacity of any ship her size. But worse still was Tarkin's realization about her new crew: They weren't mere shipjackers; they were, as Vader had intuited early on, dissidents. Partisans with a deadly agenda to fulfill.

Flights of ARC-170 and V-wing starfighters, like swarms of stinging insects, were accelerating from the station's launch bays in search of the veiled thing that was pummeling their nest. Keeping to the edge of the battle to avoid being inadvertently targeted, Vader abruptly veered the *Predator* starboard in an obvious attempt to parallel the curving storm of destruction the *Carrion Spike* was sowing.

Tarkin saw a rash of melt circles erupt along the station's already pockmarked hull, an efflorescence of globular explosions.

Vader changed vectors and decelerated to match the *Predator*'s speed to that of the *Carrion Spike*. "We have you now," Tarkin heard him mutter.

Through the viewports, he could see the ARC-170s and the V-wings playing a dangerous game with their opponent, speeding directly into hails of energy bolts in the hope of forcing the *Carrion Spike* to betray her location, and sacrificing themselves in the process.

His hands tight on the yoke, Vader called out, "Sergeant Crest, prepare to fire."

The stormtrooper's voice crackled from the cockpit nunciator. "Standing by, Lord Vader. But we have no visual on the target."

"Follow the tracers back to their source, Sergeant, and pour all the power of those quad lasers toward the point of origin."

"Shots in the dark," Tarkin said.

"Only from your vantage," Vader said; then he took his hands from the steering yoke and turned to him to add: "Your ship. Flank speed."

Tarkin pulled the copilot's yoke into his lap and began to slalom the *Predator* through the debris field spewed by the crippled station. At the same time, Vader swiveled to position himself at the controls for the forward guns. Wary of allowing the ion engines to overheat, Tarkin slued the ship through clusters of slagged alloy, incinerated starfighters, and tumbling bodies.

Far to starboard the explosions were thinning. The *Carrion Spike* had enough firepower to destroy the entire station, but the dissidents were tapering off the attack, perhaps to reserve energy for future targets. Was that the goal? Tarkin wondered. To use his ship to inflict as much damage as possible?

The thought of having the *Carrion Spike* leave such a legacy hollowed him.

"Commence fire," Vader said.

Hyphens of raw energy surged from the *Predator*, the chuddering of her reciprocating quad lasers loud in the cockpit. Ahead, fire spattered against the *Carrion Spike*'s ray and particle shields, and for the briefest instant the ship was revealed. Quickly, then, the *Predator*'s beams were streaking into empty space.

Tarkin yawed to port, hoping to evade the *Carrion Spike*'s response, but the shipjackers yawed with him and their first salvo nearly overwhelmed the *Predator*'s inferior shields. Tarkin pushed the yoke away from him, skimming the atmosphere of Galidraan III with the *Carrion Spike* hewing to his trajectory and preparing to pounce. In the grip of a second barrage, the *Predator* shook in his grip and the console lights began to flicker.

"Drop behind them," Vader said.

Tarkin rushed a deceleration burn and starboard feint, hoping to trick the shipjackers into overflying the *Predator*. Instead the *Carrion Spike* leapt and spun through a half turn—which Tarkin grasped only when he saw a tempest of energy beams converging on the cockpit.

Tarkin's sudden swerve and spin almost threw Vader from his chair.

"They're employing the pintle guns," Tarkin said in a rush. "They'll burn right through us." He risked a glance at Vader. "We've one chance to survive this. Redirect all power to the aft shields."

Vader took Tarkin at his word, and the *Predator* slowed significantly as a result. The *Carrion Spike*'s beams found their mark, all but driving the smaller ship forward.

"Shields at forty percent," Vader said.

Tarkin pulled on the shuddering yoke, taking the *Predator* into a sudden climb, but there was no escaping his own ship. Another barrage rattled the *Predator* to her rivets.

Vader slammed his fist on the console. "They have jammed our instruments. Shields at twenty percent."

A powerful explosion aft worked its way forward to the cockpit, conjuring fire from the sparking instruments, stripping the ship of shields and propulsion, and leaving the *Predator* dead in space.

———

"Damage assessment!" Teller called toward the audio pickup as he scrambled to his feet in the *Carrion Spike*'s command cabin. Still strapped into the pilot's chair, Salikk was in the midst of bringing some of the stunned systems back to life, tufts of his fur wafting through the cabin on currents of recycled air.

Anora's voice issued through one of the speakers. "Air lock controls for the escape pods are fried."

"We're not going to be needing the pods, Anora. Move on."

Hask's voice was the next to ring out. "Fire in cargo hold three has been extinguished."

"Lock down the hold and disable the exhaust fans," Teller said quickly. "I don't want us venting any smoke or fire-suppressant foam." Clapping grit from his hands, he dropped himself into the comm officer's chair. "Cala, where are you?"

The speaker crackled. "Aft maintenance bay. The hyperdrive generator seems to be operable, but it's making some awfully strange noises. Don't know what it will do when we jump. Can't now, anyway, until self-diagnostics are complete."

"How long?"

"Ten minutes. Fifteen at the most." Cala's forced exhalation could be heard through the speaker. "They knew just where to hit us, Teller."

"Of course they did—it's Tarkin's ship!"

"And they tracked us through hyperspace again."

Salikk spoke before Teller could reply. "The station has launched another squadron of starfighters. They're flying search formations, radiating out from the *Parsec Predator*."

Teller called up a magnified view of the incapacitated ship. "I was hoping they'd mistake the *Predator* for us, but Tarkin must still have limited comm." He shook his head in vexation. "We must have put on quite a show for the station personnel."

"The starfighters," Salikk repeated.

Teller watched the ARC-170s and V-wings begin to fan out. "Do we have sublight?"

"We do. But I'm worried those starfighters will sniff out our ion signatures."

"Worry more about Vader. He's probably guiding them right to us." Teller thought for a moment. "Take evasive action. Full silent running."

Salikk glanced at him. "Shouldn't we finish them off? I mean, when will we have another chance like this—to kill two of the Empire's chief commanders?"

"They're replaceable."

"Tarkin, maybe. But Vader?"

"For all we know the Emperor has a dozen more like him in deep freeze. Besides, we need to make the most out of this ship while we've got her."

Salikk nodded. "I reluctantly agree."

"Reluctance is fine." Teller swung toward the audio pickup. "Doc, where are you?"

"Cargo hold one," Artoz said. "And there's something here you need to see before we go to lightspeed."

Teller looked at Salikk. "You okay here?"

"Go," the Gotal said, fairly bleating the word.

Teller pushed himself out of the chair and hurried through the command cabin hatch into the afterdeck. Racing through the conference cabin, he took the starboard connector to the turbolift, only to find it unresponsive. He hurried back to the main cabin and took the emergency stairwell down one level to the engine room, then wormed his way through a narrow cofferdam that accessed the cargo holds. As he came through the hatch of cargo hold one, he saw Artoz crawling out from around a large black sphere set into a hexagonal dais that took up most of the hold.

"What's so important I need to see it?"

The Mon Cal got to his big feet and gestured to the sphere. "This."

Teller regarded the sphere from top to bottom. "Yeah, I saw this during our initial recon. What of it?"

"To begin with, do you know what it is?"

"Cala thinks it's a component of the stealth system—"

"No, it is not," Artoz cut in. "If the cloaking device was powered by hibridium, then yes, that would provide a possible explanation. But this ship's stealth system runs on stygium crystals, which obviates the need for a device of this sort."

"Okay," Teller said in a tentative way.

Artoz indicated the sphere's vertical seams. "The hemispheres are designed to separate longitudinally, but I can't find a control panel or any way to prompt the device to open."

Teller walked partway around the sphere. "You think it's housing a tracker of some sort?"

"Our scanners haven't detected any."

Teller made his eyes bright with mystification. "So?"

"I think this *is* the homing beacon."

Teller gaped at him.

"What I mean to say is that I think this belongs to Vader, and that Vader was able to follow us to Fial, then Galidraan, by tracking his *property*."

Teller's brow wrinkled. "Look, he may be more machine than man, but—"

"We've combed the ship forward-to-aft and belly-to-spine and found nothing in the way of a locator capable of tracking us through hyperspace."

Teller's comlink chimed before he could answer.

"The hyperdrive generator's completed its self-test," Cala updated. "It's still protesting, but we should be good to go."

"Then get down here." He commed the cockpit. "Salikk, navigate to the jump point, but hold there until I give you the word. We've got something to take care of before we go to hyperspace."

"Understood," Salikk said.

"Oh, and one more thing: Destroy Galidraan's hyperspace buoy on the way out. We don't want anyone following us this time."

Vader stood unmoving at the *Predator*'s forward viewports, the scarlet light of emergency illuminators reflecting off his helmet, the black orbs of his helmet mask seemingly fixed on the escaping *Carrion Spike*.

"Galidraan Station is dispatching a shuttle and readying their fastest corvette for pursuit," Tarkin said from the copilot's chair. "Sergeant Crest reports three dead."

"Your ship is still in the system," Vader said slowly. Then, turning his head, he barked, "Squadron Commander, are you hearing me?"

A warbling voice drifted from the cockpit nunciator. "Loud and clear, Lord Vader. Awaiting your orders."

"Commander, direct your starfighter squadron toward the bright side of Galidraan Four's outermost moon."

"My scanners aren't showing anything in that vicinity, Lord Vader."

"I will supply all the targeting data you need, Commander."

"Affirmative, Lord Vader. We're keeping the battle and tactical nets open."

Tarkin pressed the padded speaker of a comm headset to his left ear. "Station navicomputers are calculating all possible egress points."

Vader clasped his hands behind his back. "The Perlemian Trade Route is a short jump from this system."

"Escape is not their intention," Tarkin said.

Vader turned away from the viewport to look at him.

"If escape were their plan," Tarkin said, "they would have already done so." He cleared his throat meaningfully. "No. They have something else in mind. Perhaps to strike at another target." Once more he pressed the headpiece speaker to his ear, then toggled a switch that routed the audio feed to the enunciator.

"—calculations are ready, Governor Tarkin," a deep voice announced. "We're transmitting them to the shuttle, so that you and Lord Vader will have immediate access to them."

"Thank you, Colonel," Tarkin said into the headset mike. "In the meantime, I want a list of local systems that host Imperial resources."

"I can provide that information now, Governor. We have a large garrison in the Felucia system. Rhen Var has a small dirtside outpost. Nam Chorios has both a mining colony and a small Imperial prison facility. We have additional outposts at Trogan and Jomark. And of course, the naval base and R/M Facility Four deepdock at Belderone."

"What do we have parked at R/M, Colonel?"

"Several CR-ninety corvettes, two *Carrack*-class light cruisers, a couple of Victories, and a *Venator*-class destroyer—the *Liberator*."

"Stand by, Colonel." Tarkin muted the audio feed and swiveled toward Vader. "Are you reasonably certain that our particle beams wounded them?"

Vader nodded.

"If the hyperdrive is damaged, they might opt to lie low to effect repairs," Tarkin said.

Vader nodded again. "Or go in search of replacement parts."

"And if they're not wounded?"

"Continue their mission," Vader said with finality.

Tarkin fell silent for a long moment. Never having had an opportunity to put the *Carrion Spike* through her paces, the recent engagement had left him with an even more profound appreciation for the ship. "Why didn't they kill us when they had the chance? Could it be they believe they were being pursued by the Sugi crime lord?"

"No," Vader said sharply. "They know that *we* are here."

"Then perhaps they didn't kill us because they have a rendezvous or a schedule to keep?"

"Perhaps," Vader said.

Tarkin swiveled in place. "Belderone?"

"Too heavily fortified—even for your corvette."

"Felucia, then—in reprisal for the way the Republic left it."

"Of no significance."

"Rhen Var is merely an outpost . . . So: Nam Chorios?"

Vader took a moment to respond. "Instruct Belderone to send the *Liberator* there."

Tarkin activated the headset microphone. "Colonel, we need to contact Belderone and Coruscant," he started to say, then cut himself off on hearing Vader growl.

"What is it?"

"Whoever they are, they are resourceful." The Dark Lord turned slowly from the viewports. "They have jettisoned the meditation chamber."

The voice of the starfighter squadron commander issued from the enunciator. "Lord Vader, our scanners have detected an object—"

"Commander, order your pilots to open fire along that vector—lasers and proton torpedoes if they have them."

"Lord Vader, we have a detonation," the commander said a moment later.

Tarkin leapt from the chair to stand alongside Vader. "Did they hit the *Carrion Spike*?"

The answer was slow to arrive. "Lord Vader," the commander said, "the enemy has taken out the system hyperspace buoy. Our sensors are also picking up wake rotation readings."

"They have jumped to lightspeed," Vader said.

Tarkin ran a hand over his high forehead. "Then they've managed to make themselves untraceable, as well as invisible."

14

A CASE OF DO OR DIE

ITS TIERED ROOF a canopy of scanner, sensor, and communications arrays, Naval Intelligence headquarters heaved from Coruscant's metallic crust as if thrust up by tectonic forces from the depths of the planet. Along with the Palace and the byzantine COMPNOR arcology—which housed the Imperial Security Bureau, the Ubiqtorate, and other ambiguous organizations—Naval Intelligence was the third point of the Federal District's supreme triangle. The fact that the shielded, hardened, near-windowless complex more resembled a prison than a fortress had given rise to speculation that its sheer walls were designed as much to keep the agency's staff of tens of thousands of military officers inside as to keep ordinary Coruscanti out.

Constructed soon after the end of the war atop monads that had once made up the Republic's strategic center, Naval Intelligence was a nexus for gathering and analyzing transmissions that poured in from across the ecumenopolis and from all sectors of the expanding Empire. And yet its operations were not conducted in complete secrecy. During the construction phase, micro-holocams had been installed in every nook and cranny so that the actions and conversations of every staffer could be monitored at any hour of the day or night; not by the members of the Senate's various oversight committees, however, but by the Emperor and the most trusted members of the Ruling Council. Everyone involved with Naval Intelligence knew that the cams were there and had gradually grown accustomed to their presence. While the officers and others no longer played to the spy eyes as they had early on, they went about their business well aware that at any given moment they might be on stage.

Just now the Joint Chiefs of the Empire's military were gathered— Admiral Antonio Motti, General Cassio Tagge, Rear Admirals Ozzel, Jerjerrod, and others—along with several top officers from COMP-NOR, including Director Armand Isard, ISB deputy director Harus Ison, and Colonel Wullf Yularen. Naval Intelligence was represented by Vice Admirals Rancit and Screed, who had requested the meeting.

With the bright light of late afternoon pouring through the tall windows of the Palace spire's pinnacle room, Sidious studied their holograms from his chair, using controls in the armrest to choose from among several cams and to provide alternative vantages. The droid, 11-4D, stood by him, one of its appendages plugged into an interface socket that routed holofeeds to the summit from what had been a Jedi communications suite in the base of the spire.

"Tint the windows," Sidious said without taking his gaze from the projected holograms.

"Of course, Your Majesty."

With the daylight dimmed, the cyan-hued holograms acquired more detail. The intelligence officers had asked for an audience in the Palace, but Sidious had turned them down. Similarly he had declined to attend their meeting virtually. As nettlesome as it was to have learned that the dissidents in possession of Tarkin's starship had embarked on a killing spree in the Outer Rim, Sidious found the cachet-driven spitefulness of the intelligence chiefs to be even more tedious. So he had dispatched Mas Amedda and Ars Dangor in his stead.

"I accept the dissidents have managed to wreak havoc in an isolated star system," Ison was saying, "but the fact remains that they brought only one ship to bear on our facility."

"One ship capable of hiding itself from scanners," Rancit said, "outmaneuvering our starfighters, outracing a Star Destroyer . . ."

"Permit me to amend my statement, then," Ison continued as Rancit allowed his words to trail off. "One fast and powerful ship. Still, they used it to launch an attack on an unimportant outpost."

"The start of a campaign of destruction," Screed interjected.

The officers were grouped around a large circular table, with Mas Amedda and Ars Dangor occupying prominent seats. Above the center of the table floated 3-D star maps, wire-frame displays, and plotting panels, some showing the locations of Outer Rim bases and installations, others the disposition of ships of the fleet, with symbols denoting Star Destroyers, Dreadnoughts, corvettes, and frigates, on down to pickets and gunboats.

"We've no proof that the shipjackers are on a campaign," Ison said, taking up the challenge. "Targeting the space station may have been their way of evading capture by Governor Tarkin and Lord Vader."

"As a diversion, in other words?" Screed said in elaborate disbelief, his ocular implant glinting in the light from the holograms. "Governor Tarkin came close to losing his life to his own ship. Given his experience and expertise, we have to assume that the *Carrion Spike* is in the hands of a very competent and dangerous group."

"I've known Governor Tarkin for over twenty years," Rancit said in reinforcement, "and I can assure you that if he considers the group to pose a serious threat to the Empire, then they are nothing less."

Ison blew out his breath and shook his head. "Repositioning our resources from Belderone to fortify a couple of minor installations was reckless. We can't run the risk of curtailing pacification campaigns or hunting down former Separatists for a strategy of defeat-in-detail at the edge of civilized space."

"And what if the shipjackers' campaign should expand into the Mid Rim?" Rancit said. "The ship gives them the ability to strike almost anywhere in the galaxy."

Ison gaped at him for a long moment. "Is it the navy's aim, then, to redeploy the entire fleet to effect system-denial to a handful of dissidents?"

"In major star systems, yes," Rancit said. "Should the situation warrant it."

Rear Admiral Motti spoke to it. "At the risk of sounding too cavalier about this, Governor Tarkin's ship does not have unlimited firepower." The traditional cut of his brown hair and the boyish features of his clean-shaven face belied an attitude of perpetual sarcasm. "Whatever course we take, the ship will eventually cease to be a threat."

"I concur," Ison chimed in. "It's one ship. I recommend we let it go."

Mas Amedda came to his feet in anger. "Clearly all of you are oblivious to the real danger posed by this group of privateers. We are not concerned about remote outposts or even important installations. The ship must be captured or destroyed because of the danger it poses to the Emperor's unchallengeable reign!"

"That is just the point I was about to make, Vizier," Rancit said when voices around the table had quieted. He was facing Amedda, but in such a way that he seemed to be speaking more to one of the monitoring cams, as if aware that Sidious was observing, and addressing him directly. "Imperial Security initially stressed that the communications cache on Murkhana could potentially be used to disseminate anti-Imperial propaganda. Now Deputy Director Ison fails to grasp that the intent of the dissidents may be to use Governor Tarkin's ship for that very purpose."

Raven-haired man's man Director Armand Isard was about to intervene when a junior intelligence officer seated at a comm board spoke first. "Sirs, sorry to interrupt, but we're receiving reports of another unprovoked attack in the Outer Rim."

"Nam Chorios," Screed said. "Just as Governor Tarkin predicted."

"No, Admiral," the comm officer said. "Lucazec."

It was General Tagge's turn to rush to his feet. The scion of a wealthy, influential family, he was tall and thickly built, with a broad face defined by long, flaring sideburns. "TaggeCo has operations at Lucazec!"

"We're in reception of a live holofeed," the junior officer updated.

Rancit had amplified an area of the star map and was gazing up into it. "They've jumped clear across the sector, inward of the Perlemian Trade Route!" He looked at Motti. "Do we have any resources there?"

Motti had a datapad in hand and was gazing at the device's display screen. "A small garrison of ground troops and a squadron of V-wing starfighters protecting TaggeCo's mining interests."

"The holofeed is streaming," the junior officer said.

Above the table's inset projector a holographic video of the attack resolved and stabilized. Centered in the field floated TaggeCo's city-sized orbital processing plant, an entire section of it engulfed by spherical explosions, the company logo effaced by melted metal. Quanta of unleashed energy were raining down on the facility, blowing chunks of it into local space. Drifting into view between the continuous barrage of beams were pieces of V-wing starfighters and prosaic ore haulers, one of which was falling toward dun-colored Lucazec in flames, its ablative shields glowing red hot. Farther below, clouds of thick black smoke were coiling into the smudged sky.

"They've targeted surface operations, as well," Tagge said, still on his feet and clenching and unclenching his hand.

Ison glanced from him to the junior officer at the comm board in visible alarm. "Who's transmitting this holovid? Is it being sent live by an orbital facility? An outlying ship?"

"The transmission is arriving on an Imperial HoloNet frequency," the junior officer said.

"Yes," Ison said, "but the point of view . . . It looks as if one of our own ships is the aggressor."

Screed and Motti traded worried glances.

In the summit of the Palace spire, Sidious sat back into his chair, folding his arms across his chest as sinuous currents of the dark side played through him, and as if he meant to contain them.

"Have you puzzled out what is happening, droid?" he asked.

"Yes, Your Majesty," 11-4D said, simultaneous with a further update from the junior officer.

"Sirs, we have confirmation that the holovid is being transmitted by the *Carrion Spike*."

Sidious swiveled toward the tinted windows, behind which the sky above and Coruscant below were the color of ash. Narrowing his gaze, he reached out for Darth Vader, whom he sensed was observing the holovid, as well.

Yes, Lord Vader, Sidious sent through the Force, *you shall have your starfighter.*

Moving with fierce purpose, Tarkin exited the *Liberator*'s hangar command post and walked briskly along the dorsal flight deck, passing starfighters and ground-effect vehicles as he closed on the shuttle craft awaiting him. The Star Destroyer's massive overhead doors were closed, and the light on the flight deck was dim. The captain of the *Liberator* was standing at the foot of the shuttle's boarding ramp. A short man with gray hair and a meticulously trimmed beard, he saluted as Tarkin approached.

"Sorry we couldn't be of more help, Governor Tarkin."

Tarkin gestured in dismissal. "You're not to blame, Commander. You came when called, and for that alone you have my gratitude."

The commander nodded. "Thank you, sir."

Tarkin extended his hand, and the commander shook it decorously. "Are you returning to Belderone base?" Tarkin asked.

"No, sir. Coruscant has ordered us to jump directly to Ord Cestus."

Tarkin's brow furrowed in question. "Why so far down the Perlemian?"

"Triage redeployments," the commander said, "as a result of what happened at Lucazec, I suppose. The same at Centares and Lantillies. No telling where your—uh, the missing ship is going to revert next."

"Perhaps," Tarkin said, and let it go at that.

He ascended the boarding ramp and walked aft, settling into a seat in the main cabin, the *Theta*-class shuttle's only passenger. High overhead, the *Liberator*'s hangar doors parted down the middle and retracted, and the shuttle rose off its skids on repulsorlift power, dropped its wings, and sped toward its rendezvous point, a pod-shaped support carrier named the *Goliath,* which had recently arrived from deepdock at Ord Mantell. Tarkin had a port-side glimpse of bleak Nam Chorios as the shuttle angled away from the Star Destroyer, the system's sun providing barely enough light to illuminate the planet let alone warm it to human standards.

Tarkin turned inward to consider the commander's remarks. Capital ships redeploying from bases as distant as Centares and Lantillies, all because of the *Carrion Spike*. He trusted that naval command knew better than to disperse the fleet too thinly, though there was no denying that the shipjackers had once again taken everyone by surprise.

That might not have been the case if Coruscant had placed Lucazec on alert, but no one, including Tarkin, had given much thought to the possibility that the dissidents would target a lightly defended TaggeCo mining concern. Entering the star system with an altered transponder signature but transmitting authentic Imperial codes, the *Carrion Spike* had opened fire on both the orbital facility and ground-side operations before Lucazec could react. Jova would have applauded the shipjackers' tactics, the idea of masking oneself in the scent of one's enemy.

He could still summon the odors of musky excretions he had been forced to smear over himself during hunts or surveillance exercises on the plateau. The rodent Jova had struck with the airspeeder one night had only been the beginning. After that had come the dizzying, often nauseating scents of sly vulpines, antlered ruminants, squat felines . . . But in countless situations the excretions had given them the upper hand, allowing them to kill or infiltrate as needed.

Except at the Spike. But of course that wasn't the idea.

At Lucazec, the shipjackers hadn't even bothered to activate the *Carrion Spike*'s stealth systems until they had reached their target. They were experimenting, perhaps in preparation for their next attack. Deflector shields had protected the mining facility for a time, but its fate had been sealed. The destruction and casualties the ship had left in her wake were consistent with what she had wrought at Galidraan.

When the shipjackers' HoloNet transmission had been received by the *Liberator,* Tarkin had tried to convince himself that it was another counterfeit, that the holovid had been cobbled together from wartime news feeds and created images, as had been the case at Sentinel and on Murkhana. In his eagerness to prove himself correct—and to the bewilderment of some of the *Liberator*'s petty officers—he had practically placed himself inside the blue holofield, searching for evidence of corruption that would have identified the feed as a fake. But he found no such signs. It had taken some time to disabuse himself of the notion that the shipjackers were deliberately provoking him, and to accept that they were merely making use of the *Carrion Spike*'s sophisticated communications suite to call attention to their agenda, as Count Dooku had managed to do early on in the Clone Wars. And like Dooku, the shipjackers had succeeded in broadcasting the Lucazec holovid live over civilian HoloNet frequencies to thousands of Outer and Mid Rim star systems before Coruscant was able to shut down vast portions of the communications grid.

Still, the damage had been done. According to the latest reports from Naval Intelligence, the shipjackers were already attracting media attention in some of the outer systems, and certain members of the Ruling Council were worried about blowback: that disaffected factions might begin to think that the Empire was vulnerable, and that imitators would spring up, convinced that they, too, could make themselves heard far and wide.

Tarkin had also learned that the contentious debate between Imperial Security and Naval Intelligence on how best to proceed had yet to subside, especially with the *Carrion Spike* on the loose once more, hiding in hyperspace or lurking in some remote or unpopulated star system. It appeared, however, that Vice Admirals Rancit and Screed were currently the gears getting the most grease, as the Admiralty had been granted permission by the Emperor to deploy forces to unprotected worlds along the Perlemian Trade Route and the Hydian Way. That, in any case, was how the *Goliath* came to be at Nam Chorios, and apparently why the *Liberator* had been deemed needed at Ord Cestus.

No sooner had the support carrier arrived than Vader had had himself ferried aboard, as it had brought from Coruscant his personal starfighter.

Tarkin had been busy since he and Vader had parted company, speaking with Commander Cassel at Sentinel Base, with intelligence assets on Murkhana, and with the commanders of Imperial posts throughout the sector; and as well with Wullf Yularen—who had his hands full keeping the peace among the intelligence agencies. Tarkin had spent the past ten hours in the *Liberator*'s data center, poring over star maps and charts and performing complex calculations.

He needed sleep, but sleep would have to wait until after he met with Vader.

The shuttle's wings folded upward as it lazed through a magcon field into the support escort's main hangar. The ship's commander and a dozen of his top officers and black-uniformed noncoms were standing eyes-front on the deck as Tarkin descended the ramp. Alongside the group stood a full company of stormtroopers, in addition to Sergeant Crest and the remaining six members of Vader's personal detail.

"Welcome aboard, Governor Tarkin," the commander said, stepping out of line to greet him.

"Good to see you again, Ros. I wish it were under better circumstances."

"We'll just have to make them better."

Tarkin smiled without amusement "Where is Lord Vader?"

"Starfighter bay. I'll escort you." The commander turned to dismiss the others, then gestured politely to Tarkin and set off across the deck.

It took only moments to reach the starfighter bay, where the commander left Tarkin to his business. Tarkin didn't need to look far for Vader's starfighter, as it was the only Eta-2 among a squadron of V-wings. The absence of color might have struck Tarkin as a dramatic choice had black not been the Dark Lord's preferred color. What's more, many pilots during the war had made an effort to distinguish themselves, so why not Vader now?

Vader was standing between the weapons arms of the craft's split prow tinkering with something, while a silver astromech droid stood by, plugged into a portable diagnostics unit. Without so much as a word of greeting from Tarkin, Vader turned and stepped out from between the forward laser cannons.

"I trust that your fighter weathered the jump from Ord Mantell in good repair," Tarkin said.

"Not entirely, Governor, but the starfighter's troubles do not concern me at the moment. What have you learned?"

Tarkin lifted an eyebrow. "An interesting question, Lord Vader."

The foul humor Vader had been in since the attack at Lucazec hadn't faded. "I am not referring to *lessons*, Governor. Do you have new information?"

Tarkin nodded. "Something we need to discuss in strict confidence."

Vader turned to respond to a series of urgent twitters from the droid, then wordlessly led Tarkin to a small unoccupied situation room adjacent to the starfighter bay. The room featured a holotable and an array of communications modules.

"Our isolation is assured," Vader said. "Now: What have you learned?"

"I believe I have discovered a way to predict where the *Carrion Spike* will next emerge."

"Your prediction will need to improve greatly on our hunch at Galidraan, Governor."

"I've removed some of the guesswork."

Vader waited.

"Several things before I speak to my forecast. First, the device serial numbers we recorded on Murkhana indicate that the components were in fact part of a Separatist communications cache confiscated by the Republic during the war and warehoused in an Imperial depot until they disappeared sometime within the past three years."

"Disappeared," Vader said. "Like the warship modules and droids you traced from Sentinel Base."

"Precisely. Sold, stolen, or perhaps given away."

"All three possibilities imply the conspiracy of insiders."

Tarkin smiled with purpose. "There's more. The dissidents' attack on the Galidraan wheel was especially well timed, in that a *Victory*-class Star Destroyer had jumped from the system not an hour before the *Carrion Spike* arrived."

Vader considered it. "The dissidents knew."

Tarkin nodded. "They may be working in tandem with a scout ship. Or perhaps with the warship observed at Sentinel Base."

"Or receiving help from the same insiders who provided them with confiscated equipment." Vader paused. "The Emperor wishes to make an example of them, Governor. But he demands that we reel *all* of them in, not simply those who pirated your ship."

"And so we shall, if my calculations are correct."

Again, Vader waited.

Tarkin prized his datapad from the pocket of his tunic and tasked it to interface with the holoprojector table. A rotund star map resolved in midair, which Tarkin manipulated from the datapad. The *Carrion Spike*'s movements were indicated by a zigzagging red line, annotated by measurements and calculations.

"Fuel consumption," Vader said after a moment.

"I should have known you'd be ahead of me."

"I am not unfamiliar with the method, Governor."

Vader didn't offer an explanation, so Tarkin went on, using his forefinger to highlight his statements.

"The ship was fully fueled when it left Sentinel Base. We didn't bother refueling on Coruscant for the jump to Murkhana, as there was more than an ample supply for the round-trip. From Murkhana, however, the ship jumped first to Fial, then to Galidraan, and then to Lucazec. We have no way of assessing let alone knowing where the corvette is at present—whether it is in hyperspace or parked in some local star system—but either way its fuel is in short supply. And unless the shipjackers have completed their mission—a supposition I find highly unlikely—fuel has to be their next priority."

Tarkin made adjustments to the star map, magnifying an area of the local sector. "Fuel requirements for the *Carrion Spike* are not ordinary, and replenishment sites out here are few and far between. In fact, calculations suggest only two options: here"—Tarkin pointed—"at Gromas, in the Perkell sector, or here, at Phindar, in the Mandalore sector."

Vader circled the star map twice before coming to a halt and looking at Tarkin. "As it happens, Governor, I am acquainted with both worlds."

Now Tarkin waited, but once more the Dark Lord offered no explanation.

"Like Lucazec," Tarkin continued, "Gromas supports a mining operation—for phrik, I believe—"

"Yes," Vader said.

"The Empire has a depot there that includes a full range of fuel options. Phindar, by contrast, was attacked by Separatists during the war, and hosts what is little more than a large tanker in fixed orbit. The property of a criminal cartel some twenty years ago, it is now operated by subcontractors as a fuel and service facility for Imperial starships."

"Two options," Vader said, "Gromas presenting more difficulties."

"The shipjackers chose Lucazec over Nam Chorios or even Belderone, and they transmitted their attack live over the HoloNet. If, then, their plan is to spread both destruction *and* propaganda—"

"Gromas would be the expected choice, if only because of its relative importance."

Tarkin nodded slowly. "It's certainly the target we should provide to the intelligence agencies."

Vader nodded slowly, in full understanding of Tarkin's implication. "I'll inform the Emperor."

"The *Carrion Spike* may already be in motion," Tarkin said, squaring his shoulders.

As if in echo of Tarkin's posture of readiness, Vader planted his fists on his hips. "Then we have no time to spare."

15

NEGATIVE CAPABILITY

THE *CARRION SPIKE* DRIFTED above a lifeless, volcanic planet in a star system designated by number rather than by name. The crew was already assembled in the conference cabin when Teller entered, wearing the uniform of an Imperial commander.

"Turn around so we can get the full effect," Anora said from one of the chairs that surrounded the cabin's circular table.

"Doesn't fit you like it used to," Cala said.

Teller stared down at himself in disappointment. "Poverty will do that to a being." He raised his head to speak to all of them. "But I've got good news—"

"Good news from a human dressed as an Imperial," Salikk interrupted, fingering the tuft of fur on his cheek. "That has to be a first."

"What did our ally have to say?" Dr. Artoz asked.

"A task force has jumped for Gromas."

Artoz's side-facing eyes grew vivid with interest. "Confirmed?"

Teller nodded once. "From multiple sources."

"Then you were right about Tarkin," Hask said.

Teller hitched up his trousers and straddled a chair. "When he was with Outland in the Greater Seswenna, they used to track pirates by calculating fuel consumption. Outland would track them to a fuel depot and swoop in. The Jedi did the same. You just have to know how much fuel a ship started out with and you have to be reasonably certain of its itinerary. Doesn't always work, but when it does, it works like a charm." He glanced at Cala. "You glad now about taking the extra time on Murkhana?"

The Koorivar wrinkled his face but nodded.

"Even with Imperials jumping for Gromas," Hask said, "every depot between here and Centares has got to be on the lookout for this ship."

Teller compressed his lips. "I never promised a sure thing. The altered transponder signature worked at Lucazec, and there's no reason to think it won't work again. To most Imperial installations, we're just another corvette running low on fuel. But that doesn't mean something can't go wrong. If that happens, we have enough fuel to jump at the first sign of trouble."

"To where, and then what?" Salikk said.

"Let's not get ahead of ourselves," Teller told everyone. "For now, we follow the plan."

Hask was shaking her head, her slanted eyes narrowed. "We should have stashed fuel somewhere. Refueled ourselves."

Teller scowled at the Zygerrian. "We broke the bank getting that shipment to Murkhana." He gestured to himself. "Like I said, poverty wreaks havoc with a diet."

Hask looked away from him, a frown contorting her angular features, so Teller turned to Anora. "Good job with the holovid. It's getting attention all over."

She shrugged. "Just doing my job, Teller. Same as ever."

Teller grew serious as he swung to Cala. "Speaking of jobs . . ."

"Done," the Koorivar said. "Although I had to spend extra time in decontamination."

"I thought your complexion looked ruddier than usual."

"No joke, Teller," Cala said. "That stint could cost me a couple of years."

"If it's any consolation, there'll be a higher cost to the Imperials."

"That part doesn't bother you at all, does it?" Hask said with a sneer. "The indiscriminate killing, I mean."

Teller frowned. "Indiscriminate? What, because not all of them are soldiers? This is where you draw the line?"

"People have to work, Teller," the Zygerrian said.

"Don't kid yourself, Hask. These aren't civilian targets. They're Imperial installations staffed by people who have bought into the Emperor's sick vision of the future—for you, your queen, me, and everyone between here and the Unknown Regions. You've seen the recruitment posters: Serve the Empire and be a better being for it! That doesn't turn your stomach? Anyone who willingly serves is a traitor to *life*, Hask. And don't tell me they don't know what they're signing up for, because it's as clear as those posters on the wall. It's enslavement, suppression, military might the likes of which none of us has ever seen." He worked his jaw. "I won't go peacefully into that future, and neither should you. Hell, why are you even with us if you haven't thought this through by now?"

Anora made a conciliatory gesture. "She knows. She just forgets sometimes." She glanced at Hask. "Don't you?"

Hask returned a brooding nod.

But Teller wasn't through. "Look, whether they're mining ore for TaggeCo or refueling Imperial warships, it comes down to the same thing: standing with the Emperor. Our high-minded leader, who on his most benevolent day is still worse than Vader. The idea, Hask, just in case you've forgotten, is to put the fear into anyone who's even contemplating joining up. To slow the death toll, Hask. And as payback. Do you get it or not?"

"I get it," Hask said finally.

Anora slapped the tops of her thighs and laughed shortly. "Teller, sometimes you are so straight out of a holodrama I can't decide whether to cheer or applaud. My production team on Coruscant would have made good use of you."

Teller glanced from her to Hask and snorted in derision. "Artists. If the Emperor has his way, you'll be the first ones targeted for eradication." He waited a long moment. "Are we done?"

Heads nodded in assurance.

Teller looked at Anora. "Speaking of holodramas, let's see how I look with red hair."

Tarkin, dressed in a black flight suit, was waiting in the hangar command center when the ship reverted to realspace at the Rimward edge of the Phindar system. Floating above a holoprojector was a one-quarter-scale holopresence of the tanker facility's administrator, a yellow-eyed, lugubrious-looking humanoid sporting a pair of thin green arms that dangled past his knees.

"Refueling has been completed, Governor Tarkin," the Phindian rasped in Basic. "The corvette is preparing to detach as we speak."

"Good work, Administrator. You performed the refueling according to my instructions?"

"We did—though it took considerable effort."

"The Empire looks kindly on those who cooperate in such matters."

"And I look forward to whatever kindness you're willing to dole out, Governor. But you should know that the ship is assailable. My workers and the stormtroopers here are more than willing to take the crew head-on."

"No, Administrator," Tarkin said in a way that brooked no argument. "You mustn't raise any suspicions. What's more, the people aboard that ship have had plenty of time to prepare for this. You and your workers would be killed."

"If you say so, Governor."

"I do say so. Have you a recording of the commander?"

The Phindian nodded his huge, snub-nosed head. "Transmitting it now."

Tarkin squinted at the hologram that appeared alongside the holopresence of the facility administrator. Dressed in an Imperial uniform, the man was tall and lean, with thick red hair and a raised scar on his left cheek that ran from the corner of a full mouth to a bionic eye not unlike the one worn by Vice Admiral Screed.

"His code cylinder identified him as Commander LaSal."

"One moment, Administrator," Tarkin said, stepping out of cam range and turning to the nearest specialist in the command post.

"Run the hologram through the roster database. If indeed there is a Commander LaSal, find out where he is currently deployed."

"Yes, sir," the specialist said.

Tarkin moved back into view of the holocam. "You were saying, Administrator . . ."

"Only that LaSal's rank plaque insignia and command cap disk looked legitimate."

Tarkin wasn't surprised. With all the shipjackers had already accomplished, forging command cylinder codes and insignias must have been child's play.

"Sir," the specialist said from his station, "the roster shows a Commander Abel LaSal deployed aboard the Star Destroyer *Sovereign*, currently docked at Fondor. But the likenesses don't match up the way they should. Shall I contact the *Sovereign*?"

Tarkin shook his head. "That won't be necessary."

The words had scarcely left his mouth when a starfighter signals officer entered in a rush. "Governor Tarkin, Lord Vader requests that you join him in the bay soonest."

Tarkin ended the duplex transmission and hurried through the hatch and across the deck to where a yellow-and-gray V-wing was powering up. The canopy was open, and a red astromech occupied a socket aft of the cockpit. Vader's black Eta-2 warmed nearby. Catching sight of Tarkin, the Dark Lord grabbed a flight helmet and life-support chest pack and carried them to him.

"Highly recommended," Vader said, handing over the gear.

Tarkin began to slip into the chest pack.

"It seems your calculations were correct, Governor."

"Yes, but coming all this way had to be a stretch for them. There's good reason to suspect that they did in fact refuel before launching from Murkhana."

"Then someone may have warned them away from Gromas."

"A point worth considering," Tarkin said. "In addition, they've betrayed themselves in other ways. Not only are they conversant with the *Carrion Spike*'s instruments, they are also well acquainted with Imperial procedure. The self-styled commander looks every bit an officer, and he used code cylinders to requisition the fuel cells." He looked up at Vader. "Some of the Empire's own?"

"The Emperor has limited patience for puzzles, Governor. Whoever they are, we need to put an end to their game."

The tanker orbited above hospitable Phindar. A lengthy cylinder of unshielded alloy, the enormous station's aft bridge was elevated above a trapezoid of shielding that protected a quartet of sublight engines and a generic hyperdrive. Pressurized radioactive gas, liquid metal, and composites were housed in proprietary sections. Extravehicular droids of several varieties carried out refueling operations by installing fresh fuel cells in starships and removing and transporting spent cells to storage bins anchored along the tanker's starboard side. The *Carrion Spike* was still umbilicaled to the station, its bow facing the huge tanker's trapezoidal stern, as Teller hastened through the docking ring air lock and into the main cabin.

"Retract the transfer tube and get us out of here," he shouted toward the command cabin.

"Trouble?" Anora asked, leaping from her chair.

Teller shook his head while he peeled the scar from his cheek and the fake implant from his left eye. "That's the problem. Everything went way too smoothly. The Phindian didn't question anything, didn't even ask about the ship or the special fuel cells."

"You said yourself we're just another corvette out here," Anora said.

"Not up close we're not." Hearing the segmented umbilical retract into the hull, Teller hurried for the command cabin, Anora right on his heels.

"Easing us away," Salikk said from the captain's chair.

The corvette lurched slightly as maneuvering jets separated it from the tanker. Teller moved to the forward viewports to sweep his gaze over local space.

"What are you looking for?" Artoz asked from one of the other chairs.

"I won't know till I see it," Teller started to say when Cala cut him off.

"Ship reverting Rimward!" He paused to study the sensors. "Imperial escort carrier. On screen."

Teller, Anora, Hask, and Artoz crowded behind Cala's chair as an image resolved of a boxy vessel with a curved upper hull and a flat ventral one. Aft, the hull extended over the carrier's engines.

"Transponder signature identifies it as the *Goliath*," Cala continued. "Capable of carrying a wing of starfighters. Armed with ten Taim and Bak H-eights and a Krupx missile delivery system. Not much in the way of shields—"

"I'm not interested in testing its mettle," Teller said.

"It could be here simply to refuel," Artoz said, sounding unconvinced.

Abruptly, the escort vanished from the screen.

"Where'd it go?" Anora asked.

And just as abruptly the escort reappeared—now visible through the forward viewports.

"Microjump!" Cala said. "And deploying starfighters!"

Teller watched as starfighters dropped from the escort's deployment chute. "V-wings, led by an Eta-Two Actis."

"Bets on who's piloting the black one?" Hask said.

Anora was shaking her head in dismay. "How did they know?"

Teller's dark eyes were wide with surprise. "Tarkin may have figured if he could scare us away from Gromas by sending ships, we'd come to Phindar."

"Or he hedged his bet," Artoz said. "Capital ships at Gromas, he and Vader here."

Teller shook himself alert. "Doesn't much matter now." He turned to Cala. "How much time do we have?"

"A quarter hour," the Koorivar told him.

"Marking that," Artoz said.

"How far to the nearest jump point?"

Salikk swung to the navicomputer. "We need to get out of the way of Phindar and the principal moon."

"Then you've got some fancy flying to do first," Teller said. "Keep us as close to the tanker as possible and protect the hyperdrive generator at all costs. A couple of errant beams and everything's toast."

"Don't we know it," Cala said.

Salikk laughed shortly and madly. "If you think that'll keep Vader and Tarkin from firing, you're your own worst enemies."

Teller ignored the remark and looked at Anora. "Get your cams ready."

"Stay on my left wing," Vader told Tarkin over the tactical net as they fairly fell out of the escort, five additional pairs of V-wings at their backs.

The mammoth cylindrical tanker was straight ahead of them, profiled against the planet and with the *Carrion Spike* just beginning to drop beneath it, the shipjackers intent on putting the tanker between themselves and the approaching starfighters. With the corvette all but wedded bow-to-stern to the tanker, there was little point in enabling the ship's stealth system.

Schematics of the *Carrion Spike*'s airframe and hyperdrive generator had been uploaded into the targeting computer of each starfighter and astromech, as well as into the fire-control systems of the *Goliath*, a precise strike from whose larger guns could be enough to immobilize the corvette.

The squadron pilots reported in by call signs—Yellows Three through Twelve—as they formed up on Vader's black starfighter and accelerated toward the tanker.

"Our goal is to force the corvette to lower its deflector shields before we return fire," Tarkin said through his helmet headset. "Once we've done so, our priority will be to target the hyperdrive generator, which is aft of the main guns along the corvette's spine."

A chorus of distorted voices acknowledged the directives.

"Affirmative, Yellow Two."

Tarkin's right hand nudged the joystick while his left made adjustments to the instruments. Little more than a single-pilot fuselage pod sitting on vertically stacked ion engines and flanked by deployable heat-radiating stability foils, the V-wing had been designed for speed and nimbleness, at the expense of a reliable life-support system or hyperdrive. Twin ion cannons bracketed the long, wedge-shaped prow. It had been years since he had piloted one, and despite the spaciousness of the cockpit and the broad view through the paned transparisteel canopy, he felt claustrophobic, strapped into the seat by safety webbing and encumbered by gloves, flight boots, and helmet. With the hinged targeting computer intruding on his port-side view, the cockpit seemed more suitable to a double-jointed Geonosian. The old Delta-7 Aethersprite was roomy by comparison, the ARC-170 luxurious. Things could have been worse, however. The *Goliath* could have been carrying a squadron of the new—and seemingly disposable—TIE fighters.

"Commencing attack run," Vader said.

With the astromech chirping commands to the inertial compensator, Tarkin fed more power to the engines to stay abreast of and slightly behind Vader, and plummeted toward the tanker. Immediately he realized that the shipjackers were not simply attempting to hide; they were executing what amounted to a slow roll that was keeping the vulnerable dorsal surface of the *Carrion Spike* facing the curved hull of the much larger vessel. As the corvette disappeared behind the port side, Vader climbed, determined to fall on the ship, only to find when he and Tarkin arrived that the *Carrion Spike* was showing them her belly rather than her spine. They unleashed a hail of ion cannon fire regardless and came about for another rapacious run, the corvette upside down on top of the tanker by then and beginning to arc down along the vessel's starboard hull, her positioning jets flaring.

Descending, the *Carrion Spike* fell prey to four starfighters, which unloaded on her, taxing the resiliency of her powerful shields but emerging from the confrontation unscathed. Not until the corvette was tucked safely beneath the tanker once more did she reply, with powerful volleys from the lateral laser cannons that caught Yellows Seven and Eight and disintegrated them.

Jinking at the outer edge of the field of fire, Vader and Tarkin followed the ship into her second revolution, hammering away at her as she crawled out from beneath the tanker, but with no tangible results.

With Tarkin still clinging to the Eta-2's left wing, Vader powered out of his dive, rolled over, and rushed to re-engage, coming dangerously close to the tanker in an effort to squeeze himself between it

and the ascending *Carrion Spike* and forcing Tarkin to decelerate
into a tandem position. Fire from Vader's ion cannons coruscated
across the corvette from bow to stern, but the shields continued to
hold, strengthened, Tarkin guessed, by rerouting power from the
cannons and sublight maneuvering jets.

The *Carrion Spike* slowed considerably as she reached the crest of
her tortuous loop, but once arrived the ship delivered a triple barrage
of laserfire that forced four of the starfighters to diverge, one of them
shearing away a piece of the tanker's elevated aft bridge before spinning out of control and exploding.

Vader's voice boomed through the net. "Yellows Three and Four,
Ten and Twelve, form up on Yellow Two and follow our attack run.
Direct continuous fire at the corvette's command center."

Tarkin mimicked Vader's evasive maneuvers while the four
starfighters raced in to join them; then the half dozen banked as one
to begin their runs. Maintaining fire discipline, Tarkin tightened his
hand on the joystick and swooped in, the astromech transmitting
targeting data to the cockpit's display screen. Beams began to find
their way through the shields and pock the corvette's gleaming hull.
One after the next, the starfighters harried the larger ship, drenching
the shields with ion fire as she dropped under the lightly armored
hull of the tanker for a third time.

"They can't hide inside those shields for much longer," Vader said
over the net. "Echelon formation on Yellow Two, and re-engage."

They launched their attack as the *Carrion Spike* was drifting up
alongside the tanker's starboard side. Tarkin's targeting reticle went
red and a laser-lock tone filled the cockpit. He dived and was going
for a kill-shot when proximity alarms began to blare, and he glanced
up in time to see six ARC-170s spring from one of the tanker's forward bays. Leaning on the joystick, he slued hard to starboard, his
shots going wide of their mark as the tactical net grew cacophonous
with shouts of caution. Vader's Eta-2 and the rest of the V-wings
fanned out in search of clear space as the ARC-170s reeled into their
midst, narrowly avoiding collisions.

"Abort the run," Vader told everyone.

Tarkin opened the battle net to the *Goliath*. "Contact the tanker

administrator. Order him to recall his fighters at once. They're creating chaos out here."

The specialist at the far end of the communications link acknowledged the request, then returned a moment later to deliver the bad
news. "Governor Tarkin, the administrator has refused the order."

"Refused? On what pretext?"

"Sir, he replies that the tanker is his property and that you are not
his governor."

"*Goliath,* do you have a clear visual on the *Carrion Spike*?"

"Affirmative, sir."

"Then ready your proton torpedoes to target the corvette as soon
as she appears at the crest of the tanker hull."

"All due respect, sir, the tanker and the corvette might as well be
joined at the hip." It was the voice of the *Goliath*'s commander. "And
with our starfighters all over the field, one stray torpedo—"

"I'm well aware of the risk, Commander," Tarkin said, giving full
vent to his anger. "Inform your casualty notification officers that I'll
assume personal responsibility for any collateral damage."

"Execute Governor Tarkin's orders, Commander," Vader said in a
calm voice that at once managed to be full of menace.

"Yes, Lord Vader. Readying the warhead launch system."

The *Carrion Spike* was just short of crowning when her ion engines blazed to life and the ship hurtled away from the tanker in the
direction of the escort carrier, firing all guns as she fled. All vigilance
abandoned, Vader and Tarkin broke Rimward in a flurry of evasive
maneuvers while lines of destruction probed for them.

Vader ordered what remained of the squadron to tighten up their
ragged formation. "Enable countermeasures and pursue. That ship
must not be allowed to jump."

But the *Carrion Spike*'s laser cannons were already beginning to
find their marks. Yellows Five and Twelve vanished in blinding explosions, adding debris to the obstacle course Vader and Tarkin had
embarked on.

Tarkin reopened the battle net to the *Goliath*. "What are you waiting for? Why aren't you firing?"

"Sir, the corvette has disappeared from our scanners!"

"Fire along the path of her last logged vector," Tarkin said. "Engage the tractor beam."

The escort carrier began firing at extreme range, its energy beams lancing off into local space.

Vader and Tarkin were still spearheading the chase when a massive, rippling explosion erupted behind them. Tarkin looked over his left shoulder to see the tanker burst open in a roiling outpouring of fire and gas that annihilated all the ARC-170s and singed the tails of Yellow Squadron's trailing starfighters. When the expanding shock wave caught up with him, it overwhelmed the V-wing, propelling it through end-over-end spins and lateral gyrations that refused to abate.

After a long moment, the starfighter's systems came back online and he heard Vader's voice over the tactical net. "The *Carrion Spike* has jumped to hyperspace."

"Anyone else survive?" Tarkin managed to ask.

The *Goliath* responded: "Two starfighters. In addition to the escort carrier."

Tarkin lifted his face to the canopy to find that he was facing what was left of the tanker, still belching fire and beginning a spiraling death plummet into Phindar's atmosphere.

What struck him, however, as he regained his senses, was that neither the *Carrion Spike* nor the *Goliath* had fired the shot that had doomed it.

HAZARD MITIGATION

THE *CARRION SPIKE* DRIFTED aimlessly between worlds in another nameless star system, an unscheduled stop this time, the result of a split-second decision on Salikk's part, executed as the corvette was scudding away from the exploding fuel tanker, chased by starfighters and with the escort carrier's cannons, tractor beam, and torpedoes desperately trying to find it.

The ordeal at Phindar had left the corvette battered, bruised, and shaken. The armored hull was rashed with melt circles, and most of the exterior lights were molten heaps. The effects of the tractor beam, which had grabbed the ship more by chance than as the result of any skill on the part of the *Goliath*'s crew, had ripped away part of the rectenna array. The interior looked as if a whirlwind had blown through, and surges of energy had fried most of the appliances in the galley and medical bay. Areas of the ship were now off-limits because of air lock damage and radiation leaks. The toilets and showers had stopped working, and emergency illumination prevailed. Most of the alarms had been disabled to prevent them from sounding. Telltales were flashing across the command center's console, and some of the comp routines were refusing to reboot. Weapons and stealth systems, sensor suite, hyperdrive, and navicomputer had fared better, but the shield generators were functioning only at fifty percent capacity.

"On the bright side," Teller was telling his fellow shipjackers, "close calls make for captivating holovids."

All six of them were in the dimly lighted command cabin, nursing their wounds when they weren't fiddling with various instruments. Anora's forehead bore a square of bacta patch, and some of her brownish curls had been clipped away to accommodate a second patch on her scalp.

"The Empire has suspended HoloNet service to most of the sector," she said in a weak, defeated voice. "I doubt our transmission reached more than half a dozen systems."

"We only need to've reached one," Teller said, trying to sound encouraging. "Give it time and the holovid will spread to other sectors."

"I didn't have a chance to edit out the lag before the tanker explosion," Hask said. "But there's one sequence showing the starfighters ganging up on us."

Cala emerged from an access hatch in the deck plates. "The explosion would have taken out the Eta-Two and all the V-wings if the charge hadn't been late in detonating. It's possible the tanker's containment bins were equipped with sensors that monitor whether fuel cells are fully depleted. A sensor in the bin might have detected the bomb and initiated attempts to neutralize or contain the detonation."

"Not our concern," Salikk said from the command chair. The low light had little effect on his ability to see, and he was scanning the instruments as he spoke. "We're lucky we got away when we did. The *Goliath* had us in target lock."

Hask fixed her gaze on Teller. "You think Tarkin and Vader would have given the order to fire, knowing they might have blown up the tanker?"

"Are you asking seriously?" Teller said.

Hask frowned. "Maybe not about destroying the tanker. But his own starfighter pilots were in harm's way."

Teller leaned back against the port-side bulkhead. "Remember what I was telling you about Tarkin's days with the Outland Regions

Security Force, and that special ship he designed with the swing and pintle-mounted front guns?"

"I remember."

"Well, he didn't only deploy it against the pirates," Teller said. "You'd think he would have blamed Eriadu's troubles on the Core Worlds, which were skimming most of the profits from the Seswenna's lommite trade. But he really had it in for the outlaws who were harassing the Seswenna. When Outland's counteroffenses stopped yielding the desired results, Tarkin decided to extend the militia's reach by targeting any groups that were supporting or harboring the Seswenna's foes. It didn't matter to him that the support groups were caught in the middle, threatened by pirates on one side and menaced by Outland on the other. Civilian casualties you might say, Hask, but not to Tarkin. They were allies of his enemies, and that meant enemies of his and deserving whatever he decided to level against them."

Teller firmed his lips and gave his head a mournful shake. "Outland was brutal in what its warships dished out. No one knows how many were killed or where the bodies were buried. But even with the flotilla they'd amassed, Outland couldn't be everywhere at once, so Tarkin came up with the idea of making the supporters responsible for their own protection by arming them against the pirates. That way, they managed to open a separate front against the pirates, and eventually turned one group of supporters against another. With everyone suspicious about who was secretly siding with or supporting whom, they began to turn on one another, out of fear of reprisals from Outland. It was a kind of mutually assured annihilation, and ultimately Tarkin rid the Seswenna of its problems."

Teller fell silent for a moment. "You never know what events give shape to someone's life, to someone's moral choices. Maybe it was centuries of having to defend themselves against the predators, or the centuries of raids by pirates, slavers, and privateers that shaped the Eriaduan character. Maybe the history of the place seeped into their genetic makeup, resulting in an appetite for violence. But even that doesn't fully explain Tarkin, because most of the Eriaduans I've met aren't anything like him."

Teller's gaze favored Hask. "When Outland succeeded in chasing

off what was left of the groups they hadn't killed, Tarkin turned his
wrath on anyone who had come to Eriadu in flight from intersystem
conflicts or in search of new lives, employment—you know, the ones
taking jobs from native Eriaduans, crowding the cities, ruining the
economy. The entire Tarkin clan waged a campaign against them. It
didn't matter if they were human or other than; the point was that
these social parasites were cheating Eriadu out of its just and hard-
won rewards, and keeping the planet from attaining the status of the
Core Worlds. By this time Tarkin was Eriadu's governor, and probably the most popular one the planet ever had. Fresh from Outland
and years of academy life, he had the support of a cabal of influential
officers who had trained to become Judicials, but in fact were just
itching for galactic war to break out.

"Palpatine turned a blind eye to what was going on in the
Seswenna—the deportations, the purges, the atrocities committed
against any who found themselves on the Tarkins' extermination list.
And not surprisingly, under Tarkin's rule, Eriadu finally achieved the
celebrity it had been clamoring for. It became the rising star, the
planet other eager-to-be-exploited worlds began looking up to. So of
course the invisible players who had put Palpatine in power were just
as eager to embrace Tarkin. Hell, he had already formed a military. It
was to Eriadu that *Coruscant* looked when embarking down the
same path. Why else do you think he attained so much in so few
years and became such fast friends with Palpatine, those senators
who were pushing for passage of the Military Creation Act, the members of the Ruling Council? Why do you think he makes such a perfect partner for Vader?"

Teller answered his own question. "Because all of them share the
same vision. They're the entitled ones who know what's best for the
rest of us—who should live, who should die, to whom we should bow
and how low." He glanced at Cala, Artoz, and Salikk. "I don't need to
remind any of you what Tarkin did at the end of the war when there
weren't Jedi around to keep a lid on the violence and retribution. We
wouldn't be aboard this ship otherwise. The Emperor is going to win-
now the populations of the galaxy until the only ones left are the ones
he can control. And he and Vader and Tarkin are going to accomplish

that with an army of steadfast recruits who might as well be clones for the little independent thinking they do, weapons that haven't been seen in more than a thousand years, and *fear*."

Teller stepped away from the bulkhead, limping slightly as he found his way in the scant light to one of the acceleration chairs. "You can think of the *Carrion Spike* as just a ship, but she's more than that. She's an expression of who Tarkin is; a small-scale example of the lengths he's willing to go. Stealth, speed, power . . . That's Tarkin, the omniscient, ubiquitous Imperial enforcer. And that's why we're turning her into a symbol of something else: of *resistance*."

Hask narrowed her feline eyes and nodded in an uncertain way. "You know, it's funny, Teller. The last time you uncorked one of these lectures, you were saying how none of those we've killed were civilians because they were serving the Empire. To me, it sounds a lot like Tarkin's targeting of anyone who was aiding the pirates."

Teller nodded back at her. "Yeah, Hask, except for one thing—"

"We're the good guys," Anora said, pinning Teller with a sardonic look.

Back in uniform and hands clasped behind his back, Tarkin stood side by side with Vader at the center of the *Goliath*'s bridge, their presence imbuing the cabinspace with a sense of uncharacteristic urgency.

"Anything?" Tarkin sharply asked the noncom seated at the communications board.

"Nothing, sir."

"Keep trying."

The escort carrier was still in Phindar space, in part so that Tarkin could iron out responsibility for the tanker's destruction with the planetary leadership. Off to his left sat the ship's ashen-faced commander, not yet over the fact that he had nearly been made answerable for the deaths of the few starfighter pilots who had survived the fierce engagement with the *Carrion Spike*.

While he didn't show it, Tarkin felt more accountable than the commander realized. He and Vader had been baited and had come close to paying the price for rushing headlong into a trap. He took himself to task for his overconfidence at having predicted where the shipjackers would turn up, and promised that he wouldn't allow himself to make the same mistake twice. That the *Goliath*'s arrival had taken the shipjackers by surprise only made their cunning escape all the more impressive.

A tone sounded from the comm board and Tarkin stepped forward in a rush, realizing at once that he had been premature.

"Report from Phindar's rescue-and-recovery operation, sir," the noncom said after listening to her headset feed for a moment. "They suspect that the tanker was destroyed by an explosive device concealed inside a spent fuel cell."

"Then the dissidents weren't merely attempting to use the tanker as cover," Tarkin said. "They were hoping to draw us in, as much to avoid having to face the storm of our unexpected arrival as in the hope that we, too, would be caught up in the explosion."

A short holovid of the clash, the ensuing chase, and the explosion had been received three hours earlier by a couple of local systems. The delayed transmission of the holovid told Tarkin that the shipjackers had waited until the *Carrion Spike* emerged from hyperspace, which also provided him with some idea of the distance the ship had traveled, though not in which direction.

Turning to Vader, he said, "Perhaps it would have been wiser to target the tanker from the start."

Vader folded his arms across his chest and shook his head. "The Emperor would not have approved."

Tarkin regarded him. It was an odd comment coming from Vader, given the atrocities he had perpetrated for the Emperor since the end of the war. He wondered if Vader was testing him, just as he felt the Emperor had been doing during their most recent meeting.

"If we aren't willing to do whatever is required," he said finally, "then we risk losing what we have been mandated to protect."

The remark paraphrased something Skywalker had said to him following the Citadel rescue. But it got no reaction from Vader beyond his saying, "You misunderstand, Governor. As I said, we need to gather *all* of them in our net."

The comm board chimed again, this time with better and more anticipated news.

"Sir, we're receiving location coordinates from the tracking device."

Tarkin didn't bother to hide his excitement. "The Phindian administrator did one thing right. I was almost certain he lied to me."

Vader nodded. "He served the Empire well in his final moments."

Tarkin stood behind the noncom at the comm board. "What is the source of the transmissions?"

The noncom waited for interface data to arrive from the *Goliath*'s navicomputer. "Sir, the source is sector-designated as LCC-four-four-seven. Parsec equidistant from the Sumitra and Cvetaen systems."

"Those are Coreward—in the Expansion Region," Tarkin said, with genuine unease.

"Yes, sir. Closest principal planets are Thustra and Aquaris."

Vader looked at Tarkin. "Now, Governor, *we* get to spring the trap."

One of the few areas of the former Jedi Temple that had not undergone renovation was the holographic galactic map, an enormous globular representation of the galaxy located mid-level in what had been the Jedi Council spire. The Order had used the map to keep track of its far-flung members; now it served to identify trouble spots in the Emperor's realm.

The Emperor had consented to allowing the members of his Ruling Council to confer with representatives of the intelligence services in the hope that Tarkin and Vader's latest strategy would conclude the search for the Moff's ship and bring the shipjackers' co-conspirators to light. While no less irritated by the fact that a group of insignificant mutants from the galactic underbelly were scurrying about trying to stir up trouble, curiosity had gotten the better of him. Mere eddies in the current of the dark side had transformed into rapids and whirlpools.

He sat in a simple chair atop a podium not unlike the one in the audience chamber, with some of his colorfully clothed advisers arrayed beneath him—Mas Amedda, Ars Dangor, Janus Greejatus, and Kren Blista-Vanee. Intelligence chiefs Ison and Rancit stood opposite the Ruling Council members, making their cases from a circular walkway secured to the curved wall of the spire at the base of the holographic globe.

"My lord, Vice Admiral Rancit and I do find ourselves in agreement on one issue," Ison was in the midst of saying. "If Governor Tarkin is going to continue to make unilateral decisions of the sort he made at Phindar, then he should be doing so on Coruscant, coordinating the efforts of the Imperial military instead of chasing his errant corvette all over the Outer Rim."

Rancit waited until he was certain that Ison had spoken his piece. "My lord, with the *Carrion Spike* now reported to be in the Expansion Region, this crisis takes on greater exigency. It's possible that the dissidents' plan calls for the corvette to be joined by the warship—"

"I'm not interested in what is *possible,* Vice Admiral," the Emperor interrupted. "I'm interested in knowing your plans for dealing with the possibilities."

Rancit bowed his head. "Of course, my lord. Though I must stress that Naval Intelligence has detected unusual activity throughout that sector of the Expansion Region, as if unknown parties are attempting to flood certain star systems with traffic."

The Emperor leaned toward him. "As you are flooding star systems with our warships."

Rancit blinked and stood tall. "My lord, we are simply attempting to safeguard our interests in those systems. Given the path the dissidents have pursued, it is—that is, we think it reasonable to assume that they are intent on targeting systems in the Inner Rim, from which potential hyperspace jump points and destinations will multiply beyond measure. We have taken the liberty of declaring some key systems no-entry zones, but the need to allocate resources to other systems grows only more complicated."

The Emperor's gaze favored Ison. "Do you disagree with the vice admiral, Deputy Director?"

"Not entirely, my lord. The increased activities Vice Admiral Rancit alludes to could be the result of holovids transmitted from the *Carrion Spike*. COMPNOR surveillance and investigation operatives in several sectors have noted an increase in both anti-Imperial pro-paganda and mobilization among malcontent groups. ISB is making arrests and interrogating prisoners in various Imperial facilities in an effort to learn the identity of the culprits. As odd as it sounds, my lord, we have also been receiving intelligence from the Crymorah syndicate, which apparently shared some nefarious affiliation with the criminal subcontractors who operated Phindar's fueling station."

The Emperor steepled his fingers. "My instructions to Lord Vader and Moff Tarkin were to make an example of the shipjackers, not to allow the shipjackers to make a laughingstock of the Empire's intel-ligence chiefs." Turning his hooded gaze on Rancit, he made a beck-oning motion with the fingers of his right hand. "Enlighten us as to what you would have us do, Vice Admiral."

Rancit cleared his throat before beginning. "My lord, rather than engage the dissidents at the present location—which Governor Tar-kin has yet to make known to us—he proposes waiting for them to plot a course to their next target and ensnaring them there."

In fact Vader and Tarkin *had* made the location known, but the Emperor kept that to himself. Instead he said: "Given that they have successfully escaped each such attempt, just how do you propose to ensnare them?"

"By utilizing Interdictor cruisers, my lord—precisely placed to yank the *Carrion Spike* from hyperspace short of its destination sys-tem and reversion point. Governor Tarkin assures us that any jump from the dissidents' current location will require at least two rever-sions to reach potential Imperial targets. Thus, Interdictors can be positioned in advance of the *Carrion Spike*'s arrival."

The Emperor looked down at Kren Blista-Vanee.

"The requested Interdictors are being developed as part of the Deep Core Security Zone, my lord." Fond of wearing flamboyant hats and frequenting the opera, Blista-Vanee was a relative newcomer to the Ruling Council, but had already proven an asset in blazing hyper-space routes into the Deep Core star systems. "I hasten to add, how-ever, that the ships' gravity well projectors have not been tested in scenarios of this sort."

The Emperor mulled it over for a moment, then looked at Rancit once more. "Tell me about these 'potential' targets."

"Permit me, my lord," Rancit said, gesturing to the star map and amplifying a portion of it. "Our main concerns are Lantillies, from which we have already repositioned many of our resources. Also, the Imperial facility on Cartao, and Ice Station Beta on Anteevy. An attack on Taanab—though on the Perlemian Trade Route—would earn the dissidents more condemnation than praise, as Taanab's agricultural projects feed billions in the Mid and Outer Rim. The same holds true for an attack on Garos, because of the university, though there is also an Imperial facility onworld." Rancit paused. "Do you wish me to go on, my lord?"

By way of answer, the Emperor glanced at Ison.

"As I've said on countless occasions, my lord, the fleet is already too scattered. On the Admiralty's counsel, the navy is now redirecting resources from as far away as Rothana and Bothawui."

"And at the risk of repeating *myself*," Rancit said, "Imperial interests must be protected."

The Emperor spent a long moment studying Ison and Rancit, stretching out with his powers to discern alignments, configurations, some syzygy of events. Then his thoughts turned to Vader and Tarkin. He appreciated how well they were working together, but he began to wonder if they were perhaps too close to the details of the dissidents' scheme to recognize their ultimate objective. One needed to have a safe remove, as he felt he had, gazing into the 3-D representation of the galaxy he had made his own. How Plagueis would have mocked him for allowing himself to become personally involved in such a seemingly trivial matter; but then his Master had never foreseen that his onetime apprentice would become *Emperor*.

With a subtle gesture he signaled Mas Amedda to join him on the podium. When the Chagrian arrived, he said: "Tell me again how the cache of communications jammers was discovered on Murkhana."

"One of Imperial Security's assets was tasked with investigating the find by his case officer," Amedda said in a little more than a whisper.

The Emperor considered this. "His ISB case officer, here on Corus-cant?"

"Yes, my lord."

The Emperor collapsed the steeple he had made of his fingers. "Summon them, Vizier. I suspect some benefit will accrue from my speaking personally with both."

17

ZERO DEFECTS

WEAPONS RECHARGED, the interior made as shipshape as possible, the *Carrion Spike* waited for instructions regarding when to launch and where to jump. From the copilot's chair Teller, back in boots and cargo pants, watched Salikk run through a preflight check of the instruments and systems. When the Gotal's hand reached the navicomputer, however, it hovered in hesitation.

"Problem?" Teller asked.

Salikk kept his eyes trained on one of the status displays. "It's probably nothing, but . . ."

Teller sat bolt-upright in the chair's webbing. "It's probably nothing, but I've had this pain in my side . . . It's probably nothing, but my girlfriend's been acting distant lately . . ." He gave his head an aggravated shake. "Whenever I hear that phrase—"

"It's the fuel capacity," Salikk cut in. "Factoring in the cells we took on at Phindar, something doesn't add up."

"That Phindian cheated us!" Teller exclaimed. "No wonder he was being so nonchalant."

Salikk's twin-horned head was shaking back and forth. "That's not it."

Teller leaned toward the console. "Maybe you didn't notice we weren't full up when we separated from the tanker."

The Gotal's head continued to shake. "I checked—at least I think I did. But even if I overlooked a detail, the discrepancy doesn't make sense."

"We had to override that tractor beam—"

"No."

Teller looked at Artoz, who was sitting quietly in the comm officer's chair, watching both of them. "Any ideas?"

The Mon Cal thought for a moment, tapping his webbed hand on the console. "The hyperdrive motivator may be addled. We could try recalibrating the synchronization relays."

Salikk forced an exhale. "It's probably nothing." His hand was reaching for the navicomputer controls again when Teller told him to hold off, and then shouted through the ruined hatch for Cala, who was in the conference cabin.

"You've gotta put the hazmat suit back on," Teller said as the Koorivar entered from the afterdeck.

Cala stared at him. "You're trying to overdose me on rads, is that it? You've decided I'm expendable."

"Calm down," Teller said, gesturing. "I just need you to go into the fuel bay and run tests on the fuel cells we took on at Phindar. You'll know them because they're Wiborg Jenssens, marked with the tanker's logo—a kind of triple S."

Cala's shoulders sagged in defeat. "What am I supposed to be looking for?"

"With any luck, nothing more than an empty or faulty cell," Artoz said.

Cala scowled. "That Phindian cheated us!"

"Let's hope so," Teller said, freeing himself from the chair's safety webbing and getting to his feet. "Come on, I'll help suit you up."

Frozen hatches and malfunctioning air locks forced them to follow a circuitous route to the fuel hold. Once sealed into the hooded, face-shielded hazmat suit, Cala disappeared through the air lock and Teller returned to the command cabin, where he found Anora seated in the copilot's chair.

"What's going on?" she asked, her words more a demand than a question.

"It's probably nothing," he started to say, then stopped himself. Enabling the intraship comlink, he said: "Cala, you inside?"

"I'm checking them now. Power-level indicators look good."

Teller had turned toward Anora when Cala added: "Wait. The sensor found one. The cell is reading empty."

"One of the Phindian's?"

"It has the logo."

"Can you remove it?"

Cala replied with a lengthy curse. "I told you we should have brought a droid along."

"I know you did, but think of the headaches a droid would have caused Salikk." Teller aimed a grin at the magnetically sensitive Gotal. "Besides, we didn't, and you're our best bet. Is the repulsorlift conveyor still in there?"

"Right where I left it after rigging the bomb."

"Task the conveyor to remove the cell," Artoz said toward the audio pickup, "and transfer it into the decontam bay so the diagnostic unit can have a look at it."

"Have a look at it how?" Cala said. "The sensor says it's empty."

"We need to open it up," Teller said.

"Are you out of your mind?" Cala barked. "Suppose there's a bomb inside?"

Teller tried to make light of the idea. "That's something only we do. Anyway, that's why you're letting the diagnostic unit do it. It'll scan the cell first."

"This is the last time I'm putting this suit on," Cala said.

"Deal. Next time I'll have Anora do it."

A gesture from her revealed her feelings on the matter.

Another curse from Cala broke the long silence. "It's not empty."

Teller exchanged nervous glances with Salikk and Artoz. "What's inside?"

Everyone stared at the command center enunciator, as if the Koorivar were there, in the command cabin.

"A device of some sort," Cala reported finally. "Nothing like I've ever seen."

"All right," Artoz said, trying to keep his resonant voice calm. "Task the diagnostic to cam the device, then run the image through the ship's library."

Cala exhaled loudly. "Hold on."

Again the intraship comlink went quiet, and Teller ran a hand down his face.

"It's probably noth—" Anora started to say when he shushed her.

"Damn, Teller, it's an Imperial homing beacon!" the Koorivar said. "Database describes it as a paralight tracker—a kind of HoloNet transceiver that parses commands from the ship's navicomputer."

Salikk swiveled to face the others, his eyes wide with astonishment. "Tarkin knows not only where we are, but also where we're planning to go. Which means we're essentially marooned, unless you want to get there by sublight, which will only take"—he glanced at a console readout—"on the order of fifty years."

"Maybe we've done enough," Anora said, touching her injured scalp. "We call it quits right here."

Teller shook his head at her. "We haven't done near enough."

Cala's distant voice intruded. "Should I disable this thing?"

"No, don't do anything just yet," Teller told him. "Let it sit in there, and get yourself forward." He glanced around the command cabin. "Let's consider this from Tarkin's side."

"Yes, why don't we," Anora said in plain anger.

"Tarkin knows we're here," Artoz said, "and he is convinced that he has a good read on our intentions."

"With good reason," Salikk said.

"He knows we're here," Teller said, thinking out loud, "but he hasn't come for us." He cut his gaze to Artoz. "Obviously he's waiting to see what we enter into the navicomputer so he can beat us there."

"So he and Vader and whoever else—maybe the entire Imperial Navy by this time—can beat us there," the Mon Cal said. "No doubt they're calculating all possible jump egresses from this system."

Teller nodded in agreement. "Of which there have to be dozens."

"Meanwhile," Salikk said, "the navy's deploying ships to every system where Tarkin thinks we'll show ourselves."

Anora looked up from studying her hands. "Is there a way to enter false coordinates into the navicomputer?"

Salikk shook his head negatively. "Not while that tracker is enabled."

No one spoke for a moment; then Teller said: "At this point, we just need to buy some time, right? So suppose we supply Tarkin with jump coordinates into a very busy star system."

Anora's thin eyebrows formed a V. "I don't see how that helps us, unless you're counting on hiding in a traffic jam."

"We supply the coordinates," Teller said, "but we don't jump."

"You mean—"

"We get someone else to do it."

Standing proudly on the elevated command bridge walkway of the Star Destroyer *Executrix*, Tarkin felt more at home than he had in years. An *Imperial*-class wedge-shaped titan, the warship had just decanted in the Obroa-skai system after a jump from Lantillies, on Tarkin's learning that the *Carrion Spike* was on her way. The panoramic view through the bridge's bay of trapezoidal windows included nearly all the ships that made up the task force. In the distance, positioned against a radiant sweep of stars, floated three Interdictor vessels, a Detainer CC-2200, a newer-model CC-7700 frigate, and—fresh from deepdock in the Corellia system and as yet untested—an Immobilizer 418. Thickly armored, the former two had downsloping bows and stubby winglike lateral projections housing quartets of gravity well projectors. The Immobilizer, by contrast, featured four hemispherical projectors aft on the ship's sharp-bowed hull. Deployed in the middle distance between the Interdictors and the *Executrix* were frigates, pickets, and gunboats. The centermost picket carried Vader, Crest—promoted by Vader to lieutenant—and some two dozen stormtroopers, who made up a boarding party, in the unlikely event that the *Carrion Spike* could be retaken without a fight or at least put out of commission rather than reduced to wreckage.

A holotable situated starboard and below the elevated command walkway displayed a 3-D chronometer counting down in standard time to the *Carrion Spike*'s estimated moment of arrival. As expected, the dissidents had jumped the ship from her original location to the remote Thustra system, and after spending several hours there had charged the navicomputer to plot a course for Obroa-skai. The ETA was based on the assumption that the *Carrion Spike* had gone to lightspeed at that moment or soon after, and on how quickly the corvette's Class One hyperdrive could deliver her. An earlier-than-expected arrival would find the ship reverting to realspace deeper in system, where other Imperial warships, including the *Goliath*, were positioned to intercept her. A more sophisticated homing beacon would have allowed Tarkin to track the corvette through hyperspace by way of S-thread transceivers, but the stormtrooper squadron assigned to the Phindar fuel tanker had had access only to a basic device that interfaced with a ship's navicomputer.

A specialist seated at a console in the most forward of the sunken data pits got Tarkin's attention. "Sir, the quarry is due at T minus one hundred twenty."

Tarkin angled the microphone of his headset closer to his mouth and opened the battle net to the task force liaison officer, who was aboard the CC-7700 frigate.

"The projectors are powering up to high gain, Governor Tarkin," the commander said. "The field will be initiated, then disabled, in an effort to keep from dragging vessels other than the quarry from hyperspace. I should caution, however, that that may be unavoidable, given the heavy traffic in this system."

"I understand, Commander," Tarkin said. "Order your technicians to be judicious, nonetheless."

"I will, sir. But the power setting of the gravity wells is dictated to some extent by the relative speed of the targeted ship, and, well, sir, to be blunt about it, there aren't many as fast as the *Carrion Spike*."

Tarkin pinched his lower lip in thought. Ideally, local systems would had been notified that Obroa-skai had been designated a no-entry zone, but naval command had opted against issuing the designation for fear of alerting the dissidents. He had other reasons for concern: chiefly the question of why the dissidents would jump to Obroa-skai, which lacked anything in the way of an Imperial target, and was known mostly for its medcenters and libraries.

"T minus thirty and counting," the specialist in the data pit announced.

Moving to the forward end of the walkway, Tarkin fixed his gaze on the trio of Interdictors. Arms folded across his chest, he counted down in silence even while the voice of the specialist was doing the same in his right ear bead.

The countdown had just reached T minus five when Tarkin was yanked forward, nearly completely off his feet. Fearing another lurch he spread his hands wide and so was kept from being slammed head-first into the closest viewport panel. Klaxons began to howl throughout the suddenly trembling command bridge as the giant ship groaned and lurched yet again in the direction of the distant Interdictors. Struggling to remain upright, Tarkin caught a glimpse of the middle-distance frigates and pickets being pulled forward, almost as if accelerating.

"Commander," he shouted into the headset mouthpiece, "the field is too powerful!"

"Working on it, sir," the commander said with equal volume. "It's the Immobilizer. The overcurrent resistors failed to prevent the gravitic systems from redlining—"

The comlink connection broke.

Close to the Interdictors, ships began to appear where there had only been star-filled space. Tarkin turned from the forward bay and stumbled back to the data pit to study the magnified view on one of the screens. First to drop out of hyperspace was an outmoded, saucer-shaped YT-1000 freighter, followed by two angular transports and a lustrous space yacht. Then another freighter winked into visibility, followed by two passenger vessels.

Abruptly, Tarkin felt as if he'd been shoved toward the rear of the bridge. With the interdiction field neutralized, the ships that had been caught in the invisible web began to whirl out of control. Two of the ships collided and drifted out of view. The magnification screen showed the sublight engines of other ships flashing, but the ships barely had a chance to flee or correct their spins when the field re-initiated, capturing them once again. Tarkin spread his legs wide in an effort to balance himself; then his eyes went wide as well as he turned to face the viewports. Listing on its port side, an enormous ship that more resembled something grown than built decanted, broadsiding the Detainer CC-2200 before careening into a spin that left its dorsal surface impaled on the Interdictor's sloping bow.

"Mon Cal star cruiser!" a voice in his ear said, loud enough to be heard over the head-splitting racket of the klaxons. "The luxury liner *Stellar Vista* out of Corsin. Approximately ten thousand aboard!"

A brief but nova-bright explosion flared in the distance, ferocious enough to leave Tarkin blinking and seeing stars that weren't there. When he was able to focus through the viewport's blast-tinting, he saw that the stern of the organically sculpted passenger ship had disappeared and that the Interdictor had been knocked ninety degrees from its former position. In moments podlike lifeboats and flocks of spherical escape pods were streaming from the stricken liner.

"The *Stellar Vista* reports that it is in imminent distress," the specialist said. "The ship's captain is requesting all the help we can provide."

Tarkin swung toward the data pits, but spoke into the headset. "Order the frigates to render assistance. Instruct the Interdictors to negate the field, and move us into a position where we can utilize the tractor beams to grab the lifeboats."

All at once Vader's voice was booming in his ear. "Where is your corvette, Governor? It is not on any of our scanners. Do you have it?"

Tarkin hurried to the edge of the walkway and gestured to one of the seated noncoms. "Have you located the *Carrion Spike*?"

The spec turned to him. "No sign of the corvette, sir. Could it be in stealth mode?"

Tarkin compressed his lips and shook his head. "Not even a cloaking device could keep it from being detected in an interdiction field."

A second spec called to him. "Sir, the task force commander wants to know if you wish the Interdictors to re-initiate the field. Some of the transports are trying to make a run for it."

Tarkin had his mouth open to reply when Vader said, "I want all those ships corralled. Hold them in place with tractor beams if you have to, but none should be allowed to leave."

Tarkin nodded to the noncoms. "Contain those vessels."

"And the lifeboats, sir?" one asked.

"We'll see to them when we can."

Yet a third specialist joined in. "Sir, one of our frigates is taking fire."

Tarkin moved farther down the command walkway to stand over her. "On screen."

A grainy image of a modified Lux-400 yacht took shape, green hyphens of laserfire erupting from the ship's well-concealed lateral cannons.

"Do we have the transponder signature of that vessel?" Tarkin asked.

"The *Truant,* sir," the tech said. "On the wanted list in several sectors for arms smuggling."

"Draw a bead on it," Tarkin commanded.

The spec relayed the command into her headset, then glanced up at him. "Our gunners report they're having difficulty finding a clear shot because of the lifeboats and the debris field."

Tarkin fumed. "Acquire it and open fire!"

He turned his attention to the screens as turbolaser beams from the Star Destroyer's starboard-side turrets found the Lux-400, and it vanished in a short-lived fireball.

"The *Truant* is no longer on the wanted list, sir. Minimal collateral casualties."

Tarkin strode forward on the walkway to the primary data pit. "Have you confined the rest of those ships?"

"They're not going anywhere, sir, and Lord Vader's picket is currently closing on the group. Still no sign of the *Carrion Spike.*"

"Do the sensors detail any instances of ships jumping to light-speed?"

"None, sir. No instances of Cronau radiation—though the interdiction field would make that a long shot, in any case."

Tarkin shook his head in bewilderment. Had the shipjackers had a last-moment change of plans? Or had they been forewarned?

"Is the homing beacon still transmitting?"

The tech attended to his various instruments. "No signal from the tracker, sir. Nothing."

So they *had* discovered it. But when?

Tarkin continued to move forward until he was standing just short of the viewports, just short of the chaos beyond. Vader's voice fractured his introspection.

"Which vessel appeared first?"

"The YT-One-Thousand freighter," Tarkin said.

"Then we'll begin with that one, since it arrived closest to the projected arrival time of the *Carrion Spike*."

"Begin what, Lord Vader?"

"The failure of the corvette to appear does not owe to any impromptu change of plans, Governor. The dissidents are trying to throw us off the scent, and I intend to search each interdicted ship until we have answers."

Tarkin watched the picket accelerate as Vader made haste for the immobilized antique, ignoring the flaming hulk of the passenger liner and the scattering of lifeboats and escape pods to all sides.

Tarkin let his gaze become unfocused, so that the stars and the strewn ships lost all definition. His thoughts returned to the plateau and the lessons he had learned. Sometimes, especially when he, Jova, and the others had gone without food for several days—and despite their best efforts to stalk faultlessly—an elusive hunt took on such desperation that the importance of *thinking* like the prey was abandoned. Vader was correct: The dissidents hadn't had a last-moment change of plans; early on they were aware of the trap being set for them. Creatures understood themselves to be most vulnerable during flight and evasion. That's when they paid strict attention to warnings issued by other animals. Fleeing for their lives, they picked up scents on the wind; they sharpened their senses, granting themselves the ability to hear and see their pursuers at great distances. They took all advantage of knowing the territory better than the ones chasing them. The savannas and jungled areas of the plateau would perk up when Jova and his band were about, because they were the intruders, and usually up to no good.

His loathing and frustration notwithstanding, Tarkin could respect the dissidents for their cleverness and foresight, but clearly their plan had been hatched with the aid of confederates, and those allies were now beginning to play their part in keeping the *Carrion Spike* from being reclaimed.

Tarkin had lost all sense of how long he had been standing in the viewport bay when Vader's fury brought him back to the moment.

"This freighter is to be tractored aboard the *Executrix* for a thorough inspection. The crew is to be kept in detention until I'm through interrogating them."

HUNG UPSIDE DOWN

VADER STOOD OMINOUSLY motionless in the illuminated cargo hold of the YT freighter, breathing deeply and looking as if he was ready to draw his lightsaber and cut everything around him to shreds. Tarkin, too, thought it unlikely they were going to discover anything of interest among the haphazardly stacked shipping crates, but he was willing to have a look nonetheless.

The foul-smelling and disheveled old ship sat in the glare of spotlights in one of the Star Destroyer's ancillary hangars, like some stultified and wary insect. Circular in design, with an outrigger cockpit sandwiched between a pair of rectangular mandibles, the *Reticent* had seen better days a century earlier, and was now barely spaceworthy. The cargo ramp beneath the cockpit had been lowered, and glow rods set up inside and out to flood the hold with light. Vader and Tarkin's cursory search had revealed consignments of tools, medical supplies, bolts of fabric, trays of gaudy costume jewelry, tankfuls of alcoholic beverages, and droid parts. Recording devices and scanners in hand, Lieutenant Crest and two other stormtroopers—all three without helmets or armored plastrons—were following Vader and Tarkin as they nosed around.

The *Reticent* was the only ship to have been sequestered following the catastrophe at the edge of Obroa-skai space. The rest that had fallen victim to the faulty interdiction field had been checked out and allowed to go on their way, which for most of them meant directly to the system's namesake planet for repairs, after collisions with escape pods and debris from the wrecked Mon Cal star cruiser. That ship and the Detainer had also been towed to Obroa-skai, with the death toll from the crash estimated at eleven hundred beings. The state-of-the-art Immobilizer whose fail-safes had malfunctioned had been returned to Corellian Engineering for reassessment. Legitimate holovids of the events had flooded the HoloNet, most of them cammed by passengers aboard the luxury liner, and by media teams who had received word from unidentified sources of an Imperial operation taking place at the periphery of the star system. As for *Carrion Spike*, she had yet to turn up in any system. By the time the task force's fastest frigate had reached Thustra, Tarkin's rogue ship had already jumped to unknown space.

Crest was reading from a datapad.

"The ship's identification signature doesn't appear to have been altered. It hasn't even changed names in decades. The crew acquired it three years back from a dealer on Lantillies. The itinerary we sliced from the navicomputer corroborates the captain's story. They jumped from Taris to Thustra to pick up replacement parts for a fleet of Sephi flyers that were sold in bulk at the end of the war to an Obroa-skai emergency medevac center."

"How was the pickup and delivery arranged?" Tarkin asked.

"Through a broker on Lantillies—maybe the same dealer in preowned ships. He gets a line on what's needed when and where and dispatches crews to make the transfers."

"The *Reticent*'s crew are freelance operators?"

Crest nodded. "They describe themselves as itinerant merchants."

"Where were they bound after Obroa-skai?" Vader wanted to know.

"Taanab," Crest said, "to buy foodstuffs. Parties at Thustra, Obroa-skai, and Taanab have substantiated all this."

"And the communications board?" Tarkin asked.

Crest turned to him. "It isn't set up to record incoming or outgoing transmissions, but the log checks out, at least in terms of supporting the captain's claims about who contacted them and where the freighter was at the time."

Vader scanned the hold, as if in search of something unspecified. "How long did they spend at Thustra?"

"Three hours, Lord Vader."

Vader glanced at Tarkin. "What, I wonder, was their rush?"

Tarkin considered it. "Apparently the goods—the flyer replacement parts—were already crated and waiting for them. The medcenter on Obroa-skai had requested that they expedite the delivery." He fell briefly silent. "The *Reticent*'s hyperdrive is vastly inferior to that of the *Carrion Spike*. No better than a Class Five, I would imagine. That means that even though they arrived in the Obroa-skai system at almost precisely the moment we were expecting the *Carrion Spike*, the *Reticent* had to have gone to hyperspace much sooner than the *Carrion Spike* would have. The timing could owe to nothing more than coincidence, but one question to ask is just what the *dissidents* were doing in the Thustra system for so many hours."

Vader had swung abruptly to Tarkin on the word *coincidence*, and now the Dark Lord was in motion, pushing crates aside as he stormed about—without actually touching any of them.

"This ship rendezvoused with the *Carrion Spike*. I'm certain of it."

Tarkin threw Crest a questioning look.

"If so, Lord Vader," the stormtrooper said, "there's no evidence of the ships linking up. No evidence in the comm board showing intership communication, and no evidence in the docking ring's air lock memory showing that the *Reticent* was umbilicaled to another ship."

Vader took a moment to reply, and when he did it was to pose a question to Tarkin. "Why would the dissidents elect to *send* us a ship, in any case?"

Tarkin smiled faintly, aware that the question was rhetorical. "To throw us off the scent, if I recall your phrase correctly. To give us plenty to deal with while they're busy making plans to strike elsewhere."

Vader turned and proceeded to the cargo hold ramp. "Let us see what the captain of this scrap heap has to say for himself."

"You are not an itinerant merchant, Captain," Vader said, gesticulating with his right hand. "You are in league with a group of dissidents intent on destroying military installations as a means of undermining the sovereignty of the Empire."

A Koorivar with a long cranial horn, the *Reticent*'s naked and shackled captain was suspended a meter overhead, captive of a containment field produced by a device whose prototype had been manufactured on Geonosis long before the war. As far as Tarkin knew, the *Executrix* was the only capital ship in the Imperial fleet to have such an appliance, which created and maintained the field by means of disklike generators bolted to the deck and to the ceiling directly above. The detention center's version of prisoner interdiction, the field required that the detainee wear magnetic cuffs that not only anchored him in place but also monitored life signs: Too powerful a field could stop a being's heart or cause irreversible brain damage. As well—and as if the field itself weren't enough—the cuffs could be used as torture devices, capable of unleashing powerful electrical charges. Vader, however, had no need to utilize the cuffs. His dark powers had the captain writhing in pain.

"Lord Vader," Tarkin said, "we should at least give him an opportunity to respond."

Reluctantly, Vader lowered his hand, and the Koorivar's ridged facial features relaxed in cautious relief. "I'm a merchant and nothing more," he managed to say. "Torture me as you must, but it won't change the fact that we came to Obroa-skai on business."

"The business of conspiracy," Vader said. "The business of sabotage."

The Koorivar shook his head weakly. "The business of buying and selling. That is what we do, and only what we do." He paused. "Not all of us were Separatists."

Tarkin smiled to himself. It was true: Not all Koorivar population centers and worlds had thrown in with Dooku. Nor had all Sy Myrthians, a pair of which made up the rest of the crew.

But why would the captain say that?

"Why do you make a point of stating that fact, Captain?" he asked.

The Koorivar's bleary eyes found him. "The Empire demands retribution for the war, and so it lumps the innocent with the guilty and holds all of us responsible."

"Responsible for what, Captain? Do you believe that the Separatists were wrong to secede from the Republic?"

"I move about to keep from having to decide who is right and who is wrong."

"A being without a homeworld," Tarkin said. "As your species was once without a planet."

"I'm telling you the truth."

"You're lying," Vader countered. "Admit that you swore allegiance to the Separatist Alliance, and that you and your current allies are the ones seeking retribution."

The Koorivar squeezed his eyes closed, anticipating pain Vader opted not to deliver.

"Tell me about the broker who provides you with leads," Tarkin said.

"Knotts. A human who works out of Lantillies. Contact him. He'll verify everything I've been telling you."

"He helped you procure the *Reticent*?"

"He loaned us the credits, yes."

"And you've been in his employ for three years."

"Not in his employ. We're freelance. He provides jobs to several crews, and we accept jobs from several brokers."

"How did you originally find your way to a human broker on Lantillies?"

"An advert of some sort. I don't recall precisely."

"This time he instructed you to travel from Taris to Thustra?"

"Yes."

"A rush job," Tarkin surmised.

"The medcenter relies on its Sephi flyers for medical evacuations."

"So, in and out," Tarkin said. "No interaction with anyone other than the provider."

"No interaction. Exactly as you say."

"And no ship-to-ship interaction."

"There was no need. The supplies were groundside on Thustra."

Tarkin circled the Koorivar. "In your recent travels, have you seen holovids of attacks launched against Imperial facilities?"

"We try to ignore the media."

"Clueless, as well as homeless," Tarkin said, "is that it?"

The captain sneered at him. "Guilty as charged."

Tarkin traded glances with Vader. "An interesting turn of phrase, Captain," Tarkin said.

Vader loosed a sound that approximated a growl. "We're not in some Coruscant courtroom, Governor. Questions of this sort are useless."

"You'd prefer to break him with pain."

"If need be. Unless, of course, you object."

Vader's menacing tone rolled off Tarkin. "I suspect that our captain will go insane long before he breaks. But I also agree that we're wasting our time. The longer we spend here, the greater the chance that the *Carrion Spike* will elude us entirely." He watched the Koorivar peripherally as he said it.

Vader looked directly at the captain. "Yes, this one is stronger than he looks, and he is not innocent. I want more time with him. For all we know the dissidents abandoned your ship at Thustra and transferred to the YT freighter. He may be one of them."

"Then someone else must have the *Carrion Spike,* as there was no sign of her there." Tarkin glanced at the captain a final time and forced an exhalation. "I'll leave you to your work, Lord Vader."

The Koorivar's anguished screams accompanied him down the long corridor that led to the detention center's turbolifts.

Teller found Anora in the corvette's darkened cockpit, swiveling absently in one of the chairs, her bare feet crossed atop the instrument console. Salikk and the others were resting, as was the *Carrion Spike,* a slave to sundry deep-space gravities.

"We're almost done," he said, sinking into an adjacent chair.

Her face fell. "There has to be a more comforting way of saying that."

He frowned at her. "You're the writer."

"Yes, but you're *talking,* not writing."

His frown only deepened. "You know what I mean. One more jump and on to the serious business."

Her eyes searched his face. "And then?"

All he could do was shrug. "With luck, live to fight another day."

She closed her eyes and shook her head. "With luck . . . There you go again, qualifying every answer."

He didn't know how else to put it; how not to qualify his remarks. In thinking about it, he recalled having made almost the same comment when the *Reticent* had jumped for Obroa-skai. *With any luck, Tarkin and Vader will dismiss the ship's arrival as coincidental, and the crew will simply be questioned and released.* But that wasn't what happened. The Imperials had seen through the ruse, the ship had been impounded, and the crew had been arrested. Word was that neither Tarkin nor Vader had been able to glean much information from them, but Teller doubted that Tarkin would leave it at that. Tarkin wouldn't rest until he rooted out connections, and once he did . . . Well, by then it would be too late.

With any luck.

The update on the situation at Obroa-skai had also included a piece of good news. The corvette's crew had been given a target to attack, which had saved him the trouble of having to choose one from among increasingly bad options. The objective was another Imperial facility rather than some more significant objective, but Teller could live with that. No one aboard the *Carrion Spike* nursed any delusions about winning a war against the Empire single-handedly. They were merely contributing to what Teller hoped would one day grow into a *cause.* That, and avenging themselves for what each of them had had to bear; payback for atrocities the Empire had committed, which had inspired them to come together as a group.

"Nice of you to give Cala the privilege of destroying the homing beacon," Anora said.

"He earned it."

Anora put her feet on the cool deck, yawned, and stretched her thin, dark arms over her head. "When do we go?"

Teller glanced at the console's chron display. "We've still got a couple of hours."

"Do you trust your contact entirely?"

Teller rocked his head. "I'd say, up to a point. He's convinced that he has as much to gain as we do."

Anora grinned faintly. "I was expecting you to add, *or lose*."

"It was implied."

"Any compassion for our stand-ins at Obroa-skai?"

Teller exhaled in disappointment. "Not you, too."

"I'm only asking."

"They knew the risks," Teller said, straight-faced.

Anora took a long moment to respond. "I know I sound like Hask, but maybe I'm just not cut out for this, Teller." She eyed him askance. "It was never an ambition of mine to be a revolutionary."

He snorted. "I don't buy it. You were fighting the good fight in your own way long before I met you. With words, anyway."

She smiled without showing her teeth. "Not quite the same as firing laser cannons at other beings or letting strangers take the fall for you."

He studied her. "You know, I'm actually surprised to hear you talk like this. You practically jumped at the chance to get involved."

She nodded. "I won't deny it. But since we're being honest with each other, I may have been thinking of it more as a career move."

"Fame and fortune."

"I guess. And like our stand-ins, I knew the risk. But I underestimated COMPNOR and the Emperor."

"His reach."

"Not just his reach." Her face grew serious. "His power. His barbarity."

"You're not the only one who underestimated him."

Anora glanced toward the command center hatch and lowered her voice. "I still feel bad about dragging Hask into this."

Teller shrugged. "We could always drop her off somewhere."

Anora's eyes searched his face. "Really?"

"Sure, if that's what she wants."

"Should I ask her?"

"Go ahead. I'll give you odds she says no."

Anora laughed shortly. "I think you're right." She fell silent, then said: "Are we going to win, Teller?"

He reached out to clap her gently on the shoulder. "We're winning so far, aren't we?"

The subsurface Sith shrine wasn't the sole area in the Palace where the dark side of the Force was strong. Rooms and corridors throughout the lower levels still bore traces of the resentful fury Darth Vader had unleashed in the final days of the Clone Wars. In one such room a human and a Koorivar knelt in separate pools of ruthless light trained on them from hidden sources in the vaulted ceiling. To Darth Sidious, however, they were not so much living beings as whirlpools in the befuddled waters he had been negotiating since the cache of communications gear found on Murkhana had been brought to his attention; obstacles he needed to maneuver past in order to reach an untroubled stretch of current.

Sidious occupied a simple chair well removed from the twin pools of light, the droid 11-4D off to one side and, slightly behind him, Vizier Mas Amedda close at hand as well. Opposite him across the barren room, a pair of Royal Guards flanked the carved stone doorway.

The Koorivar—Bracchia—was an Imperial intelligence asset assigned to Murkhana; the human—Stellan—the Koorivar's Security Bureau case officer stationed on Coruscant. Sidious already knew all he needed to about their separate backgrounds and records of service. He sought nothing more than to observe them through the Force, and to evaluate their responses to a few simple questions.

"Koorivar," he said from the chair, "you served the Republic during the war, and more recently you provided some assistance to Lord Vader and Governor Tarkin on Murkhana."

Light reflected off the Koorivar's spiral horn as he lifted his head a bit. "I helped them rid Murkhana of arms smugglers, my lord."

"So it seems. But tell us what you told them at the time about your initial survey of the HoloNet jamming devices."

"My lord, I stated that I did not chance upon the devices on my own, nor was I cognizant of any rumors indicating that such a cache existed in Murkhana City. I was merely executing a directive I received from Coruscant."

Viewing him through the Force, Sidious saw the eddying waters began to relax and surrender themselves to the current.

"Case officer," he said to Stellan, "by 'Coruscant' he means *you*, does he not?"

"Yes, my lord. The investigation was carried out at my request." A thickset human man of indeterminate age, he had brown wavy hair and large ears set low on a blockish head.

"Then tell us how you came to learn of this cache."

The man lifted his nondescript face to the light, squinting and blinking in puzzlement. "My lord, forgive me. I assumed you were aware that the information was provided to ISB by Military Intelligence."

Sidious's pulse quickened. Instead of smoothing out, the hydraulic tightened on itself and began to spin more rapidly, as if summoning Sidious to follow the swirling funnel beneath the surface to whatever irregularity below had given rise to it.

It may as well have been the dark side that rasped: "Explain this."

Humbling himself, the case officer lowered his head. "My lord, Military Intelligence was in the process of conducting an inventory of caches of armaments, vehicles, and supplies that had been left abandoned during the war on a host of contested worlds, from Raxus all the way to Utapau. In the case of the HoloNet jamming devices, MI wasn't certain if the cache had been on Murkhana for several years, or if it was of more recent origin, and worthy therefore of further investigation. Given that an investigation of that sort fell outside its purview, MI relayed the matter to Imperial Security."

"To you," Sidious said.

"Yes, my lord, I received a crude holovid that showed the devices."

"A holovid? Cammed by someone in Military Intelligence?"

"That was my assumption, my lord. I didn't see the need to pursue the matter, nor did the deputy director. We simply instructed . . . Bracchia to conduct a survey."

Sidious thought back to the initial briefing that had taken place in the audience chamber. Defending ISB's apprehensions that the jammers could be used to spread anti-Imperial propaganda, Deputy Director Ison had wondered aloud why Naval Intelligence was suddenly so troubled by the cache when on first learning of it they had expressed no such concerns. None of the admirals—not Rancit, Screed, nor any of the others—had replied to Ison's question.

Without taking his eyes from the case officer, Sidious said in a low voice, "Droid, locate this holovid sent by Military Intelligence to ISB."

OneOne-FourDee extended its interface arm into an access port behind Sidious's chair. After a long silence, the droid said: "Your Majesty, I find no record of the holovid."

"As I suspected," Sidious said. "But you will find it in ISB's archives."

Another moment passed before 11-4D said, "Yes, Your Majesty. The holovid is archived."

And when projected, Sidious thought, it would show corruption of a telltale sort. Because the holovid was counterfeit; faked by someone with access to Imperial codes and to devices capable of subverting the HoloNet.

Deep beneath the surface he had found the irregularities responsible for the turbulence above. And it was apparent now that they were closer at hand than even he had realized.

FOOTPRINTS

IN THE MOST SECLUDED of the *Executrix*'s several tactical rooms, Tarkin closed myriad programs running on the immense battle analysis holotable, and entered a restricted Imperial code that tasked the projector to interface with the HoloNet. He then submitted himself to a series of biometric scans that allowed him to access a multitude of top-secret Republic and Imperial databases situated on Coruscant. He had already issued orders that he was not to be disturbed, but he double-checked that the door had sealed behind him and that the tactical room's security cams were offline. He called for the illumination to dim, set himself atop a tall castered stool within easy reach of the table's complex controls, and allowed his thoughts to unwind.

The Star Destroyer was holding at Obroa-skai, awaiting redeployment orders from Coruscant, now that the Emperor had given Vice Admiral Rancit command of the task force created to capture or destroy the *Carrion Spike*. Only a few hours earlier the dissidents had attacked an Imperial facility at Nouane, a client-state system in the Inner Rim. To Tarkin, the dissidents' choice of targets seemed as illogical as would have been their showing up at Obroa-skai. But with major systems becoming so heavily reinforced, perhaps the choice merely reflected the fact that their options were dwindling. At Nouane the rogue ship had been prevented from inflicting serious damage and had nearly become a fatality. The win had gone to Rancit, who through a painstaking process of elimination had predicted where the *Carrion Spike* would strike and had dispatched a flotilla in advance of the corvette's arrival. Even stealth had failed to allow the corvette to evade a continuous onslaught of long-range lasers. From what Tarkin had been given to understand, there was good reason to believe that the *Carrion Spike* had sustained heavy damage before a last-ditch retreat to hyperspace. The rumor mill had it that Rancit's assignment—some called it a promotion—was an indication of the Emperor's disappointment with Tarkin, but Vader had assured Tarkin that the Emperor was merely trying to free him from having to wear too many hats. Tarkin was to leave the chase to others for the time being, and devote himself instead to ascertaining the dissidents' ultimate objective.

And so he was.

When stalking game on the plateau, Jova would tell him that a careful study of prints on a trail could reveal not only the species of animal that had left them, but also the animal's intentions.

With a flourish of input at the holotable's keypad, Tarkin created an open field above the table and instructed the computer to render his voice into lines of text and place them in order in the field. Then he turned slightly in the direction of the nearest audio pickup.

"Access to confiscated warship modules, Separatist weapons, and HoloNet interrupters—either through salvagers, crime syndicates, or other sources," he began. "The ability to make use of purchased or pirated Separatist technology. The ability to transmit real-time holovids through the HoloNet, and the ability to create and transmit counterfeit holovids by accessing public HoloNet archives and other media sources. Knowledge of the existence of Rampart and Sentinel bases. Knowledge of Lieutenant Thon's assignment to Rampart Base. Knowledge of the existence of the *Carrion Spike*, and familiarity with her sophisticated systems. A crew of spacers conversant with Imperial procedures and with a knowledge of Imperial facilities. Possible assistance from Imperial assets with high clearance."

One by one the lines of text appeared in the field and Tarkin studied them for a long moment, his elbow planted on his raised left knee and his chin cupped in his hand.

Vader's interrogation of the *Reticent*'s crewmembers hadn't resulted in anything more than heart failure for the freighter's Sy Myrthian navigator. However, as a recompense of sorts, the Dark Lord had received a significant piece of information from one of his sources inside the Crymorah. A lieutenant in the crime syndicate claimed to have negotiated a deal with Faazah—the Sugi smuggler on Murkhana—for a supply of custom fuel cells, which had been shipped to the planet shortly before Tarkin and Vader's arrival. This in itself wasn't entirely surprising, considering that the *Carrion Spike*'s stop at the Phindar fuel tanker was evidence enough that the dissidents had added fuel to the ship before absconding with her. What *was* surprising was that the deal for the fuel cells had been arranged through an agent on Lantillies, whom Tarkin suspected was the same human the captain of the *Reticent* had named as their broker.

Knotts.

Tarkin instructed the HoloNet database to launch a search for Knotts, and in moments the hologram of a silver-haired human with a deeply lined face was rotating in place above the projector. Knotts had a world-weary look Tarkin associated with veteran soldiers who had seen more than their share of tragedy. Extracting the holoimage, he saved it off to one side of the table and regarded it in silence while machines hummed, chirped, and beeped around him.

What he read in the concise précis accompanying the holoimage supported the fact that Knotts had resided on Lantillies for some fifteen years. Digging a bit deeper, Tarkin was able to retrieve Knotts's documents of incorporation, his Republic and Imperial tax records, court proceedings of his divorce agreement, even images of the modest apartment he owned on Lantillies. Native to the Core, he had relocated to the Outer Rim and established himself as a middleman, bringing clients in want of goods or services together with groups of freelance spacers who could fulfill those needs. He was something of a dispatcher and an agent, taking what struck Tarkin as a fair credit percentage on each transaction.

The eyes-only Coruscant databases—which Tarkin hadn't had reason to access since his days as adjutant general of the Republic Navy—provided a more complete and compelling portrait of Knotts. Yes, for fifteen years he had operated a profitable if minor Outer Rim enterprise, but during the Clone Wars he had also functioned as a subcontractor for Republic Intelligence, responsible for the covert transport of arms and other materials to resistance groups operating on Separatist-occupied worlds, one of which happened to figure prominently in Tarkin's past, as well: the Mid Rim moon Antar 4.

Tarkin sat taller on the stool. The discovery of Knotts's secret past stirred a memory of the excitement he had felt on the plateau when encountering a sudden, unexpected turn along a game trail. Had his quarry gotten wind of him? Had a different threat presented itself? Was his prey keen on reversing the situation by circling behind to stalk him in his own tracks?

Antar 4 had been a member of the Republic almost from its inception, but the Secessionist Movement that preceded the Clone Wars had created a schism among the moon's indigenous humanoid Gotals and given rise to terrorist groups aligned with the Separatists. Shored up by the Republic, Gotal loyalists had managed to retain power until shortly after the Battle of Geonosis, when the moon had fallen to Separatist forces and, for a brief period, become a headquarters for Count Dooku. Tens of millions of Gotal refugees had fled to their colony world, Atzerri, replaced on Antar 4 by an influx of Koorivar, Gossams, and other species whose homeworlds had joined the CIS. As a result, the moon became a political imbroglio, and had spawned one of the first resistance groups, made up of loyalist Koorivar and Gotals whom the Republic supported with tactical advisers and secret shipments of arms and matériel. Though the resistance was successful in carrying out hundreds of acts of sabotage, the moon remained in the grip of the Separatists for the length of the war.

Tarkin recalled the Koorivar captain's words to Vader: *Not all of us were Separatists.*

With the deaths of Dooku and the Separatist leadership, and the deactivation of the droid army, Antar 4—like many CIS worlds—had soon found itself in the Empire's crosshairs. More to the point, in the crosshairs of Moff Tarkin, who had been given Imperial orders to make an example of the moon. No attempt was to be made at repatriation, nor was Tarkin to waste time sorting the Separatists from those resistance fighters and intelligence operatives waiting to be exfiltrated to safety.

COMPNOR did its best to cover up the fact that many Koorivar and Gotal loyalists had been swept up in the arrests, executions, and massacres, but the media eventually got hold of the story, and for a while the Antar Atrocity had become a celebrated cause in the Core—this despite the swift disappearances of many beings who had attached themselves to reporting on the story. Instead, the disappearances so fueled the public's hunger for details that the Emperor decided to remove Tarkin from the controversy by assigning him to pacification operations in the Western Reaches and had ultimately installed him as commander of the bases servicing the deep-space mobile battle station project, replacing Vice Admiral Rancit, who was reassigned to Naval Intelligence.

In thinking back to that period, some four years earlier, Tarkin recalled the case of two Coruscanti journalists who had risen briefly to the forefront among a host of anti-Imperial irritants. A quick search of the HoloNet archives conjured their holograms, which Tarkin placed above the table alongside that of Knotts. In the Coruscant database, Tarkin located intelligence reports detailing their activities.

An attractive, dark-skinned human woman with blue-gray eyes, Anora Fair had been the most vocal and volatile of the Core media correspondents who had fixated on the events at Antar. An ambitious journalist, Fair had already attracted attention for her probing interviews with Imperial officials and her editorials critical of Imperial policy, as well as of the Emperor himself. Her unrelenting reports on the Antar Atrocity had been brought to life with holographic recreations of arrests and executions, produced and directed by a rubicund Zygerrian female named Hask Taff, whom many a pro-Imperial pundit had deemed "a master of HoloNet manipulation."

It was clear to COMPNOR that the two of them knew more than

they could possibly have known without the help of an intelligence community insider, and suspicions at the time had focused on a disaffected former Republic station chief named Berch Teller.

A HoloNet archive search for Teller came up empty, but an access-restricted database search returned a decade-old image of a rangy, dark-haired human with thick eyebrows and a cleft chin. Extracting the hologram, Tarkin placed it alongside those of Anora Fair and Hask Taff, then changed his mind and moved Teller's hologram to the center, with Knotts—the broker—to one side, and the two media professionals on the other.

Tarkin contemplated the arrangement and was pleased. With each new set of prints, the trail was beginning to surrender its secrets.

Captain Teller's intelligence network résumé indicated a long and distinguished career. Early in the Clone Wars, Teller had been involved in covert operations on a host of Separatist worlds. That, however, paled in comparison with the fact that Teller had been one of the intelligence officers who had debriefed Tarkin following his rescue and escape from the Citadel, with the plans to a secret hyperspace route into Separatist space.

He and Teller had history.

And there was more.

Assigned to Antar 4 in the war's final year, Captain Teller had helped train and organize Gotal and Koorivar partisans into well-armed resistance groups, which had carried out raids, destroyed armories and spaceports, and generally made a nuisance of themselves for the governing Separatists. Sensing what was in store for Antar 4 after the war's abrupt conclusion, Teller had appealed to his superiors in the intelligence agencies to arrange for the extraction of his principal assets before Tarkin could bring the hammer down on the moon. Republic Intelligence had tried to provide aid in the form of documentation and transport, but COMPNOR, by then on the rise in the Imperial hegemony, had refused to intervene, and so many of Teller's operatives, despite their long-standing loyalty to the Republic, had been arrested and executed.

The Imperial directive to make an example of the moon had made perfect sense to Tarkin at the time. He wasn't a retributionist; it was simply that separating friend from foe would undoubtedly have allowed many Separatists to flee into hiding. Eliminating them en masse on Antar 4 was preferable to having to hunt them down later, in whatever remote regions they found shelter. His actions had conveyed a message to other former CIS worlds that defeat didn't grant them absolution for their crimes, or assure them that the Empire was ready to welcome them back into the fold with open arms. The message had to be made clear to Raxus, Kooriva, Murkhana, and the rest: Surrender all former Separatists, or suffer the same fate as the population of the Gotal moon.

Still, Tarkin could see how a Republic officer like Teller might feel betrayed to the point where he would attempt to wage a campaign of revenge against all odds. The military was filled with those who refused to accept that collateral damage was acceptable when it served to further the Imperial cause. In the absence of order, there was only chaos. Did Teller expect an apology from the Emperor? Compensation for the families of those who had been unjustly executed? It was witless thinking. Multiply Teller by one billion or ten billion beings, however, and the Empire could face a serious problem . . .

He continued to peruse Teller's résumé, wading through the dense text that scrolled in midair in front of his eyes. By the time Teller had made his appeal to his intelligence chiefs, he had already been reassigned to head up security at—

Tarkin stared at the words: *Desolation Station.*

The clandestine outpost responsible for overseeing much of the research for the deep-space battle station.

But Teller wasn't there for long; he had vanished shortly after the events at Antar 4 and hadn't been seen since. Some in Military Intelligence believed that he had been assassinated by COMPNOR agents, but others were convinced that it was Teller who had not only fed information about Antar 4 to Anora Fair and Hask Taff, but also been instrumental in spiriting the media partners to safety hours before they were to have been disappeared by COMPNOR.

Tarkin eased off the castered stool and began to pace the length of the massive table, all the while regarding the four projected holo-images. Was it possible that some or all of them were involved in the pirating of the *Carrion Spike*? He stopped to mull it over, and shook his head. The odds were good that Teller and Knotts knew each other, in that they had answered to the same case officer at Republic Intelligence; also that Teller had approached the journalists with his story. But none of the four was a starship pilot, much less an engineer capable of managing the corvette's sophisticated instruments and systems.

Returning to the stool, Tarkin re-summoned the lengthy file devoted to Antar 4.

The Republic databases were difficult to navigate, as much of the information had been deleted or redacted, or was in the process of being altered and "reinterpreted." Once he had successfully wormed his way into the appropriate archives, however, he was able to narrow the parameters of his search for Republic assets associated with the resistance. Ultimately the distant computers provided the names of several of Teller's partisan subordinates who had escaped execution on the moon and were at least worthy of consideration. There was, for example, a Gotal starship pilot, identified in the archives only as "Salikk," and a Koorivar munitions and surveillance expert listed only as "Cala."

Tarkin extracted holoimages of the twin-horned humanoid and the single-horned near-human and placed them on the far side of the holograms of Fair and Taff; then, changing his mind, he moved them to float between those of Teller and Knotts.

A tremor of excitement coursed through him.

He propelled the castered stool to the HoloNet array and contacted the escort carrier, *Goliath,* ordering the specialist he eventually spoke with to forward from the ship's database a record of his transmission with the Phindian administrator of the fuel tanker. When the recording arrived, he extracted the image of the scar-faced, red-haired human who had requisitioned fuel cells and ordered the computer to compare the hologram of Teller to the bogus Imperial commander with the ocular implant.

In short order, text flashed above the holotable between the two holograms:

MATCH: 99.9%

Tarkin's jaw fell open in wonder as he stared at the man who had stolen his ship.

Shifting his gaze between his dictated text and the holograms of the suspects, he began to think through everything from scratch.

Yes, Teller could have learned about the *Carrion Spike* during his short tenure at Desolation Station. And it would have been easy enough for him to persuade "Salikk" and "Cala" to join him, since he had probably been responsible for exfiltrating them from Antar 4—just as he'd been responsible for saving the lives of Fair and Taff by whisking them from Coruscant. At that point, Teller would have had a pilot, an operations and munitions specialist, and two HoloNet experts.

Tarkin ran a hand down over his mouth and took hold of his chin.

Something was missing; some*one* was missing.

He reentered the top-secret database to scan the few reports he could access relating to Desolation Station.

Teller wasn't the only being who had disappeared from the secret facility. Motivated by grievances against the Empire, many had fled and become fugitives. The count was so high, in fact, that COMP-NOR had compiled a most-wanted list of missing scientists and technicians who had held high-priority security clearances. The disappearances were often offered up as an explanation for harassment attacks against Imperial bases and installations.

Tarkin scrolled through the list several times, returning after each read-through to a Mon Cal starship systems engineer named Artoz, who had gone missing shortly after Teller. "Dr. Artoz," as he was apparently affectionately known, was a former member of the Mon Cal Knights, a group that had fought against his planet's Separatist-aligned Quarren. Artoz certainly would have known about the *Carrion Spike,* as parts for the corvette's stygian crystal stealth system had been manufactured at Mon Cal shipyards after the concept-design team had given up on attempts to utilize hibridium.

Tarkin blinked, rubbed his eyes, and stared at the midair holograms.

What about Bracchia, the Koorivar asset on Murkhana? Was he involved in the plot, despite the part he had played in procuring a replacement starship?

Were the Crymorah crime families involved?

What about the crew of the freighter *Reticent*? Had they perhaps been aboard the cobbled-together warship that had attacked Sentinel Base?

Then there was the matter of the warship itself. Who had funded the purchase of the modules, droids, and starfighters? Where and by whom had the ship been assembled? Just how wide reaching was the conspiracy? Did it involve only former Republic Intelligence operatives, or did it penetrate Imperial agencies, as well?

Sentients, like animals, have their fussy behaviors, Jova would say. *Learn the particulars of one, and you begin to understand the entire species.*

If Tarkin's hypothesis about Antar 4 being the nexus of the conspiracy was correct, could the involvement of the *Reticent*'s crew owe to something as simple as having lost friends or relatives to the mass executions? Relatives who were perhaps affiliated with Teller's partisans?

Tarkin continued to scan the 3-D images.

If he was right and he was actually looking at those who had stolen his ship and discovered how to replicate the Clone Wars Shadowfeeds, then as it happened they were not former Separatists nursing a grudge against the Empire, but rather former Republican *loyalists* with a vendetta.

Supreme Chancellor Palpatine's onetime allies had become the Emperor's new foes.

Saving his research to an encrypted file, Tarkin thought: *The trail continues beyond where you lose it.*

Were the dissidents leading him on a chase calculated to disguise their actual objective?

The thread that had begun to unspool at Sentinel Base could end at only one point.

The *Carrion Spike* stumbled out of hyperspace to an interstellar reversion point ten parsecs from Nouane. The near miss in the autonomous region had left the corvette so rattled that, for a long while, the damaged navicomputer couldn't even establish where the ship was. It was easier now to list the instruments that were still functioning than those that were damaged beyond repair.

"We have two forward laser cannons and one starboard battery," Cala reported to the others in the corvette's main cabin, where Artoz was tending to Salikk's facial injuries. "Shields are down to nothing. Hull armor's the only thing protecting us from a collision with space dust. Hyperdrive motivator is marginal, but probably good for one, possibly two more jumps—"

"One is all we need," Teller said, while the ship groaned like a wounded animal and Salikk's shed fur wafted in all directions.

"Stealth systems and sublight drives are hit or miss," the Koorivar continued. "Same with communications and the HoloNet."

Hask gave her pert-eared head a woeful shake. "We don't come off very well in the vids the Empire released of the Nouane engagement."

"There go our ratings," Artoz said.

Anora scowled at him and threw Teller a peeved look. "So much for trusting your ally to hold up his end of the bargain."

"I said I trusted him up to a point," Teller shot back. "If I trusted him entirely, we wouldn't even be having this conversation."

The remark was not an exaggeration. Had the *Carrion Spike* decanted in the Nouane system at the anticipated reversion point, she would have been instantly annihilated by Imperial fire. Instead, Teller had had Salikk decant the ship deeper in system, as far from the capital ships as was feasible. Regardless, they had been forced to make a run for it without firing a beam at the star system's Imperial facility, its inconsequence notwithstanding. Boxed in and pounded by laserfire, they had jumped to lightspeed with a maneuver that in itself had been no mean feat.

"Besides," Teller went on, "he had to make it look real."

Anora loosed a bitter laugh. "They weren't just making it *look* real, Teller. Face facts: We've been betrayed."

Teller snorted a bitter laugh. "Probably. But in the end it won't matter." He looked at Salikk, then Artoz. "Is he going to be all right, Doc?"

"I'll live," Salikk said for himself. "At least for long enough to finish this."

"The autopilot also survived," Cala said.

Teller blew out his breath and nodded. "Then we're good to go on that score. Plus, we've been assured of clear skies."

"As long as he's still convinced we're on our way," Anora said.

Teller nodded. "The *Carrion Spike* will arrive on schedule."

"You realize that the Empire won't rest until we're found and dealt with," Artoz said.

Hask glanced around. "Assuming anyone's figured out who we are."

"I wouldn't put it past Tarkin and Vader—not with the *Reticent* crew in hand." Teller compressed his lips. "Even if not, we'll be given up at some point."

Cala grinned. "Fortunately, we've all grown accustomed to looking over our shoulders."

THE CARRION SPIKE

ON THE COMMAND WALKWAY of the *Executrix*, Tarkin waited for Vader to conclude a private holocommunication with the Emperor.

"Vice Admiral Rancit is convinced that the dissidents intend to attack the Imperial academy at Carida, martyring themselves in the process," Vader said when he emerged from one of the data pits. "The vice admiral has been given permission to redeploy as many vessels as he sees fit, and he himself will be commanding all elements of the task force."

Tarkin scoffed. "The dissidents' last stand?"

"Someone's last stand," Vader said. "The Emperor has given careful thought to your premise that his onetime allies have now become his foes."

"I'm relieved to hear that, Lord Vader. Then we three are in agreement?"

Vader nodded solemnly. "We are."

Tarkin smiled in a self-satisfied way. "A shuttle is waiting to take you to the frigate."

Vader nodded again and started to move off, only to stop and turn back to Tarkin. "Tell me, Governor Tarkin, why did you choose to name the corvette the *Carrion Spike*?"

Tarkin allowed his surprise to show. "The ship is named for a unique geographic feature on Eriadu, Lord Vader." When he realized that Vader was waiting for a more complete explanation, he said, "Allow me to accompany you to the shuttle bay."

As they set off side by side, Tarkin began to tell Vader about his annual visits to the Carrion Plateau as a teenager, about the tests he had endured there, and about the training he had undergone at the hands of his wilderness-experienced elder relatives and various guides. Vader paid close attention, interrupting him several times to ask for clarification or additional detail. As Tarkin obliged, one part of him took note of how strange it felt to be having an actual dialogue with the Dark Lord. In the recent days they had spent together, their exchanges had been limited to a few sentences, and more typically had been one-sided. Vader's mask was responsible for some of that, complicating the process of conversation. But just now Vader's frequent downward glances suggested that he was actually listening; so Tarkin went on talking, opening up about his experiences on the plateau while they continued down the *Executrix*'s broad central corridor toward the waiting shuttle.

"By the time I was sixteen, I had come to know the plateau almost as well as I knew the grounds of my parents' home in Eriadu City," Tarkin said. "There was one area that we avoided, however—a vast stretch of savanna interrupted by stands of thick forest. It wasn't precisely off-limits. In fact, on several occasions I understood that my uncle was taking us well out of the way simply so I could get a glimpse of the territory. Each time he did so he would explain that we were not alone in being the plateau's reigning predators. And while there was no denying that our blasters were capable of eliminating all competitors, an act of that nature would have flown in the face of keeping the plateau pristine. One goal of the training was to help me understand how to place myself at the top of the food chain through fear rather than force, and how best to maintain my position. The territory we always seemed to skirt was there to provide me with another lesson, as it was ruled over by our chief competitors on the plateau, a one-hundred-strong troop of especially vicious primates."

He paused to glance up at Vader. "Are you familiar with the veer-mok?"

Vader nodded. "I've had some experience with the species, Governor."

Tarkin waited for more, but Vader said nothing. "Well, then, you know how ferocious they can be on their own, let alone in a group. There's scarcely a creature they can't outwit or outfight when they set their minds to it. But the species on Eriadu is probably not the one you are familiar with. The Eriadu veermok stands a meter high, but is sleek-skinned rather than woolly, is social rather than solitary, and is ardently territorial. It has adapted to the dry conditions of the plateau, rather than to swamps and moist woodlands. Like the more ordinary species, it has razor-sharp claws, equally sharp teeth in its canine muzzle, and the strength of ten humans. Its powerful arms and upper torso appear made for climbing, but the Eriadu veermok is generally not arboreal. Like all its brethren, however, it is a swift and voracious carnivore.

"At the center of the terrain the troop controlled stands a one-hundred-meter-tall hill that more resembles a rock fortress. Crowning it is a four-sided spire of black volcanic glass, some twenty meters high and flat at the top. A time-eroded shaft of quickly cooled magma, to be sure, as are the boulders that support it."

Vader looked at him. "The Carrion Spike?"

"Just so," Tarkin said. "Without Jova having to say as much, I began to grasp that the Spike was to be the site of my final test."

Vader interrupted his rhythmic breathing to make a sound of acknowledgment. "Your trial."

Tarkin nodded. "I was in the midst of my second season on the plateau when Jova first pointed the Spike out to me, but my . . . trial, as you say, wouldn't take place for four years to come. When that time arrived, he explained what was expected of me: I merely had to spend an entire day at the Spike, on my own. I would have neither food nor water, but I would be allowed to carry a vibro-lance of the sort we used in some of our hunts."

"A vibro-lance," Vader said.

"An electroshock weapon longer and lighter than the force pike. It has the same vibro-edged head but is balanced in such a way that it can also be hurled like a spear. Mine would be primed with a limited number of charges, though Jova didn't specify how many. In any case, if I could accomplish that—spend a single day at the Spike—my final test would be behind me, and I would no longer be compelled to visit the Carrion Plateau, unless of course it was my desire to do so."

"You must have thought it a simple task," Vader said.

"Initially, indeed," Tarkin said. "Until Jova allowed me to observe the hill and the spire through macrobinoculars."

"Your eyes were opened."

"Jova said that I could take as much time as I needed to assess the situation and decide on a course of action, and I spent the better part of my sixth season on the plateau doing just that. The first order of business was to get to know my enemy, which I did over the course of the first couple of weeks. I would conceal myself in areas of forest or in the tall savanna grass and observe the routines of the veermoks, which rarely varied from day to day—or perhaps it's better to say night to night, since that was when they would emerge from their hill caves and set out on communal hunts. The feasting that resulted from their hunts would continue for most of the night, sometimes at the site of their kills or sometimes back at the caves, where the females fed their gray-skinned young. With the return of the light and the heat, the males would ascend to the top of the hill and sprawl on the rocks at the foot of the Spike, which I was never able to get a good look at, even through the macrobinoculars, as the hill was the tallest feature for kilometers around in every direction. Midafternoon, the veermoks would make their descent, gathering at a watering hole to drink before repeating the entire routine.

"The water hole became my preferred place for observing them, and it was there where I began to get to know some members of the troop individually. Their dominant member was a dark-striped male, large and battle-scarred, to whom I gave the name Lord. During my weeks of stealthy observation, I saw him challenged at regular intervals. Sometimes the fights would be to the death, but more often

Lord would allow challengers to limp away in shame but remain part of the troop. Since it was impossible to defeat him, there was much competition among his subordinates to get close to him. In some sense, the fights were as much about training as they were displays of supremacy. Lord was teaching the weaker males, aware that he would eventually have to yield his position for the sake of the troop. The rest understood this and as a result followed his lead in all matters. I don't think the species is capable of abstract thought, much less truly sentient, but they do communicate with one another through a complex language of displays and vocalizations.

"There was a second male that caught my attention—a younger and smaller veermok who always seemed to be in Lord's shadow, so that was how I began to think of him. Shadow would tag behind and watch Lord from a respectful distance. Sometimes Lord wouldn't abide the scrutiny and would run Shadow off; at other times he tolerated the younger veermok's attempts to learn from him. What interested me most, however, was that Shadow had a following of his own, a subgroup of some eight young males who accompanied him wherever he went. Lord tolerated them as well, so long as they kept their distance, which they always did, retreating if he so much as turned in their direction.

"It was at the water hole that Shadow and his group began to take an interest in me. They observed me observing them, and began to study me as something curious that had showed up at the edge of their carefully defined domain. Sated from the previous night's hunt and having dismissed me as a threat, they demonstrated no immediate interest in killing me. At that point in my life, I had never heard of a veermok being domesticated, but I had heard of people who used the creatures as watchbeasts, and I imagined that it was possible to enter into some sort of partnership with them. I thought that perhaps I could make use of them as allies of a sort, either when I was at the Spike or in making my escape; and so each day I would try to edge closer to them, only to have them challenge me on every occasion, forcing me back across the invisible line of their hunting grounds.

"When I determined I had seen enough, I set myself to the task of thinking through the separate challenges I faced: getting to the top of the hill; climbing the Spike; and getting away—assuming I even survived the ordeal. Neither Jova nor any of the others offered help.

"Getting to the hill was going to require nothing more than moving while the veermoks were in the caves. I would emerge from the copse of forest closest to the hill, cross an expanse of savanna, and pick my way through the boulders to the top. There would be no shade and no rest, and some of the crevasses between the boulders appeared deep enough to swallow me whole. If I wasn't safely at the top by the time the veermoks emerged from the caves, I'd likely be torn apart on the hill.

"The Spike itself presented problems of a different sort. The edges of the black glass column appeared sharp enough to cut through cloth or hide or human flesh. So I devised a strap made from a duranium-threaded belt I found among replacement parts for the old speeder we used from time to time; and from that same belt I also fashioned thick soles for my boots and protective pads for my hands. I knew that even the veermoks' muscular legs weren't powerful enough to propel them to the top of the Spike, but there was still the matter of my remaining on the flat summit for the entire day. Especially after Jova allowed that the veermoks might delay their nocturnal hunt until they had dealt with me. The vibro-lance was meant to counter that eventuality, though the lance wouldn't contain enough charges to kill or stun all of the males. Worse still, they weren't frightened of the vibro-lance. In run-ins we'd had with solitary veermoks, they had evinced no fear even of blasters and had often proved agile enough to dodge beams. Add to this that I would have to scramble down and fight my way to the bottom of the hill and cross the savanna in darkness. That was where some of my predecessors had failed their initiations. Jova said that I would see what remained of their bones scattered about, as if the Spike were some sort of Tarkin reliquary.

"To provide myself with an advantage, I spent days working with a shovel—while the males were lazing on the hill and the females were in the caves tending to the young—to excavate a series of traps and pits along what would be my escape route, some little more than deep holes, others with floors of sharpened stakes.

"Then the day came.

"I made my crossing through the tall grass and scampered up onto the porous, fine-grained rocks. One slip and I could have broken an ankle or become permanently wedged between the boulders. Venomous insects attacked me from hidden nests; stinging ants streamed out from hills of their own making; serpents rattled in forewarning. The heat beat down on me. Nature had conspired to make the hill a last stand against technology and civilization; a place engineered to test a sentient's resolve to conquer and survive. But I endured.

"The Spike loomed above me like a lightning rod, a solidified puddle of black glass at its base. I threw the strap around it, planted the thick soles of my boots against the edges, and hauled myself up centimeters at a time. The ascent took much longer than I had anticipated, and I had scarcely reached the flat, slightly angled top when the first of the veermoks arrived.

"Seeing me there sitting cross-legged atop the Spike, the vibrolance hanging over my shoulder, they began to hop and circle round in mounting, growling agitation, uncertain, perhaps awaiting instructions from Lord. Alone among them, however, Shadow merely sat on his haunches to watch me, communicating with members of his clique by clacking vocalizations. Finally Lord made his appearance, gazing up at me with fury in his eyes—and what struck me as hatred at having to be put to a test so early in the day. I wondered if some of my ancestors had survived by killing the dominant veermok, thinking that would dissuade the rest. But I didn't believe that would work; not with Shadow standing by to assume leadership.

"As if by the power of voice alone he could dislodge me from my perch, Lord barked louder than the rest combined. After all, it was incumbent on him to deal with this intruder. But before he had a chance to act, Shadow issued another series of vocal clackings that prompted his followers to launch an attack on the Spike from all sides, their lethal claws scoring the volcanic glass with a sound that made every nerve in my body jangle. As if intent on splitting my attention, some feinted while others leapt as high as their legs could carry them. They roared and gnashed their big, triangular teeth, but I refused to give in to fear. Moreover, something unusual was going on. The attacks by Shadow's minions were chaotic, nothing at all like the well-coordinated exercises I had watched them utilize during hunts. The turmoil sent Lord into a rage. Desperate to restore order, he batted at the young males who were charging back and forth or trying to gain purchase on the glass. He drew blood from a few but was unable to control them.

"I glanced at Shadow in time to hear him issue a low, warbling groan, and at once the young males turned on Lord with teeth and claws set to one purpose. For a moment the old veermok champion seemed too confused to respond, almost as if the communal attack violated their code of behavior, some etiquette particular to the species. Quickly, though, he realized that he had to fight for his life, and he gave himself over to defending himself, killing three of the young males before the rest finally got the better of him. And throughout it all, Shadow didn't move a muscle."

"An assassination," Vader said. "With you providing the necessary distraction."

Tarkin nodded. "An opportunity they had long been waiting for."

"And the pretender—Shadow?"

Tarkin forced an exhale. "I gave the veermoks a moment to laud their new leader, then I hurled my lance and promptly killed him.

"I might as well have dropped a bomb on the hill. One moment the young veermoks didn't know what to make of their victory in overcoming Lord; now they behaved as if they had nowhere to turn. Without a leader, a true inheritor, they fell victim to a kind of bewildered grief, an almost existential despair. They dropped to their bellies and stared up at me in almost docile expectation. I didn't trust them, but I had no option but to descend the Spike at sunset, and when I threaded among them to retrieve my lance from Shadow's inert body, not one of them loosed even so much as a growl, and they actually followed me down the hill."

"What was your uncle's reaction?" Vader asked.

"Jova said it was good to see me in one piece, particularly since he and the others had wagered that my bones would be joining those of my ancestors." Tarkin paused before adding: "The following morning, the veermok troop abandoned the hill and the Spike. They left the plateau and weren't seen again."

"They failed to realize what they would bring down on themselves by turning on their leader," Vader said.

"Precisely."

"Then you are the last Tarkin to have passed the test."

Tarkin nodded. "That particular test, yes."

By then they had reached the shuttle bay. Tarkin walked alongside Vader to the foot of the ramp.

"Safe journey, Lord Vader. Be sure to give the pretender my regards."

"Rest assured, Governor Tarkin."

With an abrupt nod of his head and a swirl of his black cloak, Vader disappeared up the ramp and Tarkin started for the Star Destroyer's command bridge.

21

DISSOLUTION

THE *SECUTOR*-CLASS Star Destroyer *Conquest* hung in fixed orbit above the Carida Imperial Navy Deepdock Facility Two, some half a million kilometers from the eponymous planet. On the bridge Vice Admiral Rancit received an update from the ship's commander.

"Sir, the *Carrion Spike* has reverted to realspace, bearing zero-zero-three ecliptic. Target is acquired, firing solutions have been computed, and all starboard batteries are standing by."

Rancit took a final look at the myriad ships that made up the task force, and turned from the bridge viewport. "Prepare to fire on my command."

"Awaiting your word—"

"Belay that command," a voice boomed from the rear of the command bridge.

Rancit, the commander, and several nearby officers and specialists turned in unison to see Darth Vader storming forward on the elevated walkway, his cape billowing behind him, a squad of armed stormtroopers marching in step in his black wake.

"Lord Vader," Rancit said in genuine surprise. "I wasn't informed you were aboard."

"With purpose, Vice Admiral," Vader said, then swung to the bridge officer. "Commander, direct your technicians to scan the *Carrion Spike* for life-forms."

The commander looked to Rancit, who returned a dubious nod. "Do as he orders."

Vader came to a halt in the center of the walkway and put his gloved hands on his hips, fingers forward. "Well, Commander?"

The commander straightened from peering at a console over the shoulder of one of the specs. "The scanners aren't picking up any life signs." He glanced at Rancit in confusion. "Sir, the corvette is deserted, and appears to be astrogating on autopilot."

Rancit shook his head in denial. "But that can't be."

Vader looked at him. "Your co-conspirators abandoned the ship before it jumped to hyperspace, Vice Admiral."

Alarm found its way into Rancit's perplexity. "My co-conspirators, Lord Vader?"

"Don't act surprised," Vader said. "This entire charade was yours from the start."

Rancit tightened his fists and worked his jaw while the warship's commander and the rest exchanged worried glances. When he began to move toward one of the forward chairs, Vader raised his hand and clenched it.

"Stay right where you are, Vice Admiral." Vader pointed his finger at the bridge officer. "Order the commanders of the task force flotilla to stand down from general quarters."

The bridge officer nodded and walked backward to the communications board. "Immediately, Lord Vader."

Vader turned to Rancit once more.

"You made a deal with some of your former intelligence assets. Displeased with certain events that occurred at the end of the war, they were seeking a way to avenge themselves on the Empire, and you provided one. You allowed them access to confiscated technologies, and you facilitated the theft of Governor Tarkin's ship after luring him into your plot with counterfeit holotransmissions. You supplied them with tactical information along the way, and by doing so you are complicit in the deaths of thousands of Imperial effectives and the destruction of Imperial facilities."

Vader paced to the viewports and returned, positioning himself a meter from Rancit.

"You assured your co-conspirators that they would be allowed to strike at Carida and continue their reign of terror. But in fact you planned to betray them here, seeing to their deaths and so eliminating everyone who had been witness to your treachery. By having predicted where they would show themselves and by having put an end to their campaign, you would have earned the approval of the Emperor and . . . And what, Vice Admiral? Exactly what did you hope to achieve?"

Rancit regarded him with sudden loathing. "You of all people need to ask?"

Vader said nothing for a long moment, then approximated a sniff. "Power, Admiral? Influence? Perhaps you simply felt overlooked, that you, too, should have been named a Moff."

Rancit bit back whatever he had in mind to say.

"If only you had been one step ahead of your co-conspirators rather than one step behind," Vader continued in false lament. "Consider how far you might have risen in the Emperor's estimation had you been able to predict that *they* would betray *you* and go on to execute the plan they had in mind from the beginning."

Curiosity seeped into Rancit's rigid expression. "What plan?"

"This system was never meant to be their final target, Vice Admiral. The deal they made with you merely gave them free rein to carry out a mission of their own. They transferred to a different ship and are now on their way to the actual target."

"Where?" Rancit asked in an insistent tone.

"That is not your concern. Understand as well, Vice Admiral, that the Emperor has long held suspicions about you. He allowed your scheme to unfold as a means of ensnaring everyone involved in your conspiracy."

Rancit's courage returned. "What is the target, Vader? Tell me."

"Your apprehension is misplaced," Vader said in a menacingly calm voice. He lifted his right hand and began to bring his thumb and fingers together, then stopped. "No. You have already determined the method of your execution."

He swung to the squad of stormtroopers.

"Lieutenant Crest, Admiral Rancit is to be escorted to and placed inside an escape pod. I will give the order to launch the pod, and Admiral Rancit, once removed to a distance from this vessel, will issue the fire order that destroys it." Vader glanced over his shoulder at Rancit. "Does that meet with your approval, Vice Admiral?"

Rancit snarled. "I won't beg you, Vader."

"It would not affect the outcome in any case."

Vader nodded to the stormtroopers, who moved forward to surround Rancit.

"One last thing, Vice Admiral," Vader said as Rancit was being escorted aft down the walkway. "Moff Tarkin sends his regards."

A warship lay in wait in the shadow of a cratered, waterless moon in a star system Coreward of the Gulf of Tatooine.

Since it was not the product of a major shipbuilding conglomerate, the vessel lacked both a name and a registered signature. It was instead a farrago—a medley of modules, components, turbolasers, and ion cannons acquired by its assemblers from Imperial surplus depots, deep-space salvagers, smugglers, and others in the business of selling stolen parts and proscribed armaments. Fittingly the ship most resembled the Quarren Free Dac Volunteer Corps's *Providence*-class carrier, but at less than half the length was stubby by comparison and did not boast an aft communications tower. Its belly housed several squadrons of droid starfighters, and its weapons were operated by computer-controlled droids, but the ship was commanded by sentients—in this case a small group of humans, Koorivar, and Gotals, along with a sole Mon Cal starship systems engineer. It was the sort of vessel that would become closely associated with Outer Rim pirates in the postwar years. And in fact, it was the same capital ship that had briefly revealed itself at Sentinel Base weeks earlier.

"We've come full circle," Teller was telling Artoz in the starfighter hangar. Dressed in a flight suit, he had a helmet under one arm and was standing alongside a warming Headhunter retrofitted with a rudimentary hyperdrive—the very model Hask had used in crafting the false holovid that had been transmitted to Sentinel Base.

For the benefit of Knotts and the handful of other sentient pilots, Artoz said, "The convoy will revert to realspace at the edge of this system and continue by sublight to the Imperial marshaling station at Pii. From there, supply ships are escorted to Sentinel Base, and finally to Geonosis."

"Not this convoy," Knotts said. The world-weary human broker had helped pilot the hodgepodge carrier from its place of concealment near Lantillies. "Rancit did us a great favor by reallocating the convoy's protection."

"He promised us clear skies at Carida and gave us just that here," Teller said. "He had no reason to believe he'd be leaving the convoy vulnerable. He was simply shuffling ships around for show."

"Any word from Carida?" Knotts asked.

"Nothing yet," Artoz said.

"The evidence trail that links him to us is too much of a maze for anyone to follow," Teller said. "Accusations will be flying every which way about our not getting apprehended, but the assumption will be that we simply abandoned the cause."

"Rancit won't be happy with being denied his expected promotion," Knotts said. "He'll be on the hunt for us for betraying him."

Teller shrugged that off and glanced at Artoz. "Any suggestion Rancit makes about our being involved in the attack on the convoy would only make matters worse for him for pulling ships away. Rancit'll be lucky to be removed from Naval Intelligence with his pension intact, let alone be in a position to pose a threat to us."

"And Tarkin?" the Mon Cal asked.

"He gets back what's left of his precious corvette," Knotts said before Teller could reply.

"Tarkin won't be held accountable for any of it," Teller added. "He's a Moff. And besides, it wasn't his idea to go to Murkhana." He shook his head with finality. "I'm guessing he retains command of Sentinel Base."

Knotts nodded in agreement. "The question is, will *he* come after us?"

"Oh, you can count on that," Teller said. "We're going to need to scatter far and wide. The Corporate Sector's probably our safest bet."

No one spoke for a long moment; then Knotts said, "Once the convoy is history, how far will we have set them back?"

Artoz replied: "Work on the hyperdrive components alone had been in progress for three years before I was sent to Desolation Station. Even with perfected plans and a redoubling of their efforts, I suspect that we will set them back four years."

Teller smiled lightly. "I wish we had a better sense of what they're up to at Geonosis."

"A weapons platform of some sort," Knotts said. "Do we need to know more than that?"

Teller looked at him. "I suppose not. If we can just keep delaying them with strikes . . . Once the rest of the galaxy gets to know the Emperor as well as we know him, we won't be alone in the fight."

Doubt surfaced in Artoz's huge, glistening eyes. "With shipyards turning out *Imperial*-class Star Destroyers, any revolt will be hardpressed to make so much as a dent in the Emperor's armor. Even if we can continue to impede construction of whatever they are building at Geonosis, something unexpected is going to have to enter the mix in order for any rebellion to succeed. Yes, people will begin to recognize the truth about the Empire, but numbers alone will never make the difference—not against the likes of the Emperor, Vader, and the military they're amassing. And don't expect the Senate to restrain them, because it is even less effective than it was during the Republic."

Teller gave his head a defiant shake. "We can either decide right now that it's hopeless and call it a day, or we can hold out for hope and do what we can."

"That decision has never been in dispute," Artoz said.

"For Antar Four, then, and for a brighter future," Knotts said.

Heads nodded in concert.

While the assembled pilots were moving toward their starfighters, Cala hurried into the hangar. "The supply convoy has dropped from hyperspace. HoloNet and communications jammers are enabled, and all weapons systems are standing by."

Knotts extended his hand to Teller. "Good luck out there."

Teller shook his old friend's hand and tugged the helmet down over his head. Turning to Cala, he said, "Tell Anora and Hask that we expect nothing less than a galactic-class holovid."

The attack on the battle station convoy was well under way by the time the *Executrix* reverted from hyperspace close enough to a small moon to all but tweak its orbit. Tarkin and several officers were at the viewports as the stars shrank back into themselves. With his booted legs spread, hands clasped behind his back, graying hair swept back from his high forehead as if blown in the wind, the governor might have been the vessel's figurehead, taunting the enemy to face off with him personally in mortal combat.

"Sir, they've jammed the local HoloNet relay," a spec reported from behind him. "That's why our alerts weren't received. For the moment our countermeasures are managing to keep the battle and tactical nets open."

"Can we communicate with any of the convoy transports?" Tarkin asked without turning around.

"Negative, sir. It's possible we're not even registering on their scanners."

"Keep trying."

The boxy cargo ships and transports that made up the convoy had drawn together to allow the escort gunboats and frigates to fashion a defensive circle around them, but enemy lasers were chipping away at the perimeter, allowing droid fighters to dart through openings and prey on the larger vessels.

"Sir, battle analysis is showing one capital ship reinforced by a Nebulon-B frigate, multiple tri-droid fighters, and three—make that four starfighters. Two friendly tugs, two escort gunboats, and more than a squadron of ARC-one-seventies are already out of the fight."

Tarkin took in the scene.

Same cobbled-together *Providence*-class warship, same swarm of

droid fighters and antique starfighters. Only this time *he* was commanding the counteroffensive, and instead of Sentinel Base the enemy's objectives were the hyperdrive components he had been worried
about since leaving for Coruscant.

Pivoting away from the viewports, he made his way down the observation gallery to watch a simulation of the attack resolve above a
holotable. The spherical defense mounted by the Imperial escorts
was being dismantled by steady fire from the warships; pieces of gunboats and frigates drifted through a frenzied nimbus of ARC-170s
and droid starfighters in pitched combat.

"V-wing fighters are away," the noncom who had followed him
down the observation gallery updated. "Tactical net is viable, and the
wing commander is awaiting your orders."

"They are to engage with the frigate and the carrier and leave the
droid fighters to the convoy escorts."

Tarkin regarded the simulation for a moment longer, then paced
forward to rejoin the officers at the viewports. By shunting ships to
systems imperiled by the *Carrion Spike,* Naval Command and Control had left the convoy defenseless; like Tarkin, taken in by the dissidents' ruse. Had he not been called to Coruscant, he never would
have allowed the convoy's defensive escorts to be redeployed elsewhere, and it irked him that he had not made a stronger case for his
remaining at Sentinel. He could only hope that the Emperor had
made a wise choice in allowing Rancit's and the shipjackers' ploy to
unspool, and that all of them were now caught up in the net. He narrowed his eyes at the enemy carrier, wondering whether the crew
that had pirated the *Carrion Spike* was aboard, or if the shipjackers
had gone into hiding after deserting the corvette.

"The enemy carrier is repositioning," the bridge officer said. "Looks
like they're trying to put the convoy between us and them."

Tarkin nodded to himself as he watched the hodgepodge ship disappear behind the convoy and—recalling the tactics the dissidents
had employed at the Phindar fuel tank—thought: *Yes, this was the
same crew.*

"Wing commander reports heavy resistance from the enemy fighters," someone behind him said. "They're having trouble reaching the capital ships. Assessment scans indicate that two of the convoy transports have sustained significant damage."

Tarkin turned to the spec. "Still no communication with the convoy leader?"

"None, sir. We can't penetrate the jammers."

That was not welcome news. Tarkin couldn't be certain which of the transports was carrying basic supplies, and which contained components critical for the mobile battle station.

Jova's voice whispered in his ear: *Only glory can follow a man to the grave.*

"Commander," he said, with an abrupt turn to the officer central to the rest, "set us on a course into the midst of the battle."

A tall man with a fringe of black hair, the commander stepped away from the viewports to approach him. "With permission, Governor Tarkin, we have no way of warning the friendlies in our path."

Tarkin firmed his lips. "They'll get out of our way or they won't, Commander."

"I won't argue with that. But even if we manage to penetrate the defensive sphere without incident, we've barely enough space to squeeze between the transports."

"We'll worry about that when we have to. I will not chase that carrier in circles." Tarkin's eyes narrowed. "Death or renown, ladies and gentlemen."

"Sir!"

As the commander left his side, Tarkin glanced at the bridge officer. "Our batteries are to refrain from firing until I give the command. Alert the wing commander that for the time being he and his pilots are our artillery. The droid fighters are slow to react to chaos. I want our starfighters to break formation and improvise, firing at will."

"Clear, sir."

Tarkin resumed his stance. This was how the Empire would conquer and rule, he thought: through might and *fear.*

The *Executrix* lumbered through the congestion of starfighters and into the thick of battle, where the cargo ships and transports were being pounded by cannon and turbolaser fire from the Nebulon-B frigate and the carrier. Explosive light pulsed blindingly beyond the viewports.

"All forward batteries are to concentrate fire on the frigate," Tarkin ordered.

Local space lit up as dozens of energy beams loosed by the Star Destroyer converged on the much smaller vessel. In moments the ship's shields were overwhelmed and the beams began to take their toll, obliterating the Nebulon's rudder-like ventral appendage, then severing the spar that connected the main body of the ship to the engine module. Cracked open, the ship spilled its contents into space and imploded, sucking countless droid fighters into its blistering collapse.

"Battle speed," Tarkin said.

The *Executrix* surged forward, slipping like a needle between two of the larger transports, its pointed bow in direct line with the enemy carrier, which seemed to rear up in reaction to the Star Destroyer's relentless approach.

The bridge officer spoke up. "Wing commander reports that his squadrons are being carved to pieces."

Tarkin kept his eyes on the carrier. It wasn't turning tail as it had at Sentinel. This was the moment the scenario would change; this was the moment the dissidents would demonstrate their unshakable commitment.

"Order the starfighters to withdraw into our wake and to protect the convoy at all costs," he said at last.

"Carrier is changing vector," the spec all but shouted into his left ear. "Flank speed at the convoy leader."

Tarkin's eyes tracked the ship's abrupt swing to port and sudden acceleration. "Ten degrees port. Starboard ion batteries go to steady fire. Race to the light of the lasers!"

If Teller wasn't careful, astonishment was going to be the death of him. The sneak attack on the convoy had commenced without incident, with several Imperial support vessels destroyed and the cargo ships themselves jeopardized, until a Star Destroyer—certainly Tarkin's Star Destroyer—had reverted to realspace and turned the battle on its ear. V-wings were decimating the droid fighters, and a Headhunter and a Tikiar had been obliterated, leaving only Teller's ship and the Tikiar piloted by a Koorivar he had trained on Antar 4. The warship itself was now pushing into the heart of the fray, as if intent on going head-to-head with the Star Destroyer, but was in fact on a collision course with the bulkiest of the cargo vessels. Energy began to coruscate across the hull as it continued its desperate charge for the convoy transports.

If it was Tarkin's aim to confound and confuse, he had done so brilliantly. The V-wing fighters were creating such chaos, it was impossible to predict what Tarkin would do next. And where a more cautious commander might have steered a course around the chaos, Tarkin was taking the massive ship right into the middle of it, placing not only himself but his own pilots and everyone else in peril.

Teller had made repeated attempts to raise Salikk and the others on the battle net without success. Abruptly, the interference abated, and Salikk's face resolved in flickering fashion on the cockpit display screen.

Teller got right to the point. "Get clear and jump the ship to hyperspace while there's still time," he told the Gotal.

"Back to you, Teller," Salikk said through a pall of smoke drifting over the warship's bridge.

"Get clear of that Star Destroyer!"

Salikk shook his head. "We're already committed."

"You'd have a better chance flying into a supernova!"

Anora leaned into cam range from behind the captain's chair. "Teller, haven't you ever seen a holodrama? You're the one who's supposed to live to fight that other day."

Teller grimaced for the cockpit cam. "I'm not the one being dramatic. I'm the one who's talking sense!"

"Listen to her," Salikk said. "For my part, I'll always be grateful for the extra years you gave me after Antar."

Teller's nostrils flared. "You dumb, flat-faced space jockey!"

Salikk ignored the insult. "I'm transmitting jump coordinates to your fighter. Ease out of the fight while Tarkin is concentrating on us. The Headhunter's hyperdrive will do the rest."

Anora nodded soberly. "Looks like we're destined to be martyrs after all, Teller."

"Over and out," Salikk said before Teller could reply.

"Carrier's shields are failing," a tech updated.

"The carrier is modular," Tarkin said. "If we can't blow it to pieces we can certainly dismantle it. Order armaments to target the assembly points."

Coherent light from the *Executrix*'s turbolaser batteries stratified local space, skewering the carrier like a beast set upon by lance-wielding hunters. Debris streamed and corkscrewed from jagged breeches in the ship's belly, and illumination systems began to wink out from stern to bow. Two modules blown from the main body pirouetted away from the ship and exploded. The sublight engines flared and died.

"Droid fighters are powering down," the tech updated. "HoloNet signal-to-noise is better than fifty percent."

"Our lasers must have found the master control computer," the bridge officer said.

Its curved bow severed and deflector shields sparking out, the carrier continued to come apart as Tarkin and the others watched, the droid fighters twirling about like storm-tossed leaves. Quartered by the Star Destroyer's cannons, what remained of the vessel listed to starboard and showed its belly to the vanquisher.

"Cease fire," Tarkin said.

The order had scarcely left his mouth when the spec spoke. "Two marks reverting from hyperspace."

For a moment Tarkin thought that he had stumbled into another trap, but then the tech said, "Star Destroyers *Compliant* and *Enforcer* from Imperial marshaling station Pii."

"Sir, we have one Headhunter unaccounted for," a second tech said. "Sensors indicate that it may have jumped to hyperspace."

"We'll find it," Tarkin said. "In the meantime, ready a boarding party. I want the carrier crew taken alive."

Standing alone at the summit of the Palace spire, the Emperor narrowed his eyes as he gazed out on Coruscant, spread below him like a stage set. The sky was clearing after a cleansing of the Federal District by weather control, and the skyscrapers and towering monads shone like new. The power of the dark side coursed through him like a transfusion of unsullied blood.

Out there were people who wished him dead, others who envied his station, and still others who wished merely to be close enough to him to sate themselves on the crumbs he brushed aside. The thought of it was almost enough to transform his disgust to sadness for the plight of the ordinary. But the wretched practices of the Republic endured: corruption, decadence, the lust for prestige. A penthouse in an elite building, a position that opened doors anywhere in the Core, collections of priceless art, the finest foods, the most able servants . . . He never had need for any of it, even when a senator, even when Supreme Chancellor, and had subscribed to luxury only to satisfy juvenile fantasies and, of course, because it was expected of him. Now he had only the dark side to answer to, and the dark side had an appetite for extravagance of a different sort.

A plot had been foiled, a distraction laid to rest. Needless energy had been expended, and resources wasted. Eventually the dark side would grant him infallible foresight, but until such time future events would remain just out of clear sight, clouded by possibilities and the unremitting swirlings of the Force. He had made himself lord of all he surveyed, but he had much to learn. Actions meant to topple him from his lofty perch wouldn't end with the successful containment of this most recent fiasco. But he would deal with any who chose to challenge him with the same precision he had applied to exterminating the Jedi. And he would not allow himself to be sidetracked from his goal of unlocking the secrets many of the Sith Masters before him had sought: the means to harness the powers of the dark side to reshape reality itself; in effect, to fashion a universe of his own creation. Not mere immortality of the sort Plagueis had lusted after, but *influence* of the ultimate sort.

As his Empire swelled, bringing more and more of the outer systems into its fold, so too would his power unfurl, until every being in the galaxy was held captive in his dark embrace.

A search of the carrier's extant module yielded thirteen dead crewmembers—humans, Koorivar, and Gotals—and twice the number of survivors, representing the same mix of humans, humanoids, and nonhumans. Tarkin stepped from one of the module's air locks as the latter group was being herded into a thoroughly ruined cabinspace by the stormtrooper squads who had captured them. The floor was awash in fire-suppressant foam, and the air reeked of fried circuitry and melted components.

Tarkin waited for the prisoners to be shackled and formed up into two lines before conducting an inspection. He began with the inner line, stopping to regard each being before moving on. As he turned to move down the outer line, a smug smile softened his expression.

"Anora Fair," he said, stopping in front of the only human female among the captives. "Though I see you've restyled your hair." Leaning back to glance farther down the line, his eyes settled on a willowy, red-furred Zygerrian female. "And you would be Hask Taff. I trust you found the *Carrion Spike* to your liking?"

Neither uttered a word or altered her forward gaze—not that he would have expected them to. A sidestep brought him eye-to-eye with a rheumy-eyed middle-aged man.

"Ah, the infamous Lantillies broker himself," Tarkin said. "Nice of you to attend, Knotts."

The broker, too, stared straight ahead and offered no reply.

Tarkin took a few more steps, stopping to look up into the face of a Mon Cal. "Dr. Artoz, perhaps?" He stepped back from the line to address everyone. "But where is Teller?" When the silence had gone on long enough, he said: "Left for dead in some other module? A starfighter casualty?" He paused, then, with an eyebrow arched, added: "Escaped?"

He gave them another long moment.

"Tell me, was it our late vice admiral Rancit who reached out to you, or did you approach him?" Tarkin glanced at Knotts. "Come now, Knotts, both you and Teller answered to him during the war, did you not? Apparently your betrayal took him by surprise, spoiling the betrayal *he* planned for *you*." Again he waited. "Nothing to say? No last moment cheers of solidarity? No verbal abuse for the Empire or for the Emperor himself?"

"You'll fall from your perch soon enough, Tarkin," Anora Fair said, skewering him with an abrupt glare. "And it won't be a soft landing."

He grinned without showing his teeth. "And here I was expecting an apology for the condition in which you left my ship."

She managed to contort her shackled hands into an obscene gesture before one of the stormtroopers slammed her in the back of the head with his blaster rifle.

"So much venom from such a lovely mouth," Tarkin said. He took a backward step to scan the prisoners once more. "Anyone else, or shall I simply assume that she spoke for the lot of you?" When no one replied, he shrugged. "Well, never mind. I'm confident that once on Coruscant we can find ways to loosen all your tongues."

22

RED, IN TOOTH AND CLAW

THE EMPEROR, Vader, and Tarkin—the Empire's newly formed dark triumvirate—met in private in the pinnacle chamber of the spire. The Emperor was in his customary chair, with Tarkin seated opposite him across the table. Vader remained standing, as he usually did when in the presence of his Master. Three weeks had passed since the attack on the convoy, most of which Tarkin had devoted to interrogating the captured conspirators and collaborators, with some assistance from Vader and ISB specialists. None had died during the process, though all had since been executed in secret. The ISB had advocated for making a public spectacle of their deaths, but the Emperor had ultimately rejected the idea, if only to deny the dissidents martyrdom. The details of Rancit's death, too, became a closely guarded secret, even among his peers in the intelligence community. But most got the message: No rank or position was a guarantee of privilege or exemption.

Everyone was expendable.

"It's clear that he felt passed over," Tarkin was explaining to the Emperor. "First he was forced to disappoint his former operatives on

Antar Four due to a squabble between Military Intelligence and the ISB, and then he lost command of Sentinel Base, which he perceived as a demotion for having objected to the actions the Empire took on the Gotal moon."

"So the plot began with him," the Emperor said.

Tarkin nodded. "In a sense. He was informed through back channels of the conspirators' attempts to procure proscribed armaments, confiscated Separatist matériel, and communications jammers. When he learned, however, that the prospective buyers were former Republic intelligence operatives, he facilitated their access to Imperial depots and armories."

"The warehouse workers and salvagers who supplied the conspirators have been dealt with," Vader pointed out, "including several scientists at Desolation Station who violated the terms of their security oaths."

Tarkin waited for Vader to finish. "We've also determined that the warship was assembled at shipyards in the Bajic sector, jointly owned and operated by the Tenloss Syndicate and lower-level members of the Crymorah syndicate. Along with those, our operatives discovered two clandestine facilities located elsewhere in the Outer Rim, both of them long abandoned. We did, however, succeed in tracing the whereabouts of some of those involved, and they have since been eliminated."

"Good," the Emperor said. "Let that be a lesson to all of them"—he narrowed his eyes at Tarkin—"including the one who apparently got away."

"The Headhunter was found on Christophsis," Tarkin said, more defensively than he had planned.

"You are certain the starfighter belonged to Teller?" Vader asked.

"His genetic fingerprints were all over it," Tarkin said.

"An intelligence officer of Teller's skill would know better than to leave his ship to be found, much less his fingerprints." Vader paused, then added: "He left us his calling card."

"He's gone to ground," Tarkin said.

Vader regarded him. "You don't believe that any more than I do."

Tarkin took a breath and blew it out. "I don't suppose I do." He paused. "Finally there is the matter of funding for the warship, droids, and other matériel. Evidence points to the fact that Rancit played a role in diverting funds allocated to Naval Intelligence's black budget, but the investigation is ongoing. Others may have been involved."

The Emperor gestured in impatience. "Was it Rancit who brought these malcontents together?"

"No, he wasn't responsible for assembling the cell," Tarkin said. "The idea appears to have originated with Knotts or Teller, or perhaps they were in league with each other from the start. But Rancit may have contributed the names of people known to be on ISB's watch lists for acts of sedition or sabotage. That may explain how the Mon Cal engineer came to be part of the cell, though it's possible that Artoz was enlisted while Teller was head of security at Desolation Station. The Mon Cal's involvement certainly explains their familiarity with the *Carrion Spike*, as well as with the convoy route."

"But not the battle station," the Emperor said.

"No, my lord," Tarkin said. "Many are aware that an Imperial construction project is in progress at Geonosis, but the mobile battle station is not in jeopardy."

The Emperor steepled his fingers and fell silent for a long moment. "I will give the matter consideration."

"Of course, my lord," Tarkin said. "For Rancit the plan entailed nothing more than allowing the conspirators to attack a few Imperial facilities. He promised them Carida, but he never had any intention of allowing them to fire on the Imperial academy. In fact, he attempted to betray them earlier by incapacitating the *Carrion Spike* at Nouane, but the dissidents managed to escape."

"What case did the dissidents make for attacking the academy?"

"That an attack would send a message to potential enlistees," Tarkin said. "But of course their principal target all along was the convoy. They were counting on the fact that Rancit would go to great lengths to assure that his subterfuge was beyond suspicion, as was his wont during the Clone Wars. Thus, the starship allocations and redeployments. We suspect that the conspirators had a short list of secondary targets, as well, and were monitoring Rancit's ship dispositions. When he inadvertently fulfilled their hope that the battle station convoy would be left relatively unprotected, their decision was made."

The Emperor's furtive smile gave Tarkin pause. Had he actually seen through Rancit's and the dissidents' schemes from the beginning? Had the events of the past few weeks been less about unmasking a cell of traitors than testing Tarkin's ability to foil the plot and to work effectively with Vader?

"Along with planning to betray two of the men he worked most closely with during the Clone Wars," Tarkin went on, "Rancit outwitted the Naval Intelligence's security cams, and also managed to dupe both Deputy Director Ison and Vice Admiral Screed."

"Perhaps I should have made him a Moff, after all," the Emperor said with obvious sarcasm. "He might have had a brilliant career, if ambition hadn't brought him down."

Tarkin adopted a tight smile. "My lord, the fact that you saw fit to promote me certainly figured into his plan to even the score, as it were."

The Emperor nodded. "Ironic, is it not, that his attempts to increase his own cachet should end up benefiting so many of his seeming competitors?"

It was true. Naval Intelligence had been folded back into Military Intelligence, and Colonel Wullf Yularen had been designated to take Rancit's place as deputy director; Harus Ison had been moved into the Ubiqtorate; Admiral Tenant had been made a Joint Chief; Motti, Tagge, and others had received similar upgrades . . . Yularen's promotion, especially, had come as a relief to Tarkin, who had feared that the Emperor might assign *him* to Rancit's former position.

"We need to tighten our hold over the Outer Systems," the Emperor continued. "You will be in charge of that, Moff Tarkin. Or should I say *Grand* Moff Tarkin."

Tarkin gaped in genuine surprise. "Grand Moff?"

"The Empire's first." The Emperor spread his sickly hands. "Was it not you who suggested the creation of oversectors and oversector governance as a means of enhancing our control?"

"It was, my lord."

"Then your wish is granted. The Outer Rim is yours to oversee—and with it, Grand Moff Tarkin, the whole of the mobile battle station project."

Tarkin rose from his chair so he could bow from the waist in frank obedience. "I will not fail you." When he looked up, he saw that the Emperor was leaning forward in his chair.

"It will be a momentous responsibility," the Emperor said, drawing out the words. "For once the battle station is fully operational, you will wield the ultimate power in the galaxy."

Tarkin's gaze moved from the Emperor to Vader and back again. "I don't believe that will ever be the case, my lord."

Considering that the Emperor had created the title Grand Moff for Tarkin, he had not been promoted so much as escalated. No secret was made of it, in any case, except regarding his oversight of the battle station project, and for the two weeks that he remained on the galactic capital following the meeting with the Emperor and Vader, he was honored and feted wherever he went.

He granted lengthy interviews to top media outlets throughout the Core, announcing his intention to embark on a tour of the major systems of the Outer Rim, beginning with his native Eriadu. None of the interviewers pressed him about where he had spent the past three years, and no one brought up Antar 4. It was as if the postwar events that had occurred on the Gotal moon had passed into ancient history—or mythology. The recent attacks on facilities in the Outer and Mid Rim, as well as the holovids that had been circulated, were made to seem part of an Imperial plan to root out dissident cells.

Tarkin was quoted as saying:

> The factor that contributed most to the demise of the Republic was not, in fact, the war, but rampant self-interest. Endemic to the political process our ancestors engineered, the insidious pursuit of self-enrichment grew only more pervasive through the long centuries, and in the end left the body politic feckless and corrupt. Consider the self-interest of the Core Worlds, unwavering in their exploita-

tion of the Outer Systems for resources; the Outer Systems themselves, undermined by their permissive disregard of smuggling and slavery; those ambitious members of the Senate who sought only status and opportunity.

The reason our Emperor was able to negotiate the dark waters that characterized the terminal years of the Republic and remain at the helm through a catastrophic war that spanned the galaxy is that he has never been interested in status or self-glorification. On the contrary, he has been tireless in his devotion to unify the galaxy and assure the well-being of its myriad populations. Now, with the institution of sector and oversector governance, we are in the unique position to repay our debt to the Emperor for his decades of selfless service, by lifting some of the burden of quotidian rulership from his shoulders. By partitioning the galaxy into regions, we actually achieve a unity previously absent; where once our loyalties and allegiances were divided, they now serve one being, with one goal: a cohesive galaxy in which everyone prospers. For the first time in one thousand generations our sector governors will not be working solely to enrich Coruscant and the Core Worlds, but to advance the quality of life in the star systems that make up each sector—keeping the spaceways safe, maintaining open and accessible communications, assuring that tax revenues are properly levied and allocated to improving the infrastructure. The Senate will likewise be made up of beings devoted not to their own enrichment, but to the enrichment of the worlds they represent.

This bold vision of the future requires not only the service of those of immaculate reputation and consummate skill in the just exercise of power, but also the service of a vast military dedicated to upholding the laws necessary to ensure galactic harmony. It may appear to some that the enactment of universal laws and the widespread deployment of a heavily armed military are steps toward galactic domination, but these actions are taken merely to protect us from those who would invade, enslave, exploit, or foment political dissent, and to punish accordingly any who engage in such acts. Look on our new military not as trespassers or interlopers, but as gatekeepers, here to shore up the Emperor's vision of a pacified and prosperous galaxy.

The media took to calling it "the Tarkin Doctrine," and some commentators began to wonder if he wasn't destined to become the new voice of the Empire.

He made it his business to meet with senators representing star systems over which he now had authority. Most seemed relieved about having to answer to him rather than the Emperor or the Ruling Council, but he made clear to one and all that he wouldn't tolerate acts of sedition or anti-Imperial propaganda, and that he would be merciless with all perpetrators.

He met, too, with the Joint Chiefs of the Army and the Navy, and with the directors and top officers in the intelligence agencies. Through them he instituted changes at Desolation Station, replacing many key personnel and altering supply schedules and convoy routes. He authorized reevaluations of every scientist and technician and established new parameters for both secrecy and security. He ordered that no convoys were to move without adequate protection. And to the dismay of countless beings in systems along the supply routes, he limited the HoloNet to Imperial use. The populations of those worlds viewed his actions as the start of an Imperial conquest of the Outer Rim.

At Geonosis, he enacted procedures that would limit contact between workers—whether contractors, employees, or slaves—and the outside galaxy; leaves were canceled and communications of any sort were strictly monitored. He reinforced Sentinel Base and the marshaling stations, and deployed patrol flotillas to the nearby systems. His most trusted officers were sent in search of pirates and smugglers, with orders to eliminate them on sight.

To complement his new station, he designed and had made a gray-green uniform whose thick-belted, round-collared tunic featured four code cylinders and a rank plaque of twelve multicolored squares, six blue over trios of red and gold. In all dealings with the Emperor he was referred to as *Grand Moff,* but for ordinary interactions with military personnel he retained the honorific *Governor.*

His agenda on Coruscant complete, he traveled from the Core to the Greater Seswenna sector aboard the *Executrix,* which was now his personal vessel—"The least the Empire can do to compensate you for the loss of the *Carrion Spike,*" the Emperor had said on awarding him the *Imperial*-class Star Destroyer. In addition to the thousands of troops and technicians who staffed and crewed the massive ship, he had a personal bodyguard of thirty-two stormtroopers who accompanied him wherever he went—or at least when he allowed as much.

Arriving by Imperial shuttle at Phelar Spaceport, he was greeted by cheering crowds, media representatives, and a military marching band. In Eriadu City he visited with family and old friends and granted more interviews. The local governor, who happened to be a relative, awarded him the key to the city and held a parade in his honor. While residing at his former home, he sat for a sculptor who had been commissioned to create a statue that would stand in the city's principal public space.

He had one last mission to carry out before he left his homeworld, and with some effort he managed to persuade his platoon of personal guards that it was an undertaking he needed to fulfill alone, as it was a kind of personal pilgrimage. The stormtroopers were not pleased, as it was their duty to protect him, but they relented inasmuch as he would be spending his time on ancestral ground. Potential assassins notwithstanding, he made no show of secrecy the morning he left for the plateau, in an old airspeeder that had gone unused for years by anyone residing at the family estate. Once removed from the confines of Eriadu City, he relaxed into the journey, almost as if in an attempt to reexperience the annual trips he had made to the plateau as a youth. He even wore clothes of the sort he would have worn in those days, more suited to a hunter or trekker than to an Imperial Grand Moff.

When after several hours of ragged flight the plateau and surrounding volcanic terrain came into view, he felt as if he had never left; and indeed he hadn't, because he had carried the place within him wherever he had ventured. He had been accused by lovers and others of being heartless, but it wasn't true; it was simply that his heart was here, in this pristine part of his homeworld. His attachment to the place was not as one who worshipped nature; rather as one who had learned to tame it. And he would leave the area unchanged, the animals and riotous growth, as a reminder of the control he exercised over it.

He took the airspeeder through several passes over the plateau, observing herds of migrating animals. The day was bright and clear and he could see in detail everywhere he looked. Ultimately he landed the antique vehicle on the savanna, close to the hill of boulders he had come to climb. He set out on foot, with the legs of his trousers tucked into his high boots and the sleeves of his lightweight shirt secured at the wrist as protection against swarms of stinging insects. Arrived at the hill, he began to pick his way up over the pitted rocks, leaping over crevasses and finding finger- and toeholds as he bouldered to the summit. The hill seemed a lonelier place without its troop of guardian veermoks, but also a more sacred one—sanctified by what he had accomplished here.

He was breathing hard when he reached the top, the hot wind blowing across the rocks and garish light reflecting from the obsidian pool at the base of the Spike. He had given thought to scaling the column but realized now that it was enough simply to stand at its base and savor his recollections. He lingered for hours, as a veermok might have, sprawled on the warmed rocks, allowing himself to become nearly dehydrated in the heat. He left as that part of the planet was slipping into darkness, carefully picking his way down the boulders, a task more difficult than the ascent. One skid, one wrong step or stumble . . .

Returned to the tall grass, he followed traces of the path left by his earlier transit, then, as if avoiding obstacles concealed by the stalks, began to pursue a more zigzag route as he neared the airspeeder and an isolated patch of forest beyond. The noise of his legs swooshing through the grass competed with the buzz and drone of insect life. Otherwise there was only the sound of his respiration and a faint echo of his movements. He was fifty or so meters from the airspeeder when he heard the sound of branches snapping and giving way behind him, and the surprised exclamation of the human who had fallen into the trap.

Pleased with himself, he stopped, turned about, and started for the pit he had excavated so many years earlier.

"Welcome, Wilhuff," someone said from the towering grass off to his left before he reached the pit.

Jova stood from where he had been hiding. He was gnarled, wrinkled, and deeply tanned, but still spritely for his age. Thirty additional years of living on the Carrion didn't seem to have done him too much harm. Parting the savanna grass with leathery hands, he began to make his way toward Tarkin, proffering a sleek blaster when they reached each other.

"He dropped this when he fell in," the old man said. "A WESTAR, isn't it?"

Tarkin nodded as he accepted the blaster, switched off the safety, and tucked it into the waistband of his trousers. "Where's his speeder, Uncle?"

Jova's crooked finger pointed east. "Behind the trees. I thought he might follow you up the hill, but he stayed at the bottom, making a little nest for himself in the grass, then tracked you when you came down and started for your ship."

Together they walked to the pit to gaze down at Teller, some four meters below them, somewhat stunned by the unexpected plunge but squinting up as their heads appeared over the rim. Fortunately for Teller, the sharpened stakes that had once studded the floor of the pit had rotted to mulch. The fall, however, had damaged some of the mimetic circuits of his camouflage suit, and he was alternately blending in with the mulch and visible to the naked eye.

"I made it as easy as I could for you to stalk me, Captain," Tarkin said, using the rank Teller had earned during the Clone Wars. "I even left my stormtroopers behind in Eriadu City."

"Very bighearted of you, Governor—or do I have to start calling you Grand Moff now?" Teller tried to get to his feet, but promptly winced in pain and sat back down to inspect a clearly broken ankle.

"I knew you were leading me on," he said through gritted teeth, "but it didn't matter. Not as long as I had a shot at getting to you."

"You had plenty of shots at getting to me, as you say. So why not when we were in the air? And why a simple hand blaster rather than a sniper rifle?"

"I wanted us to be looking each other in the eye when I killed you."

Tarkin grinned faintly. "Sadly predictable, Captain. And so unnecessary."

Teller snorted. "Well, this old fossil would probably have killed me before I got off a shot, anyway."

"You're right about that," Jova said good-naturedly.

He and Tarkin stepped back from the rim. Jova stomped down an area of razor grass with his wide callused feet, and they sat facing each other.

"Were you surprised to hear from me, Uncle?" Tarkin asked.

Jova shook his hairless, nut-brown head. "I knew you'd return someday. I had to renovate some of your old traps. Lucky you recalled where you dug them." He paused to grin. "Though I don't suppose luck has much to do with anything."

Tarkin gazed around him. "I remember my time here like yesterday."

Jova nodded sagely. "I've tried to keep abreast of your career. Haven't read or heard much about you the better part of three or four years now."

"Imperial business," Tarkin said, and let it go at that. "But whatever success I've achieved is to your credit for mentoring me. My memoir will make clear your contributions."

Jova gestured in dismissal. "I don't need to be singled out. I prefer being more of a phantom."

"Phantom of the plateau."

"Why not?"

Tarkin got to his feet and returned to the rim of the pit. "How's the ankle, Captain? Swelling, I would imagine."

Teller's glower said it all.

"Need I remind you that we fought on the same side in the Clone Wars?" Tarkin said. "We fought to prevent the galaxy from splintering, and we achieved our goal. But where I've put that war behind me, you appear to be still waging it. You'd have the galaxy fracture again?"

"You haven't put it behind you," Teller said. "That war was nothing more than a prelude to the war the Emperor always had in mind. Subjugating Separatists was practice for subjugating the galaxy. You've known all along. And this time you're going to crush your opponents before they have a chance to organize."

"That's called pacification, Captain."

"It's rule by fear. You're not just demanding submission, you're generating evil."

"Then evil will have to do."

Teller stared up at him. "What transforms a man into a monster, Tarkin?"

"Monster? That's a point of view, is it not? I will say this much, however: This place, this plateau is what made me."

Teller considered it, then asked: "What is the Empire building at Geonosis?"

Tarkin showed him a faint grin. "Unfortunately, Captain, you are not cleared to know that. But I'm willing to make a deal with you. I'm certain you'll have a difficult time extricating yourself from this trap you stumbled into—what with the depth of the hole and now a broken ankle. But should you succeed, you will find your blaster, just here on the rim." He made a point of setting the weapon down. "The most dangerous of the Carrion's predators don't appear until nightfall. They'll sniff you out, and . . . Well, suffice it to say you don't want to loiter down there. Of course, even if you manage to get out, it's a long way to the edge of the escarpment." He paused in thought, then added, "I'll have Jova park your speeder at the base of the plateau. Should you make it off Eriadu alive, look me up and I'll reconsider what I said about Geonosis."

"Tarkin," Teller said, "you will die horribly because you deserve nothing less. The more you try to coerce the disadvantaged to play by your rules, the more they will rebel. I'm not the only one."

"You're hardly the first to prophesize my demise, Captain, and I could certainly make an equally dire prediction about your death.

Because here you are, trapped in a deep hole and crippled, and that's precisely where I intend to keep the others of your ilk."

Teller smiled with his eyes. "Then if I can escape, the rest will."

Tarkin returned the look. "That's an interesting analogy. Let's see how it plays out in real life, and in the long run. Until then, farewell, Captain."

Jova stood up as Tarkin approached, gesturing with his stubbled chin to the hole. "Broken ankle or no, he seems capable enough to escape. Do you want me to keep an eye on him, perhaps provide a hint or two of the lay of the land to better his chances?"

Tarkin stroked his jaw. "That might be interesting. You be the judge."

"And if he makes it down off the plateau in one piece, and to his speeder?"

Tarkin mulled it over. "Learning that he's actually at large will keep me on my toes."

Jova smiled and nodded. "A good strategy. We're never too old to learn new tricks."

The epicenter of a bustling throng of construction droids, supply ships, and cargo carriers, safeguarded by four Star Destroyers and twice as many frigates, the deep-space mobile battle station hovered in fixed orbit above secluded and forbidding Geonosis. When viewed from mid-system or from even as close as the asteroid belt that further isolated the planet from celestial interchange, one could be fooled into believing that the irradiated world had added another small moon to its collection. Still youthful, the spherical station had yet to grow into the features by which it would be recognized a decade on. The northern hemisphere focus lens frame for the super-laser was scarcely more than a metallic crater; the Quadanium hull, a mere patchwork of rectangular plates, so that one could see almost to the heart of the colossal thing. The sphere's surface city sprawls and equatorial trench might as well have been dreams.

By the time Tarkin arrived, at the conclusion of his travels through the Outer Rim systems, some of the hyperdrive components had been installed, but the station was far from being jump-ready. Nevertheless, work on some of its array of sublight engines had recently been completed, and those were ready to be tested, if only to determine how well the globe handled.

The project's chief scientists and engineers had taken Tarkin on a tour of finished portions of the station that had lasted a week, and yet he still hadn't seen half of it. From the interior of a repulsorlift construction craft, his guides had pointed out where the shield and tractor beam generators would be installed; they had laid out their plans for housing a staff and crew of three hundred thousand; they had described gun emplacements, mooring platforms, and defensive towers that would stipple the gray skin.

Tarkin was in his glory. If he felt at home on the bridge of a Star Destroyer, here he felt *centered*. The station was a vast technoscape, ripe for exploration; an unknown world awaiting his stamp of approval and his mastery.

While most of the construction work was done in micro-g, omnidirectional boosters supplied standard gravity to a large cabinspace near the surface that would one day become the overbridge, with designated posts for Tarkin and various military officers, a conference room featuring a circular table, a HoloNet booth dedicated to communicating with the Emperor, and banks of large viewscreens. There, in the company of the station's designers and construction specialists, Tarkin gave the order for the sublight engines to engage.

A faint shudder seemed to run through the orb—though Tarkin thought that the vibration could easily be the effect of exhilaration coursing through him in a way he hadn't experienced since his teenage years. Then, with almost agonizing sluggishness, the battle station began to leave its fixed orbit. Ultimately it surpassed the speed of the planet's rotation, emerging from the shadow of Geonosis and moving into deep space.

BOTTLENECK

John Jackson Miller

"AMBUSH!"

The driver's warning was hardly necessary—not when the Imperial troop transport was already off-kilter, knocked sideways by the impact of hate on eight thunderous legs. A second monstrosity, five meters tall, struck from the darkness. Prodded by its feral Tsevukan rider, the slick-skinned kivaroa rammed the transport hard. The repulsorcraft flipped over and splashed into the swamp, shedding the stormtroopers riding in its exposed exterior racks as it tumbled.

The impact snapped the driver's restraints, sending her smashing headfirst into the ceiling of the command cabin. The harness of her passenger held—but as brackish water gushed in through the shattered viewport, there was no way he was going to stay buckled in for long. Wilhuff Tarkin, Grand Moff and governor of the Outer Rim for the Galactic Empire, had many things on his agenda. Drowning in a fetid bog wasn't one of them.

Unhooking his restraints, Tarkin struggled to get his bearings. He was uninjured, but in the darkness with water rising, he was forced to feel around for the escape hatch. He hadn't yet found it when another of the angry Tsevukan natives outside obliged by ramming his beast into the damaged hovercraft, knocking it back upright.

Tarkin landed atop the motionless driver as the emergency lighting flickered on. Was she dead or unconscious? He didn't know, nor was there time to find out. Shoving her crumpled body out of the seat, he quickly grabbed the throttle. The repulsorcraft's engines, still running, whined with acceleration. The Grand Moff had no idea where he was going, but moving was better than sitting still. The transport clipped something ahead—another kivaroa, whose rider went flying into the muck.

Good riddance. Tarkin found his comlink. Before he could call for help, stormtroopers aboard speeder bikes screamed past, firing their vehicles' blasters. As the Tsevukans and their beasts charged off into the night, the Grand Moff determined his location by satellite and drove the battered transport the last kilometer to his destination.

The garrison was the last stop on his tour of Tsevuka, the Empire's newest Outer Rim possession. He'd thought an overland transit between its outposts would be more efficient—but clearly, the natives were not as pacified as his general here had led him to believe. The great Empire, menaced by mindless creatures aboard beasts of burden lurking in swamps? *Ridiculous.* It was foremost on Tarkin's mind as the base commander dashed up, wearing an expression between concern for his superior and outright panic.

The latter was the right choice. Removing his soiled jacket, the Grand Moff let his aggravation show. "Where was the patrol, Commander? There should have been more troops stationed along this route!"

"I don't have enough people for that detail." The commander swallowed hard. "Or in general."

"Nonsense. Recruiting has been going well."

"If you'll forgive me, sir, that's the problem. I've got troopers taking shifts because there aren't enough suits of stormtrooper armor to go around."

Tarkin had no patience for this. "Take it up with requisitioning."

"I have. They don't have enough either. The Empire's just—well, it's grown too fast."

Tarkin scowled. "The Empire is doing what it should, Commander. But perhaps some inside it are not." He called for his shuttle before leaving to seek a clean uniform.

"So we are punctured by the speed of our success," the Emperor said.

Sitting in his office aboard the Star Destroyer *Executrix,* Tarkin nodded. He had said something similar to open the holographic call, but Palpatine had put it more bluntly, as he often did. "It seems to be so," Tarkin replied. "My forces in these sectors rely on output from Gilvaanen, on the Inner Rim. But armor production there is only up fifty percent this year—half what is required."

The jungle world of Gilvaanen had been a smallish thorn needling Tarkin for some time. Private corporations, most employing Ithorian colonists who'd settled there long before, handled most of the armor production. To Tarkin, the way to improve output was obvious. "The corporations should be dissolved and production brought fully under Imperial control."

"*Your* control, you mean," the Emperor said, a trace of impatience in his voice. "You've said this before. But I'm not convinced it is the right path—and neither is Count Vidian."

Vidian. Tarkin watched as the count, an up-and-comer in Imperial administration, appeared in the hologram alongside the Emperor. He had been there the whole time. It had to be Vidian: No one else looked like that.

Deformed years earlier by some malady, the count had remade himself in more ways than one. The fiftyish man's destroyed face had been replaced with a pallid, featureless mask of synthflesh stretched across metal and reconstructed bone. His artificial eyes seemed to burn, macabre yellow-on-crimson orbs that provided him with data networking in addition to sight. But those were only the start of his enhancements. Surgeons had encased his battered organs in a powerful cybernetic body, protecting him not just against age and illness but also most kinds of physical harm. There was no telling how long Vidian might live—or what he might do.

And he had already done so much. A cutthroat financier in the last years of the Republic, Vidian had built a cult around his management ideas and his forceful artificial voice. Now, he was continuing his role as a corporate fixer, operating as one of Palpatine's efficiency specialists. It was his word that had kept the corporations in control of Gilvaanen's production.

"Profit is powerful," Vidian said, his perfectly modulated digital voice amplified just enough to avoid offending the Emperor. "Financial reward—and the illusion of competition—can motivate in ways force cannot."

Tarkin sniffed at the suggestion. "You're playing games when the growth of the Empire is at stake."

"There are occasions where state control is preferable, and I have recommended it," Vidian said. "But rivalry has made the armor sector a high-innovation zone. Imperialize, and you could end that." He looked to the Emperor. "Gilvaanen is in my portfolio, Your Highness. I can go at once to sort out the troubles."

"Not good enough," Tarkin said. "Count Vidian should have acted before. I must insist on a stronger hand."

Vidian faced Tarkin and flexed his metallic fingers. "Whole industries have seen how strong my hand is, *Grand Moff.*" He barely hid his disdain in saying the title. "Your military might only exists because of the production *I* have wrested from the—"

"Enough." The Emperor seemed amused rather than angry. "Rivalry indeed produces better results—by raising the penalty for failure." He looked to Tarkin. "Grand Moff, I am directing *both* of you to Gilvaanen. You will work together to find what's gone wrong with armor production—and you will see the targets met. Or I will know the reason why."

Tarkin bowed his head. "By your command."

The Grand Moff knew he would do as commanded, of course; the Emperor's choice of agents was his prerogative. Tarkin would work with Vidian. But too much was at stake for him to permit delays from some nuisance interloper.

He would find out what he was up against.

———

"Forget the old way!"

Vidian was a man with *two* false faces, Tarkin saw as he watched one of the slogan-spouting count's motivational holos. He'd requisitioned them to see more of what he was up against. Vidian wore a ruddy, healthy face in his bestsellers, thanks to image trickery. The holographers had also changed his garish eyes to look natural: magnetic and brown. It was no secret that Vidian had a reconstructed face, of course; his rebound from illness was part of his legend. But the frightening visage he wore in person was almost certainly part of the true story of his motivational success. That record, leavened with lesser-publicized outbursts of violence in the name of efficiency, had made him as popular with the Emperor as he was with the people.

Tarkin was surprised how little else was known about the man. Several of Vidian's Republic-era corporations still supplied the Empire, but conflict of interest was hardly scandalous anymore. He had no friends, no living relatives: He lived for work, surrounded mostly by aides on his base orbiting Calcoraan. He kept his most trusted lieutenant, Everi Chalis, constantly traveling on assignment. It all meant few people knew the real man, a fact that might be meaningless—or suspicious. Yes, Vidian was an early and vocal proponent of the Empire, but Tarkin wondered about his loyalty.

Where there are two false faces, perhaps there are more.

A chime sounded. Tarkin froze the holo. "Yes?"

"We've arrived at Gilvaanen," said the ship's executive officer. Commander Rae Sloane stepped into the room and looked at the hologram. "Were the research materials satisfactory?"

"Sufficient." Tarkin templed his fingers. "I won't have time to study everything. How would you summarize his recent Imperial career?"

"He's a miracle worker. He got the Gozanti freighter program launched on time, and under budget—and straightened out several shipyards. He's an icon in his community."

"He's in *my* community, now." Tarkin dismissed the hologram and looked up to see the young woman standing inside the door. "Something else?"

"This is my last flight on *Executrix,* sir. I have made captain."

"At your age? Admirable." But not surprising, Tarkin thought. A natural at starship navigation, Sloane had graduated high in her class at the Imperial Academy on Prefsbelt—and as a lieutenant, had studied navigation with the legendary Pell Baylo's last class of cadets. "Where do you go?"

Sloane shuffled uncomfortably. "I . . . do not know, Governor. I will be returning to Coruscant to await an assignment. But there are more captains than postings, right now."

"And you expect me to recommend you for one?"

Dark eyes widened. "No, sir, I wasn't asking—"

He stood to leave. "Accept no favors, and you'll never owe any."

Blasterfire resounded through the halls of the factory. The stormtroopers flanking Tarkin quickly moved in front of him, raising their weapons in defense. But the hammer-headed Ithorian at the reception desk stood and waved his spindly arms. "It's normal," he said, pointing to double doors behind. "She's expecting you."

As the doors opened, the shooting continued. Tarkin saw the source: three Ithorians fired blasters at close range at a bipedal figure standing atop a fancy antique desk. It was a human woman, as near as Tarkin could tell, but she was wearing a black helmet designed for something with two very large, bulbous cranial lobes—as well as a bulky triangular breastplate that was ably absorbing the Ithorians' shots.

Over the din, the Ithorians' target noticed Tarkin and his escorts and raised a hand. The Ithorians stopped firing. Her helmet removed, Tarkin saw the perspiring face of a brown-haired woman in her late sixties. She smiled. "Welcome, Grand Moff." She wiped sweat from her brow. "Sorry, there's not much air in this helmet."

"Thetis Quelton, I presume." Tarkin stepped into the office as the Ithorians stored their weapons in a cabinet. He was rarely amused by shows for his benefit—but from what he understood, this was vintage Quelton: testing systems herself.

She clapped the breastplate. "Not even singed. It's rare—confiscated from some species called the Pikaati. I have a full suit at home."

"Hmm." Tarkin had heard she was eccentric, a collector of all things historical—and the exotic suits of armor lining the office walls showed it. As the Ithorians helped Quelton down and out of her gear, he walked to the window and got his first real view of Gilvaanen. A once-lush jungle world, it was quickly being reshaped into its role for the Empire. Forests were being clear-cut for their trees' elastic polymers, while the mountains beneath them were being stripped for materials for ceramic composites. Gilvaanen was the perfect place to make suits of armor.

The Pikaati outfit removed, Quelton swore at her aides. "What are you standing around for, oafs? Get back to work!" The Ithorians mawkishly withdrew, careful not to jostle her historical displays. Tarkin dismissed his troops.

Quelton deposited the alien helmet on a shelf. "The Pikaati did nice work. There should be some ideas I can wrest from it."

"Surely there are more orthodox ways to study armor," Tarkin said.

"You've got to wear it to believe in it," she said. She approached another display, a massive maroon suit that once protected a six-legged beast. She ran her wrinkled hand lovingly along the ornate metalwork. "It's remarkable, isn't it? From an archaeological find; I had it restored. It shows that armor is common to sentients throughout history. Either as protection from elements or the void or enemies, all beings have designed things to protect themselves."

"Yes, yes," Tarkin said. "But while you amuse yourself, your Empire's troops go without on the Outer Rim."

She took a cloth and began shining the giant display piece. "Quelton Fabrication isn't your problem."

"You don't grasp the trouble you're in." Tarkin crossed his arms. "The production shortfalls—"

"—you told me about in your message. And the *other fellow* told me earlier."

"Other?"

"She refers to me," announced a voice from outside the office. Tarkin recognized it—but moments passed before Count Vidian entered. The cyborg's augmented hearing was acute. And just as impressive was the man himself: Dressed sparely but richly in a ruby tunic and black kilt, Vidian had metal limbs that glinted beneath the office lights. He bowed perfunctorily. "Good of you to join us, Grand Moff."

"When did you arrive?" Tarkin asked.

"Midnight. I've been here since, reviewing the facility and its workers." He turned his glowing eyes on Quelton. "I have just sent you a list of seventeen different practices that should be revised for maximum efficiency."

Quelton picked up a datapad from her desk. "So you have."

"And the employee break room should be converted to warehousing."

Tarkin raised an eyebrow. "You allow your employees leisure?"

Quelton laughed. "I scrapped breaks soon after I contracted with the Empire."

"Old news, Grand Moff." Vidian walked to the desk. "You must sanitize the room before using it for storage. The filtration system in my artificial lungs detected several different biological agents there."

Quelton was unruffled. "The Ithorians tracked them in, however long ago. It's a jungle planet—or it *was*. You've already seen that the fabrication area, with the actual armor components, is sterile."

Tarkin looked wryly at Vidian. "That should satisfy our safety inspector."

"I am no mere—" Vidian started in aggravation, before stopping. He returned to his list, rattling off other recommendations. The Grand Moff recognized the act: Vidian was trying to establish territory, to show he knew more. Now he led Tarkin and Quelton from the museum she called an office onto a tour of the inefficiencies he'd found.

Tarkin thought Vidian a self-impressed popinjay, but Quelton seemed dazzled by him, remarking offhandedly to the Grand Moff about the wonderful work Vidian's armorers had done. For her part, Quelton seemed to match Vidian's brusqueness with the Ithorians on her factory lines. Was it a show for the inspection? The creature Quelton smacked with her baton probably didn't think so.

At last, Tarkin tired of the pantomime. "These are changes at the margins," he said. "Gilvaanen is underproducing by far more than this."

"Battles are won at the margins," Vidian said. "I would expect a military man to know that."

Tarkin didn't rise to the bait. "I want Quelton's answer."

"It's not us," she said, pointing out a window. "Cladtech's the problem."

Tarkin knew the name. Quelton's rival across town, Cladtech had the lucrative contract to do final assembly of all interior armor parts. "Problems with the workers' guild?"

"Ithorians all," Quelton said, not hiding her disdain as she walked toward a large door. "Staging slowdowns over this or that."

"Rubbish," Vidian said. "The guild was dissolved years ago."

"Cladtech's owner tolerates their nonsense. He's one of *them*. Meanwhile, my armor plating is piling up at the loading docks." Quelton touched a control, and the door lifted, revealing exactly that. "I want to outfit your army, Grand Moff. I need you to help me do that."

Whatever it was in years past, Cladtech appeared to Tarkin to be inferior to Quelton's firm. Shabbier and unkempt—and that described its employees, too. The ones on the job, at least: Several had staged a sick-out on learning the Empire was inspecting. And where Quelton's harsh treatment had made her staff work faster, Mawdo Larrth, Cladtech's owner, treated his people more gingerly.

"They do good work if I leave them alone," the maudlin Ithorian said, looking over a railing at the factory floor. Machines were running, but not every one was fully staffed. Larrth said the employees had been "working to rule," doing what their contracts required and no more.

"Void the contracts," Tarkin said. "This is a military necessity."

"Then they'll all walk," Larrth said, his electronic communicator giving his translated voice the sound of defeat. "No one *has* to assemble armor for a living."

"That can change." Vidian said. "And how are they coordinating their protests? You already banned outside contact between workers."

"My people settled this world," Larrth said. "The connections of community run deep with Ithorians. I can't stop what is said at the supper table."

"You can add shifts and make the workers take their suppers here," Vidian replied.

Larrth's head bobbed as he evaluated the idea. "I don't think the workers would go for that."

"Who asked *them*?" Tarkin brushed at his shoulders. The oppressive heat in the factory was threatening the creases in his uniform.

"I apologize for the discomfort," Larrth said. He gestured to the machines below. "The injection molds run hot, and your orders have had us working double shifts. They never cool except during work stoppages. I power down then—the energy to run them would break me."

Vidian focused on the workers below. "Your average worker has been here eighteen years, correct?"

"The crew chiefs for thirty," Larrth replied. "There's a lot of experience here—it's why the work that gets done is quality. But it also explains the unrest. People remember when things were . . . *different*."

Tarkin turned his attention to the far doorway. "They will soon forget," he said. The doors opened, and a team of stormtroopers entered, accompanied by several black-clad officers. Tarkin greeted them. "The personnel section is to the right," he said. "The information should be there."

Larrth was surprised. "What's happening?"

"Imperial Security Bureau officers," Vidian said of the darkly attired figures. He looked to Tarkin, puzzled. "You called the ISB?"

"And supplemented with stormtroopers from *Executrix*," Tarkin said. "We will identify all truant workers and bring them in. They will not depart this facility again until their quotas are met."

"It must be convenient, traveling with your own army," Vidian said tartly. "You must've called them before our tour started."

"Quelton said there was labor strife here," Tarkin said. "That's reason enough."

"My review is not complete," Vidian snapped. "I will call agents in myself—but when *I* deem them necessary."

"Oh, they are necessary, regardless of your opinion." Tarkin looked

on, indifferent. He and Vidian had disagreed several times over tactics since their first meeting; he wasn't going to be delayed any further. He gestured for the ISB agents to proceed. Larrth, fretful,
followed the new arrivals.

A commotion rose from the factory floor. Stormtroopers entered,
raising their weapons at any Ithorian workers who happened to be
away from their machines. Frightened, they returned to work. Vidian
clapped his metal hand on the railing, denting it. He looked back at
Tarkin. "This is not the way."

"We broke the guilds in this industry for a reason, Count." Tarkin
looked over at him. "The Emperor cannot brook any rival power centers to form."

"Agreed," Vidian said. "But this lacks finesse."

"Finesse? You may seek marks on style, but I—"

"*Precision.* Punitive acts should be targeted at the poorer-
performing, like that hapless CEO. We must carve away the scar tissue and leave muscle."

Tarkin thought it an amusing analogy for a man whose anatomy
was mostly mechanical. But he did not respond. He turned to follow
the agents.

"Tarkin!"

The sound from far down the hall caused the Grand Moff to look
up from his work, but he did not respond. Both desk and office had
that morning belonged to one of Quelton Fabrication's vice presi-
dents, whom Thetis had fired peremptorily to give Tarkin temporary
space and to show she was willing to cut fat. "*Tarkin!*" Vidian said
again, now in the doorway.

"I will not be addressed in that fashion," Tarkin said, eyes returning to his work. "I don't care who you think you are."

"I've received word from my aide on Calcoraan, Everi Chalis.
You've been making inquiries into my background."

"Like the Emperor, I am interested in all things in the Empire."
Vidian had continued to spar with him all week, repeatedly interven-
ing to try to protect Cladtech workers he seemed to think had value.
Tarkin thought such concern was misplaced. Indeed, suspicious.

"After your outbursts in defense of the striking Ithorians, I wanted to know what kind of man I was dealing with."

"You could buy one of my holos. It would save time."

"I have seen them," Tarkin said. He lifted a datapad. "I have also seen here a response from one of your other underlings. He suggests my curiosity is justified."

Vidian paused. "Baron Danthe?"

"The same."

The cyborg laughed. "Baron Danthe is a lying, disloyal hypocrite—and jealous of my position. In the business community, and now the Empire."

"A wonder you allow him to work for you."

"As you well know, we are not always given the choice of whom we work with."

"Just so." Tarkin smirked. He, too, thought Danthe was a lying, disloyal hypocrite, an opinion formed after their sole holographic encounter that afternoon.

"I have no time for political games," Vidian said, artificial voice booming. "This is about finding the most efficient path to what the Emperor wants. Indeed, what he demands." He stuck a metallic finger in Tarkin's direction. "You've been interfering with my directives all week. You're outside your department—and beyond your competence. Now step away."

Tarkin simply stared at the cyborg. "Do those tactics work on the laborers?" he drily asked. "Because I assure you, they have no effect on me."

"Step away, Grand Moff. I will fix this planet, myself!" Vidian spun on his heel and departed.

Tarkin clasped his hands and thought as Vidian's clanking footfalls receded. The Grand Moff knew what his bailiwick was, but he had often found that others did not. Both the aristocracy and the industrialists retained some power within their spheres, and that muddled things. Vidian belonged to both classes and had a mandate from the Emperor.

Tarkin had no doubt whose side Palpatine would take in any conflict. Perhaps Vidian thought the same. If the count wanted to test their assumptions, so be it.

A knock outside his open door broke his concentration. "Excuse me, Grand Moff," Quelton said.

"Yes?"

"There have been whispers of something on the factory floor here," she said. "Something . . . well, *treasonous*. You may want to check it out . . ."

The ISB station chief walked through the night toward Tarkin. "We have them, sir. There's no escape."

"Go in."

Tarkin watched as floodlights activated, illuminating the back alleys of Gilvaanen's capital. The building ahead was dilapidated, an abandoned factory. No right-minded Ithorian would come to such a place at night. That so many had done so confirmed Tarkin's suspicions. Quelton's information was accurate. Stormtroopers emerged moments later to address him. "Secured, sir. You may enter."

Inside, beneath the harsh lights of the security forces, more than a dozen Ithorians knelt, their elongated heads casting grotesque shadows across the dump of an office. "All supervisors of the Cladtech factory line," the ISB chief said. "The meeting is illegal."

Tarkin took the chief's datapad and read from the list of names. He had seen most of them before: workers Vidian had identified as Cladtech's best. They were here preparing another strike, this one in response to Tarkin's measures earlier in the week. There was only one thing to be done. It would send Vidian into a rage, he knew—but there was no other option. Resistance could not be tolerated. "Eliminate them."

Ignoring the shocked responses from the Ithorians, Tarkin turned toward the exit. The first blasters were being raised when sounds of a commotion came from the doorway to the street. The Grand Moff heard shouts—and then took cover as a human form went flying, hurled violently into the room from outside.

It was another ISB agent, Tarkin saw—and his assailant entered a moment later. "Stop this!" Vidian demanded, the volume of his neck-mounted public address system at maximum. "I tracked someone here—and I appear to be just in time. Do *not* kill these workers!"

Tarkin emerged from cover, disgusted. "This is a military operation, in conjunction with the ISB," he said, brushing himself off. "It is definitely not—what was your term?—*your department*."

"I said stop!" Vidian said, his voice's volume lowered but his demand no less emphatic. He barged into the space between the stormtroopers and the terrified Ithorians, who now cowered on the floor. He turned, bringing his armored form between the troopers and their prisoners.

Tarkin stared, stunned. He'd wondered about Vidian's loyalties—but this was shocking behavior the Emperor would never accept. *Very well.* "We see whose side you're on." Wondering how armored Vidian's body really was, he looked to the stormtroopers. "You have your orders. You will—"

Vidian threw up his hands—but in disgust, not surrender. Spotting an overturned desk at the far end of the room, he charged toward it. Servomechanisms in his arms easily allowed him to lift its weight, revealing the hiding Ithorian figure huddled beneath. "I'm not the sympathizer. *He* is!"

Larrth?

"He's in league with his own striking workers?" Tarkin watched as Vidian grabbed the Cladtech owner and pinned him against a wall. "How did you know?"

"I heard him breathing," Vidian said, before taking Tarkin's meaning. "I was reviewing my recordings and struck on something Quelton said: 'He's one of *them*.' I'd thought it the remark of a bigot—but it made me look at the records I collected at Cladtech in a different way." He glared at Larrth. "You said you cut power to the machines whenever there was a work stoppage. Your energy consumption records confirm that."

Larrth whimpered in fear. "They're too costly . . . to idle . . ."

"Those same records also confirm that you took them offline an hour before the shifts even started—before you knew a strike was coming!" He shook Larrth violently. "Do you have premonitions? Or did you know?"

"He knew," Tarkin said, eyes narrowed. "Explain."

Vidian loosened his grip on Larrth for a few moments. "What you've been asking . . . of my people . . . is impossible," Larth said between coughs. "Letting them strike . . . was the only way . . . to give them a break . . ."

"You acquiesced to revolt and thought it mercy," Vidian said. "But you made a mistake. You were sacrificing profit already to collude with the unionists. But in trying to save a few thousand credits, you gave yourself away. That's why I tracked you here."

It made sense to Tarkin. He gestured to the stormtroopers—but before they could advance, Vidian brought his mighty hands together, snapping Larrth's neck with a sickening crunch.

"Much more efficient," Vidian said, releasing the Ithorian's limp form. He turned back to look at Tarkin—who nodded slightly and opened his palm. *Try it your way.*

Given permission, Vidian turned on the remaining Ithorians. "You are not under arrest—and you are not fired. You will go back to work immediately and meet our production targets. If you fail, everyone you supervise will die."

Terrified, the work supervisors rose. Stormtroopers hustled them from the room. "I think production will improve now," Vidian said. "And I have some ideas on what we can do for management."

"We'll talk," the Grand Moff said. The count turned for the exit, and Tarkin followed. *Perhaps I underestimated you,* he thought.

Once Tarkin gave it his grudging approval, Vidian proposed a free-market solution that absolutely delighted Thetis Quelton.

"Cladtech is hereby merged with Quelton Fabrication," Vidian said. "And the final assembly contract is now yours."

Tarkin had seldom seen anyone so pleased. Quelton had inhabited Larrth's old office mere moments before she started barking out orders over her comlink to staffers at her own plant. "We'll have this place shaped up in no time. And the Outer Rim will have all the armor it needs."

"We need more all the time," Vidian said.

"I guarantee it," Tarkin added.

But the woman seemed invigorated by the challenge—and excited to begin taking over her dead rival's operations. "It's a good old historic building," she said. "Just needs some work. It's important to keep the past alive."

"Older is not better," Vidian said.

"I know your motto," she said mildly, before sitting down at Larrth's desk. Within moments, she was immersed in the new reports.

Yes, Tarkin saw sabotage in Quelton's tipping him to the secret meeting; he wondered how long she had suspected Larrth was in league with the unionists. Vidian had seen nothing disloyal in it: a little self-interested patriotism. He'd speculated it would give Quelton more space for her burgeoning collection of useless historical relics. The cyborg prepared to leave for Quelton Fabrication, to help coordinate transition on that end.

"Count, wait outside for a moment," Tarkin said. Puzzled, Vidian withdrew as the Grand Moff turned back to Quelton. "Thetis," Tarkin called.

She looked up at him, startled to hear her first name. "Yes?"

"I leave in the morning—and it seems a celebration would be in order. I would like to see these historic suits of armor you spoke of."

"The ones in my parlor at home?"

A trace of a grin crossed his face. "You needn't move them. I could come to dinner." He looked about. "If it wouldn't delay your work here."

Quelton smiled. "Of course. I have so much more, there—artifacts from this and a dozen other worlds, all fascinating. I'll have the droids put together something nice to eat. Shall we say in four hours, at my estate?"

Tarkin nodded, and listened as she told him where to find the place. He already knew, of course; it was his business to know. Quelton returned to work.

Stepping out, Tarkin saw Vidian waiting. His electronic ears had picked up the whole conversation—and it clearly amused him. "So this is what you do? Award lucrative contracts to wealthy women and invite yourself over?"

Tarkin gave him a deadly look. "Keep your indecorous remarks to yourself. I have something for you to look into . . ."

At most mansions Tarkin had visited, butler droids had greeted him. He wasn't surprised in the least when an armored Pikaati warrior opened Thetis Quelton's door. It was the woman herself, wearing the gear she'd told him about. "I told you I had a full suit." Apparently, Quelton had no fear of appearing the peculiar tycoon before him.

Helmet under her arm, the woman in her lumbering armor led him on a predinner tour of her home. Hall after hall held pieces of the past on Gilvaanen; how people had lived there since the planet's settlement. And her massive parlor was her office display writ large, a museum of military history.

Tarkin took an interest in that, of course, but he was in fact biding his time. She was still in the Pikaati gear, atop a dais showing off an ancient suit of armor for some mammoth creature, when the Grand Moff received the message he was waiting for.

"I neglected to mention that Count Vidian will be joining us."

Quelton looked down at him, startled, before her face brightened. "That's wonderful. I have so much to ask. How they rebuilt his body is something of a legend in my circles."

"He has superior capabilities, to be sure." Tarkin paced the floor below. "And whatever else is in Vidian's legend, I've seen that his reputation as a turnaround artist is well earned. But no one is my equal when it comes to spotting loyalty."

"How do you mean?"

"Larrth was right about how Ithorians stick together," Tarkin said. "Stern disciplinary measures from a human executive should have at least sparked *some* opposition. And yet protesters never troubled your firm. There had to be a reason." He stopped beside a shield on a display. "You have been your workers' protector. Your dislike of them, your harsh treatment: They're a sham. Don't deny it. ISB interrogators have heard it from the captured. You are no more devoted to profit than Larrth was."

"You think I was putting on a show this week? Maybe I was harsher than I usually am, because of the inspection." She chuckled. "And I tipped you to their meeting. How prolabor could I be?"

"True, your tip put Cladtech in your hands—and that's what I believe you were really after. I know you're not in it for the money. Oh, you *did* want money—to spend on this ludicrous collection of yours, and to thwart Imperial attempts to eliminate the past on this world. We know about those efforts."

"I care about the past, yes—and my planet. But that's normal, for a property owner."

"Then shall we talk about the abnormal? We looked at your bid for the most recent stormtrooper armor-assembly contract. It was irrationally low—you would have lost millions of credits had you won."

"I was trying to undermine a competitor."

"You would have undermined your own firm at those prices. It's why the Empire rejected your bid, a year ago. And you certainly couldn't afford to buy Cladtech outright—and we know you tried. So why did you want that contract so badly?"

"So *these* did not go to waste." The answer came not from Quelton— but from Count Vidian, who stepped through the far door. Between his left thumb and forefinger, he held a round black ring, less than a centimeter thick.

"I can't see from here," Quelton said. "What's that?"

Vidian laughed. "You should know. There were *twenty-seven million* in your factory, waiting to be shipped to Cladtech's assembly center.

Tarkin nodded, satisfied. "Where were they?"

"She was manufacturing them in an area off the Quelton employee break room," Vidian said, "where my lungs had sensed antigens before." He approached Tarkin with the small ring. "It's a grommet for a stormtrooper helmet. It helps form the seal inside an atmospheric transduction nozzle. Possibly the lowest-tech item in the entire assembly—and it must have cost her millions."

Tarkin took the ring and eyed it. "You've had it analyzed?"

"It's quite clever. Alone, it is uninteresting even under close analysis. But when the helmet is worn, the wearer's breath awakens and circulates the tiny spores infused in the ring." Vidian gestured to the foliage outside the window. "They're native to this planet, and cause a disease of the windpipe, known only to jungle explorers. They call it—"

"*Bottleneck*," Quelton said. She took a deep breath and exhaled. "But it was soon to have another name: *stormtrooper's lung*."

Tarkin marveled at the tiny ring. "Ingenious. Because the rings are installed inside the armor, it would be beyond filtration. The armor's pathogenic response systems would see nothing at all."

"And neither would we, for some time," Vidian said. "Bottleneck isn't deadly. But it is debilitating."

"Keeping your thugs from hurting anyone else," Quelton said, turning to face the giant alien suit of armor behind her on the dais. "It would slow the Empire's conquest of the Outer Rim faster than anything."

"It would've been found," Tarkin said, clutching the ring in his fist. "And traced back to you."

"But not before it crushed recruiting. 'Join the Empire and suffer.' Not much of a slogan, is it? But then, it's what you offer the galaxy now." She looked around at the armor on display. "The warriors who fought in these suits had one thing in common. They were all defending their homeworlds against invaders—protecting their cultures, their histories. Gilvaanen was a peaceful world, with a people with a magnificent past. And you've ruined it. You've burned and you've buried, without a care to what you were throwing away." She turned and glared at Vidian. "I don't want to 'forget the old ways,' Count. Some of them were better!"

Vidian looked at Tarkin. "Another dissident! How novel. What a puddle of unhappiness this planet is."

"The ISB has been studying her communications since I first suspected her," Tarkin said. At their mention, several agents entered at the far end of the parlor, flanked by stormtroopers. He looked up at her. "We know you have spoken with other radicals offworld—but that you had cut off contact several months ago."

"They didn't approve of my plan," Quelton said, as the stormtroopers advanced toward the steps to the dais. "They don't know you like I do."

"We'll find out—when you tell us of them," Vidian said.

"I don't think so," she said, eyeing the advancing troopers. "I can still protect something." She put the Pikaati helmet back on her head. But this time, she activated the seal, which gave a low hiss. The stormtroopers raised their weapons—but Quelton wasn't moving to attack. Her armored form shook violently, causing her to tumble from the dais onto the parlor floor.

Vidian rushed to her side. "She's having a seizure!"

He began to work the helmet's fastener—before Tarkin put his hand on the cyborg's arm. "Don't. She's already dead."

"Dead!"

Tarkin nodded. "The Pikaati breathe hydrogen cyanide. The helmet flooded as soon as she activated the seal. Open that, and you could put the rest of us in danger."

Vidian stood and regarded the body. "You never expected her to tell us anything, did you?"

"We saw all we needed to in her communiqués," Tarkin said. "Her contacts abandoned her. The trail was old." He mused over the corpse. "But I was interested to see what she would do in her defense. True rebels are rare specimens. It pays to learn how they think."

It was worth a moment's contemplation—but only a moment. "Now," he said, rising, "we have another corporate vacancy to discuss . . ."

The Emperor's holographic form shimmered in Quelton's former office. "Report."

Count Vidian wasted no time. "I concur with the Grand Moff's plan, Your Highness. Gilvaanen should be 'imperialized.' "

"You had rejected that before. You now agree?" The Emperor seemed mildly surprised.

"I do. All parts of the armor-production chain will be brought under the Imperial Department of Military Research." Vidian sat motionless. "It will be a lengthy transition; I am placing Everi Chalis directly in charge."

The Emperor calculated for a moment. "A reduction in portfolio will free you for other activities."

Vidian was quick to suggest some. "I've noted inefficiencies in Star Destroyer resource production. I can put them aright with a tour of mines and processors."

"Not very glamorous work."

"But necessary." Vidian paused, before continuing. "It would entail relevant sectors being placed under my authority. And military support to enforce my edicts."

The Emperor looked to Tarkin. "This meets with your approval, Grand Moff?"

"It does." Tarkin straightened. "I propose a Star Destroyer be seconded to Count Vidian. I would detach one from my own complement for his use."

A pause. Then the Emperor gave a chuckle, a dark throaty thing that chilled even those familiar with it. "I sense a bargain here, gentlemen."

Tarkin and Vidian looked to each other. "Efficiency is what we *all* crave," the Grand Moff said.

There *had* been a bargain. Tarkin had decided it was pointless to make an enemy of Vidian when a simpler solution existed: making sure their zones of influence didn't overlap. Vidian had come to the same conclusion, offering to trade his oversight of Gilvaanen for a number of franchises Tarkin didn't care as much about. If the count's actions led to Star Destroyers being produced faster for the Outer Rim, it would be more than worth letting him have one today.

Tarkin had offered Vidian his choice of veteran captains, including several with experience escorting leaders of industry under the Republic. That's when Vidian surprised him by requesting the greenest captain on the list. "Remember my motto," Vidian had said. "I would rather have the aid of someone new, someone with no attachment to past practices."

In other words, Tarkin had thought, *you want someone you can push around. Very well.*

Aboard *Executrix,* he awarded the assignment. And the recipient could not have been more surprised.

"But *Ultimatum* is to be assigned to Yale Karlsen," Rae Sloane said. Not only was he already a captain, he was much senior.

"I have detached Captain Karlsen to the construction committee, which needs his wisdom." It had required only a minute to arrange. "Karlsen will take *Ultimatum* in time. But the ship's mission must proceed."

Sloane, who had been sitting upright in the chair across from Tarkin since being invited in, sat back as she began to comprehend the tasks before her. Tarkin spelled them out. "You'll have your hands full preparing the ship for flight. She is your responsibility, for however long you have her. The same can be said of your passenger, when he joins you."

"Count Vidian," she said, half whispering. "I'd be escorting one of the Emperor's troubleshooters."

"I'm told you once flew with the Emperor himself, and Lord Vader."

"I was merely present, sir." She paused, before straightening. "But I believe Lord Vader would endorse my performance."

That's some claim, Tarkin thought. It was daring enough that it was probably true—in which case she might not be the pushover Vidian expected. That was all well, too. For while Vidian offered no threat to him now, it couldn't hurt to have a check against him for the future.

"To your command, Captain Sloane." They stood—and Tarkin offered a last piece of advice. "Count Vidian's eyes never close. And neither should yours."

STAR WARS®: A NEW DAWN

John Jackson Miller

For a thousand generations, the Jedi Knights brought peace and order to the Galactic Republic, aided by their connection to the mystical energy field known as the Force. But they were betrayed—and the whole galaxy has paid the price. It is the Age of the Empire.

Now Emperor Palpatine, once chancellor of the Republic and secretly a Sith follower of the dark side of the Force, has brought his own peace and order to the galaxy. Peace, through brutal repression—and order, through increasing control of his subjects' lives.

But even as the Emperor tightens his iron grip, others have begun to question his means and motives. And still others, whose lives were destroyed by Palpatine's machinations, lay scattered about the galaxy like unexploded bombs, waiting to go off. . . .

Years earlier . . .

"It's time for you to go home," Obi-Wan Kenobi said.

The Jedi Master looked at the blinking lights on the panel to his right—and then at the students watching him. The aisle between the towering computer banks in the central security station was designed for a few Jedi doing maintenance, not a crowd; but the younglings fit right in, afraid to jostle one another in the presence of their teacher for the morning.

"That's the meaning of this signal," the bearded man said, turning again to the interface. Rows of blue lights twinkled in a sea of green indicators. He toggled a switch. "You can't hear anything now, or see anything. Not here in the Jedi Temple. But away from Coruscant, on planets across the galaxy, those of our Order would get the message: *Return home.*"

Sitting on the floor with his classmates in the central security station, young Caleb Dume listened—but not intently. His mind wandered, as it often did when he tried to imagine being out in the field.

He was lean and wiry now—ruddy skin and blue eyes under a mop of black hair. He was just one of the crowd, not yet apprenticed to a mentor. But one day, he'd be out *there,* traveling to exotic worlds with his Master. They'd provide peace and order for the citizens of the Galactic Republic, defeating evil wherever he found it.

Then he saw himself later as a Jedi Knight, fighting alongside the Republic's clone warriors against the enemy Separatists. Sure, Republic Chancellor Palpatine had promised to resolve the war soon, but no one could be so rude as to end the war before Caleb got his chance.

And then, finally, he dared hope he would become a Jedi Master like Obi-Wan—accepted while still young as one of the wise sages of the Order. Then he'd *really* do some great feats. He'd lead the valiant battle against the Sith, the legendary evil counterpart to the Jedi.

Of course, the Sith hadn't been seen in a thousand years, and he knew of no shadow of their return. But in his ambitions Caleb was no different from the younglings around him, whatever the gender, whatever the species. The adolescent imagination knew no bounds.

The sandy-haired Jedi Master touched the panel again. "It's just in test mode now," Obi-Wan said. "No one will respond. But were there a true emergency, Jedi could receive the message in several ways." He glanced down at his listeners. "There is the basic alert signal. And then there are other components, in which you might find more detailed text and holographic messages. No matter the format, the basic purpose should be clear—"

"*Go home!*" the collected students shouted.

Obi-Wan nodded. Then he saw a hand being raised. "The student in the back," he said, fishing for a name. "Caleb Dume, right?"

"Yes, Master."

Obi-Wan smiled. "I'm learning, too." The students giggled. "You have a question, Caleb?"

"Yes." The boy took a breath. "Where?"

"Where what?"

The other pupils laughed again, a little louder this time.

"Where's home? Where do we go?"

Obi-Wan smiled. "To Coruscant, of course. Here, to the Jedi Temple. The recall is exactly what it sounds like."

The teacher started to turn back to the beacon when he spotted Caleb Dume jabbing his hand in the air again. Caleb wasn't one to sit in front for every lesson—no one respected a teacher's pet—but shyness had never been one of his afflictions.

"Yes, Caleb?"

"Why—" The boy's voice cracked, to mild chuckles from his companions. He glared at the others and started again. "Why would you need all the Jedi here at once?"

"A very good question. Looking at this place, one would think we had all the Jedi we need!" Obi-Wan grinned at the students' Masters, all standing outside in the more spacious control room, looking in. Out of the corner of his eye, Caleb could see Depa Billaba among them. Tan-skinned and dark-haired, she had shown interest in taking him on as her apprentice—and she studied him now from afar with her usual mostly patient look: *What are you on about now, Caleb?*

Caleb had wanted to shrink into the floor, then—when Obi-Wan addressed him directly. "Why don't *you* tell *me*, Caleb: What reasons would *you* expect would cause us to recall every Jedi in the Order?"

Caleb's heart pounded as he realized everyone was watching him. In his daily life, the boy never worried about being hassled for sounding off; the kids he regularly trained with knew he never backed down. But there were students in the gathering he'd never seen before, including older ones—not to mention the Jedi Masters. And Caleb had just blundered into a chance to impress a member of the High Council in front of everyone.

Or it was a chance to founder on the question, and take their abuse. There were so many possibilities—

Including a trick question.

"I know the reasons you'd call them back," Caleb finally said. "*Unexpected* reasons!"

Riotous laughter erupted from the others, all semblance of respectful order disappearing at Caleb's words. But Obi-Wan raised his hands. "That's as good an answer as I've ever heard," he said.

The group settled down, and Obi-Wan continued: "The truth, my young friends, is I simply don't know. I could tell you of the many times over the course of the history of the Order when Jedi have been called back to Coruscant to deal with one threat or another. Some perilous times, which resulted in great heroics. There are truths, and there are legends touched with truth, and all can teach you something. I am sure Jocasta, our librarian, would help you explore more." He clasped his hands together. "But no two events were alike—and when the signal is given again, that event will be unique, too. It's my hope it will never be needed, but knowing about it is part of your training. So the important thing is, when you get the signal . . ."

". . . *go home!*" the children said, Caleb included.

"Very good." Obi-Wan deactivated the signal and walked through the crowd to the exit. The students stood and filed back out into the control room, appreciating the wider space and chatting about their return to their other lessons. The field trip to this level of the Jedi Temple was over.

Caleb stood, too, but did not leave the aisle. The Jedi taught their students to look at all sides of things, and the thought occurred to him there was another side to what they'd just been shown. Brow furrowed, he started again to raise his hand. Then he realized he was the only one left. No one was looking, or listening.

Except Obi-Wan, standing in the doorway. "What is it?" the Master called out over the din. Behind him, the others quieted, freezing in place. "What is it, Caleb?"

Surprised to have been noticed, Caleb swallowed. He saw Master Billaba frowning a little, no doubt wondering what her impulsive prospect was on about now. It was a good time to shut up. But standing alone in the aisle between the banks of lights, he was committed. "This beacon. It can send *any* message, right?"

"Ah," Obi-Wan said. "No, we wouldn't use it for regular administrative matters. As Jedi Knights—which I very much hope you will all become—you will receive such instructions individually, using less dramatic forms of—"

"Can you send people away?"

A gasp came from the group. Interrupted but not visibly irritated, Obi-Wan stared. "I'm sorry?"

"Can you send people away?" Caleb asked, pointing at the beacon controls. "It can recall every Jedi at once. Could it warn all of them away?"

The room behind Obi-Wan buzzed with whispered conversations. Master Billaba stepped into the computer room, apparently wanting to put an end to an awkward moment. "I think that's enough, Caleb. Excuse us, Master Kenobi. We value your time."

Obi-Wan wasn't looking at her. He was staring back at the beacon, too, now, contemplating. "No, no," he finally said, gesturing to the crowd without turning. "Please wait." He scratched the back of his head and turned back to the gathering. "Yes," he said, quietly. "I suppose it could be used to warn Jedi away."

The students fairly rumbled with discussions in reaction.

Warn Jedi away?

Jedi didn't run! Jedi rushed toward danger!

Jedi stood, Jedi fought!

The other Masters stepped in, beckoning to Obi-Wan. "Students," said one elder, "there's no reason to—"

"No *expected* reason," Obi-Wan said, pointing his index finger to the air. He sought Caleb's gaze. "Only what our young friend said: unexpected reasons."

A hush fell over the group. Caleb, reluctant to say anything else, let another student ask what he was thinking. "What then? If you send us all away, what then?"

Obi-Wan thought for a moment before turning toward the students and giving a warm and reassuring smile. "The same as any other time. You will obey the directive—and await the next one." Raising his arms, he dismissed the assembly. "Thank you for your time."

The students filed out of the control room quickly, still talking. Caleb remained, watching Obi-Wan disappear through another doorway. His eyes turned back to the beacon.

He could sense Master Billaba watching him. He looked back to see her, alone, waiting in the doorway. The frown was gone; her eyes were warm and caring. She gestured for him to follow her. He did.

"My young strategist has been thinking again," she said as they stepped into the elevator. "Any other questions?"

"Await orders." Caleb gazed at the floor, and then up at her. "What if orders never come? I won't know what to do."

"Maybe you will."

"Maybe I won't."

She watched him, thoughtful. "All right, maybe you won't. But anything is possible," she said, putting her arm on his shoulder as the door opened. "Perhaps the answer will come to you in another form."

Caleb didn't know what that meant. But then it was Master Billaba's way to speak in riddles, and, as always, he forgot about them as soon as he stepped out onto the floor where the young Jedi trained. On any given day, room after room would see the mightiest warriors in the galaxy teaching the next generation in lightsaber combat, acrobatics, hand-to-hand fighting—even starship piloting, using simulators. Every discipline imaginable where a kinship with the mystical Force, the energy field all Jedi drew upon for strength, could come in handy.

And those he saw were just a tiny fraction of the Jedi Order, which had outposts and operatives throughout the known galaxy. True, the Galactic Republic was at war now with the Separatists, but the Jedi had thwarted threats for a thousand generations. How could anyone or anything challenge them?

Caleb arrived in front of a room where his classmates were already at work, sparring with wooden staffs. One of his regular dueling partners, a red-skinned humanoid boy, met him in the doorway, training weapon in hand. He had also attended the lecture. "Welcome, Young Master Serious," he said, smirking. "What was all that back there with Master Kenobi?"

"Forget it," Caleb said, pushing past him into the room and reaching for his own training weapon. "It's nothing."

"But wait!" The other boy's free hand shot up into the air, mimicking Caleb's questioning. "Ooh! Ooh! Call on me!"

"Yeah, you're going to want to focus, buddy, because I'm going to whip your tail." Caleb smiled and went to work.

THIS IS OBI-WAN KENOBI
REPUBLIC FORCES HAVE BEEN TURNED AGAINST THE JEDI
AVOID CORUSCANT, AVOID DETECTION
STAY STRONG
MAY THE FORCE BE WITH YOU

PHASE ONE:
IGNITION

"Emperor unveils ambitious plan for Imperial fleet expansion"

"Count Vidian contributes star power to new industrial inspection tour"

"Leftover unexploded ordnance from Clone Wars remains a concern"

—headlines, Imperial HoloNews (Gorse Edition)

CHAPTER ONE

"SOUND COLLISION!"

Only a moment earlier, the Star Destroyer had emerged from hyperspace; now a cargo ship careened straight toward its bridge. Before *Ultimatum*'s shields could be raised or cannons could be brought to bear, the approaching vessel abruptly veered upward.

Rae Sloane watched, incredulous, as the wayward freighter hurtled above her bridge's viewport and out of sight. But not out of hearing: A tiny scraping *ka-thump* signaled it had just clipped the top of the giant ship's hull. The new captain looked back at her first officer. "Damage?"

"None, Captain."

No surprise, she thought. It was surely worse for the other guy. "These yokels act as if they haven't seen a Star Destroyer before!"

"I'm sure they haven't," Commander Chamas said.

"They'd better get used to it." Sloane observed the cloud of transports ahead of *Ultimatum*. Her enormous *Imperial*-class starship had arrived from hyperspace on the edge of the appointed safe-approach lane, bringing it perilously close to what had to be the biggest traffic jam in the Inner Rim. She addressed the dozens of crewmembers at their stations. "Stay alert. *Ultimatum*'s too new to bring back with a scratched finish." Thinking again, she narrowed her eyes. "Send a message on the Mining Guild channel. The next moron that comes within a kilometer of us gets a turbolaser haircut."

"Aye, Captain."

Of course, Sloane had never been to this system, either, having just attained her captaincy in time for *Ultimatum*'s shakedown cruise. Tall, muscular, dark-skinned, and black-haired, Sloane had performed exceptionally from the start and ascended swiftly through the ranks. True, she was only substituting on *Ultimatum,* whose intended captain was serving on assignment to the construction committee—but how many others had helmed capital ships at thirty? She didn't know: The Imperial Navy had been in existence by that name for less than a decade, since Chancellor Palpatine put down the traitorous Jedi and transformed the Republic into the Galactic Empire. Sloane just knew the days ahead would decide whether she got a ship of her own.

This system, she'd been briefed, was home to something rare: a true astronomical odd couple. Gorse, out the forward viewport, lived up to its reputation as perhaps the ugliest planet in the galaxy. Tidally locked to its parent star, the steaming mudball had one side that forever baked. Only the permanently dark side was habitable, home to an enormous industrial city amid a landscape of strip mines. Sloane couldn't imagine living on a world that never saw a sunrise—if you could call sweating through an endless muggy summer night *living.* Looking off to the right, she saw the real jewel: Cynda, Gorse's sole moon. Almost large enough to be counted in Imperial record keeping as a double planet with Gorse, Cynda had a glorious silver shine—as charming as its parent was bleak.

But Sloane wasn't interested in the sights, or the travails of all the losers on Gorse. She started to turn from the window. "Make doubly sure the convoys are respecting our clearance zone. Then inform Count Vidian we have—"

"*Forget the old way,*" snapped a low baritone voice.

The harshly intoned words startled everyone on the bridge, for they had all heard them before—just seldom in this manner. It was their famous passenger's catchphrase, quoted on many a business program during the Republic days and still used to introduce his successful series of management aids now that he had moved on to government service. Everywhere, the Republic's old ways of doing things were being replaced. "Forget the old way" really was the slogan of the times.

Sloane wasn't sure why she was hearing it now, however. "Count Vidian," she stated, her eyes searching from doorway to doorway. "We were just setting up our safety perimeter. It's standard procedure."

Denetrius Vidian appeared in the entryway farthest from Sloane. "And I told you to forget the old way," he repeated, although there was no doubting everyone had heard him the first time. "I heard you transmit the order for mining traffic to avoid you. It would be more efficient for *you* to back away from *their* transit lanes."

Sloane straightened. "The Imperial Navy does not back away from *commercial traffic.*"

Vidian stamped his metal heel on the deck. "Spare me your silly pride! If it weren't for the thorilide this system produces, you'd only have a shuttle to captain. You are slowing production down. The old way is wrong!"

Sloane scowled, hating to be talked down to on her own bridge. This needed to seem like her decision. "It's the Empire's thorilide. Give them a wide berth. Chamas, back us a kilometer from the convoy lanes—and monitor all traffic."

"Aye, Captain."

"Aye is right," Vidian said. Each syllable was crisply pronounced, mechanically modulated, and amplified so all could hear. But Sloane would never get over the strangest part, which she'd noticed when he boarded: The man's mouth never moved. Vidian's words came from a special vocal prosthetic, a computer attached to a speaker embedded in the silvery plating that ringed his neck.

She'd once heard the voice of Darth Vader, the Emperor's principal emissary; while electronically amplified, the Dark Lord's much deeper voice still retained some natural trace of whatever was inside that black armor. In contrast, Count Vidian had reportedly chosen his artificial voice based on opinion research, in a quest to own the most motivational voice in the business sector.

And since he had boarded her ship with his aides a week earlier, Vidian had shown no qualms about speaking as loudly as he felt necessary. About *Ultimatum,* her crew—and her.

Vidian strode mechanically onto the bridge. It was the only way to describe it. He was as human as she was, but much of his body had been replaced. His arms and legs were armor-plated, rather than synthflesh prosthetics; everyone knew because he made little effort to hide them. His regal burgundy tunic and knee-length black kilt were his only nods to normal attire for a fiftyish lord of industry.

But it was Vidian's face that attracted the most awkward notice. His flesh lost to the same malady that had once consumed his limbs and vocal cords, Vidian covered his features with a synthskin coating. And then there were his eyes: artificial constructs, glowing yellow irises sitting in seas of red. The eyes appeared meant for some other species besides humans; Vidian had chosen them solely for what they could do. She could tell that now as he walked, glancing outside from convoy to convoy, ship to ship, mentally analyzing the whole picture.

"We've already met some of the locals," she said. "You probably heard the bump. The people here are—"

"Disorganized. It's why I'm here." He turned and walked along the line of terminal operators until he arrived at the tactical station depicting all the ships in the area. He pushed past Cauley, the young human ensign, and tapped a command key. Then Vidian stepped back from the console and froze, seeming to stare blankly into space.

"My lord?" Cauley asked, unnerved.

"I have fed the output from your screen to my optical implants," Vidian said. "You may return to your work while I read."

The tactical officer did so—no doubt relieved, Sloane thought, not to have the cyborg hanging over his shoulder. Vidian's ways were strange, to be sure, but effective, and that was why he was on her ship. The onetime industrialist was now the Emperor's favorite efficiency expert.

Gorse's factories produced refined thorilide, a rare strategic sub-

stance needed in massive quantities for a variety of Imperial projects. But the raw material these days came from Cynda, its moon:
hence the traffic jam of cargo ships crisscrossing the void between
the two globes. The Emperor had dispatched Vidian to improve
production—a job for which he was uniquely qualified.

Vidian was known for squeezing the very last erg of energy, the
very last kilogram of raw material, the very last unit of factory production from one world after another. He was not in the Emperor's
closest circle of advisers—not yet. But it was clear to Sloane he soon
would be, provided there was no relapse of whatever ailment it was
that had brought him low years earlier. Vidian's billions had bought
him extra life—and he seemed determined that neither he nor anyone else waste a moment of it.

Since he'd boarded, she hadn't had a conversation with him where
he hadn't interrupted at least a dozen times.

"We've alerted the local mining guild to your arrival, Count. The
thorilide production totals—"

"—are already coming in," Vidian said, and with that, he marched
to another data terminal in the aft section of the bridge.

Commander Chamas joined her far forward, many meters away
from the count. In his late forties, Chamas had been leapfrogged in
rank by several younger officers. The man loved gossip too much.

"You know," Chamas said quietly, "I heard he bought the title."

"Are you surprised? Everything else about him is artificial," Sloane
whispered. "Ship's doctor even thinks some of his parts were volun-
tarily—"

"You waste time wondering," Vidian said, not looking up from
where he was studying.

Sloane's dark eyes widened. "I'm sorry, my lord—"

"Forget the formality—and the apology. There is little point for
either. But it's well for your crew to know someone is always
listening—and may have better ears than yours."

Even if they had to buy them in a store, Sloane thought. The ragged
fleshy lobes that had once been Vidian's ears held special hearing
aids. They could obviously hear her words—and more. She approached him.

"This is exactly what I'd expected," Vidian said, staring at whatever unseen thing was before his eyes. "I told the Emperor it would be worth sending me here." A number of underproducing worlds that manufactured items critical to the security of the Empire had been removed from their local governors' jurisdictions and placed under Vidian's authority: Gorse was the latest. "Messy work might have been good enough for the Republic—but the Empire is order from chaos. What we do here—and in thousands of systems just like this one—brings us closer to our ultimate goal."

Sloane thought for a moment. "Perfection?"

"Whatever the Emperor wants."

Sloane nodded.

A tinny squawk came from Vidian's neck-speaker—an unnerving sound she'd learned to interpret as his equivalent of an angry sigh. "There's a laggard holding up the moonward convoy," he said, staring into nothingness. Looking at her tactician's screen, Sloane saw it was the cargo vessel that had bumped them earlier. She ordered *Ultimatum* turned to face it.

A shower of sparks flew from the freighter's underside. Other vessels hung back, fearful it might explode. "Hail the freighter," she said.

A quavering nonhuman voice was piped onto the bridge. "This is *Cynda Dreaming*. Sorry about that scrape earlier. We weren't expecting—"

Sloane cut to the point. "What's your payload?"

"Nothing, yet. We were heading to pick up a load of thorilide on the moon for refining at Calladan Chemworks down on Gorse."

"Can you haul in your condition?"

"We need to get to the repair shop to know. I'm not sure how bad it is. Could be a couple of months—"

Vidian spoke up. "Captain, target that vessel and fire."

It was almost idly stated, to the extent that Vidian's intonations ever conveyed much genuine emotion. The directive nonetheless startled Chamas. Standing before the gunnery crew, he turned to the captain for guidance.

The freighter pilot, having heard the new voice, sounded no less surprised. "I'm sorry—I didn't get that. Did you just—"

Sloane looked for an instant at Vidian, and then at her first officer. "Fire."

The freighter captain sounded stunned. "What? You can't be—"

This time, *Ultimatum*'s turbolasers provided the interruption. Orange energy ripped through space, turning *Cynda Dreaming* into a confusion of fire and flak.

Sloane watched as the other ships of the convoy quickly rerouted. Her gunners had done their jobs, targeting the ship in a way that resulted in minimal hazard for the nearby ships. All the freighters were moving faster.

"You understand," Vidian said, turning toward her. "Replacement time for one freighter and crew in this sector is—"

"—three weeks," Sloane said, "which is less than two months." *See, I've read your reports, too.*

This was the way to handle this assignment, she realized. So what if Vidian was strange? Figuring out what the Emperor—and those who spoke for him—wanted and then providing it was the path to success. Debating his directives only wasted time and made her look bad. It was the secret of advancement in the service: Always be on the side of what is going to happen anyway.

Sloane clasped her arms behind her back. "We'll see that the convoys make double time—and challenge any ship that refuses."

"It isn't just transit," Vidian said. "There are problems on the ground, too—on planet and moon. Surveillance speaks of unruly labor, of safety and environmental protests. And there's always the unexpected."

Sloane clasped her arms behind her back. "*Ultimatum* stands at your service, my lord. This system will do what you—what the Emperor—requires of it."

"So it will," Vidian said, eyes glowing blood-red. "So it will."

Hera Syndulla watched from afar as the scattered remains of the freighter burned silently in space. No recovery vehicles were in sight. As unlikely a prospect as survivors were, no one looked for any. There were only the shipping convoys, quickly rerouting around the wreckage.

Obeying the master's whip.

This was mercy in the time of the Empire, she thought. The Imperials had none; now, to all appearances, their lack of care was infecting the people.

The green-skinned Twi'lek in her stealth-rigged starship didn't believe that was true. People were basically decent . . . and one day, they would rise up against their unjust government. But it wouldn't happen now, and certainly not here. It was too soon, and Gorse was barely awake politically. This wasn't a recruitment trip. No, these days were for seeing what the Empire could do—a project that suited the ever-curious Hera perfectly. And Count Vidian, the Emperor's miracle man, practically begged investigation.

In previous weeks, the Imperial fixer had cut a swath through the sector, "improving efficiency." On three previous worlds, like-minded acquaintances of Hera's on the HoloNet had reported misery levels skyrocketing under Vidian's electronic eyes. Then her associates had simply vanished. That had piqued Hera's interest—and learning of the count's visit to the Gorse system brought her the rest of the way.

She had another contact on Gorse, one who had promised much information on the regime. She wanted that information—but first she wanted to check out Vidian, and the system's notoriously anarchic mining trade offered her a variety of chances to get close. Industrial confusion, the perfect lure for Vidian, would provide excellent cover for her to study his methods.

Emperor Palpatine had too many minions with great power and influence. It was worth finding out whether Count Vidian had real magic before he rose any higher.

It was time to move. She picked out the identifying transponder signal of a ship in the convoy. One button-push later, her ship *was* that vessel, as far as anyone trying to watch traffic was concerned. With practiced ease, she weaved her freighter into the chaotic flood of cargo ships heading to the moon.

None of these guys can fly worth a flip, she thought. It was just as well it wasn't a recruiting trip. She probably wouldn't have found anyone worth her time.

CHAPTER TWO

"LOOK OUT, YOU BIG IDIOT!"

Seeing the bulky thorilide hauler coming right at him, Kanan Jarrus forgot about talking and abruptly banked his freighter. He didn't waste time worrying whether the bigger vessel would veer in the same direction: He took his chance while the choice was still his. He was rewarded with survival—and an alarmingly up-close look at the underbelly of the oncoming ship.

"Sorry," crackled a voice over the comm system.

"You sure are," Kanan said, blue eyes glaring from beneath dark eyebrows. *I see that guy in an alley tonight, he'd better watch out.*

It was madness. Cynda's elongated elliptical orbit meant that the distance between the moon and Gorse changed daily. Close-approach days like today made the region between the worlds a congested demolition derby. But the appearance of the Star Destroyer and its destruction of the cargo ship had created a stampede in space. A race with two terrified groups bound in opposite directions, hurtling toward each other in the same transit lanes.

Normally, Kanan would be the one pushing the limits to get where he was going. That was what kept him in drinking money, the main reason he had a job. But he also prided himself on keeping his cool when others were panicking—and that was surely happening now. Kanan *had* seen a Star Destroyer before, but he was pretty sure no one else around here had.

Another freighter moved alongside. He didn't recognize this one. Almost shaped like a gem, with a bubble-like cockpit forward and another for a gunner seated just above. It was a nice ride compared with anything else in the sky. Kanan goosed the throttle, trying to pull alongside and get a glimpse at her driver. The freighter responded by zipping ahead with surprising speed, claiming his vector and causing him to lay off the acceleration. He gawked as the other pilot hit the afterburners, soaring far ahead.

It was the one time he'd touched the brakes all trip, and it was instantly noticed. His comm system chirped, followed by a female voice, sounding none too happy. "You there! What's your identifier?"

"Who's asking?"

"This is Captain Sloane, of the Star Destroyer *Ultimatum!*"

"I'm impressed," Kanan said, smoothing the black hairs on his pointed chin. "What are you wearing?"

"*What?*"

"Just trying to get a picture. Hard to meet people out here."

"I repeat, what's your—"

"This is *Expedient,* flying for Moonglow Polychemical, out of Gorse City." He rarely bothered to activate his ID transponder; no one ever managed space traffic here anyway.

"Speed up. Or else!"

Kanan sat lazily back in his pilot's seat and rolled his eyes. "You can shoot me if you want," he said in a slow almost-drawl, "but you need to know I'm hauling a load of explosive-grade baradium bisulfate for the mines on Cynda. It's testy stuff. Now, *you* might be safe from the debris in your big ship over there, but I can't speak for the rest of the convoy. And some of these folks are hauling the same thing I am. So I'm not sure how smart that'd be." He chuckled lightly. "Be something to watch, though."

Silence.

Then, after a moment: "Move along."

"Are you sure? I mean, you could probably record it and sell—"

"Don't push it, grubber," came the icy response. "And try to go faster."

He straightened one of his fingerless gloves and smiled. "Nice talking with you, too."

"*Ultimatum* out!"

Kanan switched off the receiver. He knew there wasn't any chance of his being targeted once anyone with a brain understood what he was carrying. For their own protection, miners only used "Baby"—the sardonic nickname for baradium bisulfate—by the gram down in the mines on Cynda. Any Imperial would think twice before targeting a Baby Carrier too close by—and the Star Destroyer captain in particular would be less apt to call on him again about anything after that conversation.

That was also according to plan. He'd rather avoid that meeting, no matter what she might look like.

He mouthed Sloane's words mockingly. *"Go faster!"* He was already flying the freighter at close to top speed. When fully loaded, *Expedient* wasn't going to give him even that much. The sarcastic name was his idea. The freighter was Moonglow's, one of dozens of identical vessels the company operated; the ships met with disastrous ends often enough the firm didn't bother naming them. "Suicide fliers" didn't stay in the game long, either, provided they survived, so Kanan had no idea how many people had flown his ship before him. Giving the Baby Carrier a name was just his attempt to give it even a single amenity.

It'd be nice, he thought, if on one of the planets he visited he could fly something with some class—like that ship that had just raced past him. But then, whoever owned it probably wouldn't let him take the liberties he did with *Expedient*. Like now: Seeing two mining haulers heading right for him, he banked the ship, corkscrewing between them. They slowed down: He kept on going. *Let* them *watch out for* me.

His carefully secured payload didn't react to the sudden motion, but the maneuver did produce a dull thump from back in the cargo area. He turned his head, his short clump of tied-back hair brushing against the headrest. Through the corner of his eye, Kanan saw an old man on the deck, half swimming against the floor as he tried to get his bearings.

"Morning, Okadiah."

The man coughed. Like Kanan, Okadiah had a beard but no mustache—but his hair was completely white. He'd been sleeping back with the baradium bisulfate containers, on the one empty shelf. Okadiah preferred that to the acceleration couch in the main cabin: It was quieter. Figuring out which way was forward, the old man started to crawl. He addressed the air as he reached the copilot's seat. "I have determined I will not pay your fare, and you shall have no tip."

"Best tip I ever got was to pick another line of work," Kanan said.

"Hmph."

Actually, Okadiah Garson had several lines of work, all of which made him the perfect friend to have, in Kanan's eyes. Okadiah was foreman for one of the mining teams on Cynda, a thirty-year veteran who knew his way around. And down on Gorse, he ran The Asteroid Belt, a cantina favored by many of his own mining employees. Kanan had met Okadiah months earlier when he'd broken up a brawl at his bar; it was through Okadiah that Kanan had gotten the freighter-pilot job with Moonglow. Even now, Kanan lived in the flophouse next door to the cantina. A landlord with a liquor supply was a good deal indeed.

Okadiah claimed he only partook of his own ferments when someone got hurt in the mines. That was a handy conviction to have, considering it happened nearly every day. Yesterday's cave-in had been so bad it kept the party going all night long, causing Okadiah to miss his shift's personnel shuttle. Baby Carriers didn't get many passengers who had any other options for getting to work, and Kanan didn't take riders. But for Okadiah, he made an exception.

"I dreamed I heard a woman's voice," the old man said, rubbing his eyes. "Stern, regal, commanding."

"Starship captain."

"I like it," Okadiah said. "She's no good for you, of course, but I'm a man of means. When do I meet this angel?"

Kanan simply jabbed a thumb out the window to his left. There, the old man beheld *Ultimatum,* looming behind the frenetic rush of space traffic. Okadiah's bloodshot eyes widened and then narrowed, as he tried to determine exactly what it was he was looking at.

"Hmm," he finally said. "That wasn't there yesterday."

"It's a Star Destroyer."

"Oh, dear. Are we to be destroyed?"

"I didn't ask," Kanan said, grinning. He didn't know how an old miner on an armpit like Gorse had come by his genteel manner of speech, but it always amused him. "Somebody got on the wrong side of her. Know anyone on *Cynda Dreaming*?"

Okadiah scratched his chin. "Part of the Calladan crew. Tall fellow, skinny Hammerhead. He's run up quite a tab at The Asteroid Belt."

"Well, you can forget about collecting."

"Oh," Okadiah said, looking again out the window. There was still a bit of debris from the unlucky freighter about. "Kanan, lad, you do have a way of sobering a person up."

"Good. We're almost there."

Expedient rolled and angled downward toward the white surface of airless Cynda. An artificial crater had been hollowed out as a landing approach zone; half a dozen red-lit landing bays had been gouged into its sides, connecting with the mining areas farther below. Bringing *Expedient* to hover over the crater, Kanan turned the ship toward his appointed entrance.

Okadiah turned his head forward and squinted. "There's my transport now!"

"Told you we'd catch up."

They *had* caught up, but it wasn't purely from Kanan's efforts. The Empire's unreasonable directive had played a role. The personnel transport Okadiah was supposed to have been on had attempted to enter the bay too quickly and had clipped the side of the doorway. Now it sat blocking the entrance, disabled and partially hanging over the edge. It was in no danger of falling, but the magnetic shield that would seal the cavern against the void could not be activated. Space-suited workers were visible in the bay, staring haplessly at the wreck.

"Move it," Kanan said over the comm.

"Stay put, Moonglow-Seventy-Two," crackled the response from the control tower at the center of the crater. "We'll get you in after we get the workers suited and off-loaded."

"I'm on a schedule," Kanan said, shifting *Expedient* out of hover mode and moving toward the entrance.

Objections came loudly over the communicator, getting Okadiah's attention. He glanced at Kanan. "You are aware we're carrying high explosives?"

"I don't care," Kanan said. "Do you?"

"Not at all. Sorry to disturb. Carry on."

Kanan did, expertly bringing *Expedient*'s stubby nose toward the exposed side of the personnel carrier. He could see the miners inside its windows, clamoring futilely at him as his ship made contact with a clang.

Expedient's engines straining, Kanan gunned the ship forward, dislodging the personnel transport from the edge. The noisy scrape reverberated through both vessels, and Okadiah glimpsed nervously back into the cargo section. But in moments both ships were inside the landing area. The magnetic shield sealed the landing bay, and Kanan deactivated his engines.

Okadiah whistled. He regarded Kanan with mild wonderment for a moment and then placed his hands on the dashboard before him. "Well, that's that." He paused, seemingly confused. "We drink *after* work, is that correct?"

"That's right."

"Entirely the wrong order," the old man said, wobbling slightly as he rose. "Let's get to it, then."

CHAPTER THREE

THE HORN-HEADED Devaronian miner charged from the disabled personnel transport across the pressurized cavern's floor.

"You punk kid!" he yelled as Kanan exited *Expedient*. "What were you trying to prove back there?"

Kanan was still in his early twenties, but he hadn't answered to "kid" ever. And certainly not when the name came from a dunderhead like Yelkin, whose job it was to drill holes for explosives. Kanan turned and walked alongside his ship, opening up cargo hatches as he went.

The muscular miner stomped after him and grabbed at his shoulder. "I'm talking to you!"

With quick reflexes, Kanan grabbed Yelkin's hand and spun around, twisting the other man's arm. Yelkin winced in pain and fell to his knees. Kanan didn't let go. He spoke in low, calm tones into his captive's pointed ear. "Your ship was in the way, pal. I have a deadline."

"We all do," Yelkin said, struggling. "You saw them shoot that freighter. The Empire's come to check up—"

"Then go faster. But don't go stupid." Kanan released his hold, and Yelkin fell to the ground, gasping. Kanan brushed off his long-sleeved green tunic and turned back to *Expedient*.

Several miners arrived at Yelkin's side. "Blasted suicide flier!" one said. "They're all cracked!"

"Someone needs to show you some manners," another said to Kanan.

"So I've heard." Unworried, Kanan looked around the landing bay. The loader droids that normally helped hadn't arrived, evidently unable to make sense out of the impromptu parking situation on the loading floor. It looked like it was going to be another one of those days when he had to do everything.

Kanan unloaded a hovercart and parked it in front of the ship. Then he began the laborious process of hefting down metal crates. Cynda's lesser gravity made the cases somewhat lighter than they had been on Gorse but no less bulky—or hazardous—to carry. Heaving the first crate, he carried it toward the milling miners.

"You're in the way," he said. "For the moment."

Okadiah appeared on the far side of the spacecraft. "Gentlemen, I think a maxim is in order: Do not aggravate the man who carries high explosives."

The miners parted, glowering at Kanan as he passed. Rubbing his arm, Yelkin snarled at Okadiah. "You take in some real pieces of work, boss."

"Like I did all of you, one time or another," the old man said. He pointed toward the south, and a bank of elevators. "Let's get the shift started. If the Empire's inspecting today, Boss Lal will be here, too. At least pretend to work." He smiled toothily. "And let me add—in honor of that poor sap outside who got himself blown to smithereens—it'll be happy hour all night tonight at The Asteroid Belt. We'll even pick you up and drive you home."

Momentarily assuaged, the miners turned and made for the elevators. Okadiah watched Kanan set a case down on the hovercart. "Still winning friends and influence?"

"Don't know why I'd do that," Kanan said.

"Ah, yes. You're not staying. Like you told me: You never stay."

"Clothes on my back," Kanan said as he turned to grab another crate. "Travel light, and death will never find you."

"I said that, didn't I?" Okadiah nodded. "You'll work the bar tonight?"

"If you can afford it."

Okadiah winked and ambled off after his co-workers. Kanan did keep the bar on occasion, but on some nights he was his own best customer. He'd also tried his hand as bouncer, although again, he'd wound up starting as many fights as he'd stopped. Still, this system had been closer to a home than any he'd known in years of wandering. It would be a hard place to leave.

But he would. The day job was wearing on him. Giving up on the loader droids ever arriving to help, Kanan finished filling the first hovercart and pushed it into the freight elevator.

As the doors closed behind him, he thought on it. He might miss Okadiah's place, yes, and he'd certainly miss Cynda. In all his travels he'd never encountered a place quite like it. The landing bay didn't look like much, but he knew to watch for the big show as soon as the elevator doors opened.

They did, a thousand meters below—and Kanan was bombarded with a coruscating display of lights and colors. He was in one of the countless great caverns beneath the surface. Crystal stalagmites climbed and stalactites hung all around. Each one acted as a prism, refracting the lights of the work crew; to move was to see kaleidoscopic change. Better still, the crystals gave off warmth, making Cynda's many oxygenated caverns as bright and pleasant as parent-planet Gorse was dark and sticky.

Back before the Empire, the place had been a natural preserve. Cynda had been the literal bright spot in the lives of Gorse's residents; tourism had been the moon's—and Gorse's—number one draw. And while Republic scientists had learned early on that Cynda's interior contained massive amounts of thorilide, no one had wanted to mine for it while the workable nightside of Gorse still held any of the substance at all. As far as Kanan knew, no one even bothered looking for thorilide on Gorse's dayside, where the heat was enough to melt any droid in manufacture.

But then, almost exactly on the day that Chancellor Palpatine proclaimed the first Galactic Empire, a report had revealed that Gorse's mines were exhausted. The refineries went idle. The Empire wouldn't stand for it—and didn't need to. Cynda was right there, readily available to exploit.

Kanan saw the results now as he pushed the hovercart from the intact antechamber into the main work area. Pebble-sized crystal fragments littered the floor, and his boots crunched as he walked. Only the big industrial lights illuminated the cavity; the ceiling couldn't be seen at all in the smoky haze above. A sickly burnt stench hung on the air.

The Empire had defiled the place, but it could hardly resist. Useful as thorilide was in its processed form, in nature it had a fragile molecular structure. Efforts to free the substance from comets, already an insanely difficult process, often resulted in the collapse of the compound into its component elements. But Cynda was the mother lode in more ways than one, for its tough crystal columns managed to preserve thorilide inside them, even when blasted from their bases. Given how the prismatic structures reacted to laser torches, blasting was the only way.

The need for explosives had given Kanan a job, but it had also given Gorsians cause to object. Some were more vocal than others. And a few were downright loud about it.

Like that guy, Kanan thought, recognizing a voice coming from the far end of the work zone. *Oh, brother. Skelly.*

"You're not listening," the redheaded man declared, gray dust puffing from his protective vest as he waved his arms. "You're not listening!"

In the perfect echo chamber the cavern provided, no one could help but hear Skelly, and if there were any stalactites left intact, Kanan half expected Skelly's voice to bring them down.

But Kanan saw that the target of Skelly's harassment wasn't paying much mind, and he couldn't blame her. A four-armed, green-skinned member of Gorse's Besalisk subcommunity, Lal Grallik was the enterprising chief of Moonglow Polychemical. Running it kept "Boss Lal" jumping from planet to moon and back. Skelly was just one more nuisance to deal with. "I *am* listening, Skelly," she said. "I could probably hear you down on Gorse."

I'm sure she wishes she were there now, Kanan thought. Short and compactly built, Skelly had one mode: intense. Kanan was vaguely aware of the fortyish man's war record as a tunneler; the scars and pockmarks on his face read like a walk through recent military history. But while Kanan felt for anyone who'd gone through all that, he had little patience for the way Skelly always talked as if he were trying to yell over a barrage. The man could outshout a jet turbine.

"I'm trying to save people's lives here," Skelly said, busy auburn eyebrows lowered in all seriousness. "Your company, too." Seeing Lal return her attention to the electronic manifest in her four-fingered hands, Skelly turned around and shrugged. "No one listens."

Kanan knew Skelly worked as a demolitions expert for Dalborg, one of the other mining concerns. Okadiah had explained that Skelly had been fired by every major firm in the last five years. The only one Skelly hadn't yet landed with was Kanan's employer. It wasn't too small a firm, Okadiah had said: just lucky. Kanan agreed. Skelly knew what he was doing with a demolition charge, but a variety of neuroses came with the package. And he always looked as if he'd slept on the floor. Even when Kanan did that for real, he made sure he looked presentable.

Skelly turned to face the Moonglow chief. "Look, Lal, all you have to do is suspend blasting past Zone Forty-Two. You and the other firms, just for a while. Long enough for me to test my—"

Lal looked at him in disbelief. "I thought you said you were giving up!"

Skelly's small eyes narrowed. "You'd like that, right? I forgot. All you guild outfits are the same. Out for yourselves . ."

Kanan tried to tune it out as he pushed his pallet past. "Coming through."

Lal, clearly pleased to have someone other than Skelly to talk to, looked down at the load Kanan was hauling and checked it against her manifest. "Glad you made it, Kanan. I heard there was some trouble out there."

"No concern of mine," Kanan said, parking the hovercart. "Here's your bombs."

"This batch goes to Zone Forty-Two," Lal said, waving some workers over. She nodded to Skelly, who smoldered as he stared at the hovercart. "Someone's favorite place," she whispered.

Skelly leaned on the hovercart handle. "I've told you, we can't keep blasting down there. Not with these—"

"Take them home, then," Kanan said, walking around Skelly. "Blow yourself up." He began to unload crates of explosives one at a time for the workers to carry away.

"Wait," Skelly said, finally noticing the freighter pilot. He stepped beside Kanan and looked back at Lal. "You'll listen to Kanan, right? He's one of your top explosives haulers—and one of my best friends."

"Right on one. Wrong on the other," Kanan said, continuing his job.

"Kanan flies with this stuff," Skelly said. "He knows what it can do. He'll tell you: Using microblasts to cut crystal is one thing, but you shouldn't use it to crack open walls! He knows—"

"I'll tell you what I know," Kanan said, turning and poking a finger in Skelly's sternum, knocking him back a step. "I have a deadline. I've got more to unload. So long." He returned to the empty cart and turned it around.

Lal stepped aside to take a call. "Imperial channel," she said, waving Skelly off. "This is important."

"This is important, too," Skelly muttered to no one. Seeing Kanan pushing the hovercart away, he started marching after him. Catching up, he tried to match the pilot's pace. "Kanan—pal, why didn't you back me up over there?"

"Get lost, will you?"

"Lost is what we'll all be if this keeps up," Skelly said, huffing and puffing. "I know what the baradium family of explosives can do. Better than anyone. I've done the yield estimates. I've even studied the seismology of this moon—"

"You must be fun on holidays," Kanan said, pushing the cart back into the elevator.

"—right down to what they never consider: the core!" Skelly kept talking as he pushed his way into the car with Kanan. "It's sturdy up here, but way down deep? This moon could snap like a protein cracker!"

"Ah."

"*Ah* is right. I knew it! You agree with me!"

"No, food reminded me," Kanan said, drawing a pouch from his jacket. "I skipped breakfast."

"I'm serious," Skelly said, reaching into his own vest. He wore a single glove over a right hand that Kanan had never once seen him use, except as a pincer: There was something gripped in it now, not much larger than a coin. "It's all on this holodisk. I've got my work right here. You know those groundquakes we get on Gorse when the moon passes close by? The only reason it isn't worse on Cynda is because the crystal formations keep the tension in check. But we keep blowing them apart! If I can get just one person to read this—"

"Why does it have to be me? I'm nobody."

"Everybody comes to Okadiah's!" Skelly said. "You're there all the time. You can talk to people."

"Why can't you?" Kanan knew why. "Oh, yeah. He banned you, for aggravating people."

"Just have a look." Skelly waved the disk before Kanan.

"Get it out of my face, Skelly. I'm serious." Kanan threw his food pouch to the deck of the pallet. Pushing back against workers for other firms always caused a hassle; Okadiah had warned him against it. But Skelly was friendless, and for good reason. Kanan was near his limit.

Skelly's face twisted into a disdainful snarl. "Yeah, that's right. I forgot. You're paid by the shipload, right? And now you're all going to be running like eskrats, because the Empire's dropped by." He got in the taller man's face. "Well, the Empire had better watch out, or it's going to have a real disaster on its hands!"

"Last warning!"

Skelly opened his mouth again—but before a syllable emerged,

Kanan's fist slammed into Skelly's teeth. Five seconds of violence later, the elevator doors opened to the landing bay—where waiting loader droids saw Kanan pushing the pallet with Skelly's crumpled body atop it.

"Good, you're here," Kanan said. He shoved the cart at them. "Put this somewhere."

As Kanan headed back to *Expedient* for another load, a dazed and flustered Skelly looked up at the puzzled droids. "Nobody listens."

CHAPTER FOUR

"I HAVE A PING ON Cynda cam five-six-oh," the operator in the second row said. "Threat to the Empire in spoken Basic. Elevator cam. Thirty-eight decibels, clearly intoned."

Across the crowded data center, Zaluna Myder didn't look up from tending to her plants. "Who was listening?"

"A transport driver."

And us, Zaluna thought to herself as she turned back to business. Her gray hand swept at the air in front of her—and a new half-meter-tall hologram appeared on one of the display platforms surrounding her work dais.

Hundreds of thousands of kilometers above Gorse, a couple of people were having a conversation in one of the lunar mining station's elevators. Or they *had* been having a conversation, until one person had decked the other. And it was all unfolding again, seconds later, in three static-laced dimensions in front of Zaluna's enormous black eyes.

Focusing on the moving image, the Sullustan woman reached for this hour's mug of caf. Now in her fifties, Zaluna spent an hour each day in the corporate gym, but she still knew it was past time to do without the artificial stimulant. On the other hand, her work had only gotten busier—and the caf was the only vice she'd ever had. She knew for certain that fact put her in the distinct minority of Gorse's residents—because in the last thirty-plus years, Zaluna Myder had seen and heard everything.

She had to. It was her job. And in the earpieces plugged into her giant shell-like ears, she heard the words that had caught the system's attention: "*. . . the Empire had better watch out . . .*"

She glanced down at the terminal operator in the second row. "The listener was a transport driver, you say. Anybody we—"

"Migrant, no record," he replied. "Nobody we care about."

Zaluna didn't need to ask whether the *speaker* was someone they cared about. His words alone were enough. The surveillance super-computers had comprehended the statement, measured it against mysterious metrics, and kicked the incident up to the Mynocks, who'd taken it to her.

Myder's Mynocks. That was what the shift on her floor was named after she rose to supervise it. She had no children or grandchildren; she hadn't needed any other family, ever. Standing here on her platform she was queen, lending her guidance to the surveillance operators and taking the occasional spare moments to tend her potted plants. She'd had the misfortune to be born onto a world where the sun never rose, but at least her office had full-spectrum lighting.

Zaluna had been a fixture since her late teens here in World Window Plaza, the upside-down and truncated cone that was still the newest building on Gorse. Transcept Media Solutions had built the structure—which had no windows at all—as a local repository for marketing data about the planet's residents. There wasn't much commerce on Gorse unattached to the mining industry, but that didn't matter: When people did leave, they took their purchasing preferences with them. And thanks to the monitoring stations it maintained, Transcept would have their profiles when they arrived elsewhere. That information was surely worth something, although who'd want it or why was a subject Zaluna rarely considered.

Few people apart from poor transient laborers left Gorse anymore, but that wasn't a concern. First the Republic and later the Empire had become Transcept clients—and Zaluna had kept her dream job. Watching and listening: That was what she'd been born to do. Not because of her giant Sullustan eyes and ears—though they missed nothing—but because as long as she could remember, she had loved to observe and absorb information.

And neither did Zaluna forget anything.

"Ah, our old friend," she said aloud as her finger movement brought the holographic image to a halt. "Skelly, no surname. Human, born Corellia, forty standard years ago. Demolitions expert, Dalborg Mining, Cyndan operation. Last known address, Crispus Commons on Gorse. Clone Wars veteran. Injured, hand replaced. Two teeth missing—"

The operator in the second row looked back at her, amused. "That's him," Hetto said. "But I haven't even pulled up the file yet."

"You did eight days ago," Zaluna said, sipping from her mug. "No need to tell me twice."

"You're scaring me, boss." Laughter came from along the lines of desks.

"You could use a good scare, Hetto. Back to work, all of you."

The operators hushed immediately—and Hetto smiled and turned back to his terminal. Over two decades she'd watched his youthful brashness turn into jaded irascibility, but he still relished getting a rise out of her.

Zaluna had never expected to command a room of any kind. The diminutive Sullustans—at just over a meter and a half, Zaluna was taller than most—were one of the least threatening peoples on Gorse, a world where folks did a lot of threatening. Long before she had been promoted to her superior position, Hetto had taken to walking her to and from her tough neighborhood. She appreciated the gesture, but in fact she faced danger gamely. Theft on Gorse was a constant, like the groundquakes that rocked the world. You might get knocked down now and again, but you simply had to get back up.

It had started before the Empire, under the Republic: The Mynocks had been tasked with screening electronic communications and certain monitored public places for "conversations suspected to pose a threat to the lives of Republic citizens." As the Clone Wars had dragged on, "the lives of Republic citizens" had evolved into "Republic security"—and under the Empire, that phrase had morphed into "public order."

No matter, Zaluna had thought. *They're just words.* She'd never had a problem with listening to those of others for a good cause. The mining business attracted a lot of rowdies, yes, but worse things grew in darkness. It was smart for law enforcement authorities to use the latest tools to keep tabs on miscreants.

And there was no shortage of things to listen for. During the Clone Wars, the Separatists had hatched many plots against the Republic; watching out for them was just common sense. Even the Republic's supposed defenders, the Jedi, had turned traitors—if you believed the Emperor's account. She wasn't sure she did, but she was fairly certain that if there *was* a plot, then someone like Zaluna had probably first flagged it.

Privacy? In her younger days, Zaluna had found it a silly concept. Either thoughts were in your head, or you let them out. The only distinction between a whisper and an intergalactic broadcast was technical. A listener with the means to hear had the absolute right to do so. Really, the *obligation* to do so—else the act of communicating was a futile one. Zaluna didn't speak her mind nearly as often as Hetto, but when she had something to say, she definitely wanted people to listen.

But times had changed. Under the Empire, words had become causes with greater effects. People she'd monitored had disappeared, although she'd never found out why. And the job had ceased to be as much fun.

Skelly's frozen image lingered there before her, his mouth stuck open mid-rant. It seemed a perfect pose—and she knew she'd see it again. Because Skelly, she knew, was red-stamped. Records digitally stamped with a red star indicated visits from Gorse's mental health authority.

"He gets any more stars, he can open up his own galaxy," she said. She took a deep breath, relieved. Red-stamped people tended to stay in the medical system, rarely escalating to anything else. They were freer with words than most, rarely intending action. And Skelly had been fun to listen to in the past, at least. She unpaused the feed. "That's that, then. I'll close out the—"

"Incoming message," Hetto said, speaking abruptly. "The official channel."

That doesn't happen every day, she thought. "Put it through!"

A macabre form appeared holographically in the space before the brown-clad supervisor. His mechanical voice spoke precisely and clearly. "This is Count Vidian of the Galactic Empire, speaking to all surveillance stations under my authority. I am launching inspections of mining operations both on Cynda and at the processors on Gorse. All such locations are now under Security Condition One. No exceptions."

Zaluna gawked at the life-sized figure. "Excuse me. *All* the mining operations? Are you aware how many—"

Count Vidian did not wait to hear her finish. The transmission ended.

Hetto spoke first, as always. "What the *hell*?"

"Yeah," Zaluna said, under her breath. Then she let out a whistle. The mining trade employed tens of thousands of people.

"Is he serious? Does he even know what he's asking for?" Hetto threw up his hands. "Maybe we need to get a red stamp for *that* guy's file. I swear, some of these Impies must be out of their minds! That, or—"

"*Hetto!*" Zaluna snapped.

Except for the low murmur of audio feeds coming from the monitors, the room fell silent. More quietly this time, she said, "We do what we're told."

Zaluna traced her jowls with her fingertips as she tried to remember the last time Sec-Con One had been invoked. It hadn't happened since the Emperor first drafted Transcept into Imperial service to deal with the Jedi crisis. It meant escalating every case under watch to the highest level—and Zaluna had a sense of what that meant.

It was nothing good.

Her eyes had returned to the live feed of Skelly on Cynda, the connection she had been about to close without action. "Bump him up, Hetto."

"But he's a red-stamp."

"Which counts for nothing today." The supervisor straightened. "Whatever his condition, Master Skelly's mouth is going to earn him some time with our friends in white."

And good luck to him then, she thought.

CHAPTER FIVE

"COUNT VIDIAN, THIS IS AN HONOR," gushed the tall cape-clad Neimoidian waiting at the bottom of the Imperial shuttle's landing ramp. Despite the short notice, every firm working the moon had sent someone to the party meeting *Cudgel,* and the director's big red eyes practically beamed with pride. "The Cyndan Mining Guild welcomes you," he said, a wide, thick-lipped smile on his noseless green face. "I'm Director Palfa. We've all heard so much about—"

"Spare me," Vidian snapped, and half the listeners on the cavern floor took a step back, unnerved. "I have a schedule—and so do you. When you bother to keep it!"

The director's throat went dry. "O-of course." The others averted their eyes, afraid to stare at the cyborg.

Good, Vidian thought.

In the waning days of the Republic, Vidian's management texts had become pop-culture hits despite—no, *because of*—his reluctance to appear on the business HoloNets. He wasn't shy or ashamed of his appearance; he just didn't like wasting his time. But while the mystique added to his public reputation, in person his physical presence was a large part of his managerial success.

The turnaround expert, he had written, *is a germ invading the body corporate. It will be opposed.* Whenever someone sought to make over an organization, entrenched bureaucrats always tried to intimidate him. But two could play that game, and Vidian had been winning for fifteen years.

The legend of Denetrius Vidian had started five years before that, on what doctors expected would be his deathbed. But he'd survived, spending his bedridden time turning his meager bank balance into a fortune through electronic trading. In time, he purchased expensive, high-tech prosthetics, crafted to his own specifications. He did not look like other humans, but then humanity had abandoned him first, leaving him to rot in that hospice.

So Vidian had optimized his physical features in keeping with his now-famous trinity of management philosophies: *"Keep moving! Destroy barriers! See everything!"* Simple rules, which he diligently applied at every opportunity.

Including now, as the coterie made for the elevators. "The tour you ordered will cover some distance," the director said. "Would your lordship like to rest first?"

"No," Vidian said, marching so quickly the others had trouble keeping up. He moved faster now than he ever had in his youth; physical age no longer mattered. Some joked that Vidian was half droid, but he knew the comparison was inapt. Droids shut down. Vidian had spent too many years lying around already. So he had compounded his successes by working 90 percent of every day. *"Keep moving: With an able body, the mind can achieve anything!"*

Leading Vidian from the elevator onto a lower floor, the director paused in his blather about Cynda's wonders. "I'm sorry," he said, presenting his comlink. "Would you like to call your vessel to report your arrival?"

"I just did, while you were prattling in the elevator," Vidian said.

Palfa seemed puzzled. He hadn't seen or heard Vidian do anything. The count had installed a variety of comlink receivers into his earpieces; by routing his artificial voice through them, he regularly placed calls without ever appearing to open his mouth. Vidian hated getting information from intermediaries, who often distorted things for their own reasons; his communication capabilities were just one more way of cutting out the middle. *"Destroy barriers: Get information directly, whenever possible!"*

"This chamber leads to one of our mining levels," the director said, gesturing to the workers hurrying around. "What you're seeing is a typical day here—"

"A lie," Vidian said, continuing to walk. "I'm reading the live feed from your reports as I speak. You've doubled your pace, but will return to mediocrity when the Empire turns its eyes away. Be assured: I will see it does not."

A rumble came from the group of mining company representatives around them. But there was no point in their arguing. With a vocal command that made no external sound, Vidian cleared the daily production reports from his visual receptors.

Years earlier, he'd realized how leaders, from floor managers to chief executives, were often blind to the basic circumstances around them. Vidian didn't want to miss a detail. His optical implants not only gave him exceptional eyesight, but also eliminated the need for vid monitors by projecting external data feeds onto his own retinas. *See everything: He who has the data has the upper hand!*

Vidian looked back at the group of worried mining officials. Many were out of breath from trying to keep up with him, including a Besalisk woman. There were several of the multi-armed humanoids working at Calcoraan Depot, his administrative hub: members of a reasonably industrious but otherwise unremarkable species. Before he gave her a second thought, freight elevators opened on either side of the chamber. Stormtroopers rushed from the cars.

Right on time. Vidian pivoted and pointed to five different corridors leading from the chamber. Without a word in response, the squads split up and headed into the tunnels.

Director Palfa was startled. "What's going on?"

"No more than I said." Vidian's tone was as casual as his meaning was ominous. "You are managers. We're helping you manage."

———

Hera wasn't about to bring her ship into the Cyndan mining complex
for an unauthorized landing. Joining the convoy, however, had gotten her close, and once out of sight of the Star Destroyer, she'd parked
in orbit. Her ship's small excursion vessel had taken her the rest of the
way to a little maintenance outbuilding on the surface.

She'd studied just enough about the mining trade to know what to
pretend to be: a maintenance tech for bulk-loader droids. The rest
she'd thought up on the spot.

"This is the wrong entrance," the guy inside the airlock had said.

"Oh, gosh, I'm sorry. It's my first day, and I'm late!"

"And where's your badge?"

"I forgot. Can you believe it? My first day!"

The man had believed it, letting her pass with a smile that said he
hoped she'd keep making wrong turns in the future. People of several
different species found Hera appealing to look at, and she was happy
to put that to use for a good cause.

But as she walked carefully through the mining complex, she increasingly realized how difficult that cause had become. Gorse and
Cynda produced a strategic material for the Empire, yes, but they
were well away from the galactic center. And yet Hera spied one surveillance cam after another—including several that the workers
clearly weren't intended to see. If Coruscant-level security had made
it out to the Rim worlds, that would make any action against the Empire all the more difficult.

Another good reason to visit my friend on Gorse after this, she
thought, darting lithely beneath the viewing arc of another secret
cam. A rendezvous with any mystery informant was dangerous; she'd
learned that quickly enough in her short career as an activist. But her
contact had proven knowledge of Imperial surveillance capabilities,
and she'd need that to get to the important stuff, later on.

Finding out more about Count Vidian's methods, though, she'd
have to do through old-fashioned skulking. He was on Cynda now,
she knew: She'd seen him once already from afar, passing through the
caverns with a tour group. It was tough to get closer. The transparent
crystal columns were pretty to look at but lousy cover.

Darting through an isolated side passage, she thought she'd found a shortcut to get ahead of him. Instead, she found something else.

"Halt!" A stormtrooper appeared at the end of the corridor, his blaster raised.

Hera stopped in her tracks. "I'm sorry," she said, putting her hand to her chest and exhaling. "You scared me!"

"Who are you?"

"I work here," she said, approaching as if nothing was wrong. "I may be in the wrong place. It's my first day." She smiled.

"Where's your badge?"

"I forgot." Dark eyes looked down demurely, then back up. "Can you believe it? My first day!"

The stormtrooper studied her for a moment—and then saw the blaster she was wearing. She moved before he did, delivering a high kick that knocked the blaster from the startled stormtrooper's hands. Seeing his weapon clatter away, he lunged for it. She easily side-stepped him—and pivoted, leaping onto the armored man's back. Losing purchase on the crystalline floor, he stumbled, her full weight driving his head into the side wall. His helmet cracked loudly against the surface, and he slumped motionless to the ground.

"Sorry," Hera whispered over the fallen trooper's shoulder. "Charm doesn't work on everyone."

CHAPTER SIX

"HURRY UP! HURRY UP!"

Skelly looked back in annoyance as Tarlor Choh rushed about the cavern, egging workers on. A tall light-skinned fellow, Tarlor was Dalborg Mining's imbecile for Zone Thirty-Nine—not to be confused with all the *other* imbeciles managing their firm's efforts in this underground pocket. There were official imbeciles in all the other zones, too, Skelly knew—and not one of them had a whit of sense.

All were currently in a tizzy. For hours, arriving workers had reported the Empire spurring them along, even circulating a tale of the Star Destroyer blowing up a freighter captain for slacking. Now word had come through Tarlor that the Emperor's top efficiency expert, Count Vidian, would be inspecting.

Skelly saw it as deliverance. The top government inspector—coming right to him? Well, not to *him*, of course, but this was close enough. And better still, it was Denetrius Vidian. A business mogul under the Republic, true, but perhaps the only one Skelly respected. Vidian fed on blundering corporations, profiting from fixing their mistakes. Vidian's famous treatise, *Forget the Old Way,* was the only business holo Skelly owned.

If Skelly could get his research to Vidian, the Empire would understand—and it surely had the power to stop what the mining companies were doing.

Tarlor loomed over him. "Skelly, get those charges set!"

Skelly simply sighed, then returned his attention to the crystal column he was kneeling beside. Having prepared a suspension of baradium bisulfate in putty, he began caking a ring of the pasty substance all around the stalagmite's base.

It was slow, painstaking work—and hard to do neatly when he was irritated at the universe and everyone in it. Kanan, of course: Skelly's mouth still hurt from the man's punch. Who did he think he was? Tarlor plagued him, too—along with all his managerial kind, especially since Dalborg had recently busted him down from explosives supervisor to lowly demolitions placement tech.

And most of all, he hated his right hand, for being useless and forcing him to do the finely detailed work with his left. He could just bear to look at the fake hand now; it had been curled into a claw most of the time since that terrible day back in the Clone Wars.

The Clone Wars were yet another thing to be upset about. Everything about that conflict had been a lie. The Separatists had been this big enemy, and yet when the Empire was declared they'd melted away as if at the push of a button. The big corporations had staged the whole thing, Skelly was sure. Wars sold more ships, more weapons, and more medical devices. And in the Clone Wars, even the *soldiers* on both sides were manufactured goods.

The Republic and the Confederacy had been partners in the same corrupt game. The Empire was probably just another iteration of all that, to Skelly's thinking; no more or less immoral. To corporate oligarchs, political allegiances were just another change of clothes. This decade, central rule was in fashion. Something else would come along soon. The beast had to be fed, with lives and limbs on the battlefield and with the sweat and blood of the workers.

The problem was that blowing things up was the only thing Skelly had ever been taught to do.

He didn't fault himself for that. He was the product of a system that built only to destroy, as he saw it. He'd learned from the best—and learned well. Everything always came down to that simple list, taught to him during his first day in military demolitions: *Pair your ordnance with your initiator. Ignition leads to reaction leads to detonation.* Whether applied to compounds of baradium or its tremendously more powerful isotope, baradium-357, those steps referred to a series of complex reactions that had the same simple result.

Now forty, Skelly thought that list also applied to life. You started with a festering problem. Someone initiated a change. The system reacted to that pressure. And then, *bang,* you had your solution. It had always been his method. He'd been the one to initiate changes, whenever possible, starting back on the battlefield. It was why he'd volunteered for everything. Whenever battlements were too dangerous to storm, Skelly risked his life to burrow beneath, planting the explosives that made the decisive opening. He did that and more.

But then had come the Battle of Slag's Pit. A foolish charge on behalf of an idiot general, hoping to use demolitions to buy a Separatist fortification cheaply. The ground wasn't firm, the explosives were the wrong kind—and Skelly had raised hell about it.

No one had listened. No one ever listened.

The general had rank. All Skelly could do was enter the breach himself, relying on his innate talent to save the day for his fellow soldiers.

It hadn't been good enough.

The Clone Wars had ended while he was comatose; he'd later learned that none of his companions had been saved. His hand was another crushing blow. The medical droids had assured the platoon they were carrying all the spare parts necessary for proper battlefield surgery. But they'd lied. They only had a Klatooinian prosthetic hand left for Skelly, which had never worked right with his human neurology. Worse, their blundering had damaged his arm to the point where a proper replacement would never work, either. Skelly had just stuck a glove on the stupid thing and tried to go on.

Poverty had followed. He'd had no choice but to return to demoli-

tions work—and there, he'd only found confirmation for all his be-
liefs about corporate malfeasance. They were just as careless as the
military types.

It would have been unbearable had his travels not taken him to
Cynda.

As someone who had spent much of his time underground, he'd
been astonished by the beauty of the moon's caverns. Thoughts that
moved too quickly through his head seemed to slow down here. He'd
imagined his role a responsible one, for a time: If the moon was going
to be exploited anyway, he'd make sure it was done in a cautious manner, protective of the world and the people working on it. Cynda had
countless caverns; it was unimaginable to think the corporations
could ruin them all.

But now, Skelly could imagine exactly that. Cynda would become
one more ripped-up place, to add to the pile of torn-up lives.

The detonator armed, he replaced the applicator in his toolbox.
One more stalagmite, ready to be decapitated. Rote work, and
boring—but nicely done. Someone had to care.

"He's over there," Skelly heard the supervisor say. He stood up
from his work on the stalagmite and turned around. There, being led
by Tarlor, was a group of four Imperial stormtroopers.

Ah, Skelly thought. It seemed soon for the inspector's advance
team to be here, but that didn't matter. "Hello!" he shouted. Toolbox
still clutched in his good-for-little right hand, he saluted with his left.
An impulse act: He wasn't part of any military organization, but their
armor looked much like that of the clone troopers he'd once served
with, and he was glad to see them, in any event. "I'm Skelly. I've been
writing to your oversight offices for months—"

"*What?*" Tarlor blurted.

"—and I'm glad to see someone's listening." Skelly looked past the
stormtroopers, who continued to march toward him. "Er, is Count
Vidian here?"

The lead trooper stopped and raised his blaster rifle. His companions did the same. "Skelly, you're under arrest."

Skelly laughed nervously. "You're joking. Why?"

"You're charged with speaking to the detriment of the Empire."

Skelly's eyes widened—and his mind raced. "Wait! Did Kanan report me?"

Tarlor shook his bald head. "He's all yours. Skelly's always been trouble—and Dalborg Mining doesn't want anyone around that'll upset Count Vidian. Please tell him we cooperated fully." He looked over at Skelly and spoke acidly: "Looks like I just won the pool. *You're fired!*"

Skelly sputtered. "W-wait. This is a mistake! And Tarlor, you don't have the authority to—"

Before he could finish, the stormtroopers began to advance toward him. "Put that toolbox down!" the lead trooper said, just steps away.

With a blaster pointed at him and coming his way, Skelly made a decision. His left hand in the air, he crouched. "Okay, fine. I'm doing it. Just give me a second here." He knelt—

—and grabbed for the remote control he'd left on the ground. He tumbled behind the crystal column he'd been working on and rolled up into a ball, covering his toolbox with his body. Before the stormtroopers could follow, Skelly pressed the button.

The baradium bisulfate affixed to the column near Skelly detonated—and the massive diamond-hard cylinder fell forward, exactly the way he'd known it would. Away from him—and toward the stormtroopers. One screamed loudly, crushed immediately by the base of the falling column. On striking the surface, the entire structure shattered into dagger-like fragments.

Skelly didn't see what happened to the other stormtroopers because he was already up and running. He sprinted into an unlit passage leading from Zone Thirty-Nine into a service shaft. He knew from memory that it led to ventilation tunnels and other routes, pathways that could take him all over Cynda's underworld.

Wheezing as he ran in the dark, Skelly tried to comprehend what had just happened. So someone *was* listening to his words, after all. But they hadn't gotten his meaning.

Fine, he thought. He recognized the feeling of the toolbox full of explosives, still clutched in his immobilized right hand, bouncing against his leg as he ran. It gave him comfort, and he smiled.

There's more than one way to send a message.

CHAPTER SEVEN

VIDIAN HAD NEVER SEEN corporate hacks scatter so quickly. Since he'd declared Security Condition One, the surveillance operators on Gorse had provided him with the names of forty-six potential agitators working in the Cyndan mines. Vidian's news that the stormtroopers were making arrests had sent the executives off to alert their employees of the new scrutiny.

Other organic beings, for their supposed sentience, were really no better than droids, Vidian thought. They could be made to act according to program.

With the right encouragement, of course. Flanked by a pair of stormtroopers, the count glared at the guild chief—the only person left on the tour. "Palfa, your members will name a morale officer in each work crew to ensure the Empire is supported in word and deed."

The director cast his eyes to the ground. "My lord, I don't know how such a program will be received. It's the kind of laborers we attract. Rough characters. It's hard to control what they think—"

"When they think at all. Drunks and brawlers don't concern me. But they aren't all harmless! Consider this report I've just heard."

Vidian paused to tune his earpiece. "An arrest attempt has been made on your Level Thirty-Nine—and the suspect responded by assaulting the troopers!"

The director shook his large head. "That's terrible. I'm sure our security personnel have caught him."

"They haven't. But my troops will." Vidian switched off his audible communications long enough to give a command. "There," he said, speaking aloud again. "I've sent your office a copy of my remedial political program. Make sure your member firms adopt it immediately."

"Yes, my lord."

"Then we continue."

The dejected director led Vidian into a work zone. Like everywhere else, this space was populated by itinerant laborers, beings only slightly more effective than droids. Some passed through with explosives for other chambers. Others stood hip-deep in mounds of shattered crystal, sweating profusely as they shoveled thorilide-containing chips into bins for shipment. Cynda's interior was naturally dry; the light haze on the air was entirely organic perspiration. Vidian was glad his sense of smell no longer existed.

The rabble with the rubble, Vidian thought. Their kind had been present on countless other production worlds he'd been tasked to straighten out, and they were terrible clay to work with. Even with the troublemakers removed, few could be taught anything new—and their lifestyles outside only served to make them less effective on the job.

But they were boundless in number, and that gave him something he could do. He walked into the workers' midst and slapped his metal hands on the backs of one laborer after another. "You. You. You. And you." Each looked up, startled by the cyborg's touch. Human, nonhuman—their only common trait was their advanced ages. "Too old. Too slow."

Ignoring the mix of angry and insulted looks he was getting from the workers, Vidian called back to the guild chief, "Palfa, another directive for your members. New age caps on laborers, effective immediately."

Palfa spluttered. "But—but they're still productive!"

Vidian turned his soulless eyes toward Palfa. "And you are being unproductive," he said, stalking toward him. "Your guild is a haven for traitors and loafers!"

"My lord, perhaps I can suggest some way to—"

Vidian didn't wait to hear Palfa's suggestion. His arm lanced out and caught the director by the collar. Yanking downward, he pulled the screaming bureaucrat's cape over his head and forced him to the rocky surface. The stormtroopers watched, blasters drawn, as Vidian rained powerful blows on Palfa's body.

The count stepped back, satisfied, as the cloth-covered guildmaster's body stopped moving. Vidian looked admiringly at his hands; they still had their sterling shine.

"My lord!" one of the stormtroopers said.

"Eh?" Vidian looked at the soldier—and then back at the group of workers he'd been standing amid. They were all staring at him. "Industrial accident," he said. "Get to work—unless I told you to get out. Your firms will find more suitable labor for you on Gorse. Unemployment in a strategic resource system is unlawful. The Empire does not tolerate layabouts."

Seeing the wary workers complying, Vidian nodded with satisfaction. *Management, the Imperial way.* It was so much more efficient than under the Republic—and it came to him easily. Firing a manager inspired only the ambitious who wanted to take his or her place. But murder motivated everyone. It belonged in every supervisor's tool kit.

He changed his audio channel. "Captain Sloane, are you listening?"

From *Ultimatum,* the captain's voice filled his ear. "Affirmative."

"Inform Coruscant that there is an opening atop the Cynda Mining Guild. I'm sure the Emperor can send us someone appropriate."

"Done. Sloane out."

Leaving the stormtroopers to mind the workers as they disposed of the body, Vidian continued his tour alone. In the next chamber, he found another work crew—and while he had no intention of personally going through and identifying every slacker, he couldn't resist when he saw a white-haired man kneeling as he cleaned his pick.

"You're definitely too old," Vidian said, grabbing at the man's collar.

"Yeah? Well, you're too ugly," the man responded before he even turned to see who had accosted him. When he did, he cried out in revulsion. "What are *you* supposed to be?"

Vidian didn't react. He read the old man's badge. "Okadiah Garson." Not one of the names on the dissident list, but it didn't matter. He was through here. "Stop gawking at me like a fool."

"Sorry." Okadiah pointed to a spot behind the cyborg's ear, where his synthskin didn't completely cover the scar tissue beneath. "It's just—you missed a spot there."

"It's not for vanity. It's for the benefit of those who lose efficiency when confronted with the extraordinary." He tightened his grip on Okadiah's collar and shook. "I find this galaxy already has enough *ordinary* beings. Maybe you'd like to have your skin removed, as well, to see what it's like!"

"Maybe you should let him go," a voice said from behind.

Vidian looked back to see a dark-haired young man standing with a heavily laden hovercart in the opening to a tunnel. He held a blaster pointed straight at the count.

"Well, well," Vidian said, not in the least concerned for his safety. "We have a gunslinger. Or perhaps we've found our missing saboteur!"

In his travels, Kanan had seen a lot of people with prosthetics. Most were decent individuals, using technology to overcome misfortune. But the cyborg that had Okadiah by the collar had really gone to town with it. He looked like a war droid playing a human at a masquerade party.

"I'm no saboteur," Kanan said, still holding his weapon. "Heard a scream—sounded like trouble. What's this about?"

"I am Count Vidian, here for the Emperor. And I am doing his work." Vidian, seeming totally unconcerned by Kanan's blaster, started to lift the writhing old man by the neck.

Kanan fingered the trigger of his weapon. He had no desire whatsoever to tangle with the Empire, much less the top Imperial in the area. He was thankful when another way occurred to him. "There's something you should know." He lowered his blaster as he trod cautiously onto the work floor. "You're about to mangle the man who knows how to mine thorilide better than anyone."

Vidian paused. "Doubtful. He can't have the strength to dig or haul much."

"He teaches those who do," Kanan said. "Moonglow's the most efficient producer for its size."

Vidian shook Okadiah for a short moment before abruptly dropping him to the cavern floor. "At last—someone who understands what's important," he said. "You're fortunate I've already beaten someone else to death today, gunslinger. I have a schedule to keep." With that, the cyborg abruptly turned and exited with his guards.

Kanan holstered his blaster and turned back to check on Okadiah. Being tended to by his fellow miners, the old man rubbed his neck and looked at Kanan. "You always have to poke the gundark."

"Just following your lead," Kanan said.

Yelkin, the miner he'd tangled with that morning, rolled his eyes at Kanan. "I don't know why you didn't shoot that creep! Someone said he killed the guildmaster!"

"I pick who I party with," Kanan said. He walked back to the hovercart and activated it. "I don't mess with the Empire—and it doesn't mess with me."

"Zone Forty-Two awaits, gentlemen," Okadiah said. "I want to be done with this day."

Far across the wide chamber, Hera lowered her electrobinoculars. She'd had a bit of luck in the last hour, when all the stormtroopers had left her area. From what she'd been able to overhear, they were all after someone who had violently resisted arrest. She was interested to learn that story, but Vidian had to come first—and so she'd kept following along, trying to find safe places in each cavernous chamber from which to watch.

She'd been unable to get within a hundred meters, but she'd seen enough to know he was a vile thing, completely worthy of an important station by the Emperor's side. She'd seen both his attack on the poor guildmaster and how his escort had reacted to it: as if managerial murder was the most normal thing in the galaxy. And she'd seen him harassing the old man, moments earlier. It was good luck that the younger guy had come along. At least someone had a spine.

Watching the dark-haired man leaving with his hovercart, Hera felt a moment's impulse to follow him. People with the will to stand up to the Empire were worth knowing. But then she remembered that this wasn't a recruiting trip. She needed to keep after her objective.

Maybe next lifetime, pal. Hera slipped down from her perch and took off after Vidian.

CHAPTER EIGHT

MORE STORMTROOPERS ran past as Kanan pushed the hover-cart down the last tunnel to Zone Forty-Two. No doubt they were still looking for the idiot who had flipped out and attacked them in Zone Thirty-Nine. Lal Grallik had popped into the work area long enough to confirm the rumor that it was, indeed, Skelly on the loose. Kanan wasn't in the least surprised—or upset. At least Skelly was out of his hair.

It wasn't unusual to see stormtroopers in the Empire. But while he had hopped around some, Kanan's travels through the galaxy had tended toward a spiraling path, moving outward from the galactic center. Core Worlds, Colony worlds, Inner Rim: Each represented a new frontier for him. And each had turned out the same, with Imperial presence starting at nil and gradually growing. Kanan sometimes wondered how the stormtrooper uniform suppliers kept up with the demand. When the Imperials reached the fringe of the galaxy, what would they be wearing?

Not that the sight of stormtroopers alarmed him. No, like the woman who had spoken to him from the Star Destroyer, they were all functionaries. Organic droids, trained to react a certain way and seek out certain targets. Vidian was maybe the most literal expression that he'd seen: all their robotic efficiency and general nastiness bound up in a mass of metal, with a little skin on top. The best way to avoid being hassled by them was simply to fit perfectly into the stereotypes they were expecting to find.

On worlds like Gorse, the Empire expected to find workers of the sort drawn to low-skill, high-risk jobs. Rowdy and rambunctious characters—just not rebellious. Threats to their own sobriety and to one another, but never to the Empire. Not politically active, or even conscious.

It happened that those were the planets Kanan found the most fun. The role of roughneck suited him. He traveled the galaxy, looking at the sights—and sometimes the ceiling, after the odd fight or drunken binge. He'd visited more places than he could remember, and, beyond Okadiah, he'd never learned the names of most of the people around him. Why bother, when you were just going to leave?

Kanan pushed the cart into Zone Forty-Two. Deep beneath Cynda's surface, it was the largest chamber yet opened—and more important, sensors had found large recesses hiding behind its walls: other areas sure to be thick with minable thorilide. For weeks, various teams had triggered controlled blasts—barely audible over Skelly's objections—trying to get at the rich deposits. In a newly hollowed alcove, Moonglow's techs were working on their own attempt.

Kanan parked his cart outside the opening and pounded on the outside wall. "I'm thirsty. Let's get this done!"

Yelkin appeared from inside the hole, now wearing a white safety vest. He frowned when he saw Kanan. "You again."

"You bet."

Aggravated, the Devaronian surveyed the load of explosives. "We're measuring the length of the borehole for the charge. It should be just a—"

"Wait," someone called from inside the carved-out area. "There's a problem."

Kanan sighed as Yelkin hustled back inside. Kanan was about to start off-loading the crates himself when he glanced back into the recess. Beside Yelkin, he saw another technician sticking a long prod into a hole drilled for explosives. Or trying to. "Something's already in there!"

Kanan's eyes widened—and for the first time, he looked down at the ground outside the short tunnel. There was something he'd seen before: small and brown, discarded nearby.

Skelly's toolbox.

Kanan yelled into the opening. *"Get out! Get out!"*

He didn't have to yell a third time. The techs were moving.

"Someone's wired something already," Yelkin said in a panic. "There's a timer! Thirty seconds—"

No disarming that! "Forget it!" Kanan yelled. "Go!"

Moonglow's demolition techs kept a portable siren in the blast area; it was right in Kanan's path. He activated it. All across Zone Forty-Two, workers charged for the exit tunnels to the west.

Ahead of him, Yelkin stumbled across the craggy surface and fell. Kanan, on a headlong run, slowed as he approached the miner—the only other soul left in the enormous crystal atrium. But Yelkin wasn't asking for help. He was pointing, instead, to something Kanan had forgotten about.

"Kanan! Your cart!"

Kanan looked back at the hovercart with its full load of baradium bisulfate—a hundred times more material than Skelly would have been carrying in his kit—and remembered the demolition guys' adage: *It's the secondary that does the damage.* His cart could bring down half the cave network.

Kanan bounded back toward the opening—and its ticking bomb inside—and seized the hovercart. Turning with it, he ran, pushing it as fast as he could across the long clearing.

Yelkin wasn't moving, he saw—he'd twisted his ankle. Kanan pointed the cart toward him as his boots pounded the surface. His voice echoed across the chamber: "Yelkin! Grab for it!"

It wasn't easy to see or hear much after that.

Light from the blast came first. Emanating into the work area from the blasting tunnel, it reflected dazzlingly off the crystal structures above and to either side of Kanan. The sound came next, a muted boom. Kanan had just reached Yelkin with the crate-topped hover-cart when the shock wave hit him in mid-stride. The cart's repulsors were still working; its front bumper caught Yelkin in the gut—and now both they and the hovercart were carried forward, Kanan's hands locked onto the handle for dear life.

Searing cracks resounded across the atrium. Kanan, now a passenger hanging on like Yelkin, knew what was next. Like icicles on a summer day, meter-wide stalactites across the chamber began falling across the ground they'd already covered. First the crystal knives—and then the rock and stone suspended above them, all plummeting into the open space.

Seeing the first shard strike nearby, Kanan hit the ground with his heels for the first time in seconds. Without thinking, he leapt.

Leapt, as he hadn't in nearly a decade, farther than any mortal normally could. Leapt, atop the crates filled with deadly explosives on the careening cart. Leapt, to where he could reach out and grab the shoulder of the unaware Devaronian, clinging for dear life.

The western opening through which the other miners had evacuated was just ahead. Pulling the hapless Yelkin fully onto the hovercart in one motion, Kanan hit the ground off the left side with his next. Guiding the airborne vehicle like a wader moving a raft, he slung the cart toward the exit tunnel. He stumbled, a step shy of safety, as he tried to follow. Twisting faceup as he dropped, Kanan hit the ground. He looked up into the onrushing mass—

—and stopped it, with his mind.

It was an odd feeling, like putting on an old article of clothing. It was like the leap, something he had sworn never to do. Not in front of anyone, to be sure.

But now he had done it. All light was gone, but he could sense the black mass of debris quivering a meter from his head, even as he heard apocalyptic clamor all around. Instinctively, Kanan dug his heels into the tunnel floor and forced himself backward, the tail of his shirt grinding against the surface until he was fully inside the reinforced western tunnel.

And then he let go. Let go with his mind, and listened as a mountain, denied, found the space where he had landed.

Vidian was in an upper chamber addressing the droidmaster and his three terrified aides when the floor fell in.

Everything went dark as Vidian, his audience members, and all their furnishings tumbled downward. The fall was brief, with the remnants of what had been the floor beneath their feet smashing to pieces on the tougher surface below. An immense jolt rocked Vidian.

Up to his hips in stone, he took a moment to regain his bearings. His eyes switched to night-vision mode, and he realized that a sink-hole had opened beneath the droidmaster's office: The walls of the room, as well as the hallway leading from it, were intact, several meters above.

Disregarding the pained cries of the others struggling in the rubble, Vidian used his cybernetic arms to dig himself out. Then he began climbing for the aperture above.

"We're trapped down here," a voice called behind him. "Help us!"

"Someone will arrive before you starve," Vidian said, reaching for the bottom of the doorway.

"But there may be aftershocks—"

"Aftershocks? Impossible. This moon's crystal columns are supposed to prevent tremors," Vidian said. The event couldn't have been natural. Pulling himself up and into the intact hallway, he began to suspect what had happened.

His anger returned anew.

In the darkness, Hera felt the world rumbling around her. She'd seen Vidian fall through the floor and disappear; she'd lingered for a few moments, hoping he was gone for good.

No luck, she thought, hearing his voice from the recess up ahead. The moon had tasted him and spat him out.

She heard voices in the hallways around her, and spied portable lights flashing this way and that. There was too much activity now—someone had kicked the insect nest. She needed to use the darkness while she could.

Recon's over, the Twi'lek thought. She turned from Vidian's chamber and ran back up the hall.

Kanan continued to force himself backward as debris struck the ground behind him. Finally, after what seemed like an eon, stillness came.

And then the work lights.

Okadiah arrived at his side and knelt. "Lad? You all right?"

Kanan coughed up dust and nodded. Blinking particles from his eyes, he vaguely saw his hovercart, its securely fastened crates of explosives still there. Yelkin lay facedown atop it, wheezing.

"What happened?" Okadiah asked.

"I didn't see," Yelkin said. He looked back at the rubble-blocked passage. "I guess we caromed into the tunnel! I thought we were goners, for sure!"

"A million-to-one shot," Okadiah said, scratching his chin. He looked at Kanan. "My boy, you *are* the lucky one."

Kanan knew he was anything but lucky. For Kanan Jarrus was Caleb Dume, the Jedi who never was.

And now, he knew, it was time to go.

CHAPTER NINE

THE FORCE WAS A MYSTERIOUS energy field that sprang from life itself; that much, every Jedi student knew. The Force could be used for many purposes: protection, persuasion, wisdom—even the manipulation of matter and the performance of great physical feats. Jedi taught younglings all of those things.

But they never taught how to make the Force go away when it wasn't wanted. That was all Caleb—all *Kanan* had wanted from the Force for years. And the blasted thing had just shown up again on Cynda. It had saved his carcass, true—but if anyone had seen, Kanan's life wouldn't be worth a Confederacy credit.

He had left a moon in chaos. Zone Forty-Two's ceiling had caved in, producing tremors that caused dangerous seams to open in some floors higher up. Thankfully, no chambers had vented to space: They were too far beneath Cynda's surface. It was a miracle no one had been killed.

Kanan didn't know if Count Vidian was still there or not, or if the Empire suspected Skelly of planting the charges that caused the collapse. It was a safe bet they did. It was mining in Zone Forty-Two that

Skelly had warned about; perhaps he'd decided to bring the roof down before anybody else did. Cynda was laced with tunnels, but the Imperials had numbers. They'd find Skelly eventually, and he'd get what was coming to him.

Kanan had used one of those back tunnels to slip away, leaving Okadiah and his crew behind. Taking little-used elevators back to *Expedient,* he'd raised ship before security knew any better. He could hear over the transceiver that departures had been grounded. He doubted it would be a problem. The Moonglow techs below would vouch for his having warned them; no one would suspect Kanan of having planted the bomb, at least. He was just returning his ship safely to home base, on Gorse, like he was scheduled to do.

And that would be it. He'd never set foot on the moon again. And tomorrow, he'd find a way off Gorse. It was time to move on.

He'd been in motion since that dark day, years earlier. The darkest of days. The day when life as he knew it had fallen apart, had been blasted apart, by something he hadn't then understood. He still didn't understand much of it. There he'd been, fourteen years old, having relied for his entire life on the Jedi Order for everything: food, shelter, education, and security. Maybe not love, but at least stability, calm, sense.

And then, all at once, the Republic and its clone soldiers had turned against the Jedi. Depa Billaba fought to protect him—and he fought to protect her. She died. He fled. She died *so* he could flee, but to what end? What did she hope for him?

The young Caleb hadn't known. He'd known only that, in the end, the Force hadn't helped her. Or any of the other Jedi he'd heard about.

It's not your friend, he'd told himself. It was one reason he refused to use it, even to make his life a little easier. He'd also refused to take up his lightsaber. He still had it: Besides the finicky Force, it was his last tie to the past. But what good were lightsabers? What good was the Force, if it allowed its most devoted followers to be cut down by rank betrayal?

"A Jedi uses the Force for guidance," his first teacher had said. *Yeah, guidance right into a freaking wall!*

The problem was that the Force couldn't be turned off like a switch. Many of the benefits it conveyed were subtle. They enhanced traits without his conscious effort. No act of will could make it stop; no lapse of belief could make it fully vanish. Kanan would always be better at some things. And that had been the problem of his life. He was still driven to take jobs that interested him, and to excel at them. That was just his way.

But excelling by too much, or for too long, risked notice. And that was something he had been told to avoid.

Obi-Wan had used the beacon to warn Jedi to avoid detection. It hadn't taken long for Kanan to understand why. For days and weeks after the Jedi generals had been cut down by their own clone troopers, the new Empire continued to hunt and kill Jedi. It wasn't just about hiding physically from the Empire. *Avoid detection* meant hiding from everyone the fact that he had a connection to the Force.

The Force was a death mark.

The early months had been a blur of terror for young Caleb. He'd lived constantly with nightmares of what could happen. The Empire had control of the Jedi headquarters. That surely included the database with whatever information the Jedi had on file for Caleb Dume. They would have learned his name, for sure, and likely had images of him taken by the training center's security cams. What else did they have? He'd racked his brain many times trying to remember what, if any, biometric information the Jedi had taken from him over the years. Did they have a soundprint of his voice? A genetic sample? It bewildered Kanan now to think that the Empire might know more about his family history than he did.

Whatever had happened to the other Jedi Knights and their Padawans, he had to assume the Emperor would have been thorough about it. They'd have found a list, or constructed one. They'd have marked off everyone who fell. And they would've known Caleb Dume did not fall when Depa Billaba did.

So in the beginning, Caleb did everything right. When he took jobs to feed himself, he made sure not to excel too far beyond the expected norm. Personally distributing his own payloads on Cynda was a holdover from that; it kept his number of flights per day to a number that was merely exceptional, and not suspicious. He'd resisted friendships and long-term romantic connections, and he'd mostly restrained his chivalrous impulses. The teenager had done all those things, for fear of a middle-of-the-night visit by stormtroopers.

But weeks turned to months, and months to years, and no one came to his home—or cot, or tent, or patch of spacecraft floor—to wake him and drag him away. And the young man now known as Kanan Jarrus discovered that carousing eliminated those worries entirely.

So he'd done more of the same. He'd drunk to forget. He'd brawled to let off steam. He'd taken the dangerous jobs to fund his lifestyle— and then began it all again. He wasn't some chivalrous nomad, skulking from planet to planet doing good deeds and leaving when things got too hot. No, he left when things got *dull*. When the drinking money ran out, or when the bar-owner's daughter suddenly wanted to marry him. Kanan didn't leave because the Empire moved in: He'd stared down Imperials like Vidian before and lived. They knew he was something to ignore. No, he left because where the Empire went, fun usually died.

And he also left whenever he got too comfortable. That was when the Force, tired of being suppressed, would sneak back like an ignored pet. He didn't want it complicating his world, making him feel like somebody's prey again. And he didn't like being reminded about what had happened in that other life.

Watching *Ultimatum* growing in his cockpit window as he headed for Gorse, Kanan thought for the umpteenth time about the text portion of the message from Obi-Wan. *Republic forces have been turned against the Jedi.* There was something in that wording: *have been turned.* It suggested that maybe the people themselves hadn't turned against the Jedi, despite the Emperor's claims to the contrary.

That might have mattered years earlier, Kanan thought, but it hardly did now.

He had always been aggravated by how little Obi-Wan had shared. It made sense that he'd been short of time. And perhaps he hadn't known much, yet, when he sent the warning. But why hadn't he sent another? If he didn't have access to the beacon on Coruscant any longer, wouldn't he have found another way to get a message out, later on?

Kanan knew the answer. *Because there probably aren't any Jedi left to contact. And because Kenobi's probably dead himself.*

At one time, those had been hard thoughts to have; now they only produced a tired yawn. He couldn't see Obi-Wan willingly hunkering down on some remote world, waiting for things to blow over. He'd have had a mission, if he were alive—an important one. He'd want people to know about it. And all the missions Kanan could imagine would have put Obi-Wan into motion all around the galaxy. No, if Kenobi lived, Kanan would have heard something.

But Kanan knew he wouldn't care even if the Jedi Master popped up in the seat right behind him. Caleb Dume hadn't yet been a Jedi Knight, and Kanan Jarrus wasn't one now. None of it affected him, need *ever* affect him. He'd been dealt his hand, and that was what he would play. Play, for as long he could keep from stupid stunts like the one he'd pulled on Cynda.

He just wouldn't play *here* anymore.

He would return *Expedient* to Moonglow; it would be a dumb starship thief indeed that would want it. He'd collect his back pay, gather his few goods before Okadiah got home, and be on his way. The Star Destroyer was still out there, he saw, but it hadn't yet barred commercial flights from Gorse. He would pick a direction and be on his—

Kanan took a second look at the Star Destroyer, now ahead and to his right. From *Ultimatum*'s underside, two four-vehicle flights of TIE fighters emerged and headed in his direction.

Snapped alert, Kanan leaned forward and grabbed the steering yoke. Which way? They were headed right for *Expedient*. The ship had a little rock-shooter of a cannon, nothing more, and the vessel hadn't been refueled since that morning, four lunar flights earlier. Kanan switched the comm system from channel to channel, listening for Captain Sloane's voice. Someone, something to tell him whether he needed to fight or fly.

The voice he did hear came from the backseat—but it wasn't Obi-Wan Kenobi, or even kindly old Okadiah. "They're not after you," it said. "They're looking for me."

Kanan looked back.

Skelly!

CHAPTER TEN

"YOU!" **KANAN GRABBED** at Skelly's collar, yanking him violently forward and slamming him against the top of *Expedient*'s dashboard. Kanan's first instinct was to deal with the stowaway—but the Imperials were still out there, still heading in his direction.

"Look!" Skelly said, gasping for breath, arms flailing.

Kanan followed the upside-down man's gaze and saw, past the TIE squadrons, a *Lambda*-class shuttle departing *Ultimatum*. As its trapezoidal wings folded into flight position, another one followed. And then another—until five shuttles were heading in Kanan's direction. Two TIEs from each group broke formation and moved to flank the shuttles as the others continued ahead, clearing the space lanes. Kanan watched, disbelieving, as the vessels passed over his head on the way to Cynda.

"I told you, they're all looking for me," Skelly said. "Not you."

"Congratulations," Kanan said drily. He didn't let Skelly up. "There's about to be a hundred more stormtroopers on Cynda, thanks to you. I'm tempted to send you back to them!"

Skelly wrested free—and Kanan gave him a hard smack. Blood spurted from Skelly's nose. "You jerk! What did you do that for?"

"You blew up Zone Forty-Two. You tried to kill us!"

"I didn't!" Skelly said, wresting free.

"You're lying!" Kanan grabbed Skelly's left arm and twisted it behind his back. Turning, he started to shove the unwanted guest toward the airlock. "They're looking for you? I'm giving you back to them!"

"Watch it! Not that arm! Not that arm!" Skelly said. Putting his free hand—his mechanical hand—before him, he grabbed on to a handle near the airlock door. After a few moments' scuffling, Kanan realized the hand was in a death grip, and that Skelly wouldn't be going anywhere.

"Fine," Kanan said. He turned and grabbed his holster, which had been hanging on the back of his pilot's seat.

Skelly looked back and sneered. "What, are you going to shoot me now?"

"Maybe."

"That's gratitude! *I saved you!*"

Kanan had the blaster fully out of the holster when he finally registered what Skelly had said. "Wait. What?"

"I saved you," Skelly said. "You and your whole rotten corporate bunch!"

"Saved—" Kanan was flabbergasted. "You brought a mountain down on my head!"

Skelly went silent.

Aggravated, Kanan stood and turned back to the controls to direct *Expedient* onto a path well away from any other convoys, Imperial or otherwise. He glanced back to see Skelly slumped against the airlock door, massaging a hand that had finally come free from the handle.

Kanan lowered his pistol but didn't put it away. Suddenly exhausted, he dropped onto the acceleration couch facing the airlock. "I need a drink," he said, rubbing his forehead. "Now, tell me this again. You were saving us by *blowing us up?*"

"I wasn't trying to blow you up. I was trying to show the Imperial inspectors we shouldn't use baradium to open new chambers. Cynda can't take it."

"You could've killed people!" Kanan said.

"No, no," Skelly said. "You Moonglow guys weren't supposed to be working Forty-Two until tomorrow. I saw Boss Lal's schedule earlier!"

"That was the schedule before the Empire got here. We were working double time. We weren't on today's schedule anymore."

"*Oh,*" Skelly said in an awkward, small voice. "Er—so, *did* anyone die?"

"Glad you care," Kanan said, reaching for his shoulder holster and putting it on. "No. Not that I know of."

"Good," Skelly said. "I was just trying to prove a point—and it worked." He tugged at his collar. "The joint caved in, just like I said. If they've told Vidian I was right, he's probably looking for me now to thank me." He gestured with his left hand to the cockpit window. "That's what all the ships are about. They think I'm down there still. Search-and-rescue!"

"Uh-huh. Which is why you stowed away, instead of staying there."

"I needed a place to wait while the Empire figured out what happened. I had no idea you'd come back so fast and take off!"

Kanan shook his head and holstered his blaster. He didn't know what to believe. But before he could say anything, Skelly got to his feet and walked forward like a man with a purpose.

Kanan stood. "What do you think you're doing?"

"What do you think I'm doing? I'm hailing the Star Destroyer!"

Kanan did a double take. "What?"

"I told you, they're looking for me." Skelly reached for a button, only to be shoved into the passenger seat by Kanan.

Reaching for the seat's restaint harness, Kanan snapped Skelly in. Then he pulled out his blaster again.

"Hey! Don't shoot!"

Kanan didn't shoot. Instead, he activated the safety and turned the blaster over in his hand. Using the butt of the handle as a hammer, he pounded Skelly's harness buckle until it was bent out of shape.

"You broke it. I can't believe you did that."

"It's not my ship," Kanan said. Or it wouldn't be, after he landed. The harness would keep Skelly in place now. "I'm not letting you hail the blasted Star Destroyer!"

Skelly shook his head. "You still don't get it." With his left hand, he reached inside his vest and pulled out the holodisk he'd shown Kanan earlier. "I just need to take this information to Vidian—"

"Vidian." Kanan sat down in the pilot's seat, his head spinning. "That weird guy the Empire sent?"

"Don't you follow the news? Vidian's a fixer. He's like me—he sees what's wrong and he takes care of it. He's probably suspending all work on Cynda right now for an investigation. All I have to do is get in touch with him, show him my facts. He'll whip those corporate hacks into shape!"

Kanan looked out at *Ultimatum,* shrinking in the starboard window—and then back at Skelly. "You really think that's what'll happen?"

"Sure. Once they see what I have to show them, they might even reward you for bringing me in."

Kanan looked back to the controls—and then up. There, from the darkness of Gorse's permanent nightside, he saw something familiar rising into space.

"There's your response," he said.

"What?" Skelly turned his head. He saw dozens of ships: empty cargo vessels, personnel transports, and explosives haulers like *Expedient.* All were headed to Cynda. "The next shift?"

Kanan laughed. "So much for the Skelly Memorial Holiday."

He turned on the comm system. The Imperial traffic was all scrambled, but Boss Lal was talking on Moonglow's dedicated channel. Work zones affected by the collapse were being cordoned off, but mining operations would continue in the other areas. "Count Vidian's orders," she said, launching into a list of rerouted landing instructions.

Listening, Skelly was dumbfounded—but only for a moment. "They've just seen what blasting in the wrong place can do. And they're keeping on?" Shaking with rage, he spat three words Kanan could tell Skelly hated. *"Business as usual."*

Kanan snapped off the comm system and stretched back in his chair.

Skelly, unable to move, stared at him. "Well?"

"Well, what?"

"Well, now what?"

"I'm going home," Kanan said.

"Home?" Skelly asked. "Where's home?"

"I'm taking *Expedient* to Moonglow's shipyard, like always. I'm going to park the ship, and I'm going to turn you over to that security chief husband of Lal's." Kanan turned his attention to flying the ship.

Skelly shook his head and lowered his voice. "Some friend you are!"

Kanan bolted upright in his seat and turned. "Let's get something straight," he said, jabbing a finger in Skelly's direction. "I'm not your friend. I'm not your accomplice, and I'm certainly not your co-conspirator. I didn't help you in this, and I am not going to help you get out of it. I'm done!"

Skelly looked at Kanan for a few moments—and then turned his head away. "Great," he growled. "It's just like always. Nobody ever—"

In the window, Skelly caught the reflection of Kanan standing up. He turned his head to see Kanan walking into the back. "Wait, where are you going now?"

"Somewhere I can't hear you."

Safely back aboard her starship, Hera sent the encrypted message to her contact on Gorse. She was more certain than ever that a meeting was necessary. That the Empire spied on workplaces in a system that produced a strategic material was no surprise. But it had no qualms about using such technologies everywhere, and her contact could tell her a lot about the latest Imperial surveillance capabilities and how to defeat them. She had to risk the meeting, whether she got another chance to spy on Vidian or not.

Hera studied the scene outside. Listening, she took everything in. The Empire was encrypting its own signals, but the mining companies weren't, and she had gotten a clear picture of the hours that had just passed on Cynda.

A miner tagged as a troublemaker or dissident had been identified by Imperial surveillance. But Skelly the demolitions guy had surprised his employers, the Empire, and everyone else by using explosives in order to escape arrest. And not long after that, the big explosion had occurred in a work area—unscheduled, and evidently far more destructive than anything to be found in normal operations.

The Empire had hustled then, sending more than half the Star Destroyer's complement of troop shuttles to Cynda. Since no medical ships were on the way from Gorse—the moon's clinic was limited— she had to assume there were no casualties. That meant the stormtroopers sure to be on the shuttles weren't part of search-and-rescue. They were there to continue looking for the bomber.

But in between the reports of the blast and the Imperial scramble, she'd noticed something else. An explosives hauler—Moonglow-72, by the call sign—had been the only ship besides hers to depart Cynda before the grounding order came. She'd seen it jerk violently when the TIE formations approached—and while the sight of the Imperial fighters might have that effect on any simple tradesbeing, the ship had flown unusually after that, as if no one was piloting. Finally, it had settled on an approach to Gorse that kept well away from the most traveled lanes.

Skelly, Hera concluded, was on that transport.

It was more than a guess, but it was hardly a scientific deduction. She didn't want to let it deter her from her real goals. Her connection on Gorse, she now saw, had just responded to confirm their meeting for later. That was the important thing.

But as she was now going in Skelly's direction anyway, Hera decided it wouldn't hurt to find out what his story was . . .

CHAPTER ELEVEN

KANAN HAD LIVED with secret stress every day for years without showing it. It was out of necessity in his case, but it was also a choice. Gloom attracted gloom, as he saw it. Acting like a victim only made things worse.

Gorse and Cynda were a case study. The gravitational dance between the two worlds put both under constant stress, but Gorse wore it worse. Cynda, with its crystal lattice innards, kept it together, foolish acts of sabotage notwithstanding. Gorse, with mud on the surface and mush beneath, suffered incessant groundquakes as Cynda made her close approach. It didn't help residents' attitudes that everyone was trapped in permanent night.

But even a rattled loser could catch a break, and Gorse got one every full moon. Cynda sat huge and glorious in the sky for standard days on end. Streetlights were doused. Crime decreased, marginally. And living on Gorse didn't seem so bad.

Cynda was a few days from full, Kanan saw as he stepped off *Expedient*'s ramp onto the tarmac. He wouldn't stick around to see it. Looking toward the cluster of low buildings ahead, he spied an approaching burly figure with four arms and multiple holsters slung around his midsection. It was Gord Grallik, Boss Lal's security chief husband. Gord was a decent sort, Kanan thought: capable, if a bit doting on his wife.

"Kanan. Heard about the collapse—glad you're safe."

"I'm staying that way," Kanan said, reaching for his ID badge. "Give my ship to someone else."

"I don't blame you," Gord said. He put two of his hands up, rejecting the badge. "You should talk to Lal first. She'd hate to see you go."

"Not changing my mind."

"Go across to Cousin Drakka's and get a meal. Lal should be down here by the time you're finished." Gord looked up at the moon and shook his head. "I'm sure she's worn out."

Kanan's mind was still back on the mention of food. He'd have to see Lal to get his final pay, anyway. Remembering something else, he snapped his fingers. "Oh, and I brought you a farewell gift."

Gord followed Kanan up the ramp into the ship. There, in the front passenger seat, sat Skelly, still bound to the seat. He had a rag stuffed in his mouth and hatred in his eyes.

"*Mmmph! Mrrppph!*"

"What in—" Gord put a hand over his own mouth.

"There's your mad bomber," Kanan said. "No bounty requested."

Gord laughed heartily. Everyone around Moonglow knew about Skelly. The security chief examined the smashed restraint buckle. "I'll have to cut him out of there."

"I suggest taking the seat out and him with it," Kanan said, patting Gord on the shoulder as he turned to leave. "You don't want the rag to fall out of his mouth. He'll just start talking again."

Count Vidian sat alone in the troop compartment of *Cudgel* as it rose from Cynda. The newly arrived shuttles had landed behind him, and there was no more point staying on the moon. The stormtroopers, including his escort, had remained to investigate.

Whatever had happened down in Zone Forty-Two, it had left several areas unworkable. If it had been a deliberate act of sabotage, Vidian's forces would find out. And if the one responsible had lived, well, he would find that out, too. Either the stormtroopers would find the culprit on Cynda, or Transcept's surveillance assets would locate him on Gorse. There was no third possibility. The Empire could not be resisted.

No—it *should* not be resisted. The Empire was the only way.

The Empire, Vidian understood, was the logical result of a thousand years of galactic government. For centuries, the Republic had expanded not through force, but by quietly exerting a powerful magnetic pull on bordering systems. The promise of trade with Core World markets had great value, and the prospect inexorably lured nonmember worlds into ever-tighter cooperation with the body.

But the Republic was often slow to invite new systems in. The addition of territories tended to diminish the political power of existing senators. New members invariably aligned themselves with blocs in their own galactic neighborhood—yet most senators who controlled the invitations represented worlds near the Core. The Republic repelled even as it attracted. And there were other constituencies that had slowed expansion. Republic bureaucrats disliked the expense of extending services and protection to the hinterlands. The result was that many useful star systems were left waiting, some for centuries, on the Republic's political doorstep, even though it came at the cost of the body's overall power.

To Vidian's mind, Emperor Palpatine had brought sanity to the Republic's growth policies. In standing up to the secessionists as chancellor, he'd signaled the Republic was no longer some social club that could be exited at will. That move had attracted Vidian's attention, and his financial support. Now, as Emperor, Palpatine had shown an eagerness—no, a *zeal*—when it came to expansion. The Core Worlds had always been the heart of the Republic, drawing nutrients from the periphery. The Emperor had taken that biological model and refined it, improved it. The Empire was growing robustly, with the fat of bureaucracy no longer clogging its arteries and veins. A single brain was directing it, not an aggregation of minds with conflicting ideas.

The Emperor had done everything right—so far. Selecting the

count to represent his interests was his best decision yet. Surely no one could be more effective in advancing the Emperor's goals. Vidian was the perfect Imperial man, seeing without sentiment, reshaping what he found, and moving on.

He had but one ritual he held to—and even it was purely practical. Seated in the low light, hearing only the normal pings from the cockpit and whirs from the Lambda's guts, Vidian commanded his lungs to let out a deep breath. His prosthetic eyes no longer had lids, nor any need for them, so he set them to display nothing. What Vidian did required as few distractions as possible.

Vidian's mind was his most powerful asset—and yet, he dealt every day with its limitations. His artificial eyeballs recorded the sights of his entire waking life, but their storage capacity was limited: The data had to be purged every sleep cycle. Where Vidian had once dreamed in images, now, when he slept, he lost them.

More invasive cybernetic technologies existed that might have given Vidian near-total recall, allowing him to process all the information he had at his disposal. But he had decided against upgrading, afraid to risk harming whatever brain chemistry gave him his extraordinary genius. An irrational fear, perhaps—but while he'd never believed in the Jedi's mystical Force, he did allow that some things might defy logic where the mind was concerned.

So every evening Vidian sat as he did now, reviewing the day's events and deciding which images to commit to permanent storage. Cargo vessels en route to Cynda, yes. The backs of others' heads in countless corridors, no.

He didn't preserve the images of the death of the guildmaster. He knew no repercussions would come from it, and he didn't take undue joy from violence, apart from the satisfaction he always felt in setting a failing enterprise aright. He saved the image of the old man he'd confronted, to remind him to follow up on the new age restrictions, but he deleted the face of the foolish gunslinger. The old man's rescuer was likely just another roisterer, too brave for sense. There wasn't anything special there, either.

But the word the man had said: *Moonglow.* That gave Vidian pause. He'd seen the name of Moonglow Polychemical for the first time while doing his advance research on Gorse. He'd paid it little mind. It was a small firm, probably a start-up—or maybe a piece of a broken-up conglomerate, being run now by its old employees. That trick never worked, he thought. Why did people always insist on trying to reanimate the dead?

Calling up the company's files over the HoloNet, however, he was surprised by its numbers. The blaster-toting fool was right about its efficiency. The firm's production targets were lower, relative to the other corporations, but it was the only one coming anywhere close to meeting them. Maybe there was something there, he thought: some ideas to steal for the other manufacturers.

Scraping ideas from the bottom of the bin, Vidian thought. It galled him that the state of things on Gorse was such that he'd have to resort to—

"Message from Coruscant, my lord."

At the sound of the captain's voice, Vidian's eyes flickered and reset themselves, and *Cudgel*'s passenger area reappeared around him. "Patch it through."

A figure appeared before him in holographic form. Rugged and sharply dressed, the blond young man placed his hands together and bowed. "Count Vidian! Wonderful to see you."

"What is it, Baron?"

Vidian had pleasantries for few—and none at all for Baron Lero Danthe of Corulag. The wealthy scion of a droid-making dynasty had a sinecure in Imperial administration but was always angling to turn it into something more, usually at Vidian's expense. As now. "The Emperor has embarked on several amazing new initiatives," Danthe said, beaming. "We need more thorilide."

"I already know the quotas—"

"Those are the old quotas. The Emperor desires more." Danthe's eyes widened with happy malice. "Fifty percent more per week."

"*Fifty?*"

"I told the Emperor you were on the scene, and that if anyone could do it, you could."

"I'm sure." Vidian knew Danthe could never have said such a thing: It didn't involve stabbing the cyborg in the back.

"Of course, if my droid factories can help in any way, you have but to—"

"Vidian out." He cut the transmission.

He was still steaming a minute later when he felt the thump indicating the shuttle had arrived on *Ultimatum*'s landing deck. There weren't any "new initiatives," Vidian knew: It was all Danthe's doing, part of his continued pursuit of the count's position in the Empire. Vidian had thwarted the upstart at every turn in the past, but this was something else. Given what Vidian had seen on Cynda, even 5 percent improvement would be a challenge.

Holding a datapad, Captain Sloane met him at the foot of the landing ramp. "You asked for updates every half hour on the chamber collapse," she said. "We've confirmed it was intentional. A blasting team located a device set by the fugitive Skelly."

Vidian wasn't surprised. "The team survived. How did *they* escape?"

"Somebody played hero," she said. "We're trying to find out how—"

"Forget it," Vidian said, looking through the magnetically screened landing bay entrance into space. After a few long moments, he nodded. "It's time for the next phase."

"Of the inspection, you mean?"

Vidian looked back at her. "Of course. It's what we're here for. The thorilide mines on the moon are only part of the problem. The refineries must be put in order. I must go to Gorse."

Sloane blinked. "I had thought you'd decided it was more efficient to meet with the planetary managers here, by hologram."

"I know what I decided. Don't question me!" A second passed, and he lowered his voice's volume. "My plans have changed. I'll need your assistance on the ground."

"I'm ... not sure what you mean, my lord. Planetary security should be able to coordinate your efforts."

"Captain, I have many more steps to take that will not be popular with the *masses*," he said, hitting the last word with particular disdain. "As we've just seen, they need to know my moves have the full weight of Imperial might." He studied her and thought for a moment before continuing. "You're helming *Ultimatum* only while Captain Karlsen is detached elsewhere, no?"

Sloane averted her eyes a little. "Yes, my lord. There are more captains than postings."

"Then we must build Star Destroyers faster. Perhaps Karlsen can return to one of those, instead—while you keep *Ultimatum*."

She looked up at him. "But he's more senior."

"I hold some sway in certain quarters. Serve me well, and you may find this a permanent position."

Sloane gulped, before straightening. "Thank you, my lord." She saluted needlessly and departed.

Vidian turned to look into space. Gorse was down there, in darkness as it always was; only the lights occasionally peeking through the clouds gave any indication that the black body wasn't just another part of the void.

Gorse had been a disappointment to him before—in ways nobody knew about. And now, it and its lazy workers threatened to do more than disappoint.

But he would deal with it. Efficiently, as only he could.

CHAPTER TWELVE

IT HAD BEEN, bar none, the worst work shift in Zaluna's memory.

The new security condition had been executed earlier, quadrupling the surveillance workload on Myder's Mynocks. Imperial security officials, an occasional sight in the elevators of World Window Plaza, were crawling all over the place—and more startling to Zaluna was the presence of stormtroopers in the building. All were following leads generated by her office and others, preparing to round up troublemakers in advance of what she'd gathered was Count Vidian's impending visit to Gorse.

There had been visits to Gorse's factories by bigwigs before, but none on this scale. Vidian's role in the Emperor's administration was no secret. He'd been a wealthy entrepreneur before joining the Imperial cabinet. The poor planet and its moon of riches were recent additions to his portfolio: He'd never set foot on Gorse before, so far as she knew. So if the security steps were exceptional, they were at least explainable. Gorse needed to put on a good show for the new boss. That the boss himself had ordered the measures was only added in-

ducement. The Sec-Con One had created a frenzy, true—but an ordered one.

While her Mynocks scanned Cynda's caverns for Skelly, Zaluna
had looked for the dark-haired character she'd seen Skelly arguing
with earlier in the elevator, in case he might know something. A
Transcept file hadn't been started on him—it took a while for migrant workers to get one—but she knew she'd seen him several times
via various cams in recent weeks. The Rugged Pilot, she'd called him:
always steering his cart and minding his own business—except when
he wasn't.

She had just found the pilot's name in the Moonglow personnel
records when she caught him on a Cynda cam, saving an old man
from abuse by the frightening Count Vidian. Vidian, who had earlier
done *something* to the guildmaster: The cams couldn't see what, but
Palfa had immediately turned up dead, and Vidian had remotely ordered the records of their meeting purged. It was the sort of thing
that happened far too frequently these days.

So for standing up against Vidian, Zaluna had decided to reward
Kanan Jarrus by leaving him alone. He'd already been intimidated
enough for one day.

Work had proceeded normally for a while. Then came news of the
explosion and collapse in Cynda's mines—and everything went berserk.

Now the Imperials were on the work floor, quizzing Zaluna and
going over recordings of events on the moon. They'd been at it for
hours. While public reports from Cynda held that the collapse had
been a natural phenomenon, the officers clearly thought a bomber
was responsible and had already taken all the files on Skelly and a
dozen other potential suspects known to have been on the moon.
Making things worse for the Mynocks was the fact that few in the
mining community seemed to believe the cover story—which just
resulted in even more borderline seditious statements for her team to
evaluate. It seemed as if every miner preparing to leave Cynda for the
day had said *something* about it in a monitored place.

And the mere presence of the stormtroopers was rattling everyone. Intellectually, Zaluna knew the white-clad figures were on the side of peace and order, but there was no doubting how intimidating they looked. What must it be like to have them come to your home or workplace? She'd always wondered.

They'd all found out. Hetto, normally a source for tiny treasons in the safety of the office or during the isolation of his walks with Zaluna, was clearly nervous. He'd said nothing since the Imperials entered the room, keeping his dark eyes fixed straight ahead on his work whenever the officers came near.

And once, as she'd walked through his aisle, he'd reached out to tug at her sleeve. "Are they talking about me?" he whispered.

"You? Why would—"

"Never mind."

She thought she knew why he was worried. If Skelly had indeed done harm on the moon, her team would get the blame for not flagging him sooner. But the remedy to that was obvious: vindication. And so she continued running her searches of Cynda's surveillance network, hoping to catch sight of Skelly.

Then Zaluna had a flash of insight. *Gorse!*

She paused her search of the lunar surveillance cam feeds and started a new scan of Gorse, instead. The routine took less than a minute to find a vocal and retinal match.

"Got him," Zaluna announced. Down on the work floor, the visiting Imperials paused in their conversations. "Skelly's on Gorse. Moonglow Polychemical's offices, over in Shaketown." It was one of the covert feeds, coming off the corporate security cams.

"Here on Gorse?" The lead officer sounded alarmed. "How did he get down to the planet?" The burly lieutenant stomped up the steps to Zaluna's dais and unceremoniously pushed past her. "Let me see. Out of my way, creature!"

Zaluna thought to stomp on the rude officer's foot. Instead she listened in on her earpiece. "They've taken Skelly into custody. The factory manager's contacting planetary security now." That was plainly the case, from the images: She and the officer could clearly see Skelly secured to a chair and being watched by a Besalisk guard. She'd seen the guard many times over the years.

The lieutenant turned and barked an order, and three of the storm-troopers left the room. "Inform *Ultimatum*," he said to one of his remaining aides as he brushed past and exited her platform.

The boss saves the day again, Zaluna thought. She exhaled, hoping against hope that the uncomfortable moments for the staff had passed. It wasn't any easier on the watchers than the watched, and she'd never seen poor Hetto looking so rattled. She turned to face his workstation, hoping to find him relieved.

She didn't find him at all.

Zaluna looked around for a few moments before realizing he was behind her, peering up at her through her shelves of plants. He'd gone around to the opposite side of the platform, out of earshot of the Imperials.

"You startled me," she said with a relieved grin. "Thinking of taking up gardening?" Hetto was trying—and failing—to be nonchalant, she thought, pawing through the soil of her yellow stasias.

"They're not leaving," he said softly.

Zaluna cast a quick glance over her shoulder. The gaggle of agents was still off to the side, talking furtively about something. She looked back at Hetto reassuringly. "Don't worry. We found Skelly again."

"That's not it." He looked up at her. "Act like you dropped something."

Hearing uncharacteristic seriousness in his voice, Zaluna lifted one of the pots from the upper surface and knelt, pretending to change the saucer beneath the plant. That brought her face-to-face with Hetto, who reached through the rails and took her hands. "Zaluna, I've . . . gotten *involved* with something. There's someone I've been chatting with on the HoloNet about—never mind. I'm meeting—*was going* to meet her tonight."

"Wait. What are you—"

He moved her hands onto the pot. "The address is on the note on the outside. Go alone. *Please,* Zal."

Zaluna looked down at the pot. Something was half buried in the soil, she saw. It resembled a data cube, a high-density storage medium. Her eyes narrowed, and she shook her head. *Some woman on the HoloNet?* "Oh, Hetto, what have you gotten yourself into?"

"Nothing you didn't know was coming." He dipped his head and spoke somberly—more seriously than she'd ever heard him speak before. "If my help's ever meant anything to you, you'll deliver this. And . . . I'm sorry." With that, he released her hands and departed from the railing.

Bewildered by the exchange, Zaluna picked up the pot and stood, looking to see which way Hetto had gone. He wasn't hard to find. The big Imperial was back again, having stopped Hetto in his tracks—and there were stormtroopers with him.

"You're Hetto?"

Hetto glared. "I am."

"You are under arrest."

"On what charge?"

"Sedition. We have a record of your comments—comments intended to disturb order." The lieutenant yanked at Hetto's shoulder. "All made while working here—*here!* You've abused the trust of the Galactic Empire!"

Hetto's upper lip curled in defiance. "Galactic Empire? I think you're confused. Didn't you see the sign on the building? I work for Transcept Media Solutions!"

"Same difference! You work for us—and we won't have traitors in our midst." The lieutenant's eyes narrowed beneath bushy red eyebrows, and he looked about suspiciously. "And what about the rest of you? Perhaps you people didn't overlook the bomber on Cynda. Perhaps you *all* looked the other way!"

A shocked rumble came from the other members of the surveillance team. Zaluna moved forward to defend her people. "Now, wait a minute! This team has done everything the Empire has ever asked of it!"

"You'd better hope so." The lieutenant sneered. "Everything that happened here today will be reviewed. If there's anything to find, we'll find it." He gestured to Hetto. "We caught *him,* didn't we?"

Hetto tried to move, but the stormtroopers grabbed his arms. His smirk disappeared. "Hear that, Mynocks?" he announced. "You're all being watched, too." He glared at the lieutenant. "Watching us, watching everyone! Well, go ahead and review all you want. Nobody here had anything to do with your stupid mine collapse—not like you care!"

"Perhaps," the officer replied. "But you know the things you've said in the past about the Empire, Hetto. And so do we."

Zaluna stepped down from her platform, almost ready to take on the stormtroopers herself if she had to. "Hetto, I swear. I didn't know anything about this!"

Hetto looked at her and nodded. "I know, Zal. This isn't the only floor in this building. These days, everyone is watched. *Everyone*. I'm just an idiot."

With that, the lieutenant pointed toward the door, and the stormtroopers pushed Hetto ahead of them. Sounds of shock and dismay came from other employees.

Hetto looked back from the doorway—but not at Zaluna. His eyes were on the yellow plant on the top shelf. And then captors and prisoner were gone.

A hush fell over the work floor.

Eyes glistening, a young woman looked up at Zaluna. "Hetto's been with us for ten years."

"Twenty."

"What'll happen to him? You must know what . . . what goes on."

Zaluna straightened, too uncomfortable to look at anyone directly. "I try not to ask. All of us here—we're a tool that can stop bad things. Like we did—*could* have done—with that event on Cynda today." She shook her head. "I don't know about the rest."

Imperial agents reentered the room. "Back to work, Mynocks," Zaluna said, sounding resigned.

But she only sounded that way. Because after a moment's thought, she marched back up to her platform—and pretended to water her plants.

It was a data cube, all right. And buried with it was a small note, quickly scrawled in Hetto's hand. It bore the name of a local cantina. And one word:

HERA.

Hera would have to work fast.

It had taken her too long to find a place to park her starship. Gorse was a patchwork world, with one dead industry layered over another. The muddy ground wouldn't permit the towering skytowers of the city-canyon worlds; that left a horizontal urban sprawl that seemed to go forever. She'd finally found a spot between some abandoned buildings. Her route here had taken her from one bad neighborhood to another.

She'd arrived at Moonglow's headquarters only in time to see a Besalisk security guard and his helpers carrying someone bound to a starship acceleration seat out of the explosives hauler she'd tracked. They'd disappeared into the factory building after that; by then, Hera was sure the prisoner was Skelly.

Hera wanted to find out more about the man, but she still didn't know whether it was worth any effort. Skelly had evidently driven the Imperials up the wall, and that was a good thing. He might know something useful. Or he might be a waste of time. Her cause required a disciplined approach—not impulsive acts. Or people prone to them.

A corporate shuttle landed, discharging a female Besalisk—the head of operations here, Hera figured. Time was running out. A choice had to be made, and soon. She could see shadowy figures beginning to gather outside the building behind her: criminals, likely, now watching her. They were talking and pointing. Whatever their idea for her was, it was certainly no good.

But she got an idea for them, first.

CHAPTER THIRTEEN

NEVER MAKE A *life-changing decision on an empty stomach.* Good advice from Okadiah. But the food over at The Asteroid Belt was only edible in theory, and while Kanan Jarrus wasn't going to change his mind about leaving Gorse, he wasn't going to have his last meal come from picked-over snack bowls atop a bar. Especially not after the day he'd had.

That meant the diner by Moonglow. Just a few meters across Broken Boulevard—no one used the official name, Bogan—the establishment had survived years of hard times in the Shaketown neighborhood not just on the quality of its food but on the strength of its chef. Drakka's volatile temper had made him notoriously unemployable at his cousin Lal's mining firm, but it—and his four almost comically muscular arms—had made him eminently capable of dispatching any troublemakers.

He also made a mean bowl of stew. "Thanks," Kanan said, taking another steaming serving.

The cook didn't respond, keeping his bony beige headcrest down over his work as four massive hands worked the pots and pans.

"I'll miss these great conversations," Kanan added.

Drakka looked up long enough to growl, a creepy sound made creepier by the way the fleshy sac beneath his mouth fluttered. Then he returned to his cooking.

That was fine with Kanan. He prided himself on making it alone. Certainly, he talked to people every day: the people he had to deal with in order to get his job done. Mostly, though, he talked to no more than he absolutely had to. It wasn't because of the secrets of his past; it just suited him. People could be real pains.

Okadiah was the exception. The old man had been friendly from the start, offering a drifter a place to stay and, later, a job. Thorilide mining had left Gorse for Cynda, but the quarries on the south side of town remained, making for a lot of cheap real estate; Okadiah had opened his cantina there, in the neighborhood known as The Pits. He'd hired Kanan to drive his ancient hoverbus, running miners back and forth between the Moonglow facility and the bar. Later, he'd recommended Kanan for the job of flying explosives for Moonglow. No one on Gorse was as kindly to newcomers.

Even so, Kanan had kept the old man at arm's length. There had been someone like Okadiah on all the planets he'd visited: the one person willing to help a stranger, no questions asked. And Kanan had left all those worlds without saying good-bye to those people.

It might have been ironic, if Kanan bothered to think much about such things. The Jedi had always preached against forming connections, to prevent their acolytes from putting too much value in any one relationship. In so doing, they had unwittingly trained their students to be the perfect fugitives, able to cut and run at any moment. As long as they didn't stop to care, they could go on indefinitely.

Even so, Kanan thought as he ate, Okadiah was a little different. Kanan had never known his father; prospective Padawans tended to get plucked from their families very young. Kanan had only known mentors, like Master Billaba—and while he didn't know from experience, he suspected parents were different. Parents taught, too, but without all the judging. Good parents, anyway. And on that score, Okadiah had probably been more fatherlike than any of the other patrons Kanan had found in his travels. Okadiah didn't mind Kanan's prickly attitude, his drinking, or the hours he kept; the old man was right there with him, some of the time. And with dozens of workers on his mining detail, Okadiah could always point to someone worse on all those scores.

But for some reason, Okadiah hadn't treated him like just another member of the crew. The old man had seen something in him—what, Kanan didn't know—and he'd done everything right. Okadiah had never tried to push his help on the drifter; he'd left it to Kanan to decide what assistance to take.

It had worked—mostly. For while Kanan had never shared any secrets about his origin with the foreman, he had stayed on Gorse longer than he'd intended. The explosives hauler, bad as it was; the home across from the bar; and Okadiah, his host: They'd all made Gorse more livable than some of the other places he'd tried.

But he'd seen all the world had to offer. And there were plenty of things he wouldn't miss. One was in the doorway behind him.

"Suicide flier! You show your face here, after the last time?"

Kanan looked up at the mirror behind the grill, already knowing the speaker's identity. "Hello, Charko," he said. He felt for his shoulder holster but otherwise didn't move.

Charko, two meters of horned Chagrian meanness, wouldn't set foot in Drakka's Diner—the cook kept not one but four big blasters behind the counter. Instead, Charko just yelled like an idiot from the open front door. "We're waiting for you, pilot. Come out and play."

The Besalisk cook swore and moved toward his blasters. Charko didn't wait around. The door slammed shut. Unconcerned, Kanan finished his stew as Drakka rounded the counter, four weapons in four hands. A fully armed Besalisk defending his business was a great equalizer.

Charko never went anywhere without at least half a dozen members of his gang, the Sarlaccs. A sarlacc was a ravenous monster that was little more than a mouth; Kanan thought the name was properly descriptive. Charko's Sarlaccs had an endless appetite for the credits of anyone fool enough to wander the streets of the industrial area.

The gang activity had provided Okadiah with a business opportunity: opening his cantina across town and busing miners safely past the trouble spots.

Three times, Charko had tried—and failed—to separate Kanan from his hard-earned credits as he'd walked Broken Boulevard. The third time, Kanan had broken off one of the horns on Charko's head; the Chagrian had sworn revenge.

"They still out there?" Kanan asked without looking up.

"They've moved up the way to talk to someone," Drakka growled. "But yeah, they're still there. Idiots." He shut the door and returned to his cooking.

Well, no sense leaving unfinished business behind, Kanan thought as he wiped his face. He pushed back the bowl with one hand and drew his blaster with the other. Kanan walked cautiously to the entrance, blaster in hand. He nudged the door open with the tip of his boot.

"Hey, ugly!" he yelled. "Where'd you go?"

Outside, he spotted Charko's unmistakable one-horned silhouette as part of a shadowy gathering up the street. There were eight or nine of them, all members of Charko's band, but they were ignoring Kanan, talking to someone else.

Before Kanan could see more, the group quickly dispersed, breaking up into groups of three and heading off into the alleys, while whomever they'd been talking to remained, twenty meters up the street from Kanan.

Wearing a black cloak that gave no indication of the person beneath, the figure stood beneath the glare of the moon, watching not Kanan, but the Moonglow facility across the road. Clearly this wasn't one of the Sarlaccs.

Something told Kanan to holster his weapon. As he did so, the watcher turned toward him—and called out.

"Excuse me!" He couldn't see the speaker's face, but the voice was female, almost melodic. "Where can I find the repulsorlift entrance to Moonglow?"

The restless ground beneath Kanan's feet rumbled as she spoke, but he didn't hear it. He was still trying to process the voice, so warm and polite it was totally out of place on a Shaketown street. It startled him so much that he could only manage: "Huh?"

"Never mind," the figure said primly. "I'll find it myself."

With a whirl of her cloak, she headed off in the opposite direction.

Kanan, who had had no mission in life, now found himself with one: seeing who it was that could be attached to a voice like that. Gorse had one last surprise in store for him after all. It didn't matter that she'd been chatting amiably with a street gang. His feet, developing a will of their own, started to move to follow.

They didn't get far, and neither did the rest of him. Cousin Drakka appeared behind him, slapping two pairs of huge grease-matted hands on Kanan's shoulders.

He'd forgotten to pay his bill.

CHAPTER FOURTEEN

"I UNDERSTAND YOU'VE CAPTURED the suspect from Cynda,"
the shimmering holographic form of Count Vidian said. "You will be
receiving a squad of stormtroopers to take custody of him shortly."

Skelly glowered. Looking through the back of the image, he could
see Vidian, but Vidian could not see him. Or maybe he could. Lal had
barely informed the authorities that Skelly was there when the efficiency expert had called. It would make sense, Skelly thought, for the
Empire to keep an eye on all the producers of a strategic compound
like thorilide.

But he didn't mind their spying. He minded the fat four-armed
fools in the room with him, who had yet to release him from the
chair—and who had decided to keep the gag on him when Vidian
called, despite his urgent muffled cries to be allowed to speak.

"Moonglow. Your firm is a newer one?" Vidian asked.

"Only under that name, my lord," Lal replied. "I have worked in
this facility for more than twenty years."

Skelly wondered if a hologram could catch how nervous she was to
be speaking to the Emperor's man. *She'd better be worried,* Skelly

thought. By the time the Empire learned what he knew, the whole Mining Guild might well be out of work.

Lal continued. "We're a smaller firm, but we've made many advances in efficiency. I assure you we knew nothing about—"

"Never mind the saboteur," Vidian interrupted. "I would see these efficiencies. I will begin my inspection there."

"*Here?*" Skelly saw Lal's eyes widening. She clasped both sets of hands together, prayerfully. "My lord—we'd like some time to prepare for your arrival. It's the end of a very long workday. I know we don't have mornings around here, but could it possibly—"

Vidian waved his metallic hand dismissively. "Diurnal cycles! So annoying. Fine. In twelve hours, then—regard it the reward for your service. But I'll show no leniency in my review because of your help to me tonight. Is that understood?"

"I would expect none, my lord. Moonglow will be ready."

"See that it is," came the cold response. "An Imperial repulsorlift will arrive in five minutes. Have the prisoner ready." Vidian vanished.

Lal sat, dumbfounded, looking at the space where the image had been. Off to the side, Skelly could see her security chief husband, Gord, scratching his head. "I thought you said you didn't think the Empire would inspect here," Gord said. "We're too small."

"I don't understand, either." Lal cast a glance over at Skelly. "I guess it's because of you?"

"*Mmmm-mmmph!*" Skelly replied.

"Oh," Lal said, flustered. "Gord, get that out of his mouth!"

Gord grumbled. "All right," he said, looming over the seated Skelly. "But I think it's a bad idea."

The rag finally removed, Skelly coughed before turning his ire on the Besalisks. "That was Vidian! Why didn't you let me talk to him?"

Lal goggled at that. "I'm already terrified of him. I definitely wasn't going to let you talk to him!" Almost in a daze, she plopped down in her office chair. "Twelve hours to get this place looking good enough for an Imperial inspection?"

Gord looked back at her. "It's all right, Lal. You run a good place. I'll get the cousins in with some mops and it'll be fine."

Skelly rolled his eyes. The security chief was moon-eyed over his wife, and their mushiness was the capper to a horrid day. "You'd better worry more about what Vidian will say after he talks to me. You and every firm that's ever used Baby to break open a wall up there."

"Forget this guy," Gord said. He snapped his fingers. "Oh, Lal, I almost forgot. That Kanan fellow said he was quitting."

Lal shook her head, disappointed. "I was afraid of that. It was the worst day ever. He nearly got killed. But I wanted to thank him—he wound up saving some of my people's lives."

"Maybe you can talk him out of it," Gord said. A buzzer sounded. "There's somebody at the repulsorlift gate."

"That'd be the stormtroopers," his wife replied. She looked at Skelly sadly. "I *am* sorry."

"Yeah, sure," Skelly said. "You guys'll be the sorry ones."

Gord whistled. Two of his Besalisk assistants entered and lifted Skelly, chair and all. They carried him into the moonlit stockyard at the side of the complex. Equipment lined the inner perimeter of the tall black fencing, with a path between large enough for a repulsortruck to arrive.

Skelly knew what to expect: He'd seen the Imperial troop transports hovering through Gorse City now and again. He hoped this time, they'd take him straight to Vidian. He watched as Gord, leaving Skelly with the other guards, stepped up to the gate and opened it.

No one entered.

Curious, Gord walked into the street. A second later, the burly Besalisk looked back and shouted to his assistants. "Guys—it's Charko! The Sarlaccs are stealing our hovertruck!"

Moving almost as one, Gord's fellow guards drew their blasters and ran out to join him. Alone, Skelly shook his head. In high-crime Shaketown, no supply delivery was safe—not even when Imperials were on the way. He heard blasterfire from the street. Maybe they'd all shoot one another.

Then it occurred to Skelly that the Sarlaccs must have activated the entry buzzer. *Why would they have done that?* Before he could consider it, he became aware of someone behind him—and something pulling at the strap on his left shoulder.

"Are you Skelly?"

"What?" He looked to his left to see a cloaked figure crouching behind his chair. "Yeah. But who are—"

"Hera," the female voice said. A green hand inserted a vibroblade under one of his restraints. "And you're leaving."

"No, wait," Skelly said. "I can't go. I have a story to get out!"

For a moment, the woman stopped cutting, as if puzzled. But only for a moment. "I can help get your story out. But you have to go!"

"Wait!" Skelly had no idea who she was, or what she was talking about. "Listen—"

"I *will* listen. But you have to go," she said, severing the last bond. She ripped the straps free. "I paid Charko for a distraction. But it won't last."

Skelly looked through the gate at the street. It was empty. But he could hear Gord and his companions running somewhere and firing their blasters, and beyond that, the low whine of a repulsorcraft.

He didn't know what to do. The stormtroopers would take him to Vidian, who had the power to stop what was being done to Cynda. But then again, they might not. And the cloaked woman had said something he wasn't accustomed to hearing.

"I'll listen," she repeated. "Go!"

Skelly looked back, only to see she was no longer at his side. Hearing footfalls heading for the gate, he forced his cramped muscles to stand. Walking painfully, he headed for the gate.

"Where can I find you?" he yelled.

The call came from over the fence, outside: "I'll find you!"

She was already gone.

CHAPTER FIFTEEN

KANAN RUSHED AROUND the corner of a building—only to be nearly run down by an Imperial troop transport. Seeing the boxy repulsorcraft careening straight at him, Kanan dived to the muddy roadway. The long vehicle passed right over him, its metallic underside mere centimeters from the back of his skull.

Now he lay in the mud at the corner of a Shaketown intersection, and there was still no sign of the woman with the alluring voice.

Picking himself up, Kanan wiped off his tunic and stood as more traffic came down the other street, this time on foot: two of Charko's gang members, barreling in his direction with big metal pry bars in their hands. The sound of blaster shots followed behind them.

Kanan reached for his weapon, only to realize the Sarlaccs weren't coming after him—and that the blaster shots were meant for *them*. The hoodlums ran past without stopping, rushing to stay ahead of their pursuers—who turned out to be Gord and his fellow guards, firing blasters.

"You'd better run, punks!" Gord yelled, firing blasters held in all four hands.

Kanan looked down the street after them and then up the route the Imperials had taken. He shook his head. *I'm too sober,* he thought. *Nothing makes sense!*

He walked around the block. At the far end of one street, he could see the Moonglow service entrance. There was no sign of any caped woman there; just the stormtroopers from before, piling out of their repulsorcraft. Kanan quickly turned away.

This was no place to stay on a fool's errand, stormtroopers or not. This end of Shaketown, he recognized, had fared badly in a recent quake; half of it was under renovation and most of it was closed down. Resigned, Kanan decided to give up and head for Okadiah's. *I'm just being silly,* he thought. *Tomorrow's moving day. Time to get packing.*

Then he heard the voice again.

"Fifty up front, fifty afterward," the woman said. "Like we agreed."

Kanan looked down the alley to see the hooded figure facing off against Charko, flanked by several members of his gang. It was like the scene Kanan had witnessed outside the diner—only not. This place was more enclosed: Construction scaffolds rose against buildings on either side of the passage. There was a new menace to how Charko's friends—a mix of tough-looking humans and other beings—stood. And Charko, clutching a bunch of credits in his hand, wasn't happy at all.

"If you've got a hundred credits, maybe you've got a hundred more," the one-horned gang leader said. He took a step forward. Towering over the short woman, he gestured to her black cloak. "You've got room for a lot more cash under there, I'll bet."

Kanan strode into view at the end of the street. "Hey, Charko! You were looking for me. Did you forget?"

Charko and his companions looked back at Kanan. "Never," the Chagrian said. "There's always time for you!"

Kanan saw blasters being raised. His was already drawn. *Six—no, seven against one. That's about right.*

But before he could fire, Kanan saw the woman suddenly twirl in place. With one swift motion, her cloak came off—and became a weapon she cast into the air like a net. Charko turned back to get a faceful of fabric, dropping his credits in the process.

The gang leader stumbled backward, victim of a high kick from his assailant. His friends turned and gawped at what Kanan now saw: a beautiful, lithe, green-skinned Twi'lek, holding a pistol in one gloved hand.

The Twi'lek shot one human Sarlacc point-blank in a single motion, and then rushed forward in the next. As the burly man fell backward, the Twi'lek used his body as a makeshift staircase, giving her the altitude she needed to leap for a horizontal strut on one of the scaffolds. Catching the bar with her free hand, she used her momentum to help her gain a perch, clinging to one of the vertical supports. Turning, she fired her blaster down into the astonished crowd.

"Get her!" yelled a female gang member. But blasterfire was coming from a second direction as Kanan, done with watching, charged into the alley. The Sarlaccs scattered, uncertain who to target first.

With an angry bellow, Charko leapt from the mud, heedless of the cross fire. Turning toward the Twi'lek's position, he slammed chest-first into one of the scaffold supports. The structure shook, and the Twi'lek woman dropped her blaster. Her weapon hand freed, she scrambled like a sand monkey higher up the scaffold—even as it began to fall.

Kanan knew he had to move. He rushed his nearest attacker and grabbed her blaster arm with his left hand. His motion directed her errant shot into the assailant approaching on his right; he followed with a head-butt beneath her chin that knocked her backward. Now he could see the raging Charko trying to upend the scaffold. He dived forward, even as the Twi'lek woman vaulted in the opposite direction high above, to the scaffold on the other side of the alley.

Seized from behind by Kanan, Charko lost hold of the scaffold support—and the whole thing started to come down, all five stories of it. Kanan saw only one place to go: the large picture window of the building the scaffold was attached to. He launched himself and the Chagrian through the window, creating a shower of shards even as an avalanche of scaffolding came down in the alleyway behind them.

Dazed, his blaster lost in the dive, Kanan struggled to regain his feet inside the vacant building, which he recognized as an abandoned cantina. The Chagrian had taken the brunt of the crash, and yet somehow the thug still stood, ready to fight it out.

"You're on my turf now," Kanan said, raising his fists. "I do all my training in bars!"

Kanan and Charko traded punches across the dark quake-damaged room. Kanan grabbed a chair; Charko did the same with half a broken table. The two carried on a parry-and-thrust battle with their makeshift weapons—it was a kind of fighting the Jedi never taught, and it suited Kanan just fine.

Blow by blow, he maneuvered Charko in front of the only remaining intact window. Winded from his exertions, the Chagrian staggered. Kanan saw his opening. A roundhouse kick sent his opponent smashing through the pane behind him.

"Are we done here?" Kanan asked, stepping up to the windowsill. Charko didn't get back up this time. But the others were still out there, Kanan remembered. He readied himself and carefully climbed out the shattered window.

There wasn't anything to do. All Charko's companions were down. Some, Kanan had taken out earlier; others, the Twi'lek had. The rest had been crushed under the falling scaffold. And the Twi'lek herself was nowhere to be seen.

Rubbing his bruised cheek, Kanan searched the wreckage for his blaster. He was in pain: the kind that would pass, but enough to make it tough to go another round with the Sarlaccs. By the time he found his weapon, however, it was clear to him no danger remained.

But something was missing from the scene. The credits Charko had dropped had been plucked from the ground, and small footprints led away from the place where they had lain.

He saw the Twi'lek's cloak nearby, pinned beneath a heavy girder. *She did leave me a souvenir, after all.* With great effort, he pulled the metal aside. He took the garment into his hands and held it up. It was a good find, he thought, as he turned to stagger out of the alley. Because he was beginning to believe she had never been there.

He stopped thinking that when he stepped out into the street—and found himself looking into her eyes.

"Ah," she said, seeing her cloak.

"Ah," he repeated. Kanan stood frozen, studying her under the bright light of the moon. She was shorter than he was, with deep green skin, full lips, and a chin that came to a pleasing point. She wore a gray pilot's cap that allowed exit for two head-tails that hung at a little more than shoulder-length. She wore a brown vest, gold-colored slacks with utility pockets, and black gloves that matched the cloak in his hands.

"I knew I'd forgotten something," she said, removing the garment from his hands so deftly he barely noticed she'd done it. Then she looked at him with concern. "You okay there?"

Kanan nodded.

"You speak Basic?"

"Words fail me."

She smiled. "So they do."

It wasn't a dig—or if it was, it was delivered so gently that Kanan chose not to notice it. He looked back. "That was something back there."

"Yes," she said, still talking in that wonderful voice as she flicked mud from the cloak. "It's a good thing I was here to save you."

Kanan's brow wrinkled, and he looked back. "Save *me*?" He pointed at the bodies. "You had a whole gang after you!"

The Twi'lek lifted the cloak to put it on. "I'd paid them to do a job for me. There was a minor pricing dispute. I could have handled it." Seeing him look back at her, slack-jawed, she bumped a gloved fist underneath his bruised chin. "You did pretty good though. I'm impressed." She studied him. "So, you just randomly go around sticking your neck out for people?"

"No!" Kanan said. "Er—almost never." He blinked as she pulled her hand back. "Wait a minute," he said, gesturing back to the bodies in the alley. "You needed *them* to do a job? For *you*?"

"*Mm-hmm.* And now it's done." She flipped the cloak back into place around her shoulders, turned, and started walking.

"I do jobs," Kanan said, tromping after her. His whole body hurt from the fight, but he didn't want the conversation to end so soon. "You need something done, I'm there."

"No, thank you," she said, continuing on. "I have stops to make."

"Wait!"

Kanan tried to follow, but his body rebelled. Wincing, he grabbed at his knee. When he looked up, she was gone again—likely down one of the side alleys.

Disgusted with the universe, he yelled into Gorse's endless night. *"What's your name?"*

For a long moment, nothing.

And then that voice again, calling back to him.

"Hera."

CHAPTER SIXTEEN

STARSHIPS WERE SETTLEMENTS in the sky. Some were villages; *Ultimatum* was a great metropolis. And yet even Star Destroyers functioned like small towns. A big sink full of gossip—and as with small towns, the contents all tended to flow toward one person, like water to a drain.

Sloane stood at the window as Nibiru Chamas, *Ultimatum*'s unofficial drain, sat casually in the chair in her office. The mining ships were continuing to shuttle back and forth between Gorse and Cynda—faster than before, of course—but her mind was on the list Chamas was reading.

"Count Vidian has designed and issued new traffic patterns for the cargo ships traveling between the two worlds," Chamas said. "He has ordered several changes to the loader droids' subroutines on Cynda that should make them more productive. He has changed the color of the plates used in the communal mess hall—"

"What?"

Chamas chuckled. "That last one is a joke."

Sloane rolled her eyes. "Continue."

"He also ordered a review of Transcept's personnel—you know, the ones who found the madman on Cynda? There has already been at least one arrest for suspicious activity."

"Thorough," Sloane said.

She was thorough, too—or intended to be. She'd been caught flat-footed by Vidian's actions on her bridge, issuing commands to *her* staff. *Ultimatum* had the authority to destroy the freighter *Cynda Dreaming;* Vidian had clearly known that. But, while she agreed with that decision, it behooved her to find out more about her visitor, and how he'd interacted with other crews. She wasn't going to be just one more mechanical arm.

"What else has he done?"

"Laid groundwork for his tour of Gorse. He has a full schedule already. He doesn't head down there for hours yet, and he's already reorganized three guilds, ordered the consolidation of several equipment suppliers into a single firm, and even shut down a medcenter, moving the patients to an institution closer to the factories so they can get back to work more quickly."

"That's it?"

"Isn't that enough? He has met several times with the aides he brought aboard and made several calls back to his main office on Calcoraan Depot. There's only one thing he hasn't done."

"Slept," Sloane said. "He doesn't have the time."

"He doesn't have a *bed,*" Chamas corrected. "The attendants changing his room found the place wrecked. The furniture, smashed."

"What? When was this?"

"After he came back from the moon—after we piped a second call to him from Baron Danthe. I think our count has a temper."

Sloane chuckled. She'd heard Vidian had a short fuse—and word back from Cynda was that the Mining Guild chief had found out the hard way. "You got him another room, I hope?"

"We have an ample supply. Don't worry, it'll all be put right before our—er, *regular captain* arrives."

Thanks for reminding me I'm just a temp, Sloane thought, walking around to her desk. But Chamas's comment brought her back to what she wanted to know. This next, she wanted to ask cautiously.

"Interesting man, Vidian—and striking that he would choose government service. You said he bought the title. Do you know where he's from?"

"His biography says Corellia. In the Republic days, he was an engineer for a small design firm that worked for shipbuilders. A cog in a small wheel. His suggested improvements were constantly rejected. Then he was struck with Shilmer's syndrome—and spent the next five years while it was eating him alive conquering the stock exchanges from a bed."

"And the firm?"

"As the *legend* goes"—Chamas said the term derisively—"Vidian's first act on regaining mobility was buying the company and putting everyone on the street. But I don't even know what firm it was. There were confidentiality provisions to the severance packages. He doesn't want anyone he's burned sniping at him, ruining sales of his next management holo."

Sloane knew Vidian didn't need the money, but she didn't have any problem with his rationale. A little revenge did wonders for the healing process. It was also a human thing—and there weren't many human things about Vidian.

"If he's from Corellia," she said, "he's probably connected in the shipbuilding sector—and the Admiralty."

It was halfway between the question she'd intended, and the matter-of-fact observation she'd wanted it to sound like. But Chamas was too sly, catching her drift immediately. "In other words," he said with a smile, "can he make your posting here permanent—perhaps by giving Captain Karlsen a cushy job at one of his subsidiaries? Please, ask him for one for me, while you're at it."

Caught, Sloane simply stared. "What's tomorrow like?"

Chamas passed her his datapad showing the stops on Vidian's planned tour of Gorse. It sounded like an exhausting day.

She was struck curious by the first name on the list. "*Moonglow.* Why start with this little one?"

"They apparently captured—and lost—the fugitive from Cynda a few hours ago."

"That'll go over well for them," Sloane said, passing back the datapad. She swiveled her chair to look again out the window at the ships heading down to Gorse. Her brow furrowed as she tried to take it all in.

"So while he's on his world tour, we play traffic officer," Chamas said, standing. "Keeping the rabble back while Vidian adds to his folktale. We should demand part of the royalties on his next holo."

Sloane smiled inwardly. She only wanted a supporting role. It was her job to help the Empire; helping to find *Ultimatum*'s rightful captain a different ship would be a nice bonus.

Stormtroopers had ransacked his apartment hours earlier. That, Skelly thought without the least amusement, officially represented the first attention the Empire had ever paid to the homes in Crispus Commons.

Crispus was a project for homeless Clone Wars veterans in the sector, an idea hatched in the final days of the Republic. The Empire had kept it going, shipping in new residents from time to time without ever adding to or improving on the complex. Skelly thought it spoke volumes about what the Republic and Empire really thought about those who'd fought against the Separatists. *Let's stick them where the sun doesn't shine.*

Skelly had stayed in the dilapidated apartment partly because it was sandwiched between Gorse City's industrial districts. That way, no matter who fired him, his commute never got any longer. But the other reason he stayed was the rusted grating behind the complex's trash bin at the far end of the rectangular exercise yard—and what lay beneath.

Certain no one outside had seen his approach, he slipped behind the bin and into the hole. He closed the grille above him. Passing through an improvised curtain, he fished for the power switch. A crackle or two later, the darkness around Skelly turned red, lit by computer monitors and a single weak overhead lamp.

It had been intended as a bomb shelter, built by the Republic as part of the Crispus project in the unlikely event Count Dooku or General Grievous took a sudden interest in destroying a retirement colony. Its permacrete walls had been a moldy mess when Skelly found the place. But he liked that it had its own generator, and the presence of a giant garbage bin in front of the grating meant he could enter and depart without anyone seeing.

All Skelly's computers were built from kits, making them safe from slicing by the powers that be, corporate or government. Only one machine was attached to the HoloNet grid, and that through a connection hijacked from an Ithorian lunch wagon that parked daily on the other side of the quad. By selecting an intermediary that was mobile and garaged somewhere else, Skelly had cut down on prying eyes and ears.

Everywhere but at work. Skelly had known some of the corporations working on Cynda had installed surveillance equipment, but he'd assumed that was just to keep an eye on productivity—and to prevent the theft of explosive material, which had once been a problem. Evidently, they were now listening in on individual conversations there, too. It was insane. Deaf to his appeals about safety, but nosing in on everything else!

Skelly quickly ate a meager meal of tinned food paste before collapsing, exhausted, on a mat on the floor. This room had been his world, his *real* world, for years. Boards mounted on one wall were covered with hand-scrawled notes about the military industrial complex, and the intricate network of who owned what. A second wall was home to his studies into the history of galactic conflicts; the sides kept changing, but the stories were always the same. Whenever titans fought, the peons did the dying.

The biggest collection of notes, however, was on the wall facing him now. Apart from the curtained opening that led to a little closet, every square centimeter was festooned with notes about Cynda and its geologic structure. Seeing it all made his gut hurt. Skelly had long feared a day like this would be necessary: a day when he'd have to risk everything to get someone's attention. But he'd been deciding things on the fly, and he worried he'd already blown it.

He'd run here from Moonglow's grounds without thinking, after a spur-of-the-moment promise from someone he'd never met—and had in all likelihood ruined his chance to talk to Count Vidian. He still didn't know why he'd fled. Yes, it was natural to fear being taken anywhere by stormtroopers; the Empire's foot soldiers had a bad habit of damaging prisoners in transit. And everyone had misread his attempt to educate them as sabotage. But Vidian was still his best chance, the only one with the authority to effect change. Would Vidian leave Gorse without talking to him? Would Vidian see him at all, now that he'd run?

Staring at his collected writings from his spot on the floor, Skelly let out a low moan. *"Nobody listens."*

"What do you want to say?"

Skelly looked up, startled, to see the cloaked figure that had rescued him. She removed her cowl. "You're her!"

"Hera," the Twi'lek corrected. "Let's talk."

CHAPTER SEVENTEEN

SKELLY SAT UP, alarmed. "How did you find me?"

Hera patted her own shoulder. "If you'll look in the utility pocket on your left shoulder, you'll find a tracking device that I slipped in when I was cutting you loose." She smiled. "I *did* tell you I would find you."

Skelly reached for his pocket and discovered a small chip. He stared at her angrily. "I don't like people spying on me."

"You're in the wrong system, then." Hera simply opened her gloved hand. "I'll take that. Thanks."

"You said my name," he said, suspicious. "How do you know me?"

"You've gotten a lot of people's attention today. I heard about what you did on Cynda. You know—the blast, while the Emperor's envoy was there." She paused, stopping to take in the many notes about the Empire on the wall to her left. "I'm interested to hear your reasons for doing what you did."

Frowning, Skelly stood up. "And why do you care?"

"I'm just . . . interested," Hera said.

Seeing her reading his notes, the redheaded human interposed himself between her and the wall. "Look, don't read my stuff. I don't know you, lady. I don't know that telling you will help anything!"

Hera looked to her right—and saw the other wall and its writings about Cynda. A glint appeared in her dark eyes. "Would you tell me . . . if I was a reporter for the *Environmental Action Gazette*?"

Skelly goggled. "I thought that had shut down!"

"Just retooling," Hera said. "You can be part of the big relaunch."

Skelly studied her. He'd never been in that HoloNet publication's audience, but it had come up several times in his research. It had put a stop to a number of bad business practices in the past.

"Come on," she said, pulling a datapad from her cloak. "I did let you go."

Skelly took a deep breath—and made a decision. "Okay."

He rushed to his wall and pointed to one diagram after another, laying out his theories. Severing a few crystalline stalactites and stalagmites was fine; those were the mere outgrowths of the physical structures that held Cynda together. It was like giving the moon a haircut. But using explosives to break into new chambers was more akin to breaking bone.

"Every chamber they discover has more thorilide than the one before," Skelly said. "And that makes them use more juice to get into the next one."

"And that causes collapses that harm workers." Hera nodded, making notes on her datapad. "While ruining a beautiful natural setting."

"Now you've got it!" Triumphant, Skelly jabbed his fist to the low ceiling.

"Okay," Hera said mildly.

Skelly's face froze. "Okay?"

She smiled gently at him. "This is not big and shocking news, Skelly," she said kindly, returning the datapad to its place. "The Empire hurts workers and ruins things. It does that all the time, everywhere."

"So?"

"You have a problem, like a billion other people in the galaxy. One day, we'll all do something about it. This is good to know, and I feel for everyone involved. But I'm not sure the time is right to do much about it."

Skelly was alarmed. "You're not going to publish—after all this? What kind of deal is this? I thought you were a journalist!"

The woman took a step back—clearly not fearing him, but simply giving him space to rave. "I'm really more gathering information right now, Skelly. Preparing for . . ." She trailed off, then nodded toward the wall with his notes about Cynda. "What you've described is bad, but it's not exactly world-shattering."

"Oh, yes, it is!" Skelly whipped the holodisk out of his vest pocket and held it between his left thumb and forefinger. "Because I believe that if the Empire keeps up, they could blow the whole moon to bits!"

Hera held up a hand. "Look, forget the hyperbole. How much damage are you talking about?"

"I'm not exaggerating!" Skelly said. Pocketing the holodisk, he turned back to the wall and began riffling through attached notes with his good hand. "The moon's already brittle. The elliptical orbit means Gorse and the sun are yanking at it all the time. Gorse releases the stress through groundquakes. But all the energy stays pent up on Cynda, because the crystal lattices go so deep—"

"The bottom line, please."

"Use enough explosives in the right spots, and Cynda could crumble like a senator's promise."

Hera stared at him for a moment. Skelly stared back.

"That's just . . . beyond belief," she said, finally. "The power to destroy a body that size? It's hard to believe something like that exists."

"It exists. It's possible. And I'm beginning to think they don't care."

Hera walked to the wall and started reading. "These notes are all over the place," she said. "I can't make sense of some of it."

"Trust me," Skelly said. "I'm an expert."

"You're a planetary geologist."

"No, I build bombs."

Hera's lips pursed. *"Oh."* She drew the syllable out.

"I know how it sounds," he said, pulling down notes and wedging them into his frozen right hand. "But it's true. The mining companies know, because I've told them. But they cover it up, because they're all part of the conspiracy."

"The conspiracy?"

"The thorilide triangle," Skelly said, astonished that she hadn't heard about it. He moved across the room to the other side, with his wall of corporate shame. "The mining firms are corrupt. They're tied up—ownership, boards of directors—with the shipwrights that have sold the Empire on one construction project after another. Oh, it's all being done in secret, but you can't keep everything secret. A billion Star Destroyers isn't enough. They're building Super Star Destroyers, and Super Super Star Destroyers, and who knows what else!"

"I see," Hera said, gingerly taking a step backward. "And how do you know all this?"

"The HoloNet!"

"Oh," Hera said. "*The HoloNet.*"

"It's all one big web, and it goes on forever," Skelly said, eyes fixing on the far wall. He stepped over to it and began fumbling with notes. "Did you know it was the moneyed interests that started the Clone Wars? There was a battle droid manufacturer that had too much inventory—"

Skelly felt Hera's eyes upon him, and the air went out of his lungs. He stopped talking. The notes, the clippings, all swam before him, not making sense.

He'd done it again.

"I'm sorry to have troubled you," he half heard her say. "Good luck."

Skelly kept facing the wall. "Look, I know what I sound like. I've been through . . . well, I've been through a lot of bad things. I get worked up. I don't always say things right. But what I know—it's still real." He took a breath. "*I'm not crazy.*"

When he turned, she was gone. He could hear light footsteps heading up the ladder. He followed—but saw nothing but the trash bin and the darkened quad all around.

Deflated, Skelly climbed back inside and shut the grate after him.

He sat in silence at the bottom of the pit. His head buzzed—and hurt, as it had been hurting for a long time. Skelly's sleep cycles had been wrong ever since moving to Gorse, and time in Cynda's always bright caves confused them further. The confusion in the notes still clutched in his malfunctioning hand were one product. But he could still focus to do some things. The data on the holodisk—that, he knew was right. It was his testament, his last chance.

Skelly remembered Vidian's call to Lal Grallik. The count was coming, yes. And Vidian could still listen, and do the right thing. But he would be bringing the rest of the Empire with him, and they could still do the wrong thing.

Skelly sprang to his feet and reentered his sanctum. Opening the curtain to the closet, he exposed his secret workbench there—and, beneath, in sealed packages, the massive stores of explosive baradium he'd smuggled out over the years. Because of his fears about blasting on Cynda, every time they'd asked him to plant charges to open up a wall, he'd used a little less. He just hadn't given them back what he didn't use.

But if they didn't listen to him now, he'd give it all back. All at once, and so they'd notice.

Yes, he would.

Hera shook her head as she stepped back onto the street.

It had been a calculated risk, freeing Skelly. Her assumption in the detour was that anyone rising up against the Empire, in any way, was worth a look. Some could be helpful. Maybe not yet, but in the movement to come. It was important to know their capabilities.

But Skelly would never be of any use, and so she mentally filed him away with dozens of others she'd met just like him. Political activism drew more than its share of crackpots. Some had been legitimately driven to madness by the forces they were fighting against; some had been damaged by war, as she suspected was the case with Skelly. Some had no excuse. But while such people were always the first to revolt, they almost never led successful revolutions. Action against the Empire would have to be carefully measured—now, especially.

Thus far, Gorse had been a bust. Sunless in more ways than one: Its people wandered robotically between the drudgery of work and the dangers of the streets, sensing neither. Even the human who'd helped her against the street gang—whom she now remembered as the man helping the old-timer on Cynda—might easily fit a ready template: the gadabout, looking for a brawl. That would be disappointing, if so, but not surprising: Like everyone else on Gorse, he was trapped in a role the Empire wanted for him. He'd never be a threat. It was too bad: He seemed to know what he was doing in a fight.

But Hera put him out of her mind. Skelly was the side trip; the real goods lay ahead. And she would find them at the establishment whose unsubtle advertisement appeared on her datapad:

The Asteroid Belt

The Pits, Gorse City • Okadiah Garson, prop.

Open all nite

Come in and get belted

CHAPTER EIGHTEEN

"HEY, LADY! I'm talkin' to you!"

The big bruiser *was* talking to Zaluna, for no one else was on the street. But she'd chosen to keep going—until he kept after her. Just steps behind her, he yelled again. "I said, I'm talking to you!"

"No, you aren't," she said, continuing to walk through the mud. "If you were talking to me, you'd use my real name."

Picking up his pace, the drunk laughed. "How'm I supposed to know who you are?"

"Precisely!" Zaluna spun and looked keenly at him from beneath her light hood. "Then you have no reason to talk to me, Ketticus Brayl. Go home to your wife and children."

Face lit by moonlight, the behemoth blanched. "Wait. How do you know who I am?"

"That's not important," she said, right hand disappearing in the long, loose sleeve of her poncho—the lightest garment she owned that would conceal her features. "What's important is that you will leave me alone."

Brayl guffawed. "And if I don't?"

"Then you'll have a talk with this." Her right hand reappeared from within the sleeve, holding a slim blaster. "Are we through?"

The drunk goggled at the weapon's sudden appearance. Then he turned away, staggering off into the steamy night. Resuming her journey, Zaluna put the blaster back in its hiding place, glad no one knew it hadn't been fired in the thirty-three years since her mother had left it to her.

It wasn't true that she knew everyone on Gorse and Cynda by sight, of course—but nearly a third of a century of surveillance had put a lot of troublemakers on her watchlists. And many of them seemed to wind up down here, in The Pits. Some miners acted as if the neighborhood, settled to be close to the old quarries, was a decent place to live now that the strip mining had long since ended. Perhaps for them, it was. But in her experience, roustabouts were trouble waiting to happen. She'd monitored too many bar fights in The Pits, watched dozens of people being shaken down on the streets for money or sport. Whatever the firms paid the miners, it wasn't enough to keep some of them from hassling good folks for cash.

Then again, if they were paid more, they'd just drink more—and that seemed to make them all the worse.

The encounter was just one more headache in a day filled with them. After Hetto's arrest, the remaining surveillance staffers at Transcept had worked their overtime in silence, everyone afraid to say anything. Every operator's background was potentially under review, if the Imperial lieutenant was to be believed. Zaluna had hoped that finding the suspect Skelly again would make up for the Mynocks' not having flagged him for capture earlier—but her hopes fell when she learned that Skelly had escaped from Moonglow's offices before the stormtroopers could arrive.

At least no one suspected the Mynocks of signaling him. The factory supervisor had spent an hour defending her security team from the stormtroopers' insults. Still, Zaluna expected difficult days ahead for everyone at the Transcept office.

And even if nothing happened, a job she'd enjoyed working at would never be fun again.

It was a strange thing. So many people on Gorse lived in fear—especially Sullustans and others of smaller stature. Yet working with the Mynocks, she'd felt somewhat immune. There was safety in isolation, security in having information. Yes, her kind of work did have the potential to create problems for others. But she'd suppressed any consideration of that on the grounds that so many of the people she eavesdropped on were bad characters, likely to hassle a poor workingwoman on a darkened street.

But.

Increasingly, there had been fewer and fewer roughnecks being targeted for snooping, and more and more people like—well, like Hetto. And now Hetto himself, who faced an unknown fate. It hadn't made sense to anyone on the work floor. Sure, Hetto had complained about working conditions and pay, but who didn't? Yes, he'd thought what the Empire had done to the once magnificent caverns of Cynda was an abomination, but that was both old news and a common feeling on Gorse.

But the data cube was another thing—and Zaluna now knew it was the reason he'd been targeted. When the shift ended, she'd fled home to see what it was Hetto had given her. He hadn't given her permission to read what was on the data cube, but it wouldn't be her first time to pry—and she had no intention of passing something along to this "Hera" person without checking it out first.

She'd used a reader she'd first owned as a teenager, safely detached from the HoloNet—and studied the contents of the data cube in her closet for good measure. The contents were encrypted using a commercial program, but Zaluna had worked several years in electronic data collection and soon found her way past the protections.

She was amazed at what she discovered. Somehow, Hetto had managed to download the files Transcept kept on everyone it had ever watched on Gorse and its moon, from way back in the Republic era to the present.

She thought for a moment this "Hera" might be from a rival surveillance firm. Corporate espionage—spying on the spies for profit. Hetto, always broke, could have been hoping for a payoff. She didn't want any part of a transaction like that. But thinking on it, she realized Transcept sold data to its competitors all the time, and sometimes on a massive scale. This act didn't seem necessary.

Looking more closely at it, Zaluna realized that the bounty of personal information on the data cube wasn't the important part. Its existence served as a guide to the state of the art in surveillance means. Every image, every voice recording, every bioscan, every electronic communication tied to names in the files was tagged with information describing how it had been obtained. With it, a reader knew the location of every surveillance point on Transcept's local grid.

Who would need something like that?

Maybe it was another Skelly, some crank or mad bomber looking to know the Empire's capabilities, in order to create more mischief. She wouldn't want to be a part of that.

But Hetto wasn't that kind of person. And that suggested someone else who might want it: someone who cared about what the Empire was doing to the people of Gorse.

Someone who cared as much as Zaluna did.

If there was a chance "Hera" was of that sort, it was worth a conversation, no matter what the danger to Zaluna. One conversation, no more; she had no desire to end up like him. But Hetto deserved that much.

It had to be done in secret, though—and that was why her destination bewildered her. *"The Asteroid Belt?"* She hadn't set foot in a cantina in thirty years, but she'd seen enough video to wonder why anyone would ever consider one a place for a surreptitious meeting. *So many eyes! So many ears!* Not to mention the sensory organs of natures she'd never imagined, belonging to all the other species that frequented cantinas.

Running on adrenaline, she'd unpacked all her devices from the training programs she'd been through years earlier, when she'd learned best practices for placing hidden cams and mikes, and for locating existing ones for repair based on their subspace emissions.

Detecting them before they detected her: That would be her edge, she thought.

She saw the sign up ahead. There was no sense waiting outside any longer. "Hetto, you poor reckless soul, this is for you." She drew the cloak tightly around her and stepped toward the building.

CHAPTER NINETEEN

THE BROKEN-TOOTHED miner spotted Kanan as soon as the pilot stomped into The Asteroid Belt. "I've been lookin' for you," the burly man snarled. "We still got a fight from last night to finish!"

Bruised and dirtied from the Shaketown episode, Kanan started to walk right by. Then his gloved hands shot out, grabbing the miner by the scruff of his hairy neck. Kanan yanked hard, bringing the man's face down with a smash onto an adjacent table, knocking cards and credits from the sabacc game there astray. The startled card players watched in amazement as Kanan pulled the dazed man off their table—and then climbed on top of it himself.

"Now hear this," he yelled to the dozens of patrons crowding the big cantina. "I have had enough of today. Anyone who hassles me goes to the medcenter."

"The Empire closed the medcenter!" someone yelled.

"Correction: Anyone who hassles me goes to the morgue. That is all." In a single swift motion, he reached down for the mug of ale by his feet—the one that had belonged to the guy on the floor. He drank the contents in one swig and stepped down from the table.

From his regular station behind the bar, old Okadiah eyed him. "You astound, Kanan. You look as though you've been through a bar fight, and yet I could swear you just arrived a minute ago."

"That's because I *was* in a bar fight," Kanan said, rubbing his jaw. "Philo's Fueling Station, over in Shaketown."

"But that's not supposed to reopen for three months."

"It'll be a little longer," Kanan said, reaching over the counter to grab a bottle.

"Hmm." Okadiah shined a glass. "One can only surmise the involvement of a woman."

"Add stupidity and mix well," Kanan said. "But what a woman. She was wearing a hood when I first saw her. But her eyes are *amazing*. And she's got moves. I'm telling you, Oke, if she were to walk in here right now—"

"I think you have your wish!" Okadiah said, pointing.

"Huh?" Kanan looked behind him, expectantly. Peering in through the partially opened door was a Sullustan woman in a rose-colored poncho. Clutching a little blue bag in her hands, she cautiously peeked this way and that.

"Hood, check. Eyes, check," Okadiah said, smirking. "But I'm not sure I'll ever understand your type."

The woman slipped inside. The door slammed noisily behind her, startling her for just an instant. But she quickly made her way to a table in the corner—and then another, and then another, working her way across the room as if she were trying to avoid being seen by someone that only she saw.

Kanan watched, puzzled. "What do you make of that?"

"Perhaps the tax agent's in town," Okadiah said.

Finally arriving near the bar, the Sullustan woman looked in three different directions. Then she bolted across the space, arriving next to the seat at the far end of the counter, near Kanan.

Okadiah bowed. "Welcome to my establishment, young lady. My friend here is a great admirer."

Kanan glared at Okadiah. "It's not her, you imbecile!"

Okadiah smiled. "Can we help you with something?"

Her big eyes looked up at Kanan—and her intense expression softened a little, as if with recognition. "There is something. The bar. Would you mind if I went to the other side of it?"

Kanan goggled. "You want to sit on the barkeep's side of the bar?"

"Kanan does it all the time," Okadiah said. "He sleeps there, too."

"Lady," Kanan said, "there are no stools on that side."

"That's okay," the woman replied, her eyes scanning the ceiling. "I don't want a chair. I want to sit on the floor."

Kanan and Okadiah looked across the bar at each other, puzzled. Then they both shrugged—and the woman darted around the opening and behind the bar. Kanan saw her disappear.

"I hate to miss anything," Okadiah said, "but a host must entertain. Jarrus, lad, hold the fort." He pitched his towel to Kanan and bowed to the huddled woman. "Let's talk again sometime," he said, exiting from behind the counter.

Kanan grabbed Okadiah's shirt as he passed. "This is weird. What am I supposed to say to her?"

"You'll be back there with all the booze. Offer her a drink. Or have one yourself."

Kanan weighed the facts and realized his friend had made an excellent suggestion. Hoisting his body onto the bar, he deposited himself on the other side of the counter. There, he saw the Sullustan woman sitting on the floor, leaning back with her head and shoulders inside the cabinet beneath the sink.

"Hey! What are you doing in there?"

"It'll be just a second," she called out.

Kanan waited. Perhaps she had a lifelong ambition to be a plumber.

She peeked out. "Excuse me. Can you hand me the cutter in my bag?"

Stupefied, Kanan did as he was asked. The little bag was packed to overflowing with electronic gadgets.

"Thank you," she said, taking the tool. A few seconds later, she emerged with a look of satisfaction. "There. Taken care of."

Kanan offered his hand to help her up. "What did you do?"

"Neutralized the surveillance cams in here," she said, getting to her feet. "Thanks for the help."

"There are cams in here?"

"There are cams everywhere," the woman said, brushing herself off. Seeming much more at ease, she removed her poncho, revealing a dark-colored outfit. "That's what I was doing when I came in—moving between the blind spots. I figured Transcept hid the transmitter relay behind the bar. That's a favorite spot for cantinas—no one ever wants to clean under the sink." She put her tool back in her bag. "I cut the power to the whole system."

Kanan looked around the room. He still couldn't see where the cams were.

"Don't worry—I made it look as if a rodent chewed into the works. Happens all the time. Someone pretending to be an ale distributor will be by next week to repair everything."

"If you say so." Kanan took a deep breath, wondering if he'd ever done anything other than get soused in the place. Knowing he hadn't, he shook off the paranoia. "How do you know this, Zaluna?"

She stared at him, suddenly serious again. Big eyes got even wider. "How—how do you know my name?"

"It's on your name badge, there," Kanan said, pointing.

The woman looked at him—and then down at the official badge clipped to her work clothes. "Oh," she said, disgusted, ripping the tag off and putting it in her bag. "I guess I'm not very good at this."

"At what?"

Regaining her composure, Zaluna glanced at Kanan and smiled primly. "I am just another customer visiting a cantina. You should pay me no mind."

"Okay," Kanan said, turning away to the bottles.

"But I could use a little more help."

Kanan looked over his shoulder. "Look, ma'am, I've had a long day. I'm really not in the mood to help anyone."

"But you will." Zaluna leaned against the bar and smiled gently. "I know you. I've seen you working—on Cynda."

"How? I haven't seen you there."

Zaluna didn't explain. "You help people. I've seen you do it before. And I saw you saving your friend from Count Vidian today."

"You saw me?"

Zaluna didn't elaborate. But she smiled, a little ashamed of what she'd revealed. "That's one of the rare pleasures of my world. You spend all your time watching for bad people, and you want to forget what you see. But the good ones, those you remember."

Kanan stared. None of what Zaluna was saying made sense. The woman, he now realized, reminded him of Jocasta Nu, the Jedi librarian. They didn't look anything alike, of course. But Jocasta always seemed to know everything, and acted like knowing everything was nothing. That was definitely in this woman's manner.

"What do you want help with?"

Zaluna looked into the teeming crowd. "I'm supposed to meet someone, but I don't know what they look like."

"You don't know what everyone looks like?"

"Not this time. And I need to keep a low profile. Can you look for me?"

Kanan looked down and put his hands before him. "Zaluna, I don't know who you are or who you think I am—but you do *not* know me. I do not go around randomly helping people!"

"That's not what I've heard about you," came a voice from the far end of the bar. *The voice.*

Kanan decided to play it cool, as he turned. *They always seek you out, brother.* "Hey there, Hera," he said, smiling confidently. "What can I get you?"

CHAPTER TWENTY

THE JEDI ORDER WAS more than an unpaid police force, more than just an exercise club that was into metaphysics. It was a way of life, based on the Jedi Code—and a lot of rules for living that weren't in the Code, that had been tacked on later. One was that Jedi avoided becoming involved in romantic relationships. Once on the run, Kanan Jarrus had found that rule pretty easy to forget about.

Hera's visit here, now, wasn't any kind of date—but she *was* a lovely woman wanting a private conversation, and from his earlier experiences he knew just the spot. The Asteroid Belt had a nice, secluded table in the back where the light was just right and where you were out of the stumbling line of the drunks and the brawlers.

But never in his past visits to the table had he brought along a short, gray chaperone—and Zaluna was talking more with Hera than he was. After being sent to the bar for something for the third time by Hera, Kanan had started to suspect that the Twi'lek really had come here looking for Zaluna after all, and not him.

The two were chatting closely when Kanan returned to the table with the coasters Hera had requested. It was time to step things up.

"You can stop talking about how much you miss me, ladies—I'm back!"

"Great," Hera said, in a tone that, for the first time, wasn't music to Kanan's ears. She seemed annoyed at having been interrupted, but he wasn't going to let that deter him.

Looking down, he saw that the chair he'd been sitting in was pushed well away from the table, out into the aisle. Hera's foot had pushed it there, he realized. *So much for gratitude over being saved.* "Standing room only tonight," he said, grabbing the chair and chuckling. "Good thing nobody else grabbed this."

"Good thing," Hera repeated.

Kanan spun the chair around backward and straddled it as he sat down, putting his chest against the back of the chair and crossing his arms over the top of it—a move intended to bring him fully into the conversation. "So what'd I miss?"

Hera looked at him with impatience—until Zaluna reached out and touched her hand. "I think you can trust him. I've watched him longer than you have. He helps people—though he makes a show of doing otherwise. He stood up to Vidian just today."

"I saw," Hera said.

"You did?" Kanan asked, slack-jawed.

Hera seemed to fret. "It's still not smart. You protect secrets by keeping the circle small."

"And you protect yourself by having a witness," Zaluna said. "I've been a professional witness my whole life. If we're really going to discuss this, I'd like one now." She regarded Kanan. "He'll do."

Kanan slumped in his chair and shrugged. "I'll do." *What's going on here?*

Hera seemed to reach a decision. She leaned across the table, her hands clasped together. "All right. I'd come here to meet this guy I met on the HoloNet—"

"Oh, well, there's your first mistake," Kanan proclaimed. "I could have told you—"

But before he could finish his sentence, Hera flashed Kanan a smile that was only slightly patronizing. "Can it wait?"

Mildly chastened, Kanan shut his mouth.

"I was looking for a man named Hetto. He and Zaluna both work for a company with a surveillance contract for the Empire. Hetto had grown worried about what he saw as abuses of authority—and he had already been in contact with other . . . *concerned parties.*"

Kanan could tell from the way Hera pronounced the words that she didn't want to elaborate too much about that. But she did say that it was Hetto she was supposed to have met until his arrest changed that.

"He was arrested for trying to meet you," Zaluna said, shaking her head.

"It wasn't just that," Hera said, sounding soothing. "You know that. Hetto was aware, Zaluna. Awake to all the things the Empire is doing. This meeting? It was him reaching out, trying to do something. You were brave to take it on yourself, to finish what he started."

"I'm not brave," Zaluna said, her voice a little shaky. "I'm an old fool. I remember too much. I remember how it was—and how it got worse, even before the Empire. I remember when people didn't kill guildmasters on a whim and walk away without a thought." Her black eyes glistened. "And I remember when my people were safe. Those employees of mine are my children, and now one of them's in deep trouble." She focused on Hera. "Will they kill Hetto?"

Hera didn't seem to know what to say. Zaluna closed her huge eyes, mournful. Kanan reached out and patted her hand. "Hey, there, maybe your friend's just in a labor camp."

"Kanan is right," Hera said, a phrase he thought sounded wonderful coming from her, whether she meant it or not. "Hetto is a talented person, and they'll want to keep him around, maybe even doing work like he is now. Just someplace else."

"Yeah, and maybe they even have daylight there," Kanan said. He smiled awkwardly at Hera and shrugged.

Recovering her composure, Zaluna reached into her bag and pulled out a data cube. It was bigger than the storage device Kanan had seen Skelly waving around. "This is what Hetto wanted you to have." She peered up at Hera. "You know what's on it?"

"I think so," Hera said. She reached into a pocket and withdrew a small reading device. "May I?"

Zaluna paused, suddenly reluctant. "This is it, isn't it? This is the moment." Glancing all around the bar, she took a deep breath. "It's exciting, almost, being on this side of the cams. You wonder who else is here."

"There's no Imperial agents here, if that's what you're asking," Kanan said. He looked back across the room. "These are all one hundred percent pure shovel-carrying drunkards. I've tussled with too many of them to think they're plants for the Empire."

Hera looked at him. "And what do *you* think about the Empire?"

"As little as possible," he said. "I could take it or leave it."

"Hmm."

She sounded disappointed, Kanan thought, but only a little. Clearly, Hera was politically aware; he knew the sort, having wooed a university woman or ten on more upscale worlds. But those women had all aggressively tried to get him to care about their causes of the week. Hera was letting him be, at least for the moment. *Good for her.*

"You can look at it," Zaluna finally decided, offering the data cube. "That's what Hetto wanted. But—maybe you'd better give it right back afterward. Okay?"

"Okay," Hera said. Taking it, she plugged it into her device and began reading. Kanan saw her eyes widening as she read, and he realized she was savoring something wonderful.

"Juicy stuff?"

"Mm-hmm." She manipulated the device for several minutes. "This is huge. It's not just the information—it's how it was retrieved. The Empire is everywhere."

"But not omniscient," Zaluna said. "Eyes and ears can fail." She nodded to what Hera was holding. "Study that long enough, and you'd see where they fall short."

"This section here. What are these names?"

Zaluna examined what Hera was looking at and cleared her throat. "That's different. Those are all the requests made on the Imperial channel to the Transcept database. People they're interested in. Background checks, video files being pulled."

Kanan took a peek as Hera paged through lists of names. He still couldn't believe any of this business was real.

"I think Hetto was downloading right up until a few minutes before he was arrested," Zaluna said. "There are some really recent ones in there."

Hera pointed to a name. "What's this very last one—*Lemuel Tharsa*?"

"That's one of the command-level requests from the Star Destroyer. Somebody important wanted to know about him."

"Command level? Like the captain? Or Count Vidian?"

"I suppose."

"And who is Lemuel Tharsa?"

"The name doesn't sound familiar," Zaluna said. She took the cube and reader from Hera and ran a search. "Someone by that name did visit the planet twenty years ago—someone started a file on him, at least. No details, though."

"Why would they be looking for someone like that?" Hera asked.

"No idea. Sorry there's not more—back in the commercial surveillance days, there were more legal limits to tracking." Zaluna passed the cube and reader back to Hera. "Of course, I probably saw the guy back then, if it was even the same person. Maybe something will jog my memory."

Kanan chuckled. "Well, you people spy on millions of people. I wouldn't expect you to—"

"Kanan Jarrus, human male, early twenties," Zaluna said, looking up at him. "Freighter pilot, dangerous cargo. Flight clearance seven. Emigrated to Gorse five months ago from—"

Kanan grabbed her wrist. "Okay, you're spooky. I get it." His mouth went dry, and he reached for his drink.

"This is good," Hera said, detaching the reader and passing the data cube back to the woman. "Very good, very worth Hetto's sacrifice—and yours. May I have it long enough to copy it? I'm busy with the reason I'm here, but for this, I'd make time."

Kanan's eyebrow went up. "I thought meeting *her* was the reason you were here."

Hera looked at him kindly. "Kanan, I appreciate what you did for me back in Shaketown—and also your hosting us here. But I've done all I'm going to do to satisfy your curiosity, so—"

"Oh, no!"

Hera and Kanan looked at Zaluna.

"He's here," the Sullustan woman said, looking into the crowd. "Why would he be here, now?"

Kanan looked around, but could only see the bustling patrons. "What? Who's here?"

"What is it, Zaluna?" Hera asked, worried. "The Empire?"

Having already made a decision, Zaluna stuffed the data cube into her bag and stood. "This is too much. I have to go." She turned from the table and headed for the side door. "Good-bye!"

Kanan and Hera looked at each other, puzzled—until they became aware of a figure in a tan overcoat standing nearby.

"Kanan! Just the guy I'm looking for," Skelly said, peering out from beneath his hood. "And I see you've met my friend!"

CHAPTER TWENTY-ONE

"*YOU! I THOUGHT I'D* gotten rid of you!"

Skelly stretched out his hands and smiled broadly at Kanan. "Hello to you, too," he said, speaking loudly. "Don't get up."

Kanan did get up. He grabbed the startled fugitive by the back of the neck and forcibly shoved him down into the seat Zaluna had been occupying. "This is a room full of miners who think you tried to crush them to death!"

"That's all wrong." Skelly started to rise. "Look, I could tell them—"

"Sit down!" Kanan barked, shoving him downward. He looked around the room to see who had noticed. Thankfully, it was chaos as usual—a term that was quickly coming to describe his entire evening.

"Why did—" Hera started to say. "Our friend, the Sullustan. She ran out of here when she saw you. Why?"

"No idea," Skelly said.

"She probably met him in an elevator once," Kanan said.

Skelly pointed at Hera with his good hand. "You should be careful around this woman, Kanan. I don't think she's who she says she is."

"Thanks for the advice. But she hasn't said anything yet."

Hera stood and glanced at Kanan. "I should see where she ran off to. I'll be back."

"No, wait." He rose and touched her shoulder. "Sit with Skelly. Make sure he doesn't do—well, anything. Anything at all."

Kanan walked quickly back along the bar. Reaching the side door, he saw nothing outside but Okadiah's aged hoverbus, parked in the moonlight.

He saw Skelly and Hera talking furtively when he returned. *Did they really know each other?*

"Couldn't see her," he announced.

Hera frowned. "She'd know Skelly was wanted," she reasoned.

"Maybe she'll come back when he's gone." Sitting down, Kanan faced Skelly. "What are you doing here in the first place? Who let you go?"

Skelly pointed. "She did!"

Kanan looked at Hera and gawked. "What?"

Hera simply nodded—and shrugged.

"When? Where?"

"At Moonglow," she said. "He was being held prisoner. I set him free."

"*Why?*"

"It seemed like the thing to do."

"What, like activating a thermal detonator?" Kanan couldn't believe it.

She seemed unconcerned. "It seemed safe. There weren't any reports of casualties from the moon—"

"I was nearly one. He's a biological weapon." He clapped his hand on Skelly's sleeve. "Now will you please get out of here?"

"I'll go," Skelly said, pulling his hand back. "But I came to see you because I need a favor."

"This should be good."

"Vidian's coming to inspect Moonglow in a few hours," Skelly said.

Hera's interest was piqued. "That's odd. I thought Moonglow was a small operation."

"I overheard him telling Lal. The stormtroopers have already put up a security cordon around that part of Shaketown. So I'll need your ID to get me onto the grounds, old buddy."

Kanan took a large swallow of his drink, then asked, "My what?"

"You said you were going to quit anyway, right? Just let me borrow your badge. I'll give it back after I've made my case to Vidian."

"I won't get it back, because they're gonna shoot you in the head! And Vidian'll have a ball watching." Kanan shook his head. "That guy's horrible."

"He's brilliant. He doesn't take any guff from corporate types."

"That's for sure," Hera said. "He kills them."

"I know a few who deserve it. From what I hear, he does what needs doing." With his left hand, he gestured to his motionless right hand. "And he's not ashamed of his cybernetics. I think he talks my language. We'll consult, like two professionals. I'll save the moon. And then I'll go."

"This is the dumbest plan I've ever heard." Kanan looked over at Hera in disbelief. "This is what you let loose."

Hera sighed. "I saw someone with a grievance. I wanted to know what it was, before the Empire rubbed him out. I wanted to know if he was worth knowing." She fixed her eyes on Kanan and spoke calmly. "You can't always guess what role someone will play."

"You can't pick your friends, you mean?"

"Oh, I'm very selective."

"I bet."

"I have high standards," Hera said. "Only very special people are going to be able to help me right now."

"Like Skelly? Or her?" Kanan gestured with his thumb to the door Zaluna had left through.

"No, probably not." She smiled charitably. "And not even you. I thank you for earlier, but you're not going to be able to help me."

"Help you do what?"

She smiled gently. "If you have to ask, you're not ready to know." She rose. "And now I really need to go. The Empire's still looking for Skelly—and if they break Hetto, they could know about my rendez-vous."

Before Kanan could respond, he heard the front door being kicked open. Two stormtroopers appeared there. Turning, he saw two more coming in through the side door.

Hera saw them, too. She sighed. "Speak of the Empire, and it will appear."

Crouching behind a garbage bin, Zaluna struggled to calm down. She'd been right to move when she did. Every Imperial on Gorse was looking for Skelly, and bounty had probably been offered. She didn't know whether he was guilty of what he'd been accused of, but she wasn't going to sit around possibly betraying the Empire while he was anywhere nearby.

Treason! That was what she'd just committed, she realized. Zaluna's breaths came quickly as she looked down at the ground and her open bag. The data cube was there, glinting in the moonlight. By showing the object and its contents to Hera, Zaluna had just thrown away thirty-plus years of faithful service—and for what? To help a woman who might be in league with a mad bomber? Skelly had seemed to recognize Hera. Had his whole tussle with Kanan on the moon been a fraud, to trap her?

Entrapment had been a concern going in, and she'd taken a few steps to prepare for that. They hadn't included an escape route on this side of the building, however. Hearing the clatter of armor as storm-troopers ran past, Zaluna looked furtively for someplace to hide the data cube or something to smash it with. There was nothing. Even the garbage bin was locked.

As the sound of another transport came from the street beyond, Zaluna saw her only possible sanctuary looming large and dark, up the alley. She picked up her bag and ran for it. Either those years in the Transcept exercise room would save her, or they wouldn't.

The clamor inside The Asteroid Belt lessened only a little as the stormtroopers—one male and three female—made their way inside, blasters handy but not raised. Kanan saw Okadiah leave his sabacc game long enough to greet them. "Welcome, Officers, welcome! Happy hour all night!"

Kanan shot a concerned look at Hera. "Only two ways out of here," he said.

"I know. I checked before I came in."

Of course you did, Kanan thought.

Skelly stood up and reached for his hood. "I've had enough of this," he said, beginning to remove his cowl. "I'm trying to see Vidian anyway. I'll just go with them!"

"*No!*" Kanan and Hera said in unison, each grabbing an arm and jerking Skelly down. Kanan yanked the top of the hood forward so it was almost covering Skelly's nose.

The stormtroopers began working their way through the room, speaking to individual patrons. The drunks weren't cooperating, and the stormtroopers weren't being gentle in return.

"Side door?" Hera asked.

Kanan shook his head. "Hear that sound?"

Hera concentrated for a moment. "Just the bar."

"There's a personnel carrier idling out there. Must be more stormtroopers."

Hera glanced at the exit. "Couldn't it be the hoverbus?"

"Different sound." Only he and Okadiah had the activation code, anyway. Kanan looked around the bar, furtively—until his eyes fixed on the short hallway directly behind their table.

Kanan glanced back to make sure the stormtroopers weren't looking his way. Seeing his moment, he stood, grasping Skelly's arm tightly. "Quick," he said, making for the corridor. "You, too!"

"But that doesn't lead outside," Hera said.

"Just follow—and do exactly what I say."

CHAPTER TWENTY-TWO

"YOU THERE!"

"Me there," Kanan said, emerging alone from the short hallway with a white towel in his hand. Less than a minute had passed—and two of the stormtroopers had reached the table he'd vacated.

"We're searching this establishment," the one with the female voice said.

"For what?"

"A spy, here to meet a traitor." The male trooper shoved past Kanan and entered the short hallway.

"You're kidding." Kanan laughed. "Have a look around," he said, picking up his empty mug from the table and rubbing it with the cloth. "If your spy's here tonight, he's blasted off his boosters!"

The female stormtrooper surveyed the cheering crowd. A blitzed Ugnaught, snout-faced and only a meter tall, was riding drunkenly around on the head of a similarly soused Ithorian. The brown-hided, hammer-headed titan had a pitcher in each long-fingered hand and was lumbering around trying to serve both himself and his small passenger at the same time without spilling any ale.

A normal night for The Asteroid Belt, in all respects.

"Maybe that's your traitors there," Kanan said, pointing to them with a smile.

"Never mind," the stormtrooper said. "We're also looking for a pilot from Moonglow. We don't have pictures of him yet, but he's a witness—the bomber stowed away on his ship. We were told he lives here."

"On the floor, maybe," Kanan said, walking to set the empty mug on the bar. "These pilots are in one night, out another." He reached for an empty bottle and pitched it in the trash. "I'm just the bartender. Can I get you something?"

From down the short hallway, the other stormtrooper called out, "There's someone behind this door!"

"Uh-oh," Kanan said, stepping lively to get there first. There was a small door to the left at the end of the corridor, and the stormtrooper that Kanan had seen earlier was about to kick it in. Kanan stepped up and raised his hand. "You really don't want to go in there."

The stormtrooper looked up at Kanan, helmeted head tilted slightly in puzzlement.

And then they all heard it: the loudest, most sickening retching sound, coming from behind the door. Something metallic inside banged loudly against the wall, and then against the door, before the horrible heaving noise began again.

"It's one of the Wookiees," Kanan said, shaking his head. "Always thinks he can handle Trandoshan ale. That stuff can take the finish off a landspeeder."

The female stormtrooper didn't turn away. "But that doesn't sound—"

She was interrupted with a horrific symphony of heaving, louder than before. Kanan looked behind the armored pair. "Bring the heavy stuff, Layda!"

"Excuse me!" Hera, wearing a long apron, appeared in the open doorway on the other side of the hallway. She exited the storage room holding a mop in one hand and a carrying case of industrial-strength cleansers in the other. While the stormtroopers watched, she set the case down outside the door and reached in to find several cloth face masks. She tied one over her face, and then another. "You'll want to get back," she said to the watchers as she placed the third shield over her mouth. "I don't know if those suits will protect you."

"*Rrrraaa-arrghh-arrggh-arrrrgh!*" came another miserable howl from behind the door. The pounding resumed.

"I think we'll move along," the female stormtrooper said. Her partner's body language showed immediate relief. "If you see any suspicious characters," she said, "call the authorities."

"Gotcha," Kanan said.

Once the front doors closed behind the stormtroopers, Kanan whipped out a key and opened the door. There, inside a small storage closet, squatted a terrified Skelly, holding a metal pail in his hands. "Was that loud enough?" he said, yelling into the pail and producing a noisy echo.

"Get out of there," Kanan said, grabbing at him. "And get out of here!"

Keeping the hood pulled low over Skelly's head, Kanan shoved him back into the main room, along the bar, and out the side door. The stormtroopers and their transport were gone; only Okadiah's hoverbus remained.

Reaching the stoop, Skelly lifted his cowl and called back plaintively. "So, do I get that ID badge or not?"

Kanan answered by slamming the door and locking it.

Hera was leaning against the bar, apron removed, when he turned.

"Nice tactics, there, Kanan." He could tell from her expression that she was impressed. "If you want them to leave, make *them* want to leave. Very smooth."

"I've got a lot of experience avoiding stormtroopers."

"Oh?" she said. "Why's that?"

"I don't like their fashion sense."

She smiled. "Come here."

Kanan did—and was pleasantly surprised when she reached out to touch him. "You've been holding out on me," she said, running her finger along the collar of his shirt.

"I'd never do such a thing." He sidled up closer to her, surprised by this new attitude. If excitement turned her friendly, he wasn't going to object. "You can have anything you want."

"Great," she said. "I want your Moonglow pass."

"I'd—" Kanan said, before her response registered. "You want *what*?"

"Your pass," she said, and jabbed her hand inside his neckline to grab at something. She pulled out a gold-colored card, secured around his neck with a lanyard. "You work at Moonglow. I didn't know that, until Skelly mentioned it. I want your pass to get on the grounds."

"I don't think you can just—"

"I've seen the gate. It's automated." She made a *swish-swish* motion with her hand. "Simple."

"Wait. Why do you want to get into the factory?"

"Denetrius Vidian."

"Ew," Kanan said. He walked back over to the bar, where many of his friends beckoned in comforting glass containers. "Believe me, sweetheart, I'm much better-looking."

"I know what he looks like," she said, following him to the counter. "He's the reason I'm here."

"That's even worse," Kanan said. He began pouring them drinks. "Look, I know there's no accounting for taste. But you're way too good for someone like him."

"I'm not in a relationship with him. I'm trying to find out why he's here."

"I'd have thought that was obvious. He's here to get more blood out of stones—or thorilide out of crystals." Handing her a glass, he joined her on her side of the counter. She was really serious about this— *whatever* that she was into. "I never have figured out why the Empire needs so much thorilide."

Hera shook her head. "That's not the mystery here. They're building Star Destroyers at a rate to put one in every home. The mystery is why Gorse," she said, "and why now."

"What do you mean?"

"They were already kicking the stuffing out of you guys to speed you up before Vidian showed up. That's why your pal Skelly—"

"Not *my* pal!"

"—it's why Skelly and a lot of people like him have been so vocal. Gorse and Cynda were not worlds the Empire was honoring with its negligence."

"Careful," Kanan said, taking the excuse to lean closer to her and show her his winning smile. "Treasonous words, there."

"I think I'll trust Zaluna's surveillance sweep. So explain to me this," she asked. "Vidian's administrative domain is centered on Calcoraan, sectors away. But lately, his whole Imperial career seems to have led him toward one goal: getting authority over Gorse and Cynda. And the second he got it, he called up an Imperial escort to take him here." She ticked off the mysteries on her fingers. "Now, does that seem strange?"

"Strange that a smart person has nothing better to obsess over than the life of some Imperial weirdo," Kanan said, shaking his head in disbelief. "Why do you care?"

"Because where Vidian goes, pain follows. Friends of mine have vanished, their worlds have suffered. But everybody wants something. If I can find out what he's after, maybe I can do something about it."

Kanan shook his head. What was she—eighteen, maybe? Taking on an Imperial power broker? "Seriously, how did you come up with all this stuff?"

"I have eyes and ears. I read. I talk to people. I listen."

"You talk to people like Skelly and Zaluna, you really are desperate. Skelly's a mess. And it didn't sound like Zaluna was looking to be a part of any of this. She was fulfilling a last request, not picking up a cause."

A distant look came to her eyes. A little sad, he thought. "No," she said, "they're not really the sort of people who could be—" She stopped herself and started again. "They're not the sort I'm looking for."

"I could have told you that. I did, in fact." He put his hand to his chest. "I'm another story. Very reliable. And I'm about to be available."

"Available for what?"

"For whatever." Kanan stood upright. "I'm leaving this planet—and I recommend the same for you. You've been fun to be around, street fights notwithstanding. Forget this Vidian business, and we can go wandering."

She regarded him with skeptical amusement. "I don't think so," Hera said. "We just met. I don't even know what you are."

"Ask anyone." Kanan waved over the heads of the drunken mob. "Okadiah! Tell her about me!"

Unseen amid the drunken crowd, Okadiah called out, "A fine pilot, an occasional humanitarian, and a somewhat tolerable houseguest. Marry him, my darling!"

"That's an endorsement?" Hera asked, straining to see where the voice had come from. "Can he even see me?"

"Doesn't matter," Kanan said. "Anyone will tell you. I can do anything."

"I don't want you to do anything."

"I know the sector. I know people. I know people who know people." He turned around. "Here, watch this. What was the name from Zaluna's list?"

"The guy the Empire was inquiring about?" She didn't miss a beat. "Lemuel Tharsa."

His eyes scanned the room. "Hang on," he said. "*Okadiah!*"

The old man stepped through the crowd toward them. "You beckoned?" Laying eyes on Hera, the old man bowed admiringly. "Oh, you *definitely* beckon."

Hera lowered her eyes and grinned.

"Did you know a Lemuel Tharsa?" Kanan asked.

"I may have known several Lemuel Tharsas. Is there a shortage?"

"He was around twenty or so years ago," Hera said. "I was wondering if you remembered who he was."

Okadiah shook his head. "It grieves me to disappoint you, my dear. But no. Never on one of my crews."

Hera nodded. "All right. Thank you."

Starting to turn away, Okadiah looked back. "Now, if he worked for the refineries or the Guild administration, I wouldn't have seen him unless he came into the bar. You might ask Boss Lal. She's a lifer at Moonglow—from back in the days when it was Introsphere. She might have personnel records."

"Thanks!"

"But please don't look at mine," Okadiah said. "I don't want you knowing I'm too old for you."

"Get out of here," Kanan said, shoving his friend away. "He's got kidney stones your age," he told Hera.

"Your remark wounds," the older man said, and drifted away.

Hera looked up at Kanan. "Well, now, I *really* want to get in over there. Will you give me the badge or won't you?"

Kanan rubbed his forehead. "I knew you were going to say that. Look, it's been a long day. In a few hours, I've got to run these people back to Moonglow for the morning shift—those that regain consciousness, anyway. I also need to pick up my final pay. You come with us. If you insist, I'll take you to the grounds and get you in." He put up his hands. "But that's it, all right? No crazy stuff."

She studied him for a moment. Finally, she nodded. "Okay. Just this one thing." She raised her glass. "And no crazy stuff. That's my motto."

Hera returned to her ship, resisting Kanan's offer of lodging at The Asteroid Belt. It turned out that "drunks sleeping on the floor" was more than a jocular expression; Okadiah Garson owned the building across the alley, where exhausted revelers, for the princely sum of a credit a head, retired to the luxury of mats on the hard floor. Kanan had offered to give her the more private room upstairs from the cantina—with him either present or absent—but she'd decided to pass. She had a lot to absorb.

Zaluna had never resurfaced, and Hera doubted there was any point in trying to make contact. If Hera had arrived earlier, or if the Sullustan woman hadn't been scared off, she might now have the data cube from Transcept, obviously a treasure trove of information on people and Imperial surveillance methods. But Hera wasn't angry at fate, or herself. Every plan ran the risk of failure due to the unexpected. Recriminations were a waste of valuable time.

But Kanan Jarrus had surprised her, and people seldom did. In Shaketown, she'd seen a brawler, a typical roughneck. But in the bar—beyond his romantic interest, which she had decided to find amusing—she'd seen him act with subtlety and cunning.

It was timely, but likely a onetime thing. She didn't expect to have a chance to find out, in any event.

No, her real quarry remained. Vidian wanted increased production from the world, obviously, but the urgency of his visit had her thinking something else was going on. If Vidian was here on a secret mission—maybe a secret mission for the Emperor—then she wanted to know.

And then there was Lemuel Tharsa. From her ship, she'd checked the public HoloNet and found Tharsa was alive and well and living offworld as a mining consultant, doing freelance work for the Imperial government. Why, then, would anyone aboard *Ultimatum* want to check out his distant past on Gorse? Might he be a potential traitor in Vidian's midst—and an ally for her, were she to warn him?

She would look for answers tomorrow, at Moonglow. She would find the truth—and the truth would tell her what to do. As it always did.

She forced herself to sleep.

PHASE TWO:

REACTION

"Emperor opens new veterans' medcenter on Coruscant"

"Hunt under way for missing after industrial accident on Cynda"

"Count Vidian arrives on Gorse for inspection tour, traffic delays possible"

—headlines, Imperial HoloNews (Gorse Edition)

CHAPTER TWENTY-THREE

FOR THE FIRST TIME since she entered the Academy, Rae Sloane was late for an appointment. But the Galactic Empire had made the schedule. It could break the schedule.

And it wasn't her fault, anyway. During the descent through Gorse's atmosphere, Count Vidian had emerged from the passenger compartment to reroute the captain's shuttle—*Truncheon*—to a location well south of the factory districts. He'd demanded a flyover of the miners' hospice he had ordered closed.

She hadn't understood the point of making such a trip, if they weren't going to land. There wasn't much to see in the dark. But then she'd seen the reason in a flash—or rather, *with* a flash, as the cube-shaped building abruptly imploded. Vidian had been busy while Sloane had slept, ordering the movement of the personnel, usable equipment, and all patients—so far as she knew, anyway—from the medcenter. With many of the just-evacuated still on the ground looking back from their transports, the Empire's demolition teams had made quick work of the building. Debris removal vehicles were already on the scene; Vidian had plans to turn the site into a more convenient fuel depot. True to his reputation, the man worked incredibly fast. Sloane could only imagine what the bewildered patients watching must have thought, watching their home coming down.

She didn't bother to imagine what Vidian had thought. The man had simply watched the collapse, emotionlessly, before returning to the rear of the vehicle. It was fine with her. Her job was making sure nothing else happened to interfere with his visit. What had happened on Cynda would not happen here.

The count had stops planned all over the muddy megalopolis, so Sloane had decided against using ground vehicles to get to them all. There would be too many routes to secure. Instead, *Truncheon* would fly from stop to stop, bringing its own complement of stormtroopers and protected by electronic countermeasures against ground-to-air attacks while in flight. Such an attack was unlikely in the extreme, but Sloane tried to think of everything.

It meant clearing landing zones everywhere and securing them. That hadn't been a problem. The captain of a Star Destroyer was a naval officer, of course, but she was also the personification of Imperial authority in the system. And while she did not have formal power over the Empire's local authorities on Gorse—except under certain circumstances—captains of capital ships were nonetheless treated like miniature governors. Few petty bureaucrats wanted to argue with someone who could put a dozen AT-ATs on the ground with a comlink call. And so Gorse's local police force had joined with the stormtroopers from the planetary garrison to make ready for Vidian's arrival.

She could get used to having this kind of authority. She certainly wanted to.

"Shaketown," she announced as the ship approached an industrial neighborhood. "Such as it is."

The place was aptly named, she decided: Sloane felt a slight quake as the ship's landing gear settled in the mud. The advance team had decided against having *Truncheon* land on Moonglow's tarmac, where it would have been parked amid explosives haulers; the fugitive had flown back on one and was still at large. Instead, the street in front of Moonglow's front gate had been cordoned off—reportedly over the heated objections of a Besalisk diner owner—to create a reception area.

Such as it is. The ramp down, Sloane surveyed the scene. Vidian's official visit—even *her* visit—on another world would have merited pomp and preparation, short notice or not. Here, there were a few temporary light stands supplementing the waxing moon—and someone had laid some planks over the muddy street. About two dozen citizens stood off to the side, flanked by stormtroopers, watching as a sad little processional approached *Truncheon*. Not the greeting she had ordered or would have liked—but she knew Vidian wouldn't care.

He appeared in the doorway behind her. She'd only known Vidian to march straight into places, not wasting any time—but here, he stood, looking up, down, and all around. And mostly at the factory across the way, where his macabre eyes lingered for long moments. She decided he was just doing whatever it was he did when he prepared to inspect a place. The man could be standing there staring at tomorrow's menu in the *Ultimatum* mess halls, for all she knew.

A tan-skinned human woman waved to them, flanked by two Besalisks. Sloane knew her from their holographic conversation as Shaketown's mayor. "Welcome, Count Vidian. Welcome, Captain. May I present Lal Grallik, chief operating officer of Moonglow Polychemical?"

Vidian broke from his trance and walked down the ramp. No hand was offered. Sloane joined him on the planking.

Lal, wearing a dark business suit, bowed and gestured to the other Besalisk. "This is my husband, Gord—head of ground security."

"I hardly think we'll need him," Sloane said, following Vidian. "And I'm surprised he would be employed here after letting the demolitions man escape." She paused to glare at Lal. "Family or not!"

The male Besalisk growled. "If you think you can do any better—"

His wife shushed him. "I'm sure there won't be any problems now, Captain. Gord's team has triple-checked every square meter of the site."

"Uh-huh." Hearing a high whine coming from the south, Sloane turned to see a weathered hoverbus setting down outside the security line. "What's that there?"

"Part of the next shift for Cynda," Lal said, smiling too broadly. "We're always working here!"

The stormtroopers waved the battered hoverbus through the check-point. The Mark Six Smoothride had already been past its life span when Okadiah bought it; where it had once flown through the skies, not even Kanan ever dared to take it more than a meter off the ground. Okadiah had been so terrified it would skyrocket off uncon-trollably that he kept a parachute under the seat. Kanan thought that an unlikely scenario. It was much more likely to die in the street, as it had for him several times. It was good for one purpose: bringing hungover miners back to Moonglow so they could earn enough cred-its to drink again.

The Imperial Lambda was parked up ahead, its mass completely blocking the entrance to Drakka's Diner. Kanan was certain the chef loved that. In front of the Sienar Fleet Systems shuttle, Kanan saw his boss's husband ambling along, following several steps behind a larger party. Spotting him drive past, Lal waved. "Hello, Kanan! Good to see you didn't quit!"

Kanan replied with a half wave—and then, seeing Vidian out there, quickly pulled his head back inside the window. He gritted his teeth. Yesterday, he had been ready to leave Gorse entirely. Today, he was willingly coming back to an armed camp. But it was just one more day, and there was an excellent reason why. Looking back down the aisle, he saw her chatting amiably with the miners. They were spellbound by Hera. He couldn't blame them.

The stormtroopers waved the hoverbus around to the service gate. The Smoothride groaned as it turned sharply, and for a moment, Kanan thought he heard a thump coming from one of the rearward compartments. It could be anything, he thought. The hoverbus was apt to die on any given trip. Even the door to the restroom was broken.

"I've been having the most lovely conversation with your young friend," Okadiah said, arriving from the back. "We have decided to vacation on Naboo. You may drive us."

"Be careful. She's a woman with a mission," Kanan said as the metal beast settled harshly in the mud. The doors opened, and his passengers filed past him. Kanan remained.

"You're not flying bombs today?" Okadiah said.

"No," Kanan said, nodding toward the back. "I'd like to show someone the sights."

Okadiah patted his shoulder. "The only job that matters. Good luck."

Kanan smiled, slowly, as the man stepped out. Okadiah hadn't seen the duffel on the floor near the driver's seat—Kanan's belongings, packed while the old man wasn't looking. He'd miss Okadiah, and that was probably good-bye. But the next chapter, he could feel, had already begun.

Even if it was starting strangely. "You really want to do this?" he asked Hera. She was at the window behind the driver's seat, looking all around.

"Yes," Hera said. "I really do."

She slipped off her cloak to reveal an all-black outfit. Good for sneaking around in a sunless place, Kanan thought—and better to look at. She checked her holster to see that her blaster pistol was secure. "I really think you ought to hang this and do something else with your time," he said.

Hera replied with a firm look. "I'm sure you have suggestions." She put out her hand.

"Fine." Kanan reluctantly handed her his Moonglow ID badge. "Wave it in front of the sensor at the inner door. I'll be parked out in the street, pretending to have engine trouble." It wouldn't require much of a lie, he knew. "When you get back, I'll get my pay from Lal and take you to the spaceport—and we'll go to any planet you want."

"We will, will we?" Hera rolled her eyes.

"That's right."

"I have my own ship." She stepped out of the bus.

Huh. That was interesting news, he thought as she disappeared through the door.

Kanan guided the hoverbus back out the gate and parked it within sight of the shuttle. Stepping out, he saw that stormtroopers and local security types were still stationed all around. It was time to start the pantomime.

And there was one small blessing: Skelly hadn't made an appearance after all. *Nobody's that foolish!*

"That's Kanan, all right." Skelly surveyed the new arrivals from his perch hidden among the chimneys atop Drakka's Diner. Only one eyepiece of his secondhand macrobinoculars displayed anything, but that was enough to show him what he needed to see.

He'd realized that he couldn't simply reveal himself. The mining company people wouldn't want him to speak to Vidian, and he didn't trust stormtroopers to deliver him after the episode on the moon. He needed to reach the man when he was alone—and that meant getting into the factory. Thorilide refineries were complicated places: a lot of huge equipment often crammed into tight spaces, offering lots of hiding places.

And Moonglow had something else: an ancient connection to Shaketown's long-abandoned sewer system. Gorse wasn't a particularly rainy place, but the underground water table rose and fell dramatically with the tides. Cynda's movements squeezed the planet like a sponge, causing puddles to spring randomly from the soil. But quake damage had rendered the sewers useless, and only people interested in such places, like Skelly, knew the sewer system existed.

And how to get into it. Prying the macrobinoculars from his hand, he stuffed them into his enormous backpack. Donning it, he found the ladder leading down into the diner's back alley. There, in the middle of a low pool of brackish water, sat the rounded cover he was looking for.

Struggling under the burden of his pack, Skelly fished for handholds around the circumference of the metal disk. He curled his fingers beneath and strained for a long minute. It wouldn't budge. He tried to stand up—only to realize his malfunctioning right hand was locked in position, with his fingers underneath the cover.

Great, Skelly thought. *What else can go wrong?*

Then he found out.

"Who's back here?" Drakka, the enormous Besalisk chef, appeared

behind him, armed—as if he needed to be—with a huge iron skillet. He grabbed at Skelly with his three free hands, trying to turn him around. Skelly felt pain in his arm as his hand, still attached to the sewer cover, didn't budge.

"Whoa, there!" Skelly said. He was trespassing, he knew—but the Besalisk ought to recognize him. "It's me, Drakka! Skelly! You know me!"

"You say that like it's a good thing!" The Besalisk continued pulling. "You're breaking into my place!"

"Whoa, no!" Skelly winced with pain. "I'm going over to Moonglow to see the Imperials!"

Drakka stopped tugging. He frowned. "I'm closed today because of those idiots." Skelly watched him nervously, for a moment, as the behemoth decided what to do.

Then he reached past Skelly and ripped the sewer cover off the hole, freeing the human's hand in the process. "Besalisks have a saying," he said. "When your neighbors trouble you, send your rodents to their nest." Before Skelly could feel relief, Drakka yanked him from the ground and threw him down the hole.

"Thanks, pal!" Skelly called up from the drenched bottom. He was lucky to have good friends who wanted to lend a hand.

CHAPTER TWENTY-FOUR

HAVING POWER TO wield on the ground might not be so good after all, Sloane thought. Not if authority meant going on mindless tours of local factories. Hailing from the industrial world Ganthel, she had seen quite enough of shipyards and loading docks. She had gone to the Academy to escape a life working at such places.

But Lal Grallik had insisted on extolling the virtues of every little thing at her company. She was leading them now into the new section, built under her watch; when Gorse ran out of thorilide deposits and mining of the moon started, a new intake center had been required. *Next she'll be showing us the janitorial closets,* Sloane thought.

The one surprising thing was that Count Vidian had said little during the tour. Strange, since he was here to issue directives, and if anyone could stop the Besalisk woman in her time-wasting palaver, he could.

A beeping comlink from the rear of the entourage stopped her instead. "Lal!" her security chief husband called out. "There's a report of someone sneaking around the plant. Personnel department."

"That Skelly person?" Vidian asked.

"They didn't see who it was," Gord Grallik said. He pocketed the comlink and turned around. "I'll check it out."

Sloane gestured to her stormtrooper escort. "Go see."

"No, no," the guard said, heading off. "This is my turf."

"It's all our turf," Sloane said. She pointed after the Besalisk. "Follow him!"

Skelly watched from his hiding place behind a moving conveyer belt. He had been lucky. An old storm drain opened up right next to one of the newer buildings; he'd had to leave his pack at the bottom to climb up, but he'd been able to dash quickly into the building.

Since then, he'd crept around the high-ceilinged facility, waiting for his chance to get to Vidian. Something had happened to cause Gord to leave, and the Imperial captain had sent her stormtroopers along. Skelly continued to creep closer. He could finally hear their conversations, even over the din of the active belts.

"—and you may find this of particular interest, Captain Sloane." It was Lal, speaking from the foot of the ten-meter-tall mass of titanium at the far end of the room. "This is our heavy-duty bulk-loader vehicle, the newest in use on Gorse. You'll find the cab interior similar to what's in some of your own armored walkers: It's the same manufacturer. If you'll step inside, I can show you."

Skelly saw the women climbing up the metal staircase and into the passenger compartment of the big vehicle. Creeping ahead, he saw Vidian unaccompanied at the bottom, pacing down the long aisle between the conveyer belts out of the women's sight. Skelly's heart pounded. Whether Vidian was alone a moment or a minute, this was his chance!

"You can come out now." The loud voice was the one Skelly had heard on a dozen management recordings. "I can hear you very well, even in a place like this." Count Vidian turned to face him. "The saboteur, I presume."

"That's not what I am," Skelly said, rising from his knees. He dusted himself off. "I'm a whistleblower, Count Vidian. I'm like you—I think the old ways of doing things have to change. I see what people are doing wrong!"

"I see someone doing something wrong."

Skelly was glad Vidian was talking. He'd heard about the man's cybernetic capabilities: Talking to Skelly meant he wasn't calling for help on his internal comlink.

"If you know me," the count continued, "you know I take problems into my own hands to solve."

"Then you want this," Skelly said, pulling the holodisk from his vest. "My research. You've got to stop the blasting on Cynda. You could tear the whole moon apart by mistake!"

"Madness." Vidian kept walking purposefully toward him. "And if it were possible, and the Empire chose to do it, we would certainly not ask your permission."

Skelly's eyes locked on Vidian's macabre visage, and he stumbled backward. *"I'm trying to help you!"*

"Help by dying." With a mighty swat, Vidian smacked the disk away. It clattered to the floor beneath a conveyor belt. The second swing found Skelly's face.

It had not been a good couple of days for snooping around, Hera thought. There was no getting near Vidian during his tour of the landing field, so she'd started in the personnel department, looking to see if Lemuel Tharsa—the person of Imperial interest, according to Zaluna's files—was anyone important. He'd never been an employee, but the man had been to Moonglow: Visitor badges had been supplied to him on several occasions more than twenty years earlier. Before she could learn more, someone had found her. That was the problem with infiltrating a working factory on a day when the Empire came to inspect. No one had called in sick.

Normally, she liked a challenge. But with the Moonglow security team going one direction and the stormtroopers going another, she'd been forced early into the skulker's last resort: the ventilation shafts. Fortunately, the new building's system was less vile than what she'd found in other factories.

Peering down through another grate, she saw the Besalisk security chief again—Gord, Kanan had called him, the administrator's husband. Gord was telling his aides they had to redeem themselves for losing Skelly the day before. Hera felt a momentary pang of guilt for getting the guy in trouble with his wife and the Empire. But it passed as Gord looked up and pointed, evidently noticing the indentation in the vent housing. That's when the blasterfire started.

Enough of this, she thought, scrambling through another tube. It was time to find Vidian.

Sloane emerged from the cab of the bulk-loader to see Vidian a few dozen meters away down on the factory floor, mercilessly pummeling Skelly. She activated the comlink attached to her wrist and pulled her blaster. "Troopers, to me!"

Vidian lifted the intruder and hurled him through the air. Limbs flailed as Skelly hurtled end over end. His flight ended violently against a control console for one of the conveyor belts.

"This is under control," Vidian said, walking casually toward the spot.

Sloane ran down the stairs anyway. She could see that Vidian's opponent was bleeding and clutching his chest. Skelly stood, facing the approaching cyborg in a daze, before desperately scrambling up the side of the control station. Leaping, he reached for the overhang above and tried to pull himself up.

"Stop!" Sloane raised her weapon.

With a burst of energy that startled her, Skelly pulled himself up and onto the moving conveyor belt. Sloane fired—but the belt carried him around a turn, and her blaster bolt only singed his shin.

Sloane looked back to see Lal, horrified and keeping her distance, up on the metal staircase. "Stop all the belts!" the captain yelled. Lal bustled down the steps to the controls.

"Too late," Vidian said, watching. The conveyor belt led back outside, to the loading area. Seeing Sloane's troopers arriving through a side hallway, Vidian pointed. "After him!"

Sloane stepped up to Vidian. "That was him? Skelly?"

Vidian nodded—and started walking back up the aisle.

"He won't get off the grounds. I'll alert everyone," she said.

"I've just done so," Vidian said, his gaze cast low. He was looking for something, she realized, at the foot of one of the conveyor belts.

"But you should go supervise. Someone in authority should be out there."

The whole episode puzzled Sloane. "What was Skelly trying to accomplish? What did he want?"

Vidian knelt. He picked up a small object from the floor. "He wanted to give me this," he said. It was a holodisk, Sloane saw. "It's of no consequence. When you find him, tell him I destroyed it. He should die knowing the futility of defying the Empire."

Kanan removed a bolt from the Smoothride's engine for the fourteenth time. Then he proceeded to put it right back.

He didn't stick his neck out for many—hardly any, really!—but there was something about Hera that had kept him from leaving. He was still working out what it was. She was beautiful, of course—but she knew how to play it cool, something he liked a lot. She also seemed reasonably competent—she'd caught on to his ruse back at the cantina right away. All good traits, suited for whatever it was she was playing at. Kanan still didn't quite know what that was, but that was all right. He could play along, as he had many times before when something or someone caught his interest for a while. He had nothing else to do.

Outside, a siren blared. Looking out from beneath the engine bonnet of the hoverbus, Kanan saw several stormtroopers on speeder bikes racing into the security zone and rushing toward the factory gates. Some were headed toward Moonglow's airfield, where *Expedient* sat parked amid a few other vehicles; others were headed for the main facility.

So much for competence, he thought. Looked like Hera was in trouble.

He slammed the engine lid shut and started to turn toward the factory. He didn't have his badge, but he knew a place around the corner where he could scale the fence ringing the aerodrome.

Reaching the spot, Kanan leapt and swung himself over the railing. Hitting the soft ground, he rolled—

—and was met by stormtrooper blasters pointed in his direction.

Harsh lights flooded the corner of the airfield, nearly blinding him. He could just make out a brown-skinned woman in an Imperial captain's uniform stepping toward him.

"And where," she asked sharply, "do you think *you're* going?"

Skelly had closed the sewer grating over his head just in time. He heard the boots of stormtroopers running past, above, even as he struggled to make his way down the iron rungs of the ladder.

Reaching the bottom, he collapsed in the ankle-deep brackish water, battered and broken. His head was bleeding, and his cheekbones felt as if they were moving beneath his skin. He fumbled with his left hand to count his teeth—and felt anguish when he realized how many were gone. He struggled to roll over, certain his ribs had been cracked.

Skelly coughed, bewildered. Vidian was supposed to be different. The rule breaker. The paradigm destroyer. He had reached the heights of both the public and private sectors by ignoring the bureaucracies and their conventions, by listening to everyone and everything, and deciding based on facts.

Yet he had turned out to be just another sadist, as deaf and blind as he had been before the prosthetics.

Seeing his pack nearby, Skelly fought through the pain and dragged his body close to it. There was a medpac in there—and more. Much more.

If words couldn't save the moon, it was time for something else!

CHAPTER TWENTY-FIVE

BESALISKS LOOKED miserable in a way that few species could, Vidian thought. With enormous wide mouths and droopy skin sacs hanging beneath, when they frowned, you could read the expression from orbit.

Count Vidian wasn't interested in Lal Grallik's embarrassment over Skelly breaking in, any more than he was interested in her apologies. The encounter with the saboteur had deterred him from his intended schedule. She had taken him without delay to the refinery building: the oldest part of Moonglow, she'd said, dating back to when the firm was part of Introsphere.

She eagerly showed him her updates—and he ignored her obvious disappointment as he just as quickly undid them, stripping away one safety practice after another. Toxic exposure was a small price to pay to meet the Emperor's quota.

Vidian hated being dependent on surface refineries for thorilide: His comet-chaser harvesters required few workers and were closer to the source. But cometary deposits were already microscopic, while the shards coming from Cynda had to be reduced to a refinable size without damaging the material within. Worse, thorilide-bearing comets were exceedingly rare, and the Empire's insatiable demand for materials had nearly swept the galaxy clean of them. It had idled many of the giant harvester vessels Vidian operated—and had given the slackers in this system job security. It would take forever to replicate Gorse's refining infrastructure on Cynda: He would be reliant on fools like Lal Grallik forever.

Thorilide was Vidian's franchise within the Empire—it, and several other strategic materials. Meeting the need for it had brought him power and position. Now he was failing at meeting his Emperor's demands. And Vidian's rivals knew it.

He'd been preoccupied since Baron Danthe's second message, the night before on *Ultimatum*. Danthe wasn't calling to tell him the Emperor was re-raising production quotas, at least, but what he'd said was almost as bad. Another comet-chaser fleet was returning to Calcoraan Depot, having exhausted what was once a rich supply of thorilide-bearing comets.

And worse, Vidian had learned next from his aides that Danthe had been whispering to the Emperor, casting aspersions on Vidian's whole production scheme. The count knew what Danthe wanted: to turn Gorse into another market for his family's manufacturing droids. Vidian had no quarrel with droids, which could in many cases be much more efficient than organics. But he wasn't about to let Danthe colonize an industry that belonged to him. Vidian had taken out his temper on his stateroom, then—but he'd longed to have Danthe's windpipe in his robotic hands.

Grallik led him to the far wall, and a narrow door. Beyond it was another large room with colossal pipes in the ceiling and the long pools cut into the floor. Long and narrow, like harvesting troughs in a farm for sea life. The droids were here, too, some shoving cartloads of crystals into the roiling green liquid, others trolling the pools with long implements.

"We're very proud of this, my lord. This is a prize project of mine—the only automated xenoboric acid bath on Gorse. The crystals from Cynda start here, and the droids do the rest."

Vidian looked down into a pool. Deep and long, a roiling cauldron with an endless appetite for matter. "And how many days do you lose from droids falling in during groundquakes? Organics would keep their balance better."

"Yes, sir. But the fumes and splashing would be dangerous—and of course, if someone went in, that would be much worse than a droid."

"Worse, how? The baths cannot be used for purification until the offending matter is consumed. Droids take much longer to digest."

Lal was struck speechless by that one. Vidian didn't care. He had a call coming in. He switched his ears to comlink mode.

"Commander Chamas aboard *Ultimatum,* my lord. Message from Coruscant."

"Patch it through."

Lero Danthe appeared before his electronic eyes. "My compliments to Count Vidian."

What was left of Vidian's vocal cords stirred in a growl, a vocalization that for him had no electronic counterpart. The young man appeared life-sized, superimposed over Vidian's surroundings: There was no holoprojector here, but it worked basically the same way. "What is it?" he finally said.

The blond baron smiled. "I've just emerged from another series of meetings with top authorities, working at the highest levels on projects of the greatest . . ."

Vidian stopped listening. He was too busy moving his head around, digitally dumping the chattering baron in one pool of acid after another.

". . . and to make it all possible, the Emperor will require an immediate doubling of thorilide deliveries. Effective immediately."

Vidian gawked. "What? *Doubling?*"

"Correct."

"A doubling of the original quotas."

"No," Danthe said, explaining as if he were talking to a child. "Your quota was increased by half yesterday, remember? So—"

"So it's really a tripling." Vidian felt his ire bubbling over, angrier than any acid bath in the room. "And you didn't argue against this? This target is impossible. The failure will be yours, too."

The baron shrugged. "I'm attached to your administration, my lord, but I serve the Emperor in all things." He paused, before continuing gingerly. "I *did* suggest a number of things I could do to help—but of course those would require putting some of your territories in my hands."

"I'll just bet you did," Vidian snarled. "This isn't finished, Danthe!"

"So what should I tell the Emperor?"

"That I'll succeed! Vidian out!"

Vidian seethed. This was deception on a grand scale. Vidian had never played games of court well; it was his biggest weakness. The other aristocrats knew it, and one had finally pounced. He was undermined, completely and totally, in a way that he hadn't experienced since years earlier, when he was a different person—

Lal stood near one of the acid baths and looked back in puzzlement. "Are you all right, my lord? You—er, haven't moved for a while."

Vidian wore no emotion, as always. The words came from his neck. "I need triple the output from this factory, immediately."

Lal laughed out loud. Immediately embarrassed, she covered her wide mouth with two of her hands. "I'm sorry. You can't be serious?"

Vidian turned and began stalking toward her. "I am always serious."

She stepped back, nervously. "We can't do that. We were struggling to meet the original Imperial targets."

"Which you never met, either." Vidian stepped up to her. Lal shook, eyeing him fearfully. "Can you meet these targets?"

"N-n-no."

"Then what good are you?" Vidian's arms lanced out, shoving Lal with his open palms. She tumbled backward into one of the boiling troughs.

She screamed, the acid bubbling all around her. "Help! P-p-please!"

Vidian turned and found one of the tending poles, constructed of material designed to withstand the chemical abuse. But instead of fishing her out, he jabbed at her, pushing Lal farther in.

"I am helping," Vidian said, electronic eyes shining. "I need this vat returned to operation. Now hurry up and dissolve."

———

Hera heard the scream.

She had been staying a step ahead of the Besalisk security chief by entering the refinery and running among the rafters. There were plenty of pipes and catwalks providing routes for one as nimble as she. She'd been hoping to double back, to finish looking for what she'd entered for—when she'd heard the cry. Horrible, unlike anything she'd ever known.

She couldn't help but run toward it.

When she arrived, it was too late. The body was visible from her high vantage point—barely—in the depths of the turbulent pool, but there was no way to get down there without falling in herself. Count Vidian stood at the edge with a tending pole. It had to be him; no one else looked like that. He watched the pool for a moment before dropping the pole, turning, and heading off.

Hera saw a place where she could safely leap down, up ahead. She started working her way toward it.

But Gord Grallik arrived first—and broke her heart.

CHAPTER TWENTY-SIX

ON THE REFINERY FLOOR, Gord Grallik wailed.

The security chief had rushed into the room, still looking for Hera. She was heading down the stairs herself when he stopped between the frothing acid pools and looked down. Hera had already seen from above that the four-armed figure in the acid was unmistakably Besalisk.

"*Lal!*" Gord scrambled around, looking for one of the acid-proof prods. By the time Hera reached the floor, he had given up. He turned to the pool, ready to dive into the acid bath and save his wife.

"Don't!" Hera called out. Skidding to a stop so as not to knock them both in, she grabbed at the security chief's left arms. "It's too late!"

Gord struggled. "I've got to!"

Hera clung to him desperately. She didn't even know if he was aware of her as he struggled to step toward the pool. He greatly outweighed her—and yet she was using every bit of her strength to keep him from jumping. "*You . . . can't . . . do this!*"

At last, Gord stopped. She didn't know if he'd finally registered her presence, realizing she would fall in, too—or if he'd simply seen again what was left of Lal. So little. *"No,"* he said in a low voice. He fell to his knees. "No."

The Twi'lek hung on to his arms. "I'm sorry," she said. She was trying to pull him back from the edge, without much success.

Gord looked at her—and anger blazed in his eyes. "Did you do this?"

"No! I swear I didn't. It was Vidian!" Hera fell away from him but did not run. "Check the security monitors. You'll see!"

Besalisk hands grabbed her. With Hera in tow and murder in his eyes, Gord moved quickly with her to the security control station at the far wall. "I'll see," he said.

Vidian stood outside the refinery and looked up at the moon. He'd killed another tour guide, yes, but there really wasn't any sense in continuing with this tour, or any other. Moonglow was the best-case operator on Gorse. Even if the Empire seized direct control of the factories—a tool in his kit that he found to be of mixed effectiveness— there was no way to make the Emperor's new quotas.

And the first deliveries were due in a week.

Vidian turned and punched the wall. His hand smashed into the permacrete, leaving an indentation. Baron Danthe was at fault for this—a supposed underling, turning him into just another worker scrambling to meet an ultimatum from above. He already knew there was no way to find enough ready thorilide in his territory, or anyone else's. Not without tearing the moon completely apart . . .

Vidian stopped. He played back what his eyes and ears had recorded from earlier, the rantings of the madman Skelly.

"You've got to stop the blasting on Cynda. You could tear the whole moon apart by mistake!"

Remembering, he reached into his pocket. The holodisk was there, the one he had planned to destroy.

Vidian strode purposefully toward a nearby office building. Yes, looking at it would almost certainly be a waste of time for a man that did not waste time. The fact he considered it at all was a true measure of the desperate situation he faced.

Sloane wasn't the first Imperial captain Kanan had met. But she was certainly the best-looking—even if she did insist on pulling that wonderful black hair back beneath the little hat. One of her aides was shining a light into his face, entirely unnecessary under the light from the moon.

"They say you got into the security zone because you were ferrying miners to work," the woman said. "If you're a bus driver, why were you trying to enter the factory?"

"Heading to pick up my pay." Hands manacled behind his back, Kanan flashed a smile at her. "If you want, once I get it I can show you the town."

Sloane's brown eyes narrowed. "Wait a second. I know you! You're that pilot from the explosives hauler. *The mouth.*"

"You've got a name for me," Kanan said, grinning. "That's great. I knew you couldn't just fly off. You came all the way down here to see me?"

Sloane stepped forward, reached around to grab his ponytail, and yanked. "Let's not be giving me jobs to do, pilot," she said, forcing him to the ground. "This little act of yours might work with some. Me, I might press you into service and set you to maintaining trash compactors. Or shove you into one!"

"Okay, okay." Kanan shrugged against the stormtrooper's hold. "But if you know I'm a pilot, you know I work here."

"With no pass for the grounds?"

"Lal Grallik knows me. Ask her."

"Making friends?" Kanan heard a now-familiar voice from behind Sloane. The captain spun without releasing him, wrenching his neck in the process. Hera stepped forward from the factory, dangling his pass in her hands. "You left your ID in the plant, buddy."

The Imperials shone their light on Hera. Sloane studied her before looking back to him. Kanan nodded, to the extent he could with the captain holding on to his hair. "Told you."

Sloane released Kanan with a shove, knocking him backward and down into the mud. She turned on Hera. "And where's your badge?"

Hera grinned. "Well, I've got to have it. How could I be in here, otherwise?"

Sloane looked to the sky and growled with frustration. "I've had enough of you people. I think we'll take you all in for—"

"*Sloane!*"

The captain checked her comlink. "Count Vidian," she said. "We're still running down Skelly—and any accomplices."

"Forget them," Vidian replied.

"My lord?"

"The inspection. Everything. Forget it all. I've seen enough here. I have a new strategy that will serve the Emperor. We need to return to *Ultimatum* right away. Gather your team and meet me at the shuttle."

Sloane acknowledged the order and deactivated her comlink. She gestured to a stormtrooper to remove Kanan's handcuffs. Another returned his blaster and holster. "Your lucky day," Sloane said.

"It sure is," Kanan said, nodding to Hera. "I've got the two of you here."

Hera rushed forward and grabbed his arm. "Thank you, Captain. We'll be going." She began pushing Kanan toward the open gate, under Sloane's icy glare. "Sorry to have disturbed you."

"Yeah, good luck with your inspection," Kanan said, before Hera forcibly shoved him out the employee gate.

Hera hustled Kanan around the corner and back to the hoverbus. She seemed perturbed. "You really don't know when to quit, do you?"

Kanan shrugged. "Hey, it worked, didn't it?" He wiped the mud off his trousers. "Being hostile or closemouthed just sets them off. The way to get rid of Imperials is to be so happy to see them that they're thrilled when you're gone. Some Imperials, anyway."

Hera put up her hands. "We don't have time for this. Something horrible happened in there, and—" She paused and looked down, choking up a little. He realized he hadn't seen her looking anything but fully in control before. Now she looked spent.

"Hey," he said, touching her wrist. "You're not kidding. Something bad?"

"Vidian killed the administrator."

"What, Lal?" Kanan was shocked. "He killed her? Why?"

"Because he could," she said, looking up and staring into his eyes. "Her husband saw it and ran off searching for Vidian. And it sounds from that comlink call like Vidian's up to something else!"

"Right about over there," Kanan said, pointing to the Imperial shuttle. Across the muddy boulevard from it, Moonglow's main gate opened. Vidian appeared there, talking with the vessel's flight crew. Sloane and her stormtroopers joined him.

"We've got to follow them," Hera said.

"I can't follow a shuttle in a hoverbus!"

"It's a Mark Six Smoothride," she said. "It'll fly!"

"About a zillion years ago," Kanan said. He looked back to see Vidian marching purposefully along the planking toward the shuttle. Sloane lingered at the gate with the others, evidently giving orders related to her departure.

And then, his eye tracing the path back to the Lambda, he saw something wedged beneath the plank nearest the ship. It looked like a small pouch, several meters away from what appeared to a sewer grating.

An *open* sewer grating.

Kanan didn't need the Force to tell him to grab Hera. *"Get down!"*

The night lit up in Shaketown. The Imperial shuttle exploded, sending blazing debris in all directions. In the street, the shock wave caught Vidian, hurling him bodily into the factory's outer fence even as a fireball blazed overhead.

Kanan caught only a glimpse of the cyborg's fate as, Hera's shoulders in his gloved hands, he dived with her behind the Smoothride. Metallic debris rocketed in all directions, some of it slamming thunderously into the hoverbus. Speeder bikes parked earlier by the reinforcements went spinning wildly; Kanan saw one impale itself in the fencing behind him.

The din subsided. Once certain Hera was all right, Kanan drew his blaster and looked cautiously around the vehicle. Up the way, Vidian was on his knees but alive, his reinforced frame evidently giving him some protection. But the street before the factory was a blazing crater—and the block of buildings behind it, including poor Drakka's Diner, was now afire. Kanan's instinct was to run toward it, to see if the Besalisk cook was all right.

But something else caught his eye first. A dark figure, scrambling out from the sewer grating he'd seen. The spot was amid the flames but untouched at the moment—and the figure was limping quickly along with a large pack on his back. *Skelly!*

Finding a functioning Imperial speeder bike, Skelly took one look back. Then he mounted it and was gone.

CHAPTER TWENTY-SEVEN

HERA CAUGHT HER breath as she reached the third-story rooftop. The buildings across the boulevard from Moonglow's headquarters weren't tall, but they all had ladders or some other kind of fire escapes. Everyone knew to expect groundquakes on Gorse. This was another story.

From a concealed spot, she looked down into the street with amazement. The Imperial vessel was still burning below, destroyed by someone they'd hurt. It was something Hera had expected to see one day, something she'd always believed was coming. Just not this soon, and not this way. She wasn't sure what had driven Skelly to do it, but he certainly had been the one responsible, based on what Kanan had seen.

Hera hadn't wanted to linger at ground level after the blast. The street looked like a war zone, and the assassination attempt was sure to send the Imperials over the edge. But she'd helped with the search-and-rescue for as long as she dared, and had to scout the best way out of the security-cordoned neighborhood. Only Kanan had any kind of permission to be on the ground anyway, and he'd hung around down there, trying to free people. She thought well of him that he'd do that. It went very much against the freewheeler mold he seemed to want to fit into.

In truth, she was still reeling from the moment in the factory when Gord Grallik had viewed the recording of Vidian killing his wife. A typical tough security guy, yet he had watched the murder as if his world were crumbling around him. It still wrenched at her heart to remember it.

But that wasn't the worst part, she now realized as she looked down at the street. Vidian, singed but apparently intact, was being hustled from the scene by his escort when Gord appeared at the gate. The Besalisk rushed forward amid the flaming embers only to be stopped by the stormtroopers. She couldn't hear him from this distance, but he was appealing to them, begging them. To arrest Vidian, she supposed. A Moonglow aide handed Gord a datapad: Hera assumed it was the images from the security cam. The frantic Besalisk showed it to one trooper after another, but they would not let him pass.

Hera didn't want to watch—there was nothing at all she could do. Not here, not now. But she made herself. Gord tried to follow Vidian anyway, only to be grabbed by the troopers. It took four of them to restrain the heavy-shouldered security chief: one for each arm.

Then they beat him. This was justice in the Empire.

When the stormtroopers parted, Hera saw Gord crawling back toward Moonglow's gate. She blinked away a tear of anger. Yes, she needed to see these things, to remind her what she was fighting for.

Hera squinted to see through the smoky darkness where Vidian had gone. She spotted him and Sloane in intense discussion, heading between a line of flanking stormtroopers on the way toward—

No, Kanan's not going to like that.

"Are you kidding me?" Having finished his search and joined Hera on the roof, Kanan stared down at the empty spot on the street. "I can't believe this. They stole the hoverbus!"

"I think they call it *commandeering on official business,*" Hera said, crouching at the roof edge and pointing east. Kanan saw the outline of the hoverbus bobbing far up the lane. "I'm sure they're headed to the Imperial spaceport to get another shuttle."

Kanan frowned. "Yeah, well, wait until they find the bathroom door's stuck." He flicked wet ashes from his tunic. He'd found Drakka pinned behind his freezer unit; it had taken long minutes to extricate him. Then the cook had stormed out, intent on giving the Imperials a piece of his mind about his destroyed business. Kanan could see from his position that the conversation wasn't going very well, but he had his own problems. "The spaceport's in Highground. How am I supposed to get over there?" It was ten kilometers away.

"I'm more interested in getting out of *here*," Hera said, rising. "An attempt's been made on an envoy of the Emperor—everyone's a suspect. We've got to get out of this neighborhood before half the Empire shows up!" She turned away from the street side of the roof. "Maybe back down those alleys to the south?"

"It's Okadiah's bus," Kanan said. "I can't just forget about it." This was the whole problem with making friends, he did not say: They made it impossible to be truly free.

He looked back across Broken Boulevard—now a more descriptive term than usual—and saw a lumbering gray hovertruck departing Moonglow's loading dock. "Hey, wait," he said, grabbing Hera's wrist before she could leave. "I think we can solve both problems at once."

He pointed to the vehicle. "That's full of refined thorilide." Even trespass, murder, and sabotage couldn't stop thorilide production, it seemed: Every six minutes another one of the transports departed the plant. "It's headed—"

"—straight to the Imperial spaceport," Hera said. "I caught that on my reconnoiter yesterday."

Their eyes met—and a heartbeat later they were running along the rooftops. Hera was fast as she was lithe, hurdling obstacles and leaping one gap after another. Every so often, she looked back to see if Kanan was keeping up.

"I'm fine," he said, keeping a few steps back. "Just trying not to run into you."

She smiled and leapt the next opening. He followed suit.

Reaching the end of the row of flats, they found a door and scrambled down a staircase. Catching their breaths in the doorway, they stopped in time to see the hovertruck move up the street toward them. A stormtrooper waved the vehicle and its golden chauffeur droid past.

As soon as the stormtrooper turned his head, Kanan and Hera bolted toward the approaching truck. Kanan leapt to the running board of the passenger side.

"I am sorry," the droid said. "Riders are not allowed on the—"

Hera, now hanging outside the other door, flicked a switch on the droid's neck, shutting him off. Kanan scrambled inside the cab, grabbed for the control yoke, and ducked. The vehicle executed a wide left turn past the last stormtrooper checkpoint; the sentry never saw the woman hanging outside. Adroitly, Hera opened the door and bumped the robot out of the way.

"I prefer driving," she said, reaching for the controls. "Nothing against you."

Kanan closed the passenger door and stretched his legs. "Sweetheart, you can drive me anywhere." He glanced back at the mess Shaketown had become. "As long as it's away from here!"

Hera had been scarcely more talkative than the deactivated droid, Kanan thought. She'd said nothing about what had gone on in the plant before she'd found Lal.

He didn't know Lal's husband well, other than that he had a short fuse and a big blaster collection. And something else. "That guy lived for Lal," he said.

"I could tell. It was rough."

Watching her, Kanan thought that must be an understatement. "Well, you found out one thing about Vidian. He's evil in a can."

"Being evil doesn't stop you with the Empire. It helps." She sighed. "I didn't even get near him this time—but I guess I found out what I came to Gorse to learn. The secret to Denetrius Vidian's efficiency is murder."

"And where does that get you?"

"Nowhere I wasn't before." She shook her head. "And all I was able to find about Tharsa was that he'd visited there a few times a long time ago. I couldn't find out anything else. First, Gord showed up, then they all started running around looking for Skelly." Guiding the hovertruck around a corner, she sighed. "I don't know what Skelly thinks he can accomplish this way. This loose-cannon stuff—it doesn't get you anywhere."

"And where are *you* trying to get?" He looked at her keenly. "I thought you were going to ditch me after you did your little break-in. And you just said your big mission is done. But here you are."

She rolled her eyes. "I'm helping you get your hoverbus back."

"Uh-huh." Kanan chuckled.

"No, no, it's the least I can do," Hera said. "You were willing to come back inside, looking for me. Unnecessary—and nearly trouble for you. But appreciated."

"Well, you're the only person on this planet I'd take that chance for." That should tell her something, he thought.

"I'm not sure I believe that. You went back to help that Besalisk cook—and Okadiah told me back in the bus about you saving him from Vidian." She smiled. "You even saved Skelly at the cantina."

He put up his hands. "Hey, everyone makes mistakes!"

"Well, we'll see," she said, and left it at that. Kanan liked the look he saw from her. It said she'd come to think he was worth keeping an eye on.

Looking out at the buildings whizzing by, Kanan laughed. "Everything that goes into thorilide—all the security—and here we've just driven off with a truckload."

"We're taking it right where it's supposed to go," she said. "And it's not like we'd find anyone to sell it to."

Kanan shook his head. "You know, I don't even know what the junk is used for."

"Thorilide?" Hera asked. "It's used in granular solid-state shock absorption. They use it on Star Destroyers to keep turbolaser turrets in place after firing."

"Loose cannons again!" Kanan chortled. "They're going to this much trouble for it?"

"They've got a lot of cannons!" Hera's eyes widened as she consid-

ered it. "A Star Destroyer requires the use of sixteen million individual components, twenty-seven thousand of which are only produced
in a single system, like Gorse." She looked at him, her face animated
with passion. "That's why the Emperor needs an Empire, Kanan. It's
like a space slug, whose only function is to stay alive. It's got to consume, and consume, and consume."

"You're starting to sound like Skelly."

"He's not all wrong," she said, guiding the hovertruck into Highground. "But he's definitely not all right."

Skelly had taken the speeder bike over rooftops to reach Highground,
flying low over their surfaces to avoid any tracking of air traffic. With
most of the Imperial attention on getting police vehicles to Shaketown, Skelly had guessed that relatively little attention was being paid
to the landing fields. Even so, he knew he couldn't simply fly the bike
over the retaining wall. And he was reluctant to dismount, because
every step he took off the bike caused him pain.

But now, in the dark at the far eastern end of the compound, his
war experience subverting barricades served him again. He'd seen
during flights to Cynda that the terrain at Highground had deep
drainage ditches leading off to the low side of the compound. It was
there, outside the wall in the darkness, that he found a culvert large
enough to accommodate both him and the speeder bike. The bars
guarding the pipe were no match for the variety of explosives he carried in his pack. It amused him that the same techniques he'd used to
mine Cynda for the Empire were now getting him onto its base.

A few muffled blasts later, he was hunched painfully low against
the spine of the speeder bike, letting it carry him and his bag of revenge through the tunnel. Inside the compound, he continued to fly
the vehicle low through the drainage canals separating the landing
areas. The lights here all pointed upward; if anyone had bothered to
look down, the sight of his head poking out of the ground and gently
sailing along might have given someone pause.

But no one saw. Now, in the shadow of the spaceport's control
tower, he waited, padding at his swollen face with swabs from the
medpac. He watched the ground transport arrival area, where every

few minutes another droid-driven hovercraft appeared bearing thorilide for the waiting Imperial freighters.

This spaceport was it, he thought. The last step before the beauty
of Cynda, crushed down and refined, left for Calcoraan Depot and
distribution to all the Empire's insane shipbuilding projects. It made
Skelly sick to see it.

Time passed. For a minute, he worried that he'd gambled wrong.
He'd assumed that Vidian, having lost one ride offworld, would come
here next. But shortly the gate opened to allow in—*Okadiah's hoverbus?*

Skelly blinked when he saw it. What was it doing here? Then he
saw a group of stormtroopers exit it, followed by Vidian and the Imperial captain. No wonder he had beaten them here, he thought. It
would take a genius of a pilot to get the Smoothride to beat a determined person on a speeder bike.

He felt his ribs shifting painfully as he huddled back against the
outer wall of the control tower. Skelly was running on adrenaline,
now—his own, and stimulus shots from the medpac. But he was un-
daunted.

He'd missed Vidian before. He wouldn't do it again.

CHAPTER TWENTY-EIGHT

COUNT VIDIAN LOOKED up past the control tower. *Cudgel* was descending from space, dispatched from the Star Destroyer to return him to orbit. He didn't want to waste another moment on Gorse. Staying on the planet was unnecessary to his plans.

And now his plans had changed. He didn't have time for the people of Gorse to shuttle back and forth, mining their moon. Even his most extreme notions, erecting dormitories on Cynda and forcing laborers to move there, would take too long. But he was now looking at another alternative—provided by the strangest source imaginable.

Skelly was deranged, just another shell-shocked Clone Wars veteran. But a quick look at the material suggested that he might have stumbled onto something useful. Vidian would need to consult with his staff and *Ultimatum*'s experts to be sure.

The commandeered hoverbus was the least efficient means of reaching the spaceport he could imagine; even Sloane's surviving shuttle flight crew hadn't been able to get it more than a meter off the ground. But he'd used the time well, explaining to Sloane his intentions. She'd reacted to his plans with caution, characteristic of the navy. He hadn't been able to find an iota of imagination in the entire service. Still, Sloane was young and ambitious—and even now, she was suggesting solutions.

"The stores on *Ultimatum* should have what you need, my lord. There's no need to involve anyone on Gorse."

"Excellent."

The gates swung wide to admit the thorilide hovertruck. The droid—reactivated but muted to prevent its nattering on about its dislike of hitchhikers—guided the vehicle inside as it was programmed to do. No sentry saw Hera and Kanan, ducked down as they were. Within moments, the big vehicle was in the parking area, queued to have its cargo placed on the freighters beyond. Poking his head up, Kanan saw that the line would shortly bring them alongside the parked hoverbus.

That was a relief. He figured he was due to catch a break.

As he dropped back down next to Hera, he chuckled. "It's always an adventure with you, huh?"

Hera smiled. "Yeah, and we're just going to pick up your ride."

"I'm carrying Okadiah's chauffeur license—I should be able to just drive back out," Kanan said. "I don't think I could've just walked up and asked them for it without them wasting my time again. And I've got places to—"

Seeing her expressionless face, he stopped. "Wait," Kanan said. "You didn't come here with me because you wanted to chat, or save me from impound hassles. You're going to go sneaking around checking on Vidian some more!"

Hera responded with a gentle smile.

"This is ridiculous!" He pointed back through the windshield at the Imperial shuttle, settling in for a landing. "Vidian's leaving. What more do you need to know?"

"Something brought him here," she said. "And something's making him leave early."

"Try Skelly and his bomb!"

Hera shook her head. "That's not it, Kanan. I saw him through the electrobinoculars as he was leaving. He's—different. Something's changed. He's got a new mission."

"How do you read the expression of a human droid?" Kanan looked to the floor in aggravation as the vehicle shuddered to a stop. Hera's was the old Jedi way of doing things, he remembered. Master Billaba or Obi-Wan or someone would get an idea in their heads and chase it all over creation, hiding in closets and creeping around ventilation shafts, spying.

Even when there was plainly nothing to see, as here. Kanan sat up cautiously, took a peek outside, and opened the door on the left side of the hoverbus. He slipped out onto the gravel surface, shielded from the Imperials' sight by the Smoothride. A moment later, Hera lightly touched the ground behind him.

"Look," he said, turning around to face her in the shadows. The space between the vehicles was narrow, and it brought them close together. "I travel alone. But I think you're fun, when you're not running off doing something outlandish." He pointed with his thumb to the hoverbus. "I'm going to take this back to Okadiah's and then I'm heading for the public spaceport. You can come along, or let me hitch a ride on whatever this ship is you say you've got. But I'm done sneaking around here—and I think you should be, too."

There wasn't anything else to say. Obi-Wan's warning and the Emperor's wrath had made him hide part of who he was. But he wouldn't live his daily life skulking about just to have a woman's company—or to support her cause, any cause. That wasn't who he was. Kanan began working his way along the left side of the hoverbus, feeling glad it had open doorways on both sides. He'd wait for Vidian to leave, and then get back to his regularly scheduled life. Either Hera would see sense, or she wouldn't.

He paused to look back. Hera was at the tail end of the hoverbus, trying to peek around at the Imperials. He shook his head. *Guess not,* he thought. *It's a shame. She was something.* Kanan put his foot on the doorstep—

—and heard shouts from the other side of the vehicle. Alarmed, he looked back Hera, but she had already turned and was running in his direction. "What is it?"

"Move!" Without a further word, she shoved him into the hoverbus. He fell onto the floor, and she on top of him. Pinned, he instantly began to formulate a response about how she couldn't live without him—when he caught a sideways glance of what was outside the door on the right-hand side of the vehicle opposite him, in the direction of the Imperials.

Vidian, Sloane, and several stormtroopers were fifty meters away, running away from the *Lambda*-class shuttle that had just landed. In the moonlight, he could just make out the sight of something being hurled toward it, from the shadows of the nearby control tower.

Krakka-boom! For the second time in a little over an hour, the populated side of Gorse saw what seemed to be the light of day as an Imperial shuttle blew apart. Kanan shielded his eyes from the flash—and then held on as the shock wave rocked the Smoothride. When he looked again, he saw debris raining all across the landing field—and then he heard it, as parts of the Lambda slammed against the right fuselage and roof of the hoverbus.

As the din subsided, Hera relaxed her hold on Kanan. "I think that's it," she said. She rose, and he followed. Carefully, they crept out of the right-hand side of the vehicle for a better look.

Fiery smoke blotted out the moon. But they could see that Vidian and all his companions, including Sloane, had been flattened by the blast, some hurled several meters. Vidian was still moving, Kanan saw, but he was definitely reeling.

"Come on," Kanan said, grabbing Hera's arm.

"Yeah, I think so!"

They'd already been bystanders to one attack. They wouldn't be able to walk out of another. But before they could reach the doorway, Kanan heard a high, whizzing whine coming at him from behind—the direction of the explosion. *More debris, now?* It didn't matter. This time, *he* threw *her* down—

—right as a mass of metal screamed just over their heads. Something slammed headlong into the hoverbus, shattering more of its windows. Kanan shielded his and Hera's heads with his arms.

When Kanan finally looked up, he saw something that rendered him speechless. It was a speeder bike, the kind Imperial stormtroopers rode. Or part of it: Its long nose had shot through one of the hoverbus windows, halting its flight and effectively impaling the larger vehicle.

Outside the hoverbus, hanging upside down from the deeply lodged bike, was Skelly, his right hand holding one of the handlebars in a death grip. He looked as if he'd been through one of Okadiah's blenders. His battered body dangled limply from the frame, and a big backpack hung precariously around his midsection, about to fall.

A subsidiary explosion went off in the field behind them—but Kanan could only look at Skelly, dazzled. The bomber opened his eyes and looked back, wearily recognizing him.

"K-k-k . . . ," Skelly said, his face swollen, his mouth bloodied. "Kanan."

"What?"

"The pack. Grab it."

Not thinking, Kanan took it and then looked inside. "It's full of bombs!"

"Not good," Hera said, grabbing his arm. Across the field, emergency crews were racing from the control tower to put out the blaze, even as Vidian stood up. Vidian hadn't spotted Kanan and the others yet; there was too much flaming debris between them. But Kanan could see the cyborg's creepy glowing eyes as he scanned the area. Fresh stormtroopers ran to the blast scene from the control tower, and several of Vidian's companions rose, looking for their weapons. Overhead, a siren blared—and the ground was suddenly awash with searchlights cutting through the smoke.

"There! At the hoverbus!" Vidian yelled, his voice artificially amplified to its loudest level.

Kanan turned toward the door of the long hoverbus, three meters away, only to see a blaster shot strike just outside the door frame. Out of the corner of his eye, he could see at least a dozen stormtroopers taking positions behind pieces of the wreckage. No one had a bead on him yet, but the vehicle was another story. Hera knew it too. Like him, she was facing the hoverbus—but while she had her hand on her blaster, she hadn't drawn it. She shook her head at him. "Wrong place, wrong time."

Story of my life, Kanan thought. In a nearly autonomic reaction, he let the bag with Skelly's explosives slip from his hands and to the ground. Nothing exploded, which he almost thought was a shame.

"Put your hands behind your heads!" came Vidian's amplified call from behind.

Above and to Kanan's left, Skelly slipped off the bike, his hand finally having given out. He landed with a thud on the gravel.

"Skelly, I'm going to die," Kanan said, glaring down at the man on the ground. "But I'm going to kill you first!"

CHAPTER TWENTY-NINE

WHEN THE OTHER GUY brought an army, it was best not to argue.
Kanan kept his face toward the hoverbus. He could hear blasters
being prepared, with more stormtroopers starting to move from
cover to cover, working their way across the airfield.

Hera hadn't budged, either, but he could see her thinking. With
the smoke blotting out the moon, the Imperials hadn't seen either of
their faces clearly yet, but that would change when he turned to
run—or fight. And the latter option seemed impossible. They hadn't
taken a shot at an Imperial in all the day's chaos, and he didn't want
to start now. The odds were just too long.

Skelly sat a meter or so away from the bag, eyeing it. Vidian, with
his sharp eyes, noticed. *"Don't touch it!"*

Kanan glanced again at Hera. *It was a good run,* he said to himself.
He started to put his hands behind his head.

"Put down your weapons!" called out another voice from behind
and to Kanan's right.

"We're not holding any!" Kanan yelled.

"I didn't mean you!" For a moment, the voice seemed strangely familiar to Kanan—until he realized it *was* familiar. Kanan and Hera looked to the right to see Gord walking purposefully from the direction of the cargo intake facility. *"I'm here for Vidian!"*

The bulky security chief was bruised, Kanan saw: Hera had told him about Gord's earlier beating. The Besalisk was also armed to the teeth, prepared to deal death with all four hands. He had come the same way they had, Kanan realized, on one of the other thorilide transports. He'd never seen the security chief looking so serious—or threatening.

"Count Vidian! My name is Gord Grallik, security chief for Moonglow. You are under arrest for the murder of our supervisor—and my wife!"

"On whose authority?" That was Sloane; she sounded stunned.

"Mine," Gord said. "Gorse City has a jail. You'll be treated fairly— more fairly than you deserve!"

"Enough of this," Vidian yelled. "Blast him!"

Gord shot first. And second. And third. Moving with startling speed, the Besalisk peppered the stormtroopers with blasterfire. The Imperials' defensive positions protected them against the hoverbus, but not against anyone coming from his angle off to their right. Before anyone fired a shot in return, Gord hurled something with his fourth hand—a sonic grenade. It detonated amid the group of stormtroopers nearest him, emitting a shriek that sent them reeling.

Hera, pulling her hands from behind her head, looked at Kanan. "Are we thinking the same thing?"

Kanan nodded. "Run!"

They began to move toward the hoverbus—only to both hit the ground as attentive stormtroopers fired at the doorway. As crimson shots struck the gravel ahead of them, Kanan scrambled for the only cover they could find: a chunk of the Imperial shuttle's sublight ion engine, which earlier had hit the hoverbus roof and rolled off.

"Time to join the party," Hera said, whipping out her blaster. She leaned over the metallic barrier, took quick aim, and fired. One of the snipers stopped shooting at the hoverbus.

Kanan looked at her and drew his weapon. He'd done his best to avoid such situations—but this jam wouldn't let go of him, no matter what. *Fine, then!* "Let's dance!"

Kanan fired. Off to the north, Gord was still letting it rip, somehow shrugging off a glancing shot to his left leg. Hera and Kanan supplied him with cross fire, driving the Imperials to move Vidian and Sloane back to a more protected position.

Continuing to shoot, Kanan grew concerned about being out-flanked on his right or attacked from behind. Things looked all clear to the south, he saw. And behind him, the hoverbus—

—was *moving*!

Kanan's eyes darted to the ground, where Skelly had lain. The bag with the bombs was gone. He nudged Hera. "The bus! It's being sto-len again!"

Imperial blaster shots glancing off it ineffectually, the hoverbus rose a meter into the air—and then slammed into the ground again, nearly tipping over. A mechanical groan sounded above the gunfire, and the vessel lifted once more. But only part of it: One back corner steadfastly refused to lift, and the long vehicle dragged it across the ground as it tried to accelerate.

Hera squinted back through the dust. "Is that Skelly driving?"

Kanan yelled back. "I wouldn't call it that!" Skelly was trying—probably with one hand and certainly in a mad panic—to make the Smoothride fly, something Kanan knew it couldn't do anymore. But at least the vehicle was taking the fire that had been meant for them.

All at once the rear corner of the hovercraft yanked free from the ground. In response, the rest of it lurched, starting a wild sideways swing in their direction. Kanan yelled, *"Look out!"*

He and Hera went flat as ten thousand kilograms of metal ca-reened just over their heads, grinding and snapping away the debris that had been their cover.

Kanan raised his head to see Gord making a running charge across the open ground toward the Imperials—wild-eyed and completely heedless of the hoverbus, now dipping low as it swung widely in an arc toward him.

"*Gord, look out!*" There was no way for the Besalisk to hear him in the chaos. The spinning bus swept through Gord's position, knocking him off balance and causing him to lose two of his blasters. Gord scrambled for them, only to take a glancing blaster shot to the chest. That provided the opportunity Vidian needed. He leapt from cover toward Gord. The dazed Besalisk raised his meaty arms, ready to put up a struggle. But Vidian charged forward, knocking his attacker to the ground.

Kanan had no shot. He winced as he saw Vidian raise his fists—and lower them, again and again. But before he could think again about the security chief's fate, the wayward hoverbus completed another revolution—and was heading back for him and Hera. She saw it, too, and was already on her feet, holstering her blaster. "Come on!"

Heedless of the blaster bolts coming his way, Kanan bolted from the ground and followed. The Smoothride yawed wildly toward them with more altitude than it had before. Hera made a running leap for its underside. Kanan followed a second later.

Hera was rewarded for acting first. She had hold of one of the support struts that made up the hoverbus's chassis. Kanan, meanwhile, had only managed to hook his right hand around one of the rings attached to the rear turbofan—putting him right in the path of the straining engine's exhaust.

The hovercraft pitched and fell again, nearly scraping the hangers-on away against a horizontal obstacle. Kanan realized only afterward that it was the outer wall of the Imperial spaceport. They were on their way—somewhere!

From behind the chunk of shuttle wing she'd been using for cover, Sloane watched in stupefaction as the lumbering metal machine improbably crested the permacrete barrier. Her comlink was already in her hand. "Everyone after that thing, now!"

Climbing out from behind the twisted wedge of metal, she dashed toward her charge. "Count Vidian! Count Vidian!"

"Yelling is unnecessary." His voice filled her with relief, for a change. But just for a moment. Vidian rose from the corpse of the

Besalisk, his regal outfit bloodied and torn. "I live, no thanks to your forces. Another bomb—and now these attackers. You call this security?"

Sloane fought the impulse to argue. It was the Imperial Army garrison's responsibility to secure the landing area, not hers—but now wasn't the time to quibble. The chase was on. Squat gray Imperial troop transports loaded with stormtroopers were already heading out the west gate, and she had more than that in mind.

"Order the local authorities to put up roadblocks at every intersection—keep them penned into Highground!" she called on the comlink. "Contact ground and satellite surveillance—make sure we know where the vehicle is at all times!"

And across the tarmac, far from the blast site, she saw something she *did* have direct control over: two TIE fighters, parked and waiting. "Get those in the sky," she called out to the spaceport chief.

"Right away, Captain!"

"There were others with the saboteur," Vidian said, looking back at officers heading for the TIEs. "That makes this a conspiracy. I want Skelly shot on sight, but bring the others to me!"

Sloane hadn't gotten a good look at the two who'd been facing the hoverbus, and she doubted anyone else had. One of the traitors had shot out the one surveillance cam covering the area; that someone had known what he or she was doing. But Skelly should stand out— and they wouldn't get far in that monstrosity they were driving.

"I want those renegades," she called out to the troopers. "Now!"

CHAPTER THIRTY

THE WAY TO CONTROL your fear of being on a ledge, Master Bil-laba had said, *is not to think about it until you are off the ledge.* Even at the time, Kanan had thought that advice could go two different ways. *Off the ledge* could mean you were safely inside—or it could mean you were plummeting. A lot of Jedi adages seemed to have that problem: They always assumed everything would work out.

Kanan wasn't assuming that at the moment. The underside of a landspeeder normally wouldn't have offered any clearance for a hanger-on—and the *Smoothride,* while designed for flight, had been little more than a landspeeder for years. Taking it more than a meter off the ground sent the thing wobbling crazily off axis to the left and right. Okadiah's drivers all knew that.

But Skelly wasn't one of Okadiah's drivers. "Look out!" Kanan called forward to Hera as the machine lost altitude. Hera kicked her legs up before they brushed the mud-covered street below. Kanan, taller, felt the front of his boots smack the surface.

Kanan strained, pulling himself upward so he could get a second handhold. Ahead, he saw Hera nimbly swinging her leg upward to catch a hanging support strut. That wasn't an option for him—not with the whirling blades of the turbofan directly ahead. He had to shift his weight and reverse his handholds, turning himself around.

Doing so, he saw the pursuers. Two—no, *three* Imperial troop transports hurtled up the dark lane in the hoverbus's wake, occasionally slowed by oncoming traffic. Skelly wasn't bothered by the traffic at all, Kanan realized: Every few seconds, the vehicle slammed off something to the left or right—or pitched upward, having simply climbed over its obstacle. Kanan had to heave his body upward each time the machine came back down to keep from being scraped off. But there wasn't any choice except to hang on—not with Imperials behind and Hera in danger up ahead.

When the first blaster shot from the twin-cannon turret on the lead transport struck a few meters shy of the hoverbus, Kanan had had enough. Seeing a slight recess just inside the rear of the under-chassis, he pitched his legs upward and caught his boots beneath the lower flange. That allowed him to reach off to a more secure hand-hold on the left, leaving the turbofan housing behind.

With as much care as was possible in the whipping wind, Kanan felt around in the darkness, then began working his way backward across the Smoothride's bottom, feeling a bit like a mynock who'd lost suction. Groaning against the strain, he heaved his body across the opening of the recess to a place he could cling to just the inside of the rear of the undercarriage.

He waited there, breathing hard, as the hoverbus pitched and rolled. Waiting was excruciating—but he had to, for the right moment. Finally it came. The hoverbus struck something hard on the left, causing it to tip almost onto its right side. Seeing air opening up between him and the ground racing beneath, Kanan rolled his body around and onto the rear bumper.

This time, the Smoothride did slam against the ground when it righted itself—and Kanan began to fall backward, off the bumper.

"I've got you, Kanan!"

Kanan looked up, astonished. Someone *did* have him. Skelly was hanging out the shattered back window, his bionic right hand clasped around Kanan's belt. Skelly screamed in agony as Kanan scrambled over his shoulders and through the open pane.

Kanan hit the back floor of the hoverbus, wheezing. But he couldn't stay. The hoverbus had struck the street—anyone beneath would have been dislodged. "We've got to go back for Hera!" he called out. Then he blinked at Skelly. "Who's driving?"

Before he got an answer, the Smoothride again bounced over something, sending Kanan sliding on his back up the aisle as the vehicle tipped downward.

Upside down next to the driver's seat, he looked up. "Sorry," Hera said, grinning. "Still getting the hang of it. But welcome aboard!"

Kanan rolled over and scrambled to his feet. He saw Skelly had somehow made it forward, clearly in great pain but unable to rest. The shorter man was sitting in the stairwell of the open left doorway, his right arm wrapped around the support rail while his other hand fished around in his bag. A moment later, Skelly slung a small pipe bomb out the door.

The landspeeders parked along the left side of the street went up in an inferno that lit the area, upending them. The shock wave caught the rear section of the Smoothride, tipping the hoverbus halfway onto its right side as it hurtled toward an intersection. Kanan grabbed for the support post as Hera ably got control, using the momentum to take the vehicle down a side street.

Skelly just grinned, showing teeth broken and blackened. He reached into his bag again.

"Can you make him stop that?" Hera called back.

"Happily," Kanan said. He stepped over and yanked Skelly's satchel from him.

"Hey!" Skelly said, reaching for it—and nearly tumbling out the open door.

Kanan grabbed him—and immediately regretted it. "I should—"

Before he could finish, blasterfire shattered the windows on the left side. Kanan ducked, trying to protect his head from the flying shards. Through the open door, he could see where the blasts were coming from: one of the Recon transports, ambushing from a side street. A second later the windows on the right exploded with fire coming from the opposite direction.

"We're in a shooting gallery!" Kanan yelled. They had to get out of here—but that meant finding out where they were. Slinging the bag over his shoulder, he pulled his blaster and scrambled atop one of the seats.

It was almost impossible, watching the world whizzing by in darkness. Okadiah had never gotten the vehicle's navigation system working: Who needed it, for runs back and forth to the bar? But Kanan searched in desperation for any landmark.

"There!" The odd shape of Transcept's World Window Plaza, lit from within and without as always, whisked past. "Go right," Kanan yelled. "The old miners' highway. Let's make for The Pits!"

The Smoothride lurched. Hera barely slowed the vehicle—and yet somehow it easily made the turn onto the entrance ramp. The old elevated thoroughfare had the benefit of limited access: Now, rather than passing side streets with Imperial gunners, they were passing buildings and rooftops on either side. They were hemmed in, true— but there was very little traffic to run into on the highway anymore, and Hera opened up the throttle. Kanan scrambled off the seat and ran toward the back.

The Recon transports were racing along behind, he saw. He removed Skelly's bag from his shoulder. There were still close to a dozen improvised explosive devices inside. Now that they were out of traffic, the odds of doing more than random property damage with them were better. He called back to Skelly, still in the middle of the hover-bus. "How do I activate these?"

"Plug in the leads and let it rip!"

Pulling out a cylinder not much larger than a shot glass, Kanan quickly snapped together the two loose wires attached to it. Looking back, he took aim. He hurled it out the rear window and watched as the jetwash took it, whisking it toward the oncoming Imperials.

Fire blossomed before the lead Recon transport. Beneath it, the highway structure, already stressed from years of quakes, shook violently. The first transport flipped trying to avoid the blast, sending the stormtroopers riding outside it hurtling away—but that was better for them, as one after another the rear vehicles slammed into it.

"Three for one!" Kanan yelled, pumping his fist.

"We've got bigger problems!" Skelly yelled.

Kanan looked forward, startled. He hadn't expected clear driving all the way ahead, but it was kilometers from another on-ramp. "There shouldn't be anyone out in front of us yet!"

But before he could run forward to look, light blazed outside the left and right windows, blinding him. Feeling a sudden rush of heat, he realized it wasn't searchlights flooding the hoverbus, or small-arms fire from the Imperials. A high whine passed overhead. "Is that—"

"*TIE!*" Hera yelled.

The starfighter rocketed over them, a white bulb sandwiched between black hexagonal wings. Kanan looked back to see the twin lights of its ion engines receding in the distance—only to feel the world move again as a second fighter, its level flight path perpendicular to the highway, began strafing them from above.

Hera banked the Smoothride violently, sending her riders tumbling. There was no protection from the TIE's attack—except for the highway itself. The Smoothride's engines objecting, Hera tilted the hoverbus ninety degrees, riding not on the road surface but rather the left retaining wall of the elevated highway. The TIE, which had been aiming low for its pass, found its cannon fire pummeling duracrete rather than its intended target.

Hera twisted the Smoothride back to level again. The TIE shrieked overhead and began to loop—and now the first attacker was back, rocketing up the highway toward them. This time, Hera slammed on the brakes, sending the hoverbus into a spin—and began racing back in the other direction. The maneuver closed the distance with the TIE that had been tailing them such that its shots went harmlessly overhead.

Kanan scrambled to his feet. Hera was the best driver he had ever seen, coaxing things he'd never imagined possible out of the Smoothride. But this couldn't go on—especially not as they were now racing back toward the Recon transports, piled up and blazing. Something had to be done.

Kanan ran forward to the front of the vehicle. Skidding to a stop, he dived to the floor right at Hera's legs.

"What do you think you're doing?" Hera asked, bewildered.

Kanan reached past her feet for something beneath the driver's seat. "This thing used to fly, remember?" He yanked loose a brown pack with straps on it—Okadiah's ancient parachute.

"You're jumping out on us?"

"Hardly!" Getting to his feet, Kanan looked to the ceiling, amidships. "Cut the throttle. When I give the signal, let loose!" He looked back. "Skelly! I'm going to need your help!"

"Great!" Skelly looked at him tiredly. "I'm going to need medication." But he got to his feet.

In the ceiling at the exact center of the vehicle was the emergency exit to the roof: not a bad thing on a planet prone to quakes and mudslides. When Skelly reached him, Kanan was balanced on one of the seat backrests, trying to force open the rusty hatch. "I need you to get up here and hold me!"

The second TIE fighter was making a run along the highway's length when Kanan emerged on the roof. There was no good chance of simply throwing a bomb at it, he'd realized. The wind took him fully as he stood. Skelly had wedged himself in the opening behind Kanan and was holding on to the back of his belt. Kanan was facing down a TIE, which was racing toward him with its lasers ready to fire while he had no weapon at all.

But he had a plan.

"Hera, now!"

Behind, Skelly yelled the call down to Hera. She hit the accelerator—just as Kanan activated the parachute. Attached to nothing, the drogue caught the wind fully and ballooned backward into the air—opening wide into the TIE fighter's path. The fighter veered right, only to find ropes and canvas snagging across its starboard solar panel. Tangled, tumbling, and blinded, the distracted starfighter pilot missed seeing the microwave tower in his path.

"*Whoa!*" Kanan said, nearly losing his footing as the ship exploded spectacularly. One down. But there was the other one to go, he saw as he turned to look forward. And between the hoverbus and the TIE fighter Kanan saw the smoking pileup that had been the Recon transports. His earlier dirty work lay before them, now, a barrier—and if Hera tried to do another 180-degree turn, he feared he'd go flying. Worse still, there were stormtroopers on the deck of the highway, having emerged from the wreckage. Small-arms fire was flashing—and they were racing straight toward it!

"Pull me back!"

Skelly wasn't in any shape to move Kanan anywhere. But he did lose his hold on the roof opening, falling down into the hoverbus, causing Kanan to tumble backward toward the hole. Catching himself, he struggled to turn himself around and lower his legs inside the hatch.

He heard something from below. "Hera says to hang on!"

Kanan, halfway in the hatch with both hands on the roof, blinked. "Hera, what are you—"

Before he could finish the sentence, the hoverbus barreled through the stormtroopers on the elevated pavement before them, sending several tumbling over the side. Sure that the hoverbus would collide with the smoking wreckage, Kanan put his arm before his face—

—and felt a tremendous surge beneath him as the hoverbus struck the impediment. Struck it, and overtopped it, its repulsorlift jets using the debris as a makeshift ramp. The Smoothride launched into the air—and came fully to life, its ancient engines remembering what they once had been able to do.

Hera had made the vehicle fly! To the stunned surprise of Kanan—and certainly to the shock of the surviving TIE pilot, who veered to avoid a collision, only to crash catastrophically into a smokestack.

The Smoothride stayed aloft, leaving the elevated highway and buffeting over rooftops. Kanan couldn't believe his eyes. Slipping inside the roof opening, he landed roughly and rushed forward to Hera. "This thing hasn't flown in years!"

"You've got to talk to it right," she said, smiling.

"I thought *I* was a good pilot. But you—you're amazing."

"Thank you. But we should probably go somewhere."

Kanan blinked. "Oh, yeah." He pointed. "Back south. The Pits, out near the cantina."

She glanced at him with concern. "We can't just drive up anywhere. They've got satellites. They'll find this thing. We'll have to find a place to ditch it."

"That," Kanan reassured her, "won't be a problem."

CHAPTER THIRTY-ONE

WORDS COULD change things. Kanan had been taught that by the Jedi, and it was certainly true when it came to a short document generated by Minerax Consulting, which had changed the face of Gorse four years before the fall of the Republic.

Thorilide mining in the system, before then, had taken place entirely on the surface of Gorse in the wide, drenched plains south of the megalopolis. Then came Minerax's survey, projecting that no more thorilide deposits of any scale remained on either side of the planet. By the time the mines started seeing proof of it, the smart credits had already moved, with producers establishing operations on Cynda. In the space of a year, the strip mines that came right up to the edge of town went from work zones under the big lights to dumping grounds in the dark. The last mine on Gorse closed the day the Clone Wars ended.

So many of the places existed—Okadiah called them "Gorse's clogged pores"—that Kanan couldn't imagine a better place to hide the hoverbus. The endless junkyard was home to many abandoned craft, large and small, including several Smoothrides; it was where

Okadiah had found the thing to begin with. Kanan had realized it was the only place they could go, after this long and difficult day, to have any chance of following one of Obi-Wan's directives.

"*Avoid detection*," Kanan mumbled.

Sliding out from under the left side of the dashboard, Hera looked up at him. "What?"

He leaned against the driver's seat. "Nothing." He shrugged. "I was just thinking—so much for keeping a low profile."

"Well, I may have killed your bus," Hera said, dousing her light. "Forget flying—I don't think it'll run again."

Kanan watched her close the equipment panel. The hoverbus had so many dents and blaster scores, he was amazed the thing hadn't spontaneously combusted.

Hera walked past the driver's seat, her arms sagging a little. She looked tired. "I don't think I've ever had a day like this."

"Stick around Gorse," Kanan said, following her down the aisle. "Every day's a trip to the zoo."

Hera confronted Skelly, who was two rows back, nursing his wounds. Her tone was chilly. "What could you *possibly* have been thinking?"

Skelly stared off in a medicinal haze. "My escape route was all planned. Your hoverbus was in the way."

"In the way of what?" Kanan asked. "Careening into the wall, instead?"

"That's not it," Hera said. "I mean taking us down a main avenue—and then throwing bombs willy-nilly. You were almost a bigger menace than the Empire."

Skelly looked hurt. "I'm trying to save people here. I tried to minimize casualties."

"You sound like you're in a war," Kanan said.

"I am," Skelly said. "It's never ended." He waved his prosthetic hand around.

Hera shook her head, and then she turned away. "Vidian killed Gord. I saw it."

Kanan nodded. "I guess he couldn't live without Lal."

"He wanted justice," Hera said in a soft voice, staring at the wall. "But expecting the Empire to prosecute one of its own is—"

"Dumb?" Skelly said, looking abruptly at her.

Hera shook her head. "I was going to say, *something we have a right to expect.* Which is why people are having second thoughts about the Empire. It's not here to help you. It only exists to help itself."

"Boy, that's right," Skelly said, rubbing his forehead. "I sure got that Vidian wrong."

Kanan thought that was a whole different subject—and that the time for talking was past. The thing now was to get moving, before the Empire put search vessels into the air. "Come on," he said to her. "We're not far from The Asteroid Belt. We can decide what to do from there."

She didn't respond. Reaching for her arm, he waved to Skelly. "You wanted the hoverbus, Skelly? Keep it. We're gone."

"Wait," Hera said. "You're just going to leave him?"

"Wrong. *We're* just going to leave him, if you're smart. I don't think anyone saw you and me clearly at the spaceport, but everybody saw *him*. And that woman and her surveillance firm—their cams are all over the city. How long do you really want to hang around here?"

Hera frowned. "But he's injured."

"Which he did to himself." Kanan looked her in the eye. "I'm not sure what you're trying to accomplish, but whatever it is, this guy isn't going to help you."

She looked at him for several seconds. For a moment, Kanan thought she was going to make a decision.

And then he heard the thumping.

It was amidships, coming from the closet-sized restroom compartment. The door frame had bent slightly as a result of the day's damage to the hoverbus, and a sliver of an opening had appeared. As he approached, the pounding grew louder.

"I know we're in a dump," Skelly said, "but that's the biggest rodent I've ever heard."

Puzzled, Kanan walked to the rear and located a pry bar. Hera and Skelly gathered near the door as he returned. "This door always jams,"

Kanan said. "And locks itself, and worse. Okadiah spent his summer vacation in there once." He shoved the bar edge into the aperture and pushed. Something snapped.

The door popped open—and a very tired Sullustan fell out.

"*Zaluna?*"

Zaluna Myder rolled on the floor, gasping and clutching her bag. "Air! Air!" She looked frazzled. She was wearing the same dark clothing from the night before, Kanan saw.

Skelly looked at her in wonder. "Were you in there all this time?"

"Through the bashing and the blasting," she said, her throat dry. "The silly door's too thick—you couldn't hear me!" Zaluna looked up at Hera and Kanan with relieved recognition. Then her eyes fixed on Skelly. "*You!*"

Skelly looked confused as the woman recoiled, sliding backward on the aisle floor. "What's the deal? I don't know you. How do you know me?"

"You're the bomber," Zaluna said, big eyes growing improbably wider. "I ran the surveillance cam that got you arrested."

Skelly blinked. "You what?" Realizing what she'd said, he rocked forward on his seat toward her. "You *what*?"

Zaluna fished in her bag and pulled out her blaster. "Keep him away from me."

Kanan slapped his hands on Skelly's shoulder and pushed him back. "He's not going to hurt you. He has Beatings One through Seven coming from me, first."

"*Three* through seven," Skelly said. "Vidian got me first. And you gave me Beating Number One back on the moon yesterday." He glared at Zaluna. "Did you see *that*, too?"

"Yes," Zaluna said, looking down. "I don't think Kanan should have hit you."

"Thanks," Kanan said. He shrugged to Hera. "See what I get for helping?"

Zaluna put her blaster away. Hera stepped over to help her up into a seat. She looked back into the cramped compartment. "You've been in there how long?"

"Since last night, when we saw Skelly come into the cantina," Zaluna said, struggling to get to her feet. "The stormtroopers were outside. I was looking for someplace to hide, and the bus was there. But I got stuck. I couldn't get a signal out—and the door's so thick you couldn't hear me."

Kanan chuckled and shook his head. "All the bombs going off, all the people shooting at us—and you were right there!"

"I wouldn't recommend it." She looked to Hera. "We'll have to discuss Hetto's data cube later. I've got to get home. I've missed work!"

Hera looked at Kanan with concern. "Zaluna, I don't know that you should go home, or back to work." Hera shook her head gently. "The Empire's not just looking for Skelly anymore. They're after this vehicle, and probably us, too—we don't know. And until we know what they think about you, it's not safe for you to go back."

Zaluna looked bereft. "I really stepped in something, didn't I?"

"It's not mud," Kanan said.

The Sullustan closed her eyes and took a few deep breaths. After a moment, she opened them again—seeming almost at peace. "All right. I've been thirty-some years on one side of the cams. It won't hurt me to know what it's like on the other side." Seconds later, she was climbing atop her seat, stretching for the domed light fixture in the ceiling. It was just within her reach. "When people run, they never run smart," Zaluna said, running her fingers inside the dome. "The secret is to make sure the watchers don't know who's running."

Hera was alarmed. "What is it? There isn't a surveillance cam on board here, is there?"

"This was once a city transport. Those were set up for commercial surveillance thirty years ago." Finding nothing, Zaluna stepped down and moved to the next seat. Climbing, she repeated the process with the next light fixture.

Kanan gawked. "Why would they bug a hoverbus?"

"In those days, to see what beverages you preferred to drink on a commute," Zaluna said, fishing around with her fingers. "These days, it's for the same reason the Empire would watch a cantina, or an elevator. To catch threats before they become threats."

Skelly crossed his arms. "Everyone who called me paranoid, the line for apologies begins to the left."

Zaluna's jowls flared upward in a Sullustan smile, and she removed a small widget from inside the fixture. "Ah. Just like I thought. One of our obsolete recorders. No live feed—it does a batch upload to the satellite once a week." She pitched it to Hera as Kanan helped her down.

Hera rolled the impossibly small recording device over in the palm of her hand. "It won't send anything now, will it?"

"No, it's disconnected from the transmitter. But I admit I'd be interested to see what's on it. I've been in the dark all day. I'd like to know what all the noise was about."

"You were better off where you were," Kanan said. "I'd like to be able to forget it!"

Hera stood in the doorway and looked at him. "Can you hide all of us at the bar until we figure out what the situation is? It's safer if we don't split up."

There was no use grumbling, Kanan realized. If there was one thing he'd learned, it was that he wasn't going to change Hera's mind once she'd decided on something. "All right," he said. "But at the first sign of a stormtrooper, Skelly, I never met you!"

"*Bastinade* is here," Sloane said, sipping from a mug and gesturing to the Lambda descending from the sky.

"Can your people keep this one from being blown up?" Vidian asked. "You only have nine more shuttles."

Sloane hid her expression behind her cup. The control tower's caf was no good, but after the last few hours, any respite was welcome. They'd lost several transports, two TIE fighters—and, worst of all, their quarry. *In* a quarry: an agglomeration of pits filled with refuse and runoff like she'd never seen. The satellite trackers had lost the hoverbus after five seconds in the place. The stormtroopers could be combing the area for months.

Until now, Vidian had said nothing about the incident, choosing instead to review the matter he'd first discussed with her back when they'd commandeered the hoverbus. A very strange matter, indeed, and one with potential ramifications for everyone who lived on Gorse. If it panned out, it might well turn more than a few model citizens into stark raving Skellies.

It probably wouldn't—but Sloane was anxious to get off the planet before something else happened. *Any more time on Gorse,* she thought as she headed for the shuttle, *and I might not even get a substitute command again!*

CHAPTER THIRTY-TWO

IT WAS STRANGE, being in The Asteroid Belt alone. No customers had arrived yet, and he didn't expect any for some time. Moonglow was undoubtedly still crawling with Imperials, and with the hoverbus out of action, Okadiah would have to find another way to get his regulars to and from the cantina.

Kanan had thought a million times about ditching the others. But he didn't want to abandon Hera, and she was convinced Skelly's capture would have led the Empire directly to them. Who knew, maybe she was right. And she wouldn't leave without Zaluna, not when the woman still had the data cube Hera wanted.

At least Zaluna had been useful, leading them on routes she knew weren't under surveillance. Once she had confirmed that the cams in the building were still dead, Kanan had sent everyone upstairs into the attic apartment. He'd lingered downstairs in the dark bar, gathering up whatever food he could find.

Kanan had left that morning assuming he'd never see the place again. Now he had no idea where he'd be in twelve hours. He didn't think anyone had gotten a good look at his face back at the Imperial spaceport, but he didn't want to count on that.

And something had to be done about his other guests.

Someone worked the lock at the side door. Kanan quickly pulled his traveling bag off the bar and put it at his feet. Okadiah walked in, looking grayer than usual.

"You're here sooner than I expected," Kanan said.

"Something's going on at Moonglow," Okadiah replied, somberly placing his jacket on a peg. "You heard about Boss Lal?"

Kanan nodded—and then shook his head. "I didn't hear the whole story. What happened?"

"They said a groundquake knocked her into an acid pool at the plant. She got too close," the old man said.

Kanan shook his head. "Terrible."

"Terrible lie, you mean." Okadiah wandered through the darkness, straightening chairs. "I've known Lal Grallik for longer than you've been alive, my boy. She knew where to walk. She stepped in front of a vicious cyborg, is all—just like the guild chief did." Pausing to wipe something from his eye, he turned. "They rerouted all our personnel transports to Calladan's field. I took a hovercab over."

"That explains the crowd," Kanan said, trying to sound normal as he looked around the empty bar. "I guess it'll be quiet tonight."

"That's one reason," Okadiah said. He walked up to the counter and placed his hands together on it. "Some *gentlemen* met me when I landed."

Kanan found a rag and began to wipe the surface. "Were they dressed in white?"

"Pretty foolish, given all the mud on this planet." The old man walked to the far end of the bar and turned. Looking back, he saw the sack stuffed with food at Kanan's feet. Evidently choosing to ignore it, he joined Kanan behind the counter. "They said the Imperials had to commandeer the Smoothride to the spaceport—and that someone stole it from there and took it for a joyride."

"Surprising," Kanan said. "You'd think a big Empire would be more careful with other people's property."

"It's a good habit to get into." Okadiah opened a bottle and set out two glasses. "Apparently whoever went on this joyride shot up a bunch of stormtroopers and did a hundred thousand credits' worth of property damage." Not looking at Kanan, Okadiah poured. "Is there something you want to tell me?"

Kanan stood, stone-faced. "No, not really."

Okadiah picked up both drinks and looked at him. "That girl isn't getting you into something?"

Kanan didn't answer.

Okadiah watched the young man for a moment, before walking up to him with the drinks. "You've always struck me as a fellow with nowhere to go, Kanan—never as a man on the run." He kept his eyes fixed on him. "Nowhere to go is better. Fewer people come around asking where you are."

Kanan nodded. "I understand," he said, taking the offered glass. He gestured to a spot beneath the counter. "By the way, if you'll check the safe, you'll find some credits. I think someone dropped them behind a table."

"Is that so?"

"Enough to put a down payment on another hoverbus," Kanan said, shuffling a little on his feet. It was half the money he'd saved. "Er—probably not as new as the one you had."

"Then at least fortune smiled on someone today," Okadiah said. He raised his glass in a toast. "May the spirit of death make a clerical error and forget you exist."

"Right," Kanan said. Then he added: "To Boss Lal."

"To Lal."

Kanan downed his beverage and placed his glass in the sink. He picked up the sack of food and made for the staircase.

The raised voices behind the door silenced immediately when Kanan knocked. The latch opened. Seeing him, Hera lowered her blaster and let him inside.

The room was a living space only in the Gorsian sense of the term. A chimney ran up through a low, slanted ceiling; from the street, there was no indication there was an upper level at all. Pipes ran along the floor, bisecting the moldy chamber. Portable lamps provided the only light. A mattress had been thrown onto some crates to create a makeshift bed.

Zaluna sat at the foot of the bed, rubbing her ankles. The compartment had been a cramped place, and she'd slept wrong—when she'd been able to sleep at all. Skelly was seated in front of a little washbasin, doing his best to clean his wounds. And Hera was holding the door, looking as frustrated as he'd seen her.

"Problem?"

"We've just been discussing the day's events," Hera said, speaking evenly. She shot a look at Skelly. "Particularly some things that could have been done . . . *differently.*"

"That's what this crowd needs—a life coach." Kanan walked past and began doling out food. Zaluna and Skelly reached for it eagerly. Kanan walked to the bed and sat down, offering Hera a seat and what remained in the bag. "Your table, madam."

After a moment, she sat with him.

All ate in silence.

"I'm serious," Hera finally said as she finished her meal. "You've been doing this all wrong, Skelly. You need to forget the old way."

"That sounds familiar," Skelly grumbled.

Kanan chuckled. "What's Skelly doing wrong now?"

"It's what I was trying to tell him earlier," Hera said, crumpling the sack. "Gord confronting Vidian. Skelly blowing up everything in sight—it's suicide. It's not the way to do this."

"To do what?"

"To run a—" Hera stopped. She took a deep breath and lowered her voice. "This is no way to make a difference against the Empire."

"They're not trying to make a difference," Kanan said, doling out the food. "They're just trying to strike back."

"And I understand that. But if the people who have a beef with the Empire act solely in their own interests, it won't do anybody else any good. In fact, it might make it harder for any kind of real rebellion to flower—"

"Rebellion?" Skelly snapped. "Who's talking about rebellion?"

Nearby, Zaluna let out a *tsk-tsk*. She spoke to the air in a lilting voice: "This is how you get in trouble."

"Nobody's talking about rebellion, that's for sure," Kanan announced. Zaluna had swept the room for listening devices, but she clearly wasn't comfortable with the words she'd heard.

Hera rolled her eyes. "No, not us. We would never. But in *theory* . . ." She said the word loudly and looked reassuringly at Zaluna.

"They *really* don't like you talking theory," the Sullustan said with a chuckle.

Hera went on. "In theory, say you did have thousands of people—no, thousands of *systems*—enraged at a hypothetical Galactic Empire in a faraway galaxy. But they're all upset over local matters, over particular grievances, and they never get together on anything. So they get no strength in numbers, no strategic advantages from cooperation. They're easy to divide and conquer. And worst of all, no common spirit ever develops."

Skelly looked back in disbelief. "You're saying we don't fight back?" His voice reverberated in the small room. "What they're doing to the moon. What they did to Lal. What they did to *me*—"

"—was horrible, Skelly." Rising, Hera walked over and put a hand on his shoulder. "But you weren't hurt by one person."

"You're right. It felt like an army."

"You were hurt by a regime. You might get vengeance against the hand that hurt you—or that killed Lal. But you wouldn't get justice. Not until everyone gets it."

Skelly's eyes narrowed, and he looked back down in silence.

On the floor, Zaluna drew yet another small device from her bag and started fiddling with it. "Checking my messages," she said to those around her. "It's safe."

Hera nodded.

Skelly stared idly at the leafy stalk of the only vegetable Kanan had been able to find in the cantina's larder. "You know, there were a lot of us that lost limbs in the war. All we wanted from the docs was to be able to do what we used to again. We didn't volunteer to be turned into murder machines." He leaned forward in a daze. "What's wrong with that guy?"

Kanan assumed it was a rhetorical question. He also realized that Skelly had taken a worse beating than he'd imagined.

Zaluna gasped and dropped the gadget she was holding.

The Twi'lek looked to her with concern. "What is it?"

Hands on her knees, Zaluna stared in disbelief at the small device at her feet. "I-I just checked in. My entire team was suspended. And when I didn't show up for my shift, so was I." Her words caught in her throat. "Thirty years with a perfect work record—gone."

Hera covered her mouth with her hand. "Oh, Zaluna, I'm sorry."

"It's more than that. The Empire knows I was friends with Hetto. They're going to find out where I was today. I'm going to lose my job—or *worse!*"

"Some job, spying on everyone," Skelly said, snapping out of his funk.

"It's important!" Zaluna retorted. "At least—it was, once. We did things. Important things."

"I don't see it," Kanan said, standing and walking over to the door. He leaned against it with his arms crossed. The Empire's snooping didn't surprise him, of course. It just seemed like a waste of time. "What's the good in watching a bunch of miserable people going about their boring lives?"

"In the old days—under the Republic—we did more than that," Zaluna said, perking up. "We found missing persons. We stopped crimes. We prevented—"

"Prevented people from questioning anything!" Skelly threw the green stalk he was holding on the floor. "You helped the Empire monitor production. Helped them bust anyone who got out of line!"

"That's *now*," Zaluna said, her voice pitched high. Her words coming fast, she faced Skelly. "Has anything bad ever happened in *your* life? Anything bad that could have been stopped, if only someone had been paying better attention?"

Skelly took a breath and nodded. "More than once."

"And you, Kanan? Is there something bad that could have been prevented if someone'd been watching over you?"

Kanan shifted. Hera had been listening silently from the corner, but now he could feel her attention focused on him. "I don't know," he finally said, hands in his pockets.

"*Everybody's* got something like that," Zaluna said. "What we do— what we did—was good." She dipped her head fretfully. "And now I'm done for."

Kanan struggled to find something to say. He couldn't think of anything. But removing his hand from his pocket, he found the recording device Zaluna had located in the hoverbus. "Unless someone wants to relive today's disaster," he said, "I'll be crushing this thing."

"No, wait," Hera said, approaching him. She reached for it. "The Imperials were driving the bus for a while earlier. Vidian, and the Imperial captain."

"I didn't hear anybody," Zaluna said, offering Hera her holoplayer. "But then, no one heard me." Hera connected the devices and cued the recording back several hours.

They sat in silence, watching the material from the hoverbus surveillance cam. By the time it was over, Kanan looked up, bewildered. "Skelly was right. *They're going to blow up the moon.*"

CHAPTER THIRTY-THREE

"*. . . SO WE DON'T have to mine Cynda at all. If what the bomber says is true, the moon could be pulverized, and its thorilide directly harvested and processed in space. No need for slow miners, or the costly processors on Gorse . . .*"

Hera shut off the recorder. She looked mystified.

Skelly was apoplectic. "*He stole my idea!*"

"Stole your—" Kanan smirked. "You *gave* him your idea. You nearly got killed giving him your idea!"

"Hey, when I told you the Empire was going to destroy the world by accident, you thought I was crazy," Skelly said. "Now we know they're going to destroy it on purpose. Looks to me I wasn't crazy *enough*!"

"So this is why Vidian left Moonglow so abruptly." Hera shook her head.

"Delusional," Kanan said. Sloane, he'd noticed, had barely said a word during the recording. He wondered if she thought Vidian was insane. "You can't just *dissolve* a whole moon!"

"You want me to show you?" Skelly snapped. "I've got loads of studies I can show you!"

"All on the wall of a bomb shelter across town," Hera said. She frowned. "I didn't believe it, either. Skelly, are you sure?"

"I'm sure! Of course I'm sure," Skelly said. He gestured to his battered face. "Do you think I would've risked all this if I weren't?"

It sounded too incredible to Kanan. Was Vidian really taking any of this seriously?

And yet, hadn't Skelly brought down several levels of Cynda's substrate just by one well-placed bomb?

"It could happen," Zaluna said. "None of the rest of you was born here. I remember when I was young, my mother used to tell me the moon was all brittle, because Gorse loves it and keeps trying to hug it too hard. And the moon keeps trying to get away."

A good metaphor for some of my relationships, Kanan thought.

"She said Cynda would one day break up and come tumbling down. We all heard that story, as schoolchildren." She chuckled darkly. "Maybe that's part of why people on Gorse live as they do—because doomsday's coming. But we were told it wouldn't happen for thousands of years, so not to worry."

Hera nodded. "But what if it happened *tomorrow*?"

The grinning young lieutenant appeared in the doorway of the captain's office on *Ultimatum*. "The projections are run, Count Vidian."

"And?"

Ultimatum's planetary science specialist saluted Sloane belatedly and read from her report. "The bomber was right," Lieutenant Deltic said, "partially. The moon Cynda might be shattered by blasts at the stress points he names, but it would require far more explosives, and of a higher grade, than Gorse has in its stores."

"I have baradium-357 in quantity at Calcoraan Depot," Vidian said, looking meaningfully at Sloane. "As well as a thorilide collection vessel, of the sort that harvests the material from broken-up comets. Would the debris field remain in orbit for sifting?"

"The highly elliptical orbit makes it unlikely that the material would form a ring around the planet," the lieutenant said. "At least some debris would be ejected from the system; some would be captured, falling on the planet. Presuming the thorilide survives, your collector would have more than enough to keep it busy." She chuck-led darkly. "The planet's another story, though."

"I don't need to hear about Gorse," Vidian said.

"I do," Sloane interjected. The lieutenant worked for *her*, after all.

"Well, first there's the direct impact—that depends on how ener-getic the initial dispersal was, and where it took place. You'd have more meteor action if the blast occurred at the upcoming perigee; less if it happened weeks from now, when the moon is farther out. The chunks won't be that large, but their composition will make them harder for the atmosphere to burn up."

"And seismic reactions on Gorse?" Sloane asked.

"Hoo boy," the lieutenant said, her expression suggesting they were well off into the realm of speculation. "Little would change at first, but the system would evolve. As the tidal balance shifted, Gorse would respond. Things could get pretty rocky."

"Groundquakes and meteor storms!" Sloane looked at Vidian. "Sounds cataclysmic."

"That's not even all," the lieutenant put in. "The planet could start spinning again."

"What?"

"The moon is a junior partner in the dance between Gorse and its sun, but an unusually important one. The dynamics of Gorse's atmo-sphere are extremely sensitive to change—it's already a miracle the dark side's livable at all!"

"The bottom line?" Vidian asked drily.

The lieutenant checked her notes. "Nothing could happen. Or you *could* see the destruction of the whole biome in ten years."

Sloane was amazed. "Ten years!"

"Or not," the lieutenant said hastily. "It's almost worth doing just to see what would happen."

"Enough," Sloane said, rolling her eyes. Glancing out at the moon, hanging large and bright outside her office viewport, she remembered something else the lieutenant had said, something earlier. "You said *if* the thorilide survives the moon's destruction. Why wouldn't it?"

"I'm not a chemist," the young woman replied. "But I know the thorilide molecule is fragile, easily prone to dissolving into its component elements. It's why Cynda's such a great source for it. The crystals that the thorilide's suspended in protect it. But there's a difference between carefully controlled blasts and what we're talking about. You wouldn't know whether the crystals would survive unless you did a test first." She paused. "Be a waste of a good moon otherwise."

Sloane glanced at Vidian, and then back at the lieutenant. "Dismissed."

The lieutenant saluted and departed. The captain looked back at Vidian. "The Emperor will expect such a test," she said.

Vidian idly studied the back of his hand. "I've already considered it. One of the specialists I brought in my entourage has assured me he can make the observations using *Ultimatum*'s sensors."

Convenient, Sloane thought.

"So we can run an experiment posthaste. We will, of course, report everything we find to the Emperor," Vidian said.

Of course. Things were moving very fast—especially considering the seriousness of what they were contemplating. "It's still so hard to imagine. Wiping out Gorse within *ten years*?"

"That's acceptable," Vidian said, walking toward the doorway.

"We would be destroying a habitable world," Sloane said, at once repulsed and amazed.

"We wouldn't be refining the thorilide on Gorse anymore, but in space, using the harvester vessels I have at my disposal," Vidian said, pausing in the doorway to look back out on Cynda. "Those with appropriate skills could apply to join their crews."

"And the rest?"

"The rest are of little use and do not concern me. They can find their own way offworld—and live to be of service somewhere else. But as of this discovery, there can be no doubt: To the Empire, their world is better off dead."

"Pending the test," Sloane said.

"Of course." He turned and left.

Hera watched as the others slept.

Only Kanan had not remained. The discussion had wandered aimlessly after the Cynda revelation, with Skelly concocting new wild theories by the minute. Zaluna, who had been remarkably resilient until now, had let her weariness feed her worry. Hera had tried to give shape to the discussions, urging practicality—and that effort, somehow, had seemed to aggravate Kanan all the more.

"Don't you care about anything?" she'd asked before he left to go downstairs.

"It's never good to care about too much," he'd said, flippant as always. "You're bound for disappointment."

Now she had to decide what she was going to do. Enough hours had passed quietly that she doubted Kanan had been identified at the Imperial spaceport; that meant there weren't stormtroopers waiting outside The Asteroid Belt. She might be able to slip back to her own ship. Zaluna had at last given her the data cube Hetto had prepared for her. That, she knew, would help other dissidents elsewhere.

And she'd learned all she expected to about Vidian—that the famous odds-beating business pundit was a murderous thug evidently willing to entertain outrageous schemes. Like Kanan, she doubted the destruction of the moon was possible; it was too big an idea, too fantastic to imagine. Engineering on that scale just wasn't done—or at least she'd never heard of it. Vidian would surely figure that out. At least while he was doing that, he wouldn't be carrying out any more sadistic "inspections." So there wasn't much reason for her to linger on Gorse.

First, however, she owed it to Zaluna to get the woman to safety somewhere, before the Empire arrested her. It certainly would: Hera had no illusions about that. And for some reason she couldn't put her finger on, she wanted to have one more talk with Kanan. He was self-centered and hedonistic, to be sure—but there had been flashes of something different, moments that made her wonder who he was and where he had come from. He was good at staying a step ahead of the Empire, and she'd seen him perform remarkable physical feats.

But none of that mattered, if the man lacked a conscience. It took more than talents to bring about a revolution. It required spirit.

And not everyone had it.

CHAPTER THIRTY-FOUR

ONE OF THE PERKS of living in a place without daylight, Kanan felt, was the large number of options it offered for those who didn't want to be seen.

A group of tourists had lost their shirts—or rather, their fine and expensive cloaks—to Kanan weeks earlier in a sabacc game. The wraps had sat useless in the cantina's storeroom ever since, unable to be pawned. It turned out that in the dark, the cloaks looked just like the robes a group of weird blood cultists wore as they wandered the streets every full moon, chanting their mantras and looking for escaped house pets to practice their religion on. Not only did the Empire tolerate the cultists, it had shut down Gorse City's animal control department to reap the savings.

Kanan had cursed his fellow players, who certainly must have known that "creepy maniac" was a fashion statement nobody wanted to make. But now he and the others put the cloaks to work. "Keep walking," he said from under his hood as he led the others up the long avenue in the industrial district. "If you see anyone, keep your head down and growl like you're hungry."

No one had bothered them. The full moon was approaching soon enough that other blood cultists were about and making for the cemeteries where they liked to hold their rites. It was a good time to be out and gruesome. Kanan had lashed his traveling bag to his back beneath his cloak; mad monks carried no luggage, and he thought the hunchbacked look it gave him was a nice touch.

"Seems to be working," he said. "We won't get away with it more than once, but it'll get us across town."

"You keep surprising me," Hera said. She was walking directly behind Kanan, keeping a careful watch all around.

"Yep, it's the whole lunatic family out for a crawl," Kanan said. "Mom, dad, grandma, and the weird uncle we keep in the basement."

"*You're* the grandma," Zaluna said.

Kanan grinned. The Sullustan woman had run out of steam the night before, but sleep had seemed to return her spirits. He still thought she was a little strange, but she amazed him nonetheless. He'd had the routine of a lifetime disrupted, years earlier—but he hadn't lived remotely as long as she had. And yet Zaluna seemed to have bounced back. He wondered what her secret was.

Skelly was in worse shape. He was moving slower, now, he saw: The latest round of meds hadn't lasted the whole walk. He was looking up at the moon as he trudged along. "You know," he said, "I think I really always wanted to be a rock guy."

Kanan looked at him. "A what?"

"A mineralogist. They used to study Cynda before they started ripping it up. I'd have had to go to school for it—everything I know I learned on my own. But coming here was nice. It showed me that the underground's more than just a place to plant mines."

"Or people," Kanan said, gesturing ahead. "Beggar's Hill, ladies and gentleman."

Beggar's Hill was no hill at all. A square clearing defined by little-traveled streets, the cemetery was populated by the aboveground sepulchers that Gorse's moist soil necessitated. Nightferns and crawling yettice had overtaken most of the ancient crypts, wearing all the names away. Catching a little light now as it did at this time of Cynda's orbit, it had the look of a peaceful grotto.

Kanan watched Hera as she stepped down the little path between the graves, moonlight in her eyes. *She really is something.*

Skelly staggered up and looked around. "I guess there won't be any place like this for Lal—or Gord. I didn't get along with them, but still . . ."

"Yeah," Kanan said, but he didn't think on it long. Wakes weren't for him. The Jedi were big on funerals, but no one had memorialized any of them. A death meant it was time for the living to get moving.

And it was. "All right, I've done what I can," Kanan said. "This is the western edge of Shaketown—Moonglow's just a few blocks away. We're in the middle of everything here. Hera, you said your ship was parked two kilometers to the west. Zaluna's apartment is two blocks to the southeast. And the nearest commercial spaceport," he said, turning and pointing north, "is ten blocks that way. So wherever you want to go, you're almost there." He took his hood down. "We're done."

Hera looked over at Zaluna, who was wandering around looking at the monuments. "Have you decided?"

"I want to go with you," she said, "in your ship." The woman gestured to the graves. "Almost everyone I've known on this planet is just a name on a screen—or a name on a stone. I don't want to work at Transcept anymore, even if they let me back. And it would be nice to see an actual sunrise someplace."

"Should we go to your place and pick up your things?"

Zaluna shook her head. "They're watching it by now. And my life wasn't at that apartment anyway." She looked up at the moon. "Let's get started."

Hera turned to Skelly. "And what are you going to do?"

Skelly opened his cloak and patted his satchel with his left hand. "I'm going to cut off this problem at the source—by blowing up the explosives plant that's near the spaceport. If they can't bring baradium from Gorse, they can't destroy the moon!"

Hera looked reproachfully at him. "You do know there are other sources of explosives besides Gorse, right?"

"If I cost them a day, it's worth it." Skelly jutted out his chin. "Besides," he said, "what else is there for me to do?"

Kanan nodded in agreement, despite himself. Skelly had just summed it up. Futile efforts—that was all anyone on Gorse had left. Kanan, of course, knew all about being cut adrift with no guidance as to what to do next. He'd figured out the secret: never again identifying with anything or anyone so much that losing it left him with no other option. But not everyone was as smart as he was.

He walked up to Hera. "So, where do you want to go after we drop her off? Wor Tandell's nice. Or there are some casino worlds I think you'd love."

Hera shook her head. "I hate to sound like that droid from yesterday, Kanan, but I don't take riders."

Her serious tone startled him. "What's that again?"

"I'm not traveling the stars looking for companions or places to see," Hera said. "I have goals. I don't need anyone who isn't interested in them slowing me down."

"But Zaluna—"

"—has performed a service to the galaxy in providing data about the Empire's methods, and needs to start a new life where she can be safe. You, as near as I can tell, roll with whatever happens—and with whoever's in charge."

"That's harsh."

"It's what I see," she said. She offered her hand. "I do thank you for what you've done. Good luck to you."

Tongue-tied, Kanan simply accepted the handshake. "Okay," he finally said. "You're sure?"

Hera nodded pleasantly, took her hand back, and turned away. "Oh," she said, reaching into her cloak. Facing him again, she withdrew a small pouch and began counting out Imperial credits. "For your help."

Kanan was startled. "What am I, a mercenary?"

"No. But I saw you putting money back into Okadiah's safe, to pay for the hoverbus." She offered the cash. "Take it. You'll go farther."

So I'm a hired hand now, Kanan thought. *Oh, well.* He took the money.

He looked at Skelly and Zaluna. "So long," he said—and walked back toward the street. It would be a long trek to the spaceport, and sweaty in the robe. He doffed the cloak and threw it into the night-ferns. He'd take his chances, as he always did.

Where the path met the street, he turned to get one last glimpse of Hera. They were all still there, getting ready to go their separate ways. He shook his head, wondering what was keeping him. Kanan Jarrus never looked back. He always looked upward, outward, following the pull of the beyond. Cynda, hanging big and bulbous, was the glowing light pointing the way to his future. Up to the sky, where . . .

The moon exploded!

The Gorse skyline lit up, awash in the light of a dawn for the first time in a geologic age. No explosion of Skelly's had lit the cityscape so, and Kanan staggered, expecting some kind of thunderous sound. But there was none. And as the flash waned and his eyes adjusted, Kanan saw that, no, the moon hadn't exploded.

But it wasn't intact, either. Near the darkened lower limb of the near-full disk, a colossal plume of white ejecta was spreading down-ward and outward. It almost looked as if Cynda was shedding a tear-drop—a teardrop a hundred kilometers across and widening as it moved.

Kanan had seen comets and meteors striking moons before. Those didn't look like this. This was an eruption. *An eruption,* on a world volcanically dead.

And he knew that spot on Cynda. He landed there every day.

He looked back at the street. All traffic had stopped. People were outside their vehicles, next to their speeder bikes, looking up in fas-cination and horror. Kanan looked past them to the big glowing clock on the waterworks building behind. It said what the sickness in his stomach had already told him: Okadiah was on shift on the moon.

Everywhere, people began talking all at once, like the buzz at a sporting event. Kanan could hear Hera's voice, too, the voice he loved hearing, calling out to him from behind. But he didn't listen. He was running to a speeder bike paused in the middle of the street, grab-bing it from the hands of its stunned rider. She and the speeder bike's owner were still yelling as Kanan tore away down the thoroughfare, racing into Shaketown.

———

The world shook beneath Skelly. To one side, Zaluna's voice was filled with horror. *"It's happening."*

"No," Skelly said, looking up in wonder as the ground rumbled. "The groundquake's just a coincidence. Call it a sympathy pang."

He had removed his hood: No one was going to be looking at him. Not now. And a graveyard seemed to him the perfectly appropriate place to be witnessing the beginning of the end of the world. He looked back at Hera as the tremor subsided. "That was nothing compared with the quakes we'll feel if they keep it up."

"The Empire's doing it," Hera said, looking up in amazement. "They really are doing it."

"You didn't think they would?" Skelly asked.

"If they can do something, they will do something." She shook her head. "I just didn't think it was possible—or that it'd happen this fast."

Zaluna tugged at the Twi'lek's sleeve. "Do people need to leave, Hera? Is something going to happen to the planet?"

"Skelly says we're okay. But we should get back to my ship, just in case." She looked back to the street. "That's what I was trying to tell Kanan." Hera had something in her hands, Skelly saw—some device she'd been struggling with since not long after Kanan fled the scene. "I've been trying to get any information I can, but there's too much interference on the airwaves."

"Everyone's talking," Skelly said.

A Recon transport drove past as if nothing were happening, aiming a searchlight in the opposite direction from them. Skelly could hear another approaching down an intersecting street.

"They're still after us," he said glumly. "Even with what's going on up there."

"Then we can't wait around," Hera said, pocketing the gadget. "Looks like your plan's been overtaken by events, Skelly. Let's head for my ship."

"To go where?" Zaluna asked.

"I can drop you both someplace safe," Hera said, removing her cloak. "But first, I may need to stop Kanan before he does something rash." She glanced up at the sky with worry. "I think I know where he's going There's only one pilot in a million that could navigate that debris up there. I'm afraid of—" She stopped herself. "Let's go." She headed down the path out of the cemetery.

Skelly tried to follow. But before he could limp to the street, the roar of engines came from above. And light. Not as bright as before, but closer, and more directed. Skelly yelled out, "The Empire's found us!"

"I don't think so," Hera said as the dark mass of a starship descended toward the street.

"Your ship?" Zaluna asked, quivering.

"It's Kanan!" Skelly exclaimed, recognizing the shape. "It's *Expedient*!"

The rear ramp descended as the mining ship settled half a meter over the street. Kanan appeared in it. "Hurry," he called to Hera. "I need you to get me to that blast site. Next to you, I'm an amateur!"

Hera gestured toward her companions. "They come with us!"

"I don't care. I've got Okadiah's team on the comm," Kanan said. "They're dying!"

CHAPTER THIRTY-FIVE

EXPEDIENT **ROCKETED THROUGH** the exosphere into space.
Kanan had guessed right. He'd missed two work shifts, but with Lal
dead and Vidian's appointed caretaker not yet in place, his ship hadn't
been reassigned to anyone. His identification had gotten him onto the
tarmac—but nobody was looking at the ground anyway. He found
that the passenger seat had been replaced, but the ship hadn't yet been
reloaded with explosives. The latter fact was helping *Expedient*'s handling enormously.

Only he wasn't the one handling it.

"Busy," Hera said, guiding the control yoke. From the passenger
seat, Kanan could see that all the traffic normally headed toward
Cynda at this hour had joined the ships fleeing it. A colossal cone of
silvery debris rose into space from Cynda's southern hemisphere,
blooming outward like an upside-down snowfall. Contact with the
fast-moving ejecta could be catastrophic, and the other freighter pilots knew it.

Kanan knew it, too, which was why he'd surrendered the controls
to Hera. After their experience on the hoverbus, he'd been left with

little doubt that Hera wasn't just a good pilot; she was great. At the moment, he was upset, not the master of his emotions—and he knew how that could compromise the focus and reflexes necessary to do the kind of piloting that was about to be required: They had to go exactly to the one place everyone else was fleeing.

"No more info on the comm," he said. There'd been nothing but static for long minutes, ever since he'd heard Okadiah's team send their distress call. The other companies' channels had similarly gone dead. Looking at the long-range scope, he could see why. The fragments emanated from a point less than a kilometer away from the main entrance to the mining complex. He couldn't make out a single landmark. What hadn't blown outward had caved in.

Hera weaved *Expedient* through the rush of oncoming freighters. Half of them didn't seem to know where they were going, Kanan thought: All were seeking refuge, either on Gorse or around it. "They're afraid it's going to happen again."

"Good bet," Hera said. "But not today."

Maybe it's just a natural disaster, he thought. That, or an industrial accident. He wanted more than anything for his worst fears to be wrong. Would the Empire—would *anyone*—really test a far-fetched theory while everyone was still at work? It made no sense. But then he looked out onto *Ultimatum,* the only ship not in motion. It simply sat, the indifferent observer at a safe distance. No rescue vehicles had been released: only probe droids, headed toward the debris field.

Hera swung the ship out of traffic and onto a wide approach vector to the moon. Kanan looked back into the windowless rear of the cockpit. Light reflecting from Cynda intensified, casting his and Hera's shadows darkly upon their passengers. Skelly sat, unusually mute and reserved, on the acceleration couch to the left, his head bowed. Zaluna was on the little chair behind Kanan's, facing in the opposite direction. Initially excited by the takeoff, she'd refrained from looking out the forward viewport as they closed in on the disaster site.

"All those people," she said in a low voice. "I watched them every day." In an odd way, Kanan thought, the woman had been going with them to work on the moon for years.

Kanan looked forward as Hera expertly brought *Expedient* into a roll. He saw the length and shape of the debris field now. "No, that doesn't look suspicious at all," she said. "It's like a funnel."

"Yeah. Channeling outward." He blinked. "None of it's falling back down!"

"It won't," Skelly said morosely. "A normal blast would emanate outward spherically. You'd have a lot of fragments raining down again. This was the result of a shaped charge—a bunch of simultaneous blasts placed to direct most of the debris up and out at escape velocity."

Kanan stared at the unnatural-looking formation. "How do you know?"

"It was my idea." Skelly groaned. "It was on the holodisk."

Kanan grew sick as he studied the sensors. "Outgassing at the main landing bay. The complex has been ruptured." He unsnapped his restraint and headed for the rear of the compartment. "I've got to get down there."

Hera punched several buttons. "I can needle us in beneath the cloud. Where do you want to go?"

Skelly unhooked himself and came forward. Studying the scene, he pointed. "The auxiliary bay!"

Half in the space suit he'd retrieved, Kanan came forward to look. "Yeah, I think you're right."

Skelly directed Hera toward a small dark indentation clear of the blast zone. The auxiliary bay had been the shipping-and-receiving area for a smaller network of caverns, long since abandoned for the richer veins of the main expanse. An airlock separated the sections, installed due to fears that the old complex might vent to space.

Now that the opposite had happened, Kanan thought, it could provide the only way in.

Hera directed the ship into a deep crater. The surface beneath was coated with ashen residue from the blast, but the rectangular opening cut into the southern wall was intact.

"Magnetic field's still holding," she said. "But it's dark."

"Lights are on a different power grid," Kanan said, putting on his boots. "Can you handle it?"

"Of course." Effortlessly, Hera guided *Expedient* toward the maw.

As the ship entered the blackness, Hera activated the exterior floodlamps. At once, the occupants of *Expedient* were bathed again in light—their own, mirroring off and coruscating through the thousand stalagmites on the cavern's ceiling.

"We saved a lot on lighting this way," Skelly said.

Zaluna leaned around Kanan's chair for a look as *Expedient* touched down. She gasped at the beauty—and then retreated into her seat as Cynda rumbled. The moon hadn't quaked before to Kanan's memory, but he didn't care. He was already donning the helmet of the environment suit. The air in the bay was fine, but what lay ahead might not be. "I'm patching my suit comm into Moonglow's audio channel. Hold station here."

"I'm going," Hera said, rising. "You've got two suits."

Stuffing a bag full of oxygen masks, Kanan shook his head. "I need you here. Someone's got to fly these guys out of this place."

She was already suiting up. "Is this a rescue or a suicide mission? Now get the ramp open, because I'm going!"

Kanan felt like an insect making its way into a pile of brambles—in the dark. That was what had become of the region beyond the reinforced airlock. Passageways that had been horizontal and shafts that had been vertical had both gone diagonal as gravity sought to fill in the gap left by the explosion.

The thorilide-rich crystals that were the Empire's goal were, in fact, the only reason there was room to move at all: Even damaged by the blast, their tensile strength was amazing, giving the place a continued semblance of structure. Kanan didn't have time to think on the irony. He kept going downward, inward, ever farther into the darkness, lit only by his and Hera's helmet lights.

Hera had somehow kept up with him, even as he'd scrambled over and under and around barriers. She was unspooling a microfilament cable they'd found in the landing bay; there was no expectation of getting back to the ship otherwise.

Kanan couldn't rely on positioning technology to guide him down here in the underworld. All he had was the distress signal in his helmet, still being weakly broadcast from somewhere in the chaos. Every so often, they had seen a sign of past occupation: a cart, smashed and sideways, or the arm or leg of a droid. But there had been no indication of life.

He found a dark triangular opening up ahead. Shining his light into it, he saw what amounted to a floor several meters down. He pulled the loop of cable he'd been carrying from around his arm and lashed it to a seemingly solid crystal support. "Wait here," he said into his helmet mike.

"No."

There was no time to stop and argue. He slipped over the side and dangled, trying to find the surface somewhere beneath him. Letting go, he hit the ground—and slid downward into the darkness.

"*Kanan!*" Hera called.

"I'm all right," he said, shining his light around where he'd come to rest. "We're getting close."

She rappelled down the cable and slid down behind him. "Close? How can you tell? It's hard to see anything!"

"I can tell," Kanan said. He pointed his light to illuminate a battered head, sticking out from the ceiling.

"Oh," she said.

"Yeah." It was Yelkin. His body was crushed, embedded in the new strata of the moon.

Kanan could tell the sight chilled Hera. It didn't do him much good, either. But as the opening started to go more horizontal, they saw more corpses, dropped like sticks this way and that amid the broken crystal columns. It was like tunneling into a graveyard. Kanan recognized a uniform next—and then a hovercart, like the one he used daily. He was in the right place.

"Kanan!" Hera called.

Crawling over a mound of debris, he found her kneeling beside a half-buried equipment console. "That's your distress beacon," she said, looking around. "But I don't see—"

"*Okadiah!*"

Kanan leapt over jutting obstacles in the dark, hurrying to a spot up ahead. It was an elevator car, diagonal but still held in shape by the frame of its onetime shaft.

Okadiah was under it. Kanan shone his light on the old man's face. Okadiah's skin was blue; his eyes and lips were covered with frost. The volume of air in the underground network was vast relative to the new vents to space, and further collapses had closed those portals off. But pressure had dropped considerably, and the air that remained was frigid. Kanan whipped his pouch open and removed an oxygen mask. Carefully wrapping it around the miner's head, he was relieved to hear the old man cough.

"Kanan—"

"Don't move," Kanan said.

"That . . . a joke? Not funny."

Kanan pulled the thermo-wrap from his bag and covered Okadiah's chest and shoulders. Then he looked to the old man's legs. They had been crushed beneath the elevator car, but not fully pinned. "Hang on!"

Kanan turned and looked for something to use for leverage. Hera was right there, gripping a tough-looking stalactite. Kanan took it from her and inserted it beneath the side of the car. "You pull him out," he said to Hera—and heaved. The mass, already lopsided, gave way in the opposite direction, tilting backward enough for Hera to slide the old man free.

Kanan collapsed, panting, on the ground next to Okadiah.

Okadiah struggled to say something. "S-s-stormtroopers . . ."

"What?"

"Stormtroopers. Came in . . . ordered us out of Zone Sixty-Six. Had their own charges . . ."

Kanan exhaled. "I knew it." Feeling strength returning to his muscles, he got to his knees. "We're going to get you out of here."

"Too . . . late," Okadiah said.

Kanan looked back at Hera. She was looking away, off into the darkness, respectfully.

"C-c-come here," Okadiah mumbled. "Where . . . I can see you."

Kanan cradled the old man's battered frame in his arms. "What is it, Okadiah?"

"Not . . . you," Okadiah said, before coughing. "The . . . *pretty one.*"

Hera stepped to the other side of Kanan and knelt. "I'm here."

"Ah," he said, smiling as if laying eyes on her were medicine enough. "You . . . listen. This boy . . . is good to have around." Okadiah coughed again, this time much more violently. "You ought to . . . stick by him. Think . . . he needs . . ."

Okadiah stopped talking and closed his eyes. The inside of the transparent oxygen mask, once fogged, went clear.

No. Kanan reached for the man's chest, certain he needed to do something, but unsure of what. He knew conventional first aid, but Okadiah's injuries seemed past that. He felt useless, as useless as he had when Master Billaba had died—and the turmoil of that moment mixed with this one, clouding his concentration. He struggled to focus—

—only to feel the gentle touch of Hera's hand on his arm. She shook her head. "He's gone, Kanan."

"I tried."

"You did," she said, her touch turning into a firm grip. "We need to leave now."

Kanan looked back at her and shook his head. "No. Not without him."

CHAPTER THIRTY-SIX

"IT'S A TRIUMPH," Count Vidian declared. "A triumph, pure and simple!"

He strode onto the bridge, holding a datapad high. He didn't need it, but not everyone had his eyes. "It's the report from my lead researcher," he said, approaching Captain Sloane. "Ninety-seven percent of thorilide molecules in the effluent remained intact. Only a small portion broke down!"

"I don't recognize the name," Sloane said, pointing to the lead researcher. "*Lemuel Tharsa*. He's aboard?"

"Part of my team. He boarded with me." Vidian glared impatiently, bothered to have had his good news interrupted. "You'll find him checked in on your ship's manifest. What difference does it make? The important thing is what he *says*."

Sloane read from the report. "'The moon Cynda may be effectively pulverized using deep-bore charges, yielding an amount of ready thorilide equating to what could be mined in two thousand years, using conventional methods—'" She looked up in disbelief. "*Two thousand years?*"

"Imagine the Emperor's response!"

"We'll have increased efficiency, all right."

Vidian looked past her to the sky outside *Ultimatum*. "What's the status of the mining cargo fleets?"

"We've ordered every empty vessel to hold position, awaiting your next command," she said, handing off the datapad to an aide. "Two hundred seventy ships, counting thorilide carriers and explosives haulers."

"We'll need them all," Vidian said. "And all the ones on Gorse. We'll be bringing back thousands of metric tons of baradium-357 from Calcoraar Depot. We can retrofit the thorilide carriers for use there."

Sloane stepped over to examine a monitor. "There also appears to be at least one intact explosives freighter remaining on Cynda."

"Hardy."

"Or foolhardy. Our sensors showed it going *to* the moon, even after the explosion. Someone was determined to deliver his payload." Sloane studied the screen in more detail, before looking up with concern. "We count thirty-six vessels destroyed in Cynda's main hangar, both personnel carriers and cargo ships. All attendant personnel presumably lost."

"Acceptable," Vidian said. "If we'd alerted the miners to our plans, you'd have seen true unrest. There'd be dozens like that bomber."

"One was plenty," Sloane said, straightening. "But won't people on Gorse wonder what happened?"

Vidian began walking back to the elevator, accompanied by Sloane. "I've prepared an alert for broadcast," he said, "calling the event a comet strike. That explanation alone accounts both for why the workers were caught unawares—and for Cynda's ultimate fate."

"Efficient."

"We won't need miners anyway, when our plan works."

The captain's dark eyebrows shot up. "*Our* plan?"

"This could be big for you, Sloane," Vidian said, standing in the lift doorway. "I'll send up final instructions shortly."

"We're ready, my lord."

Vidian nodded, stepped back, and watched as the door closed in front of him. He could no longer smile, but he felt it. It *was* a triumph.

But not pure and simple. He hadn't told Sloane everything. Certainly, destroying the moon would help him meet the Emperor's goal now—but later was another story. That little inconvenient distinction had been revealed to him in the past hour, and he had shared it with no one.

He'd expected such an eventuality, however, and he had a means of dealing with it. It would get him past this crisis—and then he would lay a trap that Baron Danthe could never escape. Vidian knew something Danthe didn't, a secret that would solve all his problems.

In one stroke he would keep the Emperor's favor—and eliminate his main rival once and for all. Efficient, as always.

Together with Hera, Kanan had managed to move Okadiah's body back up the long and twisted route to the still-pressurized auxiliary bay. There, after removing their environment suits, they'd found Skelly and Zaluna outside the ship. Skelly was lying on his back, looking up at the lights, as Zaluna wandered as if in a daze, marveling at the kaleidoscopic effects.

"I watched the place on the cams for years," she'd said. "But I never imagined anything could be so beautiful."

Kanan had considered taking Okadiah's body back to Gorse for burial. But on reflection, Cynda seemed a much more fitting resting place for his friend. He and Hera had found a side grotto, where they laid the body down and covered it with rocks.

With the damage to the complex, Kanan couldn't imagine anyone mining the moon again, not in the normal way. That meant the Empire had gone all in on the moon-shattering scheme.

"You're blinking," Skelly said, looking up at Kanan.

Kanan noticed the flashing light on the device on his belt. "Call coming in." It was strange to see, now, of all times. "It's my Moonglow pager."

He activated it, and Vidian's voice echoed through the massive chamber. "Attention, all traffic associated with the Mining Guild. All empty mining cargo ships on Gorse or in orbit are instructed to follow *Ultimatum* to the Calcoraan system. All off-shift pilots on Gorse are ordered to report and fly whatever vessels are available."

Skelly sat up. He gawked, trying to calculate. "That's got to be a thousand ships!"

The transmission continued—only now, it was Sloane speaking. "This alert is for Gorse Space Traffic Control. No other traffic of any kind is allowed to depart Gorse until further notice. The space lanes must be kept clear until our return. We're leaving a TIE patrol to enforce the restriction." The message ended.

"No one can leave Gorse?" Zaluna asked, fretful.

"And if we go back, we're stuck," Skelly said. "So much for warning people."

"What is this about?" Kanan asked. "What's Calcoraan?"

Kneeling near the exit to the landing bay, Hera looked through the magnetic shield and out to space. "It's Vidian's base of operations. A nerve center, a supply hub for the Empire in this sector."

Skelly snapped his fingers. "Three fifty-seven!"

Kanan blinked. "What, *baradium-357*?"

"It's in my research," the bomber said. "I ran the numbers on the worst case, what it would take to blow the moon apart. Plain old baradium bisulfate can't do it, not even a thousand ships full. But the isotope could. That's the evil stuff, weapons-grade."

You're the expert, Kanan thought. "And they've got it there."

"They invented it there," Hera said, walking over to join them.

Zaluna spoke in a worried voice. "So what do we do?"

No one said anything.

Kanan finally shrugged and gestured to *Expedient*. "We *could* do what they want us to do."

Hera turned to face him. "Yeah?"

"That's an explosives hauler. I'm a pilot for one of the mining firms. You just heard my orders. We can't go anywhere else, more than likely—not without a fight." He put his hands before him, palms upward. "So we go."

"We follow Vidian?" Skelly's eyes narrowed. "What would we do?"

Kanan glowered at him. "We're not blowing the place up, I'll tell you that!"

"But *maybe*," Hera said, "maybe we won't have to."

Kanan looked at the ship, considering the possibilities.

"We can't decide to go without everyone's consent," Hera said. "That's the Empire's way."

Kanan looked back at her in disbelief. "What, you want a vote? We can't exactly sit around in a circle debating all year."

Hera walked into the middle of the group, addressing each of the three as she turned. "Listen, I think we all understand the stakes—at least, I hope we do. You know the Empire needs to be stopped here, and you've also got individual reasons to care. But for us to have any chance of working together, we've got to be united. We've all got to see the same big picture."

Zaluna watched her. "Tell us."

"I've been around to see it. All across the galaxy. This is an Empire motivated by greed—that delivers injustice. That rules through fear—and that prospers through deceit." Hera started counting on her fingers. "Greed, injustice, fear, deceit. You can see them here, can't you?"

"They've certainly got the greed part down," Skelly said, looking up at the ceiling. "I can't believe what they've done—what they're going to do to this place. And for what?" He waved his good hand. "Whatever. I'm in. And I think if Gord Grallik had lived, he'd go with you on the injustice part."

Hera nodded. She turned to Zaluna next. "Do you want to go home, Zaluna? Because if you do, we all will. No one will judge you."

Zaluna didn't say anything for long moments.

Finally, summoning the words, she spoke. "You know, I always liked to tell myself I was a brave person. But the fact is, I've been a coward," she said, looking down. "The place I felt safest was in a place where I could watch over others. But it's changed. Hetto, Skelly—they're far from the only ones. I've seen *hundreds* of people arrested. Based on things I heard them say and do." She shook her head. "And I never saw any of those people on the screens again. Nobody comes back!"

"The Empire doesn't keep watch in order to protect, Zaluna. It keeps watch to scare."

"I know. *I've* been the terror." Eyes full of defiance, she looked over at Hera. "I don't want to make innocent people afraid anymore. And I won't let *them* do it, either."

Hera smiled gently. Kanan knew Hera didn't want to show it, but he could tell she was immensely proud of Zaluna.

"We . . . we won't have to hurt anyone, will we?" the woman asked.

"Not if we can avoid it," Hera said.

Now she turned her eyes on Kanan. "And what about you?"

"I lost track," Kanan said. "What did you leave me with, injustice?"

"Deceit," Skelly offered.

"Well, I think I've got that covered," Kanan said, gesturing. "All those bodies down there. Nobody had to be here."

He was scratching his beard, deciding whether to offer anything else, when the next words came out anyway. "And they're not the only friends of mine that the Empire's deceived."

Hera studied him, perhaps deciding whether to ask him to elaborate. Instead, she smiled a little. "So what do you suggest doing about it?"

"Something." Kanan paused. "I don't know what. But somebody sucker punched a friend. I won't let that pass."

"Good enough." Hera stood up straight and gestured to the ramp. "It's your ship, Captain."

"You're the pilot."

"And you're the tactician." She grinned. "Let's see what you can do."

It was more than a risk, Hera thought: Going to an Imperial depot at this stage of her project bordered on madness. The Empire, as yet, hadn't identified her. Getting tagged now would be just as bad as getting caught.

But what was happening to Gorse and Cynda was beyond serious. It was the sort of thing she'd vowed to stop someday. The day had just come early—too early, before she'd assembled a capable team. Not exactly the new dawn she'd had in mind.

Skelly would have been arrested if she'd left them behind on Gorse, she still believed; that could have put the Empire on her trail. But he wasn't revolutionary material. And Zaluna had resolve now, but she would be out of her depth soon.

No, it was Kanan she wanted to see in action. She watched him from the pilot's seat, as he punched hyperspace coordinates into the nav computer. He seemed different to her now. Not obsessed, as Skelly seemed—but focused, directed. She'd seen him act that way in short bursts when heroism was required; now it was a sustained effort. It was clear that what had happened on Cynda had affected him deeply.

She hadn't lied earlier. She did want to see what he could do. But she was more interested in seeing what he *would* do.

PHASE THREE:

DETONATION

"Count Vidian leading Mining Guild in heroic effort to stabilize moon"

"Blast investigators turn eyes to mining firms"

"Tourism industry watchers suggest busy season for travel ahead"

—headlines, Imperial HoloNews (Gorse Edition)

CHAPTER THIRTY-SEVEN

A CHILD'S SNOW GLOBE, filled with blood. That was how one of the first visitors to behold Calcoraan had described the world. It was a wonder anyone had ever returned, given that description—and Rae Sloane agreed.

Looking out from *Ultimatum*'s bridge, she saw a planet that heaved and churned crimson, the result of a planetwide ocean thick with chromyl chloride. There wasn't anything living down there—not on a sea where a drop of water could unleash not one, but two potent acids. But both the liquid and the ocean floor beneath it held uses for starship manufacturing, and so Calcoraan Depot had been constructed in orbit to service the many robotic factories already in space.

It was just another bizarre stop on what had, for Sloane, become a tour of the galaxy's strangest planets. The Empire tended to like these punishing environments, she thought, like an extremophile bacterium in a volcanic rift. It made sense to her, philosophically: True power could only be claimed by those brave enough to go and get it.

And Gorse could soon become another hellish place, losing what little livability it had.

Calcoraan Depot was Vidian's design and domain, and the thing seemed an architectural expression of his philosophies. The vast polyhedral hub of the depot sat like the biggest atom in an extensive molecule, connected to all the orbital factories by a triangular lattice grid of passageways. New supplies kept moving through those tubes to the hub and its main warehouse or directly to departing vessels for snap delivery. The hub's central position also gave its occupants a view of everything around, including the approaching flotilla of cargo ships from Gorse. *Keep moving! Destroy barriers! See everything!* was fully at work in Vidian's station.

Sloane could see Vidian's minions fully at work, too, on a curious giant of a spacecraft at the far end of the sprawling complex. Vidian was over there now, overseeing final preparations and calling every thirty seconds to inquire as to when the rest of the cargo fleet would arrive from Gorse. It was a ship like none Sloane had ever seen. Seven bulging black spheres connected on a long axis, it looked like a segmented insect. But where a bug might have had legs, the vessel instead had long antenna-like structures running from the frontmost pod backward the entire length of the vessel.

"*Forager,*" the science officer said excitedly. "That's a real beauty."

The captain nodded. Lieutenant Deltic got on her nerves, but Sloane had ordered her here anyway. She felt she needed to understand the process she was being asked to protect. "What are those long things along the spine?"

"Electrostatic towers—sixteen of them." The lieutenant fidgeted with the pins on a hat gone lopsided. "They'll fan outward when it's in operation to become the spokes for the collection wheel. I saw a ship like that in action once. It just plows through the debris field, snapping up all the goodies."

"The goodies?" Sloane shook her head. "I don't think I can handle all this technical jargon."

"The thorilide molecules. They're drawn to the spokes and shunted inside the vessel. There are automated processing centers in each of those big pods—taking the place of much of what the refineries on

Gorse would've done. Just above the thrusters, that tail-end pod has the landing bays for shipping the stuff out. They'll churn out more pure thorilide in an hour than the miners did in a month."

Sloane nodded. The vessel was heavily shielded, as anything that barged into asteroid fields and comet tails needed to be; the turbolaser cannons on the outside of each pod and on the forward command hub probably also cut down on damage from errant debris. Once *Forager* was in place, Gorse would have its own Calcoraan Depot—for as long as the thorilide lasted.

Which seemed to be forever. The lieutenant was dizzy with her math again. "Even if ninety percent of the debris were to strike the planet, that machine could supply a *hundred* Empires the size of ours for a century!"

"There is only one Empire," Sloane said sternly. Then she looked at the lieutenant. "Ninety percent of the debris falling? Is that possible?"

The younger woman shrugged. "I told you. Might be a drop, might be a deluge." She grinned. "We have a betting pool going on down in Planetary Sciences. If something takes out the World Watch Plaza building in Gorse City in this calendar year, I'm taking my shore leave on Alderaan!"

"Dismissed," Sloane said. *Out the airlock,* she wanted to add.

Still, she'd found out what she wanted to know. It was amazing, seeing up close the work involved to source and service just one component of the Imperial arsenal. And this was just one of countless facilities. How many other projects were out there, similar to what Vidian had in mind? How many had he run, and how many was he running personally?

Playing bodyguard to an efficiency expert hadn't interested Sloane in the beginning. But now she saw clearly that her mission was, in large part, about the basic business of the Empire: to keep going. To keep growing. It all suggested to her that Vidian, in his eccentric way, was as vital to the Emperor as Lord Vader—and that escorting Vidian was easily more important than chasing down pirates on the Outer Rim. Things had to be built.

All interstellar empires rose and fell, ultimately, on their ability to deliver on this one simple, unexciting thing: logistics. Her military history studies had told her of the war forges of the ancient past—she didn't doubt that Vidian had studied them, too. He could well be the great armorer of future legend—and she, his preferred deputy.

It was just still a little surprising to her that an entire planetary population might wind up between hammer and anvil. Even as motley a group of specimens as lived on Gorse. The workers on her homeworld, so much closer to the galactic center, were much better behaved.

Commander Chamas approached from the door to her ready room. "I see Lieutenant Strangechild has left you in peace."

Sloane rolled her eyes. "You want something?"

"You have a call," her first officer said. "I think you'll want to take it. A very important person."

"Vidian again?"

Chamas smirked. "A different important person."

She had seen him once at the commencement ceremonies at the Academy. He'd stood on the stage and shaken some hands. Not hers, but she could hardly forget him. Baron Lero Danthe spent more on a suit than her family spent on its house on Ganthel.

"My lord," she said. "To what do I owe the honor?"

"You and your crew do the honor, by your service," the young man said, bowing. "I heard about the attempts on Count Vidian's life. I was calling to thank you for protecting him."

"Most generous." Extremely so, considering the bad blood she'd heard to exist between Vidian and his subordinate in the administration. "They haven't made the saboteur who can foil the Empire."

The golden-haired man smiled. "Very glad you're on our team."

She liked hearing it. They were separated by title and fortune, but she and Danthe represented the New Imperials—the media's catchphrase for the first generation of people to ascend to adulthood under the Empire. With few exceptions, her naval superiors were part of a class that had struggled to reach the top, only to see all the rules change; now they were spending every waking moment trying to keep pace. Perhaps not Vidian, she thought. But it was tiring dealing with them all. The Empire would be a better place once people her and Danthe's age were in charge.

But in the military as in government, the time of apprenticeship had to be respected. She knew Danthe was already fabulously wealthy, having inherited control of a firm manufacturing heavy-duty droids for use on fiery worlds like Mustafar. But Vidian's holdings were wider, his name already established. And given the cyborg's health, she couldn't imagine him handing off power for decades to come.

Not that the young man wasn't eager. "The count hasn't had time to fill me in on this special project of his involving Cynda. How would you say it's faring?"

"I couldn't judge, my lord. I'm simply the escort."

"Hmm." Danthe frowned ever so slightly, before brightening. "Well, I am sure you will do well in that. I want you to know, Captain, if you ever have the smallest need, please contact me immediately. My people will put you through directly."

"I . . . thank you, my lord." The transmission ended.

Vidian, now Danthe? Were all interim captains this popular with the elite?

CHAPTER THIRTY-EIGHT

THROUGH HIS OWN reflection on the passenger-seat window, Kanan beheld the whole of Calcoraan Depot. He'd seen other such sights in his travels: enormous examples of Imperial ingenuity and excess. They seemed to get bigger every year.

But his focus was on his reflection—and the question he now asked himself. *Caleb, what are you doing?*

He hadn't gone by that name in years, and he didn't consider it relevant to the person he was now. Yet whenever Kanan stuck his neck out further than was comfortable, Caleb Dume was usually the culprit. Caleb, the little Jedi cut off before his date with destiny, his career as a galaxy-saving superhero stunted. He couldn't believe now that he'd ever been that person. That kid didn't know what real life—or real fun—was like. That boy was a nobody, a never-was. An unwelcome squatter in the back of his gray matter. Whenever Kanan had an idea that Caleb Dume would have agreed with, it was usually better to stay inside and order a double.

As much as the Emperor, Caleb was responsible for making Kanan's early adolescence miserable with his constant regrets. Caleb was all counterfactuals and what-ifs, all mental replays of the deaths of Depa Billaba and the other Jedi, always looking for some way disaster could have been averted. It was just as well that he was avoiding other people then, because it had made the young fugitive unbearably morose. While the other teenagers in the hangouts he'd tried to blend into were thinking about podracing, he was off in the corner trying to figure out how Jedi Master Ki-Adi-Mundi could have better protected himself on Mygeeto, or Master Plo Koon on Cato Neimoidia. Every name he'd found out about in those days had just set the whole thing off again, making it impossible for him to forget.

A waste of time. Except for one thing: All that thinking and hiding in those early days had trained him to analyze situations quickly and thoroughly. The tactical smarts Hera seemed to like had sprung from there. In that case, he thought, there was one good thing that had come of it. Because looking at her in the pilot's chair now, he determined that he'd follow her anywhere.

If he didn't get her killed first. Or if she didn't do the same to him.

Hera was chipper as she braked *Expedient.* "Told you we'd catch up," she said as the ship neared the tail of the freighter convoy. It had been open to question whether they would arrive at all. *Expedient* had left Cynda just as the straggler freighters were following *Ultimatum* into hyperspace. Kanan, who had never used the ship's hyperdrive before, had worried that it might not work at all. Ships on the lunar run were there for the very reason that their long-haul days were past. But the fact that none of the other ships was better off made them catchable for the right pilot, and Hera had talked nicely to *Expedient,* getting her way. She did that a lot.

It had worked that way with him, too. He liked that Hera had direction and drive. All women were magical creatures to Kanan, but there were happy forest nymphs, and then there were wizards. There was so much more to Hera, and it might take days or weeks or years to find out what was motivating her.

Time, he had—but he wouldn't stick around long if it meant constantly letting Caleb Dume call the shots. Hera had seemed to sense that old dutiful instinct in him, and had gotten him to come this far by appealing to it. The problem was, that person was someone he'd

never really been, and could never be again. Okadiah's death deserved an answer, yes, and Gorse needed to be protected if possible.
But both were responsibilities of a kind he had avoided for years. He
intended to keep avoiding them.

Hera was clever, and pretty, and he loved her voice. If the only way
to keep hearing it, though, was to play at her cloak-and-dagger
games, he might have to be on his way, with thanks for the memories.

"Okay, you're up," Hera said.

"Hmm?"

"I'm not the pilot of record," she said, sliding out of her seat. They
were approaching the outer security perimeter, an invisible energy
shield surrounding Calcoraan Depot. TIE fighters circled the station,
demarcating the location.

"Right." Kanan squeezed past her—a not unpleasant experience—to take his usual seat. Grabbing the control yoke, he slowed
Expedient to a stop just short of the barrier indicated on his views-
creen.

A gruff female voice came across the comm system. "What's your
identifier?"

"Moonglow-Seventy-Two," Kanan replied.

"Not anymore."

The response startled Kanan for a moment. "What do you mean?"
He pushed a button. "Here, I've switched on the ID transponder. You
can see who I am. I'm from Moonglow—"

"And I said not anymore," the woman answered. "You're now Imperial Provisional Seventy-Two. Name, license, and personnel."

"Kanan Jarrus. Guild license five-four-nine-eight-one." He paused
to look back. "Passengers, three laborers."

"That's two more than you're supposed to carry."

"We'll get loaded up faster," Kanan said. "What do you care?"

"Not at all. Continue on your heading to landing station seven-
seven. Follow the lights, and go slow."

Kanan did so. *Expedient* cruised into one of the largest assort-
ments of starships he'd ever come across. Every Baby Carrier he'd
ever seen in the skies between Gorse and Cynda was here, and more
from elsewhere. And yet, unlike on the lunar run, all the ships were

moving in an orderly and precise fashion. He soon realized why, as *Expedient* shuddered and he felt the control yoke go dead in his hands.

"Tractor beam parking attendants," Kanan said. "Nice. I hope we won't owe anyone a tip." He sat back, a passenger again like all the others.

Hera watched as *Expedient* circled the facility. "Are we going to have a problem getting back out?"

He shook his head. "Doubt it. These beams are for traffic manipulation. This place is so well protected, they wouldn't need tractor beams rated to yank fleeing ships from the sky."

"That's a relief."

Kanan stood up to stretch his legs—and thought back. There was one thing the controller had said that had disturbed him. "Weird. They changed our call sign."

"I know why," Zaluna called. Kanan turned to see her on the chair across from Skelly. As soon as they'd left hyperspace, she'd gotten her datapad out and started looking for news on the public channels. "They changed your name because there is no more Moonglow."

"What?"

"Moonglow has been blamed for the big blast on Cynda."

Across the aisle, Skelly gawked. "That's not true!"

Zaluna shook her head. "It was a Moonglow team that found your first bomb, remember?"

Kanan rolled his eyes. "I was there. Don't remind me."

"I was in the Transcept monitoring room when the word went out on that," Zaluna said. "They called it a natural occurrence, so nobody would get spooked about the mining company's practices—"

"Or would see that a dissident existed," Hera put in.

"Right. Now they've totally changed that story, saying that the collapse earlier this week and the giant explosion were both Moonglow's doing. The company has been dissolved, with its assets placed under Imperial control."

"Nothing like stomping all over someone's good name after you've killed them," Kanan said. Lal Grallik had been nice to him. Count Vidian was starting to roll up some big numbers in the debt column.

Expedient traced a long arc toward a massive disk-shaped landing station connected by huge spars to the rest of the facility. Several open ports revealed a sprawling loading area.

The comm system came to life again as the vessel cruised into the landing bay. "On landing, debark and begin loading product as it arrives on the conveyers. Take standard precautions—you're on our turf now."

"Great," Kanan said when the transmission ended. "Now I guess I work for the Empire." He looked to Hera. "What's the plan?"

"The plan is, you do what they tell you," she said, standing up and checking her comlink. "Load the ship. And wait for my call."

Kanan's eyes widened. "Wait. You're leaving?"

"That's right," she said, adjusting the blaster in her holster. "I'm going to destroy the station."

CHAPTER THIRTY-NINE

KANAN NEARLY FELL OVER Hera's feet trying to get between her and the door. "Destroy the station?" He couldn't believe his ears. "I thought you were all about being careful and undercover. Now who's the loose cannon?"

"I know what I'm doing." Hera looked directly up at him and explained, a little less patient than she had been until now. "Cynda isn't just some little rock in the sky above Gorse, Kanan. I read up in the ship's gazetteer while you were sleeping. Zaluna was right. It's a rogue planet that entered the system and got captured—massive enough they might start revolving around each other in a million years, if Cynda doesn't break up first."

She pointed her thumb toward the aft of the ship. "But you saw how many starships are here. They're going back to break up the moon for sure, and not in a million years. They're doing it *now*. The people down below on Gorse are in danger *now*. So something has to be done *now*."

Kanan refused to budge. "Here I thought *I* was the suicide flier."

"I call it logic." She crossed her arms and tapped her foot on the deck. "Now, are you going to get out of my way or not?"

Shaking his head, Kanan stepped away from the airlock door.

She looked back at the others. "I'm sorry things worked out this way. If I don't make it back, you should try to warn people somehow. Then Kanan can take you someplace safe." She paused. "Somewhere besides Gorse."

Kanan looked at Zaluna, who was clutching her bag tightly to her and shaking her head over the thought of losing her homeworld. "The Jedi used to take care of these things."

The remark startled Kanan. Jedi were a topic people weren't supposed to speak of. "What do you know about the Jedi, Zaluna?"

"More than that silly story the Empire put out about them." She looked up wistfully. "I saw Jedi in action, you know, long before you were born. If innocent lives were threatened, they would figure out what to do. Even in a no-win situation."

Hera nodded. "We could use one, now."

"Or maybe it's time for people to be their own Jedi." Emboldened by the subject she was speaking on, Zaluna looked confidently from Hera to Kanan. "They weren't gods—just people like us, who saw a need. If they could find a way, I'm sure we can."

Maybe, Kanan thought.

And then it came to him.

"Wait," he said, as she started to work the door handle. "Let's say you somehow blow this whole monstrosity up. Are there other depots like this?"

Hera looked back at him, nodded. "Not exactly like this, but there are stockpiles in every sector."

"So if the Emperor thinks having a bunch of easy thorilide is worth ruining the Gorse system already, wouldn't he just try it again?"

"I imagine so."

"Then I don't get what you're trying to accomplish," Kanan said. "You're the one that thinks futile gestures are stupid."

"I'm buying time."

"For what? Is it worth sacrificing yourself to delay the inevitable?"

Hera shrugged. "I don't want to sacrifice myself, no. But you're describing a situation where we just sit back and let the Empire do whatever it wants."

"No, no. There's another answer. It's not enough to prevent it now. *We've got to make them never want to try it again.*"

Kanan's mind raced. Hera watched him, curious. "Go on."

He began talking, not yet sure where he was going. "Okay, look. The Empire didn't even have this fool idea until they got it from Skelly—"

"Fool that I am," Skelly interjected bitterly.

"—and then they tested it, back there with that big blast. But how did they know the test worked—that it didn't destroy the thorilide it freed?"

"I saw probes searching the debris," Hera offered.

"So did I," Kanan said. He began pacing. "Vidian wouldn't just demolish a moon without the Emperor's say-so. He'd have to send a report." He paused and snapped his fingers. "So we send another report—or 'fix' the one he's about to send."

"Yeah, just let me at it," Skelly said, interested. "I can throw cold water on the whole thing. I'll say crushing the moon will ruin what they're going after!"

"So we say the test didn't work." Hera nodded. "It would cause confusion—maybe slow them down until we can warn people. But can we make it look legitimate?"

"No problem," Zaluna volunteered. "Where would something like that be kept?"

"With Vidian," Kanan said. He scratched the side of his head and looked at Zaluna. "Would you be able to find him using the station's surveillance?"

"Maybe," she said. Then, "Yes. Just get me to a terminal I can slice."

Hera seemed pleased. "I like it better than blowing the place up. But this will be harder than just me sneaking around. Skelly's known, and we may be, too, for all we know."

Kanan nodded. Then something told him to turn around. Outside, a flash of color caught his eye. "Wait," he said, recognizing what it was. "Look!"

Hera and Skelly joined Kanan far forward and looked out onto the landing deck of the shipping node. A dozen other freighters—Baby Carriers and former thorilide haulers alike—were parked with their ramps down. Under the watchful eyes of ranks of stormtroopers, individuals short and tall descended from the vessels, all wearing head-to-toe coverings in fluorescent orange.

"Hazmat suits," Hera observed.

"We're here to load baradium-357, all right," Kanan said. "That's *Naughty Baby*."

Supporting himself against the back of the passenger seat, Skelly nodded. "It's like we guessed. They need the big stuff to destroy the moon. I ran the numbers on it in my report—wishing I hadn't."

Hera stared. "What are the suits for? Does it blow up if you *breathe* on it?"

"That's not the reason for them," Skelly said, hobbling back to his seat. "The canisters have an outer shell full of toxic coolant. Nasty stuff, if it leaks."

"Will it kill you?"

"Maybe. But *you'll* kill a bunch of people first. It's psychoactive—produces irrational violent impulses."

Kanan laughed. "Check around your house for some, Skelly. It'd explain a lot." Then something dawned on him. Kanan snapped his fingers and turned. *Expedient*'s supply cabinet was between the forward compartment and the cargo area. Opening the door, he beheld his own supply of bright orange outfits, hanging neatly from a rack. Masks sat on an upper shelf. "I've seen these in here but never used them."

Hera stood before the door and stared. "You've got your own wardrobe?"

Kanan removed a suit. "That's Lal's thinking. We never knew what we'd be carrying from day to day, and she didn't want anyone getting hurt. The suits are meant to be thrown away, so they're cheap enough. And one-size-fits-all. Or most, anyway."

Efficient, Kanan thought, though he decided against mentioning that Vidian would probably approve. He looked back to Skelly and Zaluna. "We'd need you both with us. It could be dangerous—"

"Tosh," Zaluna said, rising. "We know what's at stake."

Skelly rolled his eyes. "Let's go before my meds wear off, and I start thinking clearly."

"Okay," Hera said, pulling down the masks. "We try this your way. But if this doesn't work out, we go back to my plan."

"Dying is never a plan. But you've got a deal."

CHAPTER FORTY

IT WAS THE RARE space station that a Star Destroyer could dock with. Among Calcoraan Depot's many arms was a long astrobridge that mated to an airlock on *Ultimatum*'s hull. Sloane figured Vidian had calculated some minuscule time savings in it.

He had met her at the connecting port. *Greeted* was too strong a word, since as usual he seemed to be engaged in silent comlink communication with someone else. Given how many sights they passed, their ride in the tramcar from node to node felt like a tour—only a tour in which the guide had almost nothing to say.

They passed an arrival area in which heavily plated robots were being disassembled. She had never seen anything like them. "What are those?"

"Droids."

"Of what sort?"

"Heat-tolerant. The depot supplies projects across the sector, not just Gorse."

She was anxious to show what she knew. "Heat-proof. Baron Danthe's firm made them, then? He holds the monopoly."

Vidian visibly bristled at the baron's name. "Yes. Many firms supply the Empire, including his."

"But those are employees of one of your firms taking them apart." She recognized the logos on the uniforms.

"Standard maintenance." Vidian accelerated the tramcar, indicating the subject was closed.

They rode on past several more junctions, offering opportunities for more glimpses of the depot's shipments and more terse exchanges with Vidian. Sloane wondered if Vidian even remembered that he had asked her here.

"It's an amazing place," she finally said. "I appreciate the opportunity to see it."

"You don't find the logistical world too tedious?" he asked as their car began to slow.

"It's what makes the Empire go."

"Agreed," Vidian said. He pointed to a small cabinet in the car. "You'll want what's in there."

Sloane opened the compartment and withdrew a transparent face mask. Donning it, she saw a sign for landing station 77 up ahead. There were hazmat-suited workers all around the floor, taking meter-high cylindrical drums from pneumatic tubes and delivering them to freighters. "The explosives," he said, gesturing. "Being loaded here and at several other nodes, for return to Cynda. Testing has shown that organics will move explosives more quickly than droids will. Fear is a useful motivator."

"Of course." She looked at Vidian, maskless. "Don't you need—?"

"My lungs have been augmented to reject poisons."

The car stopped, and Vidian stepped out onto the shipping floor. Sloane followed.

"The explosives must be deposited deep within Cynda using shafts drilled at precise locations." He paused and looked at her. "My prep teams are already en route to the moon, but your military engineers could help speed things along."

Now we're to it, Sloane thought. "Of course. They're at your disposal."

"Fine." A red-clad human stepped forward to Vidian, offering him a datapad. The count passed it to Sloane. "Convey these instructions to your crew."

As a pair of workers passed carrying drums, another tramcar arrived from a different direction. Vidian gestured toward the loading floor. "I must finalize my report for the Emperor. Stay and educate yourself." He walked toward the vehicle. Then he paused and looked back at her. "It's good to have an ally in the military who understands what I'm doing."

It was the closest thing to warmth she'd seen from him. She bowed her head. "Your lordship commands."

"That's our boy," Kanan mumbled as he set a canister on the deck of the loading floor.

Hera nodded, anonymous in her orange getup but for the big bumps on the loose-fitting head covering where it protected her head-tails. "He hasn't sent the report yet," she said, her lovely voice muffled by the mask. "More luck that he'd drop by here!"

"If you can call it that."

"Skelly!" Hera called out.

Kanan pivoted to see the hooded Skelly limping through the crowd of busy workers toward Vidian. Worse, he was carrying his pouch of explosives. His blood running cold, Kanan picked up the baradium canister and started walking quickly in that direction.

Skelly was a dozen meters away from Vidian's back and reaching for his bag when Kanan interposed himself. He shoved the canister into Skelly's hands. "Here you go, buddy. Back to the ship."

Skelly, his expression invisible through the opaque faceplate, seemed poised to keep on going. "Don't you see?"

Vidian? You bet, Kanan wanted to say. Instead, he twirled Skelly around. He nodded to one of the stormtroopers standing guard. "Sorry. Big place. Easy to get turned about."

Skelly resisted as Kanan pulled him away from the tramline. Vidian was in the car already, seemingly none the wiser. "Skelly, have you lost your mind?"

"But he's right there, Kanan!"

"Not now!" Kanan pulled him back across to where *Expedient* was parked. "You want to blow us all up?"

"It's him or us."

"That'd be him *and* us," Hera said. Stepping over, she took the canister from Skelly's hands while Kanan pulled the bag off his shoulder.

"Watch him," Kanan said, turning to *Expedient*'s ramp. "I'm putting this where he can't get it."

Kanan shook his head as he locked the sack of bombs away. Time had only seemed to magnify the injuries Skelly had suffered at Vidian's hands; it was getting harder to get the guy to see reason through his pain. As he disembarked, Kanan saw that Hera had stationed Skelly by the ramp with a datapad, pretending to take inventory. That was the best place for him, right now.

Zaluna approached carrying a canister as gingerly as she might carry an infant. "Will they blow up if you drop them?"

"Just a little," Skelly said.

"He's kidding," Kanan said. "But if you do, make sure that hood is secure." He didn't want to imagine Zaluna on a chemically induced killing spree.

Minutes later, Hera returned from a nonchalant walkabout of the loading floor. "Okay, Vidian's gone to the hub," she said in a low voice. The layout was on Skelly's datapad now, having been downloaded from a nearby terminal by Zaluna—but it had taken too long to get, and *Expedient* was nearly fully loaded. They'd be expected to leave the station after that.

"We need to slow this down," Hera added. "And I don't know how we can get over there."

Kanan suppressed a chuckle. "And you were thinking you were going to have the run of the place."

"I'm not taking this bunch through the ductwork," she said, looking about. "And the stormtroopers are everywhere, making sure we're where we're supposed to be."

Kanan looked back the way Vidian had departed. There were three parallel portals there: a service hallway, with the canister-delivering pneumatic conduit on the left and the tramcar tube opening on the right. Kanan put his finger in the air. "There's the answer," he said. "We change where we're supposed to be."

Before she could ask him anything, Kanan stepped away.

Whistling to himself, he casually strolled over to the conduit where canisters, gingerly moved along on a gentle cushion of air, appeared in the loading area. Glimpsing left and right and seeing no one looking, Kanan disappeared up the service tunnel.

He saw there what he'd seen when walking past earlier: a spindly-looking silver droid, minding the controls on the outside of the tube. Kanan walked past to a maintenance door on the tube's exterior. With a twist, he snapped the hatch open.

"Wait!" the droid chirped. "You can't do that!" It clanked toward Kanan—who then grabbed it, shoving it bodily into the meter-wide tube. With a shove, he jammed its torso backward, fully lodging it inside. Then he slammed the maintenance panel shut.

The blockage light was already flashing outside the opening when he stepped back out onto the loading floor. Kanan looked at the light and swore loudly. "The stupid thing's stuck."

Workers gathered at the opening. Sloane marched over. "What's going on here?"

"I'll tell you what's going on," Kanan said, peering up the dark opening. "Your dumb droid's messed up the whole works!"

Sloane waved her hand dismissively. "Someone send for a repair crew."

"Yeah, you do that," he replied, pleased as he backed out that she could not see through the faceplate of his hazmat suit. He turned away from the group and marched back to *Expedient*.

"Wait," the captain called. "Where do you think you're going?" But Kanan was already heading up the ramp.

When he returned, he saw Sloane waiting with an armed storm-trooper. "Coming through," he said, pushing *Expedient*'s spare hover-cart down the ramp. Smaller than the one he'd ridden to survival on Cynda, it bounced on the air as he pushed it toward Sloane's feet. "I've got a deadline, lady. Move it."

Sloane stepped back, seemingly surprised by his presumption. "What are you doing now?"

"You're paying us to move this stuff," Kanan said. "If your depot can't bring the junk to me, I'm going to it." He looked back at Hera. "Come on, Layda. Bring your cousins."

Hera saluted and gathered the others. They followed Kanan and his hovercart toward the service hallway, even as other loaders on the floor got the same idea and went for carts of their own.

Sloane shrugged in irritation and stepped back. She looked at the stormtrooper beside her. "This is not what I went to the Academy for."

CHAPTER FORTY-ONE

SKELLY LEANED BACK against a pillar, wheezing. "Next time . . . we take the tram."

"Yeah, that wouldn't be suspicious," Kanan said, pushing the cart up another seemingly endless hallway. They hadn't encountered anyone but service droids like the one he'd accosted, but the distance was the real test. They'd gone from one node to another, working their way toward the hub.

He looked down at the hovercart in annoyance. *I thought I gave this up when I quit Moonglow!*

Walking alongside Kanan, Hera paused and looked back. She pulled on his arm, and Kanan turned to see Skelly sitting in the middle of the floor. "I'm fine," the bomber said. "Just . . . come back . . . for my body."

He looked at Hera. He couldn't see her face, but he could imagine the expression of concern. This wasn't going to work. They'd both realized on the trip from Cynda that Vidian had injured Skelly more than he was letting on; he'd gotten this far by doping himself from the medpacs, but he was starting to fade.

Kanan stopped and turned the empty cart. "Here," he said, helping Skelly climb onto the flatbed. "You make one crack about me being your nursemaid, and I'm dumping you on the floor."

"Check." Skelly collapsed flat on his back.

Hera looked up at the fat disk on the ceiling up ahead. "What have you got, Zal?"

"These are Visitractic 830 factory surveillance cams," Zaluna said. Walking in front of the group, she waved one of her devices like a dowser with a divining rod. "Quality stuff—only a few on Gorse. They're not used for facial recognition. More to make sure the product keeps moving."

"Can you kill them?"

"I'm freezing them before we come into view. As long as nobody's walking into the scene around us, it won't look odd."

"You can do that?" Kanan asked. "I thought you said they were quality cams."

"They are," Zaluna said, unsnapping and removing her hood. "But nothing leaves a cam factory without a defeat code. Too many embezzling executives have been caught by their own technology. When I was younger, we used to use the codes to mess with other operators. You'd learn about them on Hetto's data cube."

Hera pulled off her head covering and smiled at Kanan. "And *that* is why I came to Gorse."

Kanan yanked his own cowl off. He was dripping with sweat. "These masks sure aren't for marathons. How far to the hub?"

Hera looked at her datapad. "Five hundred meters to another junction, then eight hundred more. There's a reason they use the chutes and conveyer belts."

"I never want to see another conveyor belt again," Skelly mumbled.

"Wait," Kanan said. "Zaluna, will your cam trick work if we go faster?"

"It's an infrared signal. It works as soon as we get into range."

"Fine. Both of you on the cart with Skelly," he said, cracking his knuckles. He set the hovercart's repulsors to maximum and grasped the pushbar. "I did this once with a ceiling falling on me. Get ready to hang on!"

Standing behind a wall of containers on the enormous warehouse floor of Calcoraan Depot's hub, Kanan decided he was done with riding hovercarts for one lifetime. The ride across Cynda's sublunar floor amid an avalanche had been harrowing enough, but by putting his formidable muscles into a running start before leaping aboard the cart's back bumper, Kanan had turned the floating pallet into an unguided missile, caroming off the walls of the hallway. Hera, sitting up front, had nearly ground the heels off her boots bringing the thing to a stop at the end of the second, longer run.

Replacing their masks on entry, they'd found that Calcoraan Depot's hub was every bit as busy and noisy as Kanan had expected. Robotic arms, vacuum hoses, and magnets were employed here, plucking materials from a forest of towering storage units and routing them to outer parts of the station. Zaluna had wryly pointed out a wire bin the size of *Expedient* that looked as if it held replacement latches for restroom doors.

"We take this place out," Skelly said, "and we can make half the Imperial fleet prop the door shut."

At least Skelly seemed to be feeling better. Kanan wasn't. They'd found a quiet spot—*quiet* being a relative term—to park the hovercart near a far wall while Hera did some reconnaissance, looking for a route to Vidian's executive chamber. Zaluna's map showed that it was somewhere through the wall but at least one floor up—but there were no details about how to get there. Gantries and catwalks leading over the main floor hadn't worked. Elevators were secured and guarded. The maintenance hatch in the wall behind him was their last chance.

Kanan stared down at Hera's hazmat suit, rolled up in a bundle on the hovercart. She'd taken off the bulky suit so she'd have more freedom of movement for sneaking around. He wondered where she was, and thought about opening the door to follow her.

Before he could act on the impulse, Hera cracked the door open. She looked frustrated.

"This is no good," she said, opening the hatch wide. The corridor behind was lost in shadows. She raised her portable light to reveal narrow apertures lining both sides of a passage that seemed to go on forever. "The entrance is at the far end, upstairs, but it's a long hallway guarded by stormtroopers. And we have to go past a bunch of Vidian's red-suits at their desks before you get to that."

"I guess we could say we were delivering lunch," Kanan said. He was about to give up when he saw something moving behind her, passing through one of the narrow openings on the right. "Look there!"

It was tall and mechanical, entering the corridor in the faraway darkness. Kanan stepped through the hatchway to get a better look. The droid had a gray tubular body and a flat head that rotated all the way around, casting a single red light about as it did.

"That's not a guard droid," Hera said, watching it disappear through a small opening to the left of the passageway. "That's a Medtech. FX-something."

"You get a lot of medical droids at an office complex?" Kanan asked. He waved to the others outside the hatch to follow him inside. "Be careful—it's pretty dark in here."

"No light, no problem," Zaluna said, big Sullustan eyes widening as she entered.

"I'll go anywhere that's not here," Skelly said, rubbing his ear. "This place is giving me a headache on top of everything else."

The door sealed, Hera led the way, creeping toward the darkened exit the droid had taken. "I didn't go this way before," she whispered.

"Allow me." Kanan drew his blaster and rounded the corner. Nothing leapt out at him. Hera's light on uniformly placed girders cast long, deep shadows across a wide circular expanse. The place was empty but for what appeared to be furnishings in storage, including a bed, several operating tables of different types, a wardrobe, and a chair large enough to be a throne.

The medical droid ignored them as they entered the area. It simply glided next to what appeared to be a console and stopped.

Skelly squinted. "What are we—"

"Wait," Kanan said. Light sliced into the area from a quadrilateral opening in the ceiling above the medical droid. With a mechanical whir, robot and console both started rising into the rafters, lifted by a hydraulic press. The rays from above illuminated the rest of the room in front of them before the door in the ceiling closed back. "We're under Vidian's health clinic!"

"Great," Skelly said, staggering in a daze toward a cabinet. "I could use a medcenter." Opening a drawer, he slumped against the side of the fixture. The others watched as he began pawing blindly at it with his gnarled right hand, completely missing the inside of the drawer.

Zaluna looked fretfully at Hera. "Is he going to be all right?"

"The faster we get in and out, the better for him." Kanan could see the Twi'lek studying the other furnishings: All were on similar platforms. "But now we've got our way in."

"You keep saying *we*," Kanan said.

"This was your idea—and the last meter's always the hardest. Besides, we've been lucky so far," she said, grinning. "Maybe he's asleep."

"Or getting a personality transplant." Kanan sighed as he pulled at the zipper of his suit. "But I doubt it. People never get what they need."

CHAPTER FORTY-TWO

VIDIAN SAT AT the center of his web and watched it all.

His home, like everything else in Calcoraan Depot, had been built to his specifications. A hemispherical room at the center of the station's hub, it was a place for him to contemplate his plans while he recuperated from the regular maintenance surgeries conducted by his medical droids. He had no need for grand windows looking outside, or giant stellar cartographic displays in the dome above him. He could make his cybernetic eyes display all the images he wanted.

Others were rarely allowed to enter, but when they did they saw only a neutral gray ceiling, dimly lit by a ring of lights. But when Vidian, chest now covered in a post-operative white robe, looked up, he saw the space station in action, as if he could see through its walls. He inhabited every corner of its durasteel frame, watching the supplies being brought in and sorted for redistribution. He saw the movements of the ships outside the station, and their destinations far beyond. The whole galaxy spread out before him, ready to be transformed by his force of will.

It hadn't always been this way. He had been powerless, once, in ways no one knew about. Vidian's official biography painted him as a heroic whistleblower for a military contractor, but in truth, he had been that most useless of creations: a safety inspector for an interstellar mining guild.

He had lived under another name, then. That was when he'd learned all he knew about the thorilide trade—and that was when he came to understand the hypocrisy practiced by those with money and power. Lives meant nothing to the manufacturers he visited, and so many of his superiors were bribed that the reports he filed were beyond pointless.

It was on an inspection trip to Gorse, of all places, that he'd finally been fed up. He decided to get in on the game, asking for and receiving bribes from several of the firms he'd visited. But before he could spend a credit, he fell ill in a mining company lobby. In the miners' medcenter, he learned his travels had caught up with him. The toxins he'd inhaled, the biological agents he'd touched in countless filthy factories had unleashed a degenerative disease, destroying his flesh. It wasn't a theatrical end, like falling into a vat of acid, but it took the same toll. Soon, all that remained of that once-energetic young man was a parched sack of organs, somehow coaxed into continued function by the efforts of the surgeons.

He'd never been much of a person, by his own admission, but now even that was gone. All that remained was a mind, trapped, with no way to reach out. He lay there lost, at the edge of madness, contemplating his existence—or lack of it. Seething with anger over the powerlessness of the life he'd led, and hatred for those who'd won while he had played by the rules. After two years steeping in the acid of his mind, he found a rudimentary way to communicate with one of the caretaker droids.

And the guild inspector's deathbed became Denetrius Vidian's birthplace.

From there, his life had progressed more closely according to the well-known legend—the only part of his biography that was remotely true. Avenging himself against the industry bigwigs required a new identity, a figure on the same level or higher. Vidian began as a cipher, a name on an electronic bank account. But soon he became the greatest corporate stalker the Republic had ever seen, all while still in the medcenter.

The Republic had protected the thorilide mining industry against corporate raiders during the Clone Wars, so instead he'd taken stakes in firms manufacturing comet-chaser harvesting vessels. He'd bought a secret stake in Minerax Consulting, pushing out reports that wiped out surface mining on Gorse and other worlds; many of the companies that he once inspected failed—including Moonglow's predecessor firm.

Revenge, perhaps, but he didn't really care. With his cybernetic prostheses, he had been mobile by then, having left Gorse and its bad memories for riches and financial fame. He had left it all behind. He'd become someone powerful, someone he had never been in his old identity—and if he did not have Palpatine's ear, he at least had his respect. The Republic was full of ill-functioning industries. Vidian was seen as the man who could fix them all.

He wasn't about to let a snotty upstart like Baron Danthe undermine him. The Emperor encouraged vigorous competition in his administration; it was a sensible strategy, forcing everyone to give his or her best. But Danthe could only tear down those more talented. The baron had desperately been searching for some weapon to use against Vidian; it was one reason the count had sought Imperial authority over Gorse. He'd managed to demolish the medcenter of his long-ago confinement—and any trace of his true past—with no one the wiser.

Still, the fool kept trying. The baron had contacted him again, earlier, fishing for information about his plans. Calcoraan Depot operators had even intercepted Danthe calling Captain Sloane, trying to get the same thing. To her credit, Sloane had told the man nothing.

There was no reason to wait any longer. Vidian stepped from the chair and sent it back down to the basement. He crossed to the secure terminal on the side of the chamber and entered his passkey. With the tap of a control, he sent the document he had prepared to Coruscant. It had been crafted with utmost care; the Emperor would support his action. Vidian was taking a risk with his present course, yes—but he'd also laid a trap, one that would take Danthe out of his nonexistent hair for good. Sloane was a part of his master plan, as were droids he'd shown her earlier.

When all was done, Vidian would remain in the Emperor's favor, and the Empire would grow, uninterrupted, because of it. And who knew? There might even be a bonus. Vidian knew the Emperor was interested in projects to create giant weapons of intimidation. He didn't know all that existed, but it was hard to hide much from someone involved in so many strategic supply networks. The destruction of Cynda, if it could be done, might be of military interest. Moons with its peculiar structure, orbit, and proximity to its parent planet were rare, but it paid to have a variety of tools in so large a galaxy.

Vidian closed out his connection with the Imperial throneworld and paused. The place was still, apart from the whirring and clacking of the FX-4, motoring between the operating table and the tall diagnostic console beside it. "I know you're here," the count said, his back to the rest of the room.

He heard nothing. And then, light footfalls heading to his left, behind the bank of computer equipment to the right of the sealed entryway. Vidian strolled casually away from the communications terminal and gave another silent order. A fresh operating table, this one with restraints, rose into view. "I've heard you since you entered, *both* of you. You rode up behind my chair." He stepped past the medical droid. "There's no surveillance in this room. It's just me. I've heard your motions, your hearts beating. I've seen your breaths coloring the infrared. Don't make me hunt you. It's tiresome."

Vidian whirled and leapt back toward the terminal on the wall to the right of the entrance. Looking over it, he beheld a crouching young green-skinned Twi'lek woman pointing a blaster in his face. "You're new," he said.

He heard someone move behind him. Vidian stood granite-still as the blow came: a metal surgical stand, smashed over the back of his head. The Twi'lek flinched as the stand's attachments broke free, clattering off the top of the console. Vidian whipped around and lunged for his attacker in one blinding motion.

"You're *not* new," he said, clutching the dark-haired man by the neck. The broken shaft of the surgical stand was still in the man's gloved hands. Vidian lifted him from the floor and looked keenly into his blue eyes. "The gunslinger from Cynda. I may have deleted your image, but I never forget a fool. I'm fascinated to learn what brings you here."

CHAPTER FORTY-THREE

CHOKING, KANAN STRUGGLED in vain to strike Vidian with what was left of his makeshift weapon. "Shoot him!" he said between gasps. "Shoot him!"

Hera did exactly that, leaning over the computer console and firing a point-blank shot into Vidian's back. Plasma coruscated over Vidian and fed into Kanan, shocking him. Through the pain, Kanan could see the robe that covered Vidian's chest was tattered, revealing a silver sheen beneath.

"I wouldn't do that again," Vidian said, ripping off the shreds of the garment with his free hand without loosening his hold on Kanan at all. "My skin graft is a cortosis mesh—a holdover from the days when I advised manufacturers in the field late in the Clone Wars. I can assure you, young lady—every bolt you fire against me will carry directly into your friend."

Kanan saw Hera stand erect, keeping her eyes on Vidian. "You want to know why we're here? Put him down!"

"Certainly." Vidian lowered Kanan—but just as the tips of the younger man's toes touched the ground, the count delivered a mighty open-handed slap with his left hand. Kanan felt his jaw nearly go sideways.

And still, Vidian continued to hold him by the throat. Kanan struggled to speak, but only unintelligible sounds came out.

Vidian loosened his hold a little. "What's that? You want mercy?"

Kanan coughed once and glared at him. "I said, 'That was a cheap shot.'"

"Glad you approve." Vidian looked back to Hera, whose eyes darted between him and the door. "You needn't worry. These walls are soundproofed, and I haven't called for help. I rarely get to entertain—I don't want anyone to interfere."

Hera looked at Vidian—and then moved, vaulting athletically over the console. She fired her blaster just past Vidian's head, purposefully missing him, as she hit the floor. She was there just a moment before bounding forward, charging toward the cyborg. Vidian, startled by the frontal attack, reached out with both arms to grasp for her, releasing Kanan in the process. Hera instantly changed her target, diving low and tackling Kanan around the midsection while Vidian's arms crossed, catching nothing. The force of her jump propelled her and Kanan to the floor, two meters behind the count.

Vidian spun, amused rather than alarmed as the two stood. "Well done."

Kanan, breathing again, pushed Hera away from him just as Vidian charged toward them. The count was a shirtless brawler in a cage, now: the sort of opponent he'd dealt with in many a cantina. Kanan met the advancing cyborg with a roundhouse kick to his lower back. It felt like kicking a sack of titanium hammers—and Kanan felt dumber than one for the attempt when Vidian snatched his leg and shoved. Kanan tumbled backward, smashing through a lab table.

Hera opened up on Vidian again, clearly convinced no one outside would respond to the blasterfire. Vidian shrugged it off and charged her. She leapt high, vaulting over his back as he dived. But this time, his legs kept their balance, and he pivoted in time to catch her by a head-tendril. Vidian yanked, hurling her violently across the room.

"Hera!" Kanan yelled, rising from the debris. Vidian had thrown Hera hard enough to smash her against the far wall—and yet she hadn't landed at all. Blue light from a ceiling-mounted stasis beam captured her in midair.

The count looked up at her in high spirits. "Marvelous! Perfect aim. Don't move, now."

Of course, she couldn't—but before Kanan could wonder what Vidian was doing with a paralyzing suspension beam in his living quarters, the cyborg was moving toward him again. "Now, where were we? I used to spar in physical therapy."

"Oh, yeah? I used to put people there." Kanan stepped gamely toward him.

Vidian lunged with his right. Kanan stepped aside just as quickly, feeling the stroke go past. Balling his gloved fist, he pounded Vidian's left ear. The rest of the man might be sheathed with something tough, but Kanan bet that Vidian needed his ears for balance like anyone else. He was right—at least for an instant, the cyborg recoiled. It gave Kanan enough time to grab Vidian violently by what passed for his ear. Whipping the count's head around, Kanan bowled forward, smashing Vidian face-first into a cabinet with a colossal clang.

Like a spring-loaded weapon, Vidian snapped back around. His face was expressionless, but his mechanical voice betrayed excitement. "Now we're to it!"

Kanan and Vidian punched at each other for long seconds. Kanan used all his speed to prevent Vidian from landing a solid blow—and all his own technique to keep from breaking his hand on the count's metallic hide. He'd battled enough tough-skinned opponents to know to avoid head-butts or anything else more threatening to him than to Vidian. But that didn't leave him a lot of options, except for trying to knock Vidian off balance.

He tried—and the room paid for it, as the two overturned cabinets and more stands in their melee. But the cyborg was just too fast.

"We're done," Vidian said, his right arm lancing out. Catching Kanan's wrist in his viselike grip, Vidian delivered a left jab to his temple. Kanan didn't see anything for a few moments after that. But he felt motion, as Vidian grabbed his tunic and shoved him.

When the lights in his mind stopped blinking, Kanan realized

Vidian had him against the main operating table. The count snapped Kanan's right hand into one metal restraint. When Kanan struggled, the cyborg smacked him again. A moment later both Kanan's hands and feet were bound to the surface.

Vidian straightened and stretched, as one refreshed. "That was invigorating." He looked around. "Any other guests? Are we done? No grieving Besalisks to the rescue?"

Seeing no other new arrivals, Vidian turned around. "Fine then," he said, facing Hera and Kanan. "It's time we got to know one another."

Kanan swallowed and looked at Hera, who, still suspended, managed to shake her head. Skelly, down in the basement level, was in no shape to do anything, and Zaluna would never come up into the middle of a fight. Nor would they want her to.

Vidian rummaged in a wardrobe. "You flew for Moonglow, gunslinger. I killed your boss. Is that what this is?" Vidian took out a gold-colored shirt and put it on. "Friendships are costly. They make you do things outside your best interests."

Kanan said nothing.

"I'm sure you'd tell my interrogator droid more," Vidian said as he walked through the mess his room had become. "And I may have another use for you."

Struggling against the stasis beam, Hera glared. "What do you mean?"

"I might let my droids practice on you." He turned to face Kanan and scratched his chin—a move that seemed more an affectation than anything motivated by an actual itch. "Can you imagine what it is to live without senses, without any means of interacting with your environment?"

"After a few drinks."

"The mind is a dynamo in the dark, an engine endlessly running, powering nothing. It thrashes in the night, seeking daylight, inventing its own." He walked around the table, looking for the surgical stand. Finding a bent tray, Vidian knelt beside it and began meticulously replacing the scattered surgical instruments on it. He held up a scalpel before his eyes. "*Controlling nothing.* Consider that! The youngling and the aged experience it—the struggle with ineffectuality. Controlling nothing is the true death."

He rose, holding the tray. "But I have come back from the dead. And through me, the Empire will control everything." He set the tray back on the stand. "You've heard my slogan, perhaps: *Keep moving, destroy barriers, see everything*?"

"You were talking on the holo in a spaceport once," Kanan said. "Nobody was watching."

"I'm not offended. A trite bit of management advice. But for one amputated from everything, it is more. It's a prescription for being." Vidian walked back to Kanan, scalpel in hand. "I was without contact for two years. Let us see what happens if you go without for ten. Who knows? You might even become interesting."

"Wait!" Hera said, still dangling.

Vidian looked over with impatience. "Yes?"

"I thought you were going to interrogate us first."

Kanan rolled his eyes. "Oh, yeah, torture me before you torture me. Wouldn't want to forget that!" What was she thinking?

Vidian set the scalpel aside. "She's quite right." He went silent for a moment. "I've just sent for my assistant. Be patient."

Another slot in the floor opened. A black, bug-eyed globe levitated upward through it. Kanan, struggling to get loose, recognized it as an Imperial interrogator droid. Their reputation was well known—and the large syringe it wielded identified it unmistakably.

"Hold still," Vidian said. "It'll be over in a second."

Kanan's mind raced as the thing approached. Master Billaba would have advised him to use the Force. *Cast the thing against the wall! Unlock your bonds! Hypnotize Vidian into taking a long walk out of a short airlock!* He'd tried never to use the Force openly in the past, yet this was serious. Kanan started to focus—

—but before he could do anything, the interrogator droid rotated just a few degrees and extended its needle right toward the injection port on Vidian's exposed neck.

"*What?*" Vidian swatted at the hovering droid, sending it tumbling into a far wall. He fell to his hands and knees.

A large door opened within the floor. Vidian's throne rose into the room. Skelly sat on it, with Zaluna standing beside it, holding the remote control for the droid.

"I don't think that's truth serum," Hera said.

"It sure isn't." Skelly patted the small mountain of vials in his lap. "I know my pharmaceuticals." He grinned through broken teeth at Vidian. "Nighty-night, sweetheart."

Lying diagonally on a separate table from Vidian, Skelly enjoyed a bacta rub from one of the count's medical droids. "I don't know about you guys," he said, "but I think we delete him. Enough's enough."

Kanan rubbed his throat. "Show of hands on that one?"

Skelly forced his right hand up with his left.

Hera shook her head. "I want to do the right thing here," she said. "I'm not against killing if it's necessary. But something strange is going on. I want to know that killing him won't cause something worse!"

"Worse than him blowing up the moon and leaving Gorse a graveyard?" Skelly asked.

Hera shook her head. "No, I mean—bad, but different. If we assassinate Vidian here and now, and we're caught, the Empire's going to think it's got a rebellion on Gorse!"

"A rebellion? *There?*" Kanan chuckled. "It's not exactly a hotbed of political thought."

"It'll get hot when the purges start," Hera said. She pointed to Zaluna, working at a console at her side. "Zal knows better than anyone—they've been taking names. It won't be random, like rocks dropped out of the sky. It'll be targeted." Hera blinked. "Or maybe it *will* be random, whole neighborhoods firebombed from orbit just to make an example!"

Zaluna goggled. "Has . . . has that happened before?"

Hera looked away. "You don't see everything," she said softly.

Silence fell across the room. Vidian had been as good as his word on a couple of things, at least: As far as they knew, no one outside had heard anything from within his chamber, and no one had seen the fight. Zaluna had already swept for cams. Kanan had wondered why

Vidian wanted protection from the eyes of his own people. But at least his room didn't suffer from lack of restraining devices. They'd move him into the stasis field if he started to stir—but according to the medical droid, Skelly's cocktail would keep him out for a couple of hours.

Which it looked like they would need. "There's no getting into this system," Zaluna said in frustration.

Hera shook her head. "Still the last passkey?"

"It's a code, entered by hand," the woman said. "He couldn't do it by voice. If there was a cam or something around here, maybe it would have seen. There'd be something I could look at. But there isn't."

The room fell silent again.

Kanan stared. "Wait a second. Maybe there is." He stepped over to Vidian and turned the man's head. There, in his left ear, he saw a small dataport. A moment's revulsion struck and passed. "All right," he said. "Who wants to download Vidian's brain?"

CHAPTER FORTY-FOUR

ZALUNA SAT AT the portable terminal next to Vidian's bed and looked back along the clear thin wire. It stretched to a dataport hidden in the count's ear. "This is the strangest thing I've ever done. And after the last couple of days, that's saying something."

Kanan laughed and moved a piece of fallen equipment that was obstructing the holoprojector. "We're clear," he said. "Show us what he's got."

"I've deactivated his eyes and ears so they're not recording, and I've also deleted his entire encounter with us," Zaluna said. "That's pretty easy. But I can only show you what he's seen in the last day—that must be this subsystem's limit." She pushed a button. "There."

The lights in the room dimmed. Across the floor from Vidian's throne, life-sized holographic images appeared, cast by the overhead emitter. The holograms were simply stereoscopic, comprising images from Vidian's left and right eyes—but they had unusual crispness and depth.

Hera shook her head in amazement. "We're seeing through Vidian's eyes!"

"Yeah," Kanan said. "Makes you want to throw up."

Zaluna forwarded and reversed the visions through elapsed time, stopping only for a fraction of a second before setting them moving again. The images came and went so quickly that Kanan was often unsure what he was looking at, but the Sullustan seemed to know. "You can watch that fast?" he asked.

"Every day for thirty years," Zaluna said, manipulating the controls. She seemed more comfortable than he'd ever seen her. "Most people's lives aren't very interesting. You learn to skip around pretty quickly."

She reached a stretch seemingly recorded recently, here in the sanctum. A data terminal came into view—the one across the room. "There," Hera said.

Zaluna was way ahead of her. "He's entering his data key," she said, framing the sequence backward. "Right . . . *here*."

Hera quickly read the code and dashed to the terminal on the far side of the room. A few seconds later, she called back happily, "We're in!"

Skelly, nicely medicated, hobbled over. "What have you got?"

"The list of subspace data messages to Coruscant," Hera said, reading. She frowned. "He's already sent the Cynda test results to the Emperor."

Skelly found a chair and pulled it up beside her. "Find the original. We'll create a revised version, saying the tests failed. We'll say there was a measurement error."

"I don't know if we can send anything. It looks like accessing the Emperor's direct channel requires a different passkey. He must have entered it earlier and logged out."

"It must have been a while earlier," Zaluna said, still searching through the images from his eyes. "There's no other code being entered."

"We can't get lucky twice," Hera said. "But maybe there's another way." Her fingers moved quickly on the controls. "Here's the file with the lunar test results. Let's have a look."

Skelly looked on as Hera began reading. After a few moments, she paused, staring at the screen in bewilderment. "This is confusing."

"I'm sure it's technical," Kanan said. "That's why we brought Skelly, to lie in their language."

"That's not why it's confusing," Hera said, exiting the document to look at another. "I can't do it."

"You can't make the change?"

"No, there's no need," she replied, both surprised and confused. "The original results *already* say that the test blast caused most of the thorilide to disintegrate. *The version Vidian sent the Emperor was a lie.*"

"What?" Kanan had begun to think a year wouldn't be enough for them to make sense of the count's world.

Hera read aloud from it. The original report said there was thorilide in the space debris kicked up by the blast that had killed Okadiah, but that much of it had been destroyed outright. An exponentially progressive decay process had been triggered in the rest; within a year of the moon's destruction, all unharvested thorilide would cease to be. And yet Vidian had told the Emperor there was a two-thousand-year supply. Hera was flabbergasted. "Why would he want to destroy Cynda when it'll ruin the thing he's there to get?"

Kanan had the same question. "Who gets to destroy something the Emperor wants?"

Zaluna looked at Hera. "You don't think . . ."

"That he's a revolutionary, like me?" Hera stifled a laugh. "I doubt it. This seems like a good way to wind up dead."

"Or with a desk job on Kessel," Kanan said.

Skelly rubbed one of his bruises. "Well, we know he's a sadistic crazoid. Maybe that's enough, in his world."

Hera shook her head. "He's not suicidal. There's got to be a reason he wants to do it, and a reason he's not worried."

The room fell silent, except for the quiet clicking of Zaluna's hologram controller as she continued to follow Vidian throughout his day.

Kanan found Vidian's chair and collapsed on it. He cast his tired gaze onto the flood of images. It was the ultimate spy tool, he'd thought—but all it had gotten them so far was the passcode. He looked down to the floor.

And then back up, where an image caught his eye. "Frame that back," he said.

Zaluna complied. "Now, there's a well-dressed man," she said. It was a young blond human, wearing regal business attire: a richly decorated suit of clothes, with gold buttons and a half cape slung over his right shoulder. But the image seemed different from the other pictures they'd seen. "The resolution of this image is different from everything else. Strange."

Hera saw the figure. "That's Baron Danthe, the droid magnate." Hera seemed to know everything, as usual, but now she seemed confused. "He's in Imperial government, too—he's Vidian's attaché, back on Coruscant. I found him in my research. He was here?"

"He *wasn't* here," Kanan said, snapping his fingers. "He looks different because he's a hologram."

"A hologram in a hologram? Shouldn't he be blue and fuzzy?"

Zaluna shook her head as she adjusted the controls. "Not if Vidian has messages piped straight to his eyes. And it's a message, all right. It looks like Vidian saved the audio from the conversation."

The images began to move, and they heard Vidian's disembodied voice. "*Baron Danthe, how can I do my work if you won't leave me alone?*"

"*I'm only the messenger. The Emperor wants immediate assurance you can make this year's thorilide quota,*" the young man said.

"*My plans will yield all the Emperor requires—providing you don't talk him into raising the totals again.*"

"*Count, I'm hurt. I would never—*"

"*Spare me. I'm about to send His Imperial Majesty the report.*"

"*Wonderful. If you would copy me on that—*"

"*I will not. This is my domain, not yours.*" A pause. "*If you want the responsibility so much, Baron Danthe, fine. After I successfully meet the Emperor's targets this year I'll ask that he transfer management of Gorse to your office.*"

"*That's generous, my lord. I don't know what to—*"

"*Say nothing. Just stay out of my affairs!*" The image of the baron disappeared.

"Boy, they don't like each other at all," Kanan said. "Did you catch the smirk on that baron guy's face? I wouldn't trust him to hold the door open for me."

"It makes sense," Hera said. "The Emperor's leaning on Vidian to make a quota, so Vidian's got to crack Cynda like an egg. He gets a year's worth of thorilide, so he makes his quota. And by the time it runs out prematurely, Danthe will be left holding the bag!"

"Evil," Kanan said, regarding the motionless Vidian. "I knew he had it in him."

"Wait a minute," Skelly said. "The Emperor wouldn't take Vidian's word on this report. Vidian's a management guy, not a scientist. What's the name on that report?"

Hera looked at the screen again. "I can't believe I missed this. *Lemuel Tharsa!*"

Kanan blinked. "That name again. Who was he?"

Hera whipped out a datapad from her pocket. "I found that earlier. According to the HoloNet, for fifteen years Lemuel Tharsa has served as chief analyst with Minerax Consulting, producing studies on raw materials for private and, more recently, Imperial government use."

Zaluna perked up. "That's the man someone on the Star Destroyer asked us about. There wasn't much on the data cube about him—just the standard bioscan at customs."

Hera looked at her. "Check Moonglow's refinery, twenty or so years ago. I found he'd been issued entry credentials."

"Ah," Zaluna said. She opened her bag and produced Hetto's data cube. Switching off the link to Vidian's visual memory, she connected the cube to the terminal she was working at. "Moonglow was Introsphere then. We were definitely monitoring the building."

Skelly rolled his eyes. "Why am I not surprised?"

"A lot of this old material hasn't been mined—we probably didn't know where to start, when the inquiry came in." Zaluna's nimble fingers flew across the console. "I'm running a visual search on the name, limited to security badges."

"What *can't* you do?" Kanan rubbed his forehead. Hiding his Force talents even from himself made a lot more sense, now.

"Got him," Zaluna said. "Here he is." The holoprojector activated again, and a human male appeared. Kanan stood and approached the life-sized image.

The biometric data Zaluna had found in the customs files said the man was just shy of thirty at the time of the visit, but he looked far older: like a harried middle manager, prematurely balding, with a few tufts of rust-colored hair hanging on. His suit was dingy, his shoes scuffed. He could have been anyone.

And yet Kanan thought there was something oddly familiar about Lemuel Tharsa. His posture, his gestures as he ranted to an executive who clearly couldn't have cared less what he was saying. "What *is* he saying?" Kanan asked.

"Looks like we only caught a snippet." Zaluna pressed a button.

"*. . . don't have to tell you people again what the guild's safety rules are. It's the same everywhere in the trade. You've been doing it wrong. Forget the old way!*"

Skelly laughed. "There's old Vidian's motto, before Vidian said it."

Kanan and Hera looked at each other, at the prone count, and then back at the image. The voice was different, for sure, but the intonation was similar. Hera rose and approached Zaluna. "You said there were biometrics on Tharsa?"

"Right here." Zaluna punched them up on the console. "We do a little work with them at Transcept. The main spaceport requires them of all arriving visitors." Kanan bristled, glad he'd arrived on a tramp freighter that avoided that routine.

"I can't believe I'm going to ask this." Hera glanced over at Vidian. "Is Vidian's biodata in that medical console?"

"It should be." Catching Hera's drift, Zaluna ran a comparison. The results appeared on her screen. "Genetic markers are identical with Tharsa's sample on entry. No way to compare eyes, voice, or prints— but somewhere in there, that's the same guy."

"Whoa," Skelly said, looking between Vidian and the image of Tharsa. He scratched his head. "No, no. That's wrong. I saw the biography piece on the HoloNet. Vidian was a defense contractor, nearly died of Shilmer's syndrome. He wasn't some safety inspector." He chuckled. "How ironic would that be?"

"Very," Hera said, studying the results. "But that's him."

Skelly was stunned. "Then Vidian's war bio was a hoax? He was supposed to have been a whistleblower, helping the troops!"

Hera gave Skelly a sympathetic look. "Come on, are you really surprised?"

Skelly threw up his hands. "It's more fun when *I* think of the conspiracies."

"So Tharsa got sick and became Vidian." Kanan crossed his arms. "Was that on Gorse, too? Are there medcenter records?"

"The Republic had privacy laws, then," Zaluna said. "It was the one place we didn't have access. The only records would be on the site."

"Or not." Hera's brow furrowed. "Vidian had a medcenter demolished on his visit. But I don't know why he'd care about covering his tracks now—or why someone on the *Ultimatum* would be asking about Tharsa."

Kanan looked at her, puzzled. "That's not the only thing I don't get. Why wouldn't he keep his original name?"

Hera thought for a moment—and brightened. "Because he wanted to keep Tharsa alive. He's still on the Imperial rolls as an adviser, remember?" She rushed back to the terminal on the far side of the room. She pointed at the screen. "And look what he's been responsible for!"

Kanan stepped behind her and read. It was a long list of things, some dated recently. "I . . . don't get it. What are these?"

Hera ran her finger down the entries on the screen. "Technical reports from Minerax Consulting. Tharsa's name is on many of them as the preparer." Her eyes scanned the titles. "There are dozens of worlds, dozens of projects. Some are things Vidian worked on for the Empire—and some are before, from back in the Republic days."

"He's his own independent auditor?" Skelly hooted. "There's an efficient way to bilk your customers. Do your own fraudulent research!" He leered at Vidian's motionless body. "I'm impressed. You're the master. Really."

Kanan nodded. Things were falling into place. If some Imperial was asking around about Tharsa, maybe Vidian had covered his tracks on Gorse to keep anyone from making the connection. Tharsa's name would still be good with the Emperor, providing he didn't suspect anything; Vidian's plan to destroy the moon would sail through.

Hera squinted. "There's another file here tagged with Tharsa's name—older, but accessed today. But I can't get it open."

"No problem," Kanan said, turning. "Zal?"

"Reporting," Zaluna said, skipping over the cable attached to Vidian's head.

Hera stood up and stepped over to Kanan. He smiled at her. "This is something, right?"

"It's something," she said, looking around at the outer doors. "I'm just not sure what."

"We send the correct version to the Emperor, that's what," Kanan said.

"Not on that system," Hera said. "And I don't exactly think the Emperor checks his own messages—particularly not ones from random dissidents."

She turned her eyes to the ceiling. She had that look again, the one that said she was five moves ahead of him in whatever game it was she was playing. He liked the look, even if it made him a little uncomfortable. He looked back. "Any luck, Zal?"

"I can't decrypt it," Zaluna said. "I'm not a slicer. Kidnap one of those next time."

Kanan looked over at Vidian. Time was running out. They could dose the count again—but someone would be around for him eventually.

Kanan looked at Hera. "You really think there's something important in that file?"

She nodded. "It's the only one protected like that. And," she added, cautiously, "I've got a feeling."

"Good enough for me," Kanan said. He walked back to Vidian's table. "Get that medical droid back over here. I've got a plan."

CHAPTER FORTY-FIVE

"STEP LIVELY, THERE! If you were loading torpedoes on my ship, I'd be launching *you*, next!"

The orange-clad workers began moving marginally faster, but now they were walking so as to avoid Sloane, negating any increase in speed. It wasn't going well. Three of the miners from Gòrse had dropped canisters, causing coolant leaks that cleared the floor for ten minutes each time. And while the repair workers had removed the fool droid that had somehow gotten itself crammed into the pneumatic tube, they had put a long gash on the inner cushioned wall in the process. Now *that* was being repaired. *Civilians!*

At least this experience gave the lie to a little of Vidian's legend, she thought. If Calcoraan Depot was supposed to be the domain of the man who saw everything and kept everything moving, he was sleeping on the job.

There'd been no sign of trouble otherwise. Aware that the bomber from Gorse might be among the workers drafted to load explosives, she'd accepted a pistol and holster from the stormtroopers. It hadn't been necessary. Neither had any of the workers tripped to what they were really assisting in: the possible destruction of their own homes. That, she thought, could get ugly.

Her comlink beeped. She reached for it. "Sloane."

"Captain," droned a familiar voice.

"Count Vidian," she said briskly. "The loading is almost complete. We'll be ready to return to Gorse shortly."

"I need you. Report to my executive chambers—alone."

Sloane's brow wrinkled. "Is it something about the report to the Emperor?"

"You could say that," came the reply. "Come at once."

"Yes, my lord." She snapped off the comlink. She was growing tired of being at Vidian's beck and call—but *Ultimatum*'s regular captain could show up to reclaim his command at any moment, sending her back to the waiting list with everyone else. She had to do as told.

She passed a lieutenant as she marched toward a waiting tramcar. "Tell Commander Chamas to monitor the loading," she said. "I'll be back shortly."

Vidian's antechamber was lavishly appointed, but the workplace's occupants seemed oblivious to their surroundings. Two dozen men and women of various species, all "enhanced" with cybernetic computer implants, wandered the opulent room like monastics, nodding as if listening to music. Not one noticed Sloane's arrival. Each was tuned in to events many systems away, all managing the flow of goods and services vital to the functioning of the Empire in Vidian's managerial domain. Sloane wondered if anybody had ever walked into an open elevator shaft while his or her mind was on moving widgets from Wor Tandell.

Identifying herself to the stormtroopers standing guard, she entered a long hallway. The double doors at the end opened as she reached them. The room beyond lay in darkness.

Sloane rolled her eyes. *More weirdness.* Taking a deep breath, she took a step inside. "Count Vidian?"

Another step—and the doors behind her clanged loudly shut. Sloane heard movement in the dark. She reached for her sidearm— only to feel pain in her wrist as someone kicked the blaster from her hands. The weapon clattered off in the dark. A lithe, shadowy figure whisked by to her right: her assailant. The captain reached again, this time for her comlink—when someone grabbed her arms tightly from behind, spun her around, and shoved.

Sloane didn't hit the floor, or anything else. She heard the hum in the air above, felt the strong pull of an invisible force holding her body in place. It was a stasis field, like the ones in her brig. The person who had pushed her walked ahead in the dark before turning and shining a bright portable light in her face.

"Captain Sloane?" It was Vidian's voice, coming from the direction of the light.

"Count Vidian? What's going on?"

The light shifted—and Sloane saw that while Vidian's voice had indeed spoken to her, the man himself was strapped to a table, motionless. The light traced slowly across the count's form. There was a dark recess in his neck ring where his electronic speaker belonged.

"Glad you got my message." This time, Sloane realized the voice was coming from the person with the portable light—and squinting, she could just make out the figure pressing something against his own neck. "Nifty little doodad. Triggered by the throat muscles."

"You impersonated him!"

"And well," the speaker said, still using the device. His light shifted back toward Vidian, and the speaker turned his back to her. "Get this hooked back up," she heard him say to someone in a different, softer voice. Someone else in the room shuffled toward the table.

Sloane strained to see, to move, to do anything.

"Release us now," she said in her most commanding tone. "You won't get away with this!"

No answer.

"The count had better be alive and unharmed, or you'll have a death mark in every system in the galaxy!"

Still no answer.

Sloane grew concerned. Fanatics like the bomber on Gorse might not care about getting away. After a short silence, she decided on another tactic.

"Look," she said more calmly, "I can get your grievances a hearing.

But that'll only happen if you let me and the count walk out of here right now."

The figure with the light directed it at her again. "Oh, don't go so soon. This is our first date!"

She recognized that voice. Gawking, she said, "You're the mouthy pilot!"

He moved the light underneath his chin and flashed a devilish smile. "Nice to be remembered."

Sloane was flabbergasted. "We checked your badge back on Gorse. Kanan something."

"Kanan Something will do." He shone the light on her again.

She put the pieces together. "A pilot at Moonglow. That's how you got here." She glared into the light. "You've wandered off the tour, mister."

"I had to see *you*," he said, voice sugary. "You missed me, right?"

"Kanan!" came a loud whisper from the shadows.

Sloane's eyes darted to the speaker. "Ah. The co-worker." She was the person who'd kicked at her, she realized. And there were other shadowy figures in the darkness, including a slender person at the table fiddling with Vidian's vocoder. "Did you *all* come with him? You're accomplices. What did he ask you to do?"

"Forget about them," Kanan said. "Haven't you figured it out? I *am* an infiltrator—but on a mission you'll approve of. I serve the Emperor." He paused, before adding: *"Directly."*

Sloane stared down at Kanan for several seconds. Then she burst into laughter. "*You*, an agent of the Emperor?"

"What?" Kanan scowled. "It's possible."

Sloane struggled to stop laughing. "I think he can do better than *you*! What do you suicide fliers do, drink your way from port to port? Did you wander off from your keeper?"

Kanan thumped his chest. "I'm a man with a mission."

"You're an oaf with a delusion. Do you know what the penalty for impersonating a personal agent of the Emperor is?"

"No."

"A personal agent of the Emperor would!"

"You're wrong. There is no penalty—because nobody would ever do such a thing." Kanan sat the lamp on the floor, angled to point up at Sloane. He walked to a control panel near where she was suspended and touched a dial. "Now listen to what's going to happen. I'm going to give you my message, and be on my way. The stasis field's timer will release you with enough time to do what you need to do, before Vidian wakes up. Is that understood?"

"Let *me* tell *you* what will happen instead," Sloane said. "You'll let me down, turn on these lights, release Vidian—and then we'll march you down to the detention block. You can do your talking to an interrogator droid."

"That would be a mistake." Kanan began pacing around the darkened room. "I have information that's vital to you—and to the Emperor."

"If you're the Emperor's agent, you're already reporting to him directly. What do you want from me?"

"Vidian controls all communications from this depot. I can't afford to have this intercepted. I need an Imperial captain, with her own resources." He looked at her cannily. "You *are* resourceful, aren't you?"

"I can tell when I'm being played." She strained against the stasis beam. "Enough of this. Someone is going to come looking for me."

"Then I'd better talk fast," Kanan said. "And you'd better listen. *Like your life depends on it.*"

CHAPTER FORTY-SIX

BACK IN HIS hazmat suit, Kanan heaved another baradium-357 canister off the hovercart and onto a shelving unit in *Expedient*. "The seed's planted."

Through her mask, Zaluna looked at him. "That was both the most exciting thing I've ever done in my life—and the most exhausting. What do we do now?"

He locked the cylinder into a magnetic support. "Ditch these forever," Kanan said, peeling off his hazmat mask and throwing it to the deck. Once the canisters were secured, the bulky protective wear could be dispensed with.

As Zaluna pulled off her mask, Kanan saw that the Sullustan woman looked winded. "I meant, what if what you did doesn't work?" she asked. "With the captain, back there?"

"Don't worry, it'll work," Kanan said, climbing out of his suit. "Sloane was sold. I could tell."

"You could, could you?" Once the airlock door sealed behind her, Hera removed her mask and frowned. "Sloane thought you were cracked."

Kanan waved dismissively. "*Skelly* is cracked. *I* sounded like a responsible adult."

"Who wanted to buy her a drink. That charm thing of yours is not for every situation, Kanan." Hera hustled past him and slid into the pilot's seat. "See to Skelly."

Skelly, facedown where he'd collapsed on the acceleration couch, feebly tried to peel off his hood with his one working hand. He finally succeeded when Kanan gave the mask a yank. The man looked rough. They'd had to load the explosives and make their way back to the ship quickly, and there hadn't been room left on the hovercart for Skelly to ride. The walk had been hard on him, and Hera and Zaluna had supported him part of the way. They'd been the last crew to make it back, just barely avoiding notice.

Skelly looked up, his face twisted in pain. "I still think . . . we should have killed him."

Kanan shook his head. He wasn't going to explain it again. He pushed Skelly upright in his seat and strapped on an oxygen mask. "Trust me, everybody. This'll work."

"If . . . it doesn't," Skelly said between breaths, "we need . . . to warn Gorse."

"What's the point?" Kanan asked, shuttling forward. "The Empire's declared full groundstop on Gorse. Nobody can take off."

"There are tunnels," Skelly said. "And bomb shelters."

"Hera tells me they make fine homes," Kanan said, settling into the passenger seat beside her. "Let's hope it doesn't come to that."

Zaluna looked forward as the engines revved. "You need to talk to everyone on the planet at once . . ."

Kanan looked back at her. "You got something?"

She shook her head. "It—it's nothing." She slumped back in her seat, weary. "We've done too much already."

Hera turned to face Zaluna. "Come on, Zal. You have a way to help, don't you?"

Zaluna let out a deep breath. "I think there's a way," she finally said. "But I can't do it with this ship's transmitter. I need something built in the last thousand years."

"Hey, I'm sure there was a refit a century ago," Kanan said, looking up at the bulkhead. He wasn't about to get defensive about *Expedient,* no matter how much he and the ship had been through. He looked at Hera. "How about your lovely ride?"

"It's got everything," she said, pulling back on the control yoke. *Expedient* heaved off the deck. "My ship should be up to date for whatever you need. If we can land on Gorse and get to it."

"We'll be shot at on the way down and up again."

"*Up* I'm not worried about." She smiled.

I have got to see this ship, Kanan thought again as *Expedient* turned in midair. "What have you got in mind, Zaluna?"

"I still have Vidian's passcode from earlier. If we can send a signal mimicking an Imperial override request, we can push out an emergency message onto every electronic system on Gorse that Transcept is spying on." She looked at Kanan with trepidation. "We'd only be able to do it once, ever. They'd close the door immediately."

"One message, then. It'll have to be enough," Hera said, guiding the ship through the magnetic field into space. "We'd have to get there and do it before he changes the passcode."

"If he doesn't realize we did anything," Kanan said. "And he won't." He gestured forward. Traffic was moving along outside the station, and he could see the TIE fighters routinely flying past. "See? Nobody's shooting us out of the sky."

"That's just because your *new friend* hasn't called out the heavy artillery yet," Hera said—

—and as she did, *Expedient* shuddered violently. Zaluna yelped. Kanan and Hera glanced warily at each other.

"Just the parking tractor beam guiding us out," Kanan finally said, nodding forward. The ship was turning, making progress toward the perimeter.

Hera took a deep breath and let out a whistle. "We'd better hope this thing lets go of us before the stasis beam lets go of Sloane."

"I'm telling you not to worry," Kanan said, leaning back and stretching his legs. "None of this is necessary. Vidian is done for. Sloane is sold."

———

"My lord! My lord!"

Count Vidian roused. Awareness always returned quickly to him after sleep, medically induced or otherwise. His eyes activated a second after his ears did, and he saw the fraught face of the Star Destroyer captain leaning over him.

"Sloane? What's going on?"

She yanked at the straps binding him to the operating table. "You were unconscious," she said, straining to remove one of the durasteel cuffs binding his wrists. "Are you all right?"

"I believe so." Whispering a command, he cycled back through everything his eyes had recorded in the last several hours. There was nothing there from the time he was under—not even any of the feedback his nightmares had been producing lately. And neither had his senses recorded anything from the hour before, during the battle with the pilot and his companions. A glitch, caused by damage in the fight?

The servos in his hips activated, and he sat up on the table. He looked around at the mess of his living space. "Someone drugged me."

"There were intruders here," Sloane said, moving to work on the cuffs holding his ankles. "They attacked me, too, when I entered. They trapped me in your stasis beam. Then they left."

Vidian looked around. "Through the floor?"

Sloane nodded. "It was dark—I couldn't see much. What did they want?"

"Me." Vidian leaned down and ripped at the ankle cuffs with his metal hands. The manacles were designed to withstand his thrashings, and yet they couldn't survive against his rising anger. "I want a full search. Lock the station down!" He opened a channel on his internal comlink and prepared to give the command.

Sloane spoke before he could. "My lord—one of them *talked* to me." Her dark eyes were full of concern. "He claimed to be an agent of the Emperor."

"What?" Vidian closed the audio channel and stared at her. "Who?"

"One of the people who waylaid me," she said.

"An agent of the Emperor?" Vidian rose from the table and stood, turning his back to the captain. "What . . . did he say?"

"A lot of nonsense. He claimed you were acting against the Emperor's interests in the Gorse project. That your plan was to destroy the moon and its thorilide, regardless of the yield."

Vidian froze. Cautiously, he turned to face her. "Most amusing. Pray tell, what reason did this mystic give for my doing such a thing?"

"It was senseless ranting, Count Vidian. I didn't listen."

"Perhaps he thinks I'm some kind of traitor? Some kind of plant in the hierarchy?"

Sloane laughed. "I think he was insane." She looked at him. "Have you called for security already, or should I?"

"I'm doing so now," Vidian said. But directing his eyes to check the station's surveillance reports, he found precious little for his staff to go on. Nothing unusual had been seen aboard Calcoraan Depot in the last few hours. He'd recognized the gunslinger from Cynda, and he'd remembered Skelly. But all the workers aboard were in hazmat masks, and the ships had already departed. Even a check of the data feeds from his medical droids in the room confirmed that their memories had been wiped.

The infiltrators were good, whoever they were.

Reports from the TIE sentries on the system perimeter confirmed that all the ships had gone to hyperspace on the same heading: toward Cynda, as ordered. If his assailants weren't still aboard the depot, there was only one other place for them.

Vidian thought quickly about his next move. He wasn't sure who his attackers were, but neither was he sure what they would say if found. All that mattered was making sure nothing interfered with the destruction of Cynda.

And he had a way to do that. "*Ultimatum* will arrive in the Gorse system before the last of the baradium haulers?"

A little startled by the change of topic, Sloane nodded. "They haven't built the freighter that can outrun a Star Destroyer."

"Good. I want your whole complement of fighters deployed, managing the final delivery. Bring in additional TIEs from here, using the

Gozanti freighter carriers. If any hauler moves a centimeter out of line, I want that ship destroyed, cargo and all. Regardless of any danger to the pilot doing the shooting. Is that understood?"

"They'll do their duty—for me." Sloane looked at him searchingly. "You think the intruders are headed for Gorse?"

"It pays to be ready." Vidian walked across the room to a fallen cabinet. Righting it, he thought about his other problem. He highly doubted the gunslinger was an agent of the Emperor; while Palpatine was fond of testing his underlings' devotion, he was never as clumsy as this. But neither could he see a bunch of amateurs successfully boarding his station, simply looking for revenge for Lal Grallik's death.

What Vidian could easily see, however, was the pilot and his friends being part of some plot by one of his many rivals. And that meant he had to be cautious. He had no idea what the pilot had said to Sloane—but he had to be certain of her loyalty, and his eventual success. "I appreciate your freeing me, Sloane. This could have been . . . *embarrassing*."

She shrugged. "My duty is to you, sir."

"Then I will do mine to you." He paused for several seconds before speaking aloud again. "I have just sent a verbal instruction to the staff at my offices at Corellia. In a few days Captain Karlsen will be receiving a very lucrative offer to join the private sector."

Surprised, Sloane put up her hand in protest. "Sir, I wasn't expecting—"

"At that time, *Ultimatum* is yours to keep."

The news appeared to take her breath away. *Good*, Vidian thought. "Return with *Ultimatum* as planned while I finish the preparations aboard the collection ship. Once the moon is destroyed and *Forager* begins to do its job, the Emperor will see the return, and our work together will be vindicated."

"Together, my lord?"

"You'll have the credit you deserve for helping to make this happen so quickly. I might even request you and *Ultimatum* be permanently detached to me." He eyed her. "Who *is* the youngest admiral, I wonder?"

CHAPTER FORTY-SEVEN

THERE WASN'T ALWAYS much to do when a ship was in hyperspace, the interdimensional realm between stars. There was even less when flying *Expedient,* a ship with no galley or living quarters. Worse, the cockpit area offered no privacy at all; Skelly was snoring away on his seats, and Zaluna, unshakable for so long, had taken to nervously fidgeting around with the contents of her magic bag. Well, even the strongest had their limits—especially when death was coming for their homeworld.

The only getaway existed in the far rear of the ship, down one of the branching aisles of the cargo hold. And there, at the far end, standing amid the shelves of secured baradium-357 canisters, waited the person he wanted to see.

"Cozy back here," Kanan said. "We could send out for flatcakes."

"Very funny." Hera held the smile for only a moment. She looked tired. "We need to talk."

"My pleasure." Kanan found a spot at the end of the aisle with no canisters on either side, creating two makeshift seats on opposing lower shelves. "I fixed the ID transponder like you asked. It'll say we're a different ship than landed on Calcoraan Depot—in case they've finally figured out we were the ones that messed with Vidian."

Hera still wore the same worried expression, he saw. "I'm guessing you had a different problem?" Kanan asked.

"It's Skelly," she said in a low voice, nodding in the direction of the cockpit. "I think he's in trouble."

"He's always in trouble."

"I think he's *dying*," she said. "The joking around is a cover. He's in bad shape."

Kanan inhaled deeply and nodded. He'd seen the same thing. "Vidian did a number on him. Broken bones, internal bleeding." He shook his head. "I caught a look at the readings that medical droid took of him. It wanted to open him up, right then and there."

"We need to get him to a medcenter," Hera said. "He's navigating on force of will alone."

"He's got plenty of that. But where can we take him? We're about to tell everyone on Gorse to run for their lives."

Hera sighed. "You're right. They come first. He's just going to have to hang on."

She looked toward the small viewport to her left, at the end of the aisle. Stars streaked by. Kanan thought she looked striking even now, facing likely defeat. "This isn't what you came to Gorse for, was it?"

She chuckled darkly. "Not even close. I've been talking to people who have grievances against the Empire—but only to find out the scope of what's out there, what's possible. I wasn't expecting to *do* anything against it. Not yet, anyway. Not for a long time."

"That's the problem with people," Kanan said. "They never need help on your schedule—only theirs."

She nodded. Then she looked back at him. After studying him for a moment, she spoke. "Where are you from, Kanan?"

"Around," he said. "You?"

"Same."

"Fair enough."

She smiled gently. "That's not what I really wanted to ask, anyway."

Kanan smirked. "Fire away, then."

"Why are you doing this?"

"Sitting with you? Wouldn't miss it."

"No, I mean *this*. Flying around fugitives and trying to take down Vidian. I know why Skelly and I are doing this," she said. "Even Zaluna. But not you."

He shrugged. "I love a party."

"Seriously."

He scratched his beard. "You were there. You saw what happened to Okadiah, and all the others—"

"And that's awful. But by your own admission, you move around. You were about to leave Gorse forever when I found you. So while I appreciate your being here, I wonder if there's something else going on." She eyed him. "I mean, you're not here for the politics."

He laughed. "Definitely not."

She smiled. "Yeah, you don't strike me as a victim of oppression."

Kanan's grin melted a little on hearing her words, and he looked away. "You never know," he muttered. "Appearances can be deceiving."

"What?"

Feeling her eyes on him, he faced her again and smiled. "Nothing. Hey, it's like I said at the start. I'm just going where you're going."

Hera's nose wrinkled. "Hmm," she said, after a moment.

"Hmm what?"

"I think I liked your first answer better."

Zaluna stood before the onrushing stars. It was an amazing spectacle, something she had never expected to see. Her salary wasn't enough to take her far, and besides, she had nowhere to go. Her office was her universe.

And now that Skelly was snoozing and Kanan and Hera were gone, somewhere in the back, this was her last chance to get it back.

Her last chance to change her mind.

She'd completely ruined her life in the last few days. She'd only wanted to fulfill Hetto's parting wish, not go running around the galaxy like some kind of secret agent. Infiltrating an Imperial depot? Tampering not just with the computers of an important official, but with his very body? Who *was* that person? It certainly wasn't the woman she'd imagined she was.

But here, she had an opportunity to undo everything. She'd seen the big red light on the forward control panel, earlier: It had signaled when the vessel was about to exit hyperspace. Dark now, it sat adjacent to the comm system—and that was something Zaluna knew how to use.

And she *could* use it, right as they reentered realspace, to contact the Empire and get off this ride.

They might still believe her. She could say she was kidnapped, forced to help the would-be radicals. Skelly and Kanan were violent characters who'd attacked Imperial agents. Hera was the mastermind, trying to lure her into betraying the Empire. Zaluna was innocent, a pawn, a foolish woman with nothing but good intentions. She could say she was trying to entrap the agitators when she got trapped herself. They'd taken her into danger. She didn't owe them anything.

And the moon might still be saved. If Vidian was doing something he shouldn't, the Empire would stop him, wouldn't it? And how was any of it her business anyway? Maybe the deadly predictions of what might happen were wrong. Who was she to second-guess decisions made from so far on high? It would be an irrational Empire indeed that would ignore its people's best interests.

Only . . . the Empire *had* done exactly that many times that she had seen. And its minions had *never* listened to anyone's defense before. They only listened to what people said about the Empire. Zaluna knew firsthand, having been the state's ears and eyes on Gorse and Cynda for years. She'd heard—but never comprehended. She watched, but never saw.

And now that was changing. The others had started her thinking.

Hera had listened patiently to Zaluna's concerns several times during their journey, and each time had spoken frankly and firmly. Fear was understandable and forgivable—and no one expected Zaluna to do more than she was capable of. "But seeing and doing nothing isn't the worst thing," Hera had said. *"The worst thing is to see and not to care."*

Zaluna had seen Imperial minions do many things. Bad things, that Transcept's watchers were ordered to look the other way on. She'd done as commanded—but it had never made sense. Wasn't being a watchperson her job? What good was being a witness if the laws could be changed at whim by the lawgivers?

Then there was Skelly. He was troubled, for sure, but she'd come to understand that he truly was interested in protecting Cynda and Gorse. The Empire cared little for those damaged by the Clone Wars, and even less for people who had qualms about its industrial activities. She could tell that for Skelly, the impending destruction of the moon was like watching death approaching for someone close to him.

And finally, there was Kanan, who seemed to go from disaster to disaster as if he were wandering from one cantina to another. Nothing seemed to touch him—yet she knew that wasn't true. Yes, he played the roustabout, working a dangerous job and pushing back against those who pushed him. But that day with Okadiah was not the first time she'd seen him come to someone's defense. They were always small acts; often, the person helped hadn't known he'd done anything. He seemed to want it that way, for some reason.

She could also tell he was tired of living the way he had been: tired of going from one pointless job to another, looking for a place where he could live his life his own way. She'd seen the look a hundred times on the faces of other migrant workers—and the Empire had made it into a perpetual state for many. Kanan was young—but his secret soul was much older. And Zaluna knew the Empire was somehow responsible.

But Zaluna had the right to a life of her choosing, too—and time was running out.

The red light on the nav computer flashed. A buzzer, half broken and barely audible, sounded. Her eyes went to the comm system controls. It would be so easy . . .

"Your only value to the Empire is what you can do for it," said a voice from behind.

Unsurprised at hearing Hera, Zaluna turned over her words in her mind. "You know," she said calmly, "Hetto used to say that exact thing."

"He was right."

Zaluna saw Hera's reflection in the viewport, against the streaming stars. She was motionless behind her, not approaching. "Aren't you afraid?" Zaluna asked.

"Anyone would be. But the Jedi had a saying about fear. It leads, ultimately, to suffering." Hera paused. "Someone has to break the chain."

"People can't talk about the Jedi anymore."

"Maybe they should."

Zaluna nodded and looked back at the control panel. "It *was* better then." She felt her strength reviving. She was more than an extra set of eyes and ears to a sadistic cyborg—and to a faraway Emperor. She was no revolutionary, but she could at least try to stop them now.

Zaluna moved her hand to the nav computer and shut off the buzzer. "I was just coming to get you," she said. Turning to Hera, she smiled. "We're here."

CHAPTER FORTY-EIGHT

KANAN THOUGHT it sounded foolish to say aloud, but leaving hyperspace was just like entering it, except in reverse. The stars through the forward viewport went from blurred lines back to twinkling dots. Only this time, few could be seen from *Expedient*'s cockpit. Cynda hung above, a brilliant crescent from their angle, while massive Gorse sat up ahead, its cities in their eternal night.

And there was something else: more TIE fighters than he had ever seen. Swarms lay ahead, peeling off in quartets as *Expedient* entered the area.

"Vector right seven-five degrees, down-axis twenty," snapped a voice over the comm system. "Follow the formation if you want to live."

Kanan flinched. This was normally when he'd give the Imperials some lip—but he wasn't flying, and it wasn't smart. Not now. Hera complied, banking the vessel and bringing it into line with a queue of ships far ahead. Each freighter had a pair of TIEs either above and below it or on either side, defining a corridor: Kanan could tell from the sensors that two flanked *Expedient,* on the port and starboard sides. Ahead, the sky went black for a moment, as the hexagonal wing of another TIE zipped past their field of view.

"They're crisscrossing," Kanan said. "Keeping us all separated."

Hera frowned. "They're limiting the damage a saboteur can do. They're afraid there's another Skelly out here."

"They'd be right," called Skelly from behind. Holding his midsection, Skelly hobbled toward the front of the cockpit. He reached for the side of Kanan's seat and missed. Zaluna hopped from her seat and grabbed onto him. Skelly seemed almost unaware of the woman steadying him. His eyes were locked on the outside. "Somebody means business."

Expedient followed the convoy across the terminator dividing Cyndan night from day. There they saw it, sitting off in space: the gang boss to their work crew. Zaluna gasped at the sight. "Another Star Destroyer!"

"No, the same one," Hera said.

Kanan nodded. It was one of the more unnerving consequences when ships of differing speeds used hyperspace. *Ultimatum* had been in their rearview cam, parked at Calcoraan Depot, when they'd gone to lightspeed; now it was sitting in front of them over Gorse, disgorging even more TIE fighters.

Hera looked in unsettled wonder. "These TIEs can't all be from the Star Destroyer. *Imperial*-class has sixty, maybe seventy."

Kanan pointed out other vessels orbiting off Cynda's horizon. Long and bulky like the thorilide cargo craft, the ships had docking ports for four TIE fighters each. "Looks like the Empire's refitting Gozanti freighters these days."

"And they beat us here, too!" Hera was as aggravated as he'd seen her. She was clearly used to flying a faster ship. "We're lucky they didn't have time for shore leave." She looked at the scanner and raised her hands in frustration. "I don't know that we can get to Gorse at all through this blockade."

"I thought you were good," Kanan said.

"Not that good. Not in this thing."

The TIEs led the convoy on a long descent path, several hundred kilometers off the surface of Cynda. Hera rolled *Expedient* 180 degrees so the ground could be seen from the cockpit. "Construction work ahead," Kanan said. He flipped a switch, triggering the viewport's magnifying overlay.

Skelly staggered forward and half collapsed against the forward panel between Hera and Kanan. Arms splayed forward across it for support, he gawked at what he saw. "We're too late," Skelly said, staring at a large metal tower on the surface over their heads.

"What? What are those?" Kanan asked. He could see at least six others, spaced seemingly randomly across the moon's surface.

"Injection sites. They're pumping in xenoboric acid, punching holes deep into the mantle. They'll run the baradium charges down on suprafilament next." Skelly looked from tower to tower. "Down below, Cynda's got flaws, just like a diamond. They'll set off the charges in a precise order, seconds apart. The primaries will cleave it. The secondaries will crush it. The tertiaries will disperse it."

Kanan stared at him. "How do you know all this?"

"It's my idea. I did it as a thought experiment—just to prove my point. It was on the holodisk." He sighed and sagged to the floor. "Why do I always have to be right?"

Hera studied the workers on the surface. "They're in a real hurry," Hera said.

"Vidian's in the hurry," Kanan said. "He's got to destroy the moon before the Emperor gets wise to what he's doing here." He smirked. "And that's who's missing. Him and his big collector ship. I told you, you just had to trust—"

"Attention, newly arriving freighters," said a familiar voice over the comm system. "This is Captain Sloane of *Ultimatum*. I have important information about a change in plans."

Kanan smiled at the others and gave a thumbs-up signal. "This is it!"

"The accident earlier this week left the moon's mines dangerously unstable," Sloane said over the comm system. "Imperial scientists have determined the only way to prevent future disasters is to release all the stresses that have built up—now, with no one in the mines. By doing so, we assure safe mining can continue, in the name of the Empire."

"Yeah, that Empire's really looking out for them," Skelly said. "They're talking our own people into committing suicide!"

"You will be guided to sites on the Cyndan surface where you will off-load and leave immediately," the captain continued.

Kanan frowned. "Wait a minute. That wasn't what she was supposed to say. She was supposed to say Vidian's a goner—and send us all home!"

"That doesn't sound like a woman who just squealed to the Emperor," Hera said.

Kanan stared at the comm system. "No, it doesn't." He shook his head.

The hyperspace anomaly alarm flashed blue and squawked loudly. Ahead, Vidian's gigantic thorilide harvester vessel appeared in the only free patch of space available.

"Welcome, *Forager*," Sloane said over the comm system. "The final freighters are here and the last charges will be injected in forty minutes. You should receive a data hookup with Detonation Control down there in one hour."

"Excellent work, Captain Sloane," they heard Vidian say. "You'll make a fine admiral one day."

Kanan looked at Hera. "This is making me sick. They're on a date."

"Jealous?"

"Blast it, I thought she'd listen!" He pounded his fist on the dashboard. "That's the Imperial way, all right. They're always stabbing their friends in the back!"

Sloane spoke again over the device, sounding more concerned. "Count Vidian, time will be of the essence. Lieutenant Deltic's staff says you will have one hour from the Detonation Control linkup to trigger the process."

"I won't need that much time," Vidian responded, drily. "I've been ready—and *Forager* will be ready."

"To collect the thorilide after he's blown most of it up—along with the moon," Skelly muttered as the transmission ended. "Senseless." He turned around on the floor and slumped with his back against the cockpit control panels. He dabbed his nose with his hand. There was blood there. "Just drop me off anywhere. Maybe I can die on Cynda before they blow it up."

Hera looked at Skelly for a moment—and then back outside. Her eyes focused on something ahead. "Skelly, why did she say there was a time limit to detonating the explosives they're planting in the moon?"

Skelly rubbed the side of his head, his eyes closed. "It's the xenoboric acid they're injecting. Wait too long and any of the junk that's left down there will eat its way through the baradium drop cables and containers. No boom then."

Hera looked at Kanan. He caught the drift. "You said there was a chain reaction here—that some of those towers were primaries?"

Skelly sniffed, eyes opening. "Yeah. Four of them."

"Which four?" Kanan asked.

"I'm trying to remember. I'd have to look." Skelly tried to get to his feet, but only fell back down on his rump. Zaluna sprang again from her seat and helped him stand, bracing herself between the two forward chairs. Skelly looked ahead and squinted at Cynda's bright surface.

"Will killing the towers stop the reaction?" Kanan asked him.

"Yeah. But those are our people down there working those sites— and flying cargo to them."

"I know." Kanan reached down for his headset and put it on.

"That's only patched into local comm traffic," Hera said. "We can't send Zaluna's warning on it."

Kanan ignored her and worked the latch on the panel in front of his knees. A door swung open, and he pulled at what was inside. Reluctant hinges cracked and groaned. With effort, Kanan craned a targeting system with handles up toward his chest.

"Do I want to know what he's doing?" Zaluna asked.

Hera stared at him in puzzlement. "I'm not sure I know, myself."

"The meteor chaser," Kanan said, waving to the ceiling. The single cannon perched above the crew compartment had a field of fire that covered a wide arc on either side and ahead of *Expedient*. "Every Baby Carrier has one. Baby doesn't like being bumped."

"Neither do I," Skelly said, looking nervously at him. "You can't expect to fight off the Imperials with that?"

"Not more than a few," Kanan said, testing his microphone. "But if I do it right, a few's enough!"

CHAPTER FORTY-NINE

THE COMMAND CENTER of the collection ship looked like a cathedral for some ancient religion. Vidian's comm station, in the middle of the room, resembled an altar. Idle comparisons, both. But the reality was not lost on Vidian. From here, he would sacrifice the moon to his Emperor, winning his favor for another year. And the ashes of the world would smother his rival once and for all.

Intentionally or not, the collection ship's designers had built a supernatural feel into *Forager*'s bridge. Situated frontward on the foremost sphere on the ship's linked series of pods, the huge round room looked ahead through tall windows that rose and curved to a ceiling twenty meters above. More consoles like Vidian's circled him like miniature megaliths in a place for idol-worshipper rites. A catwalk two stories up ran around the front arc of the room, providing additional workstations between the windows for Vidian's droids and cybernetically enhanced assistants. He could see the metallic figures moving back and forth on the decking, digital priests backlit by the shining moon.

"Spokes deployed, my lord," one of them said. "We are ready for the collection process to begin."

Vidian nodded. It was up to Sloane and her people now. Switching his visual feed from cam to remote cam, he looked approvingly on the Cynda work sites. Sloane had done a remarkable job, throwing *Ultimatum*'s thousands of staffers at a project that, days before, had been a fantasy on a holodisk from a deranged assassin. Now they were thirty minutes away from doing something that still existed only at the outer edges of Imperial capability: the destruction of a moon, and perhaps the world below.

It had been critical to get Sloane's cooperation early on. Any extra time, any deliberation would have brought the Emperor's corps of engineers into the picture, and they would have questioned the yield from the test blast. Vidian could use Tharsa's name to falsify a report and defraud an ambitious captain, but more would be difficult. And this couldn't wait. As Vidian cycled his messages before his eyes, he saw not just more from the nuisance Danthe, but several from the Emperor's inner circle. All were almost comically urgent, suggesting that if Vidian didn't deliver thorilide in record amounts instantly, the entire Imperial fleet would have to be mothballed. The baron had really gone to work on the Emperor's people.

Well, he would finish it soon enough. He would deliver thorilide beyond anyone's fantasies—and then stick the grinning Danthe with a ticking bomb.

One of Vidian's cybernetic aides stepped forward. "Something's coming in, master, on the Mining Guild channel."

"Eh?" Vidian whispered commands until the sound reached him.

"—don't know what's going on. Feeling so . . . weird. These blasted Baby canisters—some of them started leaking these, I don't know, these *fumes* . . ."

"What's this nonsense?" Vidian said aloud.

"—don't know how it happened. Faulty loading, faulty material, faulty something—just like everything in this wretched job. I've hated it all, y'know." The voice went from woozy to bitter. "And I've hated all of *you*."

"It's one coming from one of the freighters," Vidian's aide volunteered. "The coolant lining the baradium-357 canisters has been known to cause psychotic episodes if it gets—"

"Yeah, you know me," the broadcaster interrupted, sounding angrier by the word. "You know my voice. I put up with all of you, for Okadiah's sake. In the mines, on the hoverbus, in the bar. Lot of bums, all of you. Think you're such *tough* guys. You make me sick!"

Vidian seethed as he recognized the voice. *The gunslinger!* "Zero in on that transmission," he ordered. "Find him!"

The speaker was raging now. "Filthy, stinking miners! I can see your ID transponders—I know who you are. Think you're hot stuff, hauling bombs. Let's see how hot *I* can make it!"

Vidian toggled his comlink mode. "Now hear this! This is Count Vidian. Disregard these transmissions and finish your deliveries! You've just heard the ravings of a crazy man, a provocateur—"

The pilot boomed in response. "I'm crazy? *I'm crazy?* Fine! I don't care about your stinking starfighters, Empire-man. I'm telling everyone—if you see me coming, run, because I'm going to blow every ship I see out of the sky! *Starting with the miners!*"

A horrific squawk erupted from *Expedient*'s comm system: Imperial jamming on the guild channel. Hera looked at Kanan, stupefied. "I thought you were going to warn them about the moon!"

"They wouldn't have believed it. *I* barely believe it. Right now, they're only afraid of the TIE fighters. But they're about to become more afraid of me!" Kanan flashed her a wild look. "I need you to fly like a Wookiee whose hair is on fire—and who thinks *everybody* lit the match. Can you do that?"

She seemed to get the idea, if reluctantly. "Got it."

He pointed at the TIE fighter beginning its intersecting run across their convoy corridor. "Dive when I signal."

The Imperial starfighter whisked into their field of view, its wings resolving into a fat hexagonal target. Kanan used it as exactly that, pulling the trigger on his gunnery controls. "Hera, now!"

Orange fire ripped from the weapons turret positioned over and behind their heads, tearing dead-center into the wing of the TIE fighter passing before them. Hera slammed the control yoke forward and hit the throttle, causing *Expedient* to dive. The TIE exploded into a blaze of bright flame above—but now Cynda was all they could see, its icy surface filling the viewport.

Zaluna lost her hold on the side of Kanan's seat and fell forward, mashing Skelly against the forward control panel. He called out in pain.

"Hang on!" Hera brought *Expedient* into a roll, bringing one of the two Imperial fighters that had been flanking them into Kanan's sights. He fired again. Hera didn't wait to see the result, moving once more to bring the ship lower. Cynda's gravity began to take hold.

Zaluna tried to help Skelly up. "I'm so sorry," she said. "I'm not used to this!"

"Who is?" Weakly trying to fend off her attempts to stand him up, he appealed to the air. "Please, just let me go sit down . . ."

"We need you here," Kanan said, struggling to find their other flanker on his scope. The TIE was shooting at them: He could see the flash of energized particles to his right. "Where is this guy?"

"Right here," Hera said, slamming on the braking jets. The glowing ionic thrusters of the third TIE appeared in the space before them. Kanan swung his targeting mechanism and hit the trigger. Hera pumped her fist as the starfighter blew itself apart.

Kanan glanced at Skelly, looking rocky as Zaluna held him up. Skelly outweighed the woman, but she was doing her best to keep him in place. Kanan implored him. "Come on, Skelly. We're there. Focus!"

Skelly squinted at the surface as Hera descended. There was a tower on the far horizon, nothing more than a needle on an ocean of white. A cluster of ships could be seen heading for the area. "That way!"

The alert clarion sounded on the bridge of *Ultimatum*. "Scramble wings fourteen, fifteen, seventeen," Sloane said. "Pursue freighter, hereafter tagged Renegade One. Take them down!"

The captain stood by the holographic tracking display and watched the action with bewilderment. She'd ordered the Star Destroyer to remain on its station, overseeing the convoy route and protecting *Forager*—but what was going on over the surface of Cynda defied belief. And it had all started with that bizarre message from Kanan.

"Renegade One is pursuing the other baradium haulers," said a fresh-faced ensign. Young Cauley had been trying his best to track the zigzagging renegade—but nothing it did made any sense.

"They're trying to destroy the freighters?"

"No, Captain. Just the TIE fighters accompanying them. The freighters should be easier targets, but it's just, well—" The headset-wearing ensign gawked at his monitor. Sloane stepped behind him to watch the chase. The runaway was peeling away the escorts of the fully laden cargo ships—and then seemingly shooting to miss, aiming just in front of the vessels.

"Harassing fire," she said. Kanan—pilot, insurrectionist, would-be Imperial agent? Whatever he was, he was definitely aboard that ship and trying to prevent the others from landing their cargo. His threatening message had set the stage for chaos. "Method to the madness. He's scaring them away."

"And doing a good job of it," Ensign Cauley said. He pointed to the screen. "He gets anywhere near a freighter and they try to peel off."

Sloane looked back at the holographic tracking display. One by one, baradium freighters were switching off their ID transponders, fearful of having Kanan come after them. It was only adding to the confusion. *Has everybody on Gorse tangled with this character?*

Cauley tapped his earpiece. "I've got a TIE pilot chasing after the hauler he's escorting now. It's fleeing, afraid of being targeted by Renegade One. Our pilot's asking if he can shoot his hauler down."

"What? No!" Sloane froze. She'd told Vidian she'd allow nothing to interfere with the explosives delivery, and they'd sent more than his project needed. But how much more? "Tell our pilot to stick with the ship he's convoying as best he can until our reinforcements arrive. Tell him if he can run interference—"

"Never mind," Cauley said, removing his headset. "Renegade One just shot our pilot down."

Sloane clenched her fists. "Pull all escort wings in that area off their duty. Send them all against Kanan!"

"Against who, Captain?"

"Renegade One!" Quaking in anger, she pointed outside. *"The guy shooting at everyone!"*

CHAPTER FIFTY

KANAN CHECKED HIS sights again as Hera banked *Expedient* into another S-turn. She'd been weaving between the injection tower on the Cyndan surface and the landing area nearby, where tracked Imperial ground vehicles were moving baradium canisters across the ice from the freighters.

He wasn't about to target anything directly: Shooting the tower, Skelly had said, might set off the world-destroying reaction by accident. And killing mining workers in the freighters or on the icecrawlers would make him no better than Vidian. Instead, he continued strafing the areas the workers had to cross, while preventing any more ships from landing. He wouldn't kill civilians, but he had nothing against scaring the daylights out of them for a good cause.

"Not exactly an ideal way to raise a collective consciousness," Hera said as he fired another volley just beneath a freighter attempting a landing.

"Recruit allies on your own time. This is getting attention, the Gorse way!"

Trouble was, he was running out of targets. "Skelly, where's the next primary tower?"

"Forget it," Hera snapped. Yanking on the control yoke, she sent a reluctant *Expedient* into a groaning upward spiral. Kanan saw why as the ship twisted: a sky full of TIE fighters, rocketing toward them.

A loud beeping noise came from his gunnery controls. The indicator said the weapons turret was overheating. He looked at Hera and shook his head. "This thing's rated to move some pebbles around. That's about it!"

"I think our engines could go at any minute." She sighed in exasperation as *Expedient* hurtled back toward orbit.

"Safest thing on board is the baradium!" It was a perversely lucky thing, Kanan thought: The many bumps, slams, and near-misses *Expedient* had suffered would have set his regular cargo off in a heartbeat. The ridiculously more powerful Baby on board at least had the benefit of containers that secured to the shelving.

Gorse appeared in front of them again, with *Forager* hanging before it. Its spokes were open, a gigantic metal bloom at the front of the vessel. Kanan blanched at the size of it. "Can we take out that thing?"

Hera checked her instruments and shook her head. "Big energy shield around it." She pointed *Expedient* outward, away from the ever-approaching wave of TIE fighters. It gave them a better look at *Forager* from the side, but that was about it. It was useless.

Kanan released the gunnery controls. He'd left imprints on them with his hands, he saw. He rubbed his forehead. "Anybody else got a plan?"

No one said anything for a moment.

Then a voice came from behind. "I think we can do Plan Two."

Kanan looked back to see Zaluna trying to squeeze past Skelly. She was looking outward, at *Forager*. "Which one was Plan Two?" Kanan asked.

"I thought Plan Two was slowing down the injection process," Skelly said, hanging on to Hera's chair.

Zaluna shook her head. "No, that's Plan Three. Plan One was informing on Count Vidian. Plan Two was warning people. Plan Three was slowing down the injection—"

"Can we stop this?" Hera pleaded. She nodded to the left and smiled politely at Zaluna. "TIE fighter fleet in two minutes, remember?"

The woman pointed ahead at *Forager*. "Okay. Look up there." Behind the rimless wagon wheel that was the collection array stretched seven globes, connected in a line. The one at the ship's front, nearest the spokes, had a lighted crew area at top—and a big round dish atop that. "That's an Imperial subspace transmitter."

"I didn't see that," Kanan said. "Good eyes."

"That's what they paid me for." Zaluna grinned. "I can tap into the Transcept systems on that thing and send our warning to Gorse. They won't know to jam that."

Kanan stared. "That ship's where Vidian is now. We'd have to get you in there to do your thing."

Zaluna shrank a little at that, but didn't shirk. "I know."

"And maybe we can even keep Vidian from sending the trigger command to Cynda," Hera said.

"Two for one," Kanan said. "Happy hour."

"You're going to want a stiff drink or two after this," Hera said, bringing *Expedient* around in a wide arc. She looked at him. "This is not what you'd consider a safe bet. Are you sure *you* want to do this?"

Kanan took a deep breath. It wasn't even a dare he'd take on his drunkest day. It was insane—but it had all been. And he had to admit he'd felt better these past few days doing something—even a stupid something—than he'd felt in years of running. "I've got nothing else to do. Let's go for it."

"All right." Hera looked at the Sullustan. "Strap yourself in, Zal. Everybody else—hang on!"

Vidian had had quite enough of people telling him what he couldn't do.

As a guild safety inspector, he'd given edicts to police but had no power to enforce them, as his corrupt supervisors constantly undermined him. He'd transformed his image and position such that no one could say no to him—and yet people tried anyway, trying to protect their old ways of doing things.

The gunslinger and his friends, it was obvious, were trying to prevent him from destroying the moon. Were they saboteurs working for Baron Danthe? The baron had set up the near-impossible production threshold for Vidian to meet; he might well fear the acclaim success would give the count. And Vidian knew the baron had spies about, inquiring after Vidian's "independent consultant," Lemuel Tharsa. If so, then Vidian was all the more ready to destroy the moon. No one would say no to him in this.

He retained the upper hand now, through his logic and careful preparations. The berserk antics of the fool pilot had changed nothing. He'd added his own precautions to Skelly's scheme, and those included dispatching more baradium haulers than were necessary. Already, the redundant vessels were moving into the area recently harried by the renegade. It would only mean a little lost time, not enough for the xenoboric acid to destroy the bombs he was implanting in the moon. It was the same kind of acid Lal had fallen into on Gorse, a refining necessity; *Forager* was full of the stuff. But it wouldn't devour his plan.

And the one random variable was about to be canceled out. The run-amok freighter was out of space to roam, hemmed in between the collector ship's weapons and the swarm of TIE fighters now arriving on the scene. He'd thought of everything. It was his strength, his power. One day, the difference between success and failure for the Empire might be a simple thing someone else would overlook. It would not be his fault, and would never happen on his watch. He would see everything, and act.

"We are at a safe distance from the target moon," he said. "Reorient to face it."

The engines thrummed, and Cynda came fully into glistening view. Vidian didn't bother to look at it for more than a second.

"Give me an update on the enemy," he commanded the nearest cybernetic assistant. Vidian never used the bald woman's name; it didn't seem necessary, after her surgery.

"The freighter has not attacked," she droned. "It is circling. Probing *Forager*'s energy shield."

"Is there a weakness?"

"No, my lord. The only gap in the energy shield is rearward, along the horizontal axis of the vessel. The thrusters produce a flux when ignited."

Vidian froze. The engines had just been activated a few moments earlier. And it was at the tail of the ship, above the thrusters, where the shipping bays sat, open to space . . .

"Proximity alarm!" the female cyborg said. "Unauthorized vessel on approach!"

Vidian was already looking at the scene, his optical feed having been switched to the rear external cams. Pursued madly by half a dozen TIE fighters—and those were just the ones in firing range—the errant freighter raced toward *Forager*'s aft. "What are you waiting for?" Vidian said. "All defensive turrets, fire!"

Outside, *Expedient* rocketed through the cross fire toward the rear of *Forager*. Rows of landing bays perched atop and tucked beneath the glowing thrusters, open to space. "An open door's as good as an invitation," Hera said.

But the freighter was going far too fast, Kanan thought. "This'll be close!"

At the last instant, Hera fired *Expedient*'s attitude control jets, spinning the vessel around 180 degrees. The ship entered the bay tail-first, piercing the magnetic screen. Hera fired the main thrusters, burning off speed—not to mention the chrome off any loader droids in their path.

Expedient struck the landing surface, scraping noisily across the deck as it slid inward. It was a long hangar, and the freighter needed all of it to slow down. Kanan clutched the armrests, knowing the back wall had to be there somewhere . . .

A violent jolt shook the vessel, rocking Count Vidian's underlings. Above, a droid slipped between the catwalk and the railing and fell to the main deck with a crash.

Vidian, prepared for the impact, was unshaken. "All troops aboard *Forager*," he transmitted, "stand by to repel boarders. Enough is enough!"

CHAPTER FIFTY-ONE

"WE'RE STILL ALIVE!"

Skelly had said it, but Kanan was as amazed as anyone. And Hera was simply straightening her gloves as if nothing had happened.

"You're incredible," Kanan said. "I'm permanently moving to the passenger seat."

"Time to get out of it." Hera stood, checked her weapons, and made for the airlock. "Come on, Zal!"

Zaluna took a deep breath and retrieved her pouch of electronic magic from behind the acceleration couch. She met Hera at the door.

Vidian was almost certainly at the head of *Forager,* where the transmitter was. "Do you have anything else aboard we can use?" Hera asked Kanan. "We don't know the layout."

"I think so." Adjusting his holster, Kanan walked down the aisle to a storage compartment. He knelt before the bin and opened it. There, beside Skelly's bag of improvised explosives, which he'd hidden for safekeeping, was part of the Cynda emergency kit: a rappelling gun with an automatic winder. He passed it to Hera.

He was about to close the bin when he glanced at his traveling pack—the one he'd carried with him when leaving Gorse. A thought occurred to him, and he unzipped it and felt around for something inside.

His lightsaber.

It was there, hidden innocuously inside the canvas carrying case for a blaster riflescope. Kanan hesitated for a moment before removing the case and strapping it to his left leg, opposite his holster. He wasn't going to use it, of course, but unlike on Calcoraan Depot, the chances of the ship being searched were pretty good. He didn't want anyone to find it.

He turned back to see Skelly watching him. For a moment, Kanan worried he would ask about the scope case—he had no rifle, after all—but he quickly realized Skelly was eyeing his bag of death.

"I'm not having you blow us all up," Kanan said. He lifted Skelly's bag. "This is coming with me for safekeeping."

"You'll blow yourself up just carrying that." Skelly forced himself to stand. "It's all right. Leave it. I'll go with you."

Kanan frowned. "You can barely walk!"

"So I can keep up the rear. Put that down and let's go."

Forager's interior was one huge automated factory floor, Kanan discovered. The seven spheres that formed the body of the ship intersected in a row, producing a single atrium several stories high that stretched forward out of sight. Vats, centrifuges, conveyor belts, pneumatic tubes—it was a Denetrius Vidian production, if ever there was one.

Standing at a railing overlooking the area, Hera momentarily marveled at the sight. "It's like someone crammed all of Moonglow's refineries into a starship."

"Hurry, so we can save the real one," Kanan said. He could see the stormtroopers down on the main floor now, running toward them from the far end. Metal stairs led down to what would be more than a kilometer of hard fighting, nearly the length of a Star Destroyer.

"Can I . . . go back . . . and get my bombs?" Skelly said, panting at the railing. He'd fallen behind twice—and simply fallen once—on the way here from the landing bays.

Kanan shook his head and looked at Hera. She was staring up at the rafters. "What have you got?"

"Things are looking up," she said, pointing. "There!"

Kanan squinted. Up top, a tramcar track suspended from the ceiling ran the length of the room between two banks of industrial lighting. Kanan's eye traced back toward his location—and the rungs of a ladder attached to the wall behind them, fifteen meters high or more. The ladder was the only route to the tramcar: There was no way the rappelling gun could carry more than one at a time.

Hera had the idea; Kanan made the plan. It was how things were working out between them. Kanan sent Hera up the ladder first, having her stop at intervals to turn and provide cover fire, if necessary, against any arriving Imperials. Then he sent up Zaluna, who went without complaint. Heights were apparently one more thing Zaluna wasn't afraid of.

Skelly was his problem. He'd figured the guy had to go up ahead of him or he'd never go at all, but it was making their progress impossibly slow. Skelly was in pain—and reluctant to use his right hand for a grip.

"Go on, Skelly!" Kanan yelled, after the third time he tuckered out.

Skelly dangled precariously, his right arm looped around a rung. "Just give me a—"

Skelly never finished his statement. Blasterfire peppered the wall around him, causing him to lose hold. Kanan grasped vainly at the man as he fell past, flailing. "Skelly!"

The man fell outward, his body slamming against the railing of the balcony they'd been standing on earlier. Limply, Skelly fell over the side and out of sight—presumably toward the factory floor. High above, Hera opened fire on Skelly's attackers.

Hanging partway off the ladder, Kanan craned his neck to see any sign of Skelly. He couldn't see anything—and now, more shooters were moving into the area. Hera called down from above, "Kanan, come on!"

Kanan scrambled up the ladder, narrowly escaping being shot several times in the process. Reaching the apex, he stepped out onto the short metal landing next to the parked tramcar. Hera was in it already, hanging over the front and looking down. "No sign of Skelly," she said. She looked back, her face fraught. "I don't think he could have survived that!"

"Nothing to do," Kanan said, piling into the tramcar with the others. "We'll look when we come back—*if* we come back. Let's move!"

Once activated by Hera, the tramcar rattled along across hundreds of meters. It rode on a single rail—probably electrified, Kanan thought—attached to the ceiling by metal framing.

Things went quietly for a minute, until the stormtroopers below tripped to where the intruders were. Then it was open season on the rafters, with blaster shots deflecting off the girders, the ceiling—even a few off the tramcar itself. Passing control of the vehicle to Zaluna, Hera and Kanan fired back, but the targets were too small and numerous. And they hadn't even traveled halfway across the factory floor.

"We've got to do something before they bring out the heavy artillery," Hera said.

Kanan nudged her. "Check that out!" He pointed down and ahead to enormous cylinders on the factory floor, made of some kind of special clear composite. Inside was liquid, a shocking green in color. "Xenoboric acid—like in Lal's factory!" It made sense: This was a thorilide refinery, after all. Kanan and Hera looked at each other, shrugged simultaneously, and then turned their weapons on the nearest vat.

Multiple blaster shots struck the container at the same place. A sick groan later, the protective material gave way, releasing a fountain of acid. A stricken stormtrooper dropped his weapon and howled so loudly they heard it near the ceiling. The vat's structure failed completely then, unloosing a gusher onto the floor. Now all the stormtroopers were on the move, rushing to alcoves to escape the effluent and throw off their boots and affected armor.

Kanan and Hera targeted another vat, and then another, as the tramcar advanced. The trick was clearing their way better than any army. He grinned at Hera, hoping to see her smile in return.

Instead, he saw her grimace as the tramcar ground to a halt. Hera moved to Zaluna's side and punched futilely at the control buttons. "That's it for the free ride," she said. "Someone knows we're here."

"I would think those guys," Kanan said, pointing down. Laser shots were striking the ceiling again, but with less accuracy than before: The shooters were all huddled on top of control consoles and other equipment, avoiding the acid flow. He looked at the tramcar's control panel. "I guess I can rewire this thing."

"I know I can," Hera said, scrambling over the side. "You keep shooting! We're running out of time!"

Kanan turned to do exactly that—when Zaluna poked him. She pointed above, to where the frame of the tramcar track connected with the ceiling. A row of girders ran the length of the line, offering a small, protected crawl space above. But Kanan realized it would be a long hands-and-knees scramble—and it would take someone small and athletic to get up there.

"I don't think I could make it up there," Zaluna said. "But one of you could go."

"We don't know how to access the global communications systems you talked about," Hera said.

"Wait a minute," Kanan said, getting an idea. "Hera, get back in!"

As she did so, he put down his blaster and reached for the rappelling gun. Anchoring his legs behind the dashboard, he leaned out and fired at one of the horizontal supports, far ahead. The hook snapped taut, and the motorized winder groaned into action. The current might have been cut from the track, but the tramcar still moved along it—if slowly.

"We're too heavy," Hera said. She looked up to a debarkation area, far ahead. "All three of us will take forever. I'll take the upstairs route."

Zaluna looked at her, face fraught. "Hera, I don't think you should go alone."

"And you shouldn't, either," Hera said. "Kanan, make sure she gets there. Get that warning message out!" She climbed onto the side of the car and leapt. Nimbly grabbing the side of one of the supports, she twisted her body around and disappeared into the small horizontal space, safe from the stormtroopers' shots.

The cable rewound, Kanan released the hook and prepared to fire again. Zaluna, looking up in vain to catch any sight of the scrambling Hera, shook her head. "We're going to have to send the message while Vidian's in the room, aren't we?"

"You've come this far, Zal. The hard part's over." Kanan grinned and fired the grapple. His Jedi teachers had warned him about lying to his elders, but he figured this time it was for a good cause.

"*Forager* reports being boarded," an ensign called from a terminal. "Incursion force small. Three, maybe four."

"Stand by." Captain Sloane walked to the junior officer's station and looked over her shoulder. *Ultimatum* was receiving some security feeds from the collection ship, but it was difficult to see much. For a moment, she thought she caught a glimpse of a running Twi'lek—and then she definitely spotted the arrogant space jockey.

She shook her head. "Is *Forager* asking for help?"

"No, Captain. Count Vidian is continuing the countdown, waiting for the final injection site to finish its work."

Sloane nodded. Vidian had his own stormtroopers and personal guards over there. It would be unlikely he would need assistance. Still, it was difficult just sitting here, not knowing what to do. It was times like this when she missed being a junior officer herself, having someone around with the answers—

"Captain!"

Sloane turned to see Commander Chamas rushing onto the bridge toward her. "What is it?"

Chamas looked pale. "We have a priority-one message for you."

Sloane stopped. "From the Admiralty?"

"No," the commander said, breathless. "*From the Emperor.*"

The captain's eyes bulged. "I'll take it in my ready room." She was already to the door by the time she finished the sentence.

CHAPTER FIFTY-TWO

COMMANDER CHAMAS APPEARED in hologram, speaking to the *Forager* command crew. "Your linkup to Detonation Control is live, Count Vidian. We read ten minutes until the last charges are implanted."

"I see it." Vidian was already watching the progress at the last injection site. "The delays that fool freighter caused weren't fatal."

He was still aggravated by the failure of *Ultimatum*'s fighters to stop the renegade, but the ship crash-landing on *Forager* hadn't cost him much. The infiltrators had found a way around his stormtroopers, but he had shut down the tramcar line. They'd damaged the refinery area, true—but he had many other harvester vessels on the way.

He looked up at the hologram. "Where is Sloane?"

"The captain is . . . *indisposed*." Chamas seemed agitated.

"She'll miss the show."

"Do you require assistance against—"

"No. *Forager* out." Vidian cut the transmission, and Chamas disappeared. The cyborg had never had any use for the man, and didn't want to talk to him any more than necessary. Not now, in his moment of success.

The sounds of blasterfire came from the southern hallway, one of three portals on the ground floor leading into the command center. Vidian switched to the security cam feed from the hallway and saw nothing unusual at all—just his stormtroopers standing guard. But something was wrong with the image. It was frozen, the soldiers halted mid-movement like statues—even as the sentries in the room with Vidian were firing through the southern door. They saw something he couldn't.

"Lower the security doors on the command floor level!"

Heavy barriers slowly descended from the door frames in the three large entryways. Still shooting at whoever was in the hallway, one of the stormtroopers charged the exit, moving to get through it before the door sealed. But a blaster shot caught him in mid-stride, and he fell on his side. The massive door came down on the soldier's collarbone. It stopped there, leaving a half-meter-high space between the bottom of the door and the floor beneath.

Vidian heard the blasterfire cease. The opening was too small for the attacker to easily exploit, whoever he was. He checked the cam feed again. It was still on the guards standing around motionless, and the door was still open in the image. "Someone's been interfering with what I can see."

A pinging noise came from his command console. A critical moment had passed: The very last set of baradium charges were being loaded onto the derrick for descent into Cynda's deep interior. He couldn't afford any more distractions. There weren't blast doors at the entrances on the upper level of his chamber, but he could place his remaining sentries up there. On his command, the stormtroopers dashed up the steps to the catwalks. That left one route into the room, by which he might root out his real enemy once and for all.

He turned to the command console, his back to the main door. This would be a simple matter.

Kanan stood on guard amid the fallen stormtrooper bodies. They'd beaten Hera here, as he expected, but there was no good way to sneak up on stormtroopers on alert. Now there was at least a way into Vidian's chamber—for one of them. "Ready?"

Looking at the fallen troopers, Zaluna shuddered. "I don't know."

"You knew you'd have to do this alone, didn't you? We can't both sneak in."

"I didn't think we'd get this far." Zaluna put the widget back in her pouch. They'd needed to defeat the surveillance cams on their approach, as on Calcoraan Depot, but the trick didn't work as well when anyone was in the frame. There was no way around that now. "Are you sure you don't want a tutorial on slicing Imperial communication systems?"

"I would if I could," Kanan said. He could hear more troops running in the hall, searching for them. "We're out of time."

"It happens."

The stormtroopers were closing in. Kanan knelt, protecting the doorway in front of her. "I'm sorry you have to do this, Zaluna. You never asked for any of this."

"Neither did you," she said, securing her pouch. "You're a decent person, Kanan, no matter what show you put on for the world. You keep being that way."

With a dutiful salute, Zaluna got down on all fours and peeked beneath the blast door propped up by the body of the unfortunate stormtrooper. She looked back and whispered, "All cyborgs, all the time. It'll be just like evading cams." Then she shimmied under the door.

The room was frighteningly large, with lots of computer consoles about. More places to hide. Zaluna crawled behind one. Vidian's cybernetic assistants were here and there, but their minds appeared to be on their work.

Zaluna quietly moved from one workstation to another, hoping the artificial ears in the room couldn't hear her joints cracking or her heart pounding. *It's just like working my way across the floor of that cantina the other day,* she told herself. It wasn't, but thinking it helped.

Finally, she found a console near the eastern wall that looked to have a connection to the comm system—and a nice little nook behind, where she could tap in and send her warning.

Text would have to do. She'd prewritten it on the tramcar ride: *"People of Gorse, beware . . ."* She would send it and hope for the best.

She was about to connect to the port when a voice came from overhead. "And here's our rodent."

Grabbed by the back of her shirt, Zaluna was yanked upward and outward. Spun about, she saw the moon outside the windows. She saw stormtroopers running down the metal steps to the main floor. And now she looked directly into the terrifying eyes of Count Vidian.

He shook the woman violently. Her bag fell open, spilling forth her blaster and all her devices. Vidian surveyed the instruments. "So they brought a slicer. I knew there was someone else." His other hand on Zaluna's collar, he brought her back face-to-face with him. "If you know about surveillance cams, you should have remembered something else: You don't always know where they are."

He turned and hurled her across the room.

In the middle of firing at oncoming stormtroopers outside the doorway, Kanan heard Zaluna's cry.

The gambit had failed. Kanan shot and shot again, putting his last attackers on the deck. Holstering his blaster, he turned to the door. It had descended farther since Zaluna had gone underneath it: The servos were grinding away, trying vainly to push through the armored obstacle.

Kanan placed his hands along the underside of the blast door and heaved upward. His muscles screamed, fighting against both the heavy door and the mechanism holding it in place. Metal groaned, and then something snapped. He forced the door up half a meter from where it had been—where it would go no farther. It was enough. He slid his legs beneath it and rolled, even as the door began to move again.

Righting himself, he saw the count stalking toward Zaluna's motionless body. Kanan stood. *"Vidian!"*

A stormtrooper charged at Kanan from the left side of the door, his blaster raised. Kanan moved like lightning, grabbing the rifle by its barrel and shoving. The soldier stumbled backward, allowing him to wrest the weapon free. Another trooper came toward him, from behind. Kanan spun, smacking his attacker in the side of the helmet with the weapon.

Vidian charged. Kanan turned the stormtrooper's rifle around. Three blaster shots slammed point-blank into Vidian's body, searing his tunic. Kanan knew that wouldn't stop him—but he had to get the man away from Zaluna. Vidian charged, grabbing for the barrel of the blaster rifle. He ripped it away and shattered it in his bare metal hands.

"Hurry up," the count said, unruffled. "I have a schedule to keep."

Kanan moved his hand to his holster before changing his mind. He'd learned something from their first fight. Instead, he dived to the side as Vidian lunged, hitting the ground long enough to leap again—onto Vidian's back.

Enraged, Vidian clawed at him, raking at Kanan's clothing. His heels digging into the cyborg's metal hips, Kanan wrapped his arms around the back of Vidian's neck and hung on for dear life.

Hera darted from hall to hall, careful to avoid stormtrooper details. They were numerous in this end of *Forager*—and apparently much exercised by her friends' earlier infiltration.

Kanan's been here, all right, she thought, peering around the corner at the bodies of stunned troopers. Other stormtroopers were tending to their companions and helping to defend their station. She wouldn't be able to follow the path Kanan had taken.

Opening a portal leading off the main hall, she stepped into a storage area full of equipment—and loading vehicles, all unattended. There were even several hovercarts like the one Kanan used on Cynda.

A power forklift caught her eye. A heavy-duty repulsorcraft, narrow enough to navigate hallways—with a cab that offered some degree of protection from attackers ahead.

Hera grinned. Driving loading equipment was Kanan's trade, but she'd show him what she could do.

Zaluna awoke to a nightmare. The sound had reached her first—Vidian stumbling about, driving his back into consoles and walls as he tried to dislodge Kanan. Horrific squawks came from Vidian's speakers as electronic circuits tried to express his animal rage.

And yet Kanan kept moving, shifting his hold every time Vidian came close to dislodging him. From headlock to arms around the cyborg's shoulders to a headlock again, the younger man squirmed in response to the count's every move.

Zaluna forced herself to sit up. Her leg hurt horribly where she'd landed—but the only stormtroopers here were on the floor. Vidian's cybernetic assistants milled about near the walls, looking on as the pair wreaked havoc on their work space. Vidian staggered past again with Kanan, nearly stepping on her. She rolled—

—and saw her pistol, on the floor where she'd dropped it. Vidian had a handhold on Kanan's left ankle now, she saw. She had to help her friend. Zaluna dived for the blaster and rose to face the count.

"Zal, no!" Kanan yelled.

Vidian swept forward, releasing his hold on Kanan and reaching for her blaster. She tried to fire—but he had hold of the barrel now. He squeezed. Zaluna saw a flash brighter than lightning as the blaster's energy pack discharged in their faces. She fell backward—and saw no more.

The flash subsided. Kanan, who had remembered what happened when blaster shots struck Vidian, had leapt clear an instant before the flash occurred. His eyes adjusting to the light, Kanan saw Zaluna collapse. "No!"

Vidian staggered, holding his face in his hands. Kanan quickly surmised the man had overestimated his ability to shake off energy attacks. Blaster bolts were one thing; power packs exploding point-blank were something else. Kanan scrambled past him to Zaluna's side. The woman was still breathing, he saw, but her face was burned.

So, he now saw, was Vidian's. Recovered, the cyborg had pulled his hands away from his face. His synthskin facial coating was charred and melted, revealing the metal man beneath. He straightened and stared down the pair.

"This ends now, gunslinger. Draw your weapon."

Kanan was about to—when he heard something else: blasterfire echoing through the huge chamber. He couldn't tell where it was coming from. Looking around, Vidian acted as if he couldn't figure that out, either—nor could he identify the gruesome, grinding sound that accompanied it.

Then everyone saw it: a massive hover-forklift powering its way through one of the upper doorways onto the catwalk above. Two hapless stormtroopers had already been collected by its massive arms—and a third, caught by surprise, tumbled backward over the railing to the command center floor.

The vehicle kept on going, smashing through the catwalk barrier. Vidian, astonished at the new arrival from above, dived to the side—even as Kanan moved to protect Zaluna. With a deafening crash, the forklift and its pinned troopers slammed onto the floor between the infiltrators and Vidian. The lifting arms snapped violently off, one nearly taking out the count's shins.

Hera clambered out of the cab. Vidian looked at her in amazement. "You!"

"That's the trick with surveillance cams, Count. You can't watch all of them at once." She drew her blasters.

Vidian started to claw his way up the pile of wreckage toward her. "You should have tried to run me down. You know your blasters won't hurt me."

"No, but this might." Hera turned and aimed each one at a different tall viewport. "These viewports aren't magnetically shielded—and these blasters are set on full power. I can decompress this whole compartment. If you make a move on my friends—or try to give the detonation command—you'll have a whole new address!"

Vidian responded with a digital snort. "And which of us do you think would fare better in such an event?" He stepped over to a console and clamped his left hand on it. "I won't be going anywhere. And my respiration is augmented already." He shook his head and let out an electronic cluck. "But I find what you've said much more interest-ing. We've come to it, at last. You want to save the moon, Cynda." He looked around at his workers—and at the few mobile stormtroopers, recovering and raising their weapons. "Tell me who you're working for, now!"

"I'm working for everyone. The people of Gorse. The people of the galaxy!"

Vidian seemed surprised. Then he laughed. "I think we have an agitator here!"

"If you destroy the moon, you'll destroy the thorilide," Hera shouted. "The Emperor won't stand for that!"

"Don't be so sure," Vidian said. "I'm smarter than you think." He turned to face the console. "I am going to do this. And then I am going to find out who each of you really is. And the Empire will de-stroy everyone important to you."

Kanan glared. "You're a little late on that one."

"And your time is running out. Four minutes until optimal deto-nation window." He smiled back at Kanan. "Shall we all wait to-gether?"

CHAPTER FIFTY-THREE

SLOANE KNEW back on Calcoraan Depot that she had walked into a trap. She just didn't know whose trap it was.

The mouthy pilot had told her about Vidian's double identity, his fraudulent test results, and his desire to make the Emperor's deadline by destroying Cynda—and Gorse along with it. She'd thought it all nonsense, and very likely some bizarre test of loyalty from Vidian. After the speaker and his shadowy companions sank into the floor on the hydraulic lift, Sloane had been ready to dismiss the entire thing.

But Vidian had laid it on too thick. He'd tried too hard to ensure her cooperation, insisted too much on speeding the project to a conclusion. Her elevation to permanent Star Destroyer captain—ahead of all the others with more seniority—was more than a bribe. It was a bludgeon, something no one could refuse.

And the suggestion that he might have some way of elevating her to admiral—her, a green captain without a permanent posting yet—was simply insulting to her intelligence and to the service to which she'd devoted her life.

Vidian, the mystery man had said, lived by terrorizing people into meeting quotas. Yet fear of loss of standing was driving him to destroy a resource that the Emperor could have expected would produce for years to come.

And Sloane believed him.

But there was no reporting the pilot's information up the chain—not the usual way. It was too explosive. Instead, she'd returned from Calcoraan Depot to *Ultimatum* where Chamas had arranged a secure connection with Baron Danthe, using the contact information the latter had provided. It was highly irregular to involve a civilian, but Danthe was the only person she knew who had a hope of directly reaching the Emperor or one of his minions.

Silence had followed, during which she'd done her job as ordered. Then, finally, she'd heard back from them in her ready room. The Emperor's people had confirmed that everything the young man said was true. And there was more.

Vidian had already launched one scheme to defraud the people of Gorse, starting before the days of the Empire. By secretly purchasing and controlling Minerax Consulting, he had issued the critical report accelerating the end of thorilide mining on Gorse. That single act damaged the guild he once worked for while lifting the interests of the comet-chaser industry, which he mostly controlled. On Gorse, mining work had literally gone to the moon then, defacing what had been a famous natural preserve.

That had been enough for Vidian, until the past week, when he returned to the system for the first time in years—and Sloane's part in it began. On his return to the system, Vidian had cut the last connection between him and Lemuel Tharsa by using her and *Ultimatum*'s power to eliminate the miners' medcenter where he had convalesced. But that matter was minor compared with the problem he faced meeting the Emperor's new production targets. The newly discovered prospect of destroying the moon for thorilide had been a sudden blessing, and his metal fingers grasped at the reed with full force. There, again, he had used Minerax to lie, asserting that the project would be a successful producer, long-term. Minerax, and its chief researcher: Lemuel Tharsa.

As Vidian had expected, Tharsa's name and reputation had been enough to gain Imperial approval for destruction of the moon. The man and his résumé were real. Hadn't Tharsa been a veteran of the Interstellar Thorilide Guild, before dropping out to change his line to consulting? And hadn't he given the okay to dozens of projects over the past several years, some of which redounded to Vidian's personal profit?

Yes, and no. Because the renegade pilot had spoken truly. Vidian *was* Tharsa. But Vidian had also kept Tharsa's name alive, using it in order to advance his goals and to enrich himself. Moreover, Tharsa's supposed existence helped hide the count's past from others, who might have found his true origin—as a functionary for a guild where everyone was on the take—less compelling than his self-scripted myth of a military ship designer who had taken on his superiors in the name of the troops.

There had been one other consequence: The Emperor hadn't known the truth, either.

Emperor Palpatine's reach and resources were immense. Little went on in the Galactic Empire that he didn't know about—usually, before it even happened. It was a good thing, and it worked to the advantage of all his subjects. But Vidian had spent well to cover his tracks. And perhaps Vidian's past image as a fame-seeking business guru had caused the Emperor to accept his identity as it was described. As long as Vidian was as effective as his reputation advertised, what difference did it make that he lined his pockets playing the show-off?

A whole lot, Sloane now understood. Because "Kanan"—the Emperor's agent, she now accepted—had, through her, supplied his master with the truth. Vidian *had* lied about the lunar test results. Before passing the report along, Sloane had *Ultimatum*'s technical staff confirm the man's claim: Within a year, the vast majority of unharvested thorilide from the moon's remains would decompose in space, destroying the Emperor's precious prize.

Vidian's aides aboard her ship—the ones that existed, anyway—had helped to rig the test, ensuring that false data would be reported. While still docked at Calcoraan Depot, her crack technicians had re-examined every probe droid in *Ultimatum*'s stores. Vidian's people had done a good job of hiding their tampering, but not good enough. In order to fast-track the destruction of Cynda, Vidian had been forced to prepare his deception too quickly.

Of course, the truth would have come out a year after the moon's destruction: Vidian had to know the result would enrage His Highness. And yet, here the count was, going ahead with the project. Sloane wondered whether the quest for revenge had driven the man mad.

But Vidian wasn't insane. He had a plan, outlined in a supplemental document given her by the stranger: an encrypted file from Vidian's computers. The Emperor's experts had cracked it just minutes before, prompting his call. Her anger rose now as she read the file.

Cynda would be destroyed, and within a year would be worthless rubble—but by that time, it would be the responsibility of someone else: likely his underling and greatest nemesis, Baron Lero Danthe. The baron would naturally point at Vidian, who would in turn blame Sloane and her demolition crews' incompetence. He would call her appointment to interim captain premature. And then he would rush to the rescue with another revelation: something so startling that she could barely believe Vidian had concealed it all this time. It was a fact Minerax Consulting had discovered fifteen years earlier, and that Vidian had bought the firm in order to bury.

The moon Cynda did have more thorilide than the nightside of Gorse. But Gorse's dayside held *incalculably* more, all buried under the blazing heat of a sun that never left the sky.

It would otherwise have been a useless bit of knowledge: Organics couldn't toil in that heat. And at the time, the suppliers of heat-resistant droids belonged on the side of the Separatists in the Clone Wars. The stuff was unreachable. And when the war ended, it left Danthe as the monopoly supplier. Such a prize would make Danthe incalculably rich and powerful, she realized. No wonder Vidian had hidden the fact.

And it further explained what she had seen on Calcoraan Depot: workers of Vidian's, trying to reverse-engineer Danthe's droids. Vidian's file described a one-year timetable for having his own droids ready to rush to Gorse's dayside, able to fill the need when Cynda's remains ran out of thorilide. In a sequence of events typical of his preference for neat solutions, Vidian would eliminate a competitor and save the day for the Empire—all while turning a huge profit.

But he would destroy Gorse's population in the process. And worse, he would ruin Sloane's career.

She wouldn't allow that. And neither would the Emperor. The Emperor had no quarrel with destroying places for short-term gains or with dealing harm to rivals. But the galaxy and all its assets belonged to him—and he alone would decide where and when such actions were taken.

That made her next command easy. Walking from her ready room onto the bridge, she knew the next moments would startle her crew as much as her would-be patron.

"Channel to Count Vidian," she said.

Chamas, looking at her with a mixture of curiosity and concern, snapped his fingers. Count Vidian's holographic image appeared.

"Ah, Sloane," he said. "You're back just in time. I'm just about to detonate the charges and pulverize the moon."

"Then I *am* just in time," she said, taking a deep breath before continuing. "*Ultimatum* technical crews—rescind the Detonation Control link to *Forager.*"

"What?" The shimmering Count Vidian looked at her in surprise—as did the very real form of Commander Chamas, standing nearby.

Sloane clenched her fist. "And all stormtroopers aboard *Forager,* in the name of the Emperor: *Arrest Count Vidian!*"

CHAPTER FIFTY-FOUR

IT HAD HAPPENED this way to the Jedi, Kanan remembered. Responding to some command from the Emperor, clone troopers had eliminated the Republic's cherished fighting force. It had been a dark day—by far, the darkest in Caleb Dume's young life. Kanan Jarrus usually avoided thinking about it.

But seeing the stormtroopers turning on their master: That was both amazing and delicious. Even if the Imperials were also pointing their weapons at Kanan and his friends. More troops hoisted open the main door, bringing the total number of white-armored guards to a dozen.

Up atop the bulk-loader, Kanan saw that Hera didn't know what to think. But there was no mistaking Vidian's reaction to the holographic captain.

"This is a rash act, Sloane. Have you lost your mind?"

"You're under arrest for multiple violations of the Imperial legal code. Falsification of testimony to the Emperor. Profiteering without permission of the Emperor. Breach of faith with the Emperor. Attempting to damage or destroy strategic assets deemed vital to—"

"The Emperor," Vidian finished, anger rising. "You dare invoke his name?" He pointed at Kanan. "These—*anarchists* have poisoned your mind against me. They're Gorse partisans, seeking to hinder our project." He looked back outside the viewports at the moon. "A project that must go on!"

"Forget it, Vidian," Sloane said. "You won't be destroying anything today."

Kanan could hardly restrain his response. His gambit had worked, after all.

Vidian stared as the pair of stormtroopers approached him, as if deciding what to do. "I don't think so," he said. He looked over to a pair of his cybernetic assistants. "Restore the Detonation Control uplink."

Sloane snapped at him. "We already disconnected—"

"You disconnected nothing. The injection towers, the logistical systems—you only installed them. My workers manufactured them— and my workers can take back control for me at any time."

"If that's the way you want it," Sloane said. "Death warrant extended to all workers on *Forager*'s bridge. Stormtroopers, fire!"

The stormtroopers executed their order—and several of Vidian's aides—immediately, at point-blank range. Vidian yelled something, but Kanan didn't hear it. Blasterfire blazing all around, he hit the deck. Scrambling behind the smashed remains of the forklift cab, he saw Zaluna. She looked rough, her face a scorched mess.

We've got to get out of here. He looked back to see Hera scrambling down the bulk-loader to the floor, dodging shots as she did. All around, Vidian's droids and aides fell.

Blaster in hand, Kanan considered joining in before having second thoughts. For an older man—if any man was still in that body— Vidian had worked into a superhuman rage. Whatever source powered the man's limbs, it had yet to run out of juice. Shaking off a blaster shot from a stormtrooper, Vidian launched himself at his attacker, crushing the man's helmet in his hands. A horrific scream later, and Vidian was on to another stormtrooper.

Kanan spotted a newly opened portal to the side. Hera provided cover fire as Kanan lifted Zaluna's body. He rushed to the exit and set her down outside the door.

"Wait here," he said.

"That . . . a joke?" she muttered.

"Sorry." Kanan turned back to face the room.

Hera, even amid chaos, remembered what they most needed to do. "The comm console," she called out, pointing past the latest melee. She leapt out from behind the forklift, even as Kanan bounded from the other side.

Vidian was already there.

The last stormtrooper had already fallen, Kanan realized too late. To a person, Vidian's workers were all down, too—just more workplace casualties in the count's machine. Only he, Hera, and Vidian remained here alive. And Vidian had just completed punching in a series of keys. "Detonation Control linkup restored," Vidian said. "Just over a minute to spare."

It was the same smug, self-satisfied voice they'd always heard from Vidian—but the man himself was much changed. His tunic was in tatters; his artificial skin and nose had been scorched off his face, leaving just a charred silver mask. Sparks flew from his mechanical joints. Yet he was unbowed. He turned back to Kanan and Hera. "I don't know what you told Sloane. But once the Emperor sees my results, it won't matter."

"Your results?" Hera yelled. "Destruction and genocide!"

Vidian snorted. "You're going about this wrong, you know. You'll never get anywhere against the Empire. You're too undisciplined, too disorganized."

"We'll learn," Hera said, brandishing her weapon. "The people will stop you. We'll stop you."

"We've had this fight before, the three of us. You don't have anything that can hurt me."

"Maybe *I* do." Kanan felt for the holder on his left leg where his lightsaber was hidden.

"Nonsense," Vidian said, waving his hand dismissively. "If you had anything, you'd have used it already. Right?"

Hera looked searchingly at Kanan as Vidian turned back to the console. Kanan began to reach for his secret weapon—but then he paused. Something, somewhere told him: *No, not that. Not now.*

Not yet.

"Forget him, Twi'lek," the cyborg said, reaching for the console. "He doesn't have what it takes to stop me."

"But I do," said Captain Sloane, hologram flickering back into view. Her expression was icy, her eyes narrow. "*Ultimatum* gunnery control, target the transmission tower and fire."

Now Kanan moved. Moved the way his instincts told him to go. He dived not at Vidian, but at Hera, bowling her over even as one of the viewports behind the count lit up like a hundred suns.

If there was a sound, Kanan didn't hear it. There was only light, and motion, and heat as *Forager* wrenched violently under the impact of the Star Destroyer's turbolaser barrage. Rolling away from Hera, it took what seemed like an eternity for his eyes to adjust. The lights were out in the command center, and Vidian was staggering around like one caught in a hurricane. Kanan realized why, looking out the windows. It wasn't just *Ultimatum,* now, but the TIE fighters pummeling *Forager*'s energy shield. The vessel was in one piece—for the moment—but every strike on the shield shook everything inside madly.

Somehow, Vidian reached the console again. Kanan was ready to go after him, even shaken—but this time it was Hera who grabbed him, keeping him down close to the floor. He saw the reason. *Forager*'s superstructure was holding, but the transmission tower, visible through the room's viewports, shook itself to pieces under a direct hit on the shield from *Ultimatum.*

Sloane had called her shot, Kanan realized. And her gunners had done their jobs.

His chance to destroy Cynda gone, Vidian howled and turned. He ran back through the main entrance, paying Kanan and Hera no mind. Finding his blaster on the floor nearby, Kanan rose to follow Vidian.

Behind him, Hera called out. "Kanan, no!" He looked back. She was still getting to her knees near the door he had dragged Zaluna through, beneath the catwalk that had been damaged earlier. "We have to get to a—"

Time stopped for Kanan. And then it started again, slowly.

He saw everything. He saw the TIE bomber outside, unloosing its torpedo at *Forager*'s energy shield. He saw the bridge shake violently, in response. He saw the heavy durasteel catwalk, already weakened from Hera's forklift entrance, snap from its moorings. He saw it fall toward Hera. Hera—not oblivious, but in no position to get out of the way.

He recognized the obstacles between them—the debris and the bodies, lying across the fastest route. Without thinking, he swept them away with his mind, clearing a path. No barrier blocked him from Hera.

And he moved. He moved faster than when he'd saved Yelkin, faster than he'd remembered moving in years. All in the hope of grabbing her and diving beneath the doorway.

Except time moved faster, too—faster than his hopes. He reached her too late, just as he'd been too late to save Master Billaba. The Force had been too late for many that day. But it was with him now, as he slid to the floor by Hera's side. Hera, knowing the danger she was in, put her hand up as if to shoo him away, to safety. Kanan looked instead upward, waving with his hand—

—and suspending the giant catwalk in midair, centimeters from his and Hera's heads.

She stared at it, dumbfounded—and then at him. Self-conscious, Kanan shoved at the air, pushing the levitated mass off to the side. It landed with a colossal crash.

Forager shuddered again under the Imperial attack. The view outside was a thing of perversely wondrous beauty, he thought: flashes of light before the moon as the starfighters made their runs. But it all paled before the look he saw here in the darkness, in Hera's eyes.

"But—" she started to say. "But you're—"

With a wry smile, Kanan put his finger to her mouth. "Shh. Don't tell anyone."

She looked at him for a long moment in wonderment before understanding came to her—and a gentle smile came to her face. She nodded. "Let's go."

CHAPTER FIFTY-FIVE

THE LIFE POD SOARED from *Forager*. Kanan hunched over the small circular viewport and looked back at the collector ship. Several other small pods were jettisoning away, he saw—and the Empire was watching every one.

"TIE fighter on our tail," he said.

"We don't have a tail. We barely have an engine." Hera guided the small stick directing the vehicle. It was about the only control she had. "I think the TIE's just following."

"I know." There wasn't anything to do. Kanan turned from the viewport and returned to dabbing gingerly at Zaluna's burnt face with a bacta-infused pad from the medpac.

Ultimatum was still pounding away at *Forager;* as soon as it finished, Kanan knew it would likely begin sweeping up all the life pods. Sloane would be looking for Vidian, but she'd find Kanan and company instead.

"You still can't see?" Kanan asked Zaluna.

"There's nothing good to see anyway," she replied.

———

Vidian waded through a river of acid. It was everywhere on the factory portion of *Forager:* ankle-deep in some places, waist-high in others. It was destroying the flooring, and had already eaten into the bulkheads below; he anticipated explosive decompression at any minute.

The crossing had started as a panicked mechanical run—and then slowed to a hideous slog as his legs wasted away to skeletal struts. His arms had been further damaged, too, in the trip. There had been no other choice, no other way to his destination.

He'd remembered something. The intruders had come in a baradium hauler. It was intact, he saw through the few still-functioning surveillance cams: ready to go. He would use it, eschewing the one-trip life pods. The freighter might be lost in the confusion, he hoped; he might be able to make it to one of the drill sites on Cynda, where there was still time to detonate the explosives and meet the Emperor's quota. He would find a way.

This was Baron Danthe's doing, somehow. It had to be. It was impossible to imagine a few would-be rebels and a substitute captain could've reduced his reputation and career to shambles. Detonating the moon, he was sure, would restore him—between the moon and the sunward side of Gorse, the Emperor would have thorilide for a thousand fleets.

And if it didn't, the freighter still had hyperdrive and a full cargo of baradium-357. That was an important resource, and something to build upon someplace else if necessary. He had come back from nothingness, before. Perhaps it wouldn't take twenty years this time.

But he wouldn't have to do that. He would finish the project.

Vidian staggered on failing limbs into the landing bay. The place was a mess of fallen beams and bulkheads—but the troublesome freighter was right where it was supposed to be, ramp open. He thought it ironic that it, of all things, would be his deliverance.

Reaching the ramp, Vidian looked out through the landing bay's magnetic field. *Forager,* tumbling out of control, now, was turning to face Cynda. Convenient for a quick trip, Vidian thought. *Efficient.*

Vidian staggered up the freighter's ramp—and then could go no farther. He looked down. There, on the landing deck slumped against the side of the ramp, was Skelly. The man was a battered, bloodied mess—and yet he had summoned the energy to reach for Vidian's leg strut as he'd walked up the ramp. Skelly clutched Vidian's onetime ankle now in his right hand.

The count tried to shake him off, but couldn't. "Release me!"

"That one . . . doesn't let go," Skelly said. He coughed. "Don't . . . mind me. I've just been . . . out here looking . . . at the moon."

"Don't get used to it," Vidian said, straining to keep climbing. But his acid-damaged legs couldn't give him any leverage.

"Sorry, Vidian. Blowing things up . . . is *my* job. Guild rules, y'know." Skelly shifted around—and now Vidian saw the device in his other hand, connected to a long microfilament line. Vidian's eyes followed the line up and into the doorway of the ship. "I told Kanan . . . we wouldn't need my bag of tricks," Skelly said. "But I didn't say . . . I wouldn't come back for it."

Realization came quickly. *"No! No, don't!"*

"I don't take orders from you." Then Skelly looked out the landing bay entrance at Cynda. He winked. "I saved you, sweetheart!"

He pushed the button.

The flash blinded Kanan at first. The explosion began at the rear of *Forager,* quickly consuming the landing decks and ripping forward. His eyes adjusting, Kanan recognized the familiar characteristic color of a baradium explosion. But this was bigger and more energetic than he'd ever seen.

"Hera, go!"

There was little she could do, except put the life pod's reentry heat shield between them and the blast. The TIE fighter pursuing them was slower to react. Superheated particles from the explosion ripped through the vessel's hexagonal wings, causing the starfighter to tear violently apart. A shock wave comprising not air but plasma and matter expanding outward from the blast zone slammed into their life pod.

Shaken by the impact, Hera fought with the controls, angling the life pod to catch the wave. All around, Kanan saw more effects of the blast. Less fortunate life pods were disintegrating, as were their TIE pursuers. And the electrostatic towers that had been *Forager*'s spokes were flung off in all directions—including toward *Ultimatum*. A long, ragged beam slammed off the surface of the Star Destroyer's hull, opening a fiery gash.

It was enough distraction for Hera, who took the chance to make for Gorse's atmosphere. She powered down the interior cabin lights, and the life pod went dark as it soared, just another piece of debris.

In the darkness, Hera reoriented the vessel so the passengers could look back at *Forager*'s remains. There wasn't much to see. Kanan had no doubt that *Expedient* with its shipload of baradium-357 was the reason. "*Very* naughty baby," Kanan said.

Zaluna shuddered. She hadn't seen the explosion, but she'd felt it. "I—I was hoping Skelly might have survived earlier. That he might have made it."

Hera held her. "It's okay. We got out. Maybe he did, too."

"No," Kanan said, thinking aloud. "He didn't."

Somberly, Hera looked out at the firestorm in space. "The landing bay must have taken a hit from the Star Destroyer."

Kanan shook his head. "No. Skelly did that."

"If you didn't see it," Zaluna asked, "how do you know?"

Hera studied Kanan for a moment. He had gone silent. "He just knows," she finally said. "He just knows."

She turned back to the controls. The life pod sank into the clouds of Gorse's endless night.

FINAL PHASE:
DAMAGE ASSESSMENT

"Emperor's robotic mining plan for dayside brings new era to Gorse"

"Baron Danthe granted oversight of industrial region"

"Vidian's HoloNet site goes dark as disease relapse claims him"

—headlines, Imperial HoloNews (Gorse Edition)

CHAPTER FIFTY-SIX

APART FROM HER promotion ceremonies, Sloane seldom had use for her dress uniform. But this night was different, and it was always night on Gorse.

The regional governor was here in the mayor's regal residence—easily the nicest place on the planet. She recognized several other Imperial captains and an admiral; he had brought with him a Moff, one of the highest authorities in the government. They were all here to drink and gab and celebrate the most important event in the history of industrial production of thorilide: the opening of the sunward side of Gorse to Baron Danthe's heat-resistant mining drones.

It was a huge moment for the world, liable to transform its economy in amazing ways. Gorse's refineries would be necessary; not even the Emperor would destroy the moon and devastate the planet for a onetime benefit when the long-term reward was much richer. And it was all being directly attributed to a discovery by Sloane and *Ultimatum*'s science team. It wasn't, of course; she had simply passed along Vidian's secret report to that effect. But she was being given the credit, and would take it—alongside her crew.

Her crew. Unrelated to Vidian's machinations, Captain Karlsen's posting had just been permanently awarded to her. She was glad Commander Chamas had sent Deltic and her co-workers home to the ship immediately after the commendation presentation, before they embarrassed her in front of anyone else. But they were her embarrassment now. *Ultimatum* was hers.

And the proceedings were only beginning. Later, they would all ride the luxurious shuttle to Cynda, restored once again to its status as a tourist destination. The zone damaged by the test blast was only one of many former natural preserves on the moon; the Empire had wasted no time in reopening another. It would be made available for visits from the rich and powerful: those who had served the Emperor well and those whose influence he sought to court. *That includes pretty much everyone in this room,* she thought.

Taking a drink from the tray of a GG-class serving droid, Sloane thought back on the events of the days since Vidian's death. An intermediary from the Emperor had met with her to follow up on the whole situation. Sloane had spoken completely and truthfully, of course, and he had seen no problem with her testimony. But he had expressed puzzlement over her tale of the young pilot, speaking to her in the dark. This "Kanan" was no agent of the Emperor's, she was told. It didn't make sense, and neither of them had pressed the issue. Did Vidian have another rival, loose, somewhere in the Imperial system? Or was it someone else entirely?

Sloane hadn't shaken the feeling that there was another player out there. Someone allied with the young pilot, pulling the strings. She wondered if she would ever find out.

There was something she *had* found out. She had learned that someone on *Ultimatum*'s senior staff had queried Transcept about Lemuel Tharsa on their arrival. She hadn't authorized it, and it made no sense that Vidian would have done it. She realized what had happened—and outside, on the balcony, she spotted the men responsible.

Nibiru Chamas drank there with Baron Danthe. Danthe saw her and smiled. He was even more radiant and robust in person, she saw. "My good captain," the baron said, raising his glass. "Please join us."

"I am yours to command," she said.

And so was Chamas. *He'd* sent the inquiry about Tharsa, she'd realized, using his authority as an *Ultimatum* officer to help Danthe investigate Vidian's phantom consultant. She wondered how long Chamas had been on the baron's payroll as informant.

Smiling darkly, Chamas raised his glass of wine to her. It didn't look like his first. No wonder, for she had supplanted his position with his patron. Danthe had been grateful, and she saw his hand in the *Ultimatum* staffing move. Perhaps Chamas had sought her chair. If so, then no matter: This was the way things worked in the Empire.

She stepped to the railing with the baron. Chamas, realizing his glass was empty, excused himself. It was humid as always on Gorse, and none of the visitors were out here—but she had gotten used to it. She looked up at Cynda, well past full now. It would continue to shine, and to set Gorse to rocking every so often. And one day, it would probably tear itself apart and rain down, as Vidian intended. But it wouldn't be in her lifetime, and tonight she planned to enjoy it.

Baron Danthe watched her as she stared up at it. "I do thank you for alerting me."

"I was alerting the Emperor."

"Of course." Danthe chuckled. "Such a life we lead. Did you ever think that stabbing people in the back would be a way to get ahead?"

"It's the way the game is played," Sloane said, a little surprised at his openness. "I prefer flying my starship."

"And defending the Empire against—*whatever.*" He grinned. "Have you learned any more about the others that were involved?"

"Nothing."

He gave a derisive sniff. "I don't think we need worry too much. A single rebellious act isn't the start of anything. This was a blip. A glitch in the system. Nothing more."

"Maybe." *Or maybe they'd awakened a sleeping gundark.*

Sloane decided there would be opportunities for advancement in a galaxy like that, too.

"To interesting missions ahead." She clinked her glass against his.

The sun rose, and nobody died. Zaluna had lived her entire life where that was impossible.

This was a different world with a different sun, and while she couldn't see it, she could feel its rays warming her body. She could feel the cool air of night gently giving way, hear the dew on the grass crunching as she walked. And all around, she could smell the flowers of the garden waking up.

Kanan had left them after their return to Gorse, thinking it best to meet again here on this sparsely populated agricultural planet sectors away. Zaluna didn't know the name of the planet Hera had brought her to, but then she'd never asked.

She was taking her first step into a new world: a world disconnected from the grid.

It still wasn't clear that the Empire was looking for her for her part in the *Forager* affair. Before bringing her from Gorse to the agrarian world on her fancy ship, Hera had stopped by Zaluna's apartment for her things. It showed signs of having been entered by the landlord, but it hadn't been ransacked. And certainly no video surveillance imagery from aboard *Forager* identifying Zaluna had survived.

The news had made Zaluna wonder. Maybe she hadn't been the focus of any planetary dragnet, along with the others. Maybe it had been all in her mind. Maybe she could've come back from her suspension and gone back to work at Transcept, as if nothing had happened.

But she couldn't. Because something *had* happened. A lot of somethings. And it meant she could never return to that life, if she even wanted to. And she didn't.

Still, she was glad that life on Gorse wouldn't be quite so bad anymore for those she'd left. The miraculous news of thorilide in quantity on Gorse's dayside meant that work was already going ahead, using legions of heat-resistant droids Baron Danthe had ready and waiting. No further damage would be done to Cynda or the places where people lived on Gorse. The miners, by far the roughest customers on the world, would migrate elsewhere. And while the refinery work would stay, the Empire now controlled its own firm in Moonglow: a place where a farsighted Lal Grallik had, in life, made safety improvements that would now become the model for all the other factories there. The Empire had gotten the efficiency it had wanted out of Count Vidian's trip after all—and yet people would be safer all around. Hera had particularly liked that thought. *"Victory through unintended consequences,"* she'd said.

The house they had found for Zaluna was abandoned and half in ruin, but it was cheap and quiet. The person Hera bought it from had said the garden out back had been planted by another older woman, long since dead; it was direly in need of care no one would give. Most of the planet's settlers had moved to places like Gorse to find work.

Brushing her fingers against the blooms, Zaluna couldn't imagine a sillier prospect.

She felt for the steps beneath her feet. There was a tree at the end of the path; walking up to it reminded her of the cemetery at Beggar's Hill, with its large monuments.

"Keep walking, Zal, and you'll bump into it."

Zaluna smiled. "You're still here, Kanan!"

"Enjoying the weather. Gorse was a steam bath." Zaluna felt his hand on her shoulder. "You doing all right?"

"Better than ever," she said. She began to walk past the tree, with Kanan's hand still on her shoulder. "What do you think of my garden?"

"It's good," Kanan replied. "You know you can get those eyes treated, right? To get your sight back."

"Like Vidian?" Zaluna chuckled and shook her head. "No, I think I've seen enough. I have a place to live, and there's a little girl who visits daily to help me with things. But I'll be helping myself soon." She gestured backward. "And look! I have a tree!"

Kanan laughed.

"I'm thinking it's Skelly's tree," she said. "A nice monument, don't you think?"

"Well, there are some twisted clinging vines over there I would have thought of instead."

Zaluna lifted her head to face the sky and sighed. "No, Skelly's ashes are probably still back there, raining down on Cynda. I think he'd like that."

Kanan didn't respond for a moment. And then: "That works, too."

She heard someone coming up the walk from the house. "I'm ready to go," Hera said.

"Always on the move," Zaluna said.

She felt Hera's hands on hers. "Are you sure this is what you want, Zal? You have skills. There are others you could help."

Zaluna shook her head. "I can't save Hetto—not now. I know what you're up against, and it's beyond me. Wherever he is, Hetto would never want me to risk my life trying to save him. And if he's in a bad place, he'd probably rather imagine me living somewhere nice like this. It's certainly better than where we were!"

Kanan laughed. "She's got you there."

Hera hugged her. "Take care—and thank you."

Zaluna walked to the edge of the gravel road with them. "And now," Kanan said, "I get the pleasure of walking this gentle lady back to this mysterious starship of hers." Kanan had been dropped off by a tramp freighter, and had yet to get a look at what she and Hera and had arrived in.

"I see," Zaluna asked. "Are you traveling together?"

"We haven't discussed it," Hera was quick to say.

Zaluna smiled. "You'd better take him with you," the woman said, "or I'll put him to work." She turned and walked back toward the garden.

CHAPTER FIFTY-SEVEN

KANAN AND HERA walked the long sylvan road from Zaluna's house.

"I think she'll be fine," Hera said for the third time. "The medic I took her to said she's healing nicely."

"Oh, sure," he replied again. They had done an excellent job of talking about nothing on the walk—indeed, since the life pod landed on Gorse. They'd parted quickly then, allowing Kanan time to leave a trail placing him on Gorse during all the previous action. Sloane might know his name, but as far as Imperial surveillance was concerned, he was just one more suicide flier who'd left Gorse when the work dried up.

They approached the small hangar she had rented outside the little town. Not turning toward him, she asked, "So what's next for you?"

"Well, you know me. A force always in motion."

"I do know you." She kept walking. "So what do you think about what Zaluna said?"

"What, going with you?" Kanan shrugged. "Well, you know what

I've said. You're great company." He eyed her. "But I don't think you're looking for a traveling companion, are you?"

"Not like that." She stopped outside the door to the closed hangar, and he did the same. She looked up at him. "What's happening to the galaxy is serious, and I mean to do something about it. If you mean only to mind your own business," she said, offering her hand, "then I wish you luck in your travels."

He looked down at her hand, and then at her. "I still haven't seen this ship."

"And you won't. The fewer people see it, the better."

He scratched his beard. "It sounds pretty large. Must be a lot on it to keep up."

She stared at him for a moment—and nodded. "Yes, there is."

"You might need a crew for something like that." He looked at her pointedly. "Not a traveling companion. Not a revolutionary. Crew." He thrust his hand into hers.

She flashed a shrewd smile—and shook his hand. "I can live with that."

Kanan turned and clapped his hands together. "Great! I just hope it's not as big a mess as the ship I just left."

"Well, you're going to love this," she said, opening the door to the hangar.

So. Kanan Jarrus was a Jedi. Or rather, he had been in training to become one when the Emperor betrayed them all.

It was just a guess. He hadn't said anything more to Hera about that moment aboard *Forager*. It was possible that he was just some random person who happened to have the ability to use the Force. Someone who, in a rush of adrenaline, had reached out to the universe for a great feat—and who had seen his prayer answered.

But Hera didn't think so. When she was a girl, the Jedi had helped her people in the Clone Wars. Although she had been too young then to remember specific events from those days, her father had told her, time and again, of the Jedi in action. Later, she'd watched many historical holos—all of them now banned—of Jedi in action. She understood that Jedi abilities weren't some suit of superpowered armor that someone could leave at home, or abandon in a garbage can. The Force influenced and enhanced every action of a person touched with it, whether they were conscious of it or not.

And no one but a Jedi could do the things she had seen Kanan do. The brawl in Shaketown, the escape on the hoverbus, the battle with Vidian—in each, she'd seen a man acting at the outer edge of human performance. And in all cases, she'd somehow thought him capable of doing even more. It seemed as if he'd identified a line that he would not cross, and had stuck to it.

Kanan had gravitated toward a dangerous calling on Gorse, because to him it wasn't dangerous. And it was a solitary trade, so he secretly could call on his prodigious talents if danger struck. She suspected that described all the odd jobs he'd taken on in his life. It was the strategy of someone trained in a certain discipline, and yet forbidden from practicing it. That, his nomadic nature, and his lack of family ties all added up.

Kanan probably wasn't yet a Jedi when the massacre came. She doubted he even had a lightsaber—all he had in the galaxy was one bag of clothing, and if he'd hidden it in there, she would never go looking for it. Hera wondered how young Jedi became apprenticed. She didn't know, and such information was harder to come by now than just about anything else.

Where had he been, when the great betrayal had happened? Who had he been with? Had someone warned him?

And did that someone yet exist?

Kanan might tell her, someday. Or he might not. She was all right with that. The Emperor had disenfranchised souls across the galaxy, people from all walks of life. A reluctant near-Jedi was just one more of their countless number. Many people would be required for a rebellion to work, all contributing their unique talents. All would be equally important, in their own ways.

He obviously liked her starship, she could see as he walked around it. That was good. He was also smitten with her, she could tell—and she was all right with that, too. She didn't want to tell him that her war had already begun, and that in war, there was no time for anything else. He would probably understand that eventually.

No, she thought, things would be fine the way they were. Kanan would be a great asset to her in the days to come even if he never returned to the Jedi ways.

But she couldn't help but wonder: *What would happen if he did?*

Kanan Jarrus was in love.

The *Ghost,* Hera had called it. It was the ship he'd admired as it passed him on the way to Cynda days earlier—and it was a marvel. Roughly hexagonal in shape, it was a light freighter with lots of modifications—all of them, as near as he could tell, improvements. The two main engines jutting out the back were top-notch pieces of equipment, better than anything he'd seen on Gorse or anywhere else. A cockpit sat front-and-center above another bubble housing a turret for a forward gunner. It had symmetry many Corellian cargo ships lacked—and even a small excursion module mounted aft.

After piloting dingy freighters and explosives haulers, after riding in nasty commercial liners and the holds of mining ships, Kanan found *Ghost* a breath of pure oxygen. He would kill to fly it—and as Hera had joked, he might have to. It was hers, all hers. That was fine. He'd welcome the ride.

A nightmare had begun for everyone, years earlier, and it continued in almost every way that mattered. The galaxy hadn't awoken from it yet, and maybe it never would. But Kanan had always been about going to perdition in style, and *Ghost* was a great way to get there.

Particularly with the company.

She was watching him as he admired the starship. Hera had hidden it well, constantly looking away or fiddling with some part—but Kanan was well trained in knowing when female eyes were on him. Things had changed there, too. Hera had been mildly curious about him before, but the events on *Forager* had definitely influenced her attitude toward him. That, or he had somehow gotten a lot more attractive.

Either reason was fine. Any excuse to be in her company was a good one, as long as she didn't push the matter. Hera knew one little thing about his past now, which was one more than he knew about hers. He hoped she'd figure out it had no bearing on who he was. If delivering pinpricks to the Empire was what gave her a thrill, he could certainly help her without getting into all that.

Perhaps the answer will come to you in another form, Master Billaba had said years earlier when he'd asked what a Masterless Jedi should do with his time. He'd sought answers in dangerous jobs and travel, in cantinas and carousing. Hera was a new and very different answer: as good a way to spend his time as any.

The people who had taught Kanan as a child had left him with a handful of skills and some parting advice. Nothing more. That had been their total legacy. Heeding their instructions was all he owed them. He would continue to avoid Coruscant, to avoid detection. He didn't understand what he needed to "stay strong" for, but he'd continue to defend himself against anyone who challenged him.

And the Force? Well, it might be with him, or it might not. Kanan would get by, either way. He always had.

He slapped the underside of the *Ghost* and winked as he made for the ramp. "Let's go somewhere."

THE LEVERS OF POWER

Jason Fry

"ADMIRAL! The rebel ships are accelerating to attack speed all along the line!"

At Lieutenant Habbel's shouted report, the faces in the crew pits of the *Vigilance* turned away from their workstations and sensor suites and up to Admiral Rae Sloane where she stood gazing through her Star Destroyer's viewports at the chaos over the Forest Moon of Endor.

Sloane knew her face was expressionless—just as she knew that her black-gloved hands were motionless behind her back, near her holstered chrome pistol, and her polished black boots were half a meter apart.

Years earlier, aboard the cruiser *Defiance,* Commandant Baylo had repeatedly lifted Sloane's chin and kicked her feet into the proper position, barking about the proper posture for an officer aboard a capital ship.

Back then, as a green lieutenant turned flight-school cadet, she'd been amused at the idea that such a thing could matter; now, she understood how much it did. Fear was a contagion, one that spread from the top ranks to those below. A bridge crew that saw its captain nervous or unsettled was more likely to make mistakes, and mistakes got people killed. Baylo had taught her not to move hastily or raise her voice unless she absolutely had to. *Let your rank do the heavy lifting,* he'd said.

Sloane turned her head and looked across the crew pit at Habbel, anxiously shifting from one foot to the other. What would Baylo have thought of him?

The elderly commandant was long dead, a mummified corpse drifting amid a scree of refuse ejected from the ship where he'd died. He'd been the product of another era and another war. But the lessons he'd taught her applied to this era and this war.

Habbel had pale blue eyes in a doughy red face bordered by gray hair. He was old-line Navy, an officer who knew the regulations and tactical manuals by heart but lacked both the touch with people and the innate feel for a ship that a commander needed. This was as high as he'd ever rise. She wondered when he'd realized it. Or if he had yet.

"Order Sapphire Leader to reposition our TIEs in a perimeter defense," Sloane told Habbel. "And send targeting solutions to the turbolaser crews."

"Aye-aye, Admiral," the lieutenant said, striding away. The faces of the men and women below turned back to their scopes. Sloane scanned the crew pits for signs of unease or anxiety. She didn't see any—the bridge crew had their orders and their routines. That was good—it was the foundation that would let them deal with the unexpected.

But there were new footsteps behind her, an arrogant drumming of bootheels. Suppressing a scowl, Sloane pivoted smoothly, fixing her dark eyes on Emarr Ottkreg before he could reach her. In addition to his many other faults, the Imperial Security Bureau agent had trouble with the concept of personal space.

Behind him came Nymos Lyle, Sloane's executive officer—and the closest thing she had to a confidant. Sloane had been disgusted when Ottkreg arrived aboard the *Vigilance*—she didn't know if that was because of the Emperor's visit to the Death Star, or if it was some new spasm of ISB paranoia. And, in truth, she didn't much care. She'd ordered Lyle to assist the loyalty officer, trusting Nymos to read between the lines and understand her real orders: *Keep him away from me.*

Which Lyle had done, to the best of his ability. But this time, the loyalty officer wouldn't be denied.

"What is it, Colonel?" Sloane asked, eyeing Ottkreg coldly.

The ISB agent looked puzzled.

"We're under attack," he said, his eyes jumping to the flashes of light outside the viewports behind Sloane.

"That's a common hazard during space battles," Sloane said.

Behind Ottkreg, one corner of Lyle's mouth twitched upward. Sloane turned away lest her own expression betray her. She shouldn't provoke the ISB agent, but it was difficult to resist.

Sloane walked toward the bow, her steps deliberate and unhurried, and came to a halt a meter from the bridge viewports. The forward part of the bridge was territory reserved for a ship's commanding officer, with junior officers approaching only by invitation or in an emergency. She knew Ottkreg wouldn't respect that tradition, but at least here the crew would be less likely to overhear whatever he had to say.

As the sound of Ottkreg's boot heels grew louder, Sloane took in the situation beyond those viewports. Below the bridge, the gray decks of her Star Destroyer fell away, tapering to a dagger point nearly sixteen hundred meters ahead. The half-completed sphere of the Death Star hung in the blackness of space, its superlaser like the eye of some malign god. And below the battle station was the green moon of Endor, a jewel set in blackness.

Sloane could see the arrowheads of other Star Destroyers to either side of her, and farther down the line the shining bulk of the *Executor,* the massive dreadnought that served as flagship of the task force.

Hurtling toward the line of Imperial capital ships was a motley assemblage of enemy starships. At this distance they were barely more than blobs of light, but Sloane could identify most of them by their outlines and the way they moved: bulbous Mon Calamari star cruisers, Nebulon-B frigates with jagged bows, even bulky GR-75 transports pressed into service.

The rebel fleet looked like a pirate horde, but she knew better than to underestimate those ships or their captains—they were capable fighters, and their belief in their cause had proven to be absolute.

Between the rival lines, sparks danced and spun. They reminded Sloane of the clouds of night-beetles in the outback of Ganthal, her homeworld. But these were rebel and Imperial starfighters, wheeling in a deadly, ever-shifting ballet.

"Admiral, why are you assuming a defensive posture?" Ottkreg demanded, spots of color in his cheeks. "Our starfighters have been chewing up the traitors—this is the time to advance and destroy them."

"No, it isn't," Sloane said. "There's no need to sacrifice Imperial pilots unnecessarily. Let the rebels burn themselves out in a futile attack on our line—while the Death Star picks them off one by one."

As if on cue, a green laser beam lanced out from the battle station below them, turning a winged Mon Calamari cruiser into a ball of fire.

"Such power," Ottkreg breathed, and there was a terrible greed in his eyes. Then he turned back to Sloane. "But surely it would be better—"

"My orders come from Admiral Piett," Sloane said, her voice frosty. "We're to hold here and keep them from escaping."

Lyle grimaced, his eyes scanning the battle around them. Sloane knew he felt the same way Ottkreg did—he hungered to see the Emperor's enemies destroyed, and chafed at having been told to stay out of the fray.

Sloane made a mental note to remind Lyle not to let his expressions betray him. But at least the younger man knew better than to question the orders of a superior. Ottkreg, on the other hand, wasn't part of the naval hierarchy. Which meant he had no such qualms.

"But why would Piett—" he began.

"He wouldn't," Sloane said sharply, thinking that Piett had long ago made his peace with irrational orders. "This is some plan of the Emperor's."

She watched Ottkreg parse those words for some sign of disloyalty. She wondered if the man found the ceaseless hunt for enemies ex-

hausting. Probably not—no doubt loyalty officers found the hunt in-
toxicating. If they didn't, they wouldn't have become loyalty officers
in the first place.

"We have our orders," Sloane said. "It's our job to accept that the
Emperor sees a larger picture, of which we are but a small part."

Ottkreg nodded, apparently satisfied by that show of fealty. Whorls
and eddies of blue energy danced in space ahead of them, marking
the impact of rebel projectiles and turbolaser blasts against the *Vigilance*'s shields. Sloane cataloged the impact points offhandedly, her
mind tracing the trajectories back to the rebel positions, calculating
range and effective firepower.

"Three Corellian corvettes," she said to Habbel. "Advise Sapphire
Leader to prepare an intercept solution if they maintain their current
course. But he's to await my order before engaging."

She knew Maus Monare—Sapphire Leader—would scowl beneath
his black helmet when he got the orders. Maus liked action.

"How do you know those are corvettes?" Ottkreg asked, looking
from Sloane to the three distant points of light.

"Springbuck, bring up the holotank," Sloane ordered a controller.

The air between Sloane and Ottkreg shimmered as a holoprojector
in the deck activated. Two blue balls appeared—images of the planet
Endor and its moon. Then came a smaller, incomplete sphere—the
Death Star. Arrowheads winked into existence—first the dagger representing the *Executor*, then the other Star Destroyers. Next came the
rebel ships, and finally the pirouetting starfighters—a full, three-
dimensional representation of the battlefield.

Sloane rarely called up the display—the label "holotank commander" had been a naval insult for generations. But if she gave Ottkreg something to look at, perhaps he'd take up less of her time with
annoying questions.

"Here's the *Vigilance*," Sloane said, then swept one hand through
the Star Destroyers. "And this is our defensive line. Up here are the
interdictor cruisers blocking the rebels' retreat. And here are those
Corellian corvettes. You can tap them to see their transponder tags,
current course, estimated velocity, and the like."

Ottkreg peered at the miniature ships. Lyle came to stand beside

Sloane, teeth chewing at his lower lip as he surveyed the rebel ships streaking toward them.

"No deflector shield in the galaxy could stop a shot from that battle station," Lyle said. "Why aren't the rebels retreating?"

"Because they're fanatics," Ottkreg sneered. "A last show of defiance, now that they know their extinction is at hand."

Sloane ignored the gloating ISB agent.

"Is that what you'd do?" she asked Lyle. "Retreat?"

"It's the only sane course of action," Lyle answered, reaching into the holotank. "If I were their commander, I'd regroup and punch my way past our interdictors here. Or scatter—give our tractor-beam operators more targets than they can handle."

Sloane nodded. "Agreed—that's what any rational commander would do. So we need to ask why they're doing something else."

See everything. That had been the motto of Count Denetrius Vidian, the efficiency expert she'd served briefly but at a critical point in her development as an officer. Sloane had loathed him, but she'd also learned from him—his mind had been ceaselessly at work, assessing situations from every angle. How many times had she seen Vidian obsess over some seemingly minor detail that had turned out to be the fulcrum on which everything shifted and changed?

"They're playing for time," Sloane said.

"What's the point, Admiral?" Lyle asked. "They've lost."

"They seem to think otherwise."

See everything. Find the fulcrum.

"Springbuck? What's the status of that B-wing squadron out there? Locate them and prepare an assessment of all potential targets for which confidence interval exceeds fifty percent."

"Aye-aye, Admiral."

"Comm, do we have an acknowledgment from Monare that he has an intercept solution for those corvettes?"

"Sapphire Flight is skirmishing with bandits in sector eight," Communications Officer Ives replied immediately. Sloane noted approvingly that she hadn't needed to look at her scopes. "But they're tracking the corvettes and prepared to intercept."

There were rebel starfighters everywhere—dodging and weaving among the larger warships, pursuing TIEs and in turn being pursued by them. They were attacking the Imperial ships of the line but not the Death Star. The battle station was still secure behind the envelope of shielding projected from Endor's green moon.

"Bridge deflectors to maximum," Sloane ordered. "Lieutenant, what's the latest from the garrison on the Forest Moon? That rebel incursion reported earlier—has it been contained?"

Habbel looked surprised—like most naval officers, he considered anything happening on a planet's surface beneath his notice. She kept her gaze fixed on him as he hurriedly found a comm officer.

"Another rebel ship destroyed!" crowed Ottkreg, staring at the Death Star. "Easier than bagging lake-divers back home on Ponda-kree. And to think this is only a field test—soon the rebel safeworlds will be our targets. Can you imagine having such firepower at your command, Admiral?"

Habbel looked up, his expression stony. Sloane knew what he was thinking—he resented the Death Star project, seeing it as trillions of credits that ought to have gone to the Imperial starfleet.

Commandant Baylo would have worn the same expression.

"An Imperial Star Destroyer is enough for me, Colonel," Sloane replied, raising her voice because she knew her crew would be pleased. But, in truth, the argument held no interest for her. *Power* was what was important—power that could be concentrated where it was most needed. The form that power took was irrelevant.

She'd been aboard the first Death Star once, at Grand Moff Tarkin's invitation. The ruthless Grand Moff had helped her get her first command, as a job captain under Vidian aboard the *Ultimatum*. She'd hated being inside the battle station because she couldn't see the stars—it had felt like being inside a metal tomb.

Which was what the Death Star had become for Tarkin. The Grand Moff had seen the battle station as a symbol. And because he believed the Empire was invulnerable, he figured the symbol of the Empire was invulnerable too. *The ultimate power in the universe,* he'd called it, while his underlings nodded proudly.

He'd been wrong about that, and it had killed him.

Baylo, Vidian, and Tarkin. All of them had shaped Sloane as a young officer, and she still thought of them often—her own retinue of ghosts, always in attendance.

"Admiral? The B-wings are engaged with the *Devastator*," said Springbuck. "If they attack us, we have targeting solutions prepared for the turbolaser crews and Sapphire Flight."

"We'll tell our children about this day, Admiral," Ottkreg mused, staring at the holotank. "The day the Rebellion died."

Sloane nodded at Springbuck, then turned expectantly to Habbel.

"The Endor garrison isn't responding to hails, ma'am," he said. "But the last word was that the insurgents had been captured."

The Forest Moon. That's the fulcrum.

"The last word?" she asked Habbel. "Keep hailing that garrison. Priority channels. I want an update immediately."

The three rebel corvettes survived the passage between the rebel and Imperial lines, their laser cannons firing continual barrages at the same point of the *Vigilance*'s protective shields. Sloane eyed the blue blur of the stressed shields. The rebel gunners were good—it was no easy thing to coordinate fire under constant starfighter attack.

But that focus and discipline hadn't helped them achieve anything. The *Vigilance*'s deflector shields were holding.

Sloane waited until the corvettes had committed to the attack, then gave Sapphire Squadron the order she knew Monare had been hungering to hear: Engage targets and fire at will.

"Tell the turbolaser crews to cover sector seven," she said, turning her head minutely toward the crew pits. "The rebel ships will break that way once Maus starts to chew them up."

TIE fighters screamed across space in trios as the Sapphires swept in from their patrol positions. Sloane counted one flight, then another, then a third, then there were too many to keep track of—the Sapphires were a swarm, their cannons spitting laserfire. A shield flared on the lead corvette, a last spasm of defensive energy before overloading and failing. Beside Sloane, Lyle muttered something, his fists clenched in front of him.

Sloane remained still, confident that Monare had also seen the shield fail. Two flights of Sapphires banked hard to starboard, coming around to target the hole in the corvette's defenses. The vulnerable ship slowed so the corvette to port could come up to assist her, but it was too late: The TIEs' questing lasers chewed through the hull, sending gouts of flame into space. The corvette's bow dipped and then she vanished in a cloud of fire and gas.

Habbel was standing a few meters away, waiting expectantly for her. She glared at him. Did he think an admiral couldn't handle two things at once?

"Something to report, Lieutenant?"

"Controllers aboard the Death Star report a renewed outbreak of fighting on the Forest Moon, led by indigenes. Contact has been lost with a number of stormtrooper units. But there's a report from the Endor garrison that the rebel attack has failed, and they're fleeing into the forests."

Sloane frowned. Even by-the-book combat operations were plagued by contradictory reports and incorrect intelligence— particularly during ground fighting. But something about what Habbel was telling her sounded wrong.

"Which report is the most recent?"

"The one from the garrison, Admiral."

The corvette to starboard broke formation, attempting to flee the TIEs. Sloane nodded as the *Vigilance*'s turbolasers opened up, stitching space with crimson fire. The corvette shuddered, her back broken, and split amidships, fire consuming the fragments. The third corvette was trying to break to port, but she saw at once that the rebel ship was doomed.

"Contact the Endor garrison personally, Lieutenant," Sloane said, turning away from the TIEs' pursuit of the final corvette. "I want a full sitrep as quickly as you can get it."

Habbel stared at her in disbelief. Ottkreg and Lyle had turned from contemplating the holotank to look at her as well. Lyle's expression was quizzical; Ottkreg's contemptuous.

"Ma'am?" Habbel asked.

Sloane jabbed her finger at the Death Star.

"Our entire purpose is to protect that battle station—and the man in its throne room," she said. "Now get me that sitrep, Lieutenant."

For years to come, Sloane's mind would come back to that moment, lingering there in anger or despair. The rebel task force had been caught between an Imperial fleet it couldn't outgun and a battle station invulnerable to attack—an instrument of the Emperor's indomitable will and his lust for vengeance.

That moment, she would come to realize, was the apogee of Imperial power.

Sloane was silent as she received the damage report. Three bow deflector generators and one dorsal unit had burned out under the rebel assault, but the auxiliary units had kicked in, and the shields had held. The Sapphires, meanwhile, had lost six pilots.

The damage to the deflector generators was inconsequential. The loss of the pilots was not, and she felt a burning anger at their deaths. She shoved it away, annoyed with herself. That was the cost of war.

Other Star Destroyers in the Imperial line had suffered far worse damage—the *Vehement* and the *Tector*-class *Harbinger* had been destroyed, while the battlecruiser *Pride of Tarlandia* and the *Devastator* were heavily damaged and not responding to hails. And the rebel assault hadn't burned itself out quite yet—Mon Cal cruisers and Nebulon-B frigates were still slugging it out with the Star Destroyers—some exchanging broadsides at point-blank range, like sea-bound armadas in a conflict from ancient history.

But the Imperial line was holding.

There was only the nagging matter of the incursion on the Forest Moon. Habbel had descended into the crew pit and was standing behind Ives, radiating impatience while the communications officer spoke into her headset. Sloane looked away. They were following her orders; there was nothing she could do but wait.

"The rebel assault was doomed from the start," Ottkreg exulted. He was standing in the holotank, swiveling his head left and right to study the holographic representation of the battle around him. "One last insignificant tantrum thrown by their terrorist movement."

He better move before that flight of A-wings flies up his nose, Sloane thought.

Sloane debated telling Ottkreg it wasn't over—not until they knew the threat to the Death Star's shield generator had been contained. She decided not to. Most likely, the confusion about what was happening on the Forest Moon was the usual fog of war. After the battle, the loyalty officer would make his reports, and it wouldn't do for Sloane to be labeled as overly cautious or doubting Imperial capabilities.

Politics is a blurred lens that obscures vision.

Had Vidian said that, once upon a time? Or maybe that had been Sloane's own conclusion, and it just sounded like one of the dead count's aphorisms.

Maybe so, Count, but I still have to deal with it, she thought.

"Prepare navigational and firing solutions for two different scenarios," Sloane told her crew. "First, a mop-up operation to disable or destroy the remaining rebel ships. Second, pursuit of the nearest concentration of enemy ships should they break off the attack and flee."

"Will do, Admiral," Habbel said.

She didn't know which order Piett would issue, but both were likely. This way, the *Vigilance* would have a head start complying with either.

"Admiral, something's happened."

The voice came from the starboard crew pit, and it wasn't the words that got Sloane's attention, but the tone. The controller—Feldstrom was his name, she recalled—sounded like he wasn't sure if he should have spoken up or not.

This time Sloane moved quickly, the report of her boot heels loud on the decking.

"I've lost my reading on the Death Star shield," Feldstrom said. "It might be a glitch, but—"

"Focus the orbital imagers on the shield-generator site," Sloane said, eyes searching the crew pits for the crewmember responsible for imaging.

Controller Heurys nodded, then looked up in shock.

"I have no uplink from the site," she said. "Visuals are anomalous—"

"Display it on the tank."

The representation of the battle disappeared, replaced by a magnified view from the *Vigilance*'s imagers. Ottkreg stepped back, trying to focus on what he was seeing, but Sloane grasped its importance instantly. A massive plume of smoke rose from the forest where the shield generator had been.

"Switch back to the main tank view, Heurys," Sloane said. "Highlight all enemy starfighters and attack craft."

The rebel starfighters were streaking toward the Death Star. Ottkreg sputtered in indignation as they vanished into the battle station's superstructure, pursued by clusters of TIEs.

Ottkreg was shouting something. Lyle looked numb with shock. Sloane ignored them, her eyes moving between the holotank and the viewports.

Hands behind the back, feet apart. The ultimate power in the universe. See everything.

"Admiral?" Ives called out. "Sapphire Leader requests permission to pursue the rebel fighters into the superstructure."

Of course that's what Maus wants to do.

"No," she said. "They're too far behind to do any good."

Ives relayed her order, then looked up again.

"Admiral, Flight Leader Monare asks—"

"He has his orders. There are more rebel fighters out there."

"Admiral, we must—" began Ottkreg.

"Silence on deck," Sloane snapped, staring out the viewports to where the Death Star hung above the lush green moon.

It was the Imperial ships that were the ones pinned in place, she realized. The heart of the Death Star—of the Empire itself—was under attack. And none of them could affect the outcome of that battle.

Sloane felt her heart start to thump more rapidly, but she knew her expression hadn't changed. And she wouldn't let it. Fear was a contagion, after all.

Her brain was already skipping ahead, subconsciously sorting through odds and eventualities. She let it do its work, tuning out Ottkreg's red-faced objections and the chatter from the crew pits.

But the conclusion she reached surprised even her.

Sloane pivoted on her heels, hands still behind her back, and regarded her crew.

"Recall the TIEs," she said.

Sloane heard her voice rise when she had to repeat her instructions. Commandant Baylo would not have been pleased.

"That order is countermanded!" Ottkreg screeched. "Send every TIE—"

"Don't forget whose bridge you're standing on, Colonel," Sloane said, her voice even but venomous. "You can tell the ISB whatever you like about my actions, but you have no authority to do more than that."

"Sapphire Flight is returning to the hangar," Ives said, breaking the silence, and Sloane nodded.

Ottkreg turned away from Sloane in disgust. Lyle sidled up to her, face pale.

"I'm not questioning your order, Admiral," he said in a low voice. "But—"

"It sounds like you're doing exactly that, Nymos," Sloane said. "There's a chance we could lose this battle. A very real chance, in fact."

Lyle looked aghast.

"But you're putting your career in danger," he said.

"My career?" Sloane replied, her voice once again louder than she'd intended. "The *Empire* is in danger."

She knew without looking that her crew's faces were fixed on her.

Always be on the side of what is going to happen anyway. That had been another one of Vidian's sayings. The efficiency expert had meant it cynically, but Sloane didn't think about it that way. It was about the importance of anticipation and seizing maximum advantage by staying ahead of events. That way you could guide them instead of remaining helpless as they guided you.

"Move to flank position on the *Executor*," she ordered, staring out through the viewports at the massive flagship. "Open a channel to her bridge and send it to my comlink. Turbolaser crews, protect our port flank. And I want all sensors monitoring the battle station—communications, power levels, everything."

If she was wrong, Ottkreg's report would ensure she'd spend the next three decades commanding a fuel tender in some armpit of an agricultural sector. But if she was right, the *Executor* was about to become the fulcrum of not only the battle but also the balance of power in the entire Outer Rim. That meant the flagship must be defended with every Imperial asset available.

Sloane didn't want to be right. But she knew she was.

The faint thrum of the decking beneath Sloane's feet changed in pitch and the *Vigilance* turned to starboard, her turbolasers spitting at the nearest rebel fighters. The *Executor* grew in the viewports until she was a bright wedge—one surrounded by flashes of fire.

Sloane turned from the viewports to the holotank. The rebel cruisers were all closing on the *Executor,* hammering her with fire from every direction.

"Helm, maximum acceleration," she ordered. "Where's that channel to Admiral Piett?"

A moment later, Sloane knew she'd never get an answer. The massive Super Star Destroyer's bow dipped and she began gathering speed, aimed like a spear at the surface of the Death Star.

"She's lost her helm," Lyle said, one hand jumping to his mouth.

The distance between the *Executor*'s bow and the battle station's surface shrank to nothing. From space, the collision looked deceptively gentle at first—an intersection of competing geometries. Sloane knew the reality was anything but—steel decks rippling and twisting, men and women consumed by fire or ripped out into space to their deaths. The *Executor*'s engines shoved her deeper into the side of the Death Star, until she paused and seemed to shudder. And then she vanished in a fountain of flame.

Sloane watched the death of the mightiest warship in the Imperial fleet, hands behind her back. Lyle had both hands on the sill of the main viewport, his head down. Ottkreg was simply staring at the place where the *Executor* had once been.

Sloane turned away from that emptiness. *The past is both ever-present and irretrievable.* Vidian, or Tarkin? She didn't remember.

"Are there any communications from the Death Star?" she asked calmly.

"The chain of command seems to have fragmented," Ives said calmly. "All orders were coming from the Emperor himself, but the overbridge says there's no response from the throne room."

"That's not possible," Ottkreg said. "There's some mistake."

"There isn't," Sloane said. "Ives, order the surviving captains to recall their TIEs and form up on the *Vigilance*. If anyone questions the order, remind them that I am now the ranking admiral."

Lyle turned from the viewport, eyes wide.

"This is madness," Ottkreg said. Sloane couldn't disagree.

"Admiral," said Feldstrom. "I'm picking up power fluctuations from the battle station."

"*Look,*" Lyle said, finger outstretched at the holotank.

Sloane looked. The rebel ships had broken off their assault on the Imperial line and were accelerating away from the Death Star.

"The cowards are running," Ottkreg said.

Sloane drew her pistol and shot the loyalty officer dead. He fell through the holotank and crashed onto the deck, rolling over so his lifeless eyes were staring up at the battle.

Sloane holstered her pistol.

"Has my second scenario been programmed?" she asked. "The one in which we pursued the rebel ships?"

"Yes, Admiral," Habbel said shakily. "The most likely outcome was a rebel retreat to the Annaj system. We've prepared navigational data for a jump there."

"Good," Sloane said. "Send the coordinates to all Imperial ships. Tell them to jump immediately."

Lyle looked down in shock at the loyalty officer's body. Sloane ignored him. There'd be time to explain later how a man so out of touch with reality would have reacted to her order that they retreat. The scenario she'd envisioned still held—except the roles played by the Imperials and rebels had changed. Every second she could act before the Empire's enemies did was now critical, and Ottkreg would have impeded her ability to do what had to be done.

When the Death Star exploded, Sloane barely reacted. It didn't matter anymore. The thrum beneath her feet rose again, and a moment later, the stars elongated into streaks, replaced by the churning chaos of hyperspace.

"We lost," Lyle said in the shocked silence on the bridge.

Sloane looked at him. She'd been running through lists of fleets and shipyards in her head, compiling rosters of admirals, Moffs, and advisers.

"The battle, or the war?" she asked.

"The battle," Lyle said, then shook his head. "*And* the war. Without the Death Star, without the Emperor . . ."

Sloane nodded.

"We did lose the battle," she said. "As for the war, we'll lose that as well if what's left of the Empire fights as if none of this has happened. If we imagine the Emperor can simply be replaced, or the threat of a fleet action alone will bring rebellious planets to heel. So our responsibility is to prevent that from happening."

"And how are we going to do that?" Lyle asked.

Sloane looked from the tumult of hyperspace to the body of Ottkreg.

"For openers, by realizing the next battle's already begun."

Read on for an excerpt from

BATTLEFRONT:
TWILIGHT COMPANY

by Alexander Freed

PUBLISHED BY DEL REY BOOKS

THE RAIN ON HAIDORAL Prime dropped in warm sheets from a shining sky. It smelled like vinegar, clung to the molded curves of modular industrial buildings and to litter-strewn streets, and coated skin like a sheen of acrid sweat.

After thirty straight hours, it was losing its novelty for the soldiers of Twilight Company.

Three figures crept along a deserted avenue under a torn and dripping canopy. The lean, compact man in the lead was dressed in faded gray fatigues and a hodgepodge of armor pads crudely stenciled with the starbird symbol of the Rebel Alliance. Matted dark hair dripped beneath his visored helmet, sending crawling trails of rainwater down his dusky face.

His name was Hazram Namir, though he'd gone by others. He silently cursed urban warfare and Haidoral Prime and whichever laws of atmospheric science made it rain. The thought of sleep flashed into his mind and broke against a wall of stubbornness. He gestured with a rifle thicker than his arm toward the nearest intersection, then quickened his pace.

Somewhere in the distance a swift series of blaster shots resounded, followed by shouts and silence.

The figure closest behind Namir—a tall man with graying hair and a face puckered with scar tissue—bounded across the street to take up a position opposite. The third figure, a massive form huddled in a tarp like a hooded cloak, remained behind.

The scarred man flashed a hand signal. Namir turned the corner onto the intersecting street. A dozen meters away, the sodden lumps of human bodies lay in the road. They wore tattered rain gear—sleek, lightweight wraps and sandals—and carried no weapons. Noncombatants.

It's a shame, Namir thought, *but not a bad sign.* The Empire didn't shoot civilians when everything was under control.

"Charmer—take a look?" Namir indicated the bodies. The scarred man strode over as Namir tapped his comlink. "Sector secure," he said. "What's on tap next?"

The response came in a hiss of static through Namir's earpiece—something about mop-up operations. Namir missed having a communications specialist on staff. Twilight Company's last comms tech had been a drunk and a misanthrope, but she'd been magic with a transmitter and she'd written obscene poetry with Namir on late, dull nights. She and her idiot droid had died in the bombardment on Asyrphus.

"Say again," Namir tried. "Are we ready to load?"

This time the answer came through clearly. "Support teams are crating up food and equipment," the voice said. "If you've got a lead on medical supplies, we'd love more for the *Thunderstrike*. Otherwise, get to the rendezvous—we only have a few hours before reinforcements show."

"Tell support to grab hygiene items this time," Namir said. "Anyone who says they're luxuries needs to smell the barracks."

There was another burst of static, and maybe a laugh. "I'll let them know. Stay safe."

Charmer was finishing his study of the bodies, checking each for a heartbeat and identification. He shook his head, silent, as he straightened.

"Atrocity." The hulking figure wrapped in the tarp had finally approached. His voice was deep and resonant. Two meaty, four-fingered hands kept the tarp clasped at his shoulders, while a second pair of hands loosely carried a massive blaster cannon at waist level. "How can anyone born of flesh do this?"

Charmer bit his lip. Namir shrugged. "Could've been combat droids, for all we know."

"Unlikely," the hulking figure said. "But if so, responsibility belongs to the governor." He knelt beside one of the corpses and reached out to lid its eyes. Each of his hands was as large as the dead man's head.

"Come on, Gadren," Namir said. "Someone will find them."

Gadren stayed kneeling. Charmer opened his mouth to speak, then shut it. Namir wondered whether to push the point and, if so, how hard.

Then the wall next to him exploded, and he stopped worrying about Gadren.

Fire and metal shards and grease and insulation pelted his spine. He couldn't hear and couldn't guess how he ended up in the middle of the road among the bodies, one leg bent beneath him. Something tacky was stuck to his chin and his helmet's visor was cracked; he had enough presence of mind to feel lucky he hadn't lost an eye.

Suddenly he was moving again. He was upright, and hands—Charmer's hands—were dragging him backward, clasping him below the shoulders. He snarled the native curses of his homeworld as a red storm of particle bolts flashed among the fire and debris. By the time he'd pushed Charmer away and wobbled onto his feet, he'd traced the bolts to their source.

Four Imperial stormtroopers stood at the mouth of an alley up the street. Their deathly pale armor gleamed in the rain, and the black eyepieces of their helmets gaped like pits. Their weapons shone with oil and machined care, as if the squad had stepped fully formed out of a mold.

Namir tore his gaze from the enemy long enough to see that his back was to a storefront window filled with video screens. He raised his blaster rifle, fired at the display, then climbed in among the shards.

Charmer followed. The storefront wouldn't give them cover for long—certainly not if the stormtroopers fired another rocket—but it would have to be enough.

"Check for a way up top," Namir yelled, and his voice sounded faint and tinny. He couldn't hear the storm of blaster bolts at all. "We need covering fire!" Not looking to see if Charmer obeyed, he dropped to the floor as the stormtroopers adjusted their aim to the store.

He couldn't spot Gadren, either. He ordered the alien into position anyway, hoping he was alive and that the comlinks still worked. He lined his rifle under his chin, fired twice in the direction of the stormtroopers, and was rewarded with a moment of peace.

"I need you on target, Brand," he growled into his link. "I need you here *now*."

If anyone answered, he couldn't hear it.

Now he glimpsed the stormtrooper carrying the missile launcher. The trooper was still reloading, which meant Namir had half a minute at most before the storefront came tumbling down on top of him. He took a few quick shots and saw one of the other troopers fall, though he doubted he'd hit his target. He guessed Charmer had found a vantage point after all.

Three stormtroopers remaining. One was moving away from the alley while the other stayed to protect the artillery man. Namir shot wildly at the one moving into the street, watched him skid and fall to a knee, and smiled grimly. There was something satisfying about seeing a trained stormtrooper humiliate himself. Namir's own side did it often enough.

Jerky movements drew Namir's attention back to the artillery man. Behind the stormtrooper stood Gadren, both sets of arms gripping and lifting his foe. Human limbs flailed and the missile launcher fell to the ground. White armor seemed to crumple in the alien's hands. Gadren's makeshift hood blew back, exposing his head: a brown, bulbous, wide-mouthed mass topped with a darker crest of bone, like some amphibian's nightmare idol. The second trooper in the alley turned to face Gadren and was promptly slammed to the ground with his comrade's body before Gadren crushed them both, howling in rage or grief.

Namir trusted Gadren as much as he trusted anyone, but there were times when the alien terrified him.

The last stormtrooper was still down in the street. Namir fired until flames licked a burnt and melted hole in the man's armor. Namir, Charmer, and Gadren gathered back around the bodies and assessed their own injuries.

Namir's hearing was coming back. The damage to his helmet extended far beyond the visor—a crack extended along its length—and he found a shallow cut across his forehead when he tossed the helmet to the street. Charmer was picking shards of shrapnel from his vest but made no complaints. Gadren was shivering in the warm rain.

"No Brand?" Gadren asked.

Namir only grunted.

Charmer laughed his weird, hiccoughing laugh and spoke. He swallowed the words twice, three, four times as he went, half stuttering as he had ever since the fight on Blacktar Cyst. "Keep piling bodies like this," he said, "we'll have the best vantage point in the city."

He gestured at Namir's last target, who had fallen directly onto one of the civilian corpses.

"You're a sick man, Charmer," Namir said, and swung an arm roughly around his comrade's shoulders. "I'll miss you when they boot you out."

Gadren grunted and sniffed behind them. It might have been dismay, but Namir chose to take it as mirth.

Officially, the city was Haidoral Administrative Center One, but locals called it "Glitter" after the crystalline mountains that limned the horizon. In Namir's experience, what the Galactic Empire didn't name to inspire terror—its stormtrooper legions, its Star Destroyer battleships—it tried to render as drab as possible. This didn't bother Namir, but he wasn't among the residents of the planets and cities being labeled.

A half dozen Rebel squads had already arrived at the central plaza when Namir's team marched in. The rain had condensed into mist, and the plaza's tents and canopies offered little shelter; nonetheless, men and women in ragged armor squeezed into the driest corners they could find, grumbling to one another or tending to minor wounds and damaged equipment. As victory celebrations went, it was subdued. It had been a long fight for little more than the promise of a few fresh meals.

"Stop admiring yourselves and do something *useful*," Namir barked, barely breaking stride. "Support teams can use a hand if you're too good to play *greeter*."

He barely noticed the squads stir in response. Instead, his attention shifted to a woman emerging from the shadows of a speeder stand. She was tall and thickly built, dressed in rugged pants and a bulky maroon jacket. A scoped rifle was slung over her shoulder, and the armor mesh of a retracted face mask covered her neck and chin. Her skin was gently creased with age and as dark as a human's could be, her hair was cropped close to her scalp, and she didn't so much as glance at Namir as she arrived at his side and matched his pace through the plaza.

"You want to tell me where you were?" Namir asked.

"You missed the second fire team. I took care of it," Brand said.

Namir kept his voice cool. "Drop me a hint next time?"

"You didn't need the distraction."

Namir laughed. "Love you, too."

Brand cocked her head. If she got the joke—and Namir expected she did—she wasn't amused. "So what now?" she asked.

"We've got eight hours before we leave the system," Namir said, and stopped with his back to an overturned kiosk. He leaned against the metal frame and stared into the mist. "Less if Imperial ships come before then, or if the governor's forces regroup. After that, we'll divvy up the supplies with the rest of the battle group. Probably keep an escort ship or two for the *Thunderstrike* before the others split off."

"And we abandon this sector to the Empire," Brand said.

By this time Charmer had wandered off, and Gadren had joined a circle with Namir and Brand. "We will return," he said gravely.

"Right," Namir said, smirking. "Something to look forward to."

He knew they were the wrong words at the wrong time.

Eighteen months earlier, the Rebel Alliance's sixty-first mobile infantry—commonly known as Twilight Company—had joined the push into the galactic Mid Rim. The operation was among the largest the Rebellion had ever fielded against the Empire, involving thousands of starships, hundreds of battle groups, and dozens of worlds. In the wake of the Rebellion's victory against the Empire's planet-burning Death Star battle station, High Command had believed the time was right to move from the fringes of Imperial territory toward its population centers.

Twilight Company had fought in the factory-deserts of Phorsa Gedd and taken the Ducal Palace of Bamayar. It had established beachheads for rebel hover tanks and erected bases from tarps and sheet metal. Namir had seen soldiers lose limbs and go weeks without proper treatment. He'd trained teams to construct makeshift bayonets when blaster power packs ran low. He'd set fire to cities and watched the Empire do the same. He'd left friends behind on broken worlds, knowing he'd never see them again.

On planet after planet, Twilight had fought. Battles were won and battles were lost, and Namir stopped keeping score. Twilight remained at the Rebellion's vanguard, forging ahead of the bulk of the armada, until word came down from High Command nine months in: The fleet was overextended. There was to be no further advance—only defense of the newly claimed territories.

Not long after that, the retreat began.

Twilight Company had become the rear guard of a massive withdrawal. It deployed to worlds it had helped capture mere months earlier and evacuated the bases it had built. It extracted the Rebellion's heroes and generals and pointed the way home. It marched over the graves of its own dead soldiers. Some of the company lost hope. Some became angry.

No one wanted to go back.

Read on for an excerpt from

AFTERMATH

---

by Chuck Wendig

PUBLISHED BY DEL REY BOOKS

PRELUDE:

Today is a day of celebration. We have triumphed over villainy and oppression and have given our Alliance—and the galaxy beyond it—a chance to breathe and cheer for the progress in reclaiming our freedom from an Empire that robbed us of it. We have reports from Commander Skywalker that Emperor Palpatine is dead, and his enforcer, Darth Vader, with him.

But though we may celebrate, we should not consider this our time to rest. We struck a major blow against the Empire, and now will be the time to seize on the opening we have created. The Empire's weapon may be destroyed, but the Empire itself lives on. Its oppressive hand closes around the throats of good, free-thinking people across the galaxy, from the Coruscant Core to the farthest systems in the Outer Rim. We must remember that our fight continues. Our rebellion is over. But the war . . . the war is just beginning.

—Admiral Ackbar

CORUSCANT

Then:

Monument Plaza.

Chains rattle as they lash the neck of Emperor Palpatine. Ropes follow suit—lassos looping around the statue's middle. The mad cheers of the crowd as they pull, and pull, and pull. Disappointed groans as the stone fixture refuses to budge. But then someone whips the chains around the back ends of a couple of heavy-gauge speeders, and then engines warble and hum to life—the speeders gun it and again the crowd pulls—

The sound like a giant bone breaking.

A fracture appears at the base of the statue.

More cheering. Yelling. And—

Applause as it comes crashing down.

The head of the statue snaps off, goes rolling and crashing into a fountain. Dark water splashes. The crowd laughs.

And then: The whooping of klaxons. Red lights strobe. Three airspeeders swoop down from the traffic lanes above—Imperial police. Red-and-black helmets. The glow of their lights reflected back in their helmets.

There comes no warning. No demand to stand down.

The laser cannons at the fore of each airspeeder open fire. Red bolts sear the air. The crowd is cut apart. Bodies dropped and stitched with fire.

But still, those gathered are not cowed. They are no longer a crowd. Now they are a mob. They start picking up hunks of the Palpatine statue and lobbing them up at the airspeeders. One of the speeders swings to the side to avoid an incoming chunk of stone—and it bumps another speeder, interrupting its fire. Coruscanti citizens climb up the stone spire behind both speeders—a spire on which are written the Imperial values of order, control, and the rule of law—and begin jumping onto the police cruisers. One helmeted cop is flung from his vehicle. The other crawls out onto the hood of his speeder, opening fire with a pair of blasters—just as a hunk of stone cracks him in the helmet, knocking him to the ground.

The other two airspeeders lift higher and keep firing.

Screams and fire and smoke.

Two of those gathered—a father and son, Rorak and Jak—quick-duck behind the collapsed statue. The sounds of the battle unfolding right here in Monument Plaza don't end. In the distance, the sound of more fighting, a plume of flames, flashes of blaster fire. A billboard high up in the sky among the traffic lanes suddenly goes to static.

The boy is young, only twelve standard years, not old enough to fight. Not yet. He looks to his father with pleading eyes. Over the din he yells: "But the battle station was destroyed, Dad! The battle is over!" They just watched it only an hour before. The supposed end of the Empire. The start of something better.

The confusion in the boy's shining eyes is clear: He doesn't understand what's happening.

But Rorak does. He's heard tales of the Clone Wars—tales spoken by his own father. He knows how war goes. It's not many wars, but just one, drawn out again and again, cut up into slices so it seems more manageable.

For a long time he's told his son not the truth but the idealized hope: *One day the Empire will fall and things will be different for when you have children.* And that may still come to pass. But now a stronger, sharper truth is required: "Jak—the battle isn't over. The battle is just starting."

He holds his son close.

Then he puts a hunk of statue in the boy's hand.

And he picks one up himself.

ABOUT THE AUTHORS

MELISSA SCOTT was born and raised in Little Rock, Arkansas, studied history at Harvard College, and earned her PhD from Brandeis University in the comparative history program. She has published more than thirty original novels and a handful of short stories, as well as tie-in fiction. She saw *Star Wars: A New Hope* when it opened, and has been a fan ever since. She is ridiculously happy to be writing in this universe.

JAMES LUCENO is the *New York Times* bestselling author of the *Star Wars* novels *Darth Plagueis, Millennium Falcon, Dark Lord: The Rise of Darth Vader, Cloak of Deception,* and *Labyrinth of Evil,* as well as the New Jedi Order novels *Agents of Chaos I: Hero's Trial* and *Agents of Chaos II: Jedi Eclipse, The Unifying Force,* and the eBook "Darth Maul: Saboteur." He lives with his wife in Annapolis, Maryland.

JOHN JACKSON MILLER is the *New York Times* bestselling author of *Star Wars: Kenobi, Star Wars: Knight Errant, Star Wars: Lost Tribe of the Sith: The Collected Stories,* and fifteen *Star Wars* graphic novels. A comics industry analyst and historian, he has written comics and prose for several franchises, including *Conan, Iron Man, Indiana Jones, Mass Effect, The Simpsons,* and *Star Trek.* He lives in Wisconsin with his wife, two children, and far too many comic books.

JASON FRY is the author of *The Jupiter Pirates* young-adult space-fantasy series and has written or co-written more than thirty novels, short stories, and other works set in the galaxy far, far away, including *The Essential Atlas* and the *Servants of the Empire* quartet. He lives in Brooklyn, New York, with his wife, son, and about a metric ton of *Star Wars* stuff.

ABOUT THE TYPE

This book was set in Minion, a 1990 Adobe Originals typeface by Robert Slimbach (b. 1956). Minion is inspired by classical, old-style typefaces of the late Renaissance, a period of elegant, beautiful, and highly readable type designs. Created primarily for text setting, Minion combines the aesthetic and functional qualities that make text type highly readable with the versatility of digital technology.